By Robert Newcomb

THE CHRONICLES OF BLOOD AND STONE
The Fifth Sorceress
The Gates of Dawn
The Scrolls of the Ancients

THE DESTINIES OF BLOOD AND STONE
Savage Messiah
A March into Darkness

SAVAGE MESSIAH

VOLUME I OF THE DESTINIES OF BLOOD AND STONE

ROBERT NEWCOMB

BALLANTINE BOOKS • NEW YORK

Savage Messiah is a work of fiction. Names, places, and incidents either are products of the author's imagination or are used fictitiously.

2007 Del Rey Mass Market Edition

Copyright © 2006 by Robert Newcomb
Excerpt from *A March into Darkness* copyright © 2006 by Robert Newcomb

Published in the United States by Del Rey Books, an imprint of The Random House Publishing Group, a division of Random House, Inc., New York.

This book contains an excerpt from the forthcoming book *A March into Darkness* by Robert Newcomb. This excerpt has been set for this edition only and may not reflect the final content of the forthcoming edition.

DEL REY is a registered trademark and the Del Rey colophon is a trademark of Random House, Inc.

Originally published in hardcover in the United States by Del Rey Books, an imprint of The Random House Publishing Group, a division of Random House, Inc., in 2006.

Map illustration by Russ Charpentier

ISBN 978-0-345-47708-8

Printed in the United States of America

www.delreybooks.com

OPM   9   8   7   6   5   4   3   2   1

This one's dedicated to Paul, Katie, Elizabeth, and Allison Iaconis.

My love to you all . . .

CONTENTS

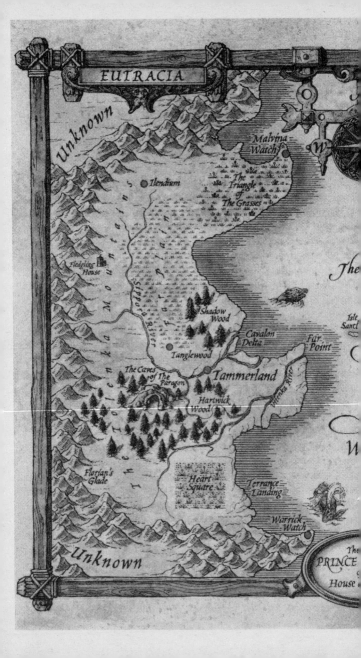

SAVAGE MESSIAH

PROLOGUE

"It is often said that it is impossible to place a value on a human life. The value of a human death, however, can be easily negotiated."

—SATINE

FROM HER PLACE AT THE PORT GUNWALE, SATINE OF THE HOUSE of Kinton watched as the demonslaver crew worked to dock the great warship at the underground pier. Tall and sinewy, with unnaturally alabaster skin and totally bald heads, the demonslavers looked more like monsters than men. They wore nothing but silver skullcaps and long black leather skirts split down the center for walking, and they looked all too ready to use the swords and tridents they kept close to hand. During the journey across the Sea of Whispers, Satine had almost grown used to the sight of them—almost, but not quite. Still, she refused to flinch under their gazes, or reveal any distaste she might feel. This sanction was too important, regardless of its unusual beginnings and intriguing development.

While several of the crew—demonslavers all—busily lowered the gangplank onto the stone pier, Satine glanced at the man standing beside her. This was the same blue-robed fellow who had approached her on behalf of his still unidentified master and who had told her not to fear his macabre crew. He had said little since they had left Eutracia. She knew only two things about him for certain: his name was Bratach, and he was of the craft of magic.

She guessed him to be about forty Seasons of New Life. He had piercing brown eyes and an aqualine nose. His close-cropped hair was dark, his mouth firm and unforgiving. He was clearly in command of both the *Sojourner* and its strange crew. Satine suspected that the small uses of the craft that he had displayed during the voyage were but a glimpse of far greater gifts. Having little understanding of magic, she could not be sure.

She followed him down the gangplank, up a series of steps, and out into the welcoming midday sunshine. Birds sang happily in the island fortress' highly manicured inner ward. Majestic fountains danced and burbled. Silently, Bratach led the way along a covered portico, into one of many magnificent buildings, and down numerous hallways, each more sumptuous than the last. Other men in dark blue robes could be seen coming and going, as well as the occasional, white-skinned demonslaver.

Finally Bratach stopped before a portal of variegated marble. Two heavily armed demonslaver guards came to swift attention. At a nod from Bratach, they swung open the massive double doors.

Although Satine was no stranger to luxury, she was stunned. The room was huge. Its entire western side lay open from floor to ceiling to reveal the sky above and the earth and the sea below. The rest of the chamber was fashioned of dark green marble shot through with swirls of the palest gray. A series of black columns rose from the floor to support the rather low ceiling. Suddenly, she was distracted by the sound of twittering laughter.

When she turned to look, she saw a group of women about her own age. They wore nothing but the flowers in their hair, and happily bathed and lounged in a descending series of ornate marble pools, where scented water splashed down from a curved trough in the wall above. Satine guessed that the women were handmaidens. But who was their mistress?

Before she could ask the question, Bratach beckoned to her. Obediently, she followed him toward the backs of two black marble thrones that sat serenely overlooking the sea below. On either side of the thrones stood a freestanding column of dark red marble, each encircled from top to bottom with garlands of Eutracian gingerlily. At the top of each column was a shallow black urn in which burned a dancing flame. The room smelled pleasantly of both the garland blossoms and the sea salt wafting in on the afternoon breeze.

From the left throne's outer edge, a bare arm appeared, red, deformed, and lacking in muscle mass. The hand was little more than a wrinkled claw, only three fingers remaining, the skin ragged and scarred. A burn perhaps, Satine thought. Then the repulsive hand crooked one of its talonlike fingers, beckoning her around to the front of the throne. After shooting a skeptical glance at Bratach, she did as she was asked.

So this was her new benefactor. She forced her revulsion aside and calmly regarded the man seated in the throne. He would have been handsome had it not been for the drastic insult to his face. His long sandy hair was pulled back from the hairline and tied behind his shoulders. His left eye was covered with a black leather patch. The rest of that side of his face was a mass of pink scar tissue, punctuated here and there by facial bones that protruded hideously through the thin membrane covering them. His right eye was hazel, and with it he stared back at her with a controlled sense of intelligence and power.

He appeared to be tall, broad-shouldered, and muscular. He wore a sleeveless, emerald-green silk jacket, matching trousers, and black leather sandals. Taken as a whole, he was, Satine was quite sure, a man to be reckoned with.

Then she looked at the woman seated by his side. She was as beautiful as the man was repulsive. Shiny brunette ringlets that hung nearly to her breasts framed the strong yet feminine face. Her eyes were level and bright blue. Like the man beside her, she radiated an undeniable sense of self-discipline. Her magnificent black, floor-length silk gown flowed over her body in an undulating river, its embroidered hem gently lapping over a pair of matching slippers. Looking more closely, Satine guessed that she was nearing the end of her pregnancy.

The man finally broke the silence.

"Welcome, Satine," he said. "My name is Wulfgar, and I am the ruler of this place—this Citadel—as we call it. I am also a fully empowered wizard." His voice was deep and commanding. "I trust your voyage was agreeable?"

"Yes," Satine answered. "Your demonslavers are most interesting."

Wulfgar smiled, and the pink scar tissue on the left side of his face moved strangely, as if it had long since ceased to be a natural part of his body. Satine found the effect both intriguing and disturbing.

"They *are* interesting, aren't they?" he answered. "Unfortunately, their numbers are now few: only enough remain to man my flagship and guard this island. But in the end, that will not matter."

He used his good hand to point to the woman seated on his right. "This is Serena, my queen. Anything you would say to me, you may also say before her."

Satine gave Wulfgar's queen a short bow.

Wulfgar regarded the woman standing before him. He had taken great pains to find her, and he needed to be sure that he had made the right choice. If for any reason she did not live up to his expectations, he would kill her and begin his search anew. But time was short, and he hoped that disposing of her would not be necessary. So far, she did not disappoint.

Tall, lean, and muscular, Satine appeared to be approximately thirty-five Seasons of New Life. She stood confidently, her legs spread a bit wide in a blatant stance of power. When she had first walked before him, he had immediately noticed her smooth, almost effortless economy of movement. Someone had trained this woman well.

She was dressed in a form-fitting, no-nonsense outfit of dull black leather. Dull, Wulfgar suddenly realized, so that it would not shine in the sun. Her black hair was pulled severely back. Her face was attractive, yet not what he might have called classically beautiful. Piercing blue eyes complemented full, red lips and a rather short nose. Her knee boots were of scuffed black leather and had seen considerable use. She wore no jewelry of any kind.

Black leather belts crisscrossed her hips, ending in double sheaths that were tied down to her thighs. Each sheath held two daggers. A soft, dark gray, hooded cloak was pushed back from her shoulders and tied loosely across her neck with a black knotted cord. The fletching of arrows and the top of a short bow peeked out just above the upper edge of the cloak; the bowstring angled down tightly between her breasts. Her hands rested casually on the dagger handles at either hip. Her face remained expressionless.

Wulfgar raised an eyebrow. Taken as a whole, Satine seemed a formidable creature indeed. He also knew that appearances meant nothing. It was her skill, stealth, and discretion that he needed most, and they would be well-tested before he could allow her to leave the Citadel alive. The stakes he was about to play for were the highest imaginable, and he had to be sure of her.

"First things first," he said. "We have been informed that your blood is not endowed. Is that so?"

"I have no idea," Satine answered. Her brow furrowed. "What possible difference could that make? No prospective employer has ever asked me that before. And over the course of my career I have had many satisfied clients, I assure you."

"No doubt," Wulfgar replied calmly. "Nonetheless, I believe I shall be like none of your other patrons. I have valid reasons for being curious about your blood."

He snapped his fingers toward Bratach. The consul walked over to Satine and reached for her arm.

Before he could touch her, Satine spun on her heels and came up alongside him. Taking his outstretched wrist, she twirled again. Using Bratach's momentum against him, she launched him up off his feet. He turned over once in midair and landed hard on his back on the unforgiving marble floor.

With a groan, he raised one arm to retaliate with some use of the craft. Satine's boot heel immediately went to his exposed throat, and her hand moved like lightning toward one of her hip daggers. The entire thing happened in the twinkle of an eye, and her emotionless expression never changed.

"Enough!" Wulfgar called. His grotesque smile surfaced again.

"I only wish to test your blood, my dear," he said. "We mean you no harm. My sincerest apologies for not informing you sooner."

Wulfgar looked at the consul lying on the floor. Bratach could have killed her with the craft, he knew. But considering Satine's amazing speed, he found himself wondering whether the consul would have even gotten the chance. He looked back at her.

"Well done, however," he added.

Narrowing her eyes, Satine raised her boot. Bratach gingerly rose from the floor.

"Now then," Wulfgar said, "please give him your hand."

Satine held out one palm.

After giving her a hard look, Bratach narrowed his eyes. A small, painless incision formed in the underside of Satine's wrist. A single drop of her blood liberated itself, and the incision closed again. The blood drop hovered in the air.

Bratach produced a vial from a pocket in his robes. Opening its top, he employed the craft to cause a single drop of red water to rise from the vial and join with Satine's blood.

Nothing happened. Releasing the hovering mixture from his powers, Bratach watched it splatter harmlessly onto the floor.

"We were informed correctly, my lord," he said. "Her blood is common."

Satine looked hard at Wulfgar. "What is all this about?" she demanded. "Do you wish to employ my services or not? Frankly, this feels like a waste of my time."

"Oh, it was no waste of time, I assure you," Wulfgar answered. "You see, some of your future targets may be able to detect endowed blood. Let's just say that given the mission you are about to undertake, that would not be in your best interests."

Thinking, Wulfgar stood from his throne and walked to the edge of the floor. A series of curved marble steps led downward, spilling out upon a terrace that overlooked the ocean. Columns lined both sides of the steps, each holding a flaming urn.

Wulfgar turned back to Satine and examined the crisscrossed belts she wore. Another test was in order, he decided.

"Let me guess," he said. "You're ambidextrous."

Satine nodded.

"A great advantage in your line of work," he mused. "Still, you will need to prove it to me."

"Very well," she answered cautiously. "What do you suggest?"

Looking over at the handmaidens, Wulfgar raised his good hand and pointed at them. Almost at once, they stopped what they were doing and came to stand in a neat row. Ten of them, their glistening bodies still dripping water. Lowering his hand, Wulfgar turned to his queen.

"You don't mind, do you, my dear?" he asked her.

With a smile, Serena shook her head. "There are more where they came from," she said.

Wulfgar looked back at Satine. "Whenever you're ready," he said quietly.

Satine didn't approve of what Wulfgar was asking her to do. But she had come a long way, and she badly needed another sanction. If this was what it took to convince him of her abilities, so be it.

"Very well," she answered. She turned to face the row of naked women. Widening her stance, she tossed the folds of her cloak over either shoulder. To Wulfgar's surprise, she closed her eyes.

"The ones on either end," she said. She took a breath and let it out slowly, calming her heart.

Crossing her arms before her, she reached for opposite thighs and grasped two of the daggers. With underhand throws, she sent the weapons spinning across the room. Her speed was so unexpected that Wulfgar scarcely saw her hands move.

With a sickening thud, the blades buried themselves in the women's foreheads. The handmaidens collapsed, dead.

Satine opened her eyes. She did not look at the results of her handiwork. She didn't need to. She turned back to Wulfgar.

"Satisfied?" she asked.

"Indeed," Wulfgar answered. With a wave of his good hand, he ordered the remaining handmaidens from the room.

"The daggers and the bow I see; surely you must have other means of assassination at your disposal," he observed. "The persons I will be sending you after will prove to be amazingly resourceful."

"I have an herbmaster in my employ," Satine replied shortly. "That's all you need to know."

Wulfgar scowled slightly, but merely turned and walked back to his throne. Satine decided that it was time for a few questions of her own.

"Just how did you find me? I have never traveled so far to consider a sanction."

Raising his mutilated arm, Wulfgar regarded his three claw-like fingers in the light of the urns. A sudden darkness came over his face; Satine found his expression unsettling. This was about much more than just politics or who controlled the craft, she realized. This was about revenge.

"Discreet inquiries were made," Wulfgar answered. He rested his ravaged limb on the arm of his throne again.

"I have servants still living in Eutracia," he added. "They sought out only the best. Your name kept appearing at the top of the list."

Wulfgar beckoned Bratach forward. The consul reached into his robe and withdrew a parchment tied with black ribbon, which he handed to Satine.

Accepting the scroll, Satine looked questioningly at Wulfgar. He nodded. She untied the ribbon and regarded the document.

"Can you kill these persons?" Wulfgar asked.

A long silence passed. Her mind racing, Satine took a deep breath. Finally, she lifted her eyes and looked Wulfgar squarely in the face.

"Yes," she answered. "You realize that these sanctions will present an entire host of unusual complications. My price will be very high."

"Of that I have no doubt," Wulfgar answered calmly.

More quiet moments passed as Satine tried to think. These would be the commissions of a lifetime, and she must be sure that the monster on the throne understood that.

"I don't think you fully grasp the nature of the task," she said. "Whoever does this job must retire from this life and go to ground forever. And that will take money—lots of it. Given the fact that I am still a relatively young woman, the sum will be huge. Despite what you see of me just now, I enjoy living in style."

Saying nothing, Wulfgar waited.

"Three hundred thousand kisa," she demanded.

"Done," Wulfgar answered immediately.

The air between them filled with an azure glow, which then dissolved to reveal several large canvas cinch bags lying on the floor.

"This represents half of the agreed-upon sum," Wulfgar said. "I will order it loaded aboard the *Sojourner* before she takes you back to Eutracia. Once there, you may hide it in any place you choose. When the sanctions are complete, I will grant you the rest of your fee."

Something Satine had once heard about wizards floated up from her memories, and she suddenly understood her mistake. Wizards cared nothing for money because they could literally conjure all they ever needed. She could probably have asked for much more. She just as quickly decided against risking the wrath of the monstrosity sitting before her by trying to amend their bargain. Then she felt something else tug at the back of her mind.

"Very well," she answered. "I formally accept the sanctions. Tell me. If you are a wizard, then why don't you do this yourself?" She paused for a moment.

"I can see the hate in your eye," she added slowly, letting her words sink in. "I know what it is to hate as well as anyone in this world. Wouldn't you prefer to see your enemies die by your own hand?" She watched the brooding darkness overtake his face once more.

"It has to do with being able to wield the craft," he answered. "After our first encounter, my enemies will no doubt be extra vigilant in their attempts to search out any unfamiliar, highly endowed blood. Besides, my consuls and I have other matters to attend to, matters that we alone must finish."

Wulfgar nodded at Bratach again. Reaching into his robes, the consul retrieved another parchment and handed it to Satine. Not standing on ceremony this time, she unrolled it. It held the likenesses of still more faces.

"You may have to dispatch these persons first in order to draw the others out," Wulfgar told her. Then the wicked smile came again. "Given the huge nature of your fee, I shall expect these initial deaths to be free of charge."

Satine rolled the two scrolls up together and smoothly placed them into her cloak. Their bargain sealed, Wulfgar looked at her with newfound admiration. Leaning back in his throne, he crossed one of his long legs over the other.

"Tell me," he finally said. "Is it true what we have been told? That given the right opportunity, you can kill anyone you choose?"

"Yes."

"Even a wizard?"

"Given the right set of circumstances, yes, even a wizard," Satine answered. "A fact it might do you well to remember, should you decide to cheat me for some reason."

Wulfgar's right eye flashed at the thinly veiled warning. Clearly, this woman was without fear. Good, he thought. She will need to be. He leaned forward in his throne.

"Succeed, Satine," he said to her, "and I shall not cheat you. Fail, however, and the price of your shortcomings will be high—much higher than you would choose to pay. No one—not even you—is beyond my grasp."

Determined to stand her ground, Satine pointed to Bratach.

"I work alone," she stated. "Keep him and the others like him away from me. I don't trust those of the craft, and I never will. If I see any of your twisted servants following me, I will abort the sanctions and kill them without thinking twice. Do you understand?"

"Agreed," Wulfgar answered. "Nonetheless, you will need to see him from time to time, to gather information. And now that our business is concluded, Bratach will see you to your quarters. You sail on the morning tide, but first Serena and I would like you to dine with us tonight. I will send one of the demonslavers to fetch you." It sounded like a polite invitation, but Satine understood it was a command.

She looked hard at the deformed man and his beautiful queen. She didn't like taking orders. But she could find no logical reason to refuse.

"Thank you," she said.

The sooner she was away from this bizarre place and attending to her new sanctions, she thought, the better.

I

⚓

DEATH

CHAPTER I

"... AND AS EACH OF YOU IS AWARE, THE STONE WE CALL THE Paragon 'conducts' its gifts to those of endowed blood by way of its twenty-five facets," Wigg told the group of keenly interested women. Out of habit, he placed his gnarled hands into the opposite sleeves of his gray robe.

"These facets allow us control of such arts of the craft as the Kinetic, the Sympathetic, the Formative, and the Causal, to name but a few," the First Wizard went on. "However, it is the Organic facet of the stone that I wish to discuss today." He withdrew his right hand and held up a long bony forefinger.

"It is this facet with which you are the least familiar," he added, "for unlike all the others, it is available only to those persons of partial blood signatures. As you look to the diagram I am about to conjure, you will notice that . . ."

While Wigg droned on, Prince Tristan of the House of Galland sighed deeply. Leaning back, he raised the two front legs of his chair from the floor, ran a hand through his long, dark hair, then crossed his arms over the laces of his black leather vest. His dreggan, the curved sword of the flying warriors known as the Minions of Day and Night, rested on the marble floor beside his chair. The black quiver that held his throwing knives lay alongside it.

On an impulse, he had decided to attend one of Wigg's lectures to the Acolytes of the Redoubt. They were the secret sisterhood of the craft, recently called to Tammerland from their various locations about the countryside. Now the red-robed women sat with rapt attention, many of them zealously taking notes in large leather-bound journals.

A short time into the lecture, the prince realized that he was already familiar with much of the subject matter, due to his recent experiences with the partial adept Abbey. He sighed again.

Of all the days to come here, he thought. Unfortunately, walking out on one of Wigg's lectures was not an option. It would send the wrong message to the acolytes, and besides, Wigg would never let him hear the end of it.

Taking another deep breath, he looked around the room.

The Redoubt, the secret underground fortress that lay directly beneath the royal palace in the capital city of Tammerland, housed many such rooms that had once been filled with eager students of the craft—before most of the wizards had been murdered and the consuls, the male counterparts to the acolytes, turned to evil. Now the Acolytes of the Redoubt sat in row after row at long mahogany tables. Before them the First Wizard lectured from a dais. A solid black panel covered the entire wall behind him. When he spoke, his words appeared in glowing azure on its surface, making it easier for the students to keep up as they took their notes. When the panel became full of Wigg's mental scribbles, he erased them with a wave of one hand, and then new words would appear.

The rest of the huge classroom was filled with more tables, bookcases, and desks. Beakers burbled and steamed, glass tubing carried colorful liquids of who knew what to who knew where, and scrolls and texts of the craft lay all about. A chart of arcane symbols took up nearly the entire wall to Tristan's right, their meanings lost upon him. Taken as a whole, Tristan thought, the place looked more like an antiques warehouse than a serious classroom of the craft.

Glancing back up at Wigg, Tristan realized that the wizard had stopped talking and was staring directly at him. Then Wigg raised his infamous, condescending right eyebrow.

With another sigh, the prince pushed his tongue against the inside of one cheek, gently lowered the two legs of his chair back down to the floor, and sat upright again. Apparently satisfied, Wigg continued with his lecture, leaving Tristan to reflect on the wizard's remarkable ability to make him feel like a callow youth rather than an adult and a prince experienced in war and the horrors of incredible evil.

Scarcely a month had passed since Wulfgar—Tristan and Shailiha's half brother—had been killed and his plan to destroy the Orb of the Vigors defeated. The Acolytes of the Redoubt had been called home to Tammerland to receive further training in the craft so that they might once more be sent forth into the countryside to perform the anonymous, charitable deeds for the citizenry that had previously been the sole purview of the consuls of the Redoubt. Many of the consuls had perished in the war against Wulfgar, their new master. Any survivors, Tristan presumed, no doubt remained at the Citadel, the island fortress in the Sea of Whispers that Wulfgar had called home.

Tristan's expression hardened. He and his friends had been successful in defeating Wulfgar and the demonslavers, but the fates of the two Scrolls of the Ancients were still in limbo. The Scrolls held the formulas for the Forestallments—the spells that could be laid into the blood signature of an endowed person, giving him or her power in the craft of magic without years of training. The Scrolls' importance was immeasurable.

The Scroll of the Vigors was now safely ensconced in the Redoubt, but in the final battle with Wulfgar it had been damaged, many of its secrets lost to the world forever. Wigg, Faegan, and Abbey continued to attempt to unravel its secrets, but the work went slowly and with frustratingly little success.

The Scroll of the Vagaries was still missing, presumably hidden somewhere at the Citadel. It had no doubt provided the formulas with which Wulfgar had attempted to destroy the Orb of the Vigors. He had very nearly succeeded. Until the Scroll of the Vagaries came into Faegan and Wigg's possession, it remained a great danger.

Tristan's mood lightened as his thoughts turned to the Conclave of the Vigors. He had ordered the formation of the Conclave just after Wulfgar's death as a replacement for the Directorate of Wizards, the previous governing body of Eutracia. Nine of his closest friends and allies now served on the Conclave with him. Wigg and Faegan, of course, as well as Tristan's twin sister, the Princess Shailiha, and his beloved Celeste. They were joined by the partial adept Abbey—Wigg's longtime love; Tyranny, the female privateer who now patrolled Eutracia's oceans with her fleet; and Adrian, the young acolyte whom the wizards had selected to represent the women of her fledgling sisterhood. The warrior Traax, commander of the Minions of Day and Night, and the hunchbacked dwarf Geldon, both of unendowed blood but great loyalty, completed the nine.

But though the Conclave was in place, and the task of rebuilding the war-torn lands of Eutracia and Parthalon had begun, Tristan had other concerns, ones that lay much closer to his heart.

His azure blood, for one. Due to the supreme quality of his endowed blood, Tristan was the only person in the world ever to employ the craft without having first been trained, or having one of his many Forestallments activated. But when he had performed that unparalleled feat—when he had employed the craft to destroy the Sorceresses of the Coven—his blood had turned a bright, glowing azure—the color always associated with any significant use of the craft. This transformation had created a host of new problems, all of which now seemed too vast and complex to overcome.

First of all, the wizards refused to train him in the arts of magic as long as his blood was blue. They also prohibited him from wearing the Paragon. Only the wearing of the Paragon would enable him to read the Tome, the great treatise of the craft. The prophecies written in the Tome stated that he *must* decipher the entire treatise in order to fulfill his destiny. Then, as the proclaimed *Jin'Sai,* or "Combiner of the Arts," he was to join the two sides of the craft for the good of the world. Should he fail or die in his attempt, it was written that his twin sister Shailiha, otherwise known as the *Jin'Saiou,* would take up the task. If he could, he would spare her that burden.

But the concern that bothered him most—the one that was never far from his heart and mind—was his love for Celeste.

She was the love of his life—a sentiment she returned with an equal if not greater ardor. They had been overjoyed when her father, Wigg, had given the prince his blessing to pursue his daughter's heart.

But soon after the physical consummation of their love, the wizards had come to them bearing devastating news. Information only then gleaned from the newly acquired Scroll of the Vigors dictated that the two of them must never be intimate again—at least until the riddle of Tristan's azure blood could be unraveled and his blood returned to red. If Celeste—or any other woman, for that matter—were to become pregnant with Tristan's seed, the resulting child would be deformed beyond description, and would also constitute a grave threat to the well-being of the craft of magic.

They had only been together once, but Tristan feared that Celeste might already be pregnant with his child. He had seen the familiar glow of the craft build around her and then vanish just after their wondrous interlude that morning beneath the great oak tree.

Since that fateful day, Tristan and Celeste's love had grown, but now they courted each other chastely, much the same way the Orb of the Vigors and the Orb of the Vagaries constantly whirled about each other but could never touch. As it was with Tristan and Celeste, so it was with the orbs: union would be devastating. While he considered the painful irony, Tristan looked sadly down at his hands.

"And because of these facets of the craft, partial adepts can also sometimes be herbmistresses or herbmasters." Wigg's voice broke in upon Tristan's thoughts. The prince looked back up at the First Wizard of the Conclave.

"Among their other varied skills, partial adepts may also practice the fine art of blaze-gazing, but this expertise is rare," Wigg went on, his words continuing to materialize on the black panel behind him. Soon he would wave his hand once more, and the writing would disappear. "Given these proclivities for such talents," he continued, "it should also become abundantly clear that—"

The classroom's double doors blew open with a deafening crash, and Faegan soared through as though his life depended on it.

It was rare to see the ancient levitate his wheeled chair, much less use it to go flying about. Something lay across his lap—something dark and charred-looking. As Faegan lowered his chair to the ground, the prince felt his stomach turn over. Lying across the old man's useless legs was the horribly burned body of a child.

"Wigg!" Faegan shouted, as he levitated the badly injured child onto a clear section of tabletop. "Come here! I need you!"

Wigg dashed from the dais. In a flash Tristan was by their sides as the two wizards called on the craft in a desperate attempt to heal the child.

The young boy looked dead, yet his chest stubbornly rose and fell in staggered, wheezing lurches. The entire top half of his torso was charred; most of his hair had been burned away. Much of his face was unrecognizable. The sickening stench of burnt flesh began to fill the room.

Sobbing openly, Faegan looked up at the prince and struggled to get the words out.

"So many . . ." he said, his body shaking. "There are so many more . . ."

Reaching up, the old wizard took hold of Tristan's hand. His grip was cold and clammy, as if some of the life had gone out of him.

"The courtyard . . ." he whispered. His hand tightened urgently around Tristan's. "You must get to the palace courtyard . . ."

His mind awash with worry for Shailiha and Celeste, Tristan ran to gather up his weapons and tore from the room.

CHAPTER II

STANDING NEAR THE BABBLING BROOK, REZNIK HEARD THE FAMILiar cry of his hungry cat. Turning, he walked over to where the beast crouched menacingly. Long ago Reznik had dug a deep circle in the ground, marking the cat's farthest range of travel. When his feet came to the edge of the ditch, Reznik stopped. Human bones, both old and new, littered the area within the circle.

A wide iron collar encircled the cat's spotted neck. A chain secured the collar to the trunk of a hinteroot tree. Reznik would never violate the confines of the cat's reach, but if she did attack him, he was confident that he could heal himself, provided the wound was not too serious. For Reznik was not only a partial adept and an accomplished herbmaster, but also an expert cutter-healer and potion-master.

Looking at the cat, he smiled. She had been with him for more than a dozen years now. She had been continually chained to the same tree ever since she was a kitten. The generous length of chain allowed her to drink from the nearby brook whenever she chose and the weather never seemed to bother her.

The cat was large—at least four or five times the size of an average house cat—with spotted tan fur and elongated, yellowish eyes with dark irises. The whiskers and eyelashes were dark and exceptionally long, as were the claws.

Reznik's thoughts soon turned from his pet to Satine. She was due to visit soon. By now she would surely need more of that which only he could offer, and he needed to have it ready. She was his highest-paying customer. He would sorely miss those gold kisa of hers should he ever lose her business.

Shaking her head and rattling the iron chain, the impatient cat snarled at him again. She was telling her master that she could smell the blood. Reznik smiled.

"Very soon now, my pretty," he cooed to her.

Turning, he walked back over to the butcher's table that sat beneath the shade of another tree. He wiped his meaty palms down the front of his bloodstained apron, then took up his favorite boning knife. In his other hand he grasped a long, cone-shaped whetstone. He carefully stroked one against the other. When he was satisfied, he bent over and set about his work. Slowly, meticulously, Reznik began boning a human corpse.

He would not need much of what lay before him. But what he did require had to be taken soon and with the greatest of care, lest it lose its potency. Placing the boning knife against the corpse's right quadriceps, he was reminded that corpses never bled when they were cut into, at least not the way a live person did.

As he removed part of the quadriceps and placed it on the table, his crooked smile came again.

And they don't complain, either, he thought.

Soon the exposed thighbone glistened wetly before him. At first glance the bone appeared to have never been broken. That was good.

Placing his knife down, he picked up a short butcher's axe. With two sure, quick strokes he severed the femur from the hip socket and then from the knee joint. He lifted the long bone from the table and placed it to one side.

Putting down the butcher's axe, he put on a pair of magnifying spectacles. Then he took up the bone again and examined it closely.

As he had expected, it was strong, and it had never seen any significant trauma. Over the course of his grisly career, he had cheated some of his other customers by using inferior ingredients. To this day, he had always gotten away with it.

He knew better than to try this with Satine. There was no more accomplished killer in all of Eutracia. Should any one of his potions not prove as promised, she wouldn't hesitate to come back and kill him. Even he would never know she was there. It would be a simple matter of being alive one moment, and dead the next. That wasn't a chance he was willing to take.

Hearing his cat growl with hunger, he grasped the bloody muscle he had just liberated from the corpse and tossed it into the dusty circle.

The cat pounced. Turning back to the table, Reznik resumed his labors.

With the small saw, he cut the thighbone in two, exposing its marrow: soft, pulpy, and yellow—exactly what he needed. As every cutter-healer knew, it was the red bone marrow of a child that was initially responsible for the manufacture of the body's blood. The marrow inevitably turned yellow with maturity. Above all, it was blood that determined so much of one's destiny here in Eutracia—and in Reznik's capable hands, sometimes the nature of one's death, as well.

He carefully removed the marrow from each of the two sections of bone and placed it in a small pan. Then he opened up the skull. When the grayish white frontal lobes presented themselves, he began to whistle happily. Nothing soothed his nerves so much as the preparation of another of his potions—especially when it was for Satine. He employed only very fresh corpses in his work for her, and only those that had perished by suicide.

Eutracian custom dictated that suicide victims should be laid to rest in separate sections of the nation's cemeteries. Though abandoned in many places, this custom of segregation was still practiced in others. When the craft had been in its infancy, many had believed that the soul of a suicide victim might not be released to the Afterlife. Few had wished to risk the chance of being placed to rest beside those who had killed themselves. Separate arrangements had therefore been made.

Ridiculous, he thought, as he continued to work. Still, he was thankful for this superstition, which proved infinitely helpful to him in his arts.

His hands had grown excessively bloody, so he walked to the brook. As he knelt down before a calm spot at the water's edge, his reflection peered back at him. He saw the face that had wrinkled and creased beyond its fifty Seasons of New Life. He also saw his shiny, bald head, the encircling fringe of gray hair drooping haphazardly to his shoulders. The soft brown eyes stared back at him with intelligence, and he could see the yellow teeth that lay just behind the full, expressive mouth. He smiled, liking what he saw.

After washing the blood from his hands, he walked over to a steaming cauldron to add the marrow and brain. He took up a long wooden staff, dipped it into the cauldron, and slowly mixed the ingredients. Then he leaned over the top and inhaled, using his well-trained sense of smell to analyze the concoction's progress.

Something wasn't quite right. Leaving the mixing staff in the cauldron, he walked back over to the table and picked up a leather-bound journal.

He thumbed through its pages, searching for the formula he needed. *Ah, there it is,* he thought. He ran his fingers down his own handwritten notes. When at last he found what was lacking, he walked over to the side of the glade that sheltered one of his many herb gardens. Fully mature gingercrinkle had a violet blossom and a clean, crisp scent, but it wasn't the blossoms he was interested in just now. He selected what he deemed to be the best example and pulled the plant from the ground.

After carefully cutting the root away, he carried it over to the stream and washed it. Then he used his mortar and pestle to grind it up. He measured out just the right amount and put it into the cauldron. Then he banked the coals, removed the mixing staff, and placed a circular lid over the cauldron's top so that his creation might simmer overnight.

There was only one more thing to do before he left the glade. He lifted the corpse from the table, carried it to the edge of the cat's circle, and unceremoniously tossed it in.

She showed little interest in it, having just eaten the muscle he had given her. Still, the body he had just tossed to her was large, and he knew that he would not have to worry about feeding her for several more days.

Reznik gathered up his instruments and his journal and began to make his way out of the glade. After taking only a couple of steps he had a sudden thought. He stopped short and turned around.

Returning to the table, he picked up the gingercrinkle blossom and placed it in one of the buttonholes of his jerkin. *Pretty*, he thought.

As he walked out of the glade, he began to whistle.

CHAPTER III

FAEGAN'S WORDS ECHOED IN TRISTAN'S EARS AS HE RAN DOWN THE hallways of the Redoubt. He skidded to a stop before the first of the several secret passageways leading to the palace above. Scrabbling at the special section of marble wall, he pulled hard, rotating it on its pivot. It opened to reveal a rough-hewn stone staircase. His weapons still in his hands, he charged up two steps at a time.

His chest was heaving when he reached the top of the steps and strapped on the baldric holding his dreggan and the quiver holding his throwing knives. Then he drew the sword, its unmistakable ring echoing in the confines of the stairway.

He held the point of the dreggan high and placed the cool, flat side of its blade against his forehead. Closing his eyes, he tried to calm his mind in anticipation of whatever might await him on the other side of the door.

When he was ready, Tristan pushed hard on the section of wall. It swiveled open easily, and he charged through the open doorway. The room on the other side was empty.

He had come up into the Chamber of Supplication, one of the many elaborate halls his late father and the Directorate of Wizards had employed in their dealings with the citizenry. The elaborate room yawned back at the prince, as if mocking him for his foolishness. Then he heard an unfamiliar noise.

At first he couldn't make it out as it wafted eerily through stained-glass windows. Tristan ran to one of the windows, pushed it open wide, and climbed through to the courtyard beyond.

Complete pandemonium reigned. The courtyard overflowed with a crushing mass of burned and wounded citizens, their cries soaring toward the heavens. Men, women, and children had already forced their way onto the palace grounds, and still more were massed in the streets beyond the drawbridge. Some of Tristan's Minion warriors were attempting to hold back the throng, but as gently as they could so as not to further harm the wounded. But the palace warriors were too few, and the crowd too large and too determined to reach sanctuary.

Tristan watched helplessly as his people died before his very eyes. Then two dark shadows crossed the grass, and the Minions Traax and Ox landed next to him.

Frantically, Tristan grabbed Traax by the shoulders. "Shailiha, Celeste, and Abbey!" he shouted, trying to make himself heard above the crowd. "Where are they? Are they safe?"

Nodding, Traax pointed to a far corner of the courtyard.

Tristan could just make out the three of them. Protected by a wide ring of Minion warriors, they were tearing bedsheets into strips and bandaging the victims as best they could.

"The warriors have strict orders to fly them to safety, should it come to that," Traax shouted to Tristan. "I tried to convince them of the danger, but none of them would leave."

Tristan looked over at Ox. He had rarely seen so much emotion upon a Minion warrior's face.

"It happen so fast!" the huge warrior said. "Wizard Faegan see first boy come through. He be burned bad. Faegan see him as he crawl across yard, and he lift chair and take him into palace. But he not see others come. Me now think neither wizard know how bad this be."

"Yes, we do," Tristan heard the familiar voice say.

Turning, the prince found Wigg standing beside him and Faegan sitting close by. Both wizards had tears in their eyes.

"The boy you tended to in the Redoubt?" Tristan asked.

All Wigg could do was shake his head.

Faegan raised his hands toward the burgeoning crowd. Tristan wondered what the crippled wizard was about to do.

Azure bolts shot from Faegan's hands toward the drawbridge, where they spread to create a glowing wall that sealed the castle entrance. When he lowered his hands, the bolts ceased. The crowd inside the palace grounds quieted. Many looked up in wonder, having beheld the majesty of the craft for the first time. Tristan turned back to Wigg.

"What has happened?" he asked.

His face dark with concern, Wigg looked at Tristan directly. "Faegan and I fear it is our greatest nightmare," he said softly. "If we're right, no power on earth may be able to stop it."

The wizard laid one hand gently upon Tristan's shoulder. "You and I must leave here immediately," he said.

Stunned, Tristan searched Wigg's face. "Are you mad?" he shot back. "Look at these people—can't you see they need our help? How can we possibly leave them?"

Faegan wheeled his chair a bit closer. His expression was as determined as Wigg's.

"Wigg is right," he said. "You and the First Wizard must depart now. There is no time to lose."

"But *why*?" Tristan asked.

"We have to know what we're dealing with," Wigg answered. "We must ascertain how much damage it has already done and where it is headed next. Faegan will stay behind to direct the aid efforts with the acolytes and Minion healers. But right now, you *must* call for a Minion litter, and a group of warriors to fly guard alongside!" The wizard's aquamarine eyes flashed.

"While we waste time arguing, I fear thousands more may be dying!" he added sternly. "Your nation needs you now as never before, and you must help her!"

Tristan looked across the courtyard toward Shailiha, Abbey, and Celeste. Blessedly, their situation seemed less dangerous now. The warriors were allowing more victims inside the circle, but only as the three women could accommodate them. Tristan reluctantly turned to Traax and nodded.

The Minion second in command was gone in a flash. In mere moments he returned with a litter borne by six warriors, as well as an additional fifty warriors to fly guard. Wigg quickly climbed aboard, anxiously gesturing to Tristan to join him.

With one last look at the horrible scene, Tristan stepped in and took the seat next to the First Wizard. He closed his eyes.

Traax barked out the order, and the litter rose into the sky.

CHAPTER IV

WIGG KNEW HOW TO FIND WHATEVER WAS ATTACKING THEIR PEOPLE. All they would have to do was follow the trail of dead bodies.

As they soared over the courtyard, Wigg shouted as much to Traax, who immediately passed the wizard's orders on to the litter bearers and guards.

Below them, the streets of Tammerland overflowed with the wounded, the dying, and the dead. Some looked up at the flying warriors and shook their fists at them. Tristan had little doubt that if they had been flying lower, he would have been able to hear their curses, as well.

Apparently many of his subjects still considered the Minions their enemy. Tristan could hardly blame them. All they knew of the winged warriors was that they had destroyed much of Tammerland, butchering, torturing, and raping the citizens in the streets and in their homes. They didn't know that the Minions were under Tristan's firm control now, no longer a threat to Tammerland and, indeed, pledged to defend all of Tristan's people.

Most of the citizenry also had no idea that the Directorate of Wizards was no more. They deserved to know that, and also to know that Tristan loved them and wanted to be—needed to be—a strong leader for them.

How can I possibly accomplish all this? he wondered. How

does one inform an entire country of so many bizarre twists and turns behind the devastation that has beset it in its recent history? Even he scarcely believed all that had happened, and he had seen it firsthand.

Disheartened, he looked down at the medallion around his neck. Taking it in one hand, he slowly closed his fist around it. The gold medallion had been given to him by his parents, just before they had died at the hands of the Coven of Sorceresses. The medal showed the lion and broadsword, the twin symbols of the House of Galland. Shailiha wore an identical one.

"It's not your fault," Wigg said quietly. Taking a deep breath, he placed his hands into the opposite sleeves of his robe. "It never has been. You must sense that. All you have ever done is protect both the citizens and the nation you care for so much. But they don't know that, Tristan. And that is because they are still without what they need the most."

Tristan did not look up. "And what is that?" he asked.

"What only you can provide," Wigg answered. "Their rightful king."

Tristan took a deep breath. For several long moments silence filled the space between him and the wizard.

"But to be king, I must wear the Paragon," he said at last. "And to do that, my blood must first revert to its natural state."

"Yes," Wigg answered heavily. "Despite whatever is causing all of this destruction, we must never lose sight of the fact that finding a way to alter your blood is paramount. If we do not figure out how to do that, then everything else we do—no matter how well-meaning—will be for naught. The *Jin'Sai* must eventually be trained, and then read the entire Tome of the Paragon. The future of our world depends upon it."

Tristan thought for a moment. "You still haven't told me what is causing all of this," he replied defensively.

Wigg took a deep breath. "If I am right, when we reach it, one look will tell us all. And if I am wrong, which is also entirely possible, then we will be seeing whatever it is for the first time. For now I would prefer to leave it at that."

As the litter continued west past Tammerland, the dark, slow-moving columns of people seemed to stretch on forever. But then he saw a break in the crowd, and for a moment his heart leapt—until the litter drew closer and he realized what he was seeing.

Directly below their flight path, a deep crevasse split the ground. It looked to be at least ten to fifteen meters deep and about one hundred meters across, a V-shaped, jagged scar that snaked its way west as far as the eye could see. Tristan guessed it was recently made: It still smoldered, gray plumes of soot and ash corkscrewing up into the air from its charred black bottom. It was a gruesome, unnatural thing, and it sent a chill down the prince's spine.

Aghast, Tristan looked at Wigg. The wizard's face was dark with worry.

Wigg stuck his head out of the litter and shouted to Traax that he wanted the warriors to change course and follow the smoldering crack wherever it might lead. Then he looked sadly down at his hands and said no more.

A great sense of foreboding rose in Tristan's chest. His gaze followed the strange, snaking catastrophe as the litter flew on toward the setting sun.

"THE OXEN ARE THIRSTY, FATHER," AARON SAID. "CAN'T WE ALL rest for a bit?"

The young man gave each of the two straining beasts a reassuring stroke on the head. The sun was going down. The day had been unusually hot, even for the Season of the Sun. They had been toiling since dawn, yet Aaron's father showed no sign of stopping. Finally Darius pulled hard on the reins that lay over his shoulders and slowed the oxen and plow to a halt.

Glad to rest, Aaron of the House of Rivenrider jumped down. Looking back, he saw the hard-won rows of rich soil that they had scratched into the earth. Before long those rows would be filled with the waving stalks of wheat and barley that he and his family would sell at the farmers' market in Tammerland.

It was late in the season to be planting. This year money had been short, and only now had they gathered enough kisa to buy the last of their seed. Still, with a little bit of luck and a great deal of hard work, they might reap enough to see them through the coming winter—especially if this year's Season of Harvest proved to be a long one.

The ox nearest Aaron rubbed his face against the young man's shoulder, nearly knocking him over. Smiling, Aaron reached out and petted one of the great animal's ears. Darius dropped the leather reins and stretched his cramped muscles. Walking up to his son, he produced a rag from his trousers for what seemed the hundredth time that day and wiped the dripping sweat from his face.

Aaron's mother, Mary, and his sister Tatiana were still bent over in the field, sowing the seeds in the freshly overturned dirt. They wore broad, straw sunbonnets on their heads, and each carried a heavy bag of seed slung over one shoulder. Sowing the seed was backbreaking work, and by now their hands and nails would be black with soil.

Leaving the oxen with his father, Aaron walked over to the edge of the field, where he could see Brook Hollow, their small village, lying in the valley below. From up here it looked like a giant patchwork quilt spread out on the ground—a quilt with the Sippora River running through it. He could see their modest farmhouse at the eastern edge of town, and their small, river-powered gristmill with which his father ground their wheat. His mother's heavy bread was the best in the world. He imagined that he could smell a warm loaf cooling on the kitchen windowsill right now.

When Aaron returned to his father, his mother and Tatiana had arrived, and his father was busy unfastening the large oilskin bags of water that the oxen always carried over their backs when laboring in the fields. With the bags came two large buckets.

Dutifully, Aaron uncorked one of the bags, filled the two buckets with water, and placed them before the oxen. The massive animals drank greedily, and Aaron smiled as he watched them.

"Sometimes I think you take better care of those animals than you do yourself," Tatiana chided him. There was a definite hint of mischief in her eyes as she peered out from beneath her sunbonnet. She was tall, pretty, and possessed endless amounts of curly red hair. Her hands and shoes were far beyond filthy. Two years her senior, Aaron loved to tease her about being his little sister. But Tatiana was quickly growing into womanhood, and he knew that he wouldn't be able to get away with that sort of thing much longer.

He gave her a mock-condescending look and pointed at her hands.

"And just how many boys will want to come and call on you with paws like that, Miss Filthy?" he shot back. "You look like you live in a pig pen! If the boys at school could see you now, you'd end up an old maid forever!" He watched Tatiana's mouth pucker up.

"That's enough, you two," their mother began. Then she stopped. At the expression on her face, they all turned back toward the field—and that was when they saw the huge shadow.

Dark and ominous, the shadow grew until it covered all of the ground around them. Then came an earsplitting noise—a great screech combined with an intensely deep howl that chilled them. Aaron put his hands over his ears, but it did little to help to muffle the noise. Looking up, he saw the source of the shadow: an enormous ball of golden light. His jaw dropped in wonder. Then, to his horror, it veered in midair and headed straight at his family.

Aaron's first instinct was to save the oxen, and he turned to unbuckle their harnesses so they could run without the awkward mass of the plow behind them. The golden orb was so close that Aaron could feel its blazing heat at his back.

As he unfastened the first of the buckles, Darius' strong hands came down on his own. Bewildered and frightened, he looked up into his father's eyes.

"Stop!" Darius screamed. "It's too late for them now! Run!"

Grabbing Aaron by the collar, Darius pulled him away from the oxen. They ran across the field as fast as they could. Aaron ran and ran until he thought his lungs might burst. Only when Darius thought his family was out of danger did they slow. They all turned to look.

The two terrified oxen desperately tried to run from the noise and the searing heat, but they were hindered by the plow, which had buried itself in the ground behind them as they ran. Aaron felt his heart shatter and steeled himself for the worst.

When the burning sphere closed on them, the two terrified animals vaporized instantly. As the fireball continued on its

way, burning a deep swath of destruction down the field, all
that remained of the oxen was a charred hole in the ground.
Gray smoke rose into the late afternoon sky almost as an after-
thought.

Running back to the crest of the hill, Aaron watched the
sphere go. It was heading directly for Brook Hollow.

The rest of his stunned family came to stand beside him.
They cried and held on to one another as they watched their
world collapse.

Focused on the unfolding catastrophe, none of them saw the
approaching litter with its phalanx of Minion warriors that flew
guard alongside.

CHAPTER V

"HOLD HIM!" SHE ORDERED THE TWO MINION WARRIORS STAND-
ing obediently by her side. Her voice could barely be heard
amid the clamor all around her. "This must be done now, lest
he die!"

Duvessa looked hard at the warriors and they grudgingly nodded back. She was well aware that they both outranked her, but
as the leader of the Minion healers, she meant to have her way.

With both Traax and the *Jin'Sai* away, she had decided that
the only two persons she would take orders from would be Faegan and Shailiha. Duvessa now knew them personally, and
counted both as friends. If Traax wanted to punish her for her
insolence to her Minion superiors when he returned, then so be
it. But she doubted that would happen, because for the last several weeks she had been Traax's lover.

The man lying on the table writhed and screamed and struggled against the leather straps that held him down. Duvessa
wished that either Faegan or one of the Acolytes of the Redoubt
was available to employ the craft. That way, the man could be

rendered unconscious before she began her work. But they were all busy elsewhere, dealing with other victims.

Had the casualty lying before her been Minion, there would be no need for the straps, and the surgery would be over by now. Minion warriors were far stronger and more stoic than most humans. Their harsh martial philosophy dictated that the use of luxuries such as sleep-herbs or painkillers was a mark of personal weakness. But the victim suffering before her was human, and Duvessa knew that according to human culture what she was about to do was savage, albeit absolutely necessary.

She looked grimly to a third warrior standing nearby. With an understanding nod, he grasped one of the torches from a nearby stand and held it toward her. Duvessa took up one of her serrated bone saws and placed its edge into the flame.

The fellow's right hand was gone at the wrist and bled still, despite the leather strap she had so tightly twisted around his upper arm. The ragged, throbbing wound had to be cleanly severed a bit higher, and that meant sawing through the bones. Then the wound's naked end would have to be cauterized. She wished she could spare the time to ply her craft upon the injuries to his face, but there were many others in even worse straits and they would have to come first.

As her saw began to glow, the man continued to bleed. Several more irretrievable seconds passed.

Seeing the hot blade above him, the terrified man screamed again. At a nod from Duvessa, the warriors tightened their grip on the patient and she began her work.

LATER, AS SHE WALKED THROUGH THE PALACE, THE SAD SCENE before her seemed like something out of a living nightmare. Night had fallen, and makeshift healing tables had sprung up in nearly every room. Some held living victims who lay waiting to be tended. Others were still occupied by the dead who had yet to be carried away. Blood was everywhere. She thought about the man she had just worked on, the one with the severed hand. He would live, but like the other poor souls who had come seeking succor, he would never be the same.

As she walked, the nauseating stench of death permeated the palace halls. In every room, torches burned brightly, pointing up macabre shadows that mimicked the necessary horrors still going on.

She lowered her head and walked on, trying to avoid stepping in blood as she searched for Shailiha and Faegan.

Born in one of the Coven's birthing houses in Parthalon, Duvessa had been raised in one of the many Minion compounds that still dotted the nation across the sea. When she grew older, she was ordered to choose a traditional Minion occupation. Many of the boys chose to become warriors. To this day, that path was forbidden to the girls, despite Tristan's new orders insisting on equality for Minion females.

Showing a natural talent for healing, she entered the healer cadres, took her training, and rose quickly through the ranks. Recently she had been promoted to the rank of premier healer. Not only was she now in charge of all the Minion healers—both male and female—but she was the first female to have ever held so lofty a station. Many males in the warrior ranks still outranked her, but given her great talent, coupled with her frequent inclination to speak her mind, they genuinely respected her.

Thousands of Minion healers served under her now, and it was quite impossible for her to know them all. Most she recognized only by the sign of their craft—a pure white feather emblazoned upon the chest of their black leather body armor. But they all knew her.

As the new premier healer, she had accompanied her fellow troops to Eutracia from Parthalon, when Tristan led the Minion forces into battle against Nicholas' hatchlings. Brin fought in that battle. Duvessa had first noticed him when his wounded wing had caught her attention. Already a fighter of some note, he was several years her junior, but he looked older. After seeing each other for a time, they married in accordance with the new freedoms granted by the prince. But their happiness was not to last.

Brin had been killed while helping his troops fight off Wulfgar's demonslaver fleet. His body had been lost at sea and was never returned to Duvessa for the traditional immolation. There had been no offspring.

Her grief at the loss of her husband was immense—at first far more than she thought she could bear. But as premier healer she had an important job to do, and there was no time for self-pity.

There had been many wounded to tend to as a result of Tristan's struggles with his half brother, and she had thrown herself into her work with abandon. By the nature of her position in the Minion hierarchy, she soon came to know Tristan, Shailiha, Celeste, Wigg, and Faegan. She had also met Adrian and Abbey, and she thought very highly of them. It was when she had joined this inner circle that she had first come to Traax's attention.

She was taken with him immediately, and he was equally interested. After the traditionally brief Minion mourning period, they began to see each other, and then finally took to sharing a bed. She knew that Traax had departed with Wigg and Tristan, and she worried about him. Although it was not uncommon for a Minion female to lose several mates during the course of her lifetime, she had no desire to experience this herself.

As she walked through the shadowy palace, she saw many red-robed Acolytes of the Redoubt. As she passed, they exchanged courteous bows with her.

During the course of the night she had seen many of the acolytes deftly employ the craft to help relieve the suffering. She still knew little about them, but she had to admit that their abilities were impressive. Sometimes she had witnessed her healers and the endowed acolytes standing shoulder to shoulder at the tables, working together. Seeing this had made her proud. Together they had finally been able to stem the massive tide of suffering. But none of them knew what terrible, unseen enemy had caused all of this, or what the future might bring.

Turning a corner and starting down another hall, she heard Faegan's voice. A door stood slightly ajar, and a soft shaft of light poured from its opening. She walked over and knocked softly. The wizard bid her enter; she swung the door wider and walked in.

Faegan was addressing a roomful of people. His black robe was stained with blood, and he looked beyond exhaustion. The Paragon hung from a gold chain around his neck. As always, he sat in his wooden chair on wheels. Nicodemus, a dark blue cat with a silver collar, lay patiently in his master's lap. On a nearby table sat the ancient violin that Faegan often played.

A fire danced merrily in the hearth, its inviting warmth belying the horrors of the grisly world that lay just outside the door. A small table at the back of the room was laden with wine, bread, and cheese—no doubt supplied by the ever-industrious gnomes, Duvessa thought.

Princess Shailiha, Celeste, and Abbey sat on a sofa along one wall. Still clad in their bloodstained dresses, they all looked exhausted. Duvessa could see that though they had tried to wash the blood from their hands, it still showed beneath their nails and in the folds of their skin. Caprice—Shailiha's giant butterfly—sat perched upon a bookcase, slowly opening and closing her yellow and violet wings. Adrian, Ox, and Geldon sat at a table nearby.

As Duvessa entered and crossed the room to pour herself a welcome goblet of wine, Faegan stopped speaking and looked at her, obviously eager to hear her report.

A dense stillness crept over the chamber as the Minion premier healer went to a chair and sat down heavily, goblet in hand. It was only after taking the weight off her feet that she fully realized just how exhausted she was. She took a long draft of the rich red wine, then removed her bloody smock and dropped it to the floor.

"How goes it outside?" Faegan asked.

"It has slowed," Duvessa answered. "Most of the major cutting has been done, and the acolytes are enacting spells of accelerated healing and pain relief over as many of the victims as they can. The Minion healers are doing all they can to help. Just the same, the loss of life has been great."

Leaning forward on her elbows, she looked straight at the wizard. She wanted answers—just as everyone else here did.

Taking a deep breath, Faegan returned her gaze. She was one

of the most handsome Minion women he had ever seen. Like Traax, she had green eyes. Her thick, dark hair was tied into a pair of braids that fell down behind her. The single, stark white feather stood out proudly on the chest of her black body armor. Her strong, sensual face stared back at him with candor, and for the hundredth time he wondered whether there was anything in the world that truly frightened her. A fitting mate for Traax, he thought.

Duvessa turned to Adrian. "Thank you for all that you and your sisters did," she said with genuine admiration. "Before we came to Eutracia, all we Minions ever saw of the craft was what the Coven allowed us to see. I used to distrust all magic, as most of my people do. Tonight I saw it used for good, and it was a welcome change."

"Thank you," Adrian said. "We did all that we could."

The acolyte had gentle brown eyes and curly, sand-colored hair. Her dark red robe, tied around the middle with a black tasseled cord, looked worn and stained. Several times that evening she and Duvessa had stood side by side, using all their gifts to try to save the same victim. Sometimes they had succeeded; sometimes they had not. Whatever had been the individual outcome, a mutual sense of respect had grown up between the two healers. Though Adrian's healing gifts were enhanced by her facility with the craft, she and her sisters still wrestled with their new lives in Tammerland, the palace, and the Redoubt. This uncertainty put her on an even footing with Duvessa.

Across the room, Shailiha looked over at Celeste, who nodded back at her. Both Wigg's daughter and the princess were eager to know where Tristan and Wigg had gone.

Her gaze hardening with determination, Shailiha folded her arms and stared at Faegan. "We all want some answers, and we want them now," she demanded. "In the space of a single night, not only have hundreds of severely burned and maimed victims come crashing through the palace gates, but both Tristan and Wigg have disappeared along with Traax and an entire phalanx of warriors!

"Where did you send them? What is it that has so suddenly attacked us?" She sat back, a look of determined expectation on her face.

Faegan knew that there would be no use in putting off the inevitable. Taking a breath, he looked down at his hands. Shailiha wasn't sure she had ever seen the old wizard so upset.

"First things first," Faegan said. He turned to face Ox.

The giant Minion shot to his feet. "I live to serve," he said quickly.

"If I know the prince at all, the first thing he will do when he arrives home will be to call an emergency meeting of the Conclave of the Vigors," the wizard said. "To have all ten members present, we must call Tyranny home. I want you to take a squadron of warriors and fly directly to the Minion outpost nearest the coast. Find out Tyranny's last position and heading, and then go after her. Tell her what has happened, and bring her here at once. Leave Scars in charge of the fleet, pending further orders. Do you understand?"

"Ox understand," the warrior said. "Everything be as wizard Faegan say."

"Good," Faegan answered. "Go now, and may the Afterlife watch over you."

After a quick click of his heels, Ox left.

"A good man . . ." Faegan said, his voice fading away as he became lost in his thoughts.

"Faegan!" Celeste called. "We're waiting!"

"Uh, er, yes—yes, of course," the wizard said. He turned his chair back to face the room. His grim look returned.

"Very well," he began. "I will start by telling you what I have already expressed to Wigg, just before he and Tristan left." He paused for a moment, as if not really knowing where to begin.

"If what Wigg and I believe is true, then we are facing a calamity of epic proportions," he said. "What we witnessed tonight may be just the beginning . . ."

In measured tones, the wizard began to explain his theories. As he did, the people before him turned to one another, aghast. Several of those with endowed blood wept openly. Those without did the best they could to comfort the others.

The wizard's talk lasted hours.

CHAPTER VI

By the time Tristan, Wigg, and the Minion phalanx saw the cause of the terrible destruction, the village of Brook Hollow was already in flames. Wigg ordered the Minions to take the litter as close as they dared.

The terrible noise shot like daggers through Tristan's ears, a plaintive screeching howl. He watched, dumbstruck, as the thing continued on its path of annihilation across the land. Then he lowered his head, as if by doing so he might somehow make the whole scene disappear.

All the death and chaos originated from the same revered phenomenon that sustained the benevolent side of the craft: the Orb of the Vigors.

Night had fallen, and the golden sphere lit up the land and heavens for leagues in every direction as it soared above the earth. So huge that it seemed to take up the entire sky, it was a wondrous, terrifying sight. Although the prince had seen the orb only a few times in his life, he was sure that it was now spinning faster on its axis than ever before. It was almost as if some form of madness had overtaken it.

Its mate—the dark, ominous Orb of the Vagaries—was nowhere to be seen. Pale white spears radiated from its center and darted off into nothingness. From a jagged tear in its lower half, the orb dripped pure, living energy. Whatever the gold stuff fell upon either vaporized instantly or was severely burned.

White-knuckled, Tristan gripped the sides of the litter. Suddenly, he understood. *Wulfgar,* he thought. This damage was a result of that night on the roof of the palace, when his half brother had tried to pollute the orb.

Tristan was about to shout his suspicions to the wizard, but

Wigg was already calling new orders to the Minions, telling them to take the litter even closer to the deadly orb. The warriors obeyed, and as they neared, the orb illuminated the litter and the straining Minions flying alongside it, turning them into surreal specters in the sky. Tristan could feel the orb's intense heat.

Then the orb's shock waves struck. The litter swung wildly, and the warriors carrying it nearly lost their hold. Twice it listed so badly that Tristan and Wigg almost fell. Finally righting the litter again, the warriors did their best to inch forward in the sky. Tristan watched in awe as they fought against the blasts that whipped at their bodies and wings.

The orb's awful energy threatened to set the litter ablaze. If that happened, Tristan thought, he and the wizard were done for.

Suddenly two of the warriors carrying the litter burst into flames. Screaming wildly, they plummeted to the scorched earth below. Warriors fell all around them now, bodies and wings ablaze as they tumbled. Tristan could only watch, horrified, and hope they died before they hit the ground.

The wizard stood up in the litter. His arms outstretched, he braced himself precariously against the bludgeoning force of the orb. The wind and heat tore wildly at his hair and robes. Tristan knew that were it not for the First Wizard's powers in the craft, he would have been blown from the litter. At first Tristan didn't understand what Wigg was doing, but then he realized that the wizard was trying to save Brook Hollow.

Tristan had seen the wizard call forth the orb several times before. But he had no idea whether the First Wizard could summon enough power to actually change the thing's course.

Just as twin azure bolts shot from Wigg's hands, a massive spray of the orb's golden energy tore into the litter and its bearers. The last thing Tristan saw before tumbling from the burning litter toward the earth was Wigg's robes catching fire.

Then he heard the wizard scream.

CHAPTER VII

PERCHED ON THE WINDOWSILL IN THE CAPTAIN'S QUARTERS OF HER flagship, Teresa of the House of Welborne—known to friend and foe alike as Tyranny—calmly regarded the Sea of Whispers. It was nearly dawn. The winds were steady, and the three Eutracian moons were high, bathing the ever-shifting ocean in their magenta glow.

Tyranny stretched her back against the window frame and ran one hand through her short, dark hair. She had never bothered preparing for bed: She still wore the high-waisted brown-and-tan striped pants and worn leather jacket that she'd put on the previous morning. Her short sword hung from her left hip and her pearl-handled dagger sat in its sheath, tied down to her right thigh. Lost in thought, as she had been most of the night, she fiddled with the single gold hoop that dangled from her earlobe.

Too often, of late, she was eschewing sleep for a night of thinking. She still could not believe her good fortune—a full fleet under her command; and official letters of marque, a pirate's dream; and the fact that she had been made a permanent member of the newly formed Conclave of the Vigors. The latter was an honor she'd never dreamed of, and she wondered how she could both fulfill her duties to the Conclave and continue to ply the waters in search of any possible surviving demonslaver ships of the late Wulfgar's fleet.

Her jaw hardened at the thought of the demonslavers. She had reasons aplenty to hate those monsters, the greatest of those reasons personal: The demonslavers had murdered her parents and captured her beloved brother, Jason. Although she had rescued him and returned him home, he would never be the same. Jason had been an expert swordsmith. After the torture by the demonslavers, his hands were ruined. He would never practice his chosen art again.

Most of her allies who had participated in the destruction of the demonslaver fleet assumed them all to be dead. Tyranny had her doubts. And as long as there was a single demonslaver still alive in these waters, she would search out and kill him.

Shrugging off her thoughts, she rose from the windowsill and crossed the cabin to her ornate desk. She took up a carved wooden box, opened the lid, and removed one of her small, dark cigarillos. Placing it between her lips, she reached for a common match, which she struck against the sole of one of her scuffed knee boots. Cupping her hands around the flame, she lit the rolled tube of dried leaves and inhaled deeply.

As she breathed out a long stream of smoke, she pulled out her desk chair and sat down. Then she reached for the open bottle of red wine atop her desk and took a long swallow straight from the lip. Leaning back in her chair, she gave herself to the seductive rocking of the *Reprise* as it plowed through the waves.

The comforting sound of ship's bells rang out on the night air. She was so used to their sound that they automatically registered in her mind, without the need to be counted.

"Ding . . . ding . . ." came the clear, bright tones. Two hours to dawn, she thought, as the last of them faded away.

She walked back over to the windowsill and sat down again. She took a pull on her cigarillo, and then flicked the ash from its glowing end into the sea before having another sip of wine.

She had begun as a pirate, and ended up . . . legal. And it was all due to Prince Tristan of the House of Galland.

Tristan had seen to it that she received her letters of marque and the one hundred thousand kisa that had been part of their bargain for taking him safely home. She was now most probably the wealthiest woman in all of Eutracia. It had also been Tristan who had given her the twelve stout, ex-pirate vessels she now commanded, not to mention her new seat on the Conclave of the Vigors. She owed him much. And she missed his company, though she would never admit it, except here, in the safe confines of her own cabin before dawn.

Taking another swallow of wine, she closed her eyes. Tristan's heart belonged to Celeste, a woman whom Tyranny had come to count as a friend. And that was that.

An urgent pounding at her door sent her thoughts flying. She knew Scars' insistent knock when something was wrong.

"Come!" she shouted.

The door swung open to reveal her first mate. At seven feet tall, he seemed to take up the entire entry. His head and face were clean shaven, and his only clothing was a pair of ripped, worn trousers. His body and face were covered with scars, the most marked of which was a prominent line that ran diagonally down over his left eye and across his cheek.

"What is it?" Tyranny asked.

Scars smiled. "The Minion K'jarr tells me that his scouting warriors have sighted a lone ship. She tacks her way west-northwest toward Eutracia, about one hour's sail from our current position."

"And . . ." Tyranny prompted.

"She is manned by demonslavers." Scars grinned widely. "She sails alone. They are either amazingly brave or equally stupid. Unless they sighted our Minion patrol—which I seriously doubt—there is no way for them to know that we are in the same waters."

Tyranny beamed. At last, she thought. She took a final pull on her cigarillo, blew the smoke toward the ceiling, then dropped the butt to the floor and crushed it out beneath her boot.

"I will speak to K'jarr immediately," she said. "In the meantime, turn us west-northwest and douse our running lamps. And make sure every ship in the fleet does the same."

Scars turned to go, and she followed him, running, up the gangway to the main deck of the *Reprise*.

AS OX SOARED HIGH OVER THE SEA OF WHISPERS WITH HIS COTERIE of warriors, his eyes scoured the moonlit waters for Tyranny's fleet. He and his troops had searched almost the entire night, and they were close to exhaustion.

Making matters worse, he was frantic over what might have happened to the prince and the First Wizard. He knew he was not among the most intellectually gifted of the Minions. Still, what he lacked in quickness of mind he felt he more than made up for with devotion and loyalty—especially where the *Jin'Sai* was concerned.

The wheels of thought ground slowly in his head. His immediate focus had to be on finding Tyranny.

He had a general idea of where to look—information supplied by one of the prince's newly constructed seaside outposts—but that still left a huge area to search.

Pulling his dark, leathery wings through the sky, Ox became more and more concerned. They needed to find Tyranny's fleet soon, for they had already flown too far from shore—long past the point of no return. It would be dawn in about two hours; he could only hope that the light would help.

Banking slightly to the left, he led his warriors in a curving turn designed to compensate for the reported movement of Tyranny's fleet. This maneuver should work, provided the privateer had not changed her course since the last heading supplied to the outpost. It was all the information Ox had, and it worried him that it might no longer be valid.

If it wasn't, they would soon all suffer a cold, watery death.

As Tyranny and Scars ran to the foredeck of the *Reprise*, a stiff, westerly wind greeted them. The moons provided excellent visibility over the ever-restless sea. But as she scanned the ocean through her spyglass, the eager privateer saw nothing.

Before she knew it, K'jarr, the Minion officer Tristan had assigned to her, was standing by her side. He looked tired and worn, and she understood that he had led the patrol that had sighted the demonslaver vessel.

"Your report," she said briskly. Despite his exhaustion, with a click of his heels K'jarr came to attention.

"She is a demonslaver ship, of that there is no doubt," he answered. "I saw the white-skinned bastards with my own eyes." Then he smiled. Exhausted as they were, he and his warriors were as eager to engage the *Jin'Sai*'s enemies as anyone aboard.

"They're about one hour's sail from our current location— provided the winds hold and they haven't changed their heading since then," he continued. "I doubt they have, since they seemed to have been tacking for the Cavalon Delta. By my estimates, we should be able to see their running lights within the next quarter to half hour."

Tyranny looked back out over the gunwale. Despite how much she wanted to engage the enemy, that a single demon-slaver ship would brave these waters alone gave her pause. Most, if not all, of Wulfgar's fleet had been destroyed. Tristan's bastard brother had been killed that same night, on the roof of the royal palace. So why would a leaderless slaver frigate ply these waters now, trying to return to a nation that would most certainly prove deadly to her? Was this the scout vessel for a new host of warships that they knew nothing about—the vanguard of another invasion force, perhaps? Suddenly, she understood.

This was no invasion. The demonslaver ship traveled alone because she had a singular mission.

Tyranny turned to Scars. "Put on all the extra sail we can muster!" she ordered. "I don't care if we crack every spar in the fleet doing it! We must not let her slip away! We will board this one, but not sink her immediately. My gut tells me that she carries secrets with her." As she looked back out to sea, another thought came to her.

"I want every ship in our fleet rigged for stealth," she added. "There must be no warning bells from the crow's nest. Send word to the fleet by whatever Minion warriors are still able to fly, rather than by signal lantern. I want quiet and darkness."

With a quick nod, her first mate went to carry out his captain's orders.

Then she heard the unmistakable flurry of Minion wings. She looked up just in time to see a number of dark, winged silhouettes crossing the luminous discs of Eutracia's three moons. She was surprised, because after K'jarr's group had landed she had sent out no new patrols. Suddenly, a mass of unfamiliar Minion warriors came half crashing, half landing onto the decks of the *Reprise*.

She finally recognized Ox. He looked completely played out, as did all of the Minions with him. Some of them were so spent that all they could do was sit or lie upon the shifting decks and try to reclaim their breath.

Tyranny and K'jarr ran to Ox. It was all the faithful warrior could do to look up at them. His expression was grave.

K'jarr helped Ox to his feet. The huge warrior could barely stand. He persevered as he wavered back and forth before her, his wings drooping behind him.

"Tyranny must come back palace," Ox said as best his starving lungs would allow. "Bad thing happen since you gone. . . . Wizard Faegan call emergency meeting of Conclave. Must go now!"

Tyranny felt a shudder go through her, but it hadn't been caused by what the warrior had just told her. It was what he hadn't said.

Reaching up, she took Ox by his massive shoulders and looked directly into his eyes. "Of course I'll come," she answered. "But why would *Faegan* call such a meeting? Why didn't the *Jin'Sai* order it himself?"

Ox looked resigned. "*Jin'Sai* and First Wizard leave palace with Traax, to chase down bad thing that kill so many people. Palace full of dead and dying." He paused to catch his breath; the wait was maddening. "Tristan and Wigg not come back. No one know if they still alive."

Tyranny stared at the Minion. "What are you talking about?" she asked.

Ox explained the situation as best he could. Tyranny blanched. K'jarr looked equally stunned.

Turning away, Tyranny walked the short distance to the starboard gunwale and rested her forearms on it, contemplating the decision she had to make. All around her, lights were being extinguished, as per her orders. Should she stay and take the prize that she was convinced might reveal so much? Or should she leave immediately for the palace as Faegan had ordered?

Scars came running. His eyes were eager, predatory.

"The crow's nest has sighted her!" he said. "She's north-northwest of us, about a half hour away. You should just be able to see her running lamps through your glass." Smiling, he handed her the telescope.

Raising the spyglass to her eye, Tyranny scoured the sea. At first she could find nothing. Then she caught a pinprick of light. She carefully twisted the cylinders of the glass. What she saw did not disappoint her.

The light from the enemy vessel's running lamps burned brightly enough to tell the privateer that she was looking at a frigate, the same vessel type used by the demonslavers. She appeared to be at full sail. Even though the ship was still too far away to tell whether demonslavers were aboard, as far as Tyranny was concerned, K'jarr's word was enough. Her jaw set, she lowered the glass and looked back at Scars.

"I want the fleet to fan out in a straight line, with the *Reprise* in the center," she ordered. "Leave just enough space between vessels for some maneuvering room, should I decide to change my attack plans. When we approach, at my order we will surround her. No other action is to be taken until I give the word for her to be boarded. As the flagship, we shall have the honor of drawing first blood. But not until we have found and secured her captain, and squeezed some answers from him. I want to know why he sails toward Eutracia without escort."

She paused as she considered her next words. "Then we will kill them all," she added.

While Scars hurried off to relay her orders, Tyranny looked back over the sea. The running lamps of the other ship slowly became visible without the aid of the spyglass. The wind rustled through her wayward hair, and a grim, determined smile came to the privateer's lips. Her eyes still trained upon her quarry, Tyranny reached down and drew her short sword from its scabbard.

SATINE WATCHED BRATACH GAZE OUT OVER THE SEA. HE HAD been doing this nonstop for the last two days, and she knew that the only reason he hadn't collapsed from exhaustion was his mastery of the craft. While he searched, the consul's hawklike face moved slowly from side to side within the hood of his dark blue robe. The westerlies were brisk, the crimson-colored sea restless as their ship made her way toward the Cavalon Delta.

So far, the voyage had been without incident. Yet as Satine approached the consul, she knew something was afoot. She had been awakened by one of the demonslavers and told that Bratach wished to see her topside right away. Pulling her gray cloak around her, she shook off her sleepiness and closed out the cold wind.

"What is it?" she asked.

At first Bratach remained silent. Then he turned toward her. He did not seem alarmed.

"We have company," he said. "I have been expecting as much for the last several days. There are a dozen frigates of the monarchy out there, coming toward us. They fly the lion and the broadsword, the battle flag of the House of Galland. They have formed an attack line, and they will soon be upon us. They sail with their running lamps extinguished." He turned his dark eyes back to the sea.

"You cannot see them yet, but I can," he added. "They mean to take us."

Satine stiffened. Twelve to one were not odds she was willing to bargain with.

"We have to run," she insisted. "We can never defeat so many, even with you aboard."

"I have no intention of trying to defeat them," Bratach responded. "Nor will we run from them. I intend to lure them in, and then go straight through their line. Besides, this is too valuable an opportunity to let pass. Much could be learned from such an experience."

Satine's eyes went wide. "Are you mad?" she nearly shouted at him.

"Watch and learn," the consul said. "Do not be alarmed by what is about to happen. Whatever you do, do not cry out. If we are to succeed, silence will be paramount. All of my demonslavers have been given the same orders."

No sooner had the consul uttered the words than Satine began to feel a tingling throughout her body. It was not unpleasant, and it provided a welcome warmth.

Then, both she and everything around her disappeared.

She looked around in terror. Staring down, all she could see were the waves as they passed by, several dozen meters below. At first she expected to fall into the water, but she did not. She stood firmly upon nothing, and she could see nothing except the three moons and the ocean they highlighted. Still, she knew she was moving with the ship by the way the deck beneath her continued to sway. It was a liberating feeling, and she wondered if this was what flying was like.

Reaching down the sides of her body, she was grateful to find that she still had substance, even though she couldn't see herself. Then she looked aft, and noticed that even the ship's wake had disappeared.

She turned to where she hoped Bratach still stood.

"I understand," she whispered. "It's marvelous."

Satine held her breath as the line of enemy frigates approached across their port bow. Dark and spectral, the looming hulls rose up out of the sea like those of ghost ships. She felt her ship tack and head straight for the center of the enemy line. But would there be enough room to pass through?

Brave as she was, she couldn't help but cringe as they neared the line of enemy ships. Reaching out, she took hold of the invisible gunwale. Her breath caught in her lungs.

They were so close that she could see the crewmen aboard the oncoming vessels. They seemed to be in great disarray, and there was much shouting. A woman stood upon the bow of what Satine assumed to be the flagship. She seemed angry beyond words as she shouted out her orders. Gripping the gunwale railing even harder, Satine knew that the next few seconds would surely determine their fate.

The enemy vessels slid by on either side, and their lone frigate slipped between the two closest ships. Satine gasped. They were so near that she could actually make out the faces of the enemy crewmen. One of them in particular stood out: a great hulking bear of a man, face, arms, and bare chest covered with scars.

Then they were past the enemy fleet and leaving it behind. Despite her distrust of the craft, this was the most awe-inspiring thing Satine had ever witnessed. Looking aft again, she saw that the distance between them and the fleet was growing quickly. There was little chance of the enemy finding them again. While she stood collecting her thoughts, she sensed that Bratach had returned to her side.

"Amazing," she said. "And very well done. But why did you risk running us so close? Wouldn't it have been safer to have outflanked them, rather than slip through their line that way?"

When Bratach finally spoke, his voice seemed to come from nothing.

"I wanted to see who was captaining the fleet, and I was not disappointed," he answered. "Tell me, did you recognize her?"

Satine realized that she did. The woman commanding the enemy fleet was one of those pictured in the parchments Wulfgar had given her that morning at the Citadel.

"I understand," she said. "Who is she?"

"Her name is Tyranny, and she is now the prince's personal privateer," Bratach answered. "My spies tell me that she is very capable. It is also rumored that she is unusually fond of the prince, a bit of information you might find useful, I should think."

Smiling to herself, Satine looked down at the waves passing beneath her feet. Being in the employ of a wizard might have its advantages after all.

She could feel the warmth of the rising sun on the small of her back. Then she felt their ship tack again, resuming their course for the delta.

As a precaution, Bratach kept their ship invisible all of the remaining way to the coast.

CHAPTER VIII

"YOU MUST EAT *SOMETHING*!" SHAWNA THE SHORT EXCLAIMED at the two worried women sitting before her.

The huge breakfast tray that Shawna had prepared sat on the meeting table before them, untouched by Shailiha and Celeste. Morganna, Shailiha's toddler, lay sleeping in her stroller by the princess' side, while Caprice sat perched on the top of the princess' high-backed chair. Shawna loved these two women, and in recent days the princess had come to rely upon the gnome wife heavily—especially as a trusted nanny for Morganna.

Shawna let go another exasperated sigh. Then she busily smoothed out her stark white apron. Her slate gray hair was tied in the back in its usual unforgiving bun, and she wore square, no-nonsense shoes, their laces tied with double knots so that they wouldn't come undone.

When Shawna's infamous ire was up, her attitude usually stayed that way for some time. By now nearly everyone in the palace could attest to that fact.

Normally, Shailiha and Celeste found Shawna's antics comic. But given recent events, they were unnerved to their very core, and neither of them found Shawna particularly amusing.

Ever since Tristan's absence on his quest to destroy the Gates of Dawn, Shailiha and Celeste had become very close, especially in their shared love for him. They both missed him terribly, and hoped against hope that he would return to them, just as he had done so many times before.

For Celeste, the pain ran deep. Not only was the love of her life missing, but her father, as well. Each of these men had only recently come into her life, and she couldn't face the thought of losing them both.

Unable to sleep, the princess and Wigg's daughter had been up all night, trying to console each other and keep fear at bay. When dawn broke, a Minion warrior brought them a message. Faegan was calling an emergency meeting of the Conclave in two hours—whether Tristan, Wigg, and Traax had returned or not. The two women could only guess at what Faegan wished to say. They doubted the news could be good.

Shailiha grasped the gold medallion hanging around her neck and held it tightly—as if doing so might somehow bring her closer to her brother, wherever he might be.

"Are you quite sure that neither of you will eat anything?" Shawna pressed, bringing the princess back to the present. Shailiha shook her head. Celeste followed suit.

With a sorrowful look, Shawna walked over and placed one of her small, gnarled hands over Shailiha's. The princess could feel the calluses on Shawna's palms, garnered from centuries of hard, honest work.

"They'll be back, just you wait and see," the gnome wife said softly. Then she thought for a moment. "Shall I take Morganna with me?" she asked. "The child will need to eat soon. And knowing how Master Faegan likes to go on and on, the meeting could be a long one." A hint of a smile crossed Shawna's face.

Shailiha found herself unable to return it. But she looked over at her daughter and nodded.

"That might be for the best," she agreed.

Turning, Shawna went to the stroller and reached up to grasp its handle. It was nearly as tall as she. When she was gone, a sad silence descended.

The chamber was spacious, constructed of a beautiful light blue marble with dark blue veins running through it. Artwork decorated the walls and patterned rugs warmed the floor. The small crackling fire in the hearth gave off a comforting aroma. But the true centerpiece of the room was the massive meeting table sitting in the middle of the floor.

Constructed superbly by Minion craftsmen on Tristan's orders, the table was Eutracian mahogany, inlaid in the center with an image of the Paragon. Each of the ten luxurious, velvet-upholstered chairs surrounding it had the name of its owner carved into its high, curved back.

Shailiha ran one hand over the highly polished tabletop, reflections from the fireplace dancing between her fingers, but she was blind to its beauty. Then she felt Celeste's hand on her arm, and she looked up.

"What is it?" she asked.

"I am not with child," Celeste said shortly.

"I see," the princess said. "How long have you known?"

"Only since this morning. I wanted to tell you sooner, but I knew how upset you already were, and I didn't want to add to your burdens. I wanted Tristan to be the first to know, but I needed to talk to someone. Do you think he will forgive me for not telling him first?"

Shailiha did her best to give her a reassuring smile. "Of course he will," she answered. "Until you tell him, it shall remain just between us."

Celeste knew that Tristan would have mixed reactions to the news—as she herself had. Both of them knew that any child conceived now, before Tristan's blood was changed back to red, would be grotesquely deformed. But they both also yearned to bring a child into the world, to love and to care for. *Perhaps one day,* she thought. They could not lose hope.

Taking a deep breath, she looked at Shailiha, only to see that the princess' expression had darkened.

"But you must tell him as soon as you can," Shailiha said. "Then your father, and Faegan. I think you know why."

Celeste knew what the princess was really trying to tell her. The azure glow of the craft had appeared just after she and Tristan had first lain together. Since she wasn't with child, the glow must have meant something else—something only the wizards would be able to unravel. Worry stabbed her heart and she shuddered.

Tyranny was fuming. As she stomped down the spacious halls of the Redoubt following behind Ox, the heels of her knee boots echoed loudly against the marble floors.

Her encounter with the slaver frigate had so angered Tyranny that she had cowed even the stalwart Ox. That anger had lasted throughout her journey back to the Redoubt in the personal litter Tristan had given her. The muscles in her jaws clenching, the privateer continued to seethe.

The demonslaver frigate had somehow escaped all twelve of her ships. *How?* She'd had the enemy vessel dead to rights. Escape should have been impossible.

There could only be one answer to how the warship had eluded her grasp, yet her mind shied away from the awful conclusion. She needed to talk to Faegan, and she needed to do it now.

When she and Ox reached the double doors of the meeting room, the two Minion guards standing on either side snapped to attention. At a nod from Tyranny, Ox left her, and the guards swung open the massive portals.

Hoping for the best, Tyranny squared her shoulders and walked in. She was immediately disappointed. Tristan, Wigg, and Traax were not there.

The other six permanent members of the Conclave waited in their respective seats. Faegan was speaking. Upon seeing her come in, he politely stopped, looked at her, and nodded. When Tyranny glanced around the room, she saw sadness and concern on every face.

Tyranny went to embrace Shailiha, Celeste, and Abbey, and did her best to offer them support. Then she took her seat.

She was painfully aware of the empty chairs on either side of her. Normally, Tristan would sit to her right and Wigg to her left. Having no one on either side gave her a strange, isolated feeling, despite the presence of the other people in the room.

Tyranny trained her wide blue eyes on the wizard. Faegan looked tired and drawn. The bloodred Paragon hanging around his neck twinkled brightly in the light of the chandelier.

She saw that both the Tome of the Paragon and the Scroll of the Vigors had been brought here, presumably for safekeeping. The massive, white leather-bound Tome sat in one corner upon a black marble pedestal, its gilt-edged pages lying open. The scroll hovered beside it in the air, spelled there by Faegan.

The scroll was half a meter wide and about one meter long when unrolled. A gold rod, with knobs on either end, ran through its center. A gold band engraved with Old Eutracian secured the tightly rolled document at its middle. Tyranny winced when she remembered how much of the precious document had been burned that night on the roof of the palace. Large sections of the fine vellum were charred and flaking. Even so, it remained magnificent. Finally she looked back at Faegan.

"There is still no word of Tristan, Wigg, or Traax?" she asked.

"No," Faegan answered. "But they are three highly resourceful individuals—especially when they are together. We must not give up hope."

"I have urgent news," Tyranny said. "My fleet sighted a lone demonslaver ship only hours ago, and she—"

She stopped cold when Faegan stiffened and cocked his head to one side.

Then a brief smile overcame the wizard's face—the first in two days. And then everyone became aware of a growing hubbub in the hallway outside. Suddenly, the double doors burst open, and Tristan, Wigg, and Traax staggered through the doorway.

All three were dirty from head to toe, covered with what looked like some sort of ash. Much of the right side of Wigg's robe had been scorched away to reveal right hand and right leg covered with red, blistered burns. Tristan looked unharmed, but his hair had been singed. Traax's long, dark hair had been burned, too, as had part of his leather body armor. All three looked exhausted.

With joyous cries and teary eyes, Celeste, Shailiha, and Abbey stood and raced to embrace the men.

Feeling a bit like an intruder on the tender scene, Tyranny lowered her head and gazed at the inlaid tabletop. She wanted to share her joy at Tristan's safe return, but that did not seem appropriate.

At last, Tristan helped Wigg to his seat, and then he and Traax sat down. Tristan smiled over at Tyranny, and she smiled back. The *Jin'Sai* nodded his greetings to the rest of the table.

Faegan placed his gnarled hands flat on the tabletop and looked at Wigg.

"You are severely burned, my old friend," he said. "But at first glance your injuries do not appear to be life-threatening. You have treated yourself with an incantation of accelerated healing, I presume? And something to help with the pain?"

Wigg reached to his left and took Abbey's hand, then nodded. He remained silent, knowing full well what Faegan's next question would be. Faegan leaned forward, his eyes shining with curiosity.

"Tell me, is it as we feared?"

"Yes," Wigg said sadly. "But I regret to tell you that there is other news, and it is equally grave."

"What is it?" Abbey asked.

"An entire village is gone," he whispered. "Brook Hollow. The energy dripping from the Orb of the Vigors burned the place to ash. Try as I might, there was nothing I could do to stop it." Taking his hand back from Abbey, Wigg wiped tears from his eyes.

"We were right, Faegan," he went on. "The Orb of the Vigors is torn—no doubt a result of Wulfgar's attempt to destroy it by polluting it with the Orb of the Vagaries. It is dripping the pure energy of the Vigors. For all I know, it may continue to do so for all time."

For several long moments there was only the crackling of the logs in the fireplace.

"How is it that the three of you survived?" Abbey finally asked.

"We lost nearly all the warriors that accompanied us," Tristan answered. "It was only by the grace of the Afterlife that there were enough warriors still alive to catch us as our burning litter went down. We were outside of the main path of the orb, and were able to build a new litter from freshly felled trees. The surviving warriors flew us home."

"What direction was the orb traveling in when you left?" Faegan asked.

"North, across the fields of Farplain," Traax answered. "Luckily, that area is largely uninhabited. But the orb's path is erratic. It's impossible to say where it might turn next."

"Do you believe that the orb has been dripping energy ever since that night Wulfgar tried to destroy it?" Shailiha asked.

"An excellent question," Wigg said. "No, I do not think so. If that had been the case, then it would have destroyed much of the palace that night, and a good deal of Tammerland, as it moved away. I believe that the orb was weakened that night, and that it finally ruptured later, in some other part of the country."

"We need to know where the orb is at all times," Tristan said. "Traax, I want you to send out several squadrons of warriors to find it. Once they have, they are to set up a chain of communication so that we will receive regular updates, just as we do with Tyranny's fleet. If the orb moves toward an inhabited place, the warriors must do all they can to warn the populace."

"That may be difficult, *Jin'Sai,*" Traax said. "They still do not trust us."

Geldon spoke up at last. "May I make a recommendation?"

"By all means," Tristan said.

"It seems to me that the Minions need someone to travel with them, to act as a human emissary on their behalf," he replied. "I would like to offer my services."

Tristan looked at the hunchbacked dwarf with true admiration. The small man with the very large heart had proven invaluable to them in the past, and Tristan was sure that this new mission would prove to be no exception.

"Of course," the prince said. "And thank you."

Unable to contain her news any longer, Tyranny spoke up.

"I know all of this is incredibly important, but so is what I have to tell you," she said.

"What is it?" Tristan asked.

Taking a deep breath, Tyranny looked around the table. "Only hours ago, a demonslaver frigate slipped through my fleet," she said. "I believe she was making for the Cavalon Delta. If I'm right, she may already be there."

Tristan's face became grave. "How can that be?" he asked. To Tyranny's relief, he seemed to be more stunned than angry. Reaching up, he ran one hand through his dark hair. "I've sailed with you, and I know how skilled you are! How could a lone frigate slip through a dozen vessels under your command?"

The muscles in Tyranny's jaw clenched. "I had her dead to rights," she answered grimly. "I ordered the fleet to fan out in a battle line and take her. There should have been no possibility of escape. As I watched her approach, she was simply there one second, and gone the next.

"Someone of the craft must have been aboard her, and caused the frigate to disappear," she added. "The same way they did not so long ago, just before we finally smashed their fleet." Sitting tiredly back in her chair, she knew that everyone around the table understood what she wasn't saying.

"Could it be true?" Tristan asked Faegan. "Could Wulfgar still be alive?"

Faegan pursed his lips. "It would explain much," he answered. "Still, that may not be the case."

"Why not?" Celeste asked.

"We believe that Wulfgar received his gifts through Forestallments," the old wizard answered, "the calculations for which came by way of the Scroll of the Vagaries. It is possible that he could also have granted Forestallments to one or more of his consuls before he came to Eutracia to destroy the orb. It could have been one such consul aboard that frigate."

He turned to Tyranny. "Don't be so hard on yourself, my dear," he said. "Even Wigg and I might not have been able to find that vessel, once she had vanished. Still, all of this doesn't answer the greater question, does it?"

"Why Wulfgar or one of his emissaries is really here," Shailiha said. "It must have to do with the ruptured orb."

Despite all of their concerns, Faegan's impish, familiar smile returned. He loved nothing so much as a good riddle, especially when he was the only one holding the answer.

"Oh, really," he teased Shailiha. "And why must that be the case?"

"He has come here to complete the job he started, has he not?" Shailiha asked. "Or he is dead, and his consuls are carrying on in his stead. Either way, they mean to finish destroying the orb."

Suddenly, Tristan knew what it was that Faegan was getting at. He looked over at his twin sister.

"They don't need to destroy the orb, Shai," he said. "Don't you see? As the Orb of the Vigors continues to drip its energy across the land, it will eventually die on its own."

He looked first at Faegan, and then at Wigg. "I'm right, aren't I?" he asked.

"In truth, we do not know," Wigg answered. "This is a calamity that we never thought we would have to face. We cannot be sure the orb will die, or whether the energy inside of it that sustains the Vigors will replenish itself.

"Either way, Faegan and I fear that without the energy of the orb to sustain the Vigors, our side of the craft will soon cease to exist," he went on. "After all, isn't that what Wulfgar wanted all along? So you see, now the real questions become not only whether he lives, but if he does, whether he knows about the continued draining of the orb."

Looking down at the table, Wigg laced his long fingers together. A grim silence fell over the room.

Tristan looked to Faegan. "What can you tell us about the orb that might help us heal the rupture?" he asked. Despite his exhaustion, his mind was alive with questions.

But Faegan was not ready to answer. "With your permission, I think we should adjourn," he said. "Everyone is exhausted, and Wigg is injured. Besides, he and I need to research this further, if we are to give you a proper answer."

Reluctantly, Tristan nodded. "Very well," he said. "But I want everyone with the exception of Geldon to stay in the palace for now." He looked at Traax. "And I want those search parties sent out immediately. For all we know, the orb could be bearing down on Tammerland this very moment."

Traax nodded. "I live to serve," came his traditional reply.

Tristan gave Tyranny a short smile. "I trust you will not mind accepting our hospitality for a while longer," he said. Not knowing quite what to say, Tyranny smiled back.

"I have one other request," Tristan announced. He looked first at Shailiha, then at Abbey and Adrian.

"The three of you have been treating the wounded in the courtyard and the palace," he said. "Have you gotten any sense of the general feeling among them?"

"We have," Adrian answered. "Most of them remain distrustful of both us and the Minions. Frankly, I can't say I blame them."

"Precisely," Tristan said. "But I think we might be able to turn this awful situation to some useful purpose."

"What are you talking about?" Wigg asked.

"Tomorrow morning I want Shailiha, Abbey, and Adrian to try to convince as many of the refugees as possible to meet with us in the Chamber of Supplication," Tristan said. "They need to be told that the heir to the throne still lives, and that I care about them. This tragedy belongs to all of us, and I want to use it to bring us all back together again, if I can. If we can convince even a few, the word will spread. I realize it will only be a small beginning, but we must try. I want everyone in this room to be there with me."

Wigg and Faegan exchanged smiles.

"Then we are adjourned," Tristan said.

As Tristan led the way from the meeting room, Faegan silently indicated to Wigg that he wanted the First Wizard to stay behind. Wigg nodded back, and then whispered to Abbey that he would meet her later in her private quarters. Abbey was reluctant to leave him, for she was anxious to examine his wounds more closely, but she knew better than to try to change his mind.

When the two wizards were alone, Faegan came straight to the point.

"There is only one way to save the orb, you know," he said.

Wigg nodded. "The Tome states that only the *Jin'Sai* may heal such damage," he said. "To do that, he must first be trained. And in order for him to be trained, his blood must first be returned to its original state. Why didn't you tell him?"

Faegan sighed. "It wouldn't have been fair," he answered. "I think we owe it to him to inform him in private. I know one thing for sure, old friend. There is far more to all of this than first meets the eye."

"Wulfgar?" Wigg asked. "Do you think he is still alive?"

Faegan sat back in his chair. Wigg could almost see the wheels turning in his head.

"I wish I knew, First Wizard," Faegan answered softly. "I wish I knew."

One of the hearth logs slipped down in the grate. Slowly it collapsed into charred ash while the two ancient mystics sat in silence.

TRISTAN ENTERED HIS PERSONAL QUARTERS, CELESTE RIGHT behind him. She watched fondly as he unbuckled his sword belt and baldric, and tossed his weapons onto a chair. Then the knee boots came off. In stocking feet, he walked to the windows and closed the draperies.

Celeste smiled. He was filthy from head to toe, and a dark growth of stubble covered his face, yet even so disheveled, he was still the handsomest man she had ever seen.

Returning to her side, he took her in his arms and he kissed her. Closing her eyes, she let herself luxuriate in his presence for a moment. How good it felt to have him back.

"Your time with the orb—was it as awful as Father said?" she asked. Then she saw his face fall, and she immediately regretted her question. His dark eyes looked down into hers with a terrifying sadness.

"Yes," he answered. "It was more horrible than you could possibly imagine. Even after seeing it with my own eyes, I still find it hard to believe. Right now, however, more discussion about the orb is not what I desire."

Celeste smiled mischievously. "Just what might you desire, my lord?" she asked. "Something that I, your humble servant, might be able to provide?" Then she remembered that the wizards had forbidden them to be together in that way.

"Sleep," Tristan answered, his eyes half closed. "I want to sleep for one hundred years."

He walked over to the huge four-poster bed and collapsed upon it, dirty clothes and all. Holding one arm out, he beckoned to her, and she went to lie beside him, her head on his chest. In the silence of the room, she could hear the comforting beat of his heart. Then she realized that there might be no better time to tell him what she must.

"Tristan," she whispered. "There is something that you need to know." Raising her head, she looked into his face. His eyes were already closed.

"Tristan?" she asked softly.

No answer came. Her prince was asleep.

CHAPTER IX

As SATINE GUIDED HER BLACK GELDING THROUGH THE BYWAYS OF Tammerland, she took in the sights and sounds of the human suffering that seemed to fill the streets. She was not surprised by what she saw, because Bratach had explained both the condition of the orb, and its expected effect. Following a discreet distance behind the carriage-of-four that the consul had hired, she quickly realized that even his detailed description had not done the situation justice.

It was afternoon in Tammerland. The gray sky threatened heavy rain at any moment. Pre-storm winds rose occasionally, picking up litter from the streets, where grim groups of citizens served in makeshift burial details, pushing wheelbarrows or pulling handcarts piled high with corpses. Arms, legs, and heads hung over the carts' lips; sometimes lifeless eyes stared out into space, giving the unnerving impression that they could still see.

Pulling her horse to a stop for a moment, Satine reached into her cloak and removed a black silk scarf. Hoping to keep the stench of death from her nostrils, she tied it around the lower part of her face. She clucked to her horse and they began moving again.

She hadn't wanted to come into Tammerland this soon. Too many people knew her here. She had hoped that this visit could wait until later, after she had drawn out her primary targets. Then she could finish her sanctions quickly and retire. But Bratach wanted to be sure that she was familiar with the address he had given her, the place he referred to as his sanctuary on this side of the Sea of Whispers. She would soon have need of it, he told her.

Narrowing her eyes slightly, she realized that she still didn't know what he had meant by that.

She remained in awe of the technique the consul had employed to slip them safely past the prince's fleet. Bratach had finally ordered the frigate anchored just off the Cavalon Delta. After augmenting his spell to keep the ship invisible in his absence, Bratach had ushered Satine and a group of armed demonslavers into a skiff, in which they had made their way up the Sippora River to the very outskirts of Tammerland proper. Only then had Bratach caused himself and Satine to become visible again. The skiff and her demonslavers had departed, heading back to the frigate waiting offshore.

Bratach's carriage stopped. Satine knew Tammerland well, for she had been raised there. But the city held bad memories, and the sooner she was gone, the better. She had two errands to perform, and then her mission could begin.

Looking around to orient herself, she found that they were on Tamarac Boulevard, one of the main thoroughfares that led to Bargainer's Square. The address she needed was just across the street.

Just as Bratach had told her, number Twenty-Seven Tamarac Boulevard seemed to be an archery shop. The sign dangling above its doors was carved with the image of a single arrow. It truly was a working place of business. But according to Bratach, the shop had a good deal more to offer her.

Without comment from its passenger, Bratach's carriage moved away. He had told her that they should never be seen together, other than in the confines of the shop. Should she need him, she could arrange to meet him through its auspices. In truth, she was glad to be rid of him. He was, she thought, little more than Wulfgar's endowed errand boy, and she disliked being told what to do by anyone, especially a subordinate. One corner of her mouth came up. Even if he *can* make ships disappear, she thought.

Glancing up and down the boulevard, she saw no one familiar. Keeping to the opposite side of the street, she dismounted and tied the gelding to a nearby rail.

She stepped onto the sidewalk, leaned up against an oil lamp pole, and cast her gaze across the street. There was no way to discern whether there were any customers inside the shop, so now seemed as good a time as any.

Slipping her hands beneath her cloak, she found the handles of her four daggers and gave them each a tug, loosening them in their sheaths.

She pushed off from the pole, removed the scarf from her face, and walked warily across the street. As she entered the shop, the little bell at the top of the door cheerfully announced her presence.

The place was spacious and airy, belying the impression of shoddiness it gave from the street. All manner of archery equipment—some quite finely crafted, even by Satine's high professional standards—lined the walls and littered the various tables. While looking over the goods with an expert eye, she surreptitiously studied the other end of the shop.

A man Satine took as the proprietor stood at the far end, behind a long wooden counter. Two patrons stood there, loudly arguing with him over the price of a dozen arrows. They were impoverished, greasy-looking men, and their manners matched their appearance. The proprietor was a short, balding man. Red garters held up the sleeves of his sweat-stained shirt. He was doing his best to keep control of the situation, but the rowdy customers were becoming ruder and more threatening with every passing second. Their speech was slurred; Satine guessed that they had been drinking.

Grabbing up a longbow from a nearby wall, Satine strode purposefully to the counter. As she approached, one of the men leered at her. Several of his teeth were missing, and she could smell the ale on his breath. Ignoring him, Satine held up the longbow.

"How much?" she asked.

"Wha-what?" the owner asked, as he turned away from the two men. He gave Satine an angry look, as though she were a nuisance rather than a paying customer.

This was getting her nowhere. It was time to let him know who she really was. Holding the bow higher, she pointed to its string.

"Is this catgut, or something else?" she asked. "I understand catgut is hard to come by these days."

As expected, she watched a surprised look come over the man's face.

"It's catgut," he answered. "Makes for the best strings, you know."

"So I've been told," she said. His coded reply had been exactly what Bratach had told her to expect. Now the only obstacles were the two miscreants standing by her side.

She placed the bow down on the countertop and slipped her hands beneath her cloak. As she did so, she sized up the situation. The man standing nearest her would have to be dealt with first. The other was a short distance down the length of the counter.

She usually only killed for money, but this was different. Not only had they both seen her here, they were unnecessary distractions. Her sanctions had to be protected, and these men were simply in the wrong place at the wrong time. One corner of her mouth came up. This would be so easy that it almost wasn't worth doing.

The nearest man turned to look at her. His angry eyes were bloodshot.

"Someone ought to teach you some manners," he snarled. Still refusing to look at him, she remained motionless. When she didn't reply, his hand started moving toward her.

When his hand was close enough, with a single, smooth move Satine turned on one heel, grasped his hand in midair, and then turned it over. She heard the bones crack.

Then she grabbed one of her daggers and plunged the blade directly into his body. With a quick, upward thrust, she sliced him open from his groin to his breast. When she felt the knife strike bone she stopped, twisted the blade upward, and thrust its point into his heart. As he collapsed, she pushed him away with the sole of one boot.

The other one was coming for her. She raised the bloody dagger over her head and let it fly. It twirled end over end twice, and then buried itself into the man's throat. As the blood burbled from his mouth, he tried to reach out to her. Then the light went out of his eyes, and he collapsed facedown onto the floor.

Silence fell as Satine removed the black scarf from her cloak. She retrieved her dagger from the dead man. After wiping it clean, she replaced the blade in its sheath.

She looked calmly across the counter to the proprietor. His mouth was hanging open.

"But . . . you're a woman!" he breathed.

"So you noticed," she shot back. "Congratulations."

Saying nothing more, she walked toward the front of the shop. First she reached up and drew down the window shades. Then she opened the door and turned its sign around, so that it now read "Closed." After turning the lock she walked back to the counter, placed her palms on it, and looked the sweaty man directly in the eyes.

"Until I leave here and these two bodies have been disposed of, you're closed," she said. "You are the consul named Ivan, I presume? If you aren't, I've just killed two men for nothing."

Slowly regaining his composure, Bratach's consul pointed down at the two corpses. "Why did you do that, you fool?" he asked. "We need no undue attention drawn to this place!"

Satine's eyes hardened. "I kill whom I choose, when I choose," she answered. Then she shrugged. "I wouldn't worry. They don't exactly look like two of Eutracia's finest. Besides, there is an easy way to dispose of this refuse, right in plain sight."

Raising an eyebrow, Ivan nervously ran one finger around the inside of his sweaty shirt collar. "How?"

"You're a consul, are you not?" she asked. "Simply use the craft to scorch their clothing and bodies. Then, under the cover of night, toss them out into the street. Believe me, no one will notice two more out there." Satine crossed her arms over her breasts and looked hard at Ivan. "Now then," she demanded. "Why am I here?"

"Bratach didn't tell you?" he asked skeptically.

"Not really," she answered. "All he said was that this shop serves as some form of refuge. It's apparent he didn't tell you that I would be a woman, either. He seems to like his little games, doesn't he?"

"Follow me," Ivan said.

He turned and walked toward the back of the shop, where he disappeared around one end of a hanging curtain. With one palm resting lightly upon a dagger hilt, Satine warily followed.

The area behind the curtain was dark and musty. The consul narrowed his eyes as he called on the craft to light an oil lamp sconce on the wall. He lifted the globe free and carried it to a door. Creaking on its hinges, the door opened slowly to reveal a wooden stairway leading downward.

The chamber below was simple and utilitarian. Ancient, multicolored bricks lined the walls. Brightly burning oil sconces illuminated the room. There was another door in the opposite wall. Several beds were stacked on the dirt floor in a far corner. Shelves were piled with dried foodstuffs and containers of water, while another area held a rudimentary wine cellar. A table sat in the center of the room, holding a half-full bottle of red wine, stained glasses, and a scattering of playing cards. The air in the room was fetid and musty.

Putting down the lamp, Ivan beckoned her to sit. Then he poured two glasses of wine. He handed her one.

He raised his glass. "To the successful completion of your sanctions," he toasted. Holding his glass high, he waited for her to drink.

"After you," she said sternly. "I insist."

Ivan smiled. "Bring you all the way here, just to poison you?" he asked. "My, but you are skeptical."

"I'm also still alive."

Smiling again, Ivan took a deep gulp. Finally, Satine followed his lead. To her surprise, the wine was quite good.

"And now to address your questions," Ivan said. Taking a deep breath, he sat back in his chair and rolled his glass back and forth between his hands.

"This room is indeed a sanctuary of sorts," he began. "It is a place where we of the brotherhood loyal to Wulfgar might hide and transfer messages of importance to one another. There is a great deal going on in Eutracia that the wizards of the Redoubt know nothing of." He took another sip of wine.

"There are dozens of these underground sanctuaries scattered across the land," he went on. "Some are in cities, and some are not. They were built more than three centuries ago, during the Sorceresses' War, by slave labor controlled by the

Coven of Sorceresses. It is even said that Failee—Wigg's late wife and First Mistress of the Coven—once held a strategic meeting here in this very room, when her forces were close to taking Tammerland.

"We mean to give the wizards yet another war. This time it shall be one that they cannot hide from behind the walls of the palace. The wizards of the Redoubt believe that all of their once-loyal consuls have fled to the Citadel. They couldn't be more wrong."

Satine put down her wineglass and leaned over the table. "Thanks so much for the history lesson," she said. "But I don't give a tinker's damn about your politics. Or who controls the craft, either. All I want is to complete my sanctions and collect my money."

"Understandable," Ivan answered, "given the fact that you possess no endowed blood. If you did, and if you had then been trained in the glory of the Vagaries, such things would mean far more to you."

"So what is this sanctuary to me?"

"Your assignments will most probably take you far afield. In addition, you may eventually be sought by the prince's forces. During that time, you may be forced to go to ground." He removed a folded piece of parchment from his trousers and handed it to her.

"What's this?" she asked.

"It's a list of both the rural and urban locations of all the other sanctuaries," Ivan said. He took another sip. "Carry it with you at all times. The list is too long to commit to memory. If you are about to be killed or captured, you must do your best to destroy it."

Satine shoved the list into her right boot without looking at it.

"We have also devised a method by which you will know whether a message awaits you, without your having to go inside. Do you remember the 'open' and 'closed' sign that you turned around just a little while ago?"

"Of course," she answered, her curiosity rising.

"Each establishment has two such signs. One printed in red, and one in black. If the sign in red is hanging in the window, then a message awaits you inside. If the sign is in black, then there is no message. Do you understand?"

Satine nodded. "But what about the rural sanctuaries?" she asked. "Surely they aren't shops as well, sitting out in the middle of nowhere?"

"Of course not," Ivan answered. "In most cases they are simple peasants' cottages. If there is a wreath of wildflowers pinned to the front door, there is a message for you inside. A bare door means no message."

"Very well," Satine said. "But I made it very clear to Wulfgar and Serena that I work alone. So what kinds of messages might I need to receive?"

"Information regarding the movements of your various targets," Ivan said. He smiled conspiratorially. "We have someone inside, one who is in a position to know such information and relay it to us."

Looking thoughtfully into her glass, Satine took another sip of wine. She looked back over at Ivan. Before she could speak, he handed her another parchment.

"Your first such message," he said quietly. "I suggest you read it now."

After reading it, she looked back into his eyes. His wicked smile had returned.

"As you can see, we suggest you start out small, so to speak," he said.

For the first time since Satine had come to Tammerland, she smiled, too. "I understand," she said. "But won't this make it more difficult to deal with the other targets later?" she asked. "The ones I am truly being paid for?"

Ivan sat back in his chair and sighed. "Perhaps," he said. "That concerns many of us on this side of the Sea of Whispers. Even so, this is how Wulfgar has ordered it. He wants them *all* dead, of course. But he wants some to suffer first as they helplessly watch their friends perish." He paused.

"We shall need a code name for you," he finally said. "These will be political killings, and the prince and his wizards have a long reach. Surely you will wish to protect your identity as much as possible."

Thinking it over, Satine had to agree. "Very well," she answered. "Use the code name 'Gray Fox.'"

A brief smile came to Ivan's lips. Looking at the color of her cloak, he understood.

"Then 'Gray Fox' it shall be," he said. "Except for me and Bratach, the other consuls shall know you by only that name."

A thought suddenly revisited Satine. "What about the orb?" she asked.

"What of it?"

"Bratach explained to me what is happening. Does that have anything to do with why I am here?"

Ivan leaned toward her. "It has *everything* to do with it," he answered. "But for our safety and your own you are to know little more of it than that, unless such information impacts your mission. Succeed in your task, and all will go according to plan." He began rolling the wineglass between his hands again as he thought for a moment.

"The wonderful byproduct of the rupture in the orb is the fact that so many wounded are rushing into Tammerland," he continued. "One of the greatest tenets of the craft states that chaos is the overriding principle of the universe. The wizards of the Redoubt are now suffering more chaos than they can effectively deal with. And it will only worsen as time goes by.

"At first, our master thought he had completely failed in his attempt to pollute the Orb of the Vigors," he said. "But when we discovered that the orb had ruptured, we immediately sent word to him. Now things have changed. While it was once our mission to destroy the orb, we must now see to it that it isn't interfered with in any way. Ironic, wouldn't you agree?"

Satine had suddenly had quite enough talk of wizards, magic, and orbs. She wanted to be gone from this suffocating place, and begin her sanctions. There were still two places she needed to go first, and she wouldn't get there by sitting here talking politics with some fat consul in a bleak cellar. After taking a final sip of wine, she stood up.

"Is there anything else?" she asked.

Ivan pointed to the closed door on the other side of the room. "Exit by that passageway," he answered. "It will bring you up into an alley several blocks from here. You will have to circle back around to collect your horse. Each sanctuary has a secret tunnel out." The smile came again. "A fact you would do well to remember."

Satine walked to the door and pried it open. A curving, brick-lined tunnel led upward. It was lit with oil sconces. She started to leave, then stopped and turned back to Ivan.

"Thank you," she said softly.

"Just do your job properly, woman," he answered back. "That's all the thanks we of the Vagaries require of you."

Turning back to face the tunnel, Satine walked in and closed the door behind her.

CHAPTER X

NIGHT HAD FALLEN AT THE CITADEL, AND WULFGAR WAS ALONE. The hour was late. His pregnant queen and her handmaidens had long since retired. Looking out over the dark Sea of Whispers from the comfort of his throne room, the bastard brother of the *Jin'Sai* found himself restless, and concerned.

While he sat and pondered, the blazing fires in the urns on either side of the twin thrones cast spectral shadows across the polished marble walls and ceilings. He heard only the distant crashing of the waves. He had grown to love this chamber, especially when Serena was by his side.

He raised his damaged arm before his good eye. The nearly useless appendage somehow seemed even more hideous in the firelight. He lowered it and silently cursed the wizards of the Redoubt, and his half brother and sister. His jaw hardened as he gazed back out over the sea.

His mind turned toward the professional killer he had hired. Satine had impressed him. Still, he understood that the assassin—no matter how deadly she might be—was only an oblique part of his overall plan. Satine was a form of guarantee that the Orb of the Vigors would continue to deteriorate.

His spying consuls in Eutracia—especially his secret servant within the walls of the royal palace—were keeping him well informed of the movements of the ruptured orb.

Nonetheless, obstacles remained, not the least of which was the considerable time involved in receiving crucial information from Eutracia. He had lied to Satine when he told her that he had only a few demonslavers remaining. There were in fact tens of thousands of them still here at the Isle of the Citadel. Those remaining slavers and the ships they manned were relaying the information back to him from his consuls in Eutracia. Still, he seethed at the slowness of it.

What worried him above all else was that his Citadel consuls had not yet discovered the formula in the Scroll of the Vagaries that he needed most: the calculations for the single, all-important spell that would ensure his victory.

The scroll's unexpected references to this all-important Forestallment had been discovered only days earlier, by his ceaselessly researching consuls and its suggested existence had come as a shock to them all. When Wulfgar had been informed, his heart had leapt for joy. He quickly realized that if it could be deciphered and then imbued into his blood, his victory over the *Jin'Sai* would be all but assured. Then, as the Lord of the Vagaries, he would reign supreme in the practice of the craft.

Soon Wulfgar meant to invade Eutracia and make the nation his. Once he had taken Eutracia, the less sophisticated nation of Parthalon would succumb easily.

Standing from his throne, he laid the mangled side of his face against the nearby marble column. The coolness of the stone always comforted his tortured flesh, but he granted himself this show of weakness only when he was alone. He had tried repeatedly to heal his body and face by means of the craft, but even his powers had proven inadequate. Since learning that his consuls might identify and decipher the Forestallment they sought, his hope for a recovery had been renewed.

Lifting his face from the marble, he thought of Serena and the unborn girl-child she carried. Serena was brave, and she loved him. But in his heart he could sense both the pain and the revulsion she tried so hard to hide. In truth, who could blame her?

She and her husband were both fervent practitioners of the Vagaries. They were also human beings who loved each other deeply. He knew that she desperately wanted to see him the way he had looked when they had first fallen in love during their early days here at the Citadel.

Even more, Wulfgar wanted his daughter to see him as he had

once been: handsome and strong, rather than the freak he had become at the hands of the wizards of the Redoubt. A deformed monster who would undoubtedly make his new daughter cry, simply by looking down into the crib in which she would soon lie.

He heard the huge double doors at the other side of the room unexpectedly swing open. Turning, he saw one of his armed demonslavers enter.

"What is it?" Wulfgar snapped.

The demonslaver bowed. "Forgive me, my lord," he answered. "But Einar has come, begging an audience. He says it is most urgent."

Wulfgar nodded. "Very well."

The demonslaver bowed again and walked back through the doors. In a few moments the visitor entered the room and approached.

Tall, erect, and almost ravenously lean, he had prematurely gray hair, which he kept tied behind his head, and bright blue eyes, which at the moment were calmly scanning his master's face. Einar was the most gifted of Wulfgar's Citadel consuls, and he was in charge of both their training and their day-to-day activities. He was also the overseer of the scriptorium, the great library that held the fortress' most precious texts and scrolls.

Then Wulfgar saw that the Scroll of the Vagaries glided along by Einar's side. An azure glow surrounded it, telling Wulfgar that the consul had been recently working with it. Normally Wulfgar would be furious that the precious document had been removed from the scriptorium without his permission. But something about the fearless look on his lead consul's face told him that he should hear what the man had to say.

Einar stopped before him, the scroll hovering just a meter or so away. Wulfgar pointed to the parchment.

"Why did you bring the scroll here?" he demanded.

"I wanted to bring you this news personally," Einar said. His eyes flashed with promise, and his gaze was steady.

"We have found the Forestallment that we seek," he said. "It's true, my lord. The calculations exist."

Wulfgar stared wide-eyed at the consul, then looked at the scroll. "Can it be true?" he asked.

"Yes, my lord. That is why I took the liberty of bringing the scroll here to you. Knowing how anxious you have been, I wanted to prove it to you immediately, and in private."

Wulfgar smiled. "Then by all means proceed."

Einar raised his hands, and the scroll began to unroll itself. On and on it went, until Wulfgar thought that it might extend itself completely. Then it stopped. Narrowing his eyes, Einar caused a specific portion of the text to duplicate itself in glowing azure and rise from the body of the parchment to hang in the air. Wulfgar walked closer and began to read the Old Eutracian text. The translation read:

> *"And it shall come to pass that the bastard sibling of the* Jin'-Sai *will one day wish to hear, rather than simply read, of the mysteries that make up his blood. And when that day comes, the calculations for such a Forestallment shall be provided herein for his use. Only he, the* Jin'Sai, *and the* Jin'Saiou *are capable of accepting such a gift, for the quality of their blood knows no equal. Therefore the* Enseterat—*or the Lord of the Vagaries, as he shall also be known—shall finally be able to commune with us, and all will be revealed."*

Inarticulate with joy, Wulfgar looked at the groups of numbers and symbols in Old Eutracian that comprised the formula for the Forestallment. The formula was both the longest and the most elegant solution of the craft he had ever seen. He looked back at Einar.

"You have analyzed the calculations?" he asked.

"Yes, my lord. I believe that the end result shall be as the scroll promises. I have never seen so involved a formula. As such, the risk of error is great. For that reason, I suggest that if my lord still wishes to go ahead, that only I perform the transferal. And that it be done here in the throne room, in the strictest of privacy. Gifting you with this Forestallment will be arduous for both of us. I do not wish the demonslavers and the other consuls to hear you, should you cry out. This is why I brought the scroll to you, rather than requesting that you come to it."

Lost in thought, Wulfgar walked the short distance over to the open wall of the throne room. He looked to the sea. The winds had risen and the froth-tipped waves were restless and angry, much like the building conflict in his heart.

Given the length and complexity of the calculations, Wulfgar understood the risk. The installation of so powerful a Forestallment in his blood would be the single most painful experience of his life—probably even more excruciating than the injuries he had suffered at the hands of the wizards of the Redoubt. Once the process began there could be no reprieve, no turning back. Even considering the unusual strength of his blood, he couldn't be sure he would survive it.

But these were risks he would simply have to take. He looked back over at the waiting consul.

"Very well," Wulfgar said. He walked to his throne and sat down.

"You don't wish to lie down, sire?" Einar asked, sounding concerned.

"Where? On the floor?" Wulfgar shook his head. "No. My throne will do."

As the consul walked to his master's side, the hovering text followed him. Narrowing his eyes, Einar caused the glowing numbers and symbols to rise to a place just above his master's head. He placed one palm upon Wulfgar's brow.

"Are you ready, sire?"

Taking a deep breath, Wulfgar closed his eyes.

"Proceed," he answered. "And may the Afterlife watch over all of your gifts this night."

CHAPTER XI

AS SATINE WALKED HER GELDING DOWN THE NEARLY DESERTED streets of Tammerland, the city seemed gray and mournful. Dead bodies littered the gutters. Rain had recently fallen. It had soaked through her cloak, and the dampness caused her to shiver. Pulling the garment closer, she rode on.

She had been navigating the streets for the last three hours. Dawn would soon arrive. With so few people out and about, it sometimes seemed that she had the entire city to herself, a sensation that she did not mind.

After leaving Ivan, she had followed the winding tunnel to a cramped, windowless shed that opened onto an abandoned alleyway. From there she had made her way to the adjoining street and back to the still-closed archery shop, where she had reclaimed her horse.

Satine had two more stops to make before commencing her sanctions, and she was on her way to the first of them—a personal job, not professional, but one she meant to see through, despite the delay it would cause.

Satine rode the twisting, dilapidated streets until she reached the dead-end alley she had been searching for. She stopped her horse and jumped down. The place was deserted. Deciding to leave the gelding in the street, she tied him to a nearby rail. Then she unfastened the worn leather satchel from the back of her saddle and quickly entered the alley. After another look around, she slipped behind a pile of trash. She hurriedly began changing her clothes in the forgiving darkness.

The woman who emerged looked far different. Her usual leather clothing was gone. Instead she wore a close-fitting outfit of black cloth. On her feet were supple black slippers. Her black scarf was wound completely around her head and face, leaving only her watchful eyes showing. Black gloves covered her hands; her long braid she neatly tucked beneath her clothing. Cloak, bow, and quiver were left behind. Her only weapons were her sword, her four daggers, and her skill. If she was lucky, they would be all she would need. If she were unlucky she would soon be dead, and it wouldn't matter.

She searched the length of the alleyway again. She was still alone. Hurrying to the other side, she flattened herself against the slick wall.

Praying it would hold, she grasped the rusty downspout with both hands and, like a spider, quickly climbed to the roof.

She took a few precious moments to look around again. Still, she saw no one. Turning north, she ran and jumped across the rooftops toward her target.

Satine knew the rooftop terrain well. She had been raised in this area of Tammerland and had played upon these roofs as a child. This night she was a child no more, and her task was deadly serious.

She knew that the sun would soon rise, chasing away her cover of darkness. If she did not reach her target in time, her chance would be lost. Once her sanctions had begun in earnest, there might never be another opportunity like this one.

Finally seeing the familiar roof up ahead, she took a flying leap between buildings and landed surely on all fours. Just as she had hoped, the nearby skylight emitted a soft glow through its frosted glass. Someone in the house beneath her had already risen, and she knew who it would be.

Moving silently to the skylight, she removed one of her daggers from its sheath and began to pry open the window. As it gave way its hinges creaked, and she winced. She replaced the dagger in its sheath, raised the window, and surveyed the room. Then she grasped the edge of the skylight, curled her supple body over it, performing a perfect forward somersault down into the waiting room below, dropping silently onto a table that stood against the near wall.

Before taking her first step down, she looked carefully around the room. Translucent paper filled the wood-framed panes that made up the four walls. The wall opposite her perch held a sliding door.

The foyer she had entered was small and unassuming. A single oil lamp glowed softly across the highly polished hardwood floor. Each of the interlocking floorboards looked perfect and smooth, just as she remembered them. But this floor held a secret.

She looked at the boards, trying to remember which of them were safe to step upon. They were each only the width of an average person's foot. Only eight of them could be traversed without emitting a squeaking sound—an unobtrusive yet effective intruder alert.

Desperately hoping that the path of the boards had not been altered since she had last visited, Satine sat down upon the table and dangled her long legs over the side. She stretched forth a slippered foot and gingerly placed it upon what she remembered to be one of the safe boards. She stayed that way for a moment, wondering whether to put her full weight upon it. Finally, she did. Nothing happened.

With a sigh of relief, she made her way across the room. Blessedly, each of the boards she chose proved to be the correct one. The final board lay just before the sliding door. That was when she heard the sound of footsteps coming down the hall on the other side.

Satine froze. What mattered now was whether the person in the hallway would stop to slide open the door. Satine could move out of view to one side, but if she did, the boards would sound. If she remained where she was and the door opened, there would be no escape.

Holding her breath, she listened intently as the footsteps slowed to a stop directly opposite her on the other side of the paper door. As she stood there, she imagined that she could hear the other person's heart beating. Steeling herself for what might follow, she curled and separated the fingers of her right hand. It would have to be done quickly, and without hesitation.

Silently, the door began to slide open.

Satine leaped into the hallway. Raising her arm, she used the claw of her readied fingers to take him by the throat. He instinctively tried to cry out, but no sound could come. She kneed him in the groin, doubling him over and eradicating his will to fight. She recognized his face, but she refused to let that deter her. Slipping quickly around him, she laced one arm under his throat and choked him unconscious. As she cradled him silently to the floor his eyes fluttered shut. The entire process had been silent, and had taken no more than a few seconds.

Satine placed the tips of her first two fingers to the side of the man's throat. His heartbeat was weak but regular. He would soon regain consciousness and, no doubt, do his best to send out an alarm. From here on she would have to move quickly.

It had not been her intention to kill the man. If it had, he would already be dead. Stepping over him, she silently made her way down the narrow hall toward the next paper door.

She removed one of her daggers from its sheath, and used it to make a short, vertical incision in one of the wall's paper panels. Holding the slit open with the blade of her knife, she peered into the chamber just beyond.

In the center of the room, Satine's true target sat cross-legged, his back to the door, upon a long, green mat. His shiny, shaved head reflected the light of the oil lamps. He wore a short white robe covered by a pleated black cloth skirt. Its ties wound around his waist and ended in a distinctive knot. He was barefoot and still, save for an occasional movement of his hands. A familiar scent drifted to Satine's nostrils, and she realized that he was taking his morning tea. She moved away from the slit.

The most difficult part would be gaining entrance to the room without him hearing her do it. The door before her was the only way in. She slid it open just enough for her body to slip sideways through the opening. Reaching behind her back, she soundlessly unsheathed her sword.

She took two measured steps forward and then stopped. Lifting the blade over her head with both hands she crept forward again, stopping less than a meter from the unsuspecting man's back. Intent upon taking his head from his shoulders with a single strike, Satine brought the sword down and around with all her strength.

The moment her blade began cutting through the air, the man leaped to his feet, faced her, and raised his hands. As the razor-sharp blade whistled around, he clamped his open palms down upon either flat side of it, halting it in midstroke. Helpless to retrieve the sword from his iron grip, Satine looked into the eyes of the man who had just bested her.

Then, smiling to herself behind her mask, she released her hold upon her sword. Just as she had been taught, she let her arms fall to either side. Her opponent smiled.

Suddenly, he tossed the weapon into the air. It turned over twice, its silver blade flashing. He caught it one-handed by the hilt. Turning it around, he handed it to her. After giving him a short, respectful bow, she took it. The man returned her bow.

"Hello, my child," he said simply. The timbre of his voice was old, calm, and reassuring. "It is good to see you again."

After sheathing her sword, Satine unwound the black scarf from around her face. "And you, master," she answered back. "I am glad to see that your skill at blade-catching has not diminished."

The old man embraced her warmly. "And had I not reacted in time, would you have halted your blow?" he asked.

"Of course," she answered. "But we both know that has never been necessary."

Smiling, the old man beckoned for her to sit with him. Satine lowered herself to the green mat.

She recognized the familiar blue and white tea service sitting before her. As the old man came to sit opposite her he offered her some, and she accepted. She took a long draft of the rich, black tea, then looked back into the wise eyes of the man she so loved and respected.

For many years Aeolus had been both her teacher and her surrogate father. Then had come that fateful day when she had finally decided to leave her post here at his school, and strike out on her own. It had been a hard decision, and she knew that the choice of her current occupation brought the old man heartache and worry. But he also knew why she had done it. In some ways, even he could not completely disagree with the dangerous path she had chosen.

The bald head that he shaved every morning glinted in the light, and his penetrating eyes regarded her calmly. The neatly trimmed gray beard was just as she remembered, and the still-muscular body that belied his eighty Seasons of New Life remained coiled and ever ready beneath the folds of his martial garments. Satine took another sip of the tea, then put down her cup.

"You heard me in the hall, didn't you?" she asked. "When I rendered Morgan unconscious."

"Truth be known, I first sensed your presence when you pried open the skylight," Aeolus answered. "After all, who could take morning tea properly with all of that infernal racket? You made more noise than a thunderbeast! I taught you better than that!" Then he looked concerned. "I assume Morgan will suffer no lasting effects?"

"No," she answered. "Although I doubt he will be pleased when he wakes up. What will you tell him?"

Aeolus smiled. "Only that upon my orders he was being tested by another student, one who shall remain nameless. Besides, his shame at having been bested will probably overcome any curiosity he might have about who it might have been.

Serves him right! He should never have been caught off guard like that. Still, I suggest that you use the front door next time. It makes things so much easier."

She smiled again. "True," she answered. "But not nearly so interesting."

Aeolus' mood became more somber. He put down his cup. "You have not visited here for more than a year," he said. "Then you suddenly appear in your combat garb, and clandestinely enter my school through the rooftop. It is apparent that you want your visit to be kept secret. Why are you here? And why do you seem so burdened?"

She took a deep breath. "I have come to tell you some things," she began. "And I need to ask for your help."

Aeolus shifted his weight and stared at her. Realizing he was not going to respond, Satine chose her next words carefully.

"After the successful completion of the sanctions I have recently accepted, I will be retiring from this life," she announced.

Looking into Aeolus' eyes, she expected to see joy at her news. She was well acquainted with how much he disapproved of her profession. Instead, she was surprised to see a look of increased concern cross her master's face.

"I would prefer that you retire *now*," he said quietly. "This very day, in fact. My opinion on this issue had not changed. But you also know that as long as I draw breath, you will always have a home here."

"Thank you," she responded. "But this last mission is far more dangerous than any I have ever accepted. The sum I demanded reflects that. With this money I can finally retire, and spend the rest of my life pursuing my other goal."

Aeolus' face darkened. "This personal vendetta of yours will never bring your father back," he said to her. "Even if you find the man who killed him. I loved Jacob as though he was my own son. You know that. He was not only my finest instructor, but also my best friend. But he's been gone ten years. You must let it go, if you are to have any semblance of a normal life. I would have thought that your years here at the Serpent and the Sword would have taught you that."

Satine looked down at the floor. "Apparently I was never destined for a normal life," she answered. "Surely you, above all people, can see that. I simply cannot rest until I find Father's killer—even if *you* have somehow made your personal peace with it."

Memories of her childhood flooded her mind. Her mother had died giving birth to her, but her father had worked tirelessly to make up for the loss.

Jacob had been Aeolus' head instructor at the martial school known as the Discipline of the Serpent and the Sword. The serpent represented the various skills of hand-to-hand combat, and the sword stood for the arts of armed combat. Satine was a master of both. As a widower, Jacob had been forced to bring his young daughter to the school with him every day. The school had quickly become her second home.

When Satine was twelve, Aeolus asked her and Jacob to move in with him full-time—a common practice in Eutracian martial arts circles. At that point, Satine began her formal training. It had even been discussed that one day her father would inherit the school from the childless Aeolus, and Satine would then become her father's head instructor. Sadly, none of that had come to pass.

In a fit of jealous rage, one of the lesser students who had been passed over for the title of head instructor killed her father in his own bed. At the time it was rumored that the murderer had been under the influence of a mind-altering drug designed to enhance one's enlightenment. He had then run away, using his considerable skills to become one with the night. Satine had given chase, but to no avail.

Satine had been twenty-five years old at the time, and her father's murder had forged within her an intense need both to find his assailant and to make the man suffer mightily before she finally killed him.

She knew that to find her father's killer she would need money, and lots of it. To acquire money, she would need a trade. The only skills she possessed that might generate such sums were her combat arts. When she made the decision to defy Aeolus' teachings of peace and serenity, she reluctantly left the school and she began selling her skills to the highest bidder.

And so she wandered Eutracia, searching for both her next sanction, and the vile monster who had killed her father. Her reputation grew quickly. Soon, rather than having to search for work, she was being sought out. In between commissions she used up every kisa of the money she had earned. She knew her quarry's name; once she had missed him at a local tavern by only a day. Since then she had not been so fortunate, and it often seemed to her that the vermin she chased had somehow disappeared from the face of the earth. But her determination had not flagged.

She looked back at Aeolus. "There is something else you need to understand," she said haltingly, unsure quite how to tell him.

"And that is?" her master asked.

"My new sanctions are to be political killings," she said. "Given how much you always supported both the monarchy of Nicholas I and the Directorate of Wizards, I thought this was something you should be aware of. You know that I have no such political leanings. But I would like to ask that, should it become necessary, I can come here to hide. Now that you have been told, if you wish to dismiss me from your life forever, I will understand." Her gaze went to the floor.

"It's true that I once favored the monarchy, and the wizards who helped to guide it," Aeolus answered. He rolled his teacup between his palms. "But times have changed. It is widely known that the prince killed his father, and that he is in league with the very winged demons that butchered so many. It is also rumored that he has caused some manifestation of magic to go about Eutracia, destroying everything in its path, and that the surviving wizards gladly serve his purposes." He raised a questioning eyebrow at her. "You have no doubt seen the bodies in the streets?" he asked. Satine nodded.

"Whether these rumors have merit is not for me to say," Aeolus stated. Then his demeanor stiffened, and he leaned forward a bit.

"The path you have chosen will be dangerous," he said seriously. "You are about to go to war with those who command the craft of magic. They are far more proficient in death-dealing than you or I could imagine. I cannot condone what you are about to do. But if you need a place to hide in order to save your own life, you will be welcome here."

Aeolus thought for a moment. "Given what you have just told me, I assume you will be visiting the community of partial adepts?" he asked.

Satine nodded.

Aeolus sighed. "Such a vile place," he said. "Are you sure that you must go there?"

"Yes," she answered. "These new sanctions will surely be the most difficult of my career."

"Will you be dealing with the rogue herbmaster, Reznik?"

"Yes," she said. "There is no other choice."

Realizing that she had accomplished everything she had come to do, Satine knew it was time to leave. She reclaimed her sword from the floor and stood. Aeolus came to his feet with her. She had almost forgotten how tall and imposing he was.

"Goodbye, my child," he said softly. "May the Afterlife watch over you."

She took both of his gnarled hands into hers. "And you," she said softly, then turned, walked out the door, and didn't look back.

The master instructor sat back down upon the floor mat and took another sip of tea. Distantly, he heard the almost inaudible sound of the skylight hinges creaking shut, telling him that his greatest student had just departed. Then the muffled sound of thunder signaled the return of the storm.

Typically, Satine had been purposefully coy about the identities of her targets. He knew that had he asked her their names, she would not have told him—and he appreciated her desire to protect him by keeping him in the dark. But he could guess. And if he was right, and her targets were those of the royal house or the wizards they commanded, he wasn't sure he could accept that.

Short of killing her, Aeolus knew that there would be nothing he could do to stop Satine, and killing her wasn't an option he was willing to consider. He understood all too well that her impending mission would soon force him to make a life-altering choice. A choice between two people he very much loved and respected.

The thunder came again, and he looked sadly down into his teacup.

CHAPTER XII

TRISTAN SAT IN A HIGH-BACKED CHAIR ATOP THE CARPETED DAIS and watched people stream into the Chamber of Supplication. A flood of terrible memories plagued him. The last time he had appeared before so many of his subjects had been on his coronation day, when the Sorceresses of the Coven had attacked. This time, although the room and the purpose of the gathering were very different, the mood was in many ways the same. As on that awful day not so long ago, these citizens gathered before him were angry, terrified, and unsure of the future. As before, they believed the craft lay at the heart of all their troubles.

The prince couldn't help but wonder whether any of these people had actually seen him kill his father, or witnessed the barbaric slaughter of the Directorate of Wizards. The terrible things he had done that day had been forced upon him, but many of these people would not know that. They no doubt had also lost loved ones to the ferocious Minions of Day and Night, long before he had become the winged warriors' new lord.

Worse yet, rumor and innuendo always tore through Eutracia like wildfire, especially where the royal family was concerned. As was always the case with gossip, much of it was sure to be outright lies. He desperately needed his subjects' trust and understanding. But he knew that securing those things would be difficult.

Tristan glanced around. The Chamber of Supplication was the second largest room in the palace; only the Great Hall was larger. He had ruled out the Great Hall as a meeting place. That was where the Coven and the Minions had first appeared and then done so much of their dirty work. Asking his already traumatized subjects to return there would have been too great a burden for many of them to bear, not to mention the effect the place would have on Wigg, the prince's twin sister, and perhaps even him.

Excepting Geldon, all the members of the Conclave of the Vigors were seated with him upon the dais. The hunchbacked dwarf and Ox had left the previous evening with a phalanx of Minion warriors to determine the whereabouts of the ruptured Orb of the Vigors. So far, no word had been received.

Abbey, Celeste, Adrian, Shailiha, and Tyranny were seated on the prince's right. Wigg, Faegan, and Traax were on his left. He had given some thought to excluding the Minion warrior from these proceedings, for Traax's presence would no doubt startle and inflame many of the attendees. Then he had reconsidered. Traax was a full-fledged member of the Conclave, and he deserved to be treated as such.

Tristan looked around the room, remembering how important this chamber had once been to his father and to the Directorate of Wizards. The Chamber of Supplication was the hall in which the king and the late Directorate had heard requests from the populace at large. This usually occurred on the first of each month. Hundreds of people had attended, each seeming to bear a request more urgent than the last.

Tristan remembered sitting here by the king's side, as Nicholas quietly considered petitions. The prince had listened intently, in preparation for when he would become king. Those days seemed far away.

The morning breeze gently moved the patterned draperies by the open stained-glass windows. Dappled pillars of morning sunshine streamed in, making the highly polished marble of the chamber shine. It was almost as if Wigg and Faegan had enchanted the room, making it eager to be of use again.

Seeing that the hall was now filled to overflowing, Tristan looked over at Wigg. The First Wizard nodded. Shailiha gave her brother a brief smile of reassurance. After taking a deep breath, Tristan stood and held his arms wide in a gesture of welcome.

"Citizens, subjects, and friends!" he began loudly. "I am Prince Tristan, son of Nicholas and Morganna, the late king and queen of Eutracia! You have been invited to this hall in peace, and no harm will befall you. I know you have many questions and concerns, and we on the dais will attempt to answer them for you. Before that begins, I must tell you the story of how and why our nation has arrived at this crossroads. It is a tale that you may find incredible. But it is true, nonetheless."

Pausing, Tristan looked out over the crowd. The faces staring back at him looked angry and skeptical, and not a few of them glowered with outright hatred. But all were silent. For the time being, at least, they seemed willing to hear what he had to say.

He went on to tell them of the attack by the Coven of Sorceresses, of how Shailiha had been kidnapped, and of what he and Wigg had suffered to bring her and the Paragon home again. He explained the return of his son Nicholas from the Afterlife, and the subsequent construction and destruction of the Gates of Dawn, followed by his son's death. Lastly he told them of the Scrolls of the Ancients, and of his lost half brother named Wulfgar, who had tried to employ the scrolls to pollute the Orb of the Vigors. He went on to say that this was the manifestation of the craft that had already wounded so many of them and caused the destruction of Brook Hollow.

He introduced each person on the dais, explaining the various contributions each of them had made in the name of their nation. By prior agreement with Faegan and Wigg, when he introduced Adrian he was careful to make no mention of the secret order of the Acolytes of the Redoubt. When he finally finished, he cast his gaze back and forth over the crowd, searching for reactions. They weren't long in coming.

The first to address him was a man dressed in modest peasant garb. He looked tired and worn, and his right hand had obviously been recently bandaged. Jumping to his feet, he raised his injured limb and pointed it at the prince.

"Liar!" he shouted loudly. "You say your newly formed Conclave wishes to protect us from the orb! But what you really want to do is to kill us all! Don't lie to us! I saw you do it, that day you destroyed Brook Hollow! You and your wizard came flying out of the east in the litter your winged monsters carried. Then I saw Wigg raise his arms and cause the orb to fly directly over the town and turn it to ash! What other cities have you ordered that abomination of the craft to destroy, while at the same time you try to blind us with your little speeches about goodwill, eh? Don't lie to me! I lost my wife and both my sons in Brook Hollow! I watched them die, helpless to do anything about it! If I thought I could get away with it, I'd kill you right now with my bare hands! You aren't half the man your father was, and everyone here knows that!"

As others in the crowd began to shout and wave their fists in agreement, the man who had just berated Tristan suddenly took a brazen step toward the dais. Traax immediately leaped to his feet and drew his dreggan.

Hearing the blade's familiar ring, Tristan snapped around. He shook his head, tacitly ordering the warrior to stand down. It was clear that the situation could rapidly deteriorate, and violence was the last thing he wanted. His face a mask, Traax finally slid the sword back into its scabbard and reluctantly took his seat.

Even though Tristan had not been prepared to hear it, sadly he had to admit that the bereaved man actually made a sort of perverse sense. Had their roles been reversed, Tristan could imagine himself coming to the same conclusion—especially considering all of the false, hateful tales circulating about him. But before he could formulate a reply, Wigg came to stand by his side.

"The truth is that I was trying to turn the orb *away* from the village, not toward it," the First Wizard said to the crowd, "but I was unsuccessful. If you choose not to believe me, there is little I can do about it. But before you make up your minds, there is something I would like to show you all."

Raising one arm, Wigg pulled back the sleeve of his robe. Despite the spell of accelerated healing he had placed over it, the skin of his arm still looked raw and painful.

"This is my reward for trying to help you," the wizard said, as he held his arm up for all to see. Lowering it again, he placed his hands into the opposite sleeves of his robe. "We must all fight this disaster together if we are to have any hope of succeeding. The rupture of the orb is the greatest threat we have ever faced, including the return of the Coven of Sorceresses."

"But I saw you kill your own father!" a woman shouted at the prince, jumping to her feet. She had two small children by her side. "You can't deny that!" Her voice was nearly hysterical. "I was there! It is said that you carry that very sword to this day!"

Looking down at her, Tristan took a measured step forward. Silence crept over the room. Reaching behind his back, he slowly drew his dreggan. As it left its scabbard, the blade sent its familiar ring through the air.

"Do you mean this one?" he asked.

Then he calmly pushed the hidden button on the hilt that was common to all such Minion swords. He felt the dreggan jump in his hand as its blade immediately shot forward by another foot. Many in the crowd jumped back in their seats.

"Yes," Tristan said. To anyone who knew him well, it was clear that his frustration was beginning to seep through. "This is the sword that I used to kill my father! I admit it. Had I not, the warrior Kluge would have killed your king slowly, hewing him to pieces." Walking still closer to the edge of the dais, the prince looked down at the woman.

"So you tell me," he said. "Given only those two choices, had it been *your* father's head upon the block, what would you have done?"

Tristan thrust the tip of the blade into the carpeted dais. The sword stood upright before him, swaying gently back and forth. When it slowed, he took another step nearer then he opened his palms, and raised them for all to see.

"Look at my hands!" he shouted. "Do you see these scars? I put them there myself, when I took a blood oath to find my parents' killers and to bring the princess and the Paragon back to Eutracia! If we are to have any hope of surviving both the ruptured orb and those who would use it against us, you must trust the Conclave!"

"And what if we do believe all of your rubbish?" another man yelled. Around him, others had jumped to their feet and were talking with one another in urgent tones.

"We don't trust the craft, and we don't trust your dealings with it!" the man went on. "The craft has brought us nothing but suffering and death, while its practitioners constantly vie for control of it! As far as we know, you may be as bad as these supposed enemies you speak of—or perhaps even worse! And pray, tell us, *my lord,* with King Nicholas now dead by your own hand, do you profess to be our new sovereign?"

Tristan lowered his head. The title of king was once something he would have done anything to avoid. Now he found that he wanted it with all his heart. He had yet to formally take the oath that would grant him that privilege. Eutracian law stated that until he did so, he would remain prince. For some time he had kept silent about his reasons for waiting. But now he decided that he should reveal his feelings both to his subjects and to the newly formed Conclave.

Beckoning Wigg closer, Tristan walked to the very edge of the platform. When Wigg reached him, Tristan leaned over and whispered into the First Wizard's ear.

A skeptical look came over Wigg's face. "Are you sure about this?" he whispered back.

"Just do it," the prince said under his breath. He held out his right arm.

A small incision formed in Tristan's wrist. Under Wigg's guidance, a single drop of azure blood rose from the wound and hovered in the air.

From beneath his robes, the First Wizard produced a small pewter vial. He opened it and caused a single drop of the red water of the Caves of the Paragon to come floating through the air toward the single drop of Tristan's blood. There was a pause, and then the two raced toward each other and joined. As they did, a hush came over the crowd.

Tristan watched as the combination of fluids twisted and then turned into his glowing azure blood signature. With a swift calculation of the craft, Wigg magnified the blood signature's size, so that everyone in the Chamber of Supplication could see it. As Tristan had hoped, the chamber was now absolutely still.

Speaking quickly into the silence, Tristan went on to explain, in the simplest of terms, what the blood signature was. He told them about how his blood had turned azure the day he defeated the Coven of the Sorceresses. At last he paused and pointed to his blood signature as it twinkled wetly in the soft morning light.

"Rather than controlling the craft, I am as much a prisoner of it as anyone, perhaps even more so," he said. "For until a way can be found to return my blood to its original state, the wizards may not train me in the arts of magic. Nor am I allowed to give the kingdom an heir." A distinct sadness crept over his face.

"One day, I shall take the oath as your sovereign," he finished at last. "But I shall refuse to do so until my blood is whole again and I can be trained in the craft, just as my late father would have been. Not until then will I presume to call myself your king."

With that Tristan dismissed the meeting. As he watched the somber crowd disperse, the remaining members of the Conclave came forward to join him.

He reclaimed his sword from the floor and returned it to its scabbard. Celeste and Shailiha each gave him a reassuring hug. Tristan looked down at Faegan, and then at Wigg.

"Do you think they believed us?" he asked.

"That is difficult to say," Wigg answered. "Some may have, but many certainly did not. They have suffered much and, until we can find a way to heal the orb, may suffer a great deal more. In my more than three centuries, I have never seen the populace more distrustful. Even during the height of the Sorceresses' War they were more trusting. I sense that they would like to believe in you, and that is what is most important. Now that the spark of trust has been rekindled, we must be careful how we fan the flame."

Faegan wheeled his chair a bit closer. "I never had the privilege of knowing your parents," the ancient wizard said in his gravely voice. "But I have no doubt that they would have been proud of what you did here today. At the very least, this is a start. Remember, even the greatest of journeys must always begin with a single step."

AT THE VERY BACK OF THE ROOM ONE OF THE MEETING attendees walked out promptly, well ahead of the other departing subjects. Quickly traversing the palace grounds and striding across the lowered drawbridge, the cloaked figure jumped upon the waiting horse and then wheeled him around.

Gathering her cloak around her, the Gray Fox galloped away, up the narrow street and on toward her next assignation.

CHAPTER XIII

WHEN THE VOICES FIRST REVEALED THEMSELVES TO HIM, HE feared he had suddenly gone mad. Then he understood. They were the result of the activation of the Forestallment.

That had been two days ago. Now, as he stood on the terrace overlooking the broad ocean, the *Enseterat* had never felt more confident or more powerful.

Just as the *Jin'Sai* had his wizards, Wulfgar now had his own allies. But his were were infinitely more powerful in their abilities to aid him. Tristan, his mind still burdened with his tainted, untrained blood, had yet to unleash such power. And the Scroll of the Vigors—the only tool that might possibly help him heal the great orb—was irreversibly damaged.

It was late afternoon at the Citadel, and the sea was high again. Seabirds swooped and called out to one another as they skimmed the frothy waves, their sharp eyes searching the blue-green shallows for their next meal. The sky was overcast and the wind blustery, and the salt-laden air smelled pleasantly of both brine and the tangled seaweed that continually washed up against the rocks of the shore.

Turning his gaze to the bay, Wulfgar looked over to the growing fleet of strong, new ships that he had only recently released from the depths where they had been imprisoned for more than three centuries. Superior to the demonslaver vessels in every way, they would prove to be the mightiest armada of the Vagaries ever assembled. Then would come the captains to sail them. Unlike the unendowed, white-skinned slavers who had failed him, these beings had once been masterful commanders of their craft.

All this was due to the new Forestallment—and the voices it had brought. Einar had promised he would hear them, but nothing in the world could have adequately prepared Wulfgar for the experience.

It had been early evening, and the *Enseterat* and his queen were taking dinner on the spacious balcony of their quarters. Wulfgar was about to ask her how she was feeling, when, to Serena's horror, he suddenly clutched the sides of his head. With a scream of agony, he fell backward, chair and all, and began to writhe uncontrollably on the marble floor. Helpless, Serena watched as Wulfgar struggled in the grip of something neither of them understood.

Then, fearing for her husband's life, she sent for Einar. But by the time the lead consul arrived, Wulfgar's pain had departed and he had calmed.

Rising from the floor, the *Enseterat* turned and looked at Einar and his wife. There was a renewed sense of power and majesty about him, a greatness that they had never seen. As though he were the only person in the world, Wulfgar silently turned his gaze away from them and out toward the shifting sea.

That was when the voices first came, a soulful chorus that overwhelmed him. Out of sheer reverence, he fell to his knees.

"Wulfgar," they began, *"you have finally been granted the Forestallment that allows us to commune with your mind."*

"Who are you?" he thought. Instinctively, he knew that he did not need to speak aloud to be heard by them.

"We are the Heretics of the Guild." The voices were melodic, soothing. *"We welcome you to our service. The pain you just endured was the result of our initial communication; you shall not have to bear it again. Despite the initial defeat of your demonslaver fleet, you have done well. The Orb of the Vigors continues to bleed, and we must allow nothing to interfere with that. Your employment of the female assassin was a wise precaution, but in the end, you shall require far more than just her unendowed skills to secure the prizes you seek. You must remember well the information we are about to impart to you, for what we grant you now will lead you to the final victory."*

The chorus faded, and was replaced by a whirling riot of azure numbers and letters roaring in his mind—all of them in Old Eutracian. He closed his eyes and stared at the glowing formulas that danced brightly against the infinite blackness behind his eyelids. Finally they slowed, and he began to grasp what they represented.

They comprised an index to the massive Scroll of the Vagaries.

Wulfgar's heart leaped for joy. Until now, both the scroll's great size and its overwhelming complexity had made it difficult to decipher. The calculations for the thousands of Forestallments it contained were recorded upon it randomly. No concern had been given to categorizing what type of gift each individual formula might grant, or what subdivision of the craft it fell into.

As a result, it took weeks for his consuls to find any particular set of calculations. But with the index at their disposal, they would be free to peruse the scroll at will and quickly make its teachings their own.

Over the course of the last two days, Wulfgar and Einar had done exactly that. The calculations that the Heretics had granted the *Enseterat* gave him the power not only to free his new fleet from the depths, but to summon the majestic beings who would man them. It would be an unparalleled force able to crush the *Jin'Sai*, his Minions of Day and Night, and the wizards of the Redoubt. But first Wulfgar had to retrieve the ships.

Wulfgar smiled. The clearing sky revealed the three Eutracian moons, their magenta glow shining down upon the ocean. He raised his hands.

Almost at once the sky crackled with azure lighting, and the Isle of the Citadel trembled before the cascades of thunder. Concentrating with all of his might, he caused the water of the bay to burble and roil.

First a ship's crow's nest appeared, breaking through the waves. The tips of several masts soon followed. Then the massive hull and superstructures emerged, their lengths awash with seawater. After more than three centuries, the great vessel finally rose to float again upon the ocean beside its sisters. Wulfgar lowered his hands and stared at the vessel with rapt admiration.

The Black Ships—the most powerful armada that ever commanded the seas.

As the thunder and azure lightning abated, Wulfgar examined the vessel. Even though he had liberated several of them by now, each time another rose from the depths his jaw dropped in wonder.

With ten full masts and spars as thick as several tree trunks combined, the gigantic black frigate was easily quadruple the size of the largest vessels in his failed demonslaver fleet. For a time her hulk rocked dangerously to and fro, as if she were trying to again become accustomed to lying atop the waves. Finally she found her natural balance and settled down, her only motion coinciding with the normal movement of the sea.

The entire ship was an inky black. Moonlight twinkled on the seawater still running off her topsides, hull, and masts. As the Heretics had told him, eight full decks lay within her, and a massive hinged door took up nearly her entire stern. It could be opened and lowered to a safe distance just above the waves—much the way a drawbridge could be lowered from within the walls of a palace. Even the frigate's massive, furled sails were of the darkest black, as were those of the other Black Ships already anchored nearby.

Wulfgar took a moment to rest before attempting to salvage another of the menacing warships.

"Well done, my lord," Einar said from his place near his master's side. "All is nearly ready. Very soon the *Jin'Sai* will finally taste true defeat, and the world will be yours. I am proud to stand by your side in this greatest of endeavors."

Wulfgar only smiled. As he raised his arms, the moonlit skies began to cry out once more with the coming of the azure lightning and the deafening thunder. The surface of the bay burbled and roiled again, and another massive crow's nest poked through the surface of the waters, searching out its freedom.

CHAPTER XIV

*"A little of this, and a little of that, shall make my concoction
   both potent and fat.
When my brew is finally done, the deaths it will cause shall
   be second to none.
Should the fixings be added too slow, or too quick,
The potion won't work, nor the healthy go sick.
So with patience and care I nimbly proceed,
And I now cast this spell, to strengthen the deed!"*

* * *

UPON COMPLETING THE INCANTATION, REZNIK LOWERED HIS ARMS and placed his face near the pungent steam that rose from the small pot atop the woodstove. Inhaling the wispy aroma, he smiled.

This batch would prove his finest yet. But before it was ready, it would need another incantation. It would also need a few more ingredients before it could rise to the level of quality demanded by Satine.

Crossing to the other side of his spacious cottage, he took down an amber jar from a shelf.

The jar was filled with Eutracian derma-gnashers that he had painstakingly netted the day before. Although not dangerous, the winged, blue-and-gold-striped insects were a great nuisance. One bite would produce itching, swelling, and redness that lasted for days.

Back at his worktable, he placed the jar down and, using one of his collection of finely honed cutting instruments, carefully enlarged one of the holes in the perforated seal that stretched tightly across the jar's top. Into the widened hole he placed the tip of the small ladies' perfume sprayer that he had purchased secondhand at a local Eutracian fair and gave the spray bulb a quick squeeze. The poison, formulated from one of his personal recipes, worked quickly. The derma-gnashers began to die and fall to the bottom.

One by one he removed them and started to dissect them under a magnifying lens. As was his habit when he was happy with the progress of his work, he began to whistle. Eventually he had what he needed—approximately one teaspoon of runny orange-red venom. He walked the stuff over to the pot and poured it in.

Then he took down a thick volume from a bookshelf. Blowing the dust off its cover, he checked the title: *Accelerants and Retardants in the Use of Potions and Poisons.* Balancing the massive book in one hand, he thumbed through it with the other. After several moments of searching, he found the page he was looking for.

He went into an adjoining room and contemplated the bottle-lined shelves. There were hundreds of containers here, each one holding a different ground herb, root, or precious oil. He found the oil of encumbrance and returned to the other room.

Looking back to the book, he ran one finger down the page until he found the line he was looking for. Carefully he measured out a portion of the violet oil and added it to the pot one drop at a time.

Reznik took a deep breath. *Almost done.* By previous agreement with Satine, he was to have a new batch ready every ninety days. He also knew that she would be here within the next couple of hours, for one of the sentries had seen her enter the labyrinth and had sent a runner with the news. Reznik wanted the formula done by the time she arrived. Satine was never one to sit in one place very long. If, for some reason, she was forced to do just that, her mood could markedly change for the worse.

For the final ingredient, Reznik walked to the center of the cottage floor, pushed the throw rug to one side, and reached down to grasp the iron ring embedded in the floorboards. With a quick tug, he pulled open the trapdoor and then let it fall over backward onto the floor. As he walked down the steps and into the darkness, he started to whistle again.

AS SATINE GUIDED HER GELDING THROUGH THE LABYRINTHINE PASsageway, a shudder went through her. She did her best to remain calm. If she didn't, she could become disoriented, take a wrong turn at some point, and die in this place. This was the only way in and out of the community of rogue partial adepts, Reznik had once told her. She hated coming here—but it was a necessary evil.

No potion she had ever found rivaled the quality and effectiveness of Reznik's. Nor had any other tool of assassination ever granted her the all-important margin of safety this one did. It had been one of the mainstays of her art for several years now. Her current sanctions would most certainly call for its use, and she had little left of her last supply.

In order to supply the community with goods, the smooth, square-cut tunnel was wide enough to accommodate even the largest of wagons and teams. But this path was meant only for those partial adepts accepted into the community and able to employ magic in order to recall the safe route through the unforgiving maze. For them, it held no more danger than a walk through a flower garden. Reznik had accompanied Satine through the many twists and turns the first few times she came. After that, he coldly told her that she was on her own, no matter how many kisa she might be willing to pay him for his services. It had only been her ability to pay such large sums that had convinced him to show her the way in the first place. The other partials had been none too happy to know that he had brought her here.

But after Reznik's payment of a few well-placed bribes, even the more distrustful had grudgingly decided to ignore Satine's occasional comings and goings. Provided, of course, that she didn't visit too often, or reveal the secret to anyone else.

As usual she had seen the sentries high atop the sheer, smooth bluff. Recognizing her, one of them waved his hand and a section of the rock wall slowly darkened to reveal the passageway. Spurring her horse onward, she nervously entered the tunnel. The darkness closed in around her as the sentry sealed the entrance again.

The tunnels were slick and sheer, about five meters high. Enchanted wall torches burned continually, producing no smoke. There were numerous intersections, each of which had to be navigated correctly. Reznik had told her that if even one wrong branch was selected, the craft would immediately sense it and arise to kill her—but he never told her what form her death might take.

While Satine's horse walked along, the clip-clop of his hooves rang out crisply, and the scent of the torches combined with the fetid smell of damp mildew clinging to the walls. Shivering slightly, she drew her gray cloak closer and began to search for the first of the marks she had surreptitiously scratched into the walls with her dagger the last time she had come here with Reznik.

But as she approached the first crossing, her heart skipped a beat and she pulled her horse up short. Even in the flickering torchlight, she could see that her life-preserving marks had been eradicated.

The partial adepts must have finally discovered her secret. Now she would have to find her way through twenty deadly intersections by means of memory alone.

Turning in her saddle, she looked longingly back the way she had come. She could wheel her horse around and leave. She hadn't been through any of the intersections yet, so going back now would all but guarantee her safety. Provided, of course, that one of the sentries sensed her presence and opened the exit. But if she turned back she would never gain her potion, which she absolutely needed to fulfill her sanctions.

She considered abandoning the mission entirely and running.

But she had already accepted partial payment from Wulfgar. Should she try to double-cross him, his wrath would be great and his reach long. She had no desire to be looking over her shoulder for the rest of her life, continually wondering when one of his vengeful consuls would suddenly come looming out of the dark.

Satine began to sweat. There was no man or blade in the world that she feared. This was different, however. The craft was at work here, and there was nothing she could do to change that. Trying to control her emotions, she looked carefully at the first of the intersections.

Four separate paths branched off in various directions. Wall torches hung at their entrances, beckoning her forward. She felt fairly certain about which path to take at this first juncture. Taking a deep breath, Satine reached down toward her right thigh and slid one of her daggers from its sheath.

She gently spurred her horse forward toward the first path on the right, reaching out as she did so to mark the wall with her blade. That should at least help guide her back during her return.

Providing, of course, she returned at all.

CHAPTER XV

WITH HIS SHORT NECK CRANED OVER THE SIDE OF THE LITTER AND the wind tearing at his hair and clothes, Geldon searched for the Orb of the Vigors. When the destroyed village of Brook Hollow came into sight, he ordered the litter down so that they might search for survivors. When his litter finally came to rest in a nearby field, the hunchbacked dwarf felt his stomach turn over as he surveyed the destruction. The accompanying Minion phalanx landed warily all around him, dreggans drawn.

Most of the village had disappeared, reduced to little more than piles of rubble. Strangely, random areas of the town stood unharmed, as though nothing untoward had happened at all. Smoke and ash swirled in the wind, occasionally blotting out the sun, and the stench of dead and burned bodies lingered with the heat.

Geldon turned sadly toward Ox. The Minion warrior was as overcome as he was.

"Ox never hear of so much bad happen so fast," he said. "Even Minion war party not able make such death in so short time."

Geldon pointed to the haphazard rows of surviving homes. "I want a group of warriors to search those dwellings for survivors. If you find any, bring them straight to me."

Nodding, Ox went to pass on the order, and several warriors immediately took flight.

Geldon removed a handkerchief from his trousers and held it over his nose and mouth as he walked deeper into town. Ox and the remaining Minions followed silently along, the still-warm cinders crunching beneath their boots.

A baby's burnt crib lay here, a father's boot there. Parts of chimneys still stood valiantly, like charred, broken fingers pointing accusingly at the sky. Those corpses that hadn't been completely consumed by the orb's energy lay all about, contorted in death, the remnants of their clothing flapping in the breeze. The charred skeletons of entire families could be seen holding on to one another.

Flies had been feasting here for some time. In the sky, vultures careened and turned.

His first instinct was to burn all of the dead upon funeral pyres. There were enough warriors to do the job, and he felt the victims deserved at least that much. But he couldn't spare the time. Tristan would be aching for a report, and they had to keep moving if they were to find the rampaging orb. Saying nothing, he lowered his head and walked on.

Then, in an open spot in the rubble, Geldon saw a small, charred body. It had been turned to ash, but the shape remained: long hair splayed out and hands stretched forth in a posture of beseeching, as though begging the orb not to harm him or her.

Kneeling down, Geldon found himself saddened, yet mesmerized. It was like looking into the recent past, and seeing a moment captured forever.

A sudden gust came up and scattered the ashes to the winds. Just like the village of Brook Hollow, the memory of the young child was no more.

Standing slowly, Geldon saw that the Minion search party was returning—without survivors. Landing in the rubble beside him and Ox, the officer in charge snapped his heels together.

"All of the standing houses are empty," the officer said. "Whoever once lived in them, do so no more."

Nodding at the officer, Geldon looked over at Ox.

"What do now?" Ox asked.

"We do what we came for," Geldon answered. "We find the ruptured orb, and we send a report back to the *Jin'Sai*. May the Afterlife grant that we find no more disasters such as this."

Turning, Geldon left the death site of the anonymous child and led the Minions back to his litter.

TWO HOURS LATER, THEY STILL HADN'T LOCATED THE ORB. THEY knew that finding it would only be a matter of time, for the destruction it left in its wake was impossible to miss. After Brook Hollow, the charred, smoking chasm in the ground was the most telling sign of its passing.

They soon came upon the place where the orb's zigzagging path entered the waters of the Sippora.

The dripping energy had apparently entered the river directly east of where Fledgling House sat quietly nestled at the base of the Tolenka Mountains. Fed by melting snows and glacial runoff, the river was notoriously cold. But as they all looked on in awe, it was clear that the mighty Sippora had been assaulted by a power that even Wigg and Faegan could not have mustered. The Sippora was *boiling* over its banks.

Multiple geysers of steaming water flew hundreds of feet into the air—so high that the flying Minions had to convey the litter farther up. As the hissing, superheated water landed again, it scorched white all of the vegetation it touched. The heavy steam rising from the river made it difficult to see, and even at this altitude it burned their skin.

The litter rocked back and forth wildly, threatening to buckle in the heat. Geldon had no choice but to order his bearers higher yet. Urgently wiping the moisture from his eyes, Geldon looked down.

Thrown free by the surging geysers, dead, stinking fish lay all along the banks. New plumes of steam and water continued to erupt. It was as if all of the various powers of nature had suddenly joined to go berserk in this one spot. But it wasn't nature that had gone berserk, Geldon realized. It was the very craft itself.

The spectacle was as hypnotizing as it was terrifying. Still, he knew there was nothing that they could do here. They needed to move on. Finally, he shouted orders to Ox, and the litter and its protective phalanx traveled north, between the base of the majestic Tolenkas and the impossible, boiling river.

AFTER ANOTHER HOUR OF FLIGHT, GELDON AND HIS WARRIORS caught up to the orb. It had finally ceased following the river and had begun zigzagging its way northwest, the telltale canyon snaking along in its wake like the blood trail of a wounded animal.

As they drew nearer, the heat from the scarred earth below became far more intense and the smoke thickened. Then they began to hear screeching and howling. The noise was deafening.

At last they saw it. Thunderstruck, Geldon watched as the wounded Orb of the Vigors burned its way across a field, and then tore into the pine forest lining the base of the Tolenka Mountains, setting fire to everything in its path and lighting up the dark forest in every direction. Undeterred by the thick trees, it crashed through the woods with offshoots of the palest white radiating from its sides. Around it, the raging forest fire leaped higher and higher. Soon the rising smoke became so thick that they could barely see what was happening. Tears filling his eyes, the dwarf lowered his head.

This was not the same orb Geldon had seen that night on the palace roof, when Wigg and Abbey had defeated Wulfgar. This was a wounded, suffering thing. Careening to and fro without reason, it screamed in pain.

Geldon had no idea whether the orb might actually be a sentient being. But right now he pitied it and wanted to help. He just didn't know how. That was when the other sounds of torment began reaching their ears.

Many of them already ablaze, beasts and birds barreled from the fiery inferno in wild-eyed panic. The hordes of terrified wildlife trampled one another as they tried to escape. Geldon had never known that animals could sound so human as they screamed in their suffering.

Now hundreds of birds—many of them ablaze—were flying out of the forest and directly at the litter and the Minion phalanx. They were a living, breathing cloud of darkness and fire.

Part of Geldon's litter burst into flames. Through the fire and smoke, he caught sight of Ox signaling to the others, and the litter lurched sickeningly upward. Holding on as best he could, Geldon felt his stomach rise into his throat.

Birds pummeled him and the struggling warriors, their beaks and claws puncturing skin. Flying with all their might, the Minions climbed faster, until they finally broke out of the swarming, dying birds.

Geldon leaned out to watch the scene below, and suddenly he understood what was about to happen.

All of the land animals so desperately trying to escape the fires were about to charge into the smoking, superheated ditch left by the Orb of the Vigors.

Their vision clouded by the smoke still spewing from the canyon, the unsuspecting creatures ran straight over the edge. Amid bloodcurdling cries and the sound of snapping limbs, they exploded into flames. After what seemed like an eternity their numbers finally thinned and it was over. A sickening stench rose from the mass grave.

Geldon looked over at Ox. Both were bloody and wounded, but alive. Looking around, he could see that they had lost some of their warriors. Those who remained alive were covered with wounds and completely spent. With a nod, he told Ox to order them down.

His damaged litter came to earth a safe distance from the forest, and Geldon set foot upon the ground on shaking legs. Turning, he looked back to find the rampaging orb. Despite all of the smoke, he could still see it: it was plowing through the woods, setting countless more trees ablaze.

As the exhausted Minions half-landed, half-fell to the ground around him, he walked as close to the smoldering canyon as he dared. He could smell the carnage.

Everything he had seen that day suddenly became too much to bear, and the waves of nausea came. This time he had no choice but to go to his knees and simply let the sickness come.

CHAPTER XVI

LOOKING UP FROM THE SCROLL HE WAS READING, FAEGAN WEARILY rubbed his eyes. "Have you found anything?" he asked.

Wigg, Abbey, Adrian, and Celeste all glumly shook their heads. They had been deep into research for two days, but the secret they were searching for had yet to reveal itself. Frowning, Faegan let go a sigh as he watched his companions go back to their studies.

Rubbing the back of his neck, he took a moment's respite to look around the great room. Nicodemus sat contentedly in his lap. Without looking down, Faegan scratched the cat under the chin.

The five of them sat at a table in the Archives—the great library of the craft, located deep beneath the palace.

The square chamber measured at least two hundred meters on each side, and was seven stories deep. Seven levels of bookshelves lined the walls, each level bordered by a walkway and railing and accessed by a magnificent set of curved mahogany stairs.

The floor and ceiling of the Archives were of dark green marble shot through with traces of gray and magenta. Several hundred finely carved desks, reading tables, and beautifully upholstered chairs were tastefully arranged on the bottom floor. Golden light was supplied by a combination of oil-lamp chandeliers, wall sconces, and table lamps, all enchanted to burn eternally and without smoke. The room smelled pleasantly of must and old parchment.

Faegan had asked the others here because they were the only other members of the Conclave of the Vigors who could read Old Eutracian, the lost language in which the Tome of the Paragon, the Scroll of the Vigors, and many of the other works housed in this room were written.

Having already read the first two volumes of the Tome, Wigg and Faegan knew that only the *Jin'Sai* would be able to save the damaged orb. But to do that, Tristan had to be trained in the craft, and *that* could not be accomplished without first finding the way to turn his incredible blood back to its proper red color.

And so had come the mind-numbing work of trying to find the answer. Both of the wizards were convinced that it lay here, hidden away somewhere in the Archives of the Redoubt. But with thousands of documents to pore over, Faegan realized that it would be akin to finding a thimble in a sneezeweed stack, as Abbey was so fond of saying. With the orb destroying everything in its path, time was of the essence.

Faegan was convinced that the answer they sought lay somewhere within the Tome of the Paragon. He could recall countless references in the Tome to Tristan's blood, including mentions of it turning azure, should the prince ever successfully employ his gifts without first having been trained. Still, the wizard had yet to recall any outright mention of how to reverse what Tristan had unwittingly done to himself.

Adding to their frustration was the fact that each of them wanted to be out in the countryside, trying to do something about containing and healing the damaged orb. Tristan was especially eager to leave the palace. But he agreed that little could be gained by going until they knew more about the disaster they faced.

By now Geldon and his party of warriors would have tracked the orb down and sent back a report. Faegan was eager to read whatever Geldon might have to say, and to learn where the orb had traveled. But there was nothing any of them could do until they had found and grasped the loose thread of knowledge they needed and pulled upon it to unravel the mystery of Tristan's blood.

Faegan gently picked the cat up off his lap and placed him on the floor. After a luxurious stretch, Nicodemus walked over to Wigg and rubbed the length of his body up against the wizard's leg.

Scowling, the First Wizard did his best to pretend he hadn't noticed. Other than whenever one of them turned over a page of crinkled text or rolled some dusty scroll open or closed, the dense silence in the room went on unabated.

Faegan finally abandoned the disappointing scroll he had been reading and wheeled himself over to a nearby table. He took up his violin and bow, placed the instrument under his chin, and began to play. When he heard the sweet, sorrowful refrain begin, Wigg raised a critical eyebrow but did not look up.

Faegan often took up his ancient instrument when he was under great mental stress. Sometimes he would simply leave it on a table and allow the craft to select the notes and seesaw the resin-laden bow. Today he preferred to play it himself, and to let his mind soar freely with the music. Wigg shook his head and sighed.

After a half hour or so, Faegan abruptly stopped what he was doing and lowered his instrument. Wigg looked up to see that a strange expression had suddenly crossed his friend's face.

"What is it?"

Faegan quickly held up one arm, indicating that he wanted silence. The others looked up to see him suddenly begin wheeling his chair about the room, much the way they themselves might pace about while trying to think. Then he abruptly stopped and quickly swiveled his chair back toward the others. He looked directly at Wigg.

"We have been going about this all wrong," he said.

Wigg raised himself up in his chair. "How so?"

Letting go a great cackle, Faegan happily clapped his palms together. "Don't you see? We've all been thinking in exactly the opposite way we should have been!"

A skeptical look on her face, Abbey leaned over and whispered to Wigg, "What's he blathering about this time?"

"What I'm blathering about, dear lady, is the route to the solution of our problem," Faegan replied happily, his wizard's ears having heard every word.

Wigg folded his arms over his chest. "Pray tell us, then."

"It's all so simple, yet at the same time so complex," Faegan answered. He wheeled himself back to the table. "If any of you commanded the gift of Consummate Recollection, you would understand."

Celeste gave her father a wry look, then turned back to Faegan. "Understand what?"

"We have been searching for references to Tristan's blood," Faegan answered. "At first glance that would seem the correct thing to do. But we were looking for a way to go *forward* to solve our problem. What we should have been looking for was an act of *reversal*."

"There are many references to acts of reversal in the Tome,"

Wigg countered. "The reversal of spells and incantations has long been one of the subdivisions of the craft. There are likely to be as many references to them as there are to anything else— perhaps even more. I understand your line of reasoning, but I fail to see how this will narrow our search."

"All of what you say is true," Faegan agreed. The self-satisfied smile crossed his face again. "But tell me, how many references could there possibly be to the supposed reversal of endowed blood? The Tome states that only the *Jin'Sai* will ever be able to make use of the craft without first having been trained. And that if and when he does, his blood will turn azure. That has of course already occurred. So it would logically follow that if I use my gift to search for the phrase 'blood reversal,' the Tome will direct us to what we are searching for." His smile surfaced again. "Or at the very least take us much closer."

Wigg rubbed his chin. He had to admit that what Faegan was saying made sense. "Then I suggest you get started," he said.

Faegan nodded. Turning his chair around, he looked over at the black pedestal that held the Tome of the Paragon. He called upon the craft, and the white leather-bound book rose hauntingly from its place. It glided across the room to land before him on the table.

Faegan then looked over at Adrian. "Please take up a quill and parchment," he said, "and write down each of the page numbers as I dictate them. It is vitally important that you leave none of them out. Do you understand?"

"Yes," Adrian said. She carefully dipped the quill into the waiting ink bottle. "I am ready."

Faegan closed his eyes. After a few moments he began to speak haltingly, naming specific volumes and page numbers. When he finished, he opened his eyes. Adrian had recorded six different references.

Faegan eagerly grabbed up the parchment and made a mental note of the numbers. He closed his eyes again. The Tome opened itself, and its pages began turning over until they stopped at the first of Adrian's references. Faegan opened his eyes.

"And now we shall see what we shall see," he said, rubbing his hands together like a schoolboy in a candy shop.

Faegan looked down at the first of the referenced pages. As his eyes ran across them, the words duplicated themselves in gleaming azure and rose into the air. One by one they joined to form paragraphs, the paragraphs forming a completed page.

As the five of them sat there reading the glowing page and the others that followed, they were astounded by what they learned.

CHAPTER XVII

AS SHE NEARED THE EXIT OF THE STONE LABYRINTH, SATINE could see natural light streaming in up ahead. She knew that she was going to be all right, but she had never been so exhausted. Her nerves had jangled and her heart had raced for the last two hours. Her face and body were soaked with sweat, her breathing was labored, and her hands shook noticeably. Taking a deep breath, she forced herself to calm down.

Somehow she had made the correct decision at each of the twenty deadly intersections, and she would live another day.

Walking her horse out of the square-cut tunnel and into the light, she raised one arm up to block the sun. She squinted, trying to reaccustom her eyes to being outdoors. Though she was about to enter a place that held no attraction for her other than the goods that Reznik provided, her nerves welcomed the change of scene.

After having been on a horse for most of the day, she decided to stretch her legs. She slid from her saddle and walked around to face the gelding. She gave his face a comforting rub. She checked her weapons, took the reins in one hand, and began walking toward Valrenkium, the village of partial adepts.

She stood upon the short rise overlooking the secret town. Coming here was dangerous, the place ugly and distasteful. This particular group of partials were among the most secretive and deadly practitioners of the craft known to man.

They called themselves the Corporeals, and for very good reason.

Reznik had told her that "Valrenkium" meant "The Parish of Death" in Old Eutracian. The partial adepts who lived here employed their skills in the organic arts of the craft to produce potions, poisons, and other means of death and mayhem. Supposedly, many of the abominations of the craft that had long plagued Eutracia could be traced back to this place.

To the casual observer, the village appeared to be much like any of the other hamlets scattered across Eutracia. Quaint brick houses stood in neat rows, their windows open. Smoke drifted lazily from their chimneys. Children laughed and played, dogs barked, and chickens ran about in the streets. Vendors sat in stalls displaying their wares. The sounds of a blacksmith's hammer could be heard, pounding out its double clang.

But as Satine drew closer, she saw the gibbets lining the road into town. The curved iron cages, barely big enough for a single prisoner to stand up in, turned slowly in the wind. As she walked by, voices called out to her. Those still possessing enough strength reached out beseechingly from between the iron bands. She lowered her head and continued on.

Other gibbets held those already past help, their bloated and rotting corpses slumped within. *They are the lucky ones,* she thought.

Captured from the countryside and brought to Valrenkium to die of exposure, many of these prisoners would be taken down only after their dead bodies had aged sufficiently for use. Like a good cheese or a keg of wine, Reznik had said once, laughing. Others were used the moment they arrived; some were allowed to live for a time, depending upon the needs of the Corporeal partial adepts.

Every time Satine visited Valrenkium, her first instinct was to cut the gibbets down and set the prisoners free. But she resisted the urge. Not only would such a move endanger her life, it would also do no good. The entire village was surrounded by the same rocky bluffs through which the tunnel had just led her, and their tops were constantly ringed with archers. She couldn't imagine herself scaling those sheer stone walls, let alone any of the weakened prisoners doing so. Besides, she needed to stay in

the Corporeals' good graces, at least through this visit. After today, the whole lot of them could go to the Afterlife, for all she
cared.

Most people in Eutracia regarded the rumors about Valrenkium and the Corporeals to be nothing more than myths,
grown stronger over time and embellished even further by the
return of the Coven of Sorceresses. But Satine knew differently.

Walking deeper into the village, Satine finally began to
hear the screams, and the telltale odor wafted to her nose.
Steeling herself, she hurried on to Reznik's cottage. Tying
her horse to a rail, she looked around warily before untying
the two heavy saddlebags she had brought with her. She slung
them over her shoulder and walked to the door, which she
opened without knocking. The familiar interior of the cottage
yawned before her. She pushed the door closed with one
boot.

Reznik was nowhere to be seen. She walked to a nearby table
and put the saddlebags down.

The place had changed little since her last visit: a mishmash of
tables, beakers, books, scrolls, and other items of the craft. An
adjoining room served as the library, its walls lined with overflowing bookcases. Beyond that lay an atrium, the sunlight
streaming in through its glass ceiling and down onto the various
plants of the craft the herbmaster cultivated. The herbs gave the
cottage an earthy smell, belying the cruel work that went on here.

Satine saw the open trapdoor in the center of the floor. She
walked over to it and looked down.

Soft light flickered on the wooden steps. The clink of glass
could be heard, as well as someone whistling contentedly. As
she stood there wondering what to do, cool air wafted up the
steps to greet her.

Finally making up her mind, she reached beneath her cloak
and placed her palms upon two of her dagger handles. All of her
senses alert, she started down.

Satine had never been down here before. In fact, she hadn't
known this room existed. The chamber belowground was larger
than the house above it. It was cold here—far colder than it
should have been for this time of year. Looking around, she
could see why.

From floor to ceiling, great blocks of ice were piled up against the walls. They twinkled an icy blue as they caught the light of the numerous table lamps. Still, there was something wrong about it all, she realized. The blocks were not melting. Nor did any water collect upon the dirt floor. Suddenly even colder, Satine pulled her cloak closer.

Reznik sat at a worktable in a far corner of the room. He wore magnifying spectacles and a woolen overcoat. He carefully examined a glass tube full of violet fluid, which Satine recognized immediately.

Hearing her approach, Reznik stopped whistling and looked up.

"Come in, come in!" he said enthusiastically. Uncoiling a little, Satine walked farther into the room.

Reznik came to greet her. After looking her up and down, he smiled.

"I expected you a bit sooner," he said slyly. "The sentry at the entrance to the tunnels sent a runner, telling me that you had finally arrived. It seemed to take you longer than usual to reach my home. There was no difficulty, I trust?"

He was toying with her, she knew. Reznik knew everything that went on in Valrenkium. If this place had a ringleader, it was he. If he hadn't been the one who had erased her marks at the intersections, he would certainly know who had.

But that was all right, she thought. After today she wouldn't need to play this vile bastard's games.

"No trouble," she said confidently. "I just took my time." Wanting to change the subject, she looked around the room. "I've never been down here. What is this place?"

"This is where I store my most precious ingredients," Reznik answered. "I keep it cold in here, so that the goods remain preserved."

Satine grimaced. She wasn't sure she wanted to know more, but her curiosity was getting the best of her. Table after table was covered with fluid-filled jars. Some contained what were clearly human body parts; others held colorful, grotesque items she could not identify.

"You use blocks of ice to accomplish this," she mused, forcing down her revulsion. "But where do you get them this time of the year? And why don't they melt?"

One corner of the herbmaster's mouth came up. "I am a partial adept, remember? My arts are organic in nature. They have to do with things of the earth, sea, and sky. For me, enchanting a few blocks of ice to remain frozen is but a small thing."

Satine looked down at the vial in his hand. "That's mine, isn't it?"

"Yes," he answered. "There are three more just like it. I believe this is the finest batch I have ever produced. I have also formulated a new enhancement for it that I am especially proud of."

She took the vial from him, walked it over to one of the tables, and held it before the light of an oil lamp. As usual, the nearly transparent fluid was a soft violet in color, but this time there were slight overtones of crimson that she had never seen in previous batches.

She didn't know much about Reznik's art, but she was intimately familiar with the formula she always purchased from him because her life depended upon it. That was why she had always insisted upon coming here to collect her goods, rather than buying them from a Valrenkian agent on the street.

She looked back at him. "You incorporated the dermagnasher venom as usual?" she asked.

"Yes. It was fresh today."

"And the oil of encumbrance?" she asked. "That is vital."

"Of course."

"The organs you used, they came from a fresh, endowed suicide?"

"Yes," Reznik gloated. "I took them and the marrow the same day the body was delivered to me."

"Good," she answered. "You have also enchanted the fluid to immediately dissolve the delivery mechanism?"

"I assume that your methods will remain the same?"

"Yes."

"If that is the case, then you will be pleased," he answered. "As usual, the contents of one of the vials has been sweetened with honey."

Satine held the vial to the light again. She gave it a gentle shake. "What are these crimson clouds I see swirling in there?" she asked. "They were never present in my other purchases."

She looked back at him with narrowed eyes. "I don't like surprises, Reznik."

"Ah," he said as he walked closer. He seemed quite pleased with himself. "That is the enhancement I told you of. Those clouds you see are a new form of preservative."

"How does it work?"

Reznik smiled. "Do you remember my once telling you that the bone marrow of a child is always red?"

She nodded.

"The marrow is red until adulthood. Then it turns yellow, signaling the end of its maturation process. The addition of the livelier red marrow will keep the fluid 'active,' so to speak, and it will therefore hold its potency longer. It was something of a breakthrough, if I don't mind saying so. I hope you are pleased."

She was, but she chose not to show it. "And the delivery systems?" she asked.

Reznik reached across the table, took up a small leather case, and handed it to her. She opened it and looked inside. As usual, all seemed to be in order.

"Well done," she said simply. "Is there anything else that I need to know?"

"Only that I wish you good hunting."

He went back to the worktable, gathered the other two vials, and gave them to her. Satine placed the three vials and the leather case into her cloak's specially sewn pockets, then retied the strings. They both turned and walked up the steps to the cottage above.

Satine opened one of the bulging saddlebags on the table. Several gold kisa spilled from it and rattled onto the tabletop. Reznik smiled.

"It's all there, I assume?" he asked politely.

"Of course," Satine answered. She pulled the hood of her cloak up over her head. She was eager to leave. She wanted to be safely through the sandstone maze by nightfall.

"In that case our business is concluded," Reznik said. He gestured to a pot that sat upon another wood-burning stove. "Unless you would like to join me in a bowl of bone soup?" he offered. "I made it fresh this morning. Some company would be welcome."

Satine felt her stomach turn over. She couldn't imagine eating anything in this place, much less wanting to know what kind of creature the bones had come from.

"Uh, er, no—no, thank you," she answered stiffly. "I need to be going."

"Suit yourself," the herbmaster said. Sitting down, he took up a broad soup ladle. He gave her another look.

"Goodbye, Satine," he said. "Until next time."

"Goodbye," she answered.

Walking out the door, she climbed upon her gelding and wheeled him around to begin her journey back. She took a final look at the brick cottage that held so many awful secrets.

And good riddance, she thought.

Prodding her horse forward, the Gray Fox began her ride back through the winding streets of Valrenkium.

CHAPTER XVIII

SADDENED AND ANGERED BY WHAT HE SAW, TRISTAN WALKED slowly among the wounded still filling the palace courtyard. The Orb of the Vigors had done this, and it infuriated him to be waiting here rather than taking some kind of action to stop it.

The sun had just started to set over the western wall of the palace. The songbirds had quieted, and the turquoise of the sky had slowly faded into the deeper indigo of evening. The stars and moons would be out soon, and with them would come the comforting chirps of the night creatures.

All about him, torches were lit, their soft glow throwing shadows across the walls and grounds. Minion healers continued to work hard tending the wounded. He had walked by Duvessa only moments ago, and they had nodded to each other. Her white cutter's smock had been covered with blood.

By now, some of the wounded had left their care. Others whose injuries made it impossible for them to travel had stayed behind. To the prince it seemed that the palace still overflowed with them. Tents had been erected for those well enough to sleep outdoors in the courtyard. They gave the entire place the chilling look of a military field hospital. In many ways, he supposed that it was.

He had tried to converse with some of the patients. A few spoke to him, but most only looked up at him in anger and distrust—as though he had somehow trapped them here on purpose. Eventually he gave up and walked on, his head lowered.

He desperately wanted to hear from Geldon, but no word had come. Tristan worried about both the dwarf and Ox. Each had saved his life more than once, and he owed them more than he could ever repay. He couldn't stop wondering where the orb had traveled after its deadly assault on Brook Hollow. Had more of his people been killed?

A sudden breeze came up, bringing with it the familiar scent of myrrh.

Smiling, he turned to see Celeste approach. She wore a light blue gown with matching slippers. A strand of freshwater pearls lay elegantly around her neck. The glow from the torches created highlights in her long, red hair. But as she came nearer, Tristan's smile dissolved. It was clear that something was wrong.

Finally reaching him, she took him in her arms and held him close. When they parted, he saw that her eyes were shining with tears. She wiped them away with one hand.

Tristan ran one of his palms across her cheek. "What is it? Has something happened?"

Shaking her hair back over one shoulder, Celeste composed herself. "Shailiha told me I might find you here," she said softly. "I need to speak to you. Is there someplace we might go to be alone?"

"Of course."

He led her around one side of the palace, through a manicured gap in a tall witherblossom hedge, and then on into another yard. They sat together on one of the marble benches that lay along the edge of the grass.

This had once been his mother's private gardens. None of the wounded were here. The gardens had long been in disrepair. Still, just being here and away from the depressing courtyard almost made Tristan forget his troubles.

When he looked back into Celeste's eyes, her anxiousness crowded in on him again. "What is it?" he asked.

Taking both of his hands into hers, she looked him in the eyes. "I am not with child," she said.

Looking down for a moment, Tristan took a deep breath. "I see." Reaching up, he placed one palm upon her cheek. "How long have you known?"

"Three days," she answered. "I wanted to tell you sooner. But you and Father had already gone searching for the orb." She looked away. "I'm sorry, my love," she said so softly he could barely hear her. "In truth, I didn't know whether to be relieved or disappointed—I suppose it is a little of both. But at least for now, it is not to be. And perhaps, worst of all, we still do not know if we can ever be intimate with each other again." She paused.

"I miss you in that way," she whispered then. "More than you could ever know."

Reaching out, he lifted her face back to his. "And I you," he said. "Have you told your father?"

Celeste shook her head. "Only Shailiha," she answered. "I needed someone to talk to while you were away. We have become close, she and I."

The moonlight showed a hint of a smile playing on her lips. "Shailiha tells me that you used to be quite a handful when you were growing up," she said. "But now between your twin sister and me, you don't stand a chance of misbehaving."

Tristan smiled back. "How true."

He took her in his arms and kissed her hard on the mouth. As he held her, he could feel her body rise up to meet his and hear her breathing quicken.

Then, summoning his will, he took her by the shoulders and gently moved her away. As he did, her head arched back, exposing her lovely throat to the moonlight. The anger he felt about his azure blood began to boil over again, and with a long sigh, he forced it back down. Eutracia needed both his and Celeste's gifts right now. Protecting his land and the craft had to take precedence over personal needs.

Bending over, he gave Celeste one last kiss—a brief one, almost chaste. Then, his arm around her waist, he walked her from the private gardens and on toward the twinkling lights of the palace.

CHAPTER XIX

"IT IS TIME TO BRING THEM, WULFGAR, AND TO BOARD THEM ONTO your Black Ships. Then only the coming of the ships' captains shall be required to launch your invasion. Bring the beasts now, and witness the majesty of their power. For they will destroy both the palace and the Redoubt of the Directorate, that vile seat of the Vigors. Load them onto the Black Ships, our son of the lower, lesser world. We will be watching."

Sleeping soundly, Wulfgar at first heard the words as if in a dream. Startled awake by the clear choir-voiced message, the *Enseterat* blinked open his good eye.

He immediately understood. Yesterday he had employed yet another of the Forestallments granted him by the Scroll of the Vagaries. It allowed him to conjure the great beasts into the world. As their gigantic shapes had taken form, even he had been awed by their splendor.

He rolled over in bed and looked into the face of his sleeping queen. Her dark ringlets were spread out across her pillow, and her face was the very picture of contentment. Beneath the elaborate quilt, he could see the swollen, impending promise of their child.

Serena, Wulfgar found himself thinking. How aptly she was named, and how much he loved her. He would soon be forced to leave her side. But this time he would return in triumph.

Wulfgar slid from the bed, put on a silk robe, and walked to the balcony. The day had broken clear and fresh, and the seabirds sang to one another as they coasted effortlessly over the waves below. Stretching the sleepy muscles in his back, he inhaled the bracing air.

He would indeed load the amazing beasts today, just as his fathers and mothers of above had ordered him to. Then he would perform the only other task remaining, and set out to make both Eutracia and the craft of magic his own.

"My love?"

Turning, he saw Serena had awakened. Propped up on one elbow, she looked at him lovingly as he stood there, the morning sun on his ravaged face. He walked over to her and sat down on the edge of the bed. He ran his good hand through the ringlets of her hair. He smiled again.

"Today is to be very special," he said softly. "The Heretics spoke to me in my sleep and told me that I am to load the beasts aboard the Black Ships. I shall need your help, for your gifts easily surpass those of Einar."

Serena smiled. "I will do all I can for you, my lord," she answered.

She rose. Placing one hand upon her abdomen, she sleepily padded her way toward the elegant washroom. Wulfgar went to the velvet pull cord and gave it a sharp tug, telling the demonslavers that he wanted breakfast. He then walked back out onto the balcony.

This would be an eventful day.

HOLDING SERENA'S HAND, WULFGAR WALKED HIS QUEEN DOWN THE wide, marble stairway leading from their throne room. It was nearly midday. The sea winds were light; the ocean was calm. As they approached the terrace at the bottom of the steps, Serena saw Einar standing there. She smiled at the consul, and he bowed respectfully.

Wulfgar gazed out at his fleet of Black Ships. Their dark, majestic shapes lay peacefully at anchor. Each time he saw them he was amazed. He had been even more awed when the Heretics told him what these warships were capable of.

He looked over at Einar. "Have the beasts been gathered?"

"Yes, my lord," the consul answered. "I suggest that we begin promptly. My ability to keep them under control is not limitless. They are immensely powerful, and equally strong-willed."

Wulfgar nodded.

Looking out over the waves, he pointed at the nearest Black Ship. Almost at once they could hear the chattering of the vessel's anchor wheel as it began hoisting the chain from the sea. Dripping, the massive, black anchor soon followed. It finally came to a halt in its holding place, just below the bow gunwale.

Wulfgar lowered his arm, took a deep breath, and then pointed at the ship again.

The gigantic vessel slowly turned until her stern was facing them. Then she moved backward through the waves and gently beached herself. The rocks lining the edge of the sea were crushed like grapes beneath her weight. Finally settling herself, she listed a bit toward her port side.

At Wulfgar's next gesture, the huge trapdoor in the ship's stern lowered itself. Unopened for centuries, it creaked loudly all of the way down. With a final groan, it, too, came to rest upon the shoreline, leaving a dark, gaping portal in the ship's hull. Lowering his hands, Wulfgar turned to his queen.

"Do you remember your instructions, my love?" he asked her.

She nodded. "I am ready."

Wulfgar looked over at Einar. "Have the demonslavers bring them out," he ordered. While the three of them watched, seven creatures appeared from around the far edge of the shoreline.

This was the first Serena had seen of them. She gasped. The monsters were each at least ten meters high. Each had dark, leathery skin that looked much like the wrinkled pages of some old, charred book. They walked on all fours, and each bore a demonslaver atop its back. They strode ponderously toward the shore. Despite their plodding gait, their inherent strength was obvious.

Their curved backs arched upward, and then down again. Their bodies were long, tall, and very deep. The rather short four legs were huge and set wide apart. They ended in massive, cloven hooves that looked as if they could easily crush anything they landed upon. Each time one of them set foot upon the earth, Serena could hear a great stomping noise and feel the ground shake.

They had long, swaying necks with broad, flat heads and deep jaw lines. The glistening eyes were dark. An equally dark slit made up the mouth, and a long, dark horn protruded from each of the creatures' foreheads. As Serena looked more closely at one of the monsters, she realized that its deadliest weapon was not its horn but its tail: thickly muscled, at least as long as the rest of the body, it ended in a gigantic paddle that swayed back and forth with the creature's plodding gait.

Serena looked again to the demonslavers sitting atop the great beasts. They used no saddles, but held reins that led to bridles on their mounts' heads. Long whips were cracked liberally to keep the lumbering giants in order.

"What are they called, my lord?" Serena asked.

"Earthshakers," Wulfgar replied. "Or at least that was what they used to be called. Their kind has not been seen since the Sorceresses' War." The *Enseterat* smiled. "What a shock it shall be when the wizards of the Redoubt see them once again. Not to mention the Black Ships that have returned them to their shores."

Just then one of the things stopped dead in its tracks and looked directly at them. Serena thought that her heart might stop. The Earthshaker opened its jaws wide and gave a bloodcurdling cry.

The awful sound was something of a cross between the growl of a dog and the scream of a terrified woman. Raising its head angrily, the great beast cried out again. The noise hurt Serena's ears. When it opened its mouth she saw row upon row of long, pointed teeth. These creatures were meat eaters.

The rebellious Earthshaker stopped crying out, but the demonslaver atop it was having a difficult time getting it to move forward and enter the Black Ship.

Wulfgar looked quickly over at Serena and Einar. "Augment me," he ordered. The *Enseterat* raised his hands. Azure bolts shot from them toward the Earthshaker and its mount.

Serena and Einar raised their arms, but waited to see what Wulfgar had in mind. Azure walls sprung up, one on either side of the rebellious monster. The twin walls created a passageway that led to the stern of the ship. Understanding, Wulfgar's queen and consul added their powers to his own, reinforcing the walls.

With nowhere else to go, the Earthshaker walked through the corridor, stepped upon the lowered doorway, and entered the ship. As it did, Serena and Einar kept the azure walls in place. Wulfgar caused the ship's stern hatch to rise up and close.

Taking another deep breath, he sent the warship sailing back from the beach and out to its original position, where its anchor rattled back down into the Sea of Whispers. The Black Ship turned gently into the wind. She tugged hard at the anchor chain, then finally settled herself.

Wulfgar turned toward his consul. "It shall be your responsibility to ensure that enough meat and water have been stored aboard the Black Ships to sustain the beasts all the way to Eutracia," he said. "They must be strong and eager when we arrive."

Einar bowed slightly. "As you wish, my lord."

Wulfgar's eye narrowed as he looked proudly at the remaining line of Earthshakers he had conjured. He turned back to his queen and his consul. They both smiled at him.

"Today we board the Earthshakers. Then I shall call forth those who shall captain the Black Ships for me," he said. Thinking of the *Jin'Sai* and the *Jin'Saiou,* he turned his gaze back out to sea. "Nothing can stand in our way now."

Wulfgar raised his arms again and caused yet another of the Black Ships' anchors to clamber its way up out of the sea.

CHAPTER XX

"GET YOUR SHOES OFF MY TABLE, YOU OLD FOOL!" SHAWNA THE Short hollered, pointing the paring knife at her husband. "Considering they're yours, only the Afterlife knows where they've been!"

Masters Wigg and Faegan had asked that food be brought to their upcoming meeting, and Shawna meant to do the best possible job of it. That didn't mean having Shannon's shoes atop the butcher's table, or the smell of his corncob pipe stinking up the palace kitchens.

She stopped slicing the treemelon long enough to reach out with her free hand and shoved Shannon's feet off the table. The gnome hadn't been expecting that.

He slid off his chair and onto the floor. His chair crashed backward against a rack of freshly polished pots and pans, and most of them went down noisily with him. Shailiha was pretty sure that one of them landed on his head.

Trying to choke back a smile, the princess put a hand over her mouth. One of Shannon's hands fumbled back up to the tabletop, then the rest of him appeared. The ever-present ale jug was still locked firmly in his other hand, and his prized corncob pipe remained clamped between his teeth—even though it was now upside down.

Angrily adjusting his black cap, he glared at his wife of more than three hundred years. Shawna stood her ground giving back as good as she got with an angry look of her own.

Shannon pointed a pudgy finger at her in defiance.

"I swear you'll be the death of me, woman!" he blustered as he righted his chair. "When you shout like that, you sound like a mare giving breached birth to a porcupine! Is making me suffer the only reason the Afterlife put you on this earth?"

"No!" Shawna shouted back. "But it's the one I enjoy the most!"

Seeing the ashes falling from Shannon's pipe, Shawna's righteous indignation went into overdrive. She dropped the knife, picked up a copper frying pan, and started after him.

Shannon could be lazy and he liked his ale far too much, but he was no fool where his wife was concerned. Backing away, he held the ale jug high, as if to ward her off.

"Out!" Shawna shouted. Without warning, she swung the heavy pan like a broadsword.

Shailiha held her breath. She didn't know whether Shawna might actually brain him with the pan. But then Morganna started to cry.

"Now see what you've done!" Shawna shouted. His eyes wide, Shannon continued to back away. "Leave here this instant, or I'll give you a goose egg the size of a Shadowood thorn apple!"

Shawna was particularly protective of Morganna, and no one knew that better than Shannon. Clutching his jug, he backed out of the kitchen just in time to narrowly avoid another swing of the frying pan.

With Shannon gone, Shawna looked over at the baby. Shailiha had already taken her up from her stroller, and the child was beginning to quiet.

Shawna took a pan from the stove and poured some warm milk into a bottle. Fastening a nipple to the bottle, she handed it to the princess. Shailiha gave the bottle to Morganna, who began to drink greedily.

"Men!" Shawna muttered as she went back about her work. "The small ones can be just as much trouble as the large ones—maybe more!"

The princess smiled. She enjoyed being in the kitchens with the gnomes, and so she had brought Morganna here to pass the time, as she and the other members of the Conclave waited for the meeting to be called.

Tristan had told them all that there would be a meeting as soon as the wizards ended their research. It was now well into the afternoon, and still the two irascible mystics had not called for them. Shailiha knew that Tristan had spent much of last night and most of today prowling the palace, trying to release his pent-up frustration.

She really couldn't blame him. She had seen the changes he had gone through, and she had shared many of them with him. She had wept for him, laughed with him, mourned with him, and been terrified for him. In the end they had always had each other, and nothing could change that. Today might prove to be one of the most important days of his life. She would be there with him, no matter what news the wizards might bring.

There was something else that had been tugging at the princess' heart—something other than their predicament concerning the Orb of the Vigors. It was a deeply personal concern. She had yet to talk to anyone about it, not even Celeste.

Despite all of the people now living here in the palace with her and her brother, Shailiha was desperately lonely.

Tristan and Celeste had found each other. After more than three hundred years, Abbey had found her way back into Wigg's heart. Traax and Duvessa seemed drawn to each other. But for Shailiha there was no one.

Her grief at the death of her husband Frederick had been all-consuming at first. She had loved him more than her life. With his passing she had thought that the secret, fiery part of her heart that could feel such love for a man had been smothered forever, and that she would never again want it rekindled.

But as time went by she felt familiar needs stirring within her once more. Was it wrong to feel this way? she asked over and over. Was Frederick looking down upon her from the Afterlife? If he was, would the presence of another man in her life hurt him?

Shailiha looked down into Morganna's face. At least Frederick lived on in their child, she thought. For now, she supposed that would have to do.

"Begging your pardons, ladies," a strong male voice said from one of the several kitchen doorways. "The wizards wish to have the food brought in so that they may start the meeting."

Shawna and Shailiha looked up to see a Minion warrior standing there. "Keep your armor on," Shawna said. "I have a few more items to prepare."

Repressing a laugh, the princess watched the gnome finish her work. Soon several silver trays lay on the butcher's table, each piled high with delicacies: roast pork with plumberry stuffing; selected fruits, vegetables, and cheeses; and one of Shawna's specialty desserts, a five-tiered, swizzle-rum and cinnamon cake, slathered with farmer's cheese frosting. It all smelled wonderful.

Shailiha wondered whether any of them would want to eat after they had heard the wizards' news. She shrugged. They all had to eat sometime, she supposed.

Finally finished, the gnome wife wiped her hands down her apron. Looking up, she cast her commanding stare upon the unsuspecting Minion warrior.

"Well, don't just stand there with your wings drooping!" To emphasize her point, she pointed a diminutive forefinger at him as though it were a deadly weapon. "Help us with these! That's why you're here, isn't it?"

The warrior stiffened. "Minion men do not do such work."

Pursing her lips, Shawna walked over to him. She barely reached his waist.

Shailiha waited. She knew that this would prove interesting.

Shawna crooked her finger, beckoning the warrior closer. As he bent over, quick as a flash she reached up and grabbed one of his earlobes. Then she gave it a savage twist. The warrior's face went red with indignation but, surprisingly, he did not move.

"Now then," Shawna said. "You can either help us carry these things to the meeting room, or I can report to the *Jin'Sai* that you chose to be *uncooperative*. Which would you prefer?"

She let go. With a sour look, the warrior picked up two of the trays as though they weighed nothing and started for the door. Shailiha placed Morganna into the stroller and took up the remaining tray. Shawna took the stroller by the handle. Then she stretched up toward Shailiha's ear. The princess bent over.

"I told you men were trouble," she whispered. Then she winked. "But if a girl knows how, they can be managed. Even the *really big* ones."

Smiling, Shailiha followed the gnome from the kitchen.

CHAPTER XXI

THE ORB OF THE VIGORS WAS SLICING A PASS INTO THE TOLENKA Mountains.

Geldon stared in disbelief.

The orb still screamed—perhaps even louder now than before. As its golden rain fell onto the granite mountains, it vaporized the stone, leaving in its wake a narrow, charred passage. The newly created canyon penetrated the slopes like a long, dark finger trying to poke its way through to the other side. The rough-hewn pass was already several hundred meters long, and the orb showed no signs of stopping or of changing course, even as it headed directly toward one of the Tolenkas' many deep, white glaciers.

His mouth agape, Geldon watched as solid, living rock was melted, and freshly carved boulders and granite shards were ripped away from the mountain. Occasionally rubble tumbled down to obstruct the pass, but then the energy dripping from the orb pulverized it, clearing the way again.

Geldon tried to recall what Wigg and Faegan had told him about the mysterious mountain range. Lining Eutracia on her entire western side, the Tolenkas had always been insurmountable. No pass had ever been found through the imposing slopes. Their peaks were so high that even the wizards could not climb them. As an experiment, Tristan had recently ordered a group of the hardiest Minion warriors to try to fly over them. They had been forced back by the thin air and the savage, icy conditions that prohibited any traversing of the peaks.

For centuries, rumors abounded about what might lie on the western side of the mountains. Some said that it was a great, dark void, and that if a man stepped too far, he would fall off the edge of the world. Others swore that it was a home to savage, inhuman creatures that would kill every Eutracian man, woman, and child if set free to roam the eastern lands. Still others maintained that the western side held the Afterlife: that the souls of their departed friends and relatives could be found there, that the howling winds that whistled down the slopes were actually the plaintive cries of the dead, and that the runoff of snow during each Season of New Life was in fact their tears, as they cried in their torment to be set free to rejoin the world of the living.

In truth, no one really knew. Wigg and Faegan did not believe such rumors. Even so, when Geldon had pressed them about it, they had abruptly changed the subject. He got the feeling they knew more, but chose not to speak of it.

Geldon looked up toward the peaks. As always, their tips were shrouded in fog. Then he looked back down at the orb, as it blasted through the icy slopes.

Suddenly a new sound could be heard: strange, more ominous than the screaming of the orb. It started softly at first, but soon Geldon felt it as much as heard it. As it grew in intensity, the litter began to shake. He looked around, trying to find the source of the sound. When he finally saw what was causing it, he knew he and the Minions would have to act quickly. They had left most of the warriors behind to eat and rest in a grassy field—and now those warriors were in great danger.

Part of the nearby glacier, melted by the heat from the ruptured orb, had sheared off and roared down the side of the mountain toward the field below. Had it been only snow, it would have been deadly enough. But this was ice, harsh, hammering, unyielding. As Geldon watched, it plummeted on down the slopes and tore into the forest, crushing the pine trees in its path as though they were matchsticks.

The smoke and soot from the orb obscured the onrushing crash of ice from the unsuspecting warriors resting in the field. Wild-eyed, Geldon looked out at Ox, and then both were barking out orders to their bearers to take them back down as fast as they could.

Folding his wings behind his back, Ox launched himself from the litter and soared downward in a near vertical free fall. He opened his wings and swooped upward at the last possible moment, then flew with all his strength as the huge chunk of glacier chased behind him.

As the litter descended, the smoke and soot obscured Geldon's vision completely. He had no choice but to hold tight to the swaying litter and hope that his bearers could find their way out of it. When he could finally see again, he almost wished he couldn't.

Ox had succeeded in ordering most of the remaining warriors into the air in time, but not all. When the massive disintegrating glacier plowed out of the smoke-filled forest, some of them had no chance. They stood there in shocked disbelief as the ice overcame them, burying them instantly. Ox and the survivors, hovering beside the litter, watched in horror as the glacier carved its way across the ground, ripping up the green turf of the fields and throwing great hunks of it dozens of meters into the air.

When its momentum finally waned, the deadly glacier slowed, coming at last to a grinding halt only meters away from the superheated canyon. The rising heat of the canyon melted the ice almost instantly, and its runoff streamed across the ground and into the recently formed gorge. Water soon flowed down the canyon like a raging river.

Taking a deep breath, Geldon looked over at Ox. Nodding back, the warrior commanded his troops to take the litter to the ground.

On shaking legs, Geldon exited the litter and looked back toward the mountains. With the avalanche over, he could once again hear the orb hacking its way through the granite slopes. He turned and walked toward Ox. He would have to return to Tammerland with this news. No note in the world could properly describe what had just happened here.

CHAPTER XXII

By the time Shailiha, Shawna, and the Minion warrior arrived at the Conclave chamber, the other members had already taken their seats. After arranging the food to her liking on a nearby table, Shawna pushed Morganna's stroller from the room. The warrior who had escorted them followed Shawna out, closing the large double doors behind him.

The mood in the room was anxious. Tristan seemed especially eager to hear what Wigg and Faegan were about to say. All the Conclave members sat quietly, waiting for things to begin. The two wizards seemed lost in thought as Shailiha took her place at the table.

Shailiha smelled the comforting scent of the burning logs as their flames danced in the light blue fireplace set into the opposite wall. The Tome of the Paragon and the partially burned Scroll of the Vigors lay upon a nearby table.

Clearing his throat, Wigg placed his hands flat upon the tabletop. He looked over at the prince.

"You and I are going to Parthalon," he said. "We must revisit the Recluse. We leave within the hour. It will be shortly after midnight when we arrive, and I suggest some Minion warriors accompany us."

Tristan looked at Wigg as though the wizard had just gone mad. "Why?"

Picturing the underground rooms of the Recluse, where he, Wigg, and Geldon had been tortured by the Coven, Tristan closed his eyes. He could see the unforgiving gibbets in which the three of them had been imprisoned, the five black marble thrones of the Mistresses, and the snarling reptilian monsters known as the Wiktors. He tried to keep the memories from flooding back—to no avail. He would never forget his torture, and his brutal violation by Succiu. And now, impossibly, the wizards wanted him to go back to the scene of those awful events.

Tristan opened his eyes and placed his forearms on the table. The only sound in the room was the gentle crackling of the fire in the hearth. After running one hand through his dark hair, he looked at the wizards.

"I assume you have a good reason," he said.

"You and Wigg must find the Scroll Master," Faegan said. "He may be the only living person who fully understands the key to changing your blood."

For a short time the room went silent again.

"Who is this person?" Celeste asked at last.

"Our research of the Scroll of the Vigors reveals the existence of one who is the Scroll's earthly master," Faegan answered. "His help could be vital—provided he still lives, of course, and that Tristan and Wigg can find him."

Abbey leaned forward. "There are several of us here who can read Old Eutracian," she protested. "So why do we need this supposed Scroll Master to aid us? Why can't we just keep reading the scroll ourselves to learn what we need?"

"Because time is working against us," Wigg answered. "We still have not heard from Geldon and Ox. We must therefore assume that the orb continues to ravage the land. Those of you who can read Old Eutracian will continue to research the scroll, but if the scroll does indeed hold the Forestallment calculations that will allow us to change Tristan's blood back to red, this supposed Scroll Master may be able to provide them to us long before we happen upon them ourselves. The scroll is huge. It could take us weeks to find what we are looking for. And what if the Forestallment we seek was in a part of the scroll that was destroyed, eh? In that case, only the Scroll Master could tell us what we need to know—if he still lives."

"But what makes you think that you should begin your search at the Recluse?" Shailiha asked.

Leaning back in his chair, Wigg let go a thoughtful sigh. "Because some of the later Forestallment calculations in the Scroll of the Vigors were in Failee's handwriting," he answered.

A hush descended over the table.

"That would mean that the Scroll of the Vigors, and perhaps also the Scroll of the Vagaries, were at one time in her possession," Tristan said.

"That is correct," Faegan answered. "They had to be, in order for her to place the Forestallments into your blood signature— and Shailiha and Celeste's—in the first place. For all we know, your blood signature may already possess the Forestallment required to change it from azure back to red. But even if that were the case, we would not know how to identify or activate it." The wizard looked away for a moment as he contemplated his next thought. "But this new set of facts also raises another puzzle."

"At what point in Eutracian history did Failee gain possession of the scrolls, and how did she get them to Parthalon?" Adrian asked, furrowing her brow. "It was always my understanding that when the Directorate banished the Coven to the Sea of

Whispers, they provided them with only a small boat and a few meager supplies. How did she do it?"

"How indeed," Wigg replied. "Not to mention the question of how the scrolls came to be back in Eutracia."

"None of this explains why you must start your search for this supposed Scroll Master at the Recluse," Shailiha repeated.

"The subterranean levels of the Recluse were Failee's private domain," Wigg explained uncomfortably. "It was where she kept not only her laboratory, but also her library. I feel it is safe to assume that she, too, would likely have been searching for the Scroll Master, and I'm hoping she might have left notes on her research—some kind of clue for us to follow."

"Do you really believe the Scroll Master might still be alive?" Tristan asked. "And what purpose did he serve?"

"Those are riddles that can only be unraveled once we arrive," Wigg answered. He looked around the table.

"Even though Tristan and I have been in that awful place before, we will still be walking into the unknown," he added. "I fear there is much more to those lower regions than we were allowed to see."

Then Tyranny spoke up. "There is still much about all of this that I do not understand," she said. "I know little of the craft, but I am trying to learn. Assuming that you two are able to find this Scroll Master and he gives you the Forestallment Tristan needs, how does that help us repair the ruptured orb?"

For the first time since the meeting began, Wigg smiled. "As you already know, Tristan's blood must be returned to its original state before he can be trained in the craft, or any of his Forestallments activated. The Tome states that only the red, trained blood of the *Jin'Sai* shall have the power to heal the orbs, should either of them ever be rent asunder. Simply put, the Forestallment we seek will grant Tristan the power to heal the orb."

Feeling as though the responsibility for the entire world had just landed upon his shoulders, Tristan looked over at the Tome and the Scroll of the Vigors.

Traax interrupted his thoughts. "I wish permission to accompany you, *Jin'Sai*. I consider it my duty."

Tristan considered Traax's request for a moment.

"No, my friend," he answered. "I have another mission for you. It is one that will prove far more hazardous than trying to look after Wigg and me in Parthalon, and it will test your loyalty, I'm afraid."

Traax automatically bowed his head. "I live to serve."

Faegan narrowed his eyes. "Just what do you have in mind?" he asked the prince.

Tristan looked over at Tyranny. "Will you accompany Traax on a mission for me?" he asked her. "I must warn you that it will be very dangerous."

"Anything. You know that," she replied earnestly.

"Ever since the orb began its rampage across Eutracia, I have had doubts about whether Wulfgar actually died that night," Tristan said. "I want you and Traax to take the fleet as near to the Isle of the Citadel as you dare. When you are near enough, I want you to send a Minion war party high over the island. If you see any surviving demonslavers, try to capture a few and return them to the *Reprise* for questioning." A smile brushed across the prince's lips.

"I am well aware of how persuasive Scars can be if left to his own devices," he added wryly. "Don't let him kill them all. I would like to question some of them myself when I return. While you are gone, the warriors accompanying you shall be under your command."

Tyranny and Traax positively beamed. They had both been longing for some real action.

"Sounds like fun," Tyranny said. She looked over at Traax. "We sail on the evening tide." The warrior nodded back.

"While you are on this mission," Tristan said to Traax, "you are to take your orders from Tyranny as you would from me."

"Yes, my lord," Traax answered.

"Taking into account the losses we sustained during our battles with Wulfgar's forces, how many combat warriors do we have left?" Tristan asked. "If Wulfgar were to return with a force equal to the first, could we beat him back again?"

Traax's face darkened. "That is difficult to say," he answered. "Combat-ready warriors usually number about one half of the total. The remainder serve in roles of support. But during the recent hostilities, we lost at least half of our fighters. And per your orders, a certain number of them remained behind in Parthalon. Even if they were brought here, their numbers are not enough to make any appreciable difference. If we could summon seventy-five thousand combat-ready troops, we would be lucky. I fear that should Wulfgar return in such strength, we would be hard-pressed to defeat him."

Tristan leaned across the table and looked at his second in command.

"Exactly," he said. "That is precisely why I must order you to do something else for me, something you may find contradictory to your nature."

"Of course, my lord."

Tristan's gaze hardened. "I want you to order the training of suitable Minion females as combat warriors," he said.

Everyone around the table was stunned—not the least Traax. Tristan had discussed this with no one, and it came as a bolt out of the blue.

Traax just sat there, his eyes wide and unbelieving.

"When they are ready," the prince continued, "I want Duvessa to serve directly under you as their subcommander. I trust her, and I can think of no Minion female better suited to the task."

Traax opened his mouth, but for a moment no sound came out. Finally he found his voice.

"But my lord . . . ," he began, trying to find the right words. "Such a thing has never been done! It is not the Minion way!"

Tristan narrowed his eyes. Several members of the Conclave held their breath.

"There is a first time for everything, and this is to be theirs," Tristan said. His tone was firm, controlled. "We need them. To do otherwise would be a shameful waste of talent. Like the healers, they are to wear a feather on the chest of their body armor to designate their status. But this feather is to be red, like the blood they may one day have to spill. Those healers who become warriors may wear both." Then he smiled. "What's wrong?" he asked. "Are you afraid they might surprise you, and prove to be better than you imagined?"

Traax took a deep breath. Despite his misgivings, he remained true to his Minion vows. He bowed his head.

"I live to serve," he said softly.

"Good," Tristan answered. "And thank you."

Traax sighed and pursed his lips.

"Then we are agreed," Tristan said to the group. "Is there anything else to discuss before Wigg and I leave for Parthalon?"

Shailiha and Celeste exchanged glances. The princess cleared her throat.

"Celeste and I will go with Tyranny and Traax," she said. As if to emphasize that she would not be dissuaded, the princess folded her arms over her breasts. Celeste gave Tristan a little smile.

The prince had been expecting something like this. Hoping for some tacit advice, he looked over at Wigg. A sour look on his face, the First Wizard shook his head. Faegan did the same. But as Tristan sat there looking at the two women, he felt his heart softening. Finally he made up his mind.

"I'll compromise with you," he said. "Shailiha, you go with Tyranny and Traax. Celeste will join her father and me on our trip to Parthalon."

The two women nodded their agreement. Wigg shook his head angrily, and the telltale vein in his right temple began to throb. Faegan did his best to stifle a smile.

Standing, Tristan adjourned the meeting. He walked to the serving table and poured himself a welcome glass of wine. As the group broke up, he saw Shailiha and Celeste saying goodbye to each other in a far corner of the room.

Suddenly Tyranny was at his side, quiet and serious. Reaching out, she touched his arm.

"Please be careful," she said. As if not quite knowing what to say next, she let go a frustrated sigh. Then she ran one hand through her hair, and her smile reappeared. "If you die over there in Parthalon, I'll kill you."

Tristan snorted, and then took a sip of wine.

"It's true that I don't relish going back into the bowels of the Recluse," he said, "but this Scroll Master doesn't sound like much of a threat. He's probably just some old hermit with spectacles. The truth is I'd much rather be going with you. I have a feeling that is where the real action will be."

Looking into Tyranny's eyes, he thought he saw a hint of moisture there. But she quickly blinked it away. She gave him a rather lingering kiss on the cheek.

"Farewell, *Jin'Sai,*" she said softly.

Before he could respond she headed for the door. Shailiha followed her, stopping to give her brother a long farewell hug. The prince hugged her back.

And you, Tristan thought, as he watched them walk away.

Taking another sip of wine, he turned his thoughts back toward the Recluse.

CHAPTER XXIII

AS SHE WALKED DOWN THE HALLS OF THE REDOUBT, THE YOUNG acolyte still found herself stunned by its beauty. Even as First Sister Adrian's assistant, she might take years to learn to navigate these multicolored hallways. In fact, she was having difficulty finding her way back to her own quarters. The hour was late, and her usual walk before retiring had turned into something more than she had imagined.

Early in her walk she had come upon Sister Adrian, and the First Sister had revealed some of what had transpired in the meeting of the Conclave. The two had chatted a while and then, after agreeing to make their morning rounds among the wounded together, they had said good night and gone their separate ways.

Now she guessed at which direction to take at yet another intersection guarded by Minion warriors. She chose rightward— and realized that she had guessed correctly. She recognized where she was. Her quarters were two doors down and on the left.

When she reached her door, she called upon the craft. Almost immediately she heard the lock turn over once, then twice more. She grasped the gold handle, gave it a turn, and let herself in.

Her sumptuous quarters still awed her. During her travels as an acolyte, she had never stayed anywhere as elegant as this. The flames in the fireplace still danced merrily, highlighting the ceiling and walls. A scented candle burned on the table by her bed.

She removed her red robe and dropped it onto an overstuffed chair. Dressed only in her silk undergarments, she slipped between the satin sheets of her bed. Life would be good here, she thought.

Lying back in the sheets, she decided to view again the amazing anomaly she had acquired just before the *Jin'Sai* and his wizards had defeated Wulfgar that night atop the roof of the palace.

Raising her right wrist, she called upon the craft. In response a small incision appeared in her skin. As it did, a single drop of her blood left the wound and came to hover in the air. The incision closed again. As expected, her blood signature formed from the freshly liberated droplet.

Her blood signature appeared proper in every respect. It was clearly right-leaning, illustrating her tendency to practice only the Vigors. It was also free of Forestallments—yet another condition the wizards had insisted upon before granting her membership in the Acolytes of the Redoubt.

Then she narrowed her eyes, and her blood signature began to twist and turn upon itself. As it did, it came to reveal something quite different from what the wizards had seen when they examined it. It now clearly leaned to the left, and dozens of Forestallments branched away from the main body of the signature. With a smile of satisfaction, she caused it to vanish.

Leaning over to one side of the bed, she blew out the candle. In the dying firelight, she committed to memory what she had just learned from Sister Adrian.

Bratach would be pleased.

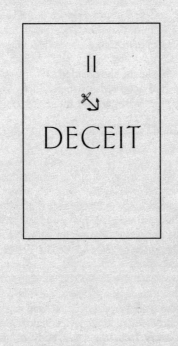

II

DECEIT

CHAPTER XXIV

TRISTAN FOUND HIMSELF LYING ON HIS BACK IN THE COOL, DAMP grass. As he sat up, he felt his head spin, but he knew from past experience that the feeling would soon pass. It was still night in Parthalon, but the orange-red furnace of dawn was already starting to creep up over the eastern horizon. As his head cleared he looked around, trying to find Wigg and Celeste.

The First Wizard lay to Tristan's left. He came up onto his elbows, then stood stiffly, shook the dew from his robe, and looked around. The twelve Minion warriors who had been selected to accompany them also began to stir.

Tristan stood, checked his weapons, then went and knelt beside Celeste in the wet grass. She wore a tan leather jerkin, black breeches, and soft brown knee boots. A sword lay at her left hip, its scabbard wet with dew. A sheathed dagger was tied down to her right thigh. He smiled as she sat up and wrapped her arms around her knees. Her hair was tousled and she looked sleepy, but she smiled back at him.

"Faegan's portal is quite an experience, isn't it?" she commented groggily.

She pushed her hair from her eyes, then swept a handful over one shoulder. When she tried to stand, she half-fell, half-stumbled against Tristan, and he steadied her.

"I don't think I'll ever get used to traveling in this way," she said.

He smiled again. "I know," he answered. "Still, it's preferable to a thirty-day voyage across the Sea of Whispers."

"Begging your pardon, my lord, but we are assembled and ready to move," a gravelly Minion voice said.

Tristan turned and saw Alrik, the officer Traax had chosen to lead the accompanying warriors. Tristan had liked him the moment they had met. At fifty-two Seasons of New Life, Alrik was a good bit older than the lord he served. His long hair was streaked with gray, but he was as sturdy as a granite boulder. A decades-old battle scar ran from his right cheekbone down to the cleft in his jaw. The eleven other warriors stood at attention just behind him.

Trying to get his bearings, Tristan looked around. He had asked Faegan to deliver them as close to the Recluse as possible, but given the great distance involved and the complex calculations required to operate the portal, such requests might mean little. Now Tristan and Wigg concluded that they did not know where they were.

Tristan addressed Alrik. "Send one of the warriors into the sky to determine our location," he ordered. "I want to be at the Recluse as soon as possible." With a click of his heels, Alrik did as he was asked.

After a short time the warrior returned. "The Recluse is due north," he said. "It is about one hour's walk from our current position. Do you wish litters constructed, *Jin 'Sai*?" he asked.

Tristan shook his head. "By the time you finished them, we'd already be there." He gave a sly look over at the First Wizard. "The walk will do us all good."

With Alrik leading them, they set out for the Recluse. Tristan and Celeste talked to each other as they went. Lost in thought, Wigg walked behind them. The rest of the Minion warriors brought up the rear. After nearly an hour they came up over a short rise, and Tristan recognized where they were.

He saw the small, lonely grave in the middle of the field. He stopped.

For several long moments Tristan didn't speak. His face a mask, he stood there, staring at the grave that had once held his only son. Suddenly understanding, Celeste remained still. Wigg placed one of his hands on Tristan's shoulder. Only the sounds of the waking songbirds and the gentle swish of the wind as it brushed through the grass interrupted the silence.

"Are you all right?" Wigg asked. There was an unusual gentleness in his voice.

"It had been my hope that we would not pass by here," Tristan answered softly, almost to himself.

"I know it's difficult," Wigg said. "But we must steel our hearts for what is yet to come."

Tristan knew that Wigg was right, but all he could do was to nod in agreement. Finally he signaled to the Minions, and the procession began moving again.

The last time Tristan had come here had been to order the Minion troops to Eutracia to fight Nicholas' hatchlings. He had also ordered the reconstruction of the Recluse, hoping one day to use the fortress as his headquarters in Parthalon. One corner of his mouth turned up at that thought. He had to admit that the reconstruction hadn't been a priority for him of late. If nothing else, this trip would serve to ascertain the progress of the Minion men and women who presumably were still at work on the fortress.

Tristan reached the top of the next hill first and looked down. The rays of the rising sun shone down on the lake below and on the island that lay in its center. Mouth agape, Tristan raised a hand to bring his group to a halt. The structure on the island was more than merely reconstructed. It was a revelation.

A long, stone arch provided the only way in or out of the castle, spanning the water from the shore of the lake to where it met the wooden drawbridge, which was flanked by high barbicans and lowered from the castle's outer wall. Minion warriors manned the portcullis, castle walls, and surrounding areas. Beyond the first two gate towers lay the single entry to the innermost sanctuary of the Recluse.

Unlike the dark and forbidding towers and outer ward, the buildings at the heart of the Recluse looked light and ethereal. Just as Tristan remembered, they were a pale, light blue marble. The turrets at the corners of the main structure were very high. As Tristan had ordered, the flags of the Coven of the Sorceresses had been replaced by new banners depicting his Eutracian heraldry—the lion and the broadsword.

Tristan continued to admire the wondrous structure. The first time he had been here, he had been its prisoner. Now he was its lord.

"It's beautiful," Celeste said. "It's hard to believe that something so lovely could have housed people so evil." She looked toward her father. He took her hand.

"Is it really true that my mother lived here for more than three hundred years?" she asked. "While I had been abandoned in the Caves of the Paragon with Ragnar?"

Wigg's face grew hard, but he answered softly. "Yes, my dear."

Tristan looked at Alrik. "I want you to fly to the Recluse. Tell them that their lord is about to arrive."

Alrik clicked his heels together. "I live to serve," he answered, and, spreading his wings, launched himself into the air.

With a nod from Tristan, the rest of the group began walking down the hill. As they approached the bridge, a contingent of warriors came striding out to meet them. Their leader was tall and a bit thin for a Minion. But the steely gaze in his eyes spoke volumes about his ability to lead. Alrik walked on one side of him; on the other was a female Gallipolai, one of the offshoots of the Minion race who were born with white wings and blond hair. Once Minion slaves, they had been freed by Tristan.

As Tristan, Wigg, and Celeste approached, the warriors all went down on one knee.

"I live to serve!" came the uniform oath.

"You may rise," the prince said.

Alrik returned to Tristan's side.

"Are you in charge here?" Tristan asked the warrior who had led the others down the drawbridge.

The Minion bowed. "Yes, my lord." His voice was strong, his manner direct. "I am Lorcan. Commander Traax placed me in charge of finishing the reconstruction of the Recluse, just after you recalled so many of us to fight in Eutracia." A menacing smile flashed across his face. "I wish I could have been there with you. We were told that a great many of your enemies died that day."

Then Lorcan looked at Wigg and bowed again. "And the lead wizard is with us as well," he said. "We are honored."

Wigg cleared his throat. "Actually, the title is now First Wizard," he said. "I would like to present my daughter, Celeste." Looking at her, Lorcan bowed once more.

Tristan regarded the Gallipolai standing by Lorcan's side. She was lovely, her long blond hair and white feathered wings luminous in the early morning light. Her cornflower-blue eyes reminded him of Narissa, the Gallipolai who had died in his arms just after he had killed Kluge, the Minions' previous commander. It had been some time since Tristan had seen a Gallipolai. He had almost forgotten how strikingly beautiful both the men and the women of their race could be.

"And who is this?" he asked.

"This is Persephone, my wife," Lorcan answered proudly. "And my assistant here."

Suddenly the warrior's face was overcome with concern. "You did give the order granting us the right to intermarry, did you not?" he asked.

Tristan smiled. "Indeed," he answered. "My congratulations to you both."

Relieved, Lorcan and Persephone beamed back at him.

"May I ask why you have come?" Lorcan inquired. "Is it to inspect the Recluse?"

"In a way," Wigg answered. "We will certainly wish to examine all of your wonderful work before we leave. But that is not the primary reason we are here. Tell me, have the chambers below the Recluse been disturbed in any way?"

"No," Lorcan answered. "Those areas are said to be of the craft. I had them sealed until further orders."

"Good," Wigg answered. "Can you please direct us to the passageway that leads down?"

"Of course," Lorcan answered. He turned and led them across the drawbridge.

There was little going on in the outer ward, but the grand foyer of the Recluse was a beehive of activity. The outside of the fortress had been completed, and the workers now directed all of their energy toward decorating the inner chambers. Artisans had turned the massive foyer into a wondrous workshop. Some of them were busy weaving carpet. Others were creating artwork or building furniture. Tristan saw that at the rate they were producing, the interior of the Recluse would reclaim its previous splendor within a matter of weeks.

Lorcan led them across the black-and-white checkerboard floor and down a long hallway, finally stopping before a pair of huge double doors guarded by two Minion warriors. The warriors snapped to attention. Lorcan turned to look at his lord.

"This is but one of many ways down," he said. "But of all the stairways leading to the lower regions, this one remains the most intact. Most of the others were damaged beyond use."

With a gesture from Tristan, the guards opened the doors. The massive hinges creaked ominously, as if to warn away anyone foolish enough to enter. A winding staircase led down into the unrelenting blackness.

"Does my lord wish the services of additional warriors?" Lorcan asked.

Tristan thought for a moment. "No. But if we have not returned after two hours, I want you to personally lead a search party for us. Do you understand?"

Loran nodded, and clicked his heels.

Walking to stand in front of the prince, Wigg looked down the curved stairway. Even his wizard's eyes could see nothing in the gloom. He turned back to Tristan.

"Some potential source of light must remain," he mused. "Even Failee couldn't see in the dark."

Tristan pursed his lips. "Are you quite sure about that?" he asked. Wigg only scowled back.

Looking down the stairway again, Wigg narrowed his eyes and called upon the craft. Almost immediately a series of wall sconces lit up, their golden glow flooding out into the hallway.

"It is wide enough to descend two abreast," Wigg said. "I suggest that I go first, followed by you and Celeste. Then the rest of the warriors follow behind you, two by two, with Alrik bringing up the rear. Agreed?"

Tristan nodded. He looked over at Celeste, who smiled at him and drew her sword.

Tristan reached behind his right shoulder and drew his dreggan from its scabbard. The warriors in his party did the same.

"Are you ready?" Wigg asked.

"Is there any other choice?" Tristan answered.

Turning back toward the stairway, Wigg took a deep breath. With careful, measured steps, he began to lead them down.

CHAPTER XXV

WHEN SHE HEARD THE SHOUT, SATINE BOLTED UPRIGHT FROM her bed.

She threw on a silk robe, quickly tied its sash around her waist, and grabbed the razor-sharp sword lying on the nightstand.

She ran to the other side of the room and tore open the door. Without hesitation she ran in the direction of the wailing that resounded through the night. The screaming voice sounded like Aeolus. As she ran, armed students of the Serpent and the Sword joined her.

Rounding the corner, she realized that the cries were coming from an already open doorway.

She skidded to a stop and took a deep breath. Then she raised the sword over her head and launched herself in.

A single candle lit the room with a soft, even glow. Aeolus sat on the bed, cradling the head of the man that lay there. Fresh, sticky blood was everywhere.

When the stricken man saw Satine enter the room, he smiled. For the briefest of moments, the light returned to his eyes. But it seemed to take all the life he had remaining. It was as if after seeing her this last time, he could finally allow himself to die.

A decisive rattle escaped his lungs, and his head slumped to the side. Satine saw that his throat had been slit from ear to ear. She looked at Aeolus, but all her master could do was shake his head.

Satine lowered her sword. She started to kneel down. Then she heard the sound of rapid footfalls on the rooftop above.

Turning quickly, she pushed her way past the others and tore down the hall. A trail of blood led her to another room. Raising her sword, she rushed in.

There was no one there. Looking up, she saw that the skylight in the ceiling was open. Its handle dripped fresh blood.

Then she heard the footfalls again—faster, louder, closer. She ran across the room and leaped atop the same table the assassin had used in his escape. She jumped up and hoisted herself through the open skylight. As she stood on the roof, the magenta-colored moonlight glinted off her blade. The night wind snaked coldly between her skin and the folds of her robe. Looking around warily, she could detect no movement or sound in the inky night.

Suddenly, there he was.

A figure swathed in dark cloth ran furtively ahead of her. Carrying a sword, he leaped from the roof she stood on and landed nimbly upon the next. Knowing she hadn't a second to lose, Satine ran to the edge of the roof and launched herself into the night.

As she flew through the air, the distance between the two rooftops somehow grew longer. It was as if the buildings were moving away from each other. Terror gripped her as she realized that she wasn't going to make it.

Tumbling helplessly toward the ground, she looked up and saw the assassin looking down over the edge of the far building. He smiled wickedly at her, his teeth glinting in the moonlight.

With a scream Satine tore off her covers and launched her naked body from the bed. She was shaking and bathed in sweat. Looking to the window, she saw that it was nearly dawn.

She got to her knees, then sat back on her heels and wrapped her arms around herself. She fought back the urge to vomit. She looked to the other side of the room. The small set of carriage bells she had tied to the door handle had not rung. It was a crude device, but effective: No one had tried to violate the sanctity of her chamber. For that much, at least, she could be thankful.

The recurring nightmare of her father's death always rattled her to the very core. Tonight had been no exception. When they had first begun, she had wondered how long they would persist, and what it would finally take to make them go away. Only as the years went on did she come to understand.

The only way she would ever be free of them would be to find her father's killer, and to see him die slowly, painfully. Only that would erase her shame at failing to catch him that horrible night on the roof of the Serpent and the Sword.

She rose and stood on shaky legs and lit a pair of candles. She carried one of them to the washstand on the other side of the room. In the mirror, the face that stared back at her was stark white, her hair matted to her sweaty skin.

She splashed some water on her face, dried herself with a cloth, then ran a hairbrush through her hair.

In the candlelight her reflection showed the tattoos on each of her upper arms. They were the twin marks of mastery from Aeolus' school: the image of a coiled serpent on her right arm, a sword on the left.

She touched the sword tattoo gently. She was proud of these markings, for few had ever attained them both. They would be with her until the day she died.

Uncoiling a little, she walked over to the window of her room in the Rooster and Finch and looked out. She had returned from Valrenkium yesterday after a hard two-day ride. Tammerland would be waking up soon, and she needed to be on her way again.

She now had everything she required to begin her sanctions, and it was time to get to work. She went to the weather-beaten wardrobe, opened its doors, and removed her clothes and weapons.

As the light of the morning sun crept over the lone windowsill, she began to dress.

"THIS IS ALL THE INFORMATION WE HAVE FOR YOU REGARDING THE whereabouts of your first target," Bratach said. He handed Satine the parchment. "It should be enough for someone of your talents."

Satine took the parchment and read it, quickly committing it to memory. She handed it back to him, then watched as he placed one of its corners into the flame of the candle on the table between them.

Bratach, Ivan, and Satine sat in the subterranean sanctuary of the archery shop. After leaving the Rooster and Finch, she had walked her horse past the shop to see whether a message might be waiting for her. When she saw the "open" sign hanging by the parted doors, she pulled her gelding up short. The words were red.

Once she had gone in, Ivan had closed the shop and led the way down the back stairs, where Bratach had been waiting.

Flicking the last cinders from his fingertips, Bratach leaned back in his chair. "So you choose to be known as the Gray Fox," he mused. "Appropriate, I must say."

He picked up a half-full wine bottle and poured himself a

glass. After pouring one for Ivan, he held the bottle out to Satine and raised one eyebrow.

Satine shook her head. "I never drink once a sanction has begun."

Bratach nodded. "So much the better." He looked at Ivan and then back at Satine.

"You dropped out of sight for a while," he said, his tone a bit darker. "We were beginning to worry. One hundred fifty thousand kisa is a great deal of money. We wouldn't like to think that you might cheat us by running away. Our master and his forces will be here soon. We shall need to know that your tasks have been completed."

"I told you that I had things to do before I could begin," she shot back. "I told your master that once I accept a sanction, I always see it through. That is exactly what I shall do."

"Good," Bratach answered.

Casting her gaze down at the ashes on the table, she decided to take a risk. "Who is your confederate inside the palace?" she asked. "How did you slip him by the wizards without detection? And how does he communicate with you?"

"Don't worry," Bratach said mockingly. "The information you receive is genuine. Finding your first target should be simple. Just follow the trail, so to speak." He leaned back again. "We shall require proof. When the job is done, bring us the head."

Standing, Satine looked hard into Bratach's eyes.

"No," she said adamantly. "That was never part of the agreement. The way I have this planned, that will be quite impossible. Besides, you will no doubt get all the confirmation you require from whomever you have inside. Take it or leave it."

Bratach looked angrily at Satine. He needed her services badly. Plans had already been put into motion that even Lord Wulfgar could not stop. The assassinations had to go forward, no matter the cost.

"Very well," he said. "But if you fail us, I will hunt you down and kill you myself."

One corner of Satine's mouth came up. She leaned over and placed her face close to his.

"That won't be necessary," she said. "If I fail, I will already be dead."

Turning away, she walked toward the stairs. Then, one boot on the first step, she turned and looked at them.

"When this first job is completed I will inform you," she said. Saying nothing more, she walked up the stairs.

CHAPTER XXVI

MEMORIES ARE STRANGE CREATURES OF THE MIND. THE THINGS that trigger them can be as varied and surprising as the experiences themselves. Like ghosts from the past, certain sights, sounds, and smells can each in their own way summon remembrances both welcome and foreboding. Just now Tristan of the House of Galland's senses told him that he wished he had never come here. He guessed that the First Wizard felt the same.

Tristan and the others followed Wigg down the curved staircase. The echoes of many boot heels striking the paved floor added to the sense of emptiness. If there was one thing in the world that Tristan could not abide, it was being confined.

They had been traveling downward for some time. The air grew colder with every step and it smelled increasingly fetid and damp—like a humid, nighttime forest overgrown with moss. Finally Wigg slowed and raised his hand. Everyone stopped.

"A landing is just beyond," he said. "Be on guard. I cannot tell whether this is an area that Tristan and I have been in before. There is no telling what we might find."

Wigg took the last few steps down. Tristan and the others soon found themselves standing upon the floor of a circular room. The prince felt his heart recoil. They stood in the chamber in which he, Wigg, and Geldon had been tortured—and where Failee had tried to convince Shailiha to become her fifth sorceress.

Letting go of Celeste's hand, Tristan turned slowly around as he took in the imposing space. There was no one else here, and he finally relaxed a little.

The white marble walls were cracked and partially tumbled down, and it looked as though the rest of the room might cave in at any moment. The black pentangle inlaid into the floor was hardly recognizable. The five black thrones that had once sat at each of the pentangle's corners had been overturned and broken, their pieces scattered about. Dust, debris, and marble shards lay everywhere.

Then Tristan saw the torture devices hanging from the ceiling on the far side of the room. Saying nothing, he slid his dreggan back into its scabbard and walked over.

He reached up and touched the black iron gibbet in which he had once been imprisoned. Its door hung open, and the chain creaked as it moved at his touch. Wigg came over and placed a hand on the prince's shoulder.

"Do you remember?" Tristan breathed. The question was unnecessary, but he couldn't help asking.

"Yes," Wigg answered.

"It was all so horrible," Tristan said, so softly that Wigg had to augment his hearing with the craft. Then Tristan walked over to the other gibbets that had held Wigg and Geldon. He touched each of them also. When he turned back, there were tears in his eyes.

"But we won," Wigg said. "Through a supreme effort of will you were able to call upon the craft without having first been trained. No one had ever done that before. You killed the sorceresses, and we brought Shailiha and the Paragon home."

Tristan nodded. Celeste walked up to him and touched him on one arm. He did his best to summon a smile for her.

"What was it that destroyed this place?" Celeste asked.

"When an endowed person possessing Forestallments dies, the Forestallments leave his being," Wigg answered. "Or so goes the theory. When that happens a great atmospheric disturbance occurs, bringing forth thunder, lightning, and wind. When Tristan killed the sorceresses, they all died at once except for Succiu. The resulting storm was so great that it collapsed the palace and ruptured the foundations of these chambers below ground."

Celeste walked over to the damaged pentangle. She thought to herself for a moment. She looked back over at her father.

"Where do they go?" she asked.

"What do you mean?" he responded.

"When the Forestallments depart a dead body, where do they go?" Celeste asked again. Intrigued by her question, Tristan also turned to Wigg.

Placing his hands into the opposite sleeves of his robe, the First Wizard scowled a bit. "We still do not know. Faegan and I believe that they don't really go anywhere. We postulate that with no living host to sustain them, they simply cease to be, like a spell that has been terminated."

Turning to check on the Minion warriors, Tristan's gaze fell upon two large, jagged sections of white marble, and he immediately recognized them. He walked over, knelt down, and touched one. It was cool and smooth, just the way it had felt that day when it had pressed so unforgivingly into his naked back.

It was the ruin of the altar upon which Succiu had violated him—causing Nicholas to be conceived—and imbued his blood with the many Forestallments his signature now carried.

As Tristan stood up, Wigg came to join him again. "Are you all right?" the wizard asked.

Tristan let go a deep breath. "No," he said, his eyes still locked upon the smashed altar. "But I will be."

"You must let it all go," Wigg said.

Finally looking away from the altar, Tristan nodded.

"Father, would you please come here?" Celeste asked.

Tristan and Wigg turned to see that she had walked to another area of the room. Several Minion warriors were there with her, and they were all looking down at the floor.

Three sets of remains lay there, nothing more than separate collections of ash that loosely resembled human beings.

"These are the remains of the Coven, aren't they?" Celeste asked.

"Yes," her father said.

"Which of them was my mother?"

Wigg pointed to the one in the middle. "There," he said. "That was Failee."

Kneeling down, Celeste looked at the pile of dark, fragile ash, tentatively reached out, and touched it. It collapsed in on itself, losing all semblance of its previous shape. After closing her eyes for a moment, she stood back up.

"I'm sorry," Wigg said.

Celeste shook her head. "You have nothing to be sorry about," she answered. "You are still here with me, and that is what matters now."

Wigg nodded, his eyes suspiciously shiny.

After a moment, he pointed to the far side of the room where the floor ended, opening the room to a lower level. "My instinct tells me that is where we must concentrate our search."

A set of stairs led downward from one side of the floor's edge. The lower level of the chamber had been Failee's area of experimentation. She had kept the Wiktors, her awful pets, down there. Tristan clearly remembered how they had clambered out of their lairs to try to kill him and the wizard after he had destroyed the sorceresses. Only at the last moment had Wigg been able to kill the Wiktors.

The area was covered in ash—evidence of Wigg's incineration of the Wiktors.

Wigg pointed to the stairs and raised an eyebrow. "Shall we?" he asked.

At an order from Tristan, the three of them started down the stairs, followed by Alrik and the warriors. For the first time, Tristan saw the numerous hallways that branched off from this lower room. The piles of dark, smoky ashes gradually trailed off toward each opening.

As Tristan walked forward, some of the ash came up over the tops of his knee boots. Occasionally a fire-bleached bone poked up to glint bleakly in the dim light. Tristan was sickened.

Dirty clouds billowed into the air as the party disturbed the remains, making it hard to see and breathe. Wigg finally ordered everyone to a halt so that the air could clear.

When they could see again, Tristan spotted a door in the far wall of the room. He and Wigg waded to it slowly so as to raise as little dust as possible. The door was made of heavy iron and painted black. Wigg stiffened, and Tristan knew that his reaction could only mean one thing.

There was living, endowed blood somewhere on the other side. Tristan glanced at Wigg, who nodded.

"The endowed blood on the other side is highly unusual," the wizard said, his brow furrowing with concentration.

"How so?" Tristan asked.

Wigg shook his head. "That's impossible to say until I confront it. I say we force the door and go in. Agreed?"

Tristan nodded and called back to Alrik to bring two warriors. The five of them shoveled the ash away from the door by hand. With each handful they removed, more caved back in again. It was filthy work, and the rising ash choked their lungs and stung their eyes.

"This is pointless," Wigg growled. "Everyone stand back!"

The First Wizard narrowed his eyes and called the craft. An azure glow began to surround the area before the door. He raised his arms and the glow formed into several thin, nearly transparent sheets of azure.

Wigg directed the sheets straight down into the knee-high ash to form a square barrier, with the door making up the fourth side. Lifting his arms again, he caused the segregated ash within the quadrant to rise into the air and deposit itself to one side, leaving a clean area before the door. Then he stepped gingerly over one of the azure panels, and motioned to Tristan and Celeste to join him.

"Are you ready?" he asked the prince.

Tristan raised his dreggan. "As ready as we'll ever be," he said grimly.

"Very well," Wigg answered.

At Wigg's gesture, twin azure bolts assaulted the door and covered it like flowing liquid. When the entire door was engulfed, Wigg raised his arms higher.

With a great creaking noise, the massive iron door began to give way.

CHAPTER XXVII

"ARE YOU SURE THIS IS GOING TO WORK?" ABBEY ASKED NER-vously. "I know how useful your portal can be, but tell me truly. Have you ever tried anything like this before?"

Faegan ignored her question for a moment. It was late af-ternoon in Eutracia and the sun was already low in the sky, the salty sea air rising to greet his senses. As busy as he had been all day and the previous night, the time had seemed to fly by.

Truth be known, he wasn't at all sure about the risk he was about to take. There was no way he could be until it was over. By then, if it had gone wrong it would be too late. But if it was successful, it could change the world.

Faegan, Adrian, Abbey, and Duvessa were in a Minion litter together, hovering in the sky near the Cavalon Delta. Ten strong warriors bore it, their wings working diligently to keep it aloft. They had been here for hours, helping to prepare the *Reprise* for sea.

After much discussion, Tyranny and Traax had decided that only the *Reprise* would make this voyage. Faegan had agreed. The rest of the fleet was to stay behind and protect the coast, should Tristan be correct about Wulfgar. This was a mission of intelligence rather than of war. They would stand a much better chance of remaining unseen if only one ship approached the Citadel.

Now the *Reprise* bobbed calmly at her moorings just off the coast. Faegan, uncertain of how the portal might affect the ship, had recommended that her sails be tightly furled, and her wheel tied off. Under Tyranny's critical gaze, everything else had been lashed down, closed, or otherwise secured.

In addition to Tyranny's regular crew, a Minion phalanx lined the deck. The war frigate lay low in the sea, her lower decks loaded with enough food and water to sustain the added number of people aboard.

"Am I sure about this?" Faegan finally said to Abbey. "No, absolutely not! But I believe my theory is valid." Looking back toward the warship, he sighed. "Would Wigg try to skin me alive if he knew? Yes. Do those brave souls aboard that ship down there think it worth the risk? Again, yes."

"But if this works, once they are through and on the other side how will they know where they are?" Adrian asked. "To have sailed there while continually marking their progress on a chart is one thing. But to be so suddenly deposited upon the Sea of Whispers so many leagues from home seems quite another."

Faegan nodded. "Tyranny came to me last night with that very concern. We decided that once they were through, the most reliable navigational aid would be her sextant. I made some modifications to it. To come home in the same manner they must reach the exact location to which the portal brought them, or they will never find it again." Faegan scowled. "My greatest fear is not whether the portal will do its job, or whether Tyranny can return to the same set of coordinates. Rather, I am concerned about the much greater amount of power needed to conjure a portal of such size and its possibly deleterious effects on both the ship and those aboard her. But if they can get through safely, they should be all right."

"I certainly hope so," Duvessa said.

Faegan looked down at the *Reprise*. "So do I," he answered softly.

TYRANNY WAS NERVOUSLY EYEING THE DECKS OF HER SHIP. "I hope your wizard is as good as everyone claims," she said to Shailiha.

Taking a deep draft on her cigarillo as though it were her last, she raised her face to the darkening sky and luxuriously exhaled the smoke. Then she dropped the remains of the cigarillo to the deck and ground it out with the sole of one of her scuffed knee boots.

Scars and K'jarr stood with her awaiting orders. It had been decided that while at sea, even Shailiha would come under Tyranny's command. This would be the princess' first ocean voyage, and Tyranny fervently hoped that the short spell Faegan had cast over Shailiha the previous night would keep her from becoming seasick. If the portal worked, they would exit only one day's sail from the Citadel, putting them right into demonslaver-infested waters. There would be no time for anyone to be ill.

Tyranny looked over at Scars. Her perpetually shirtless, muscle-bound first mate smiled in response. He was more than ready to intercept however many of Wulfgar's demonslavers they could find.

"Is everything in place?" she asked.

"Yes, Captain," he answered. "All of the sails are furled and double-tied. All of the hatches are closed and locked; the ship's wheel is tied off, and the rudder secured. All of our crew members and as many of the Minion warriors as possible have gone below. We're as ready as we will ever be."

After giving Scars a nod, Tyranny turned to K'jarr. "And your warriors remaining above decks, they are lashed to the gunwales and masts?"

"Yes, Captain," he answered. "We only await your command to begin."

"Very well," Tyranny said. "It's time."

K'jarr walked over to the foremast, followed by Scars, Tyranny, and Shailiha. The women watched as Scars tied K'jarr to the mast. Then Tyranny did the same for Scars, pulling the knots as tight as she could. When she was finished, she looked up at them both.

"Good luck, gentlemen," she said. "The Afterlife willing, we'll see you on the other side."

Taking Shailiha by the arm, Tyranny walked her to the prow of the ship, where she tied the princess securely to several iron rings that had been screwed into the gunwale just for this purpose. Once satisfied, she did the same to herself, as best she could. She looked over at Shailiha.

"I fear we may be in for a very rough ride," she said. "Even Faegan isn't sure how long it will last. Not exactly the most genteel way to take your first sea voyage, is it?"

"True." Shailiha did her best to smile. "But I trust in Faegan. What shall be, shall be."

Tyranny nodded. She looked up into the sky near the bow of the ship and called down the warrior who had been hovering there, waiting for her command. He was by her side in an instant.

"Tell Master Faegan that all is ready," she ordered.

The warrior clicked his heels together. "I live to serve," came the reply, and he launched himself toward the litter. From their places in the bow Shailiha and Tyranny could just make out Faegan's form. They watched the wizard raise his hands.

Almost at once the *Reprise*'s anchor rose from the seafloor, its chain clanking as the anchor wheel took up its length. Then the anchor slipped itself up and into its mooring station. The unfettered *Reprise* drifted freely. That was when the howling began.

Just forward of the bow, a huge azure portal formed. Its swirling vortex was as tall and as broad as the ship.

Then the howling increased. Shailiha thought her eardrums might burst, and suddenly felt terrified. She had been through one of Faegan's portals before, but it had never made noise.

As the vortex engulfed the bow of the *Reprise,* Shailiha began to feel the effects of the portal making her sleepy and dizzy. She tried to call out to Tyranny, but she couldn't make her mouth work, much less make herself heard above the din.

Her head slumped to her breast.

Far above, Faegan and the others watched as the shrieking, whirling azure portal swallowed up the warship and then disappeared.

STUNNED, BRATACH LOWERED HIS SPYGLASS. HE STOOD UPON THE INvisible frigate, his endowed blood shielded from Faegan's senses, savoring the marvelous coincidence that had seen him checking his ship and its demonslavers the same day Faegan had used his portal. Initially, his interest had been piqued by the sight of Tyranny and the Minions making preparations to get under way. Then, when Faegan had unexpectedly appeared in a litter overhead, he knew he would simply have to stay to learn what he could.

What the crafty, crippled old wizard had just accomplished was impressive. Bratach could not be sure where the *Reprise* was going, but he had his suspicions. Still, if the plan was to attack the Citadel, why send only one ship? The Minion force aboard her was not sufficient to seize the island. Why weren't the First Wizard and the *Jin'Sai* aboard? But in the end, none of that mattered. Even if that was where the *Reprise* was headed, Bratach had no way to warn his lord in time.

Looking back to the sky, he saw Faegan's litter depart for Tammerland. As the litter shrank against the sunset, another thought occurred to him. Faegan had been very clever—but not quite clever enough. Now Bratach knew Faegan's secret of the portal. When his master arrived, together they would turn it against their enemy.

Smiling, Bratach turned and walked down the deck, feeling his way along the invisible gunwale until he found the gangway. He walked carefully down the stairs and went to confer with his demonslavers.

MORE THAN HALFWAY ACROSS THE SEA, AN AZURE RADIANCE GREW and grew until the portal's swirling vortex formed and the deafening howling began. It was night and the seas were high. The sky was cloudy and threatening. In the distance the first branches of lightning were visible, scratching their way closer across the darkness.

Like some plague-ridden ghost ship from the past suddenly returned to haunt the present, the *Reprise* was vomited from the portal's mouth to land harshly upon the waves. Its job done, the portal vanished.

The ocean tossed the ship back and forth mercilessly. One of her masts was cracked and her bowsprit was gone. Her sails still furled and her ship's wheel tied off, she was helpless against the sea.

Then the first of the stressed planks in her keel suddenly let loose. Seawater rushed in. The storm arrived and the rain began in earnest, bringing with it thunder and lighting. White-capped waves rose higher as the storm-tossed ship began to list from the water invading her belly. Despite the storm and the ship's violent rocking, none of those aboard had yet awoken from the passage through the portal.

Her head lying upon her chest and the gold medallion around her neck swinging back and forth in the relentless rain, Shailiha of the House of Galland slumped forward in her bonds.

Then lightning clove the mizzen mast in two. When it came crashing down upon the deck it fell upon deaf ears.

CHAPTER XXVIII

LYING ON HIS BACK BEFORE THE CAMPFIRE, WITH HIS HEAD propped up on a log, Geldon contemplated all of the amazing things he had witnessed over the course of the last several days. In his heart he had to admit that none of it was good.

They were close to Tammerland. They had stopped to make camp just west of Tanglewood, near the still-smoldering canyon that the rampaging orb had gouged into the earth. The note he had sent by Minion messenger would soon reach the wizards. But after seeing the orb cut through the Tolenka Mountains, he knew that he had to return there to observe it again, if he was to have any hope of ever properly describing it. The wizards would have many questions. He hoped he could answer them.

He had wanted to leave Ox in charge of the Minion party remaining with the orb, but the huge warrior wanted to see Tristan again. Geldon had finally relented and left an officer of Ox's choosing in charge. His orders were to send a warrior to the palace immediately should there be any change in either the condition of the orb or its direction of travel. Thrilled to be in charge of his first command, the young Minion had clicked his heels sharply.

The destruction of Brook Hollow, the encounter with the birds and animals fleeing the forest fire, and then his escape from an onrushing glacier had all taken their toll upon Geldon's nerves. That was to say nothing of watching the orb cut through solid granite. It would be good to be back in the palace again, he thought, and to sleep in his own bed.

He smiled. He could already picture the vein in Wigg's forehead throbbing, and Faegan as he sat there calmly in his chair on wheels, stroking his dark blue cat while the two wizards listened to his every word.

He took another long pull of akulee from the carved stone jug he held. The Minion ale was exceedingly strong. Since traveling with the Minions, he had developed a taste for the bitter concoction. Taking another sip, he promised himself that he wouldn't become drunk.

The night was clear, and a million stars competed with one another for space in the heavens. A stag had been hunted down and killed by two of the warriors; the slowly roasting venison smelled wonderful as a cook turned it on the spit. The flickering firelight showed up the sides of the dozen or so tents that had been erected.

Geldon could occasionally see flying warriors on patrol, their dark silhouettes flashing spectrally across the faces of the three Eutracian moons. The mighty Sippora River babbled happily by only a few meters away. For the first time since leaving the palace the dwarf was beginning to feel relaxed.

Ox came over and sat down heavily in the grass. He picked up the akulee jug, took a long drink, and then wiped his mouth with the back of one hand.

Smiling at Geldon, he handed the jug back. His mood more sanguine than it had been in days, Geldon took another swig.

"Warriors say for one your size you drink akulee good," Ox said in his broken Eutracian. "You also brave. If you be bigger and have wings, you make good Minion."

Looking back into the fire, Geldon laughed.

Another warrior walked up. In his hands he held a plate that was piled high with freshly cooked venison. With a bow, he placed it on the ground between them, and Ox and Geldon ate greedily, washing the meat down with gulps of akulee.

The sound of music suddenly surprised Geldon. Looking around, he saw a warrior sitting on a tree stump near the edge of the camp and strumming a lyre. The melody that wafted through the air was lovely. Then the warrior began reciting something as he played. Other warriors gathered around him, listening with rapt attention.

Geldon turned to Ox. The Minion scowled.

"That be H'rani," he said, chewing and talking at the same time. "He always be playing that thing."

"What is it that he is reciting?"

"It be love poem," Ox answered. Yet another hunk of meat went into his mouth. "He write himself."

Even more interested, Geldon sat up a little. He knew that the Minions were great builders, shipwrights, and warriors. But he had never known any of them to demonstrate a talent for the finer arts.

"He's very good," Geldon said. "We should thank him."

Taking up the jug again, Ox drank for what seemed forever. Some of the ale ran sloppily down his chin and onto his black body armor. Finally he stopped and wiped his face. A loud wet belch followed. Smiling, Geldon shook his head a little.

"No need thank H'rani," Ox answered. "Thank *Jin'Sai*."

"What do you mean?"

"Ever since *Jin'Sai* free female Minions and Gallipolai that day in Parthalon, they act strange. Females want men come court them before take as wife. But Minion warriors not know how. For centuries they only take. Some like new ways, some not. All females seem to like much better. Ox find it all strange. But is law of *Jin'Sai*, so all males respect it." Ox looked critically toward H'rani.

"It said that H'rani soon ask for hand of Gallipolai," Ox added, his mouth twisting with mild disgust. "That she like this thing with lyre. One of acolytes give H'rani lyre and show him how play. Then he make up poem. Other warriors hear him, and now want also learn." He shook his head with a derisive snort.

"You don't seem to approve," Geldon said lightly.

"Ox believe it be embarrassing for true Minion warrior."

Geldon smiled. "What's the matter?" he asked. "Don't you think that a Minion can be a warrior and a poet, too?"

With a dissatisfied grunt, Ox started tearing into another piece of meat. Geldon settled back to listen to the music.

So much is changing, the dwarf thought.

TRYING HER BEST TO EXERCISE PATIENCE AND CONTROL, SATINE realized that she had only a few more meters to go.

As she lay upon her belly in the dewy underbrush, she raised her eyes a fraction and quickly noted her bearings. She had been crawling through the thick undergrowth for nearly an hour, and time was precious now. At any moment her target might move, rendering all of her painstaking work meaningless.

Her black combat clothing was soaked through. Clenching her jaw, she fought back the urge to shiver.

As she had traveled north on horseback she had followed the scar in the earth left by the orb, just as Bratach's note had told her to do. Coming up over a ridge, she had seen the Minion campfires burning in the valley below. She also knew that she would never be able to cross that much illuminated ground without being seen. Another way would have to be found.

Leaving her horse behind, she selected only what she would need to do the job. She placed the items into a waterproof oilskin bag. After changing into her dark clothing, she slung the bag over her back and crept down the rise to stand on the banks of the Sippora.

She slipped silently into the river and began wading north along the bank, heading upstream. With only her nose and eyes above the surface of the water, the going was very hard. Twice she had been forced to stop and rest, clinging to vines that lined the shore. Twice she had been forced to submerge entirely, when Minion patrols appeared overhead. Every bone in her body ached from the cold, but her discipline held.

In the end it had been worth it. She was now only about fifty meters from the camp. Suddenly the sound of music came to her ears, and she paused for a moment to listen. She smiled. The noise was welcome; it could do nothing but help her.

She slithered like a snake up the western side of the riverbank and entered the dense undergrowth. There she silently crawled forward, one agonizingly slow meter at a time. Then she heard voices that were all too close, and she froze.

At least two Minion warriors walked through the shorter grass on her left. They couldn't be more than four or five meters away. Satine slowly moved her hands down toward the daggers on either side of her thighs. Then the warriors' voices went still, and she sensed that they had stopped.

Praying that they hadn't detected her presence, Satine controlled her breathing and calmed her heart. If she had to attack them she would. But that might alert the entire camp—in which case, she'd be done for.

As she lay there awaiting her fate, the wind swished the grasses to and fro. She felt as though Eutracia's three moons conspired to shine their light down upon her alone. Despite the chill of the night air and the cold, wet clothing sticking to her skin, beads of sweat began to form beneath her black mask and run maddeningly down her face. Still, she did not move.

Suddenly she heard the sound of streaming water. She listened as it went on for a bit. It finally ended. Satine allowed herself a slight smile. With nature's call having been answered, the warriors began to move again, laughing as they went.

A few moments later, she risked raising herself up on her hands to look. She watched them enter the camp and blend in among the other winged ones. She also noted that her target was still in the same place. Thanking her good fortune, she lowered herself back to the ground and resumed her slow forward crawl.

After another half hour of slow progress, she stopped on a short rise that overlooked the campsite. The foliage surrounding her was high, keeping her well concealed, but she would soon be discovered if she did not quickly finish her business.

The huge bearded warrior and the hunchbacked dwarf sat side by side, eating and drinking in the light of the fire. The smell of roasted venison made her stomach growl. She was less than ten meters from the edge of the camp.

Reaching behind her, she grasped the oilskin pouch and placed it on the ground. She opened it and removed four items.

The first was a small leather case. Two dull wooden tubes followed. Inside, the fine, aged Eutracian maple had been carefully polished smooth. Grasping the first of them, she inserted one of its ends into the end of the other, making sure that it seated properly. Then she placed the joined tubes on the ground beside her.

Next she opened the case. It separated like two halves of a book. It protected the vial of violet fluid she had purchased from Reznik, as well as a set of darts. Short and slim, they had been charmed by Reznik to dissolve immediately upon impact, while the insect wings attached to them were charmed to stay attached in flight. She smiled at the cleverness of it all.

She selected one dart, carefully opened the vial, dipped the tip of the dart into the poison, and then closed the vial again. She placed the dart into the near end of the tube and replaced the tube on the ground. She was nearly ready.

She took up the fourth item. It was a small, forked twig cut the day before from a hinteroot tree. She placed it on the ground just forward of her head. She looked back down into the campsite. Blessedly, nothing had changed.

She took the branch and pushed one end of it into the ground. The Y-shaped fork pointed upward. Closing one eye, she then twisted the branch in the ground until it was facing just right. She reached back for the tube and gently placed its far end into the crook of the upright branch. Her target sat just beyond.

Finally ready, Satine closed her eyes. She took several deep breaths and then she held the last one in. She placed her mouth against the near end of the tube, took careful aim, and waited for the wind to abate.

The grasses surrounding Satine stopped swaying. Her time was at hand. She remained immobile, lying as silent as death as she sighted the blowgun on her victim. Using everything she had, she expelled the air from her lungs into the tube.

After a final look, the Gray Fox smiled. Then she collected her things and began slinking back the way she had come.

WHEN HE FELT THE BITE GELDON INSTINCTIVELY REACHED UP AND slapped himself on the side of the neck. Looking down at his hand he saw a small bit of his own blood and the remains of smashed insect wings. Scowling, he wiped his hand down the length of his trousers and then looked over at Ox. The Minion was still eating.

"I've just been bitten again," Geldon grumbled.

The side of his neck began to itch, and he scratched it. He could feel the usual bump on the skin begin to rise. He had been bitten several times since coming to live in Eutracia, and he found it annoying.

"What is it that they call these things again?" he asked.

In between bites of the venison, Ox grinned.

"They be derma-gnashers," he answered. "They be pesky, but they not be dangerous."

"Wigg and Faegan should rid the land of these nuisances," Geldon groused as he settled back down against the log. He scratched his neck again. Attempting to ignore the bite, he turned his attention back to the warrior playing the lyre and reciting the love poems.

As he did, a warrior walked up and tossed another log upon their fire.

* * *

GELDON SAID GOOD NIGHT AND RETIRED TO HIS TENT. FULL OF meat and swill, Ox happily fell asleep by the fire. Several hours passed as the moons chased each other across the sky.

But when the screaming started the entire camp came alive.

Ox was on his feet immediately. He turned around, frantic, unable to find the source of the noise. Then Geldon came tearing out of his tent. His eyes bulged; his face was so red Ox thought it might burst. In his hand he held a dagger, which he waved all about like a madman. He was only half clothed.

Glaring at the warriors, he began screaming vulgar, insulting epithets at them. Ox and the others simply stood there, staring at him. Never in their lives had they seen anyone in command of the Minions act this way. It seemed that the dwarf had suddenly gone insane.

Geldon's rantings became even more abusive. He waved the knife faster. Uncertainly, Ox took a tentative step forward. Holding the knife higher, Geldon backed away like a cornered animal.

"What be wrong?" Ox asked, holding out his hands. He looked Geldon up and down again. "You be ill?"

"No, I'm not ill, you winged moron!" Geldon snarled at him. Reaching up, he wiped some of the sweat from his face. A bit of foam dripped from one corner of his mouth. Then a wicked smile came.

"And none of you abominations of the craft can stop me! If any of you come closer, I'll kill you all, I swear it!"

More confused than ever, Ox searched Geldon's face. It was the face of one who had lost all reason.

"What you want do?" the great warrior asked.

Geldon lowered the knife for a moment and a brief look of calm passed over him.

"All I want you to do is watch, you ignorant bastards," he hissed. "Watch and remember."

Before Ox could move, Geldon raised his dagger and plunged it into his own right eye.

He didn't scream, tremble, or complain. As the fluid from his injured eye snaked down his cheek, the other eye closed, and he began to fall forward.

He was dead before he hit the ground.

CHAPTER XXIX

TRISTAN WATCHED ANXIOUSLY AS THE BLACK IRON DOOR, CREAK-
ing on its hinges, grudgingly opened in response to Wigg's
azure bolts. Complete darkness reigned on the other side. No
sound came from the depths.

The prince, Alrik, and Celeste waited for Wigg to lead them
in, but the wizard showed no signs of moving. Tristan narrowed
his eyes to try to see into the room beyond, but nothing was visible in the inky darkness. Awaiting their orders, the rest of the
warriors stood staunchly behind them in the knee-deep ash.
Wigg finally turned to face everyone.

"I suspect that there will be enchanted lamps in there, just as
there were here," he whispered. "After I light them I will go in
first—followed by Celeste, then the prince, and finally the warriors." Tristan started to object, but Wigg quickly raised his
hand, cutting him off.

"If I am correct and these were once Failee's personal research chambers, then there are bound to be safeguards of some
sort. I want Celeste to follow me because of her prowess with
throwing azure bolts. Magic will be far more effective in this
place than any metal weapon ever made, I assure you!" Then he
looked past Tristan to his daughter.

"Sheathe your sword," he whispered. "It will only interfere
with your use of the craft." Celeste did as she was told.

Wigg turned back to face the darkness. Raising his arms, he
called the craft again. Light slowly began to build on the other
side of the door and gradually flooded out over the dark gray
ash. Wigg carefully walked through the door. The others followed close behind.

Tristan felt as if he had been here before. But that was impossible, he thought, as he looked around. Then he realized why it

all felt so familiar: the place was like a miniature version of the Archives of the Redoubt.

The room was large; its ceiling very high. Several closed doors were visible in its stone walls. The many wall sconces Wigg had illuminated burned brightly, giving everything an eerie, almost sterile feel.

Lining the walls were tall bookcases packed with texts, scrolls, and parchments. Worktables sat here and there littered with tools of the craft: tubes, beakers, and charts of esoteric symbols. The air was dusty and dank.

Walking over to what had apparently been Failee's desk, Wigg sadly ran one of his long fingers across the wood. His fingertip traced a telltale line in the dust. He sighed, and a distinct shininess appeared in his eyes. But, true to form, he collected himself. Placing his hands into the opposite sleeves of his robes, he lifted his head and resumed his examination of the room.

Tristan couldn't quite escape the feeling that there was something wrong about the room, as if significant parts of the puzzle were still missing. He lowered his dreggan and, accompanied by Celeste, walked over to Wigg.

"Are you thinking the same thing that I am?" he asked.

Wigg pursed his lips. "If you're saying that there must be more to all of this than just what we see here, then, yes, I am," he said. Wigg looked over at one of the closed doors in a far wall. "Our search for this so-called Scroll Master may prove to take far longer than we imagined—if he is here at all. There is no telling how large this place might be."

Suddenly, with a great bang, the door they had used to enter the room swung shut. Several warriors ran to it and tried to pry it open again, but even their combined strength couldn't budge it. A terrible stench filled the air.

Glowing azure ooze began to run from the gaps between the walls' stone blocks. As more and more of it appeared, the awful stench, like that of decaying flesh, became overpowering. Transfixed, they watched as winding rivulets of the stuff snaked to the floor and gathered into separate, undulating puddles.

The ooze kept coming. A few puddles became dozens of

pools, and the smell became so unbearable that Tristan placed his free hand over his nose and mouth. It did little to help.

Stunned, he looked at Wigg. The wizard's face was white. Pointing toward the mysterious puddles, Wigg snapped his head toward Celeste.

"Use your bolts!" he shouted. "Destroy the pools! If they all come to life in this enclosed space we will never make it out alive!"

Raising his arms, Wigg sent bolts flying against the largest pool, which exploded into nothingness. Then he attacked another, and another. Celeste did the same. The bolts flying from her fingertips were even more explosive and earsplitting than her father's. But as Tristan struggled to look through the haze created by the powerful bolts, his heart sank.

More puddles were continuing to form on the floor. There was no way that Wigg and Celeste would be able to destroy them all.

Motioning to his warriors to stand just behind him, Tristan grasped his dreggan with both hands, spread his legs slightly, and raised the heavy sword over his head.

The first puddle took shape, a head rising up from the undulating ooze. It glowed azure, just like the pool that was giving it birth. The head was long with a curved snout and slanted, yellow eyes with black irises. Leathery wings sprouted from the spiny back; its body was squat and powerful. A snaking, forked tail whipped back and forth, and short, humanlike arms sprouted from either side of its torso. Hands formed, and then powerful rear legs, and the creature stood up ominously to face them.

It was easily the size of an average human. The seven dark talons at the end of each hand looked as though they could tear a man in half with a single swipe. Arteries and veins pumping black blood lay just below the surface of its translucent skin.

It turned its head and looked at them calmly for a moment. Then it opened its mouth, snarled, and launched itself straight up into the air. As it rose it turned itself over to land upside down on the ceiling. Somehow it simply hung there, defying gravity. Snarling again, it ran across the ceiling as easily as if it had been on the floor.

Stunned, Tristan watched helplessly as it tore across the room. Then it stopped, and flipped over to fall back down. As it fell, it swiped a taloned paw at a Minion warrior, breaking his neck.

Blood rushing from the gaping wounds, the Minion fell to the floor. Landing on top of him, the hideous beast let go another awful snarl, shook its head, and took a ripping bite out of the warrior's broken neck.

Two of the warriors standing nearby raised their dreggans to strike it down. But with lightning speed it launched itself into the air again, this time opening its wings as it went. It flew across the room, landed solidly upon the far wall, and clung there, looking down at them. It shook its head, blood running from its jaws, and hissed another savage warning.

Twirling around, Tristan saw that the other puddles had now birthed more of the awful monsters.

One of the creatures snapped open its wings and launched itself at the prince. Dreggan held high, Tristan waited until the last possible moment, then swung the heavy sword for all he was worth. As the blade whistled around it took off one of the thing's lower legs, and the monster cried out in pain. Black blood spurted from its wound.

Undeterred, it backed away in the air and attacked once more. Tristan forced himself to wait again, then lifted the point of his sword and impaled the thing through the chest. Black, sticky blood ran down over his hands. The stench was nauseating.

Impaled upon Tristan's dreggan, the beast screamed and lashed out with its talons, scratching him across the face. With every ounce of his strength, Tristan thrust the blade higher. The light went out of the creature's eyes.

Dropping the point of his sword to the floor, Tristan pushed the corpse off his blade with one foot. Trying to catch his breath, he turned to look around the room.

The Minions were battling ferociously, but the creatures had the advantage of being able to run across the walls and ceilings. Amid all of the confusion, Tristan had no way to tell whether his warriors were prevailing.

Cutting another of the screaming things down out of the air, Tristan glanced frantically around, searching for Wigg and Celeste.

The wizard and his daughter were hovering high in the air near the ceiling. Whenever a monster attacked, Celeste killed it. The ends of her fingers were scorched black, and she looked near the point of total exhaustion.

Behind her, Wigg was using the craft to seal off the spaces between the bricks in the walls. Little by little he succeeded in using an azure force to blanket the cracks, and keep any more of the oozing fluid from entering the room. If he could finish in time, they might all have a chance at survival.

Another of the things flew at Celeste from her blind side. Realizing that she didn't see it, Tristan tossed his dreggan into his left hand, reached behind his right shoulder, and grabbed one of his throwing knives, which he let fly straight for the creature's head. He held his breath as the silver blade spun across the room.

The knife blade pierced one of the monster's outstretched wings, pinning it to one of the bookcases.

Screaming, it tried to remove the knife, but it couldn't reach it. As it hung there struggling, its black blood ran down the spines of Failee's cherished books.

Finally, the room began to quiet. With the exception of the creature nailed to the bookcase, all of the monsters looked to be dead. But so were a good number of the Minion warriors.

Exhausted, the Minions began tending to their wounded. Tristan wiped his sword blade clean, slid it back into its scabbard, and tried to catch his breath.

Wigg and Celeste descended to the ground, and Tristan realized that it had been Wigg who had been keeping her in the air.

She walked weakly to the prince, and he held her. She felt heavy in his arms and he knew that she was close to passing out. He pushed some of her red hair away from her face, and she managed to give him a brief smile. Tristan looked over at Wigg.

"I think you have some explaining to do," Tristan said.

"First things first," Wigg answered. Reaching out, he lifted one of Celeste's eyelids and peered into her eye. Then he placed his palm on her forehead. He closed his eyes. After a few moments, he nodded.

"She will be fine," he said. "She has overtaxed her gift. She is still unaccustomed to using her powers for such a sustained period. But that will come with practice." Then he took up one of her hands and examined her scorched fingertips.

"She possesses the greatest ability with azure bolts that I have ever seen," he added. "If we can one day safely activate the rest of her Forestallments, she will truly be a wonder."

"First Wizard, if you please!" Alrik shouted. Wigg went to the stricken warriors and employed the craft to help them as best he could.

Celeste looked up into Tristan's face. Her smile was stronger this time, and she stood on her own. Then she stretched up and gently kissed the scratches on his cheek.

"I should come on these adventures of yours more often," she said. "Especially if it means ending up in your arms."

Smiling, he stroked the side of her face.

Wigg and Alrik appeared by Tristan's side. "How bad is it?" the prince asked.

Alrik scowled. "At least half of them were injured," he said. "Several of them are beyond hope. The First Wizard was kind enough to grant those three painless deaths." The wizard concurred with a nod.

Tristan lowered his head for a moment as he thought. "Have the dead and wounded escorted back to the surface," he ordered. "I want another dozen fresh warriors to join us down here. We don't know what may still await us." With a click of his heels Alrik left to attend to his new orders.

An angry scream came from the other side of the room. Whirling around, Tristan saw that it had come from the lone surviving creature still pinned to the bookcase. He exchanged glances with Wigg and Celeste, and then they all walked over.

The beast had lost a great deal of blood. It had to be nearly dead, yet it found the energy to snarl at them again, red Minion blood staining its open mouth.

Studying it, Wigg placed his hands into the opposite sleeves of his robe.

"It's called a Wingwalker," he said. "Like the blood stalkers and Screaming Harpies, it was one of the Coven's tools during the Sorceresses' War. I have not seen one for more than three hundred years. Unlike the stalkers, these creatures are not particularly intelligent. Nor do they command the power of speech. They were conjured strictly for killing. They were a blunt instrument to be sure, but they were also particularly effective." He looked at the prince. "Does it seem familiar to you in any way?"

Tristan nodded. "They look something like Wiktors."

"Correct," Wigg said. "My guess is that Wiktors are early descendants of the Wingwalkers. From Wingwalker to Wiktor—and then, eventually, through Failee's magic, Minion warriors." He turned and looked back over to where the warriors were standing. "But I wouldn't tell *them* that," he whispered.

"How did they know we were here?" Celeste asked.

Wigg looked back at the door through which they had entered. With a great collective effort the Minions had finally succeeded in opening it again.

"Most likely that door was charmed to react to any blood passing through it other than that of the Coven," he answered. "In turn it signaled the release of the Wingwalker fluid from the walls."

Tristan indicated toward the azure energy still coating the walls. "You will continue to enforce that spell?" he asked.

Wigg smiled. "That would be a good idea, don't you think? When time permits I shall dissolve the barrier one bit at a time. That way the warriors can dispatch any remaining Wingwalkers one by one as they begin to form. But now I need to finish one more task."

Removing his hands from the sleeves of his robe, Wigg pointed at the surviving Wingwalker. It looked back at him with venom in its eyes and then let go a bloody scream of defiance.

A narrow band of azure light shot from Wigg's fingers and raced across the room to strike the beast in the chest. The Wingwalkers' skin and muscle began to melt away, until all that was left was its seared white skeleton. The First Wizard slowly lowered his hand.

Wigg seemed about to speak again when something made

him stop and tilt his head this way and that, as if seeking the source of a sound only he could hear.

Looking around in concern, Tristan noticed that one of the doors on the other side of the room stood ajar. An azure glow silently filtered in through the opening.

Then Wigg cocked his head to the side again, listening hard.

"Do not follow me," he ordered Tristan and Celeste. Before they could muster a reply, he was crossing the room.

Wigg pointed to the partially open door. Unlike the others, it opened easily for him. Azure light shone on his face and robe.

Then a voice came from the other side, just loud enough for Tristan and Celeste to hear.

"Wigg . . . is that really you?" The words coming from the other side were struggling and soft-spoken. "How . . . why . . . ?"

Wigg's mouth fell open and his face blanched. As the breath rushed out of him, he bent over in shock. For a moment it looked as though his knees might give way. Then he regained control and stood upright again.

Without turning to look at Tristan or Celeste, the First Wizard walked slowly, numbly, through the doorway and into the azure light.

CHAPTER XXX

SOMEONE SLAPPED HER ACROSS THE FACE. PULLING AWAY, SHE frowned and tried to go back to sleep. Then she was slapped again, and someone began shouting at her. She should never be awakened this way, she thought. Didn't they know she was a princess? And why was she so cold and wet?

Then the insistent voice came again: "Shailiha! Wake up! We're in trouble!"

Then came another stinging slap across the face. The princess of Eutracia finally opened her eyes—and realized that she was still tied to the gunwale, slumped in her bonds. She raised her head and looked up blearily, trying to remember.

It was night and a sea storm was raging. The *Reprise* seemed helpless and crippled as the wind tore at her. Parts of her foremast and its rigging had come down, and now it rolled back and forth across the pitching deck. The rain came in unrelenting sheets, and the ship bucked wildly upon the waves. Crewmen and warriors, their shouting drowned out by the howling wind, worked frantically to regain control of the vessel.

Her vision clearing, Shailiha recognized Tyranny standing before her. The privateer was soaked to the skin. There was a look of desperation on her face that the princess had never seen before. Removing her dagger from its sheath, Tyranny quickly cut Shailiha's bonds.

As she struggled to stand on her own, the princess found the lingering effects of passing through the portal and the bucking of the ship nearly debilitating. Helping Shailiha to find her sea legs, Tyranny held her shoulders. Shailiha placed her mouth next to Tyranny's ear.

"What happened?" she shouted against the howling wind.

"We're taking on water!" Tyranny shouted back. "And this storm isn't helping! The stress of going through Faegan's portal must have weakened the hull! We have a great deal to do if we are going to survive this!"

Shailiha looked over at the scorched foremast to which K'jarr and Scars had been tied. What was left of it rose awkwardly toward the sky, like a tree that had been hit by lightning.

"K'jarr and Scars!" she shouted. "Are they . . . ?"

"They're alive!" Tyranny shouted back. "But when the mast was hit, it gave them a rude awakening!"

Tyranny pointed down the length of the deck. Knotted lifelines had been tied between each of the masts to help the crew walk along the decks without being thrown overboard in the storm.

"Follow me!" she shouted. "Whatever you do, don't let go of the ropes! If you go overboard now we will never find you!"

Shailiha followed Tyranny as best she could. The decks were slippery with rain and they pitched constantly, making her fall down more than once. They reached, then passed the first mast, and she followed the captain on, hand over hand along the knotted rope.

Finally Tyranny reached a deck hatch. It was open and several canvas tubes snaked up out of it. Their ends lay unseen over the starboard gunwales. Letting go of the rope, Tyranny went down the stairway first. Shailiha followed.

As the stricken war frigate bucked and pitched, it was all the princess could do to keep herself from being repeatedly thrown against the walls of the stairway. It was drier here, but not by much. The strange canvas tubes stretched down the staircase. Tyranny grabbed a swinging lantern from its hook on the wall and held it before them.

Two more decks down, Shailiha could hear shouting and the sounds of men at work. As she descended into the chamber behind Tyranny, they stopped midway down the staircase. The privateer held the lantern high. Shailiha could see immediately that they were in for the fight of their lives.

The room was large and had been cleared of its cargo. Seamen and Minions were working frantically to stem the seawater that rushed in through the rent in the *Reprise*'s hull every time she tipped to starboard. At least one of the hull planks was gone, perhaps more.

About a dozen warriors and crewmen stood shoulder to shoulder in waist-deep seawater as they struggled to repair the damage. Watching some of the warriors work mechanical pumps, Shailiha suddenly realized what the canvas snakes were for.

Frantically they pushed up and down on the pumps' wooden handles, sending bursts of seawater shooting up and through the canvas tubes that made their way to the decks above. The warriors were barely holding their own. Each time they seemed to gain a little against the rising water, the ship would roll to starboard again and more would come rushing through the jagged tear in her side.

The *Reprise* pitched high in the bow and Shailiha almost fell from the stairway. Tyranny grabbed the collar of her jerkin and pulled her back.

While the warriors pumped the seawater out, Tyranny's crewmen tried to repair the hull. A massive corkscrewlike device rested upon the shoulders of several of the men. At each end of the giant screw sat a very large, flat iron panel. One of these was placed against a sturdy, upright timber in the center of the room. The other was pointed toward the rent in the hull.

Shailiha watched as several crewmen placed thick wooden handles into holes in the sides of the giant hardwood screw. As a group they began turning them. The flat iron panel at the end of the screw slowly made its way toward the broken hull.

Some crew held high fresh boards cut to cover the hole in the hull. As the screw turned, it would force the iron panel against the boards and hold them in place. Other crewmen stood by with trowels full of pitch and tar, ready to seal off the joints between the boards. As the warriors manned the pumps and the crewmen turned the screw, Shailiha held her breath.

Just as the screw began to seat itself against the freshly cut planks, the *Reprise* rolled to starboard again. Another rush of water flooded in, knocking the men over and causing them to drop the screw and the boards.

As the men tried to stand, it was plain to see that the ice-cold water was even higher now, and that the situation was quickly becoming hopeless. Soon other sections of this deck would be engulfed, and the *Reprise* would almost certainly go down. Shailiha looked over at Tyranny. The privateer's expression was hard.

"Scars!" Tyranny cried out.

At the sound of her voice the gigantic first mate looked up and saw the two women standing halfway down the stairway. It took several precious moments, but he finally managed to wade over to them.

"We aren't going to make it, are we?" Tyranny shouted, raising her lantern a bit.

Without answering, Scars turned back to look at the rent in the hull. They heard a harsh, tearing sound, as yet another plank flanking the damage came loose and flew into the room. More seawater flooded in behind it. It was now nearly as high as the crewmen's chests.

Scars turned back to his captain. "Our problem isn't so much the damage as it is the storm!" he shouted back at her. "If the ship wasn't rocking back and forth so badly, we might be able to repair her! But the situation only grows worse. If we do not succeed very soon, she will surely go down!"

For several moments Tyranny did not speak. Then she seemed to make up her mind. "I am going topside!" she shouted. "I will unfurl the sails! Then I'll do what I can to heel her over! When you feel her come hard to port and the damage to the hull rises clear of the waves, you must hurry! I don't know how long I'll be able to hold her over in these winds!"

Scars looked horrified.

"Captain, you can't!" he shouted back. "In a storm like this you must leave the sails furled and allow her to nose into the wind! It's the only way she'll survive the stresses! You know that! Raising the sails now could rip every remaining mast from the ship and tear the hull in half!"

By now every man and warrior in the chamber had stopped what he was doing and strained to hear the argument above the raging storm. Looking down into the rapidly flooding chamber, Tyranny scanned the workers, taking a moment to stare into the eyes of every man there. Handing the lantern to Shailiha, she placed her fists akimbo.

"This is not up for debate!" she shouted at them. "True, what I propose may not work! But if we don't try, what do you think will happen, eh? At best you have one more chance to succeed! And if you don't, we're all food for the fishes anyway!" Then her expression softened a bit, and she looked down at Scars.

"Don't fail me," she said. She turned and pushed Shailiha back up the stairway.

When they reached topside, the storm was raging worse than ever. Glancing around, Tyranny spotted one of her officers and headed for him. Snatching the lantern from Shailiha, Tyranny shoved it into the man's hands, then put her mouth to his ear.

"I want every sail unfurled—now!" she shouted. "Be quick

about it! This is a matter of life or death!" His mouth hanging open, the officer looked at her as though she had just gone mad.

Tyranny reached down to her thigh, drew her dagger, and placed its blade at the man's throat.

"Now!" she barked. "Or I'll throw you overboard myself!"

With a quick nod, the officer went to give the orders.

"You're with me!" Tyranny shouted to Shailiha. Together they made their way astern, toward the ship's wheel, which was still tightly bound with rope.

"Stand clear!" Tyranny shouted. Shailiha did as she was told.

Tyranny raised her face to the storm and watched with hope as the sails came down. The wind tore at them relentlessly, threatening to rip both them and the masts they were attached to away from the *Reprise* and out into the darkness of the sea. Then the sails filled and the frigate lurched forward, bounding uncontrollably through the waves. Taking a deep breath, Tyranny knew it was time. Removing her sword from its scabbard, she held it high and then brought it down with all her strength against the rope binding the ship's wheel.

Finally free, the wheel spun madly, its spokes a blur as the ship's rudder struggled to find its equilibrium in the raging currents. As the wheel settled down, Tyranny motioned for Shailiha to come and join her. They each took hold of it. Tyranny looked up at the straining sails and back at Shailiha.

"Now!" the privateer shouted. "And with everything you have!" Straining against the wheel, the two women began to turn it with all their might.

With an agonizing groan, the *Reprise* did her best to heel over toward the port side. As she started to come about, Tyranny and Shailiha turned the wheel over even harder, and the great ship screamed as though she were about to come apart.

Knowing there was nothing else she could do, Shailiha closed her eyes. She thought of Tristan and Morganna. Then the great ship lurched, and another of the masts came tumbling down.

CHAPTER XXXI

EYES CLOSED, FAEGAN SMOOTHLY STROKED THE STRINGS OF HIS centuries-old violin. As the sorrowful melody rose into the air, he focused on the many problems plaguing his nation. He had been playing and thinking for more than an hour now, yet no concrete answers had come to him. Too many pieces of the puzzle were still missing.

He suddenly sensed an extra weight upon the scroll of his violin, and felt an unexpected breeze caress his face. With a short smile he stopped playing and lowered his bow. He opened his eyes.

Caprice, Shailiha's yellow and violet flier of the fields, perched upon his violin as if to tell him not to worry, that everything would be all right. The wizard found such a thought to be a very tempting luxury. But then his mind started to work again and he sighed sadly.

"You're lonely for your mistress, aren't you?" he asked. Caprice slowly opened and closed her wings one time: Yes.

He smiled. Although Shailiha and Caprice were oftentimes inseparable, the princess had chosen to leave the flier behind when she left on her mission with Tyranny.

"I know," Faegan said. "I miss her, too."

The wizard sat on the balcony overlooking the aviary of the fliers of the fields. This was perhaps his favorite place in the world. He often came here to be alone and to think. Located in the depths of the Redoubt, the aviary was more than three stories high and filled with soaring fliers of all the colors of the rainbow. Oil sconces on the light blue marble walls gave the chamber a soft, welcoming feel.

Faegan gave the violin a gentle shake, and Caprice launched

herself into the air to rejoin her fellows. As she went, Faegan's sadness returned.

He hadn't come here to punish himself, although that was what sitting here alone had come to feel like.

He was worried for all of those who were now so far afield. Geldon's note, which had arrived the previous night, had done nothing to assuage his fears about the rampaging orb. He feared for Wigg, Tristan, and Celeste, as they probed the depths of the Recluse. But he was most concerned about the welfare of Shailiha and Tyranny, and all of the other brave souls aboard the *Reprise*.

He knew that the theory behind transporting something so large was basically sound. He was also reasonably sure that his calculations for the ship's destination in the Sea of Whispers were accurate—at least to within a league or so. But when the portal had swallowed up the ship, his blood had run cold.

He had never known the vortex to make any sound whatsoever, much less the terrible screeching noise he had heard that day. He had come to the conclusion that this had been because of the portal's unusual size, and there was absolutely nothing he could do about it for the time being. But still he worried. Sending the ship through a portal had been his idea.

On top of all those concerns, something even worse gnawed at his conscience and his sense of personal honor.

Because he had broken under Wulfgar's torture, the Scroll of the Vigors had become damaged. And as long as Wulfgar—who, he was sure, still lived—possessed the Scroll of the Vagaries, their trials and tribulations might never end.

He looked down at the simple black robe that covered his partially destroyed legs and memories of the excruciating pain Wulfgar had caused them came flooding in. A lone tear traced its way down his cheek. Taking a deep breath, he looked out over the fliers again.

He suddenly sensed familiar, endowed blood on the other side of the doors behind him. Sitting up a bit straighter in his chair, he cleared his throat and quickly wiped the tear from his face.

He heard the doors open. Swiveling his chair around, he

found Abbey standing there. Her face was white and her hands trembled. She had been crying.

"What's wrong?" he asked.

Abbey took a few tentative steps. She kneeled down and took one of his gnarled hands into hers. Her hands still shook.

"You must prepare yourself, for I bring terrible news," she said, her voice breaking.

Faegan swallowed hard. Rather than ask her again he simply waited, his heart in his throat.

"Geldon is dead," she said.

For several long moments the wizard sat there in his chair, frozen in the moment.

"How?" he asked at last. It had been a struggle to get the word out. "Was it the orb?"

Abbey shook her head. "No. I think you had best hear the tale from Ox. Even after witnessing Geldon's death, the Minions don't understand what happened. It seems to be a puzzle that only a full-fledged wizard or sorceress might unravel." She paused. "But I'm afraid there is even worse news," she said softly. "And this does have to do with the orb."

Not altogether sure that he could bear any more bad tidings, Faegan looked back out over the aviary. His hands tightened around the violin. "What is it?"

"Ox says that the orb has changed course," she answered. "It has struck the Tolenka Mountains and is heading west. It is literally carving a pass through the peaks. If it burns all the way through to the other side—"

"I am well aware of the prophecy," he answered, cutting her off. His voice was little more than a whisper.

He covered his face with his hands. Then, taking a deep breath, Faegan did his best to gather himself up and speak again. But in the end all he could do was nod. Without a last look at the fliers, he gave his chair a push and followed Abbey down the hall.

After Ox told Faegan of Geldon's strange and terrible death, the wizard gathered up Abbey, Adrian, Ox, and Duvessa in a special room in the Redoubt. Also present was Vivian of the House of Wentworth, Adrian's assistant in the sisterhood.

Vivian was rather short, with curly blond hair and a kind, intelligent face. The dark red robe of her office fell loosely over her slim body. Faegan was not well acquainted with the young woman, but what he knew of her he liked. Given the nature of the tragedy, he thought it fitting that she join them.

Faegan had gathered them here because he knew that a grisly service would have to be performed. With Wigg in Parthalon, only he would be able to do it.

The room in which they stood was called the Cubiculum of Humanistic Research. Here, the consuls and the late Directorate of Wizards had done extensive study of the human form and how it related to the science of the craft. Due to their understandable worry regarding the ethics involved, the Directorate had debated for nearly a decade before finally voting to build it. When construction was done, a strict policy had been established that the research conducted here was to take place only upon subjects who had already died, and only for the explicit benefit of the Vigors.

The room held several examination tables. Side tables bearing metal instruments stood next to many of them. Glass cabinets lined the walls. The floor was brilliant white. Everything sparkled with cleanliness.

On the table before Faegan lay Geldon's dead body, covered by a black sheet. Ox had immediately ordered it packed in ice from one of the mountainside glaciers. He had then had it flown back to the palace as fast as possible. That had been good thinking and Faegan had told him so. Now, narrowing his eyes, Faegan used the craft to activate an azure field around the table that would preserve the corpse for as long as necessary.

Faegan sadly looked up at Ox. Minion warriors supposedly never cried—at least that was one of the legends they chose to propagate. But on more than one occasion today Faegan had seen the tears in Ox's eyes, and he understood. Ox just nodded back.

Faegan found the tale of Geldon's death as difficult to believe as everyone else. For Geldon to suddenly commit suicide was completely out of character—especially since his coming to live with them here in Eutracia.

"Are you quite sure that he seemed perfectly normal before he killed himself?" the wizard asked.

Ox nodded. "He worried about orb, but all of us be. We eat and drink much. Then he go to sleep in tent. Ox fall asleep by fire. But when Geldon wake up in middle of night, he be crazy. He come out of tent, waving knife. He say many bad things— things Ox never hear him say before."

"And then?"

"Then he stab himself with knife. Geldon must want die that night. Ox swear as Minion warrior."

Faegan managed a slight smile. "No one doubts your word, my friend."

Frustrated, he rubbed his face. After levitating his chair to a more appropriate height, he grabbed one corner of the sheet, then paused and looked over at the others.

"You might want to prepare yourselves," he said gently. Then he slowly pulled the sheet away from the corpse and let it fall to the floor.

There was no disputing that the naked body was Geldon's, or that the hunchbacked dwarf was dead. Ox had wisely left the knife undisturbed, its handle still protruding from the ravaged eye socket. Vitreous fluid and blood had dried splattered upon Geldon's face. The body was white and cold.

Faegan took hold of the knife handle and, with a quick, sure pull, removed it from Geldon's head.

The wizard held the bloody knife to the light. Turning it over, he examined it closely. Try as he might he could find nothing out of the ordinary about it.

"Was the knife his property?" he asked Ox. "Or did it belong to someone else?"

"It be his," the warrior answered. "He bring it from Parthalon."

"I see," Faegan answered. "This is all so puzzling. What I can tell you is that this knife has not been charmed in any way. This weapon is only the instrument of Geldon's death, not the under-lying cause." He placed the knife on a side table.

"Before he died, did he complain of anything?" Faegan asked. "Was he ill in any way?"

Ox shook his head. "He complain about derma-gnashers," he said. "He be bitten on neck. I laugh at him. But that close to for-est, we all be bitten."

Faegan nodded. Turning the dwarf's head to one side he saw the small lump indicative of a derma-gnasher attack. The area was red and swollen, and he could see where the dwarf had scratched it.

Faegan then closely examined Geldon's nails and the inside of his mouth; he saw nothing untoward. Shaking his head, he looked down at the bite again. He asked Abbey to come closer and pointed to the bite.

"As a practicing herbmistress, do you see anything unusual there?" he asked.

Abbey bent over to look.

"No," she said flatly. "The bite seems to be of no consequence."

"I agree," Faegan answered.

"May I examine the wound?" Duvessa asked. Faegan nodded.

Coming around the table, Duvessa put her hands behind Geldon's head and raised it upward. She placed one eye very near the damaged socket and examined it closely. Finally she placed the head back down upon the table.

"There is nothing inconsistent here," she said. "I have seen it before. Death is instantaneous. Still, none of this answers the larger question—just what possessed him to do it?"

"What indeed?" Faegan repeated. He looked back over at Abbey, Adrian, and Vivian. His face was stern.

"In order to learn more I will be forced to do a necropsy," he said. "Because I have not done one since the Sorceresses' War and Wigg is not here to help, assisting me has now become your job. Abbey, I want you to keep an especially sharp lookout for anything of the organic facet of the craft that seems to be unusual, especially regarding Geldon's unendowed blood. Duvessa, you will assist me with organ removal. Every cut you make must be clean and sure, if we are to ever find the answer to this. As for Adrian and Vivian— well, let's just say that this shall be the sisterhood's induction into this particular art of the craft." Then he looked back down at the corpse and laid one hand tenderly upon Geldon's shoulder.

"Are you all with me?" he asked. "Given his many sacrifices for us, we owe it to him to find out what truly happened." Without hesitation each of the women agreed.

"I have request," Ox suddenly said.

"What is it?" Faegan asked.

"On behalf of other warriors, I ask you grant him Minion funeral pyre when you done. He deserve it."

Faegan thought for a moment. "Very well," he answered. "But only after we have finished—and not before the other members of the Conclave have returned to the palace and paid their respects."

Ox nodded. "Minions thank Faegan," he said.

Faegan reached over to a nearby table and took up a small, razor-sharp knife. Its blade glinted in the light. Looking back down, he suddenly remembered the first crudely written note he had received from Geldon by way of a Parthalonian racing pigeon. He remembered how it had excited him to have finally found a friend from across the sea. Tears came again, and he brushed them away with a forearm.

Reaching down, he placed the blade of the knife against the cold, white flesh.

LESS THAN AN HOUR LATER, VIVIAN WALKED ALONE THROUGH THE palace halls. She had told Faegan that the necropsy had made her ill and that she needed to get some air. Understanding, he had granted her permission to leave.

Quietly she made her way up out of the Redoubt and through the Hall of Supplication. As she walked among the healing stations, the midday breeze wafted pleasantly through the open windows. She continued on through the great room and out into the courtyard beyond. Pausing, she took a deep breath. She hadn't really been ill, but the fresh air rejuvenated her just the same.

Many Minion tents still stood here to shelter the wounded. More often than not, the stricken citizens looked up at her with gratitude as she walked among them. Unlike the way many of them felt about the prince and the rest of his entourage, they all seemed to have great respect for the kindly women in the red robes. To keep up appearances she stopped to speak with several of them before walking to the drawbridge.

As she strolled under the portcullis and started over the moat, the warriors standing guard came to attention and smartly clicked their heels. The assistant to the First Sister was an important person, after all.

She nodded back politely and pulled the hood of her robe up over her head. Turning right onto the nearest street, she continued on her way and became one with the crowd.

Most of the bodies had been removed from the streets, but an odd sense of fatalism lay over the city, combined with an atmosphere that was almost festive. It was almost as if everyone was waiting for the rampaging orb to reach the capital and destroy everything in its path, a dread anticipation that brought with it a sense of abandon.

This once-fashionable, quiet section of the city was deteriorating into another Bargainers' Square—complete with whores of both sexes, drunkards, and scoundrels of every kind. Had she not possessed her skills of the craft, Vivian would have been reluctant to venture here alone. Peering out from the shadows of her hood, she walked on.

The street ended in a roundabout surrounding a small fountain. A number of people loitered there, but she could afford to be patient. She sat down on the ledge of the pool to wait for the right moment.

At last, she slipped one hand into the pocket of her robe and withdrew a small handful of wheat grains taken from the palace kitchens. She kept her hand closed tightly around them and closed her eyes.

The faintest hint of azure escaped from between her fingers, then faded. Shifting her weight slightly, she released the grains into the water and smiled.

The dwarf was dead, the method of his death stymieing even the wizard Faegan. Clearly, Satine had succeeded with the first of her sanctions. Soon Bratach and Ivan would know, and would send Satine toward her next target. Then their master and his army would return from across the sea, and everything would change.

Her task here complete, the acolyte stood and stretched. As she started back to the palace, she smiled. Truth be known, she had been intrigued by the necropsy. Perhaps she would watch the rest of it after all.

CHAPTER XXXII

WULFGAR, SERENA, AND EINAR STOOD TOGETHER AT THE WEST-ern shore of the Isle of the Citadel, the rays of the rising sun just beginning to emerge at their backs. As he cast his gaze out over the Sea of Whispers, Wulfgar thought of the orders the Heretics of the Guild had imparted to him the previous evening.

He had been with his beloved queen. It was early evening at the Citadel and the stars were just coming out. Seated in the throne room, the two of them had been happily considering names for their unborn daughter. Then the familiar feeling had come over him. Without speaking the *Enseterat* rose from his throne. Understanding what was happening, Serena watched in awestruck silence.

The Lord of the Vagaries walked to the open section of the wall and went down on his knees. He lifted his face to the heavens. As he did, the beautiful choir of voices came to him once more.

You have done well, the Heretics told him. *You have raised the Black Ships, and you have conjured the beasts that will help you lay waste to the lairs of our enemies. It is now time for you to raise your other endowed servants from the depths. Of the hundreds condemned by the Coven of Sorceresses, only seven remain strong enough to rise and serve you. The calculations required for this feat are to be found within the Scroll of the Vagaries. To secure them, employ the index forestalled in your blood. Once your servants are among you, you may begin your campaign to rid the world of the Vigors and all those who would practice them.*

I will obey, Wulfgar responded silently.

For the rest of the night, the *Enseterat* searched. Activating the proper Forestallment, he mentally scanned the scroll's index. Thou-sands of glowing numbers and letters floated before his mind's eye.

Finally he found the ones he was looking for. Now knowing the locations of the calculations in the massive scroll, Wulfgar read them aloud while Einar recorded them on a piece of parchment. As he looked out over the sea, Wulfgar held that same parchment in his hand. After more than three hundred years of imprisonment, the onetime servants of the Coven would rise to serve *him*.

Serena touched her husband's good arm.

"Forgive me, my lord," she said. "But what is it that the Heretics have asked you to do? You have yet to tell me."

Wulfgar smiled. Then he looked down at the parchment.

"Watch and learn, my love," he said and began to recite the calculations in Old Eutracian.

As the sea before them began to burble and roil, Serena thought she must be seeing things. She looked over at Einar, but her husband's lead consul said nothing.

Then ghoulish faces appeared, rising to the surface of the sea and Serena understood. They were the Necrophagians—the Eaters of the Dead. Wulfgar paused in his incantation and lowered the parchment.

Seven faces lay just beneath the surface of the waves. Their skin was a putrid gray-green. Their eyes and mouths were no more than dark holes in their faces. The faces were covered with boils, and the awful moaning they made was the most plaintive sound Serena had ever heard. It was as if they were in some form of mortal agony and begging to be released from it. Wulfgar raised the parchment once again and resumed reading the calculations aloud.

The heavens began to tremble and azure lightning ripped across the morning sky. Thunder tore through the air. The wind howled, causing the sea to crash against the shore. The *Enseterat* dropped the parchment to the ground and raised his hands to the sky.

Lighting bolts shot down to strike the faces in the sea. The shoreline began to shake, and the waves crashed even harder. Fearing for her unborn child, Serena placed a hand over her abdomen and stepped back.

As the wind raged and the lightning cascaded across the sky, the faces in the water slowly submerged. Then the heavens quieted and an eerie calm descended. The Sea of Whispers became as smooth as glass. The seven Necrophagians were gone.

Serena stepped back to her husband's side. "What has become of them?" she asked. "Are they dead?"

Wulfgar did not take his eyes from the sea. "Quite the contrary," he said. "In fact, they are even more alive than before. And they owe it all to me, their new lord. Behold."

He walked to the very edge of the water and raised his arms again.

"Come to me," he said.

Seven heads broke the surface of the sea. Each wore a long, arched, black hat, folded up along one side and adorned with a long red feather that pointed rearward. Below the hats the heads were mere skulls, the bone blackened. Some showed cracks here and there. Their lidless eyes glowed an eerie green. Below the eyes, nasal cavities lay exposed. Lipless mouths showed teeth of the purest white, in sharp contrast with the rest of the macabre faces.

Bodies rising from the sea, they stepped silently onto the shore, the tatters of what looked like ancient military uniforms flapping in the breeze. Their boots and long capes were black, their breastplates tarnished silver. Each wore a sword, a dagger, or both.

They came to stand in a line before their new lord. Then they dropped to one knee and bowed their dark, dripping heads. With a shudder, Serena turned to her husband.

"They look like the officers of some long-defeated army," she said.

Smiling, Wulfgar looked over at his queen. "Well done, my love," he answered. "That is exactly what they are."

He turned back to his new servants. "You may rise," he said. They stood.

As the seawater dripped from them, Serena wondered what purpose these creatures were to serve. She knew her husband would tell her in his own good time.

With a menacing smile on his face, the *Enseterat* turned and led his wife, his consul, and his new officers back to the Citadel.

CHAPTER XXXIII

ALL OF HIS SENSES ALERT, WIGG TENTATIVELY WALKED INTO THE large inner chamber. It smelled damp and musty, as though its door hadn't been opened for centuries.

There were more tables and bookcases, and tools of the craft lay scattered about. At least two dozen small alcoves lined the walls. Within each, a raggedly clothed skeleton hung chained to the wall, its bones slumped to the floor in an awkward posture. Wigg could not be sure what had killed these poor souls, but he had a fair idea of who had been responsible. Then he heard the pleading voice once more.

"Wigg . . . is that you?"

He walked deeper into the room. In an alcove in the far wall lay a chained woman, curled into a fetal position, shaking. Her once colorful gown had long since become faded rags, and her blond hair was snarled. She was filthy, but not emaciated. From the ceiling, a cone of azure light shone down upon her, bathing her in its glow.

Wigg finally recognized her and tears welled up in his eyes. He slowly went to one knee and looked into her face.

"Jessamay?" he said. He reached out to touch her.

"No!" she shrieked.

Like a cornered animal, she retreated farther into the alcove. She shook harder. She pointed to the cone of azure light.

"If the boundaries of the glow are improperly violated, I will die!" Lowering her head, she began to cry.

After a time she raised her face. "Please, you must believe me," she whispered.

Still stunned, Wigg sat back on his heels. "Jessamay, it is really you?" he asked softly. The woman nodded.

"But how—why are you here?" he stammered. It was all he

could do to get the words out. "The Directorate thought you dead."

"Death would have been preferable," the woman said. "Failee brought us here. We were the subjects of her experiments. I am the only one who survived."

On all fours, she carefully inched closer to the edge of the azure light. As if still unable to believe who she saw, she searched his face again.

"Wigg . . . ," she whispered, "after all this time. . . . You look much older than I remember. But it is you, just the same." Then she suddenly bolted upright and panic stormed over her face.

"You must leave here at once!" She looked frantically around the room. "If the Coven finds you, they will kill you on sight!"

Wigg smiled. "It's all right," he said. "The members of the Coven have been dead for many months. Their ashes lay just beyond this door."

At first she looked at him as if he had lost his mind. Then, realizing he spoke the truth, she smiled and tears of joy ran down her face.

"Wigg, are you all right?" Tristan shouted. Wigg turned to see Tristan and Celeste entering the room. The prince had apparently ordered the Minions to remain behind.

"I'm sorry, Father," Celeste said. "I know you told us to wait, but we were worried about you." They came to stand next to the wizard.

The moment Jessamay saw Tristan she took a short breath. She went to her knees and lowered her head to the floor. Tristan looked over at Wigg. The First Wizard seemed as surprised as he was.

"Do you know this woman?" the prince asked.

Wigg nodded. "Her name is Jessamay, of the House of Finton," he said. "She is at least as old as I am." Then he looked back down at her.

"Why do you bow to us, Jessamay?" he asked.

Slowly she lifted her head and said, "The *Jin'Sai* has finally come! Thank the Afterlife!"

Wigg inched a bit closer.

"Yes," he said. "Both the *Jin'Sai* and the *Jin'Saiou* were delivered to us thirty-two years ago, and they are safe. So are the

Paragon, and the Tome. This is Prince Tristan of the House of Galland. The woman is Celeste, my daughter."

Then he more closely examined the azure light that imprisoned Jessamay.

"This is a sorceress' cone, isn't it?" he asked. Jessamay nodded.

"I have not seen one for more than three hundred years," Wigg mused. "Did Failee conjure it?"

"Yes."

"What are you talking about?" Celeste asked.

"The sorceress' cone was a device used by the Coven during the war," Wigg said. "It works somewhat like a wizard's warp, except that if a person tries to enter or exit the cone without knowing the spell of protection, he or she will be quickly burned to death."

Wigg looked into Jessamay's face. "How long have you been here?" he asked.

Jessamay bit her lip and pulled the remnants of her ragged gown closer.

"I have been here in the Recluse ever since Succiu returned from her recent mission to Eutracia," she answered. "But I have existed in this cone for almost four centuries."

Stunned, Tristan felt the breath go out of him. "How is such a thing possible?" he asked.

Wigg looked down at Jessamay again. "Failee enhanced your time enchantments with a charm of endurance, didn't she?" he asked. Jessamay nodded. She began to cry again.

"What are you talking about?" Celeste asked.

"It is but one of many enchantments that can be added to an already existing spell," Wigg answered. "In this case the charm allows the subject to live without the need for food, air, water, or sleep."

Tristan scowled. "I don't understand," he said. "That sounds more like a blessing than a curse."

Wigg's face darkened. "Once imprisoned inside the cone, if the subject's time enchantments are then graced with the charm of endurance, he or she will continue to survive within its confines forever. No one need ever return to care for her, or to feed her. This allows for total, permanent isolation. To further enhance the effect, Failee would sometimes cause her subjects to endure extreme heat or cold. Or she would cause the chamber to become lightless, forcing her victims to face their endless torment in the dark. Then she would simply leave them to suffer their fate for all of eternity."

The First Wizard looked grimly at them both. "Could either of you imagine a worse fate?" he asked.

Looking back at Jessamay, Tristan felt his hatred of the Coven rise again. Given the seemingly never-ending effects of their horrific deeds, he often found it difficult to believe that they were really dead. His admiration for the woman trapped in the light grew.

"We're wasting time," Wigg whispered. "We must free her, and get her to the surface. Her sanity hinges upon it if, indeed, she is not mad already."

Celeste looked at her father with concern. Tilting her head toward the far side of the room, she beckoned Tristan and Wigg to accompany her.

"What is it?" Wigg asked.

"Do you really think that freeing her is wise?" Celeste asked nervously. "She already admits to having been experimented upon. How do we know that she hasn't somehow become another of Failee's traps?"

Wigg gazed sadly back over at Jessamay. Her eyes looked frightened, but hopeful. He turned back to Tristan and Celeste.

"I understand your concerns," he said. "We knew that this trip would have its dangers. Freeing her is simply the right thing to do." His expression darkened. "I know that if our roles were reversed, she would attempt it for me," he added quietly. "Can I do less?"

Tristan took a deep breath. "Very well," he agreed. "Free her if you can. But before that, please tell us something. Just who was she, all of those years ago?"

Wigg looked back to the cruel, azure prison. Tears welled up in his eyes again.

"She was quite simply the bravest woman I ever knew," he said. "If it hadn't been for her, I wouldn't be here today."

Saying nothing more, he walked back to Jessamay. Tristan and Celeste followed.

"I am going to try to help you," Wigg told her. "Tell me, do you still command any of your gifts?"

Jessamay shook her head. "My powers deserted me the moment Failee forced me into the cone."

Thinking, Wigg pursed his lips. "Do you know the calculations required to dissipate the cone?" he asked.

"No," she said. "But you may be able to find them in Failee's grimoire."

Wigg's jaw dropped. "Do you mean to say that you know where it is?" he breathed. "I hadn't dared hope that we might find it."

Jessamay nodded again. "I saw her remove it from its hiding place many times. It should still be there."

"Where is it?"

"Walk to the chandelier nearest the door," she said. "Conjure an azure beam, and then use it to pull the chandelier down a bit. The grimoire will be revealed."

Wigg hurried over to stand beneath the chandelier. Raising one hand, he produced a beam. It rose from his fingertips and secured itself around the base of the fixture. Then the wizard drew back on the beam and the chandelier lowered. The beam disappeared.

There was a grating sound, and then one of the blocks in the wall slowly pivoted to reveal a dark space behind it.

Wigg walked over and looked inside. At first, all he could see was blackness. Conjuring some light, he looked in again. His face lit up with joy as he pulled out a book. Cradling it in his arms, he walked to a nearby desk and set it down.

The book was large, bound in tooled leather that shone a deep, lustrous red. Wigg carefully opened it. The ancient, gilded pages made crinkling sounds as he turned them over.

"What's a grimoire?" Tristan asked.

"It is a book of magic," Wigg answered, as he scanned the pages. "They contain the owner's favorite spells, incantations, calculations, and formulas. Sometimes they have even been known to record personal correspondence. Failee destroyed her first grimoire near the end of the Sorceresses' War, to keep it from being captured. That was a great loss for the Directorate. This second book is also Failee's. I can tell by the handwriting. This grimoire may contain all of the knowledge she amassed after she was banished to Parthalon, and perhaps a good deal more. Finding it is a great victory."

"Can you use it to free Jessamay?" Tristan asked.

"Perhaps," Wigg answered, "assuming that Failee properly

recorded the calculations that will reverse the spell. She was nothing if not thorough." He turned another page.

"Now give me some peace and quiet," he said gruffly.

Tristan smiled over at Celeste and she grinned back.

While they waited, the prince looked back at the woman trapped in the light and thought about all of the history she must have seen. He wondered what her importance might have been to Wigg and the Directorate. Jessamay had said that she had been brought here by Succiu after the Coven's attack on Eutracia. Had she known his parents? Or Faegan?

"I have it!" Wigg shouted.

As he picked up the book, Celeste took him by the arm.

"Please be careful, Father," she said. Wigg nodded.

"I want you two to stay here," he said. Then he winked at them. "Don't worry. I may be more than three hundred years old, but I still have a few tricks up my sleeve."

Holding the open book in his hands, he walked back to the cone of azure light. He looked into Jessamay's eyes.

"I am going to try to free you," he said. "But first—can you manage to cut yourself slightly with your manacles?"

Jessamay nodded. "You wish to be sure that it's really me, don't you?" she asked.

Without waiting for an answer, Jessamay carefully used the edge of one of her manacles to scrape the skin of the opposite wrist. Then she did it again. She started to bleed.

Tilting her hand slightly, she allowed a few drops of her blood to fall to the alcove floor. As they landed, they began twisting themselves into matching blood signatures. Coming as close as he dared Wigg bent down and looked at them. Satisfied, he stood back up.

"It's really me," Jessamay said. "I swear it to you."

"I know," Wigg answered.

"Please promise me something," she said then.

"Anything."

"If you see your efforts failing, you must improperly violate the boundaries of the cone and let me die. I would rather join the Afterlife than spend one more moment as Failee's plaything."

"I promise," Wigg answered gravely.

Holding the grimoire before him, he started to read the passage. Tristan and Celeste held their breath.

At first nothing happened. Tristan looked at Celeste, wondering whether the incantation was going to work. Then the cone began to change.

As Jessamay slinked fearfully toward the rear of the alcove, droplets of azure energy began to run down from the cone's apex. Their paths crisscrossed as they descended in snaking, undulating streaks, and the cone slowly vanished from the top down. Wigg continued to recite the incantation until the prison of light was gone. Only an azure pool remained on the floor.

Wigg closed the book and pointed at Jessamay.

"Spread your arms and close your eyes," he ordered.

She obeyed, and the rusty chains binding her to the wall rattled.

A bolt of azure light streaked from Wigg's hand. The chains attached to Jessamay's right manacle exploded in a cloud of smoke. Then he did the same to the ones on the other side.

"Tristan," the wizard called out, "come here."

Tristan and Celeste walked to his side. Wigg handed the grimoire to the prince.

Stepping forward, Wigg looked into Jessamay's eyes. She was crying freely now and she was barely able to stand. Wigg took her into his arms and carried her out of the alcove.

"You must take Failee's blood criterion and signature scope!" Jessamay said urgently, her voice a rasping whisper.

Wigg looked around. "Where?"

She waved an arm weakly in the direction of one of the tables. "There," she said.

Although confused by her request, Wigg barked out the order to Tristan, who went to gather the tools. "But why—" Wigg began. He was interrupted by the sudden squeal of rusty hinges.

Tristan spun around. Just as before, the iron door on the far side of the room had begun to close.

Horrified, he shoved the grimoire into Celeste's hands and ran. He reached the door and tried with all his strength to stop it, but he couldn't. Through the narrowing gap he could see and hear Alrik and his warriors on the other side.

Shouting frantically at one another, several of the Minions grasped the edge of the door and pulled against it. But even their combined strength could not overcome the craft.

Tristan let go just in time to save his fingers from being

crushed. But some of his warriors were not so fortunate. Even as the door closed with a final bang, they never gave up. Severed fingers fell to the floor at Tristan's feet.

His chest heaving, Tristan turned away from the door. Then he froze. The pool of azure liquid left by the cone was growing . . . and fast. "Look out!" he shouted.

Jessamay in his arms, Wigg turned around. "I should have known!" he exclaimed. "It's another trap!"

The fluid was nearly at their toes now.

"Take Jessamay!" Wigg ordered. Handing Celeste the blood criterion and signature scope, Tristan took the sorceress from Wigg. Then Wigg snatched the grimoire from his daughter.

He raised his hands and the glow of the craft appeared. In a moment, Tristan felt his body growing lighter. Soon his toes were off the floor. Wigg raised his hands farther, and they all levitated toward the ceiling.

Tristan looked down at the floor and saw, to his horror, that the fluid was increasing in volume. The temperature in the room was rising; steam began to roil. Rushing waves of the fluid began noisily overturning the furniture.

Two of the bookcases tumbled down. As furniture and books swirled in the strange fluid, they caught fire, sending acrid smoke toward the fugitives hovering near the ceiling.

The fluid was already halfway to the ceiling. Tristan found it difficult to breathe. Coughing, he struggled to hold Jessamay higher. There was now very little space between his head and the ceiling.

He looked toward Celeste. There was so much steam and smoke that he could barely see her face. Then he smelled burning leather. Looking down, he saw that the fluid had reached the toes of his boots.

With his last bit of strength he lifted Jessamay higher. She screamed as the searing, smoking fluid began to reach them. Tristan looked frantically over at Wigg, to see the wizard desperately trying to decipher a page of the grimoire.

The smoke and the heat were suffocating, and Tristan felt close to passing out. He knew he could hold Jessamay for only a few more seconds. Leaning close, Celeste kissed him goodbye.

CHAPTER XXXIV

"PUT YOUR BACKS INTO IT!" SCARS SHOUTED AT THE TOP OF HIS lungs. Even his booming voice could barely be heard above the raging storm. "Pump those handles with everything you have and turn that screw quickly! This is our last chance to stay alive!"

As the *Reprise* heeled hard to port, the Minions and Tyranny's crewmen struggled to repair the great ship. Scars watched anxiously as his men turned the screw and K'jarr's warriors manned the pumps. He knew Tyranny wouldn't be able to hold her over for long, and they had to get the fresh boards into place before she righted again.

The frigate groaned in protest. Scars cast his gaze upward. He couldn't imagine what it must be like above decks. He knew the ship wouldn't be able to take much more of this.

With one of its flat iron braces firmly against a supporting timber, the screw inched the opposing brace toward the damaged hull. Crewmen were busy hammering the fresh-cut planks into place. Finally the brace seated, and the crew slathered on pitch and tar, covering the gaps between the planks. Scars barked out orders, spurring the men on. Their lives depended upon the next few moments. Scars knew they needed just a little more time, if only their captain could give it to them. Then he felt the heavy ship come to starboard again, and he knew he had a decision to make.

As the *Reprise* came back over, the shifting stress on the hull would transfer through the screw and against the timber. The already weakened timber might well break under the strain. If it did, the freshly seated planks would cave in again, and this time all would be lost.

There were only two choices, and neither was good. He could

order the screw removed to protect the mast, and hope that the hull would hold on its own; or he could leave the giant screw in place, and hope that the mast didn't buckle under the stress. Once the tar had dried, the screw could be removed. Over time, the seawater on the outer side of the hull would swell the fresh wood and seal the boards together, ensuring the job.

But the pitch had just been applied, and they were clearly out of time. As his crewmen began to counterturn the screw, Scars made his decision. He pointed at them.

"Belay that!" he shouted at the top of his lungs. "Leave the screw as it is! The timber will just have to hold!"

As the *Reprise* settled back down to starboard, they all held their breath.

Seawater slammed against the fragile repairs, and the *Reprise* let go another tortured groan. The men watched in horror as sharp, twisted bits of timber popped and splintered away to splash into the shoulder-deep seawater. The beam actually buckled a bit, as the ship came over hard. Then the *Reprise* settled and once again angled into the wind. The mast and the hull repairs held.

The Minions and crewmen cheered. But the next few moments were important, and Scars had no intention of letting them be wasted.

"Stop celebrating like a pack of fallen virgins!" he roared at them. "There is still work to do!" He raised a beefy arm.

"You men, there. Tighten up that screw until the slack has been taken up! And keep those pumps going until the cabin is completely dry! Slather on that pitch and tar until not a drop of seawater can come through! This night is not yet over!"

Looking over at K'jarr, Scars finally allowed himself a smile. The exhausted Minion warrior smiled back.

"Let's go topside!" Scars said. "The captain will need a report!"

They waded through the water and started up the gangway. Scars was desperately worried about what they would find above.

As they reached the deck, they could see that the storm had abated. With its passing, the first welcome rays of dawn crept over the horizon. Between the storm and the stresses of Faegan's portal, the *Reprise* had suffered badly.

Two of her masts were down, their splintered pieces rolling to and fro across the deck. The sails and sheets that had fallen with them lay in ruins. Many of the sails still aloft had great tears in them, and much of the rigging had come down. The bowsprit was missing altogether. The ship wandered east-northeasterly.

Looking back to the ship's wheel, they saw that the boatswain had at some point taken control from the captain. He struggled to keep her on a steady course. Most of the crew and warriors who had been below were now topside, hurrying about their duties. Knowing that his captain would be sure to ask, Scars ordered an immediate count of the crew and warriors.

But they could not find Tyranny or Shailiha. Fearing the worst, Scars shouted out their names. After a time he and K'jarr engaged several warriors to help them search.

Soon one of the warriors called out. Scars and K'jarr ran to the aft starboard gunwale and found the women there.

Shailiha lay prostrate on the deck. There was a bleeding gash on her forehead. Although Tyranny did not appear to be injured, it was clear that she was both physically and mentally exhausted. Both women were soaked to the skin, shivering. Tyranny was using a cloth to staunch the princess' wound.

Calling for a Minion healer, K'jarr knelt beside her, and was heartened to see that Shailiha was alert. When she saw him, she managed a smile through the pain. K'jarr took her hand.

"How bad is it?" he asked the captain.

"The wound is deep," Tyranny said. "When the second mast came down, part of it struck her. Even so, she refused to let go of the wheel. If it hadn't been for her persistence, I doubt I could have held it over by myself. We owe her much." Then she stood.

"Where do we stand?" she asked Scars.

"The rent in the hull has been repaired. The screw is still in place, and the new planks seem to be holding. I believe the breach was caused by the added stresses of Faegan's portal." Scars surveyed the damage around him. "But it seems that the rest of her hasn't fared so well."

"Have we lost any people?"

"I don't know yet," Scars said. "They are doing a count as we speak."

Turning east, Tyranny saw the rising sun. She looked back at Scars.

"Take the princess to my quarters," she ordered. "Have the Minion healers tend to her there. As soon as she has been treated, I want a report on her condition. And bring me the teak box I keep there. You know the one. Then I want a full report on our damage. We still have a mission to perform, and I intend to see it through."

She cast her gaze back over the mangled ship. "We might be down, but we're not out," she said. A hint of a smile crossed her face. "It will take more than the miscalculations of some crazy old wizard to sink the *Reprise.*"

Scars smiled back. He picked up the princess as if she weighed nothing, turned, and carried her below decks. As the war frigate plowed her errant way east, Tyranny and K'jarr remained silent.

Scars soon reappeared carrying a large teak box. He set it upon the deck. Tyranny bent down to open it. K'jarr raised an eyebrow.

"What does it contain?" he asked.

"My navigational tools," the privateer answered. "Faegan supposedly made some alterations to them, so as to make my job easier. I can only hope that the wizard's calculations for my sextant were better than the ones he used to alter his portal," she added dryly.

The sextant was a triangular-shaped affair made of shiny brass. At one end there was a small, horizontally mounted telescope. The telescope faced two mirrors mounted on the opposite side of the apparatus. The bottom portion of the instrument was curved, and it was marked off in degrees. A lever led down from the apex of the sextant and counted off the degrees at its pointed end.

Tyranny gazed eastward through the telescope, focusing it upon the horizon. Then she moved the lever in order to align the two mirrors with both the horizon and the rising sun. Taking the sextant from her eye, she noted the number of degrees indicated by the lever. A worried look came over her face.

She reached into the box and removed her charts. She closed the lid, then spread the charts out upon it. Using her dagger to point to a position on the chart, she looked back up at Scars and K'jarr.

"It's just as I feared," she said. "By my reckoning we are a good forty leagues northwest of where Faegan's portal was supposed to deliver us. I cannot be completely sure. Now let's see what Faegan's way of doing things has to say," she said skeptically.

Tyranny pushed the point of her dagger through the chart and into the teak box, so that it was now standing upright at the location she had just calculated. Holding the sextant with one hand directly over the center of the chart, with her free hand she reached into her jacket and removed a small piece of parchment. She held it up.

"Ristutatem appricitamitat onovenatu!" she read loudly.

Almost at once her sextant began to glow with the craft. When she released it, it hovered in the brisk sea air. Then it turned in the direction of the sun. K'jarr and Scars watched in awe as the lever on the sextant began to move of its own accord. The lever seesawed back and forth a bit before it finally settled down.

Without warning, a slim azure beam suddenly shot from the base of the sextant and burned a small "X" into the parchment. Then the beam disappeared. Tyranny took the sextant from the air, and the glow surrounding it disappeared.

"How did you do that?" K'jarr asked. "It was my understanding that your blood was not endowed."

Tyranny smiled. "It isn't," she answered. "Faegan enchanted the sextant before we set sail. It responds to my voice, rather than my blood. Provided I say the Old Eutracian command properly, the sextant will do the same thing for me every time. At first I thought the old wizard was going to suffer a nervous breakdown, trying to teach me the words. He finally gave up and wrote them down for me instead." She shoved the parchment back under her jacket.

She studied the chart. The charred "X" was about ten leagues away from the calculations she had just made manually. That put their position slightly closer to the planned exit point from the portal. Running one finger southeast across the chart, she pointed to the Isle of the Citadel. She looked up at K'jarr.

"Can a warrior scouting party make the flight there and back?" she asked.

K'jarr examined the chart, then turned to stare up at the sky, noting the direction and strength of the wind.

"Yes," he answered, "provided I send our most gifted fliers. The wind will be in their faces on the outward leg. But if it holds, it will be at their backs for the return trip. Do you wish me to lead them?"

Tyranny nodded. "Make your course southeasterly. I want you to fly high and survey the Citadel without being seen. Make a count of any demonslaver vessels you might encounter. If you can capture a demonslaver, do so. Go now."

K'jarr bowed, and with a click of his heels, he was gone.

She was about to speak to Scars when she saw a female Minion healer approach. The white feather of her craft stood out proudly on her black body armor. She came to stand at attention.

"Permission to speak?" she asked. Tyranny nodded.

"I have just tended to the princess," the healer said. "Her wound will heal. She will remain dizzy for another day or two, but she should suffer no lasting effects. I have given her something for the pain. I suggest she remain in bed until tomorrow."

"Very well," Tyranny answered. "And thank you. Please remain by her side until I order otherwise." With a short bow, the healer went back to her patient.

"I want that damage report as soon as I can get it," she said to Scars. "We need as much speed and maneuverability out of this wallowing whale as she can muster."

Scars nodded. "We will do all we can, Captain," he said.

Tyranny nodded and her expression softened. "I know," she said. "Now go."

When Scars was gone, Tyranny opened the teak box again. Reaching in, she removed one of her cigarillos and a common match. Then she walked over to lean her tired body against the gunwale.

Hearing the familiar sound of Minion wings, she looked up to see a party of six warriors leaving the deck. They flew in the shape of an arrowhead, with K'jarr at the lead. After circling the ship once, they turned southeast.

Tyranny watched them until they disappeared. Then she stabbed the cigarillo between her lips, struck the match against her scuffed knee boot, and lit the tobacco. Taking a welcome lungful of smoke, she raised her face and blew it back out into the air. The spent match went over the side.

She looked with sadness down the length of her mangled flagship, thinking about her mission. Its beginning had not been auspicious.

CHAPTER XXXV

SURROUNDED BY FIGHTING AND SCREAMING, DUVESSA KNEW that she was close to defeat. Her muscles burned and sweat dripped maddeningly down her face, threatening to obscure her vision. It was just before dawn, and the glow from the torches surrounding the battle sent their shadows dancing eerily across the uneven killing ground. She knew better than to risk trying to see how her allies were faring. One mistake like that could cost her dearly.

Just as her enemy's sword came whistling around again, Duvessa raised her dreggan high and parried the strike vertically. The blades of the two weapons clanged together with such force that sparks flew. Summoning all of her strength, she turned and slid the edge of her blade down along her opponent's, forcing his guard down. Sensing an opening, she pointed her sword toward her enemy's throat and lunged forward.

With a wicked smile her opponent stepped to one side, banging his blade down upon her weapon with everything he had. He stamped down upon her sword blade, pinning it to the ground. Then he struck her in the face. The sudden blow made her drop her weapon.

Kicking her dreggan away, her enemy whirled around behind her. He kicked her viciously in the back. Thrown face down into the dirt, she tried desperately to think.

"Kneel," the harsh voice commanded.

She had no choice but to obey. As she came to her knees, she dragged her right palm across the ground, filling her hand with dirt. She knew the killing blow would come any moment now.

Holding her hands at her sides, she forced herself to look up into her killer's eyes. With another smile he raised his sword high, its blade glinting briefly in the torchlight. Duvessa held her breath.

Just as the sword reached its apex she rolled to one side, throwing the dirt into his face. He cried out, and she pulled her dagger from its sheath.

She came to her feet and ran behind him. Grabbing his hair with her free hand she yanked his head back and pulled the blade of her dagger across his throat.

"Enough!" the Minion head instructor shouted.

At his sharp command, all of the warriors stopped fighting. Their chests heaving, they lowered the points of their dreggans to the dirt. Duvessa wearily recovered her weapon.

"You're learning!" the instructor shouted to the group at large. "But each of you has a long way to go before you can claim the rite of ascension. That is why we train as realistically as possible. Remember, only fully realized death blows are not permitted."

The instructor's name was Baltasar. Walking over to Duvessa, he smiled at her.

"Well done," he said. "Any trick that helps you stay alive is by definition a good one. Still, a Minion warrior should never find herself on her knees. With practice, your hands will become accustomed to retaining your weapon as it is struck by another. Even so, I must applaud your resourcefulness."

Duvessa gave him a slight bow. "Thank you," she answered.

Baltasar gave her a reassuring look. "I know that being chosen by the *Jin'Sai* to lead this new group of female warriors is a heavy burden," he said quietly. "I also realize that each of you is eager to prove herself. And being Traax's mate means that you—even more than the others—shall have a great deal to live up to. You must be the best of them. That is why I push you so hard."

"I understand," she answered.

Baltasar pointed to the white feather emblazoned on the chest of her body armor. "If you become as good a fighter as you are a healer, I think this new force shall be in very capable hands."

After giving her another brief smile, he turned to speak to

some of the other female candidates about their progress. At the same time the male Minion warriors they had been sparring with offered their guidance, as well.

Duvessa looked over at the warrior she had just bested. He was still trying to clear the dirt from his eyes. She sheathed her dreggan. Taking a cloth from beneath her armor, she told him to look up at the stars. She gently wiped away the dirt.

"I'm sorry," she said.

"Don't be," he answered. "You won, and that is what matters. Serves me right for assuming that you had given up! Like Baltasar said, any device that keeps you alive in combat is a good one. Had you really meant business with your dagger, I would be watering the ground with my blood."

After giving the warrior a respectful nod, Duvessa went to sit down upon a nearby stone wall and rest.

This area and several others like it had been turned over to the advanced martial training of female warriors. Since the unexpected order had come from the *Jin'Sai,* hundreds had volunteered. For the last several days the instructors had rousted the recruits from their beds several hours before dawn. Then had come the training lectures, followed by the grueling hours of live practice. They had not complained.

She knew that they weren't ready for their rites of ascension. She also knew that not a single woman who had volunteered for these special phalanxes would give up until she had completed the course.

Looking wearily out over the training field, Duvessa understood how much every woman here aspired to wear the red feather—and serve under her command. It would be a heavy responsibility, but one that she welcomed.

Lost in her thoughts, she didn't see Abbey until the herbmistress was standing right in front of her.

Abbey sat down on the stone wall. During her time here at the palace, Duvessa had come to like Abbey very much, and to respect the talents of the kindly partial adept. As she looked at her now, she could see that the herbmistress was concerned.

"What is it?" Duvessa asked. She immediately thought of Traax. "Has there been word from Tyranny?"

Abbey shook her head. "Not that I know of," she answered. "Faegan wishes to see you, me, and Adrian in the Redoubt. He told me that it is important." She gave Duvessa a short smile. "I'm afraid your breakfast will have to wait."

Duvessa stood. After a last look at the phalanxes-in-training, the two women began the walk back.

As Faegan sat waiting in the Cubiculum of Humanistic Research, he was overcome by several separate but equally compelling emotions. The first was an overwhelming sense of sorrow over Geldon's death. The dwarf's body, preserved by the craft, still lay on the examination table under the black sheet. The necropsy that Faegan had performed had been painstaking. More than once the wizard had been forced to stop what he was doing, wipe away his tears, and force himself to continue.

Another emotion stirring within him was pure, unadulterated wonder. The necropsy had revealed a great deal about the nature of Geldon's death. He knew he had to share what he'd learned with those Conclave members who remained at the palace. As an experienced herbmistress, Abbey's counsel might be particularly helpful.

A third emotion had crept in as his examination progressed. It was a deep sense of anger directed toward whoever had done this to his friend. He still did not know why his friend had been killed, but he meant to find out.

When the three women filed into the room, they could all sense Faegan's outrage. The wizard was without question the greatest living scholar of the craft, and they knew him for his kindness of heart. But this seemed to be a different Faegan. This Faegan wanted revenge, and he clearly meant to have it.

"Please forgive the hour," he said. "I know it is very early. What I have to tell you simply couldn't wait."

Faegan beckoned Duvessa, Adrian, and Abbey to sit at a nearby table. He wheeled his chair over to join them.

Several texts and scrolls lay there. Two other tools of the craft sat next to them. One of them was a blood criterion, used for measuring the quality of endowed blood. The other was a signature scope. Its purpose was to identify the lean of a blood signature. When the women were seated, Faegan placed his gnarled hands flat upon the tabletop.

"I know what killed Geldon," he said.

"You mean why he committed suicide?" Abbey offered.

"No," Faegan answered flatly. "I mean what killed him. Geldon was murdered."

"How can that be?" Duvessa asked. "Several dozen Minion warriors saw him plunge the knife into his own eye. Surely you don't think they are lying?"

"No, no, of course not." Faegan shook his head. "Geldon used the knife, all right. But he was compelled to do it. As I suspected, the craft is afoot here. This particular use of magic is one of the most devious and clever that I have ever seen. So clever, in fact, that I nearly missed it."

"What are you talking about?" Adrian asked.

"When faced with such a difficult problem, it is always best to start with what one knows," Faegan answered. "Geldon was of unendowed blood. Despite all of the problems we are wrestling with, he seemed to be happy. He was one of the most resilient men I ever knew. He had to be, to survive as long as he did in the clutches of the Coven. Suicide was simply not in his nature."

He took up a parchment and laid it flat. The paper held an unidentified blood signature.

"Despite the fact that he was unendowed, this showed up in his blood," he said. "He acquired it just before he died. When I first saw it, I couldn't believe my eyes."

Abbey picked up the parchment. The blood signature was "complete," meaning that it showed evidence of both the mother and the father. Therefore, whoever had possessed this signature was of fully endowed blood. She placed the parchment back on the table.

"I mean no disrespect, but what you are saying is quite impossible," she argued. "Blood simply cannot be changed from unendowed to endowed."

"It wasn't," Faegan answered. "But that does not mean it cannot carry the signature of another for a time, if they are mixed somehow. Take a look at this list of foreign matter I found in Geldon's blood." He unrolled another parchment and handed it to her.

"Please read it aloud," he asked.

Abbey looked down the page. "This list shows human brain matter, human yellow bone marrow, human red bone marrow, derma-gnasher venom, root of gingercrinkle, and oil of encumbrance. There are also a few other trace elements mentioned here." With a puzzled expression, she looked back up at Faegan.

"How on earth did he manage to get all of these ingredients into his bloodstream?" she asked. "I have never come across such an unusual concoction in all my life."

"He didn't put them there," Faegan answered. "Someone else did. Geldon was poisoned. I don't have quite all of the pieces to the puzzle yet, but I'm close."

"But what makes you think he was poisoned?" Duvessa countered. "After all, they were a long way from home. Isn't it possible that through some quirk of fate he ingested these things naturally?"

Adrian shook her head. "Gingercrinkle, perhaps," she said. "And even the oil of encumbrance. But human brain? Bone marrow? Impossible." The First Sister of the acolytes looked at Faegan.

"It was the derma-gnasher attack, wasn't it?" she asked. "It had to be. He consumed what the others did. These things couldn't have been in the food or drink, or they would all be dead. And the derma-gnasher puncture was the only insult to his body—other than the damaged eye, of course."

Faegan nodded. "Well done," he said. "When I did the necropsy, you may remember that I took a cross section of tissue from the area surrounding the bite mark. The ingredients listed on the parchment were found in far higher concentration there than anywhere else in his body. The bite was therefore the poison's point of entry."

"So what does all this mean?" Abbey asked. "That we have a swarm of infected derma-gnashers infesting Eutracia? With everything else that is going on, I cannot believe that Geldon's death was so random an act."

"Nor do I," Faegan agreed. "This is what I think happened. I believe this potion was concocted by someone of the craft. The blood signature that appeared in Geldon's blood was obviously not his, as his blood was not endowed. Given the bite on his neck, the derma-gnasher venom was to be expected. I still don't know what the actual delivery system was. It may have been an enchanted derma-gnasher, trained to do its master's bidding. Or it could have been something else entirely—like a blow dart, for instance, disguised with the venom to throw us off. But coming that close to a Minion camp unseen would take skills of the highest order." The ancient wizard paused for a moment as he collected his thoughts.

"The entire mixture was enchanted," he went on, thinking out loud. "And if the brain and bone marrow came from a person who had committed suicide, then a special enchantment might well revive a desire to take one's own life. Transferred to a living host, the poison then becomes active. The subject goes mad, and he or she commits suicide involuntarily."

"But why include the oil of encumbrance?" Abbey asked. "That would only seem to weaken the potion, rather than strengthen it."

Placing one hand under his chin, Faegan thought for a moment. "True," he said. "But oil of encumbrance's true nature is to delay the effect of other ingredients. For example, if you wish to make a slow-acting medicine, oil of encumbrance would be the perfect additive."

"But why would the assassin wish to slow the process?" Duvessa asked.

"For one reason only," Faegan answered. "To allow him time to get away. Just imagine how perfect it all is! First, the victim is surreptitiously poisoned. The poison goes to work slowly. Several hours later the victim is seen raving like a lunatic and commits suicide before a group of witnesses. Foul play is never suspected. The entire event is chalked up to madness, and by then the assassin is long gone. The only other mark on the body is the derma-gnasher attack, and everyone else near him also has those." More amazed than before, Faegan sat back in his chair.

"It's as monstrous as it is brilliant," he breathed. "And it means that there is an assassin of the highest order lurking about Eutracia. One who is in league with someone of the craft. Or these two vast talents may reside within a single person. Either way, we are now forced to assume that the members of the Conclave have been marked for death."

"But how would he or she possibly know who the members are?" Adrian asked. "All of our meetings have taken place here in the Redoubt. And the Conclave was formed only several months ago."

Faegan looked back at her with knowing eyes. "Tristan's meeting with the citizens in the Hall of Supplication," he said. "If you remember, he not only introduced each of us, but he also went so far as to explain our various roles. I would not be surprised to learn that Geldon's killer had been sitting there the entire time, sizing us up."

He let go a deep breath, then looked back over at Geldon's corpse again.

"Our enemies have planned exceedingly well," he said. "But who is this assassin, and who of the craft is he in league with? This formula was mixed by an expert, I assure you."

Suddenly Abbey stared at the wizard as though she had just seen a ghost.

"What is it?" he asked her.

"Do you suppose . . . ," she said softly.

"Suppose what?"

As if not knowing how to begin, Abbey took a deep breath. "Fifty years ago—long before Wigg brought me back to Tammerland—a badly wounded man stumbled onto my cottage. He had been savagely tortured, and he was delirious. Several of his fingers had been cut off. I took him in. But by then a massive infection had set in, and there was little I could do for him. Still, he told me a few things before he died."

Faegan leaned closer. "What did he say?"

"He told me that he was a Valrenkian," she said.

Faegan sat back in his chair. "Did you believe him?" he asked.

"At the time I thought it was his delirium talking," she answered. "But as the years wore on, I came to believe it. It was a deathbed confession. Why would he lie?"

"Why indeed," Faegan mused. Then his expression changed and he looked sternly at her. "Why didn't you report this to the Directorate?"

Abbey pursed her lips. "You don't know what things were

like then," she said defensively. "You were still in Shadowood. The partials had been banished for nearly three hundred years. Worse yet, before I left, Wigg granted me the time enchantments. That was strictly against Directorate policy. Had I suddenly returned, they were sure to find out. He would have lost his seat on the Directorate, or worse. Despite what he had done to me I still loved him. So I stayed away."

Faegan gave a little smile of understanding. "Did this man say anything else?"

"He wanted to repent," she said. "When he wished to leave that life, they refused. They told him that once you were accepted into their midst, you were a Valrenkian until death. They tortured him, but somehow he managed to escape. But he did also say that he was sorry for the things he had done. And then he whispered the most telling thing of all."

"And that was?"

"That they were a secret society of partial adepts. The last thing he said to me was that they were of the Vagaries, and that they used human and animal body parts in their work. They survive by selling their dark wares throughout Eutracia. Sometimes they kidnap citizens, and other times they rob graves for their raw materials."

Faegan closed his eyes. "So it's true after all," he said softly.

"Who are the Valrenkians?" Duvessa asked.

Opening his eyes, Faegan looked over at the Minion. "Until this moment, I believed them to be more myth than flesh and blood," he answered. "Now I'm not so sure. Legend says that they were originally formed by the Coven of Sorceresses. They were supposedly converted to the Vagaries, and then taught their grisly trades. Right or wrong, these rumors were one of the major factors in the Directorate's decision to banish the partials."

Faegan looked back at Abbey. "Did this man tell you where their community was located?"

Abbey shook her head. "But if what we surmise about Geldon's death is true, then a clue to their whereabouts might be right under our noses."

"What do you mean?"

"You said that one of the ingredients in the poison used to kill

Geldon was gingercrinkle, did you not?" she asked. Faegan nodded.

"Gingercrinkle grows only in one place," she went on. "On the southwestern border of Hartwick Wood. Trying to send out search parties to look for this assassin would be pointless. We don't even know what he or she looks like. But if the killer acquired this potion from the Valrenkians, then that would be a good place to begin our search. If we can find them, they might lead us to him."

Faegan looked down at his hands and then back up again. "This issue of the gingercrinkle will probably be a mere coincidence," he said. "But in good conscience I cannot let it go unexplored."

Silence fell over the room for a time as the wizard carefully considered his options. He finally looked over at Duvessa.

"Go and fetch Ox," he said. "I have a new mission for the Minions."

CHAPTER XXXVI

WHEN TRISTAN FIRST HEARD THE INCESSANT POUNDING, HE THOUGHT he must be dreaming. Then he saw that the rising azure fluid licked the soles of his boots. His feet burned, and he knew it was the end.

Even though he was close to passing out, something made him look upward. Marble dust fell onto his head and into his eyes. He still heard the muffled sound of hammering, but he couldn't imagine how or why.

Then a wide crack snaked jaggedly across the ceiling. Several others followed. With a great tearing sound, a chunk of the ceiling suddenly fell away, barely missing the four of them.

Hands quickly reached down and grabbed them. With an upward heave, they were all suddenly hauled to the relative safety of the floor above, and then dragged away from the edge of the smoking hole. As Tristan tried to understand what had just happened, Jessamay fainted in his arms.

At least fifty Minion warriors stood there, chests heaving. They held iron mallets. The floor of the room was a broken, smashed disaster. Celeste and Wigg stood weakly next to the prince as they all tried desperately to catch their breath.

Tristan felt his legs start to buckle, and one of the warriors took Jessamay from him. Then he and Celeste suddenly felt strong hands under their shoulders, helping them to remain upright. One warrior took the blood criterion and the signature scope from Celeste and placed them on the floor a short distance away.

Wigg seemed able to stand on his own. Through blurry eyes, Tristan watched the wizard walk back over to the gaping hole in the floor.

With Failee's grimoire still in his hands, Wigg looked down. The ever-increasing azure fluid was still swirling upward. He opened the grimoire, and searched through it. Finally finding what he wanted, he held the book in one hand, raised the other, and began reading aloud from the text.

Almost at once an azure glow surrounded the hole in the floor. The deadly fluid in the room abated, and then finally disappeared altogether. Closing the book and lowering his arm, Wigg let go a sigh of relief. He walked tiredly back to the others.

The wizard examined Tristan and Celeste, and told them that they would be all right. Then he placed one hand upon Jessamay's forehead. In a few moments she began to stir.

Tristan looked around to see Alrik standing there. What the prince could see of the room looked bleak and unfurnished. The Minion officer smiled broadly.

"Thank you," Tristan said thickly. His head was still swimming, but he was starting to feel better. He brushed the marble dust from his hair and clothing. "Where are we?"

"We are still below ground," Alrik said. "When I saw the iron door close I immediately ran, ordering my warriors to follow me. We grabbed our tools, and we barely arrived here in time. But as you can see, fifty Minion warriors with iron mallets are a force to be reckoned with. The floor did not want to surrender to us, but we finally broke through."

"You weren't able to find the counteracting spell in time, were you?" Tristan asked Wigg.

The First Wizard shook his head. "If it hadn't been for the Minions, we would be quite dead by now. I considered trying to use the craft to blow a hole in the ceiling, but by then we were too close."

"What about all of Failee's texts and scrolls?" Tristan asked. "Have they been destroyed?"

Wigg nodded sadly. "But we still have her grimoire, and her blood criterion and signature scope," he answered. Looking down at the leather-bound volume in his hands, Wigg ran one palm over its cover. "If I could have saved only one thing from that horrible place below, it would have been this."

Jessamay groaned. She still lay in the arms of one of the warriors. Her eyes fluttered. Wigg walked over to her and, gently lifting one of her eyelids, peered into her eye.

"She will be all right, but she has been through a great deal," he said. He looked around the room for a moment, and then back at the prince. "We need to get her back up to the Recluse."

Tristan took Celeste into his arms. He searched her face. "Are you all right?" he asked.

She coughed and scowled a bit. "I think so," she said. She looked around the room again. "But let's get out of here."

Tristan looked back at Alrik. "Escort us back to the surface," he ordered. Then he smiled. "This time, we'll follow you."

Tristan picked up Failee's rescued instruments. With a click of his heels, Alrik led the way out of the room.

The walk back to the surface took some time. When they finally reached the first floor, everyone was glad to take a deep breath of fresh air. Wigg ordered Alrik to take them somewhere where Jessamay could be made comfortable. After another short walk, Alrik stopped before a door.

"This room should serve your needs," he said.

Handing the instruments over to Wigg, Tristan took Jessamay back into his arms. "You may leave us now," he told Alrik. "And you may dismiss your warriors. But we shall need some food and drink brought to us. I have no idea how long we might remain."

Alrik clicked his heels. *"Jin'Sai,"* he said.

As Alrik went about his orders, his warriors obediently following, Tristan carried Jessamay through the open doorway.

The renovated room was spacious and well-appointed. Wide balcony doors lay open to the outdoors, letting in golden rays of sunlight and a cool, welcome breeze. Patterned carpet lined the floor, and a large, four-poster, canopied bed stood against one wall. An ornate writing desk and matching chair sat on the far side of the room, and a door across from it was open to an elaborate washroom.

Celeste carefully placed the instruments on the desk, while Tristan laid Jessamay down on the bed. As Wigg sat on the edge of the bed, his daughter came to stand near him.

Wigg placed one palm upon Jessamay's cheek and smiled. "You're safe now," he reassured her. "After all of these years, you can begin to live for yourself again."

Jessamay shook her head, and her eyes filled with tears. "I can feel my powers starting to return," she said softly. "And there is something I must tell you."

Smiling again, Wigg took his hand from her face. "Your time enchantments are still in place," he answered. "There is all the time in the world to tell us about your experiences with Failee. Rest assured, we want to hear them all."

"No, no. You must listen to me," she protested. "You must examine my blood signature again."

Wigg took one of her hands into his. "There is no need," he said. "Don't you remember? I already examined it, and I am convinced. What's the matter?" he chided. "After all of this time, have you somehow managed to forget who you are? I certainly haven't."

Jessamay began shaking her head violently. She tried to rise up from the bed. "You don't understand!" she insisted. "You must reexamine my signature now, this instant! And this time use Failee's signature scope! I must know if it's true! The very future of the craft depends upon it!"

Wigg pushed her back down onto the bed. "Very well," he said, "if that's what it takes to make you lie still. But after that, you must get some rest."

Narrowing his eyes, Wigg caused another incision to appear in Jessamay's wrist. A single drop of blood rose from it, and then the wound closed. The blood drop came to hover in the air before the wizard, where it twisted itself into the same blood signature they had all seen before. Wigg looked up at the prince.

"Please see if there is any parchment in that desk," he asked.

Tristan walked over and he looked through the newly made drawers. He found a small piece of parchment and placed it on the desk.

Staring at the hovering blood, Wigg commanded it to glide over to the desk. It gently landed upon the parchment. Leaving Jessamay's side, the wizard walked to the desk and sat down.

Confidently, Wigg casually positioned the tripod directly over the blood signature, then looked down through the lens secured at the top.

He took a quick breath. He looked in shock at Jessamay. Upon seeing his reaction, she covered her face with her hands and began to cry even harder.

Wigg's face was blanched and his jaw was working. But in his completely astonished state, no words came. Finally he found his voice.

"But this is impossible . . . ," he said, so softly that Tristan and Celeste could barely hear him. "This violates every established precept. . . ."

With shaking hands, Wigg readjusted the scope. He looked again. His expert eye remained glued to the lens for a long time. As Jessamay watched in fear, her sobbing continued unabated.

CHAPTER XXXVII

AS SERENA SAT AMONG HER HUSBAND'S NEW SERVANTS, SHE FELT a shudder go through her. Were they dead, alive, or something else, she wondered. Even given her immense skills of the craft, she could not tell.

But at least she could understand Wulfgar's vision of the future—the vision that had been imparted to him by the Guild of the Heretics, and that he had at last explained to her.

The meeting room was large and well appointed. Ten sat at the table: herself, Wulfgar, Einar, and the Council of Seven, as her husband called his new servants. A pair of armed demon-slavers stood guard on the other side of the closed double doors. Two candelabras on the table threw their flickering light over a sumptuous spread of food and wine. In the far wall, a fire danced merrily in the hearth. Its smoke smelled familiar and comforting.

Taking up her wineglass, Serena refocused her attention on Wulfgar's words.

". . . each of you will captain a Black Ship," he was saying. "You will command not only the Earthshakers assigned to your vessel, but also several full legions of demonslavers. Tomorrow you shall practice the sea maneuvers that you once carried out centuries ago, albeit for a very different cause. I wish to be sure that the legends of your prowess are still true." As he spoke, the ravaged half of his face contorted grotesquely.

"When we finally launch the war against Eutracia, several of you shall march your forces north to ensure the continued self-destruction of the Orb of the Vigors," he went on. "That is our chief concern. The rest of you shall aid me in the attack upon the royal palace. We shall destroy the Conclave of the Vigors, my half brother's Minions of Day and Night, and the Redoubt of the Directorate. When our victories are secure we will then turn our attention east, toward Parthalon. Compared to Eutracia, Parthalon will collapse like a house of cards."

"A question, my lord," one of the seven captains said.

It was the first time Serena had heard any of them speak, and it surprised her. Like the others, his glowing eyes and white teeth shone in his black skull.

"And that is?" Wulfgar asked.

"Are we to assume that any opposing force nearing the orb—especially that which might be commanded by the wizards or the *Jin'Sai*—is to be obliterated?" the captain asked.

Wulfgar smiled. "Indeed."

Then the Lord of the Vagaries leaned over, and placed both

his hands upon the table. His single eye seemed to take everyone in at once. Even Serena found it unnerving.

"But hear me well," he added quietly. "The *Jin'Sai* and the *Jin'Saiou* are not to be killed. I have my own plans for my dear half brother and sister. Any of you who disobey this order will again find himself imprisoned in the sea—this time for all eternity."

The captain bowed his head slightly. "We understand, my lord," he answered. "All shall be as you order."

Serena watched as one of the Council lifted a goblet of wine in one skeletal hand and drank greedily. Some of the wine dribbled sloppily from his lipless mouth, running down his chin and onto his lap.

Unable to help herself, Serena continued to stare. He looked much like the others. Between the rents in his clothing and the spaces between his black ribs, she could see his esophagus undulate, and the swallowed wine swell his stomach. She watched transfixed as his dark heart beat, and his equally black lungs expanded and contracted with every breath.

Picking up a napkin from the table, he politely patted the wine from his teeth and chin. Amazed, Serena felt as though she was having dinner in a graveyard, with all of the interred risen from the ground, to join in the feast.

Wulfgar stood and trained his gaze upon the first of his captains. "Come to me," he said.

The bizarre servant did as he was told.

"Kneel," Wulfgar ordered. The captain did so.

"Give me your sword."

The captain drew his weapon. It hadn't been freed for centuries, and it made a grating sound when it cleared its scabbard. Even so, the blade gleamed brightly in the lamplight. Bowing his head, the captain respectfully offered the weapon to his lord.

Taking the hilt in his good hand, Wulfgar held the sword to the light. Then he looked at those assembled at the table.

"So that your service to our cause shall have greater meaning for us all, I wish to know each of you by your family house," he said. He looked back down at his kneeling servant. "What was your family name, before your enemies condemned you to the sea?" he asked.

"Merriwhether," the captain answered.

Lowering the tip of the sword, Wulfgar pointed it toward the scabbard at the captain's side. Suddenly, a small, azure bolt of lightning launched from the tip of the weapon. Striking the scabbard, it etched the captain's family name into it. The script was elegant. The lightning disappeared, and Wulfgar raised the sword again.

"Arise, Captain Merriwhether," he said. "Welcome to the Council of Seven."

He handed the weapon back, and with a short bow, the captain stood and sheathed his sword.

As Serena and Einar watched Wulfgar repeat the process with each of the six other captains, Serena took care to remember their names: Merriwhether, Duggan, Sebastion, Grindoff, Cathmore, Ballard, and Garmane.

As they stood before her husband, Serena felt another twinge of her nerves. But this time, she knew, it was caused by her absolute certainty of the success of their mission, and her undying love for her husband. She knew that the *Enseterat* would return to her in victory.

Wulfgar raised his wine goblet.

"A toast," he said.

As Serena and Einar stood, all lifted their glasses.

"Tomorrow I shall order all of the demonslaver frigates into port, so that they will not interfere with your maneuvers," Wulfgar said. He raised his wine goblet higher.

"To the successful sea trials of the Black Ships!" he proclaimed.

As Wulfgar took a draft of wine, his Council of Seven cheered.

CHAPTER XXXVIII

BEATING HIS DARK WINGS THROUGH THE SKY, OX BLESSED THE good weather. A dozen stout warriors made up the arrowhead-shaped formation flying in his wake.

Ox and his phalanx had been searching for several hours. So far, they had seen nothing out of the ordinary. Truth be told, he wasn't really sure what he was looking for. Even Faegan hadn't been able to help very much when he gave the Minion his orders.

The wizard had done his best to explain, but the supposed existence of the Valrenkian community was not a simple concept to grasp, even for someone with a quicker wit than Ox. Faegan told him to scour the southern border of Hartwick Wood. Once there, he was to closely examine any villages or random groups of people he came across. If the warriors found a community that looked suspicious, they were to try to take a suitable prisoner. If the wizard's interrogation of him revealed nothing, he would, of course, be returned. So far, though, they had seen nothing unusual in the two hamlets they had searched. Only the Minions themselves were out of the ordinary: frightened citizens had scattered wildly when the warriors swooped low to take a look.

It was nearly midday, and the skies were clear. To scan as much territory as possible, Ox had taken his warriors very high. It was cold at this altitude, and frost had begun to form in their beards and hair.

Looking down, Ox could see the gentle curve of the Vitenka River. From its mouth at the coastal city of Far Point, it meandered southwest along the edge of the forest. In the distant south lay Heart Square, the fertile plain that always yielded so much wheat and barley. To the west of Heart Square the Vitenka would eventually split, its two branches reaching south toward the lower reaches of the Tolenka Mountains.

Thinking of the Tolenkas, Ox's mind turned to the Orb of the Vigors. He was no longer able to see the broken orb, but he was fully aware that it was still blasting its way through the granite peaks. He wondered what had become of the Minion party he and Geldon had left there, to watch the orb.

Ottikar, Ox's second in command, advanced to his side and pointed to the ground. Ox looked down again and saw a large, jagged circle of sandstone bluffs. Their wide, flat, tan-colored tops reflected scattered deposits of quartz. Inside their walls sat a small village, its inhabitants mere fly specks at this altitude.

As Ox looked closer, he began to see why Ottikar had brought this place to his attention. As best he could tell, there was absolutely no way in or out of the community.

Examining the stark bluffs again, he saw people standing atop them. Ox recognized guards when he saw them.

"Tell others stay here and circle," he shouted to Ottikar. "Then come back. You and me go down and look."

Nodding, Ottikar flew to rejoin the group. Moments later, he was by Ox's side again.

"Follow!" Ox ordered his second in command. "It not normal have no way in or out, or have guards atop walls! We try find reason!"

Folding his wings behind his back, Ox rolled over into a nearly vertical dive. The wind tearing at his face, he pointed himself toward the village.

Ottikar narrowed his eyes. Snapping back his wings, he followed his commander down.

HIS NAME WAS UTHER, AND HE PRIDED HIMSELF UPON BEING ONE of the most savage Valrenkians. Because of the very high quality of his goods, he was also one of the wealthiest. The care and expertise he commanded in the preparation of his dark wares was second only to that of Reznik. It was often whispered among the Corporeals that Uther had long wished to usurp Reznik's place as their leader, and that he was willing to do anything—including murdering the revered herbmaster—to accomplish his ends.

Everyone knew that Reznik was aware of Uther's designs upon his position. They also understood that the wily leader of the Valrenkians would not be easily killed. And so they waited and watched, to see which of the two would prevail.

The front room of Uther's cottage, like Reznik's house, was filled with beakers, bottles, and books. Numerous fluid-filled jars held human and animal body parts. Uther watched his young apprentice cutting the toes off a corpse that had just been taken down from one of the street gibbets and grimaced. The boy was doing a terrible job of it. Many Corporeals did not appreciate the value of a good brace of toes, but Uther did. He shoved the boy aside and snatched away the knife.

"You ignorant bastard! How many times must I show you?" He waggled the knife in the apprentice's face. The boy blushed.

"Take each toe off at the joint nearest the foot!" Uther instructed. "Otherwise you run the risk of rendering the entire appendage useless! I didn't age this endowed corpse just so you could come along and butcher it! Now watch me again!" Muttering under his breath, Uther placed the razor-sharp blade against the lifeless skin.

Before he could begin, they heard a commotion outside. Looking out the windows, Uther saw people gathering in the street. That was unusual enough to warrant looking into it.

Uther dropped the knife. Running his hands down his bloody smock, he hurried out the door. His confused apprentice followed.

The crowd in the street was growing, talking, pointing up at the sky. Looking up, at first Uther couldn't see what was commanding their attention. Then two dark forms appeared, seeming to plummet right out of the sun.

Uther had heard of the winged ones who had accompanied the Coven upon its return to Eutracia. He also knew of the rumors claiming that these creatures were now under the command of the prince. But, like the others here, Uther rarely traveled beyond the walls of the bluffs and until this moment had never seen one of the Minions of Day and Night. A cottage door banged shut, and he turned to see Reznik run over to join the stunned crowd.

At the last possible second, the two plunging forms abruptly pulled out of their dives. Snapping their wings open, the Minions leveled out and soared through the streets. The Valrenkians began to scatter.

Uther and his apprentice turned to run back to the cottage. But the apprentice tripped over his robe and Uther went down on top of him. As he hit the ground, he felt his ankle snap.

His apprentice scrambled his way out from under him and, with no regard for his master, ran into their cottage and slammed the door. Uther heard the lock in the door turn over. He looked frantically back to the sky, but saw nothing. The street had become deathly still.

Uther rose to stand on his good foot. Then he saw the two dark shadows tear across the ground toward him. He tried to run, but his bad foot collapsed painfully under him and he landed in the dirt again.

Uther watched in abject terror as the warriors soared down. In perfect unison, they leveled out on either side of him and expertly scooped him up, each holding one of his arms. Uther screamed, and tried to break free.

The next thing he knew was a meaty fist smacking into his face—and then nothing.

Finally seeing that it was safe, Reznik and a few others tentatively left their houses. They watched as the dark forms in the sky grew smaller, finally disappearing in the northeast. No one needed to tell Reznik who had sent the Minions, or where they were off to.

As he looked back down to the street, he couldn't escape the feeling that Satine was somehow the cause of this. Then he looked back to the sky, and another disturbing realization crossed his mind.

The wizards knew about them now, and they would be back. When they came, Valrenkium would have to be ready for them.

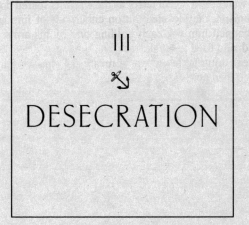

III

DESECRATION

CHAPTER XXXIX

"The pollution that shall ravage the land will be never-ending, unless the Jin'Sai *or the* Jin'Saiou *can summon the power to stop it. For the calamity shall be of the craft, and far beyond their wizards' abilities to control."*

—PAGE 333, VOLUME I OF THE
PROPHECIES OF THE TOME

TRISTAN SHOT CELESTE A QUIZZICAL LOOK, THEN WALKED OVER to Wigg. An eerie silence still commanded the room.

Wigg's eye was still trained upon the lens at the top of the signature scope as though he thought that if he stared at the blood signature long enough, he might somehow change what he was seeing. Tristan placed a hand upon the First Wizard's shoulder.

"Wigg," he said quietly, "are you all right?"

Wigg looked up at the prince. It was plain to see that he was overcome.

"What's wrong?" Tristan asked.

"It's her blood signature," Wigg breathed. He looked over at Jessamay. "You knew, didn't you?" he asked. "That's why you wanted me to use the scope."

Jessamay nodded.

Sensing Jessamay's pain, Celeste walked over and put her arms around the older woman. Jessamay gave Celeste a startled look. Then she looked back at Wigg. A strange mixture of sadness and surprise had suddenly come over her face. Celeste held Jessamay closer.

"What did you see through the scope?" Celeste asked her father.

Wigg sighed. "Do you remember my telling you that blood

signatures lean either to the left or to the right?" he asked. Tristan and Celeste nodded.

"If the signature leans to the right, then its owner is induced to practice the Vigors," Tristan said as if reciting a lesson. "And if it leans to the left, the Vagaries. The lean is determined at birth, and it is immutable."

Wigg nodded, then shook his head in wonder. "Jessamay's signature displays no lean whatsoever," he said.

Tristan scowled. "But you said that was impossible!"

"That's right," Wigg said. "And until this afternoon, that's what I believed. But the proof is right here, on this table."

He went to sit on the bed. As Celeste moved aside, he took one of Jessamay's hands.

"Failee did this to you, didn't she?" he asked. "It was part of her experimentation."

Using her free hand to wipe away her tears, Jessamay nodded.

"It was so horrible," she whispered. "I was the only one who survived. Even so, Failee hadn't quite finished her work."

"What do you mean?" Tristan asked.

"Failee was trying to convert her signature from right-leaning, to left," Wigg answered for Jessamay. "But you killed the First Mistress before it was done."

He shook his head. "Jessamay and the others were here the entire time we were. They were only two rooms away, and we never realized it. If only we had known . . ."

He looked back down at the terrified sorceress. "I'm right, aren't I?" he asked.

"Yes," she said. "Failee wished to convert disciples of the Vigors to willingly serve the Vagaries by altering their blood signatures," she said. "Had she completed her work, our world would be a far different place. During her last session with me, she bragged about how close she was."

"Who were the other subjects in the alcoves?" Celeste asked.

Wigg's mouth suddenly fell open and he covered his face with his palms. He shook his head gently.

"They were my other female officers of the Black Watch, weren't they?" he asked, his voice muffled by his hands.

Jessamay touched Wigg's face. "Yes," she answered. "She never told us what became of the male Black Watch officers she captured. Killed, presumably. We females were brought here by Succiu, when she returned from her raid on Eutracia. Failee gloated about it, telling us that she now possessed not only us, but the Paragon and the *Jin'Saiou,* as well. She said that nothing could stand in the way of her creating her fifth sorceress. Katherine, Jessica, Phaedra, Mallory—" Her voice broke. "Not all of us, but many. You and the other wizards no doubt thought us killed in battle. But we were here, suffering under Failee's hand. The bones of my Black Watch sisters lie in the alcoves below."

"What is the Black Watch?" Tristan asked.

Wigg rubbed his face. "The Black Watch was an elite fighting force formed during the height of the Sorceresses' War," he said. "Each officer was endowed. They were trained in the craft as best we knew how during those early days of the war—and all were devoted to the Vigors. They commanded handpicked Eutracian citizens who had volunteered for hazardous duty. Using hit-and-run tactics, the Black Watch came to be the scourge of the Coven." He paused for a moment, looking up at the prince.

"As the commander of all the forces fighting the Coven, I also oversaw the Black Watch. Jessamay was my most accomplished commander. We fought side by side many times. She saved my life twice."

He looked back down at Jessamay. "There is still something I do not understand. That was more than three hundred years ago. In between your capture and Succiu's bringing you here, where were you kept?"

A dark look came over Jessamay's face. "We were held prisoner in individual sorceress' cones, deep in the Caves of the Paragon," she answered. "For nearly three hundred years we lingered there, under Failee's charms of endurance. During the Coven's banishment, we were watched over by a mad, half-human, half–blood stalker named Ragnar."

For several long moments no one spoke. Tristan took Celeste's hand. They had both been scarred by Ragnar, but his treatment of Celeste—three hundred years of abuse and torture—was by far the worse.

Another sudden look of understanding crossed Wigg's face.

Staring out at nothing, he slowly nodded his head. Then he balled his hands up into fists.

"Of course!" he whispered. "So that is how Nicholas managed it! I should have guessed sooner!"

"What?" Tristan asked.

"Nicholas' conversion of the consuls," Wigg answered. "We were never sure how he enticed them to the Vagaries. Now we know."

Tristan nodded. "Failee must have finished her research at some point, and recorded the calculations in the Scroll of the Vagaries," he mused. "But I obviously killed her before she could complete the spell upon Jessamay—or Shailiha and me, for that matter. Then the Scrolls somehow came into Nicholas' possession. He used the same calculation to convert the consuls, before he hid them in the Gates of Dawn."

"During my time with her, Failee talked about the Scrolls, and the science of Forestallments," Jessamay said. "Where are the Scrolls now?"

Tristan exchanged glances with Wigg. "The Scroll of the Vigors is safe in Eutracia," he said. "But the Scroll of the Vagaries is in the possession of . . . other forces. And I fear we have not heard the last of its new owner."

Jessamay took hold of Wigg's robe. Her eyes searched his face.

"I must speak to you alone," she said. "It is vital. I mean no disrespect to the *Jin'Sai* or to your daughter, but you must grant me this request."

Wigg smoothed her hair. He nodded.

"Very well," he said, "if it means that much to you."

Wigg looked over at Tristan and Celeste. Tristan nodded, and escorted Celeste from the room. Then Wigg turned back to his old friend.

"First I must ask you a question," he said. "I must admit that we did not come here searching for you. We came seeking someone else. Someone known as the 'Scroll Master.' Do you know anything about him?"

"I do," Jessamay said. "From what Failee said, it sounded as if he resides in Eutracia, where he guards something called the Well of Forestallments. I will gladly tell you what I know of that later. But right now you must let me speak. When I tell you, you will understand why."

"What is it?"

Jessamay looked away for a moment. When her gaze returned to him, her eyes were again full of tears.

"Your daughter is dying," she whispered.

For several long moments Wigg felt frozen in time. As his mind started to work again, he stared blankly at Jessamay. Anger boiled up within him.

Suddenly he grabbed Jessamay by the shoulders. His powerful aquamarine eyes seemed to bore right through her.

"You lie!" he shouted.

Jessamay turned her face away.

"You couldn't possibly know such a thing! You have been locked away for nearly three centuries! Celeste is fine!"

"Please, Wigg, you must listen to me!" Jessamay said quietly. "You have no idea how much it hurts me to tell you this."

Coming to his senses, Wigg let her go. "Forgive me," he said. "But I love her more than my life. What you are saying simply cannot be true." He looked longingly back at the door his daughter and the prince had just gone through.

"I know," Jessamay said. "But she is slowly dying, just the same."

"How could you possibly know this?" Wigg asked.

"When you examined my blood signature, you saw the many Forestallments there?"

Wigg nodded. "I presume Failee added them."

"That's right," Jessamay answered. "I have no idea what unrealized gifts they may one day hold," she said. "But before she died, Failee activated at least one of them."

"What is it?" he asked.

"I am able to examine a person's blood signature without first making them bleed," she said.

"But that's impossible," Wigg argued.

"No, it isn't," Jessamay answered. "At least not for me. The place in the body the blood comes nearest the surface is one's eyes. You need only look into a mirror to know that I am right. I can examine the blood signature in the veins that run through the whites of a person's eyes."

"Amazing," Wigg said. "But why would Failee want to perfect such a gift?"

"Think of the tactical advantage," Jessamay said. "By simply looking into someone's eyes, you could quickly discern whether he or she was of the Vigors or of the Vagaries. If we had had that skill during the war, Failee's spies would have been of no use to her."

Nodding, Wigg closed his eyes. "Of course," he whispered. "But what does all of this have to do with my daughter?"

"When Celeste held me, she was near enough for me to look deeply into her eyes. She is blessed with time enchantments, is she not?"

Wigg nodded. "She is nearly as old as you and me."

"Her blood signature is eroding," Jessamay said. "I believe it has had recent union with blood far stronger than hers, blood that must have been tainted by the craft. It is overcoming her signature and slowly destroying it. At least one-third of it has already vanished. The tainted blood has left minute traces of azure in its wake. And although she may not have told you, Celeste is no doubt weaker and fatigued. If you don't believe me, you need only examine her blood signature yourself to know that I am right."

She took her old ally by the hand. "In an endowed person without time enchantments, this would simply result in his or her loss of the craft," Jessamay said. "But in Celeste's case—"

"As her blood signature dies, so will her time enchantments," Wigg acknowledged. He covered his face with his hands again. "As they do, she will become dust upon the wind."

Beside himself with pain, he looked into Jessamay's eyes. "Is there any way to save her?"

Jessamay shook her head. "I do not know," she answered. "Such intricacies of the craft are beyond my knowledge. I can only tell you what I see. But it would seem that if whatever caused this could be made whole again—untainted, as it were—and united with her blood once more, there might be a chance. But your daughter's time is running short."

Wigg stood upon shaking legs. Looking out but seeing nothing, he shuffled over to the balcony doors.

He knew what had polluted his daughter's blood—and what had caused the azure glow that surrounded her after she and Tristan had made love. Somehow, Tristan's altered blood, carried into her with his seed, had been absorbed into her body. And now that tainted blood was killing her.

Wigg closed his eyes. *In the end, it didn't matter whether my daughter carried Tristan's child or not,* he thought.

But then he was struck by a glimmer of hope. If Tristan's blood could be restored to its original state and he again had union with Celeste, perhaps the effects might be reversed, and she could be saved.

But the secret to Tristan's blood remained as elusive as ever. Through an innocent act of love, the *Jin'Sai* had unknowingly begun the death of not only the love of his life, but his mentor's only child. And the First Wizard felt powerless to stop it.

As Wigg looked out over the balcony, a cool breeze caressed his face. Birds sang. *My only child is dying before my eyes,* he thought. *Yet outside the birds are singing.*

In a fit of rage, Wigg fell to his knees, raised his face to the sky, and screamed at the heavens.

CHAPTER XL

K'JARR'S ENDURANCE WAS EBBING. IF HE CONTINUED THE SEARCH for the Citadel much longer, his war party would not be able to make it back to the *Reprise*. Still, his sense of duty to the *Jin'Sai* made him press on.

It was early evening, and the three moons were out. The moonlight gave the warriors a better view, but the wind was against them and the sky was partly cloudy, making it difficult to survey the ocean below.

K'jarr had taken his six warriors as high as he dared, nearly starving their lungs of air. He was about to order them to descend a bit when he saw flickering lights in the distance and finally got his first glimpse of the Citadel.

K'jarr took a quick breath. He had never seen such an imposing structure. Even the royal palace in Tammerland was no match for this.

The island fortress of dark gray stone rose straight up out of living rock. The irregularly shaped shoreline held a deep port, and at the island's eastern end he thought he could see herds of corralled livestock. The Citadel's numerous towers rose majestically into the sky, their curved walls dotted with elaborate stained-glass windows and connected by interlacing bridges and catwalks. As the magenta moonlight and the fortress' torches conspired to reveal the Citadel's secrets, K'jarr again considered his plan.

He knew that the easiest way to capture a demonslaver would be to snatch one up from a patrolling vessel, rather than from the relative security of the island. He and his warriors would circle as long as possible, and with any luck be able to single out a patrolling frigate. They would wait aloft until her demonslaver crew had gone below decks, leaving only a few night sentries topside. Then he and another warrior would swoop down and silently scoop up one of the guards.

But as K'jarr surveyed the island's port, his heart sank. It seemed that every demonslaver frigate was at anchor there, just off the shore. As he scanned the ocean surrounding the island, he could find no patrolling ships.

He immediately became suspicious. He turned to look at his six warriors and, waving them onward, led them in a wide, banking curve toward the far end of the island.

It was there, just off the northern coast, that K'jarr and his party finally saw Wulfgar's seven Black Ships.

The ships were easily four or five times the size of the largest vessels they had ever seen. The sea wind filled their dark sails to the straining point. As the menacing warships bounded through the waves, K'jarr could make out hundreds of chalky-skinned demonslavers swarming over their decks. Then suddenly, the ships all came about and sailed back in the opposite direction.

K'jarr knew that Tyranny's lone flagship, faced with such enemy ships, would have no choice but to cut and run. Despite the size and weight of these monstrous black vessels, he doubted that even the *Reprise* could outdistance them.

The demonslaver crews repeated their turning maneuvers several more times. It was almost as if they were preparing for something, K'jarr thought. Then the warrior understood: The ships were conducting trials of some sort. And once their master was satisfied, these warships would be loosed upon Eutracia.

K'jarr looked quickly toward the heavens. He knew that if he and his group stayed in any one part of the sky too long, the moonlight might reveal them. Finding a suitable cloud, he waved his warriors a bit higher. The fluffy cumulus was just what they needed. It was slowly heading northwest, and soon it would be directly over the fleet.

The Minions all came to hide in the base of the cloud. Peering through the light layer of mist, they watched the warships with awe.

Aboard the lead vessel K'jarr saw what appeared to be a black skeleton standing arrogantly in the prow. The skeleton was dressed in some sort of ragged military uniform. A torn, black cape hung down its back, twirling in the wind.

Then K'jarr blinked, and the skeleton was gone. K'jarr rubbed his eyes then looked again. The bizarre form did not reappear. Surely the moonlight was playing tricks on him.

Suddenly, the seven Black Ships formed a straight battle line in the sea. As the lead ship gained slightly on the others, an azure glow surrounded her, and K'jarr knew that the craft was in play. With no help from any of her crew, each of her massive sails began to furl itself until it was tightly wound and tied off against a spar. Without aid of the wind, the ship's bow raised high, then plunged mightily back down into the sea. K'jarr expected her bow to rise up again, but it didn't.

Instead, the bow continued to plow deeper into the waves. As it did, the dark hull pitched upward to nearly vertical, and the stern of the great ship rose high into the air. As K'jarr watched her sink, his breath caught. The ocean quickly engulfed her decks, and the entire vessel was swallowed by the sea.

As the ripples closed in and the sea calmed, the magenta moonlight revealed no trace of the ship.

"One of their great ships has just sunk," one of K'jarr's officers said. "It would seem that they are not so invincible after all."

His eyes still locked upon the six other vessels, K'jarr shook his head.

"No," he answered quietly. "She did not sink. She *submerged*." He pointed to the next ship. "Watch," he whispered.

The glow of the craft appeared once more. Just as the first ship had done, so did the second. One by one, the five others followed suit with perfect dives into the deep. The glow of the craft slowly retreated and the sea calmed again. The warriors hovered, speechless.

The cloud that hid them was thinning, and they would soon be exposed. K'jarr knew that they would not be able to capture a demonslaver. Worse yet, if they did not start back now they would perish in the sea before reaching the *Reprise*. The unbelievable things they had witnessed had to be relayed to Tyranny and the princess, whether they took a captive or not.

K'jarr gave the order to retreat. Leaving the security of the cloud, one by one the warriors turned west, each hoping that he could reach Tyranny's flagship before his strength gave out.

AS HE WATCHED FROM THE SHORE WULFGAR PACED NERVOUSLY, his full attention upon the restless sea. Bratach and Serena stood waiting nearby. The cool evening wind swirled about them, and Serena pulled her shawl closer.

An area of the sea suddenly became disturbed. Soon the ocean was alive and roiling. Without warning, the first of the Black Ships exploded from the depths.

Her bow shot to the surface, and the rest of her massive hull followed. With a gigantic crash she landed solidly upon the ocean. The demonslavers aboard her appeared to be unaffected by their ship's recent maneuver. Wulfgar watched as, seawater dripping from her black masts and decks, she rocked back and forth, finding her equilibrium. Then her black sails unfurled. As they caught the night air, they snapped open sharply, and the warship began bounding across the waves.

From his place in the bow, the macabre figure of Captain

Merriwhether grasped a line to steady himself. He then pulled his sword from its recently engraved scabbard. As he held the centuries-old weapon high, the crimson moonlight glinted off its blade. Smiling, Wulfgar raised his good arm in response.

Just as the first ship had done, each of the other six vessels exploded from the depths. Then, one by one, they turned and sailed off.

Once they had passed, Wulfgar turned toward Einar and Serena. The moonlight tinted his ravaged face pink. Taking his queen by the hand, he smiled.

"Tomorrow I sail for Eutracia."

CHAPTER XLI

STARING OUT OF HIS HIRED CARRIAGE-OF-FOUR, BRATACH couldn't help but feel a swell of pride. So far, all was going according to plan.

The assassin Satine had begun her sanctions, the Orb of the Vigors continued to spew forth its deadly energy, and the royal palace was in a state of uproar. By now, not only should his master have conjured forth the Earthshakers and summoned the Council of Seven, but the Black Ships should also be in his service. Unless Bratach missed his guess, Wulfgar would be sailing for Eutracia any day now.

As he watched the Eutracian streets slide by, one corner of Bratach's mouth turned up. There was very little—if anything—that could stop them now. Soon the Vigors would be extinguished, the royal house and the two wizards dealt with, and the coming war fought and won. Then the *Enseterat* would stride the earth like a colossus and control the fate of the craft for all time.

Bratach had purchased secondhand the dark, shopworn trousers and simple peasant shirt he wore, along with the dirty knee boots, so as to better fit in with common Eutracian society.

Having worn the dark blue robe of a consul for most of his adult life, he felt strangely out of place in these pedestrian clothes. But the last thing he needed was to be publicly greeted by another onetime consul of the Redoubt—even though Nicholas had made them all brothers in service to the Vagaries.

The thought of Nicholas saddened him. Other than the *Enseterat,* he had never known such a perfect being. Nicholas had come heartbreakingly close to achieving his victory, only to perish upon his masterpieces, the Gates of Dawn. But this time they would not fail, and the *Jin'Sai* would pay dearly.

Suddenly the carriage came to a halt, returning Bratach's thoughts to the present.

"This is it!" he heard the driver shout down. "That'll be two kisa, if you please."

Bratach swung open the carriage door and stepped into the busy street. After gazing about for a moment, he found what he was looking for. Smiling to himself, he walked toward the driver and quickly conjured several kisa. As he drew them from his pocket, the newly created coins sparkled brightly in the sun. He handed four of them up.

"Here are two extra," he said. "Wait for me nearby. I won't be long."

Greedily fingering the golden coins, the driver smiled. "Very well, sir," he answered.

"Don't stray far. I'll be right back."

As Bratach watched, the driver took his carriage around the corner. Then Bratach looked around. What he was searching for was down the next street to the left. Eager to reach his destination, he set off.

It was still morning and the sun shined brightly. As he entered the busy roundabout, he was at first dismayed to see the place so full of people. But he was resigned to wait as long as necessary. As it had the days before, the fountain in the center splashed happily.

Walking over to a nearby vendor, he surreptitiously conjured several more kisa and exchanged them for a massive, freshly roasted turkey leg. Chewing like a contented peasant, he walked to the fountain and sat down upon its edge.

By the time the turkey leg was gone, the crowd surrounding

him had thinned out a bit. Shifting his weight slightly, he placed one hand down into the cool water. He looked around once more and closed his eyes.

He removed his hand from the water and peered down. As he did, he employed the craft to cause a small area of the surface to calm. He smiled as he read the message that had formed from the grains Vivian had left there yesterday.

It is done, he read.

After scanning the remainder of the message he closed his eyes again. The grains vanished and the water stirred once more.

Wulfgar's consul stood to walk back to his carriage. Finding himself in a particularly cheerful mood, he decided to do some shopping before heading back to meet Ivan.

As Bratach's carriage approached the archery shop, he saw that the "Open" sign hanging in the window showed red letters rather than black. Before leaving for the roundabout he had ordered Ivan to display it, hoping that Satine would see it and enter. If Vivian had known about Geldon's death as late as yesterday, it was possible that the dwarf's killer had by now returned to the city.

Bratach entered the shop, his package under one arm. The little bell over the door cheerfully announced his presence.

One customer was at the counter, talking with Ivan. The fellow was trying to decide whether to purchase arrows fletched with highland goose quill or the teal feathers of a three-winged triad lark.

As usual Ivan was sweating heavily, his red sleeve garters ringed with perspiration. When he saw Bratach he gave a short nod. Bratach nodded back. Deciding to wait out the customer, he wandered about for a bit.

Finally the customer paid for his arrows and left. Ivan locked the door behind him, turned the sign around to read "Closed," and drew the window shades. Then he looked at Bratach.

"She's downstairs," he said.

"Good," Bratach answered.

He went to the back of the shop and down the hidden stairs, Ivan following.

Satine was sitting at the table, her long legs propped on it. As Bratach walked in she regarded him calmly. He placed his package down, and then he and Ivan sat.

Bratach poured a glass of wine. After taking a long draft, he addressed Satine.

"My confederate in the palace has confirmed that the dwarf is dead," he said. "Congratulations."

A smile crossed Satine's lips. "Of course he's dead," she answered. "I never miss."

She reached into her cloak and removed the two parchments that Wulfgar had given her that day at the Citadel. Removing her legs from the table, she sat upright, unrolled the documents, and unsheathed one of her daggers. With four quick, expert cuts, she excised Geldon's likeness from the scroll. Holding the picture to the candle, she watched it turn to ash. As she let the last bit of it flutter away, she rubbed her fingers together.

"One down," she said.

"Indeed," Bratach answered. "However, for the time being you are to do nothing." Casually, he began to unfasten the package's wrapping.

Satine narrowed her eyes. "And just why is that?" she asked. "I don't like sitting around, waiting for your orders. Even if you are of the craft."

"For the simple reason that my spy tells me there are no available targets just now," Bratach answered.

He reached into the package and produced a small wheel of cheese, a blood sausage, and a loaf of gingerwheat bread. He placed them on a plate that looked something less than clean, took up a knife, and cut a wedge of the cheese. He offered it to her. Satine shook her head. He took a bite, chewed thoughtfully, and then took another sip of the wine.

"It seems that, at the moment, all of your targets are either safely ensconced in the palace or out of the country altogether," he mused. "Common sense dictates that we wait—at least until my spy informs me of a more promising opportunity."

Satine looked hard at Ivan, then at Bratach. "If common sense had anything to do with this, I would never have accepted these sanctions in the first place," she argued. "I'm strictly in it for the money. The sooner I finish, the sooner I collect the other half." She leaned back in her chair again. "The palace walls mean nothing to me," she went on. "And my blood is not endowed. Unless I'm careless, the wizards and the acolytes will not detect my presence. And I'm never careless."

She pointed down at the parchments. "If I can manage it, who do you want disposed of next?"

As he took another sip of wine, Bratach considered her words. What she proposed was risky. But the idea of killing one of them right under the wizard's noses was tempting. If Satine could accomplish it, Wulfgar would be very pleased. And then Bratach, as Wulfgar's loyal consul, could take the credit. With the return of the *Enseterat,* there would soon be a new order in the land, and Bratach had every intention of standing with those at the very pinnacle of power. Such an audacious act might help accomplish that.

"Very well, then," he finally answered. "You may try. I can help your cause by providing you with detailed plans of the palace and the Redoubt. This must be planned exceedingly well, Satine. You must not fail us."

"I never fail," she answered. "But you have yet to tell me which one of them to kill."

With the point of his knife, Bratach pulled the parchments closer. Pursing his lips in thought, he looked down at the likenesses. Then made his choice and stabbed the knife through the drawing and into the tabletop.

"This one," he said. He looked over at Ivan. "A fitting choice, don't you think?"

Ivan smiled. "By all means," he answered.

Bratach looked back over at Satine. "As long as you are here, we might as well fill you in," he said. "Ivan, fetch me some parchment."

After some rummaging around, Ivan returned with several sheets and placed them on the table. Bratach looked down and narrowed his eyes. Fascinated, Satine watched as the consul began to burn an image of the first floor of the palace into the sheet.

In the end, it would prove to be a very long day.

CHAPTER XLII

EVENING CAME TO PARTHALON, THE INDIGO NIGHT A COOL, COM-
forting blanket. Having left Wigg and Jessamay to themselves,
Tristan and Celeste walked side by side through the winding
halls of the Recluse. This was one of the few times they had
been alone in recent days, and they were thankful for the opportunity. They stopped in the grand foyer.

Torches flickered, throwing shadows across the walls and
checkerboard floor. Yet another team of Minion men and
women were busy building furniture, weaving rugs, and creating art for the still-unfurnished rooms of the Recluse. As he
walked through the great chamber, Tristan couldn't help but
wonder how he would employ such a massive building, now
that it was so close to being completed.

Alrik presented himself to the prince. Placing his fists upon
his hips, the warrior smiled broadly.

"Wonderful, isn't it?" he asked. "I estimate completion
within two fortnights. Does the *Jin'Sai* have any other specific
orders for the Recluse afterward?"

Shaking his head, Tristan sighed. "I was just thinking about
that," he said.

"There is something else it would be my honor to show you,"
Alrik said. "In addition to the Recluse, we have completely re-
built the horse barns. I think my lord and his lady would find
them interesting."

At the mention of the Recluse stables, Tristan's face lit up.
Horsemanship had always been one of his and Shailiha's greatest joys. The chance to see what the clever Minion carpenters
had done with the barns seemed just the tonic he needed. He
glanced at Celeste.

"I'd love to," she said. Smiling, she laced one arm through his.

The two of them followed Alrik out of the Recluse and back over the drawbridge.

As they went, Tristan was reminded of the day Geldon had stolen a team and wagon from the Coven stables, so that they could race back to the Ghetto of the Shunned. It would be good to see him again when they returned to Eutracia.

At the end of the drawbridge, Alrik led them around one side of the Recluse. At the sight of the refurbished stables, Tristan's heart began to lift.

At least a dozen large paddocks surrounded the stable buildings, lit by flickering torches. The split-rail fences had been painted bright white, and beautiful horses milled about within their confines.

A large brick building sat in the center of the manicured grounds. Looking closer, Tristan saw that his family crest had been painted on its double doors. Several smaller buildings were attached to the central one. Even the royal stables in Tammerland, before their destruction, could not have surpassed these.

"It's magnificent," he told Alrik. "I hadn't expected this."

Alrik's chest swelled with pride. He gestured to the doors. "If my lord will allow me?"

Tristan nodded. "By all means."

Alrik pushed the doors apart, and familiar equine smells and sounds greeted them.

Stalls of highly polished wood lined both sides of the barn. Horses neighed and snorted as the three of them walked into the barn's cool darkness.

Turning to his right, Tristan walked over to one of the stall doors. A bay mare stepped forward and stuck her head out over the top. Neighing softly, she shook her head, sending her mane flying about. Smiling, Tristan grasped her bridle and rubbed her forehead.

"Are they all this magnificent?" he asked.

Alrik smiled. "Indeed they are. They have to be, to qualify for this place."

Then the Minion did something strange. After turning to Celeste, and giving her a quick, conspiratorial wink behind Tristan's back, he nodded toward the rear of the barn. Celeste turned to see that a large group of warrior stable hands had quietly gathered, all on bended knee, their heads bowed.

Celeste gave Alrik a quizzical look. But before she could speak, the warrior placed a forefinger against his lips. Still confused, she nodded back. Alrik turned back to the prince.

"If my lord would allow me, there is something else that I would be pleased to show you," he said.

"Of course," Tristan answered, his full attention still upon the mare. "What is it?"

"It is my understanding that the *Jin'Sai* recently lost his favorite mount," Alrik said gently. "Is that true?"

His back still to them, Tristan lowered his head. "Yes. Pilgrim was killed during our battle to secure the Scroll of the Vigors. There will never be another like him."

"With all due respect, my lord, you may be in error."

Turning around, Tristan scowled at him. "What do you mean?" he asked.

Alrik turned and gestured to the kneeling warriors at the other end of the barn. As he did, they rose, and their ranks slowly parted. One of them walked forward leading a horse.

The magnificent black stallion was easily as tall as Pilgrim had been, but he looked younger. His mane and tail were exceptionally long. Large, spirited eyes sat on either side of his wide, beautifully shaped head. As he walked, taut muscles swelled beneath his shining coat. He wore a highly polished black bridle and saddle. The pure silver hardware of the horse's tack was adorned with the lion and the broadsword.

Tristan had always believed that he would never again see a mount as magnificent as Pilgrim. But standing here in the light of the torches, he knew he had been wrong.

"We understand that we cannot replace Pilgrim," Alrik said humbly. "It would be presumptuous of us to try. But on behalf of myself and the Minion stable hands, please accept this stallion as a token of our admiration and our loyalty. Trained by the best of our handlers, he is the finest horse in all of Parthalon."

Tristan didn't know what to say. He looked at Alrik and Celeste, and then back at the stallion again. Fighting a lump in his throat, he walked over to the horse and accepted the reins from the groom. As he stroked the stallion's neck, the horse rubbed his head against his new master's shoulder. The bond was immediate. Tristan looked at the warriors again, and then to Alrik.

"I accept," he said softly. "And thank you."

Alrik and Celeste joined him. Celeste put out a hand to stroke the horse's silky nose.

"How did you know I was coming to Parthalon?" Tristan asked.

Alrik smiled. "We didn't," he answered. "We have been training this stallion for months in the hope that you would soon visit. As the First Wizard and I walked over the drawbridge together and into the Recluse, it was he who mentioned that you had lost your previous mount. So you see out of darkness there comes a bit of light."

Celeste smiled at Tristan.

"He's beautiful," she said. "What will you call him?"

Tristan looked back down the length of the barn, and to the torches that burned so brightly. As they cast their flickering shadows across the walls, he made up his mind. He turned back to Celeste.

"I will call him Shadow," he said.

Tristan placed a foot in the stirrup and swung himself up into the saddle. The leather was soft as butter, and he immediately felt comfortable. Shadow began to dance about beneath him, telling his rider that he was eager to go. The prince easily stayed with him. He smiled.

"If you will excuse us, Shadow and I are going to get to know each other better," he said. He looked at Alrik. "You will see that Celeste is safely escorted back to the Recluse?"

Coming to attention, Alrik clicked his heels. "On my life," he promised. The prince nodded back gratefully.

Saying nothing more, Tristan wheeled Shadow around. Without looking back he galloped the stallion out of the barn and into the moonlight.

CHAPTER XLIII

"NOW THEN," FAEGAN SAID. "LET'S BEGIN, SHALL WE?"

The wizard had chosen this chamber of the Redoubt because it had gone unused for centuries. It was dark and unfurnished, save for the simple table and five chairs he had requested. Moisture seeped freely from the walls. Mildew had crept in long ago, making the place smell musty and abandoned. A single wall torch burned quietly.

Faegan, Abbey, and Adrian sat on one side of the rectangular table. Next to Faegan was Lionel the Little—the wizard's herbmaster and the trusted keeper of the herb cubiculum in Shadowood. Since arriving at the height of their trials with Wulfgar, Lionel had stayed on at the palace.

The Valrenkian captive sat across from them. Bound to his chair by a wizard's warp, he glared at Faegan with venomous eyes.

The prisoner was of average build. He appeared to be about forty-five Seasons of New Life. His blond hair was thinning at the top, and he still wore his bloody butcher's smock. A purple bruise had risen on his jaw from Ox's blow; his broken ankle had been set by the wizard. He had remained unconscious all of the way to this room.

After placing him in the chair and securing him with the warp, Faegan had carefully examined the Valrenkian's blood signature. Sure enough, it revealed him to be a partial adept. The abbreviated signature had possessed curved lines, indicating that the man's gifts had been inherited from his mother rather than his father. His examination complete, Faegan had then employed the craft to rouse the man.

Summoning all of the saliva he could, the Valrenkian spat at them, then sneered arrogantly.

"What do you want with me?" he growled. "I demand to

know why I have been brought here!" Pausing for a moment, he looked around the bleak, unforgiving room.

"Wherever this might be," he added nastily.

"Where you are is not important," Faegan said. "We require answers from you. We can either do this the simple way—with me asking the questions and you answering them honestly—or we can proceed the hard way, through my use of the craft. First of all, you are a Valrenkian, are you not?"

The man just spat at them again.

"What is the name of the assassin who was hired to kill the inhabitants of the royal palace?" the wizard pressed. The prisoner again remained silent.

Abbey placed her mouth near the wizard's ear. "This is getting us nowhere," she whispered. "Time is precious."

Faegan nodded. Narrowing his eyes, he called the craft. Almost at once the Valrenkian's eyes widened with surprise.

"What are you doing to me?" he shouted.

"Enhancing your willingness to comply," Faegan answered calmly.

The man's head suddenly snapped back and his eyes opened wide. Abbey realized that Faegan had just successfully entered the Valrenkian's mind. The captive's rebellious attitude might remain, but now he would be forced to answer their questions—and truthfully.

"Let's try again, shall we?" Faegan asked. "Are you a member of the rogue Valrenkian community?"

"Yes."

"What is your name?"

"Uther, of the House of Kronsteen."

"Tell me, Uther of the House of Kronsteen, what is the name of the assassin hired to kill those living at the royal palace?"

"The only assassin I know of is called Satine. She buys her wares from Reznik."

"So this assassin you speak of is a woman?"

"Yes."

Thinking for a moment, Faegan sat back in his chair. "Who is Reznik?" he asked.

"He is a most accomplished Valrenkian. He leads us. Satine buys the tools of her trade from him."

"Where is Satine now?" Faegan asked.

"I don't know."

"You have seen her?" Abbey asked.

"Yes. She visits roughly every three moons, to purchase fresh goods from Reznik."

"Please describe her," Abbey asked.

"Satine wears black leather clothing and a gray cloak. Her dark hair is long and braided. One of her arms is tattooed with a serpent, the other with a sword. She carries four daggers and a short bow. It is said that she has additional weapons at her disposal, but I don't know what those might be."

Faegan lifted his eyebrows. "How is it that you know about her tattoos?"

"Last year, one hot afternoon during the Season of the Sun, she rode into Valrenkium with her cloak removed. Her shirt was sleeveless."

"What goods does she purchase from Reznik?" Adrian asked, leaning forward and resting her forearms on the table.

"I do not know," Uther answered. "That is kept strictly between Reznik and her."

"Who is her next target?" Faegan asked.

"I do not know."

"Tell me about the Valrenkians," Faegan said. "Is it true that you practice the Vagaries?"

"Yes."

"The Minion warriors said that human body parts were in evidence in Valrenkium, and that people were being systematically tortured and killed," the wizard said. "Is this true?"

Uther managed a slight smile. "Yes," he answered. "We sometimes kidnap people for our needs. Some of us also unearth corpses from graves. We sell our endowed wares to the highest bidder. Those of us who practice this subdiscipline are also known as Corporeals."

Angrily, Faegan thought of Geldon lying dead on the table, and the manner in which he had been killed. "Does Reznik use dead bodies in his work?" he asked.

"Yes," Uther said. "He sometimes employs the bodies of suicides. He pays more for those—especially if the corpse's blood was endowed. A grave robber secures them for him."

Sighing deeply, Faegan nodded. It was becoming clear that his analysis of Geldon's death had been correct.

Faegan was quickly developing a better understanding of the assassin. She was a cold, ruthless professional who would stop at nothing to complete her job. Clearly, she was rarely equaled for cunning and inventiveness, and despite what they had learned, finding her would remain next to impossible. He wondered who her benefactor was.

Looking at the captive, Lionel the Little slowly removed his spectacles and wiped his face with one hand. After repositioning his spectacles, he cleared his throat.

"Are there women and children in Valrenkium, are there?" he asked harshly, in his peculiar way of speaking.

"Yes."

"Are all of the adults willing practitioners of your dark arts?" Lionel asked.

"Of course," Uther answered. "Why else would they be there?"

"What about the children?"

"Until they are old enough to learn our secrets, the children are innocents. They begin apprenticing at the age of seventeen."

"Tell us more about the people you abduct," Lionel said. "What do you do with them, what do you do?"

"We use their body parts to produce our wares. We do not always kill the women that we take. Sometimes we hold the more attractive ones for . . . other purposes." Uther smiled again.

"During the Sorceresses' War, it was rumored that the occasional gnome woman was also taken," he added. "It is said that they were particularly prized. Some of them even came to like it."

Surprising everyone, Lionel tore from his chair and launched himself at the Valrenkian. With a crash, they both went down to the floor. Screaming, Lionel began pummeling Uther's face.

Knowing how difficult it would be for Faegan to stop the gnome while also keeping his hold on Uther's mind, Adrian lifted one hand. An azure bolt shot from her fingers, striking Lionel squarely in the back. Using the bolt to take hold of him, she smoothly levitated him back toward the table.

His face beet red, the squirming gnome was returned to his seat. With another bolt, Adrian carefully righted Uther's chair.

The Valrenkian's nose was bleeding, and two of his teeth were on the floor. She had to admit that she wasn't sorry.

Faegan looked harshly at the gnome. "Must I place a warp about you, as well?" he asked angrily.

Folding his arms over his chest, Lionel glowered at Uther. "I'm sorry, master, yes, I am," he said. "But you know better than most about the injustices that have been inflicted upon us gnomes over the centuries, yes, you do."

Unafraid, Lionel looked into the wizard's eyes. "When we are done here, all I ask is a few moments alone with this animal."

As much as Faegan would have liked to, he couldn't permit such a thing. He knew that Lionel understood that, too. He placed one hand on Lionel's shoulder.

"Tell me," he asked softly. "Do you wish to become like him?"

Lionel remained silent. Faegan resumed his questioning of Uther.

"Other than the bluffs that surround Valrenkium, what defenses do you have there?" he asked.

"Endowed archers stand atop the walls," Uther answered. "The only way in or out is through a maze of sandstone tunnels. The entrance must first be revealed by one of us. To safely navigate the tunnels, you must know the way. Inside, one wrong turn and you're dead."

"What else?"

"Creatures," Uther said softly.

"What kind of creatures?" Abbey asked.

Uther shook his head. "You may force my mind all you wish to, but I cannot answer that. Only Reznik knows. He alone controls them. Some say that these beasts were first conjured by the Coven. Legend says that the creatures are immortal."

Deciding to end the interrogation for the time being, Faegan raised one arm. The Valrenkian's eyes snapped wide open once more.

"You will remember nothing of what happened here," Faegan said. "In addition, you will not remember being taken from your home. Should you attempt to use any of your gifts of the craft, you will find yourself powerless to do so. Do you understand?"

Uther stared blankly out at nothing. "I understand," he whispered.

The wizard snapped his fingers. Uther slipped back into unconsciousness, his head slumping forward onto his chest. His breathing became deep and rhythmic. Blood dripped lazily from his wounded mouth.

Faegan glanced over at his friends. They looked stunned.

"I didn't know you could do that," Abbey said.

Faegan gave her a short smile. "You still have much to learn," he said. "This kind of thing is relatively simple to accomplish when the subject is a partial adept. But trying to make it work on a full-fledged wizard or sorceress is another thing altogether."

"What shall we do?" Adrian asked. "While we sit here, innocent people are being tortured. Even worse, the Vagaries are being practiced."

Faegan laced his fingers together.

"There is only one thing to do," he said quietly. Pausing for a moment, he glanced at their captive.

"I am taking the Minions back to Valrenkium," he said. His expression hardened.

"And this time," he added softly, "their mission will be quite different."

CHAPTER XLIV

FLYING SOME DISTANCE AWAY FROM TRAAX, DUVESSA COULD SEE his dark form highlighted by the setting sun.

Duvessa and Traax each led a sizable phalanx of warriors. The wizard's litter followed a short distance behind, borne through the air by twelve stout warriors. Ox flew in the lead, guiding them toward their destination.

Though Duvessa's female fighters had not yet passed their rites of ascension, Faegan had asked for volunteers from her group to participate in this urgent mission. He had told them that now, in actual combat, they would earn their red feathers. Duvessa was proud of her women: There had been no shortage of volunteers.

Ox raised one hand, and the entire war party slowed to hover in the air. When Faegan's litter caught up, Ox pointed toward the southwest. "Valrenkium be just beyond border to Hartwick Wood," he said.

Faegan nodded. "Well done," he said. He looked at Traax and Duvessa.

"Remember your orders," he said sternly. "I want everyone to land swiftly, ready to fight. This Reznik must surely have assumed that we would return in strength, and he has had ample time to make plans of his own. There is no telling what awaits us down there." He paused for a moment. "May the Afterlife look over us all."

Faegan cast his gaze into the distance and used the craft to make out the sheer sandstone bluffs. Closing his eyes, he hoped against hope that he was doing the right thing. Then he nodded, and the twin phalanxes regrouped and began to pick up speed.

As they approached Valrenkium, they saw no archers atop the bluffs. The dark entrance to the tunnels Uther had described lay open, but Faegan knew better than to enter.

Soaring over the bluffs, he ordered the phalanxes to descend into the heart of Valrenkium. Dreggans drawn, four thousand anxious warriors landed quietly in the village square. Faegan's litter came to rest near Duvessa, Traax, and Ox. As the wizard levitated his chair out and onto the ground, the Minions fanned out.

Valrenkium seemed deserted. The wind whistled hauntingly through the streets, whirling up little maelstroms of debris. Many of the buildings' doors banged open and closed in the wind, adding to the nerve-racking tension.

Down the single road that led out of town, the gibbets were empty. Blood still dripped slowly from many of them as they creaked to and fro. Scowling, Faegan looked over at Duvessa and Traax.

"Start kicking in doors," he ordered sternly. "Before we leave, we must be sure that no one was left behind. If you find any evidence of the craft—no matter how small—send for me at once."

Feet and fists flying, the Minions began barging through doors and windows. As time went by, the groups returned one by one to say that the buildings were all deserted, barren of people, even of food and drink. All of the tools of the Valrenkians' craft—the herbs, roots, and precious oils—were also missing. After more than an hour of searching, Traax, Duvessa, and Ox walked back over to the litter.

"We're too late," Traax said angrily, sheathing his dreggan.

"What are your orders?" Duvessa asked the wizard.

Looking around, Faegan took a moment to think. He was angry with himself. Perhaps the only opportunity he would ever have to crush the Corporeals had slipped right through his fingers. He hated to admit it, but it was unlikely that such a chance would ever come again.

Trying to decide what to do, he looked to the sky. Darkness was falling quickly.

"There's nothing more we can do here," he concluded. "Make ready to leave for Tammerland. I want to have as many warriors guarding the palace as we—"

The first explosion was loud and grating—like stone grinding against stone. Then came another, and another. Dust-colored smoke filled the night air. The crashes came so quickly that they became an earsplitting wall of continuous noise. Faegan looked up and his mouth fell open.

From the tops of the bluffs surrounding the village, huge fingers of living stone shot into the air. Like tentacles, they grew out from one side of the bluffs, bridged the space above the village, narrowly missing the roofs of the buildings, and stopped at the other side, where they fused with the living rock of the far bluffs. They were numerous and spaced less than a foot apart.

When the noise finally stopped, the warriors and the wizard stared up through the smoke. From bluff to bluff, a latticelike arrangement of stone columns crisscrossed the entire area above them. Faegan was stunned. The dense smoke and the amazing speed with which the things had formed had given him no real opportunity to act. He was forced to admit that Reznik had easily tempted them all into a trap.

Suddenly, there was a scratching, grinding noise. Although softer, it was no less nerve-racking.

The sides of the bluffs began to move, sections of the walls morphing into cones. A blazing torch appeared within each one;

the many flames easily illuminated the entire square. While the captives stood there in wonder, silence reclaimed the village.

"How is this possible?" Traax asked. "I thought partial adepts couldn't summon such immense power."

"Impressive," Faegan answered quietly as he continued to examine the structure that imprisoned them. "Partial adepts are the undisputed masters of the organic realm of the craft," he added. "Stone and fire are certainly a part of that world. Partial adepts may possess only partial blood signatures, but that does not necessarily mean the quality of their blood cannot be high. Now the question before us is one of escape."

Traax snapped open his wings and flew the short distance up to the stone grid. He slid his dreggan from its scabbard and hacked his blade several times against one of the newly formed bars. The sword had no effect. Faegan motioned to Traax to move aside.

The azure bolts that streamed from the wizard's hands were perhaps the brightest the warriors had ever seen. While Faegan strained to hold the bolts securely against one of the stone bars, dense smoke rose. Finally tiring, he lowered his hands. When the smoke cleared they could see that aside from black singe marks, the stone hadn't been affected at all.

"There must be another way out of here," Traax protested. "No cage in the world can hold this many Minion warriors against their will."

Faegan pursed his lips. "I fear this one can," he replied. Looking back toward the tunnel exit, he shook his head. "Uther told us that the only other way out of here was the tunnel," he added. "He said that it is full of danger. 'One wrong move and you're dead,' was how he described it."

"Still, there seems no other choice," Duvessa countered. "The food and water are all gone. Forced to stay here long enough, we'll all starve to death."

"I'm aware of that," Faegan said ruefully. "I'm also beginning to acquire a better sense of this Reznik fellow. I don't believe he meant for us to simply starve to death. No, I fear that the worst of our troubles are yet to come."

No sooner had the wizard finished his sentence than the ground began to tremble. Stunned and confused, the warriors anxiously looked around and many drew their swords. Soon the ground shook so violently that they all found it difficult to remain standing. Some of them took to the air, to hovering just above the quaking earth. The warriors responsible for Faegan's litter quickly bore it aloft.

Then, with great heaving motions, the earth began to open. Dust flew high as the square-shaped sections of ground slowly levered themselves upward like trapdoors. The openings revealed darkness below. All went quiet again, but Faegan knew the silence was not to last.

When the rumbling began, Faegan tried to shout to Traax, but the noise drowned out his voice. More of the warriors left the ground, but more than half of them were still earthbound when the first of the beasts came charging up out of their lairs. Furious, the screaming, grunting monsters ripped into the warriors.

Faegan raised his arms and shot bolts squarely into the back of the first creature, tearing it to bits.

Urgently looking around, he gasped as dozens more of the earthen doors released hundreds of the terrifying beasts.

Each creature was about the size of a full-grown deer. They ran on all fours, easily leaping a dozen feet or more in a single bound. Their heads were like those of wild boars, with long snouts, slanted red eyes, and almond-shaped ears. Their bodies were stout and their short legs powerful, ending in sharp, cloven hooves. Their hides were covered with long, sharp spines. Curved tusks bracketed their mouths.

Duvessa called out orders to her warriors, but she could not make herself heard above the sounds of the attack. And then one of the creatures charged at her and she had to focus on defending herself.

Forcing herself to wait until the last moment, she swung the heavy sword with all her strength. The tip of the dreggan slashed across the monster's throat, releasing a torrent of blood. When the screaming beast went down onto its front knees, she raised the dreggan with both hands and plunged the blade into the top of its skull. Pulling the bloody sword out, she quickly looked around and her gorge rose.

The monsters weren't simply killing the Minions. They were devouring them. All around her fallen warriors screamed as the dark beasts tore into their flesh, the powerful jaws driving those long teeth through the toughest Minion body armor as if it weren't there.

Nearby, one of the monsters was attempting to take a bite out of one of Duvessa's warriors. Duvessa rushed over and slashed her sword across the back of the thing's neck, then quickly backed away. Turning its head toward her, the beast cried out. But despite its bleeding wound, it eagerly went back to devouring its victim. Duvessa struck it once, twice, a third time, and finally severed its head.

Duvessa looked down into the eyes of the fallen warrior. The woman's body was torn wide, and she was moaning in pain and fear. When she saw her leader standing over her, she calmed a bit. With a trembling hand she reached out, grasped Duvessa's blade, and used her last bit of strength to place the dreggan's tip against her throat. Her gaze was beseeching.

Understanding, Duvessa nodded. Knowing it would be the quickest, surest way, she felt for the hidden button in her sword hilt and pushed it. With a clang the dreggan's blade launched its extra foot, ending the warrior's life.

It was all Duvessa could do to force down the vomit. Trying to collect herself, she turned back to the battle. Soon more of the awful things fell to her swinging sword.

From his litter in the air, Faegan did his best to destroy the beasts as they exited the dark holes in the earth. Given their great numbers, even he couldn't kill them all. He had lost sight of Traax and Ox, but he knew that the officers were doing all that they could. Those warriors who had managed to lift into the air before the beasts struck were having a better time of it. But the majority of the warriors had remained on the ground. Many of them were dead, the beasts hungrily tearing away chunks of their flesh.

Having landed, Traax suddenly found himself facing three of the snarling things at once. His back up against a building, he had nowhere to go. He knew that if he tried to concentrate all of his efforts on killing one of them, the other two would eventually find an opening and rush in.

He swung his dreggan in slashing arcs, trying as best he could to keep the things at bay. His hands covered with blood and his shoulders nearly ready to give out, he knew that if someone didn't come to his aid, the monsters would soon rip into him.

Suddenly a small group of warriors led by Ox descended behind the beasts. They raised their dreggans high and began to hack at the monsters. After what seemed like an eternity, the creatures' mangled bodies lay dead between them.

Traax nodded at Ox and his troops in thanks. His arms covered with blood, Ox grinned.

The fighting had by now all but ended. Exhausted warriors walked among the dying creatures, finishing them off with their quick, hard sword strokes. Smoke from Faegan's bolts lazily wafted into the air. The smell of fresh blood was everywhere. Looking up, Traax could see the wizard was safe in his litter.

Suddenly he thought of Duvessa. Sprinting through the square, he frantically called out her name.

He found her leaning against the side of a building. She was bloody and dazed, but she seemed unharmed. He ran to her and took her into his arms. In a rare public display of Minion affection, Traax unfolded his dark wings and he gently wrapped them around her, silently telling her that it would be all right.

Saying nothing, she laid her head upon his chest. As he brushed some of her hair from her face he whispered that she had earned her red feather several times over today, here in the bloody square that had taken so many of their comrades' lives.

Faegan's litter descended and he examined the scene. The indestructible stone bars were still firmly in place overhead. Everywhere he looked, dead warriors, beasts, and the body parts of both lay scattered across the killing field. So much blood had been spilled that it was hard to find a patch of ground that wasn't a muddy red. He lowered his head, overwhelmed by guilt.

When he looked up he saw Ox, Traax, and Duvessa slowly approaching. Taking a deep breath, he did his best to collect his thoughts.

"What *were* those things?" Traax asked. He lowered the tip of his dreggan to the bloody ground and leaned his weight upon its hilt.

"They were either some abomination that Reznik conjured to

guard this place or the work of the Coven, left over from long ago," the wizard said. "We may never know which."

"What are your orders?" Duvessa asked.

Faegan thought for a moment.

"Duvessa, I want you to start organizing the treatment of the wounded," he ordered. "You have permission to follow Minion custom and grant a quick, merciful death to those you deem beyond help. Take a count of how many casualties we have sustained. Ox and Traax, loot the buildings of anything you can find, the heavier the better. Pile it all atop those earthen doorways. If more of those monsters wait below, I want to do everything I can to keep them from rising up. I will use the craft to help hold the doorways closed, but there are far too many of them for me to do the job without help. Go now. We have no time to lose."

Each of the Minions offered a tired salute and walked away to carry out the orders. Levitating his chair from the litter, Faegan settled it upon the blood-soaked ground.

He looked up at the stone bars. His powers had already proven useless against the latticework. Even if more warriors from the palace flew to their aid, he doubted it would help. If his gifts couldn't break the bars, no number of Minion warriors would be able to do so.

His mind turned to the members of the Conclave no longer in Eutracia. Trapped as he was so far away from Tammerland, the originating point of his portal would be very different. The formulas for its successful operation would need to be altered, but he had none of the necessary calculating tools with him. He could neither help the other Conclave members nor escape this place with his warriors. How foolish he had been to not anticipate such a crisis! He should have brought the tools with him. Angrily, he pounded the arms of his chair.

Tyranny and her group could, of course, sail home, but it would take far longer. He also knew about the Minion vessels anchored off the shore of Parthalon. That meant that Wigg, Tristan, and Celeste could do the same as Tyranny. But for them to sail home would take longer still, and the Sea of Whispers was a dangerous place.

Making matters worse, he had no clue about what other horrors Reznik might have arranged for them.

Seething at his own stupidity, he hardened his jaw.

When he had interrogated Uther, he had neglected to demand the safe route through the tunnel maze. His plan had been to simply fly into Valrenkium, and then out again. His trust in the abilities of the warriors, his own gifts in the craft, and his desire to see these wrongs ended quickly had led them here, to become trapped like rats. He would not underestimate Reznik again.

Looking into the distance, he could just make out the dark, square-cut exit in the bluffs. It was an all too tempting trap. Wherever Reznik had gone, he surely hoped that Faegan would be desperate enough to enter, followed by what was left of his ravaged Minions. Reznik's trap was perfect.

Turning away from the tunnels, the crippled wizard covered his face with his hands.

CHAPTER XLV

"AND I SAY YOU'RE WRONG!" TYRANNY BELLOWED AT THE CHA-grined Minion warrior. Her chin stuck out like the prow of her flagship. "What you're telling me is impossible! No vessel ever built could do such a thing! When a ship goes down, she goes down for good, and that's the end of her!"

Tyranny stomped angrily across the floor of her stateroom and took a cigarillo from the box on her desk. She shoved it between her lips, struck a match, lit it, and then took a quick lungful of smoke. When she turned back to K'jarr, she gave him a look so cold that it could have frozen a bucket of seawater.

K'jarr pursed his lips. The last thing he wanted to do was to offend Tyranny, but the truth was the truth. He turned his palms up, pleading.

"I can only tell you what I saw," he said quietly. "The seven ships were each at least four times the size of the *Reprise,* perhaps larger. They went down bow first. After a time they surfaced again, some distance from where they had submerged. They looked none the worse for wear. Their speed beneath the waves was at least as great as it was afloat. They are as black as night. Had I been alone, I would have thought it all a bad dream. But each of the warriors accompanying me saw the same thing."

Letting go a defiant snort, Tyranny looked over at Shailiha and Scars. Not knowing what to say, they remained still. The privateer ran one hand through her tousled hair and began angrily pacing back and forth, puffing on her cigarello as she went.

"The men who supposedly captained these submersible vessels, they were black *skeletons,* you say? And they didn't drown when they submerged with their ships?"

As she strode back and forth the heels of her knee boots thumped on the hardwood floor. She glared at K'jarr as though he had just been released from some Minion home for the deranged.

"Yes, captain," K'jarr answered. "They each wore a tattered uniform that I found eerily familiar." Pausing for a moment, he gave Tyranny a thoughtful look. "Perhaps these skeletal captains didn't need to survive their sea trials after all," he mused.

Tyranny stopped pacing. "What do you mean?"

K'jarr took a deep breath. "Perhaps they were dead already. They certainly looked like it."

Sighing, Tyranny closed her eyes and rubbed her brow. It wasn't bad enough that her damaged frigate wallowed like a harpooned whale through demonslaver-infested waters. Now she had to contend with this outlandish tale. Worse yet, the warriors had come home empty-handed. But she knew that the warrior had no reason to lie. She looked back at K'jarr.

"Do you have anything else to add?"

K'jarr shook his head. "Only that you must believe me," he said. "I'm telling you the truth."

Sighing, Tyranny shook her head. "You are dismissed."

With a click of his heels, K'jarr crossed the stateroom and left. The intricately carved door closed quietly behind him.

Tyranny went back to her desk and sat down. Sensing that it

was going to be a long night, she reached for the wine bottle sitting there and poured herself a glassful. She lifted the bottle toward Shailiha and Scars, who sat in twin chairs opposite her desk. When they nodded, she poured two more goblets full. Then, crossing one of her long legs over the other and placing them atop the desk, she exhaled a long billow of bluish smoke.

For some time, the only sounds disturbing the quiet of the stateroom were the creaking of the ship and the splashing of the waves, just below the open stained-glass windows.

"You were hard on him," Shailiha said quietly. "Despite what you might think of his story, I have never known a Minion warrior to lie."

Tyranny sighed. "I know," she answered. "But—do you really believe the wild story he just told us?"

Shailiha leaned forward and placed her wineglass on the desk. The wound on her forehead was purple and swollen, and she was tired.

"You are new to the wonders and the horrors of the craft," she said. "In the right hands, magic can do amazing things. Not all of them are good."

"So you believe him?"

"I think it's too dangerous not to," the princess answered.

Tyranny looked over at Scars. "And you?"

The gigantic first mate shrugged his shoulders. "I have seen far fewer uses of the craft than the princess. Those I have witnessed have astounded me. I don't think it impossible. But I will tell you one thing for certain." He emptied his wine goblet in a single swallow and placed it back on the desk. His expression darkened. "If what K'jarr says is true and we meet those Black Ships on the open sea, there will be no hope for us. We must do everything we can to avoid them."

Tyranny stood up from her chair. She walked to one of the open windows and angrily tossed her spent cigarillo into the sea.

The last day and a half had passed quietly enough. While the *Reprise* lumbered southeast, her crewmen and the Minion warriors were doing everything they could to repair the mangled ship.

A new bowsprit had been carved and mounted, most of the damaged rigging had been replaced, and the canvas-masters were busy mending the sails. The repairs to the hull were holding. Still, the damage to the fallen mast could only be repaired in port. Until it was replaced, the *Reprise* was much slower than she had been, and that continued to worry her captain. But for the most part the warship was again seaworthy. So far, no other vessels had been sighted.

Tyranny knew she had three choices. First, she could continue their mission to capture a demonslaver. But given their reduced speed, that would prove problematic. Second, they could return to Faegan's portal, wait for its daily opening, and use it to go home. Doing so would probably cause further damage to the ship, but they would presumably be delivered so close to the shore of Eutracia that it wouldn't matter. Third, they could sail home without the aid of the portal. The voyage would take quite a bit of time, and sailing home would be fraught with dangers, not the least of which were the strange Black Ships K'jarr had mentioned—if they truly existed.

As she thought over her options, Tyranny gazed out the window. Darkness was falling, the sea calm. She finally nodded. When she turned back to Shailiha and Scars she was smiling slightly.

"Is Faegan's other spell still working?" she asked the princess.

Before departing Eutracia, the crafty wizard had not only enchanted her against seasickness, but also enveloped her in a spell that would cloak her endowed blood from practitioners of the craft. As long as the spell was working, she would feel a slight but not unpleasant tingle in her left hand. She held her hand up and rubbed her fingers against her palm.

"Yes," she answered. "I think we should continue our mission. Tristan wants a demonslaver." A sly smile crossed her face. "Let's go get him one."

"I agree," Scars interjected. "We didn't come all this way just to turn tail and go home. Besides, it's been too long since I've broken the bones of some of those white-skinned bastards. I'm eager for some exercise."

Tyranny nodded. "Very well, then. But we cannot take the *Reprise* much closer to the Citadel for fear of being seen. We'll have the Minions fly us in and back out again." She looked closely at Shailiha. "Are they strong enough to carry us?"

"When the Gates of Dawn collapsed, Ox carried Tristan all

the way home to Tammerland," the princess said. "But Ox is extremely strong. K'jarr would know the answer better than I. He has already made the trip to the Citadel and back. He could also select the best fliers."

Remembering the other gift of the craft that Faegan had so wisely conjured for them, Tyranny smiled. Lashed to the deck above and covered with a massive oilskin, it had remained safe through the storm.

"If we have enough warriors who can carry us, and Faegan's device works properly, then each of the warriors will only have to fly half the journey at a time," she mused. "We are closer to the Citadel than we were when Traax and his party left. Our odds are better now, and it's a chance worth taking.

"Do you have a feel for the weather?" she asked Scars.

The first mate pursed his lips. "K'jarr says that there is a fog bank building to the east," he answered. "My sea bones agree. It should help hide us. But if it doesn't clear on our way home, finding the *Reprise* could become very difficult."

"It's a chance we'll have to take," Tyranny answered. "Go topside and tell K'jarr of our plan. Have him select seven additional warriors for the trip. They will have to be the best, because they literally will have our lives in their hands. We will sail one more day southeast, then fly to the Citadel tomorrow night. This will not only give K'jarr and Shailiha another day of rest, but it will also bring us closer to the fog bank."

Scars nodded to his captain and departed to carry out his orders.

Taking another sip of wine, Shailiha regarded Tyranny thoughtfully.

Tyranny raised her eyebrows. "You have something on your mind. Do you have concerns about the mission? If you do, now's the time to say so."

Looking down, Shailiha rolled the wineglass between her palms. Something had been bothering her for some time. At last she looked Tyranny in the eyes. "It's not the mission I'm thinking of."

"What, then?"

"You love him, don't you?"

Sighing, Tyranny looked down at the deck. When she raised

her face, it showed a rare vulnerability. "Am I really that transparent?"

"Perhaps only to me," Shailiha answered. "No one else has mentioned it. I speak of it for two reasons. The first is that I want you to know that I understand. I care for him in a different way than you do, of course, but I know how easy it is to become attached to him. Trust me, I've seen it before."

Smiling wryly, Tyranny shook her head. "I have never known a man quite like him," she said. "I wish you could have seen him that day I rescued him from the slaver ship. He was filthy and wounded, but the moment I saw him, he stood out from all the rest. As I came to know him, he captured my heart as no other ever has."

After an awkward silence, Tyranny spoke again. "You mentioned that there were two reasons for discussing this. What is the other?"

"I want your promise that you will do nothing to interfere with the relationship between my brother and Celeste," Shailiha said bluntly. "They have only recently found each other, and they love each other deeply. Ever since the return of the Coven, his life has been very difficult. And her life has been a nightmare from the day she was born. I don't want you to harm whatever joy they have been able to pluck from the ashes."

Tyranny walked back over to the window. "You needn't concern yourself with that," she said.

Despite the courage in the privateer's voice, Shailiha could tell that it was difficult for her to get the words out. When Tyranny turned around, the princess saw the shine of unshed tears, but they were quickly blinked away.

"Some time ago, I decided not to try to get in the way," she said softly. "Because of your brother, I am a member of the Conclave and the captain of Eutracia's fleet. They are positions I do not take lightly. I owe Tristan more than I could ever repay. And regardless of my personal feelings for him, I am also very fond of Celeste. You have my word."

"Thank you," Shailiha said. Standing, she turned toward the door.

"Just the same, there is something else you should know," Tyranny added. Raising her eyebrows, Shailiha looked back at her.

"If for any reason Tristan and Celeste are no longer together, my promise is rescinded." A crafty smile crept across her face. "I'm no thief, but I remain a privateer."

Shailiha couldn't help but smile back. "Agreed," she said. She strode to the door and left the room.

CHAPTER XLVI

THE SUN WOULD SOON RISE, SATINE REALIZED. IN ANOTHER FOUR hours or so, she would be discovered. She didn't need that much time to complete her next sanction, but she appreciated the margin of safety. The nighttime sky was cloudy, and for that she was also thankful. Moonlight would have proven a deadly adversary.

From her place in the bushes, Satine watched carefully as a pair of stern Minion guards strode in opposite directions along the base of the castle wall. The light from their nearby campsites sent the patrolling warriors' shadows crawling across the dark gray stones, adding to her tension. Despite the bravado she had displayed for Bratach, this would be the most dangerous sanction of her career.

Lying upon the dewy ground, the Gray Fox watched as the two warriors reached the limits of their patrols, smartly turned, and approached one another again. She had been watching them for some time now, so as to make sure that there would be no sudden change in their routine. She had chosen this section of the palace wall because it was the most remote, and therefore less guarded.

As they neared, the warriors took no heed of one another. When no more than a foot separated them, they stopped, spun briskly around, and then walked away once more. They would do the same thing over and over again until they were relieved.

The next time the warriors met and turned, Satine began

counting to herself. She continued to count until the warriors reached the lengths of their patrols; at forty, they did an about-face and walked back.

Looking at the top of the wall, she knew that what she had planned would be difficult. When the guards met and turned again she began to count again, this time looking at the area between her hiding place and the base of the wall. Still counting, she visualized her run, and her ascent to the top. When she envisioned herself on top of the wall, she had reached forty-one. But by then the unsuspecting warriors had already met and turned yet again.

Satine sighed. There would be barely enough time, and even then it would have to go perfectly. If she made any noise or didn't move swiftly enough, the Minions would notice her, and both her mission and her life would come to an abrupt end. Her run would have to be silent, her throw perfect, and her climb swift. Bringing the rope up after her quickly enough was yet another concern.

Unlike the night she killed Geldon, Satine was dressed in peasant garb. She wore a short tunic, brown breeches, and a pair of very worn knee boots—all purchased that morning at a secondhand shop. A battered leather belt was cinched around her middle. She wore no hat; her dark braid was tucked inside the neck of her tunic. Except for a single hip dagger, she carried no weapons. She felt naked without them, but for her plan to work, she had to appear as one of the innocent citizenry in all respects.

She had wound white bandages spotted with blood around both her left forearm and her right thigh. The stray dog she had killed earlier that day had gone quietly, and it was his blood, rather than her own, that adorned her bandages.

She reached around to the leather bag slung across her back and felt for the small grappling hook. It came out easily, along with the black knotted line tied to it. After slowly coiling the line, she laid the neat circle of rope by her side. Using both hands, she quietly snapped open the three-pronged hook and laid it alongside the rope. Then she looked back to the wall.

As expected, the two warriors were still marching their mind-numbing drill. She would give them two more passes, she decided, and then she would make for the wall. She waited patiently, her heart hammering in her chest and her muscles coiled and ready.

The warriors approached again, and then turned away. Reaching out for the handle of the grappling hook, she waited. She coiled the free end of the rope around her left hand.

Again the warriors came. Once she left the security of the bushes, there was no going back. As the warriors approached one another for the final time, she started counting.

One.

The moment the warriors turned and started back, she left the bushes. She ran lightly but quickly, her boots hardly making a sound as she raced for the wall. At the same time she began to swing the hook, letting the line out bit by bit as she went. When she was just over halfway there she sent the hook flying, and she prayed.

Ten.

Her throw was perfect. The hook caught securely to the top of the wall with barely a sound. To make sure of its purchase she gave it a sharp yank, and it held. Bracing her feet against the wall, she began her climb upward, hand over hand against the knots in the rope. Using every ounce of skill and strength she possessed, she made her way quickly, like a spider.

Twenty-six.

The height of the wall seemed greater now that she was upon it, and the rope began burning her naked palms. The climb was tougher than she had envisioned, and her time was running out.

Thirty-four.

Scrambling as fast as she could, she finally neared the top. The last few knots dug viciously into her hands, and the sweat burned her eyes.

Thirty-six.

With a final heave she lifted herself atop the wall. But the knotted rope still dangled in plain sight, its end swinging gently in the wind.

Thirty-eight.

She reached down and gave the line a silent snap. The end obeyed, and flew up to reach her. She grabbed it with one hand and quickly pulled the line up. Then she lay as still as death on top of the dirty wall.

Forty.

The pacing warriors met in the center, turned, and then walked away again.

Closing her eyes, Satine sighed with relief. But this was no time to tarry. She lifted the hook free of the wall and turned it around to secure it against the other side. She took a moment to look down. There was no one about. She lowered the rope, then started down.

When she reached the inner ward of the palace, she snapped the rope again and lifted the hook free. It fell securely into her outstretched hand.

She closed the prongs of the hook and rewound the line. She removed the leather bag from across her back, taking out several small items, which she placed into her tunic. She then returned the hook and line to the bag and closed it.

With her dagger, she dug a shallow hole and buried the bag. If her plan worked, she wouldn't need it again. Replacing the dagger in its thigh sheath, she pulled Bratach's map from between her breasts. Looking around, she verified her position.

Hundreds of fires cheerfully burned before the tents of the sleeping wounded. Even at this time of night, many of the palace windows were lit from within. Minion guards patrolled among the tents, but they now held little fear for her. After all, she was no more than one of the hundreds of other wounded citizens who had yet to leave the security of the palace.

She pulled her braid free. Mindful of her pretended wounds, the Gray Fox walked out onto the palace grounds with an exaggerated limp.

The manicured grass was wet beneath her feet; the crisp evening air smelled pleasantly of the smoke rising from the campfires. A moon had emerged from behind the clouds. Satine was surprised by how many people still milled about at this hour. Yet another advantage, she thought. The larger the crowd, the easier it would be to become lost in the scene.

As she walked among them, she smiled and nodded. An elderly man of about eighty Seasons of New Life offered her a mug of warm ale and a seat beside him before the warmth of his fire. He wore a blood-soaked bandage around his head, and his creased face showed the creeping fatigue of his years. Satine smiled and graciously begged off, saying that she had no wish to disturb his sleeping family. Nodding, he bid her on her way.

After strolling between the tents for a time, she found a small clearing and stopped to look across the ward to the drawbridge. As she expected, the massive wooden gate was raised and locked. Several Minions stood guard beside it.

Should more of the wounded arrive, the warriors would of course lower the bridge to allow them entrance. Otherwise, during the night the bridge would remain raised in the interests of security—especially with the wizards away. Her timing couldn't have been better. Smiling to herself, she changed direction and walked toward the castle.

She had heard that much of the great structure's interior always remained lit at night. Given the large number of wounded still being tended inside, she was sure that it was illuminated even more than usual. Walking up the granite steps, she saw that the entire place seemed much more like some huge hospital than it did a royal dwelling. She crossed the giant patio, then entered the Chamber of Supplication.

The beds of the wounded filled the checkerboard floor, the hall having been reclaimed as a healing ward soon after the prince had given his speech to the citizens. She smiled briefly to herself. Bratach's suggestion that she attend had been invaluable. She continued on between the beds.

Minion healers, the white feather emblazoned upon their body armor, tended the wounded. The place smelled of blood, antiseptic, and freshly bleached linen. Acolytes of the Redoubt helped the healers, the azure glow of the craft sometimes surrounding the beds and the victims lying upon them. Standing torches and wall sconces threw flickering light across the walls, creating magnified shadow vignettes of the ongoing pain and suffering. Low moans and the urgent orders of the Minion healers and the acolytes rose into the air.

To Satine's relief, no one took any particular notice of her as she made her way among the beds. When she reached the far wall of the room she walked out into a long hallway. "Twenty more paces and you will see an alcove," Bratach had told her. "Stop there to consult your map."

She continued on, the crowds thinning as she went. The farther she proceeded into the castle unescorted, the more likely she was to be questioned by an acolyte or a Minion guard. She understood perfectly why Bratach had not told her the name of his confederate here. Should she be captured and later forced to talk by the wizards' use of the craft, he would lose only one, not two valuable allies.

Soon the alcove loomed. She looked up and down the length of the hall, then stepped in. The arched niche was fairly shallow and didn't provide much cover, but she wouldn't need to be in it for long. An oil sconce attached to the wall overhead granted her a small amount of light. Just below it hung an oil portrait of the prince, presumably painted during his younger, happier days. She snorted a soft, derisive laugh down her nose as she again removed the map from its hiding place.

After another hundred paces or so, she would take the hallway on the left, which led to the sleeping quarters. She would need the third door on the right.

She put her map away and peered out into the hallway. Satisfied that no one was near enough to concern her, she strode down the hall.

That was when she heard the crisp strikes of boot heels. Minion boot heels—she was sure of it. Looking around, she saw no place to hide.

Because surprise would be on her side, she might be able to kill them before they could react—except that the only real weapon she carried was her dagger; the items in her pockets needed to be saved for use on her target. Besides, if she killed them, their bodies would be evidence that an intruder had been in the palace. She couldn't afford that. She would simply have to try and bluff her way past them.

Then she remembered something she had seen on the map. She took it out, tore away a small section, and hid the rest away. Taking a deep breath, she walked on.

When the patrolling warriors came around the corner, she literally walked into them. Assuming a look of astonishment she held up her hands in a gesture of surrender.

"What are you doing here?" one of the guards growled. "This area is off-limits to the general populace."

He was especially tall, even for a Minion, and he was glaring at her. The other warrior had red hair, and his gaze was no less suspicious.

Satine quickly shifted her expression from one of astonishment to that of apology. "I'm here on behalf of Sister Katherine," she said, desperately hoping that her ruse would work. "I was walking through the Chamber of Supplication when she asked me to fetch more linen and to tear it into bandages," she went on. "They need them immediately, and they cannot spare a healer to fetch them. I was glad to help."

Holding up the section of map, she gestured at it. "She drew me this map, but I think I might have gotten lost anyway," she added anxiously.

Giving them no time to think, she pointed urgently down the hall. "She told me that there was another linen closet, a little farther down." Without asking permission, she began limping away. "It's this way, is it not?" she demanded, as she brazenly kept on going.

The taller warrior turned to look at his companion. He shook his head.

"There must have been another influx of wounded," he said. "The healers have reached the point where they need extra help."

Seizing the initiative, Satine put a worried look on her face as she continued to limp down the hall. "You're holding me up!" she fairly shouted at them. "People are bleeding to death! Now, is the linen closet down this way or not?"

The tall warrior nodded. "It's near the next corner. The door should be unlocked. But be quick about it, woman."

With a wave, Satine turned her back to them and hurried down the hall. Only when the sound of the warriors' boot heels became distant enough did she finally turn around and look. The patrolling warriors were rounding the next corner, moving out of sight.

Stopping for a moment, Satine leaned up against the cool marble wall. She closed her eyes and did her best to calm her heartbeat. Nearly there, she thought. Hiding the torn map again, she walked on.

The corner she was looking for was just ahead. She slowed her pace, rounded the corner, and crept silently to the third door on the right. She placed her ear to the door. Silence.

She dropped to the floor, turned her head, and peered through the narrow gap under the door. Only moonlight illuminated the room.

She stood, reached into a pocket, and produced a pair of narrow iron tools, each about as long as her hand. One had a flat end, the other a hook. Slipping them both into the keyhole, she worked them carefully back and forth until she heard the lock quietly turn over. She placed the tools back into her pocket.

After checking to make sure she was still alone, she grasped the gold, cantilevered handle and gave it a turn. She gently pushed open the door. To her great relief, the hinges did not creak. She silently stepped into the room and closed the door behind her.

Moonlight drifted in through the open stained-glass windows. The figure in the four-poster bed lay unmoving. Satine quietly crept to stand by the side of the bed. Identifying the face in the moonlight, she smiled.

From her pockets, she produced one of the vials she had purchased from Reznik and a short line of string with a small, lead plumb bob in the shape of a teardrop tied to one end.

She held the vial to the moonlight and gave it a gentle shake. The violet fluid and the magenta swirls blended quickly.

She carefully opened the vial. Her nose picked up the scent of the Eutracian bees' honey she had ordered the fluid laced with. Unrolling the line, she let the plumb bob drop to a point directly over the victim's lips. She placed the open end of the vial near the other end of the string, and very carefully poured a small amount of the fluid onto it. As the violet liquid silently crept its way down the string, she watched and waited.

Soon the fluid gathered on the bob and started to form a perfect droplet. Holding the line steady, she watched the droplet grow in size until it finally became too large to sustain itself. It fell directly onto the victim's lips, not an iota of it wasted.

The sleeping person scowled then unconsciously licked the sweet poison. Another drop soon followed. Again it was automatically licked into the waiting mouth.

Satine closed the vial and silently returned both it and the plumb line to her pockets. She made her way to the door, then turned around to take a final look at the sleeping figure in the bed. Her victim stirred, then lay still.

Satine opened the door and peered out. No one was about. She slipped out and headed back the way she had come.

Her limping walk back to the courtyard was uneventful. She did not see the warriors who had stopped her in the hallway, nor did she pause to speak to anyone else. Soon she was outside again threading her way between the tents of the wounded.

She looked at the sky. Dawn would arrive soon. There was still one more task to complete, and she would need to hurry.

As she casually limped back over to the remote section of wall by which she had arrived, she removed her dagger. Quickly she buried the plumb bob, the lock picks, and the deadly vial. After scraping the dirt back over the hole, she wiped her hands down the length of her trousers and limped back into the camp.

The drawbridge was still up, but she was not concerned. She knew that it was lowered each day at dawn to allow the wounded to pass in and out of the courtyard. The warriors would take little notice of someone who was mostly healed and wanting to be on her way.

As she wandered through the camp, she again came upon the old man who had spoken to her. He smiled, the creases in his face showing in the glow of the firelight.

Sitting down on the stump beside him, Satine smiled and told him that she was finally ready for that mug of warm ale.

CHAPTER XLVII

HIS NAME WAS DAX. AT THIRTY-TWO SEASONS OF NEW LIFE HE was relatively young to be a Minion officer. His bravery and skill in the aerial campaign against Nicholas' hatchlings and the recent sea battles with Wulfgar's demonslavers had quickly brought him to the attention of his superiors. With that had come a well-deserved promotion.

Now a captain, he had been honored when Ox selected him to command the warriors left behind at the base of the Tolenka Mountains. It was his task to observe the rampaging Orb of the Vigors and to send regular reports to the Conclave. Eager to make his mark, Dax took his first command seriously.

After the departure of Geldon and Ox, his first order had been to move the camp farther away from the newly created canyon. The intense heat lingering there had vastly accelerated the deterioration of the animal carcasses that lay within. His greatest concern had been disease, but the rising stench alone was enough incentive to move. As it was, even from the relative security of their new campsite, he could sometimes detect the telltale odor of rotting flesh.

Near dawn, Dax stood up from his camp stool and slowly stretched his wings. He did not look like a typical Minion. Clean-shaven like commander Traax, he was fairer than most. His eyes were a rare light blue and he had light brown hair and wings. Although still unmarried, he hoped to one day take a mate and have children.

Rufio, his aide-de-camp, lay asleep at the edge of the campfire, an empty akulee jug by his feet. Twenty years Dax's senior and possessing the battle scars to prove it, Rufio was a great bull of a warrior. He was nearly as large as Ox, and his loyalty was just as unshakable.

As the sun scratched its way up over the eastern horizon, the camp bugler sounded his horn and the troops woke up and exited their tents. Shortly, the usual sounds of grumbling and the smell of warm food began to greet Dax's senses.

He suddenly noticed shadows passing over the grass. Looking up, he saw the night patrol returning. Dax picked up his dreggan and he secured the weapon's baldric over one shoulder. After checking the blade to make sure it wouldn't stick in its scabbard, he attached his returning wheel to his belt. Smiling, he gave Rufio's meaty shoulder a short kick.

"Wake up! The patrol has returned."

With a groan, Rufio rose up onto his elbows. Grimacing, he narrowed his dark eyes against the rising sun. Then he looked at the akulee jug and he shook his head regretfully.

Eager to speak with the leader of the patrol, Dax walked over to where the warriors would land. Rufio slowly stood to find his head still swimming. Stretching his muscles, he stiffly followed along.

The six exhausted warriors landed. Their wings drooped, and their bodies and faces were blackened with soot. It was all their leader could do to snap his heels together in the customary salute. They carried extinguished torches, which they unceremoniously dropped to the ground. Concern showed on the leader's face.

"What of the orb?" Dax demanded.

"The situation has changed," the lead warrior answered. "The orb is still carving into the mountainside, its pace unchanged, but it has now traveled far enough so that the entrance to the pass may be seen. In my opinion you should view it for yourself, sir. No words of mine could do it justice."

Dax nodded his approval. "Very well. Take your warriors to the camp. Eat, drink, and rest. I will return shortly."

Grateful for the respite, the tired warriors clicked their heels, then turned and walked the short distance back to camp.

"Are you game for a little sightseeing?" Dax asked Rufio. A teasing smile crossed his face. "It would do you good!"

Still trying to clear his head, Rufio pulled on his beard. He knew he hadn't really been asked a question; he had been given an order. He clicked his boots.

"As you wish, Captain," he answered. At Dax's order, he picked up two of the torches the others had left behind.

Taking a few quick steps, Dax snapped open his wings and he launched himself into the air. Rufio followed.

They headed northwest, toward the place where the ruptured orb had first made contact with the forest. They soon found themselves over the steaming canyon. Trying to avoid the stench, Dax took them higher.

Steaming water still filled the ugly gouge in the earth. Thousands of bloated animal carcasses bobbed aimlessly, making the flooded canyon seem even more crowded than before. Scavenger birds circled above, banking to descend and collect their next meal.

The two warriors landed at the edge of the decimated forest at the base of the Tolenkas. In every direction, vast areas of timberland had burned to the ground. The smoldering soil that had once sustained the trees was as black as night. Here and there wisps of dark smoke rose lazily into the sky. Devoid of both animal life and the majestic forest, the entire area was eerily quiet. Taking to the sky, the two warriors flew west again, climbing up the rising sides of the mountains.

As they went higher, the charred remains of the forest gradually disappeared to reveal the stone base of the Tolenkas. Following the darkest part of the destruction left by the orb, Dax's gaze soon fell upon another canyon, this one carved out of the rock.

He and Rufio descended carefully. Just as the patrol leader had told them, the pass was magnificent. Its floor was jagged, uneven, and at least thirty meters wide. Its scarred walls rose vertically, their tops lost somewhere in the ever-present fog. Hissing steam poured from jagged cracks in the walls and floor. The warriors could soon feel the heat beginning to seep into the soles of their boots, and rivulets of sweat crept down beneath their body armor.

A limited amount of sunlight filtered through the fog. As Dax looked down the length of the canyon, he could see no end to it. Great explosions of rock could be heard in the distance, testament to the orb's continued success at the task that humanity had never been able to accomplish. The ground shook slightly, causing the occasional rockslide. This was a dangerous, evolving place, and Dax knew they would have to be very careful if they were to stay alive.

The Minion captain slid his dreggan from its scabbard. Rufio followed suit, then handed Dax one of the torches. Their senses alert, the two warriors began walking into the passageway.

The interior of the pass was darker than it had seemed from the outside. Dax ordered Rufio to light the torches, and shortly they were able to continue on, bright lights held high.

The deeper in they went, the hotter it became. Sweat ran freely down their bodies, and the soles of their boots were almost too hot to stand upon. Dax took to the air, and Rufio followed.

Dax realized that the heat would soon force them to turn back. Even so he pushed forward, trying to learn as much as he could. From the moment he had entered the pass, something told him that exploring it could be even more important than viewing the orb.

Dense smoke gathered, irritating their eyes and lungs. The heat was nearly unbearable; the sounds of the screaming orb and falling rocks were deafening. The canyon floor and walls shook much more violently now, and the warriors had to watch carefully for constantly falling shards of rock.

As Dax was about to order Rufio to turn back, the sounds and tremors calmed. The smoke began to lift, and the ground finally stopped shaking. Suddenly the way forward had become a bit clearer.

Holding his torch in one hand and his dreggan in the other, Dax stopped to hover in the air. Rufio came up alongside, and both gazed intently down the length of the canyon.

Through the gloom, Dax thought he saw a pinprick of light. As if it had a life of its own, its sparkling radiance started coming closer. It grew quickly, and with its speedy approach the deep, rumbling sounds started again. Faster and faster it raced toward them.

Dax suddenly realized that it wasn't a pinprick of light at all, it was a wall of glowing azure, and it was barreling straight at them. It stretched from one side of the pass to the other, and when Dax looked up, he saw that its top was lost in the fog above.

Dax knew little of magic, but his instincts told him that the thing was lethal. "Fly!" he screamed to Rufio. "Fly for your life!"

Without knowing how deep the pass was, they had no choice but to turn around and fly back in the direction from which they had come. They immediately dropped their torches and sheathed their dreggans. Pulling on their wings with all their strength, Dax and Rufio frantically made for the exit.

They didn't dare turn and look, for that would only slow them down. But even without checking, Dax could sense that they were losing ground.

The sides and floors of the canyon shook violently with its approach. The noise had grown so all-encompassing that the fleeing warriors thought their eardrums might burst. Great chunks of rock tore loose and plummeted from the walls, threatening to strike them down at any moment. As Dax and Rufio finally neared the exit, they redoubled their efforts and prayed for speed and safety.

The azure wall now only meters behind, Dax plunged through the exit first. Hoping that the wall would stay on a linear path as its energy exploded from the canyon, he veered to the right.

Always the slower, Rufio had not been able to keep up with Dax's blistering pace. Dax heard him scream and turned to look.

When the azure wall reached the exit, it came to an abrupt, unexpected stop. As it did, the entire mountain range seemed to shake. The exit was blocked by an azure barrier, which pressed against the walls of the pass, sending shards of granite falling in every direction. The earth shook for a few moments more, and then everything fell silent.

Rufio screamed again. Dax's jaw fell open.

Rufio was trapped in the azure barrier. He had been caught while flying through; only his head, shoulders, and arms protruded. Eyes bulging, the warrior struggled desperately, crying out in pain as the azure wall slowly sucked him backward. With no thought for his own safety, Dax flew to him.

Screaming, Rufio reached toward Dax. Dax took Rufio's wrists and pulled as hard as he could. But to no avail: Rufio was being engulfed.

Out of sheer desperation, Dax let go and drew his dreggan. He hacked at the azure wall. To his horror, his blows had no effect. His blade simply disappeared into the wall, much as if he had been striking at the surface of a pond. Each time his dreggan left the barrier, the wound it left behind immediately sealed itself.

The azure had pulled Rufio in up to his shoulders now. Grabbing Rufio's wrists again, Dax pulled with all of his might, but there was no resisting the power of the craft.

With a bloodcurdling scream, Rufio's head was finally sucked into oblivion. Straining mightily, trying to fly backward, Dax did his best to keep hold of his friend. Only when his own fingers were nearly touching the deadly wall did he finally let go.

Rufio's hands disappeared, and the wall sealed itself after them.

Stunned, Dax hovered there. The azure barrier had made no sound, had given no quarter. And now Dax's best friend was gone. For several long moments Dax lowered his head in mourning.

The exhausted Minion slowly drifted to the ground. He now believed that if he didn't touch the wall, it wouldn't harm him. But he was no fool. He didn't trust his theory enough to put it to the test.

Had the circumstances been different, Dax would have thought the wall incredibly beautiful. Smooth as glass and stretching toward the heavens, the azure light was shot through with white flashes of energy. It made no sound as it shimmered there, nor did it advance or retreat, but the light it emitted surged powerfully back and forth, as though it were begging to be unleashed.

Dax knew that there was nothing more he could do. Another party of warriors would have to be sent out immediately to watch this deadly new phenomenon, and a message would have to be sent to the *Jin'Sai* at once.

Sadly he turned his gaze to the spot where Rufio had disappeared. The wall showed no trace of having engulfed him. With no body to immolate, it had been the worst possible of Minion deaths.

Launching himself into the sky, Dax turned toward the campsite. As his wings pulled him through the air, he did not look back.

CHAPTER XLVIII

"IT'S TRUE, DAUGHTER," WIGG SAID, HIS VOICE CRACKING. "YOU are dying, and we must return to Eutracia as soon as possible. It is now even more important that we make Tristan's blood whole again—not only to heal the orb, but to save your life." Wigg looked at Jessamay, who nodded.

"Jessamay believes that only another physical union with Tristan—after his blood is healed—might reverse this process," the wizard said. "After examining your blood signature, I agree. I wish things were different."

It was early evening in Parthalon. Wigg, Jessamay, Tristan, and Celeste were sitting quietly on the balcony of Jessamay's quarters in the Recluse. Three tension-filled days had passed since Wigg had learned the terrible news.

His first instinct had been to return everyone to Eutracia immediately. But Jessamay had been too weak to risk taking her through Faegan's portal. Now, at last, she finally felt well enough. Tomorrow they would travel back to the place where Faegan's portal opened each day at noon, and they would go home.

Tristan sat holding Celeste. His face was grief-stricken as she sobbed, her head buried against his shoulder.

Wigg had just broken the terrible news. He had put that task off until he could examine Celeste's blood signature for himself. Two days earlier he had obtained a drop of his daughter's blood under the weak pretext of checking to see that her Forestallment remained intact after the scorching of her fingertips. When he had examined her blood through Failee's signature scope, his world had fallen apart.

Nearly one-third of Celeste's blood signature was already gone. Glowing, azure bits—traces of Tristan's blood—coursed ominously within the bloodlines of the signature. Wigg had never seen anything like it. It was almost as if the azure bits were devouring his daughter's signature little by little.

Frustrated, Wigg shook his head. In truth, the only reason he hadn't told Tristan and Celeste right then and there was simple— he hadn't known how. It had taken all his courage to finally speak.

Tristan's eyes were red and shiny, and he pulled Celeste a bit closer to him.

"This can't be happening," he said. His voice shook with every word. "Please tell us that this has all been some kind of mistake!"

With a heavy sigh, Wigg placed his hands into the opposite sleeves of his robe. "I wish I could. But everything I have just told you is true. As her signature disappears, her aging will accelerate. When the signature is finally gone, there will be nothing left to sustain her time enchantments. Remember, despite how she looks to us, and how much we may love her, she is nearly three hundred years old."

Celeste looked at her father. Trying to collect herself, she wiped away her tears. "Isn't there anything we can do?" she asked. Her voice sounded very small.

Jessamay went to sit beside Celeste and took her hands. "There is hope," she said. "But first we must return to Eutracia. Our answers lie there."

The effects of Failee's magic now gone, Jessamay looked like a different person. After she had bathed and washed her hair, she had gratefully donned a spare dress of Failee's. It hung a bit loosely, but it would do for now.

Tristan guessed that Wigg must have granted Jessamay the time enchantments when she had been somewhere around thirty-five Seasons of New Life. She was pretty, with blue eyes and a seductive figure—a far cry from the chained, cowering wretch they had seen found trapped in Failee's research chambers. Her long blond hair was naturally curly and fell to her shoulders. Her color had returned, and with it much of her strength. There was a kind, candid demeanor about her that the prince found comforting.

Still, none of these things told him how powerful a sorceress Jessamay might be. Nor did he fully understand the ramifications of her having a blood signature that showed no appreciable lean. But since Wigg seemed to trust Jessamay implicitly, Tristan decided to put away his misgivings, at least for the time being. Right now, Celeste was his most immediate concern.

"How long does she have?" he asked the wizard.

Wigg shook his head. "I can't answer that. All we can do is monitor her condition through regular examinations of her blood."

Tristan looked back at Celeste, and a terrible memory struck him. When his son Nicholas had been draining the Paragon of its power, Wigg and Faegan had begun to age prematurely and lose their gifts. Had they not been able to stop Nicholas when they did, the wizards would have turned to dust.

Beside himself with grief, he lowered his head. After a few

moments he looked back at Celeste. When he searched her face this time, he could see the truth of it.

Her appearance was already changing.

He had noticed it before, but had simply chalked it up to the immense stress they had all been under. She was still beautiful, but slight crow's-feet had appeared at the corners of her eyes, and lines had formed around her mouth. While they had walked to the Recluse stables two nights before, he had noticed that her gait was a bit slower, and that one of her ankles seemed to bother her. And he had assumed that the dark circles beneath her eyes were simply from lack of sleep. But now he knew differently.

His heart breaking, he stood and went to the balcony railing. Celeste followed. Summoning her composure as best she could, she laced one arm through his.

"I did this to you," he said after a long silence. "You have every right to hate me for it. Your life has always been difficult, and loving me has only added to your burdens. I'm so sorry."

Reaching out, she turned his face to hers. "You didn't know. It's as much my fault as anyone's." Then she let go and turned to look out over the balcony.

"I've changed already, haven't I?" she asked. "I'm aging. Don't tell me tales, my love. I've seen what is happening to me."

Her tears came again, and then she blurted, "Will you still love me?"

Her question broke his heart. He gently placed his forehead against hers. He could smell the lovely, familiar scent of myrrh in her hair. He pulled her closer.

"Always," he answered.

After thinking to himself for a moment, he finally made a decision. Squaring his shoulders, he turned to leave.

Celeste was puzzled. "What are you doing?"

"Something I should have done long ago," he answered.

Walking across the room, he went to the door and opened it. The two warriors standing on the other side immediately came to attention. Tristan whispered something to one of them. After clicking his heels, the warrior left his post. Tristan shut the door.

As the prince walked back to the balcony, Wigg and Jessamay gave him curious looks, but he ignored them. Returning to Celeste, he went to one knee and looked up into her face.

"Will you marry me?" he asked simply.

Celeste's face exploded with joy. "Yes," she answered, her voice cracking with emotion. "A thousand times, yes!"

Coming to his feet, Tristan turned to Wigg. "As First Wizard of the Directorate, you were empowered to perform marriages, were you not?" he asked.

Tears glistened in Wigg's eyes. "Indeed I was."

"Good," Tristan said, "because I respectfully request your daughter's hand."

It took Wigg several moments to find his voice. "Granted," he said.

Wigg and Jessamay came to hug them both. Only moments later, there was a knock at the door. Tristan nodded to Wigg, and the wizard went to answer it. The warrior had returned. He held a box in his arms.

Tristan beckoned him inside. The warrior walked to the prince and handed him the box.

"Is it all here?" Tristan asked.

"Yes, my lord."

"Then you are dismissed."

With another click of his heels, the Minion left the room.

"What is it?" Jessamay asked.

Tristan opened the box. It contained several finger rings and two freshly wound crowns of laurel leaves. He smiled at Celeste.

"These rings belonged to your mother," he said. "I guessed that if her wardrobe was still here, her jewelry might be, too."

Celeste looked at her father. Wigg's eyes were wet, but he smiled as he nodded back.

The ring Celeste chose was a deep blue square-cut sapphire surrounded by Parthalonian diamonds. Tristan took it from her and put it in his pocket. Then he removed the laurel wreaths. He placed one on Celeste's head, and he put the other on his own. He removed his weapons and placed them on the balcony floor, then took Celeste's hand. As he did, he felt it tremble slightly.

Wigg and Jessamay came to stand before them. Tristan and Celeste went slowly to their knees. They closed their eyes.

Reaching out, Wigg placed an ancient hand atop each of their heads. For several moments quiet reigned, the only sounds the rustling of the trees and the soft calls of the night creatures.

In quiet, measured tones, Wigg began to recite the ceremony.

CHAPTER XLIX

WHEN THE PAIR OF PATROLLING WARRIORS FIRST HEARD THE laughter, they thought little of it. With so much activity in the royal residence these days, all manner of noise had become commonplace. The distant laughter waxed and waned, but as the Minions continued down the corridor, it grew louder. The two warriors stopped and looked at each other.

"Do you hear that?" Oleg asked.

Nodding, Justus quickly held up one hand. He turned his head, trying to determine where the laughter was coming from, but with all of the traffic in the hall, he couldn't tell. Finally he indicated that they should walk on.

As they went farther, the laughter grew even louder, and its timbre changed from lighthearted to delirious. The warriors realized that something was very wrong. Then the screaming began.

Drawing their dreggans, the warriors started to run. Following the frantic screams as best they could, they eventually skidded to a stop before the door to one of the many personal chambers. From inside came the sounds of breaking glass, and for a few moments the screaming became much worse. Then they heard a series of soft thuds, and things went eerily quiet.

Without hesitation, Justus kicked the door. After another kick, the sturdy Eutracian oak gave way and the door banged open. Dreggans held high, the warriors rushed into the room.

The Minions were no strangers to death, but they were unprepared for the sight that greeted them. After making a quick search of the adjoining rooms, they sheathed their weapons.

"Go find Abbey and Adrian," Justus ordered. "And have a guard detail posted outside the door. Be quick about it!" With an obedient click of his boot heels, Oleg hurried away.

Sighing, Justus shook his head. He crossed the room, parted the drapes, and opened the windows. The sunshine only accentuated the ghastliness of the scene.

ALONE IN HER CHAMBERS, ABBEY POKED HER FORK AT HER BREAKfast of spotted quail eggs. Shawna had cooked them just the way she liked—slow-fried in a generous portion of fatback. The accompanying hog loin strips and dark gingerwheat toast all looked delicious, but she couldn't bring herself to eat any of it.

Exchanging her fork for a teacup, she took a sip of the dark, rather bitter brew. She had made the nerveweed tea herself, hoping it would calm her. The cup was still warm in her palms, and the tea felt good going down.

Deciding to abandon her breakfast for good, she stood and walked to her dressing table at the other side of the room. The image reflected in the mirror showed how tired she was from worry and lack of sleep. Sitting down, she picked up her brush and began absentmindedly running it through her hair.

She feared for everyone who had left the palace, but Faegan's group concerned her the most. They had been away far too long. Given the large number of warriors involved, they should have made short work of the Valrenkians and returned home by now. With each passing moment her worry increased.

With so many members of the Conclave gone, she knew it would be up to her to come to the aid of the crippled wizard and his warriors. In one hour, she was to meet with Adrian in the Conclave chambers. Abbey had an idea, but she would need Adrian's help to carry it out.

When she heard the insistent banging on her door, near panic gripped her. Dropping her brush to the table, she shot to her feet and whirled around.

"Enter!"

The door opened to reveal a Minion warrior. His chest was heaving.

"What is it?" she demanded.

Still trying to catch his breath, the warrior made a quick explanation. Abbey immediately tore from the room, and the two of them ran pell-mell down the corridor.

When they reached the chamber, the doorway was ringed with guards. Brushing them aside, Abbey rushed in.

Sister Adrian was already there. Her face was pale and drawn. Vivian and the warrior Justus stood beside her. No one spoke as Abbey took in the grisly scene.

Lionel the Little was dead. He was naked and blood still dripped from his body. A crude hangman's noose had been fashioned from his bedsheets and looped tightly around his neck; the other end was firmly tied to one of the room's chandeliers. Several tipped-over chairs lay near his dangling feet. Abbey realized that he would have needed them all—one stacked atop the next—to have reached the chandelier.

His neck was clearly broken, and his swollen, discolored tongue protruded grotesquely from between his teeth. The bedsheets creaked softly; the breeze coming through the open windows slowly turned his compact body in circles.

In one hand, the gnome still clutched the jagged neck of a broken wine bottle. Wounds on his torso suggested that he had used it to try to disembowel himself.

Justus stepped forward. "This is exactly how we found him," he said. "I did not touch anything other than the windows and drapes, because I was sure you and the wizards would wish to view the scene intact."

Nodding, Abbey walked closer to the swaying corpse. "You did the right thing." She turned back to Justus. "You are sure that there was no one else here with him?"

Justus nodded. "I searched the adjoining rooms, and the windows were all locked from the inside. This appears to have been a suicide. Before Lionel died, his screams sounded insane—just as they say Geldon's did."

"Cut the body down," Abbey ordered. "Take it to the Cubiculum of Humanistic Research. Adrian and I will be along shortly."

Justus and Oleg took the body down from the chandelier, wrapped it in a blanket, and then carried it from the room. Abbey turned to Adrian and Vivian.

"Do the two of you understand what this means?" she asked. Adrian nodded. "Satine has just claimed her second victim."

Vivian scowled. "Who is Satine?"

"I'm sorry," Abbey said. "I thought that by now Adrian might have told you. Satine is an assassin we believe has been hired to kill members of the Conclave. Apparently, she's targeting more than just us." Abbey paused, noting the look of shock on Vivian's face.

"But this recent attack means far more than that, I'm afraid," she went on. Walking to the windows, she looked out over the palace grounds.

"What do you mean?" Adrian asked.

Abbey turned around. "Don't you see? Satine was somehow able to breach the palace walls. She slipped by all of the Minion guards and she killed one of us right under our noses! This was as much an insult to us all as it was an act of assassination. She is as good as telling us that we're not safe—even here in the palace! When we examine Lionel's body, I'll bet my life that we find the same pollutants in his bloodstream that we discovered in Geldon's."

"We should close the drawbridge and make an immediate search," Adrian insisted. "We already know what she looks like. Perhaps she's still here."

Abbey shook her head ruefully. "Trust me, she's long gone. It is far easier to depart this place in the daytime than it is to sneak in at night. My guess is that she waited, then simply sauntered out through the gate this morning with the usual smattering of wounded well enough to leave. How clever! Tell me, can you place the same azure field around Lionel's corpse that Faegan did for Geldon's?"

"Yes," the First Sister answered. "But it will not be as strong. If a necropsy is to be performed, it will have to be soon."

Abbey looked over at Vivian. "If you will excuse us, the First Sister and I were about to meet in the Conclave Chambers. We have much to discuss. Please stay here and see if you can discover anything else that might help shed some light on what happened."

Vivian bowed slightly. "Of course."

After the other women left the room, Vivian's face darkened. She had not attended the interrogation of the captured Valrenkian, and yet Adrian and Abbey had spoken of Satine as though the assassin's identity was something Vivian already knew.

Abbey was no fool. Had the herbmistress' comments about

Satine been merely an oversight, or something else? As she continued to gaze out the window, Wulfgar's servant came to several disheartening conclusions.

Not only had the Gray Fox's identity been uncovered, but Vivian would have to be even more careful from here on. She must immediately return to the fountain in the middle of the square. Her thoughts turned to the message she would be forced to leave in the burbling water.

Bratach would not be pleased.

CHAPTER L

SHAILIHA SHIVERED. IT WAS PAINFULLY COLD AT THIS ALTITUDE, and more than once she had been forced to wipe frost from her hair and eyelashes. She and Tyranny wore heavy cloaks to help ward off the weather. As usual, Scars was dressed only in his torn trousers. Smiling, Shailiha shook her head. Like Ox, he never seemed bothered by the weather.

K'jarr and three other handpicked warriors—Crevin, Micah, and Lan—sat quietly beside them. Six additional Minion bearers bore the litter though the nighttime sky. When they landed, Tyranny wanted the four idle warriors to be fresh. All their lives would depend upon it.

They had entered the fog bank two hours ago. Once there, Tyranny had carefully consulted her enchanted sextant, and then told the warriors to change course slightly. She had been eager to confirm the additional enchantments that would allow the sextant both to operate in the fog and to read the stars as well as the sun. She had been greatly relieved when it worked as promised.

The mist surrounding them was wet and dense, making it impossible to watch the ocean sliding by below. But K'jarr had a considerable talent for dead reckoning, and he was reasonably sure about when to order their descent. Until that time they would take advantage of the welcome cover. It was not their intention to immediately approach the fortress.

The previous day had passed calmly enough, giving the *Reprise*'s canvas-masters a chance to finish repairing her sails. The frigate now had more speed, but she still lumbered more than Tyranny liked.

Before leaving the ship in charge of her boatswain, Tyranny had ordered that the frigate sail in circles, always staying near the same relative position. If the raiding party was to find the ship again, this would be crucial.

Shailiha looked over at Tyranny. The privateer's expression was grim. Other than when she gave directions to the warriors, she had said little. Shailiha couldn't help imagining that the captain was thinking of Tristan, and of the private conversation the two of them had shared in Tyranny's stateroom.

The princess rubbed her fingers together. The tingle in her hand told her that Faegan's spell was still working. *May it continue to hold,* she thought.

K'jarr leaned toward Tyranny. "It is time!" he shouted. Tyranny nodded back. K'jarr gestured to the warriors carrying the litter and they started down.

When they broke through the bottom of the fog, they saw that the Sea of Whispers was calm. From this distance, all they could see of the Citadel was a smattering of twinkling lights that floated ephemerally above the waves.

The litter descended in a tight spiral. When they were no more than a hundred meters or so above the waves, the warriors widened the spiral and held their altitude. Tyranny nodded to Shailiha and Scars.

Tyranny, Scars, and the princess stood up, as did the four waiting warriors. The two women removed their cloaks and checked their weapons. Crevin and Micah lifted Tyranny and Scars into their arms, and K'jarr took Shailiha. She wrapped her arms tightly around his neck. By previous agreement, the princess would go first.

K'jarr climbed onto the sturdy sidewall of the litter, snapped open his wings, and promptly stepped off. The warriors carrying Tyranny and Scars went next. Lan followed.

At first Shailiha was sure that she was about to die. The wind tore at her hair and clothes, and K'jarr had difficulty stabilizing his flight. He finally leveled out and soared low over the waves, waiting for the others to join them. Soon the four warriors closed ranks, waiting for the next stage of their plan to unfold.

The litter and the other warriors broke free of the fog. Fanning their wings to gentle the descent, the bearers dropped the litter atop the waves then landed themselves, one by one, and climbed inside it.

Shailiha listened as Tyranny shouted out a series of commands in Old Eutracian. The litter began to glow. Shailiha winced, knowing that this might give away their position, but it couldn't be helped. Faegan's enchantment would hold the litter in the same place on the sea, so that on the return leg of their mission they could find it again.

Watching the glow fade away almost immediately, Shailiha breathed a sigh of relief. As long as night reigned, the litter would prove nearly impossible to see. Once Tyranny was again within the prescribed range of the spell, she would utter another set of orders, and the litter would glow once more. It was imperative that they return from the Citadel before dawn—otherwise, the litter would prove an all-too-vulnerable target.

Satisfied, Tyranny ordered the others to form up on Crevin, and they flew toward the Citadel.

There was still a good bit of distance to cover, and the tension-filled trip took some time. As they neared the island, Tyranny ordered the warriors to take them higher, so that she could better scout the terrain.

There was no fog here, and the moonlight revealed the Citadel in all its menacing splendor. Several slaver frigates patrolled the sea around the horseshoe-shaped bay at the island's southern end, where the rest of the demonslaver fleet lay quietly anchored. But there was no sign of the Black Ships, or the skeletal captains K'jarr had warned them about.

After carefully surveying the island, Tyranny ordered Crevin to lead the group down. They landed behind some rocks, on a part of the shore that closely bordered the fortress' walls.

The Minions lowered their passengers to the ground. As the warriors closed their wings, they and the women drew their swords. Scars smiled and cracked his knuckles. The only other sound was the restless sea, its waves crashing over and over against the rocks. About a hundred meters ahead, the Citadel beckoned.

The ground rose dramatically, ending at the sheer rock walls surrounding the fortress. Demonslavers patrolled the guard paths at their tops. Tyranny looked over at the warriors.

"Crevin and Micah, I want you to circle around the walls as far as you dare," she whispered. "See if you can find a way in. The rest of us will wait here. Be quick."

The two warriors ran to the base of the wall, then crept away in opposite directions.

Her hand clenched tightly around her sword, Shailiha watched the warriors disappear into the darkness. Despite the coolness of the night, her palms had become moist, her mouth dry.

After what seemed forever, the warriors finally returned. Crevin shook his head.

"I searched as far as I dared," he whispered, "but the wall looks impenetrable and impossible to climb. I believe that the southern gate we saw from the air is the only way in or out."

"I agree," Micah said. "Gaining entrance to this place will be difficult." The warrior smiled, his teeth glinting in the moonlight. "But not impossible."

Tyranny understood what Micah was saying. To capture a demonslaver, they would have to take to the air again. It was risky but there seemed to be no other choice.

Looking back at the fortress, Tyranny noticed a square stone structure atop the spot where two angled sections of wall joined. A soft, golden glow came from its windows. She assumed that it must be a guard post of some kind. After thinking for a moment, she whispered her plan to the others. They nodded back.

Crevin hoisted Tyranny into his arms again. Snapping open his wings, he made a short run along the shore and then launched himself into the air.

He flew as fast as he could toward the wall, then spiraled upward, staying close to the fortress. When they neared the summit he slowed and hovered again. Very carefully they peeked over the top of the wall.

There was no one there.

Landing upon the rampart, Crevin set Tyranny on her feet. After a signal from Tyranny, Micah flew up to join them. They made for the stone structure at the corner and flattened themselves up against it. The wooden door was slightly ajar; light poured softly from its windows.

Laughter came from inside. Tyranny carefully raised her face to the window and glanced in. Ducking back down, she whispered a quick set of orders to the warriors, and they nodded back.

Tyranny positioned herself before the door, quickly pushed it open, and rushed in. The warriors were right behind her.

Four demonslavers sat at a table, drinking and playing cards. When the one nearest the door grabbed up his sword and rose from his chair, Tyranny swung her weapon at his throat. She meant to behead him with a single stroke, but her blow landed short. The tip of the blade slashed across his windpipe, and dark blood rushed forth in a geyser. Dropping to one knee, she swung the blade around again, taking off one of his legs. As he collapsed to the floor, she plunged her sword into his heart.

While another slaver swung at Tyranny with a short sword and Micah battled the third, Crevin tried to follow Tyranny's orders and choke the last one into unconsciousness.

Tyranny barely avoided the demonslaver blade as it whistled around. For several moments the battle seesawed back and forth, their blades striking so viciously against one another that sparks flew. Then the slaver suddenly stopped fighting. His eyes went wide. For a moment he stared into space. With a crash he fell face down onto the table, then slid to the floor, Micah's dagger sticking out of his back.

Tyranny looked around. The first slaver Micah had been struggling with lay dead in the corner, awash in his own blood. Crevin had succeeded in rendering the last one unconscious. Still seated in his chair, the slaver's head lay slumped over the table.

Lowering her bloody sword, Tyranny walked to the door and poked her head out. Atop distant sections of the wall, she could just make out more white-skinned demonslavers treading the guard path. No alarm had gone out. She was grateful that the thick stone walls of the guardhouse had muffled most of the noise. Then she heard the soft flurry of wings, and Lan and K'jarr landed with Scars and Shailiha. Tyranny urgently waved them inside and shut the door.

Scars walked over to the unconscious demonslaver. Casually lifting the creature's head by one earring, he examined its face. Then he let go and with a thud, the demonslaver fell back onto the table. Scars smiled at Tyranny.

"It isn't fair of you to hog all of the fun, Captain," he whispered.

Ignoring him for the moment, Tyranny ordered Crevin and Micah to opposite windows of the guardhouse to watch for approaching demonslavers. Then she smiled at Scars.

"Sorry you missed all the excitement," she said. "But you'll get your chance. I've decided we're going farther."

"What are you talking about?" Shailiha protested in a whisper. "We have what we came for. We should leave right now, while we still can!"

"I'm not leaving until I know more about this place," Tyranny replied.

The princess was dumbfounded. What Tyranny was saying made no sense.

"Are you mad?" she asked. "What could you possibly hope to accomplish—other than getting us all killed?"

Tyranny glared at her companions.

"Listen to me—all of you!" she said quietly. "I have no more wish to die than you do. But we've managed to come this far, and I say it's worth the risk to try to go farther. This citadel has been the source of all of our troubles, has it not? This is the chance of a lifetime, and we owe it to the Conclave to try to learn everything about this place that we can!"

Then she gave Shailiha a conspiratorial wink. "Besides," she added, "you know as well as I that well-behaved women rarely make history."

Shaking her head, Shailiha obstinately pointed to the unconscious slaver. "What can we possibly learn about the Citadel that he can't tell us?"

"That's what I want to find out. But I do agree with you about keeping our prize safe." Tyranny looked over at Micah. "I want you to fly him back to those high rocks on the shore. For the time being, you should be safe there. If we have not joined you in two hours' time, do your best to fly the slaver to the litter. I know it will be difficult to locate, but if you are forced to leave the island without us, we are probably all dead anyway. Then I want you and the others to try to make your way back to the *Reprise,* and from there to Faegan's portal. Go now. And good luck."

Micah lifted the demonslaver. K'jarr took his place at the window. After a silent nod of farewell, Micah carried the slaver through the door. They heard a few short steps, followed by the familiar sound of wings.

Shailiha glanced skeptically at K'jarr. The look on his face told her that he was as unsure about Tyranny's plan as she was. Scowling, the warrior returned to his surveillance.

"I know you have your doubts," Tyranny whispered. "Just answer one question. If the *Jin'Sai* were here, what would *he* do?"

"That doesn't matter now," K'jarr whispered back. As he turned back toward them, the look on his face was grim. "While we have been standing here talking, six slavers approach! I suspect they are coming to relieve the ones we killed."

With no time to lose, they lined up in threes on either side of the door. Silently cursing Tyranny's decision, Shailiha grimly raised her sword.

Soon the approaching slavers' footsteps could be heard. They grew louder. Then they stopped. An ominous silence descended.

As Shailiha tightened her grip upon her sword, the rusty hinges of the guardhouse door squeaked.

CHAPTER LI

AS THEY WALKED TOGETHER, ADRIAN LOOKED WORRIEDLY AT Abbey. Lionel's death had hit both women hard. There had still been no word from Faegan's group. Ottikar said he could easily find Valrenkium again, but if Abbey's hunch was right, getting there would be only half the battle. With every passing moment, her concern for the wizard and his warriors grew.

Adrian carried a basket containing a quill, a bottle of ink, and several rolls of blank parchment. Abbey held a flask of green liquid. She had spent several hours preparing it, using Faegan's stores of herbs and precious oils, and she would be the first to admit that she couldn't trust its effectiveness. Not only had the formula been complex, but it had been gleaned solely from memory. Without Faegan or Lionel to help her, the process had been difficult.

At their destination, they found the door guarded by a quartet of stern-faced warriors. The Minions snapped to attention.

"There have been no incidents, I trust?" Abbey asked.

The warrior in charge shook his head. "Another pair of guards has been with him the entire time. There has been no trouble."

He unlocked the door and swung it open, and the two women walked into the room.

The chamber was spacious and tastefully decorated. A table laden with food and drink sat in one corner. There were no windows and no balcony; the only door was that which they had just come through.

Uther limped about the room like a wounded tiger. The two guards assigned to him sat quietly nearby, watching his every move. Uther's face was bruised and there were gaps in his teeth where Lionel had knocked two of them out during their brief scuffle. *I wish Lionel could see that,* Abbey thought.

When he heard the women enter the room, Uther swung around. He pointed an accusatory finger at them.

"Who are you?" he shouted. "What is this place, and how did I get here? What happened to my face?"

He started to approach the women, but the two warriors intervened. At a gesture from Abbey, the Minions halted, stopping just short of taking hold of him. Uther glowered at the acolyte and the herbmistress.

"And most important," he breathed, "how is it that I no longer possess my gifts of the craft?"

For a moment, Adrian found his questions odd. *Surely he must already know,* she thought. Then she remembered that Faegan had wiped Uther's mind clean of certain memories; in addition, should he try to use the craft, he would find himself powerless. He would presumably stay that way until Faegan ended the spell.

"We'll be the ones asking the questions," Abbey answered. She ordered the warriors to move the room's writing desk and chair to the center of the floor.

"Sit down at the desk," she ordered the Valrenkian.

"No!" Uther growled. "Go to the Afterlife, bitch!"

Abbey raised an eyebrow. Looking over at the two warriors, she snapped her fingers. The Minions grabbed the Valrenkian and dragged him across the room, lifted him high, and smashed him down into the chair. Dazed, Uther shook his head.

"Bind him," Abbey ordered.

The Minions produced a length of rope and tied Uther securely to the chair. As his consciousness cleared, he glared back at the two women with venom in his eyes.

"Who are you?" he asked thickly. "What do you want?"

"We want some answers," Abbey said. "And you are going to give them to us. As a wizard friend of mine is so fond of saying, we can either do this the hard way or the easy way."

"No." Raising his face, he spat at them.

"Suit yourself." Abbey looked over at the warriors. "Do whatever you must to open his mouth."

The warriors took hold of Uther's head. Struggling wildly, he screamed. When he managed to bite one of them on the hand, the warrior laughed and swiped the Valrenkian hard across the face. Then they wrenched his head back and forced open his jaws. Blood dripped from one corner of Uther's mouth.

Abbey didn't like using violence, but if the Valrenkian wouldn't cooperate, he left her no choice. She opened the bottle of green liquid and poured it down his throat. Uther coughed and then quieted. His head lolled, and his eyelids drooped heavily.

"What is it that you just gave him?" one of the warriors asked.

Abbey bent down and closely examined his eyes.

"It's a crude form of truth elixir," she said. "And it appears that it's beginning to take hold." Relieved, she walked back over to stand next to Adrian. "Your turn," she said.

Adrian closed her eyes and raised her palms. Almost at once, Uther was engulfed in azure haze. His eyes widened, and his head snapped back.

"You have succeeded in entering his mind?" Abbey asked. "And he will do as he is asked?"

Adrian nodded. "But not to the same degree that Wigg or Faegan could manage," she answered quietly. "We can only hope that combining your liquid with my use of the craft will be enough to get what we need."

"Then we'll start with a few test questions, to which we already know the answers," Abbey whispered. She returned her gaze to the prisoner.

"What is your name?"

Uther was still staring blankly into space. "Uther—Uther of the House of Kronsteen."

"Are you a Valrenkian?"

"Yes."

"Do you practice the Vagaries?"

A cruel smile came to his lips. "Yes."

"Do you know a fellow partial adept named Reznik?"

"Yes."

Deciding he was telling the truth, Abbey stepped closer.

"Other than scaling the bluffs or traveling through the stone maze, is there any way in or out of your village?"

"Only by flying in," he answered thickly. "But people can't fly. Only birds, insects, and your grotesque servants can fly." The smile came again.

"Tell me about the sandstone maze," she asked. "Do you know the way in and out?"

"Of course."

"The safe route is committed to your memory?"

"Yes."

Abbey nodded at Adrian. The acolyte walked to the desk and put down the basket she carried. She removed the writing items and set them before Uther. She opened the ink bottle and placed the quill into it. Then she unrolled the parchments and flattened them out. As though Adrian didn't exist, Uther gazed at nothing. Adrian returned to Abbey's side.

"Free his arms," Abbey ordered.

The warriors freed his arms but passed several coils around Uther's chest before reknotting the rope. Even so, the Valrenkian didn't move.

"There is now paper and ink before you," Abbey said.

Uther looked down dumbly at the items lying there. He nodded.

"Draw a map showing the safe way in and out of the stone maze," she said. "Leave nothing out. Do you understand?" Hoping against hope that he would comply, Abbey held her breath.

"Very well," Uther answered.

Numbly, he took up the quill and began to draw.

For Abbey and Adrian, the time passed with agonizing slowness. Trying to rid herself of nervous energy, Abbey walked to the other table and poured herself a glass of wine. They waited impatiently, listening to the scratching of Uther's quill. Finally he put it down and stared blankly into space once more.

"It is done," he said.

Abbey and Adrian walked to the table and stared down at the drawing. Sure enough, it was a map of the maze—complete with arrows pointing toward the passageways that would presumably lead one safely into the village. After blowing on the map to dry the ink, Abbey rolled it up and asked Uther, "How do I know that your map is valid?"

"I would stake my life on it."

For the first time since entering the room, Abbey smiled. "That's not a bad idea," she mused. She turned to the guards.

"Go and find Ottikar. I want him and an entire phalanx of armed warriors ready to depart at once." She pointed to Uther. "And bring the captive along. I have something special in mind for him."

The warrior nearest them snapped his heels together and untied the prisoner. As the two women walked to the door, Adrian asked Abbey, "You're bringing Uther with us? True, my spell still affects him, but I thought you told me that your potion wouldn't last very long."

Abbey gave her a wink. "Unless I miss my guess," she said, "it won't have to. In fact, I'm counting on it."

More confused than ever, Adrian followed Abbey down the hall.

CHAPTER LII

As Vivian approached the far end of the palace courtyard, she nodded to the warriors guarding the drawbridge. Even though she was in a hurry, she kept her pace slow and deliberate. The warriors smiled and snapped to attention as she walked by.

Pulling the hood of her red cloak up over her head, she exited the grounds and wended her way down one of Tammerland's busier streets. Only when she knew she was out of sight of the palace did she change direction and pick up her pace.

This time she would have both good and bad news for Bratach. He would be pleased to hear that Lionel the Little was dead, but Satine's identity had been revealed, and Vivian could see no end to the trouble this news might bring. Who could have imagined that one of the Valrenkians would be captured and interrogated? Silently cursing, she hurried on.

It was now late afternoon, the sun just low enough to play hide-and-seek among the higher rooftops. Shafts of fading sunlight sliced down into the alleyways, and the air felt warm and humid. Some of the food vendors were busily closing up their carts as they stopped work for the day. Little by little, enticing aromas faded from the air.

But for each cart that departed, a tavern lamplight came alive, signaling the change of venue for the pleasure-seekers who frequented this part of town. Soon the mood in the streets would turn even more drunken and dangerous, she knew.

Her stomach growled, reminding her that she hadn't eaten for hours. She stopped to buy a bag of freshly boiled peanuts from a crippled, blind vendor about to close up his cart. Two blocks later, her fingers covered with oil and her belly quieting, she found herself reminiscing about how she had met Wulfgar.

Even though their meeting had been brief, she had immediately become his—heart, mind, and soul.

Like the other women of her kind, she had been silently called to the Redoubt through a process of the craft known as the River of Thought. At that time the wizards, the *Jin'Sai,* and the *Jin'Saiou* had been locked in mortal conflict with Wulfgar and his forces. Like the other women of her sisterhood she had immediately felt the River's irresistible call, telling her to end her current duties and make her way to Tammerland. The women had been ordered to gather in the Hall of Supplication. Wigg and Faegan were already there, waiting for them. After showing the wizards the tattoo of the Paragon on her shoulder, each sister was asked to perform some small act of the craft. Next, their blood signatures were compared to those in the palace records and examined for any evidence of Forestallments or other tampering. Only then did Wigg induct them all into the newly formed Acolytes of the Redoubt. Finally they were shown their new home—the magnificent secret hallways and chambers lying deep below the palace.

Vivian had been overjoyed. To gather with her sisters to study and practice the craft had long been her greatest dream. But then Wulfgar had come to her. He had introduced her to a totally different dream—one for which she would willingly discard her previous vows. Suddenly, the newly formed Acolytes of the Redoubt had become the object of her undying hatred, something that she would now do anything in her power to destroy.

The meeting between Vivian and Wulfgar had occurred on the night Wulfgar's demonslavers attacked the palace. The royal residence was in turmoil, and those Minion warriors remaining were clearly losing the fight. Tristan, Shailiha, Wigg, Abbey, and the bulk of the warrior forces were away, trying to hold off Wulfgar's fleet. Of those able to wield the craft, only Faegan, Celeste, and the acolytes remained behind.

Frantic to help, Vivian and the other sisters had left the Redoubt to go to the aid of the warriors. Vivian had been hurrying toward the door of her chambers when it suddenly opened of its own accord. Strangely, no one stood on the other side. Shaking her head in confusion, she started to leave. That was when Wulfgar materialized before her. The magnificent

Scroll of the Vigors also appeared, hovering gently by his side.

On trembling legs she retreated into the room, almost falling as she stumbled against a nearby chair. The imposing man walked purposefully into the room, the Scroll following him. Without looking back, he caused the door to close. Then Vivian heard the lock turn over, telling her that she was his prisoner.

She had no idea whether the man before her was friend or foe. He was tall, with long, sand-colored hair and commanding hazel eyes. She tentatively decided that, since he had access to the Redoubt and was obviously in possession of the Scroll, he must be some unknown ally of the wizards. She couldn't have been more wrong.

The man smiled at her. His mesmerizing gaze seemed to look right into her soul.

"Who . . . who are you?" she asked.

The man clasped his hands together. "I am Wulfgar," he answered. "I am your new lord."

At the mention of his name, Vivian's blood ran cold. The enemy of the Vigors that everyone was trying to vanquish stood here, in her personal chambers! But why?

Stunned, she took another step back. She tried to speak, but the words wouldn't come. Finally, she found her tongue.

"What do you want of me?" she asked, her voice breaking. "Where are Faegan and Celeste?"

Wulfgar smiled. "I have just come from a meeting with them," he answered. "After the application of some rather inventive persuasion, the wizard finally gave up the hiding place of the scroll. Celeste tried to resist me, and for that she paid dearly."

Vivian's knees buckled and she half-sat, half-stumbled into the chair. Tears welled up in her eyes.

"Are they dead?" she asked.

"The wizard is alive, but very much the worse for wear. As for Celeste, I have no idea. Nor do I care. I do not wish to speak of them. I wish to discuss you and your future in the craft."

"What are you talking about?"

"I have sought you out for a particular purpose," he answered. "You should be honored. Tell me, what is your name? Do not lie, for I shall know."

As if it could somehow grant a modicum of safety, she retreated a bit more into the chair. "Vivian," she answered. "Vivian, of the House of Wentworth."

For a moment Wulfgar searched her face. Then he smiled again.

"As I walked in invisibility through the Redoubt, I searched for unusually gifted blood," he said. "That is what brought me to your door, Vivian. Do you know that the quality of your blood is quite high? Whosoever of the acolytes would become my servant must have the quality of blood equal to the tasks that shall be asked of her. Sister Adrian—your would-be leader—would have been my first choice. But she is already above ground, among the others of your sisterhood. And for obvious reasons, what must be done to turn you to my cause can only occur in private. You are my second choice, Vivian."

As she began to understand Wulfgar's horrible plan, her fear was slowly replaced by anger. She raised an arm and pointed at him. A narrow beam of the craft shot from her fingertips and barreled straight for his heart.

Slowly, Wulfgar smiled and raised one hand. The azure beam crashed against his palm. The beam fizzled, then dripped harmlessly to the floor. Wulfgar lowered his hand.

"Do not try that again, Vivian," he said. "I have taken pains to find you, and my time grows short. Soon I must complete my business with the Orb of the Vigors. I do not wish to kill you, but if you try my patience again, I will not hesitate to do so."

"What do you want of me?"

Wulfgar pursed his lips in thought.

"I believe that my plan for the orb will succeed," he said. "But if for some reason it should not yet I survive the day, I wish to leave someone here who is loyal to my cause. Such a person could be of great help to me in the future. The recently departed son of the *Jin'Sai* knew the value of an alternative plan, should his first one fail. His was to leave the Scrolls of the

Ancients in the base of the Gates of Dawn. This very moment one of them floats by my side, while its mate is safely ensconced elsewhere. So you see, my child, Nicholas' lessons were not lost upon me."

He took another step closer. Vivian cringed.

"The small legacy of the craft that I plan to leave in my wake will be you, my dear," he added.

Wasting no more time, Wulfgar pointed at her and enveloped her in a wizard's warp. She struggled to break free, but it was hopeless.

He walked closer. Placing his hand upon her forehead, he smiled down at her. She tried to scream. She couldn't.

"There, there," he cooed softly. "Do not fear, my child. You are about to receive the greatest of gifts. I shall redeem you from the twisted mire that is the Vigors, and deliver you to the light." Wulfgar closed his eyes. An azure glow surrounded them both.

Exquisite pain coursed through her, and her body jangled like a marionette's, dancing convulsively upon some unseen master's strings. Her blood pounded so hard through her veins that she could hear her own heartbeat. Her eyes rolled back in her head, and foam dripped from one corner of her mouth. The torment was unrelenting and all-encompassing. Finally it stopped. Wulfgar removed his hand from her forehead and the glow disappeared. She was drenched in sweat, but otherwise felt unharmed.

"Rise and face your new lord," he said.

Vivian smiled as she stood up from the chair. She had never before felt so alive. Raising her arms over her head, she stretched her lithe body like a cat. Wulfgar saw that her gaze held nothing but adoration for him.

"Whom do you serve?" he asked.

"Only you, master."

"And which side of the craft do you cherish above life itself?"

"Only the Vagaries."

"Extend one arm. I must be sure of my work. Do not be afraid. I will temporarily enhance your vision, so that you might see what I see."

Vivian held out one arm. Narrowing his eyes, Wulfgar caused a small incision to form in the soft underside of her wrist and a single blood droplet to well from it. The droplet hovered in the air and immediately began to twist itself into her blood signature.

As she watched it revolve before her eyes, Vivian gasped. Her blood signature had been altered. It now tilted slightly to the left, indicating her new proclivity to practice the Vagaries.

Satisfied, Wulfgar caused the blood signature to vanish and the incision to heal. Vivian stared at him with rapt admiration.

"How is this possible, master?" she breathed.

"In truth, I cannot take the credit," Wulfgar answered. "Your conversion was accomplished via a little known but immensely powerful Forestallment, handed down by Failee, Wigg's deceased wife. Ironic, wouldn't you agree?"

Vivian nodded.

Wulfgar explained her new role as his spy here in the Redoubt. He taught her how to mask her blood signature with an image of her old one. He told her who Bratach was, and described his role in their cause. And he taught her how to use the grains of wheat to leave secret messages in the fountain. Satisfied, he had then taken his leave of her to go to the palace roof to confront the Orb of the Vigors.

Wulfgar had not succeeded in polluting the orb that night. But upon reading the first message left for her by Bratach, Vivian had been overjoyed to learn that her new master had survived, and that he would soon return.

Setting aside those memories, Vivian turned another corner to find herself in the roundabout, where the indigo of the coming night played deftly upon the fountain and its dancing waters. She walked to it and sat down upon its edge.

This time she didn't have to wait for the traffic in the roundabout to lessen. There was no one there to see her take the grains of wheat from her pocket, or notice the narrow bands of azure escaping from between her fingers.

The azure slowly died, and Vivian placed her hand into the water.

CHAPTER LIII

AS THE DOOR HINGES CREAKED, TYRANNY REALIZED HER MISTAKE. In their haste to prepare an ambush for the approaching demon-slavers, she and her little band had neglected to drag the dead slavers along with them. The monsters they had killed still lay sprawled across the stone room.

As soon as they opened the door, the arriving demonslavers would surely see their fallen comrades, and any hope for surprise that Tyranny might have had would vanish in a flash.

Tyranny looked desperately at Scars. He grimly shook his head, telling her that it was too late to do anything about it. Swallowing hard, Shailiha raised her sword a bit higher.

Suddenly they heard a slaver call out, from somewhere along the guard path.

"You, there!" the voice shouted. "No rest for your group yet! Get back to your posts and stay on patrol!"

Still as death, the little war party in the stone room waited and listened. Then they heard some grumbling, and the door was pulled shut. The slavers' footsteps retreated into the distance.

Lowering her sword, Tyranny let go of the breath she had been holding. She closed her eyes for a moment. Then she looked over at Shailiha and winked.

Shailiha uncoiled a little and shook her head, but though she tried to scowl, she couldn't hold back a smile.

Placing one finger over her lips, Tyranny cracked open the door and peeked out. Then she shut the door and turned to the others.

"Those slavers are back on patrol," she whispered. "Now is as good a time as any to get going!"

Shailiha shot her a look. "Don't tell me you still mean to take us into the Citadel!"

Tyranny nodded. "Indeed I do! But we can't remain there for as long as I'd hoped. If these dead slavers weren't due to go on duty quite yet, it certainly can't be long from now. Once someone finds these bodies, this whole place is going to erupt. We have to go now!"

She opened the door and cautiously ventured out. The others followed silently. Glancing at the sky, the privateer winced. The clouds had departed, and the three red moons blatantly cast the invaders' dark shadows across the guard path.

Their only option now was to have the Minion warriors fly Tyranny, Shailiha, and Scars down into the courtyard.

K'jarr hoisted Tyranny into his arms. Then he suddenly froze, and his eyes widened. In the haunting moonlight, Tyranny could see the blood draining from his face.

"What are you waiting for?" she whispered urgently.

Letting go with one arm, he pointed out to the ocean. "Look! Perhaps now you'll believe me!"

Twisting around, Tyranny gazed out over the moonlit water, and her own eyes widened in terror and amazement. "Get us out of here right now!" she ordered. "Over the ocean, not down into the courtyard!"

Snapping open his wings, K'jarr took several running steps and launched himself into the air. The others followed.

But as the Minions' shadows rolled across the guard path, one of the distant, patrolling demonslavers saw them. He shouted an alarm. In mere moments the Citadel erupted into pandemonium as armed demonslavers began to pour out of the buildings below.

K'jarr started to carve out a turn that would take them all back to the litter, but Tyranny stopped him.

"No!" she shouted urgently. Removing one arm from around the warrior's neck, she pointed down to the sea. "Take us there! We must see this!"

Obeying at once, K'jarr changed course. As they watched, a large area of the sea roiled and burbled. Then a dark crow's nest broke through the waves. The Black Ships were surfacing.

Amid upheavals of dark seawater, all seven vessels burst from the ocean at once. As one, their black sails snapped open and the warships lurched forward, bounding across the waves.

Her mouth hanging open, all Tyranny could do was to hold on to K'jarr and stare at the vessels, awestruck. K'jarr stopped to hover, and the warriors carrying Scars and Shailiha came up alongside.

Each of the deadly looking vessels was easily five or six times the size of the *Reprise*. White-skinned demonslavers poured over their decks. In her current condition, Tyranny's flagship didn't have a chance of outrunning them, and the privateer knew it.

"Get closer," she ordered.

As she and K'jarr neared, Tyranny got her first glimpse of one of the Black Ships' skeletal captains. He rode the bow of his surging ship, holding on to the rigging with one fleshless arm. His bones were as black as the vessel that carried him. His tattered uniform seemed somehow familiar, but she couldn't place it. His eyes glowed with an eerie green; his teeth were white against the black of his skinless head. The moonlight glinted off the blade of the shiny sword he held aloft.

The nighttime sky began to glow with azure for leagues in every direction, turning night into day. Swiveling her gaze back toward the Citadel, Tyranny squinted against the brilliant light.

Two men and a woman stood on the shore. From this distance Tyranny couldn't identify the obviously pregnant woman in the red gown, or the fellow in the dark blue robe. But she knew the other man—the one in the emerald-green silk jacket and matching trousers. It was Wulfgar.

The *Enseterat*'s arms were raised, the glow streaming from his open hands setting the night sky wildly alight.

Before Tyranny could order K'jarr and the others to flee, Wulfgar pointed in their direction. A narrow beam shot straight at them. Tyranny had never seen a bolt of the craft launched from so far away.

The three warriors scattered frantically, the bolt narrowly missing them. As it roared past, Tyranny could feel its heat and wind tear at her hair and clothing. The force of the blast turned K'jarr over. With Tyranny holding on for dear life, he tumbled nearly fifty meters before stabilizing himself again. Trying to take stock of her surroundings, Tyranny saw that the other warriors still carried their passengers. Blessedly, none of them seemed to have been hurt.

More azure bolts coursed through the air. Tyranny could see that the unknown man and woman were adding their own magic to Wulfgar's. Soon the sky was full of the deadly streaking shafts.

"Get us out of here!" Tyranny screamed. "Back to the litter!"

With Tyranny, Scars, and Shailiha holding on tight, the three warriors turned and flew northwest as fast as their wings could take them. As they put some distance between themselves and the Citadel, the onslaught of azure bolts finally stopped.

Thinking that they might finally be safe, Tyranny sighed in relief. Then she looked down again, and a chill went through her.

The seven Black Ships were chasing them.

The pursuing warships sailed in a straight battle line. Their speed was amazing, but they were not quite able to maintain the pace of the flying warriors, and they slowly lost ground. At first Tyranny was elated. But even Minion warriors would eventually tire, she realized.

The Black Ships remained on course like a pack of dogs following a scent. Then she saw azure again—not in the sky, but upon the sea. The Black Ships were glowing.

She watched in awe as the mighty vessels took on the color of the craft. The aura started at the vessels' sterns, slowly engulfing each ship as it moved toward the bow and replacing black with the most brilliant hue of the craft she had ever seen.

Tyranny had to admit that the vessels were magnificent. She looked over at Shailiha and Scars and saw that they were equally entranced.

Suddenly she heard a great rumbling. Louder and louder it became, until she realized that it was coming from the vessels.

The Black Ships were rising from the water.

At first she thought she was seeing things. She blinked her eyes and looked again, but the scene remained the same. Seawater ran from the ships' bottoms as they rose about ten meters above the waves. Their speed increased. Tyranny looked over at Shailiha. Her face grim, the princess shook her head.

The Black Ships were gaining on them. Tyranny knew that the litter couldn't be far away now. But if she caused it to glow, the ships' captains would surely see it. If the Black Ships destroyed the litter, not only might they lose the remaining Minions, Micah, and the captured slaver, but the enchanted sextant would be lost as well. Worse yet, they still had to return to the *Reprise* well ahead of their pursuers, and Faegan's portal would be leagues away from there, if it opened at all.

Then she remembered something she had so glibly asked all of the others not so long ago, back inside the demonslaver guard-house. If the *Jin'Sai* were here, she wondered, what would *he* do?

Panic gripped her; she had never been so unsure of herself in her life. Turning, she gazed forward and searched for the tiny litter.

Suddenly she remembered the last command in Old Eutracian that Faegan had written down for her. He had told her to use it only in the direst of emergencies, for it would be difficult to control and he couldn't guarantee how long it might last. Now it seemed their only hope. But first they would have to reach the litter well ahead of the Black Ships. Behind them, she could see the dark hulls looming ever closer.

The chase was on.

CHAPTER LIV

AS FAEGAN SAT ALONE IN THE CHILLY, SUBTERRANEAN ROOM, HE pulled the shawl closer around his shoulders. One night and much of the next day had passed since he and his group had been trapped here in Valrenkium, and he could still see no way out of their troubles. The blue-tinted blocks of ice standing against the walls twinkled back at him, only adding to his sense of outrage and disgust.

He had ordered the entire village searched once more. This time, Reznik's cellar had been discovered. Now one of Reznik's handwritten texts lay open in the wizard's lap. He was hoping that he might find notes to guide him in removing the strange stone lattice that entrapped them. So far, he had had no luck.

Faegan was beginning to develop a feel for Reznik and his ways. Like Satine, Reznik was not only ruthless but also an expert in his chosen field. There would have been nothing, Faegan realized, that Reznik would have loved more than to add another insult to the wizard's defeat.

In his haste Reznik had been unable to take everything. It was Faegan's guess that he had hidden much of what remained here in this cellar, where he hoped it wouldn't be found. As Faegan examined the grisly treasures of the craft, he was forced to admit that despite how much he hated what had gone on here, the tools and texts of the Valrenkian's various subdisciplines were fascinating. If Faegan and the warriors could escape this place, he had every intention of taking Reznik's possessions back to the Redoubt for further study.

The wizard sighed. This room—nay, this entire village—was a gigantic shop of horrors. He hadn't seen this much evidence of twisted, secret torture since the Sorceresses' War, and he hoped he would never have to again. Worse yet, he had not succeeded in his goal of wiping out the Valrenkians.

He would give anything to know where these abusers of the craft had fled. He knew that there were greater problems in the realm to worry about, but no matter how long it might take, he would personally hunt down the Corporeals and kill them all. Not only because of their crimes against humanity, but also for their crimes against the craft.

But first he and his warriors had to escape this place.

He frowned as he remembered the old wizards' axiom about survival. Popular during the Sorceresses' War, it was called the Rule of Threes. Even wizards and sorceresses could survive without air for only three minutes, without water for three days, and without food for three weeks. Had he brought the right tools of the craft with him, he might have been able to conjure some food. But as it was, it seemed they were to remain desperately hungry. Fortunately, they had found a working well at one end of the square, so at least they would be spared dying of dehydration.

The stone lattice still spanned the entire village. He didn't dare venture into the trap-filled maze, the only other way out of this madhouse. Some of the warriors had volunteered to brave it, to see if they could make it to the other side. The offer had been tempting, but in the end the wizard's heart couldn't allow it.

But what worried him the most were his fellow members of the Conclave who were no longer in Eutracia—Tristan, Wigg, and Celeste in Parthalon, and Tyranny and Shailiha somewhere out upon the Sea of Whispers. By now they might all desperately need his help to return home, and he couldn't give it.

Finally his frustration got the better of him. In a rare display of anger he threw the text he had been reading across the room. When several of Reznik's macabre bottles shattered, it did his heart good.

"I surrender!" a voice boomed from the other side of the cellar.

Wheeling his chair around, Faegan saw Traax descend the steps. There was an unexpected smile on the warrior's face. Faegan scowled.

"It would be a shame to kill me, wizard, for I bring good news!" Traax said. When he reached the dirt floor, he planted his hands on his hips and his smile widened.

"What is it?" Faegan asked skeptically. His gray-green eyes narrowed. "Don't tell me you've found a way out of this zoo!"

"Perhaps! Abbey, Sister Adrian, and Ottikar have found us! The captured Valrenkian Uther is with them! He must certainly know how to navigate the maze!"

His heart leaping, Faegan tossed the shawl aside, levitated his chair, and sailed up and out of the cellar. Traax quickly followed.

The scene in the square was jubilant. It was midevening, and the torches were lit. The warriors had gathered on one side of the square, and they cheered as they looked up through the stone latticework. Duvessa and Ox beamed at Faegan and Traax as they approached. Looking up, Faegan smiled. He couldn't have hoped for more.

Just beyond the latticework, Abbey and Adrian stood in a Minion litter borne aloft by six stout warriors. The women were smiling broadly. A phalanx of warriors surrounded them, and off to one side, Ottikar and another warrior held Uther between them by his wrists.

Apparently the Valrenkian hadn't been given the comfort of a litter. He dangled precariously, the torchlight showing his face red with anger and embarrassment. The warriors in the village shouted invectives at him, many of them calling for his head. For the first time since entering the village, Faegan smiled.

"This seems a fine mess you've gotten everyone into!" Abbey shouted down at him. Despite the seriousness of the situation she couldn't resist poking some fun at him. "Do you mean to say that even your powers cannot break these stone bars?"

Folding his arms over his chest, Faegan scowled. Levitating his chair he soared as close to Abbey and Adrian's litter as the lattice would allow.

"That's exactly what I mean!" he answered gruffly. Then his face registered concern. "Have you heard from Tristan and Wigg, or Shailiha and Tyranny?"

The women's faces turned grim. "There is no word from them," Abbey answered. "But that does not mean that there is reason for alarm." Then she bit her lower lip and looked down at her hands.

Sensing trouble, Faegan leaned forward and peered through the latticework. "What is it? What aren't you telling me?"

"I am sorry. There is no other way to say it. Lionel the Little is dead."

A hush went over the crowd. Duvessa looked to Traax, who took her hand. Ox raged silently, his face red.

Stunned, Faegan sat back in his chair, staring out at nothing. Then he closed his eyes. First Geldon, he thought, and now Lionel. No one on either side of the stone lattice said a word.

Finally Faegan balled his hands into fists, pounded on the arms of his chair, and opened his eyes. His entire body trembled with fury.

"Satine?" he whispered.

Abbey nodded. "We believe so. We won't be sure until you perform the necropsy. Before we left the palace, Sister Adrian conjured a preservative field around the body. Lionel's symptoms were the same as Geldon's—madness followed by apparent suicide. If it was Satine, she crept right by the Minion guards and somehow poisoned Lionel in his sleep."

Several more moments of silence passed.

"How did he die?" the wizard asked at last.

Abbey took a deep breath. "He hanged himself."

Uther began to laugh out loud. His jaw hardening, Faegan turned his deadly gaze toward the Valrenkian. Ottikar and the other warrior struggled to hold on to the prisoner as pandemonium erupted on both sides of the latticework and several free Minions tried to attack the Valrenkian.

"Stop it!" Faegan shouted. "Don't you see? We need him!"

Realizing that his raspy voice was being drowned out by the incensed warriors, the wizard extended one hand and sent an explosive bolt skyward, shooting between the stone bars. The warriors gradually calmed.

Faegan glared at them, then pointed at Uther.

"We need his knowledge of the maze!" he shouted. Then he leveled his iron gaze on the Valrenkian once more. "But once we are free," he added, "I just might hand him over to you."

Uther sneered haughtily at the wizard. "No, you won't! It's common knowledge that every member of the late Directorate took a vow against murder! Stop bluffing! It will do you no good!"

Faegan's return glare was as cold as ice.

"You're wrong, Corporeal," he growled. "I was never a member of the Directorate. I suffer no such restriction. Your comrades have conspired in the murders of two people I loved very much. If you wish to see another day, I suggest you cooperate."

Stunned, Abbey looked over at Adrian. Neither of them had ever seen the wizard so angry. Would he really kill Uther in cold blood? Abbey decided that it was time to intervene. She removed the parchment from within her robe.

The wizard's eyes narrowed. "What's that?"

Abbey passed it through the bars.

"It's Uther's guide through the sandstone maze," she answered, then she and Adrian explained how they had induced him to draw it for them.

Faegan unrolled the map and examined it, then looked back at the women.

"Well done," he said. "But how do we know it's valid? He may be trying to trick us."

"We believe it to be accurate," Adrian answered. "But we think it best that *you* enter Uther's mind, just to be sure."

Faegan nodded. He looked at the two warriors still dangling Uther in the air. "Hold him tightly," he ordered.

Ottikar gave the other warrior a nod and they put a bit more distance between them, tightening the stretch on Uther's arms. The Valrenkian winced.

"Good," Faegan said. He closed his eyes.

Smiling, Adrian and Abbey waited. Any moment now the Valrenkian's head would snap back and his eyes would widen. And then they would have their answer.

But as the moments went by the women began to wonder, and then to worry. Uther seemed completely unaffected. No azure glow appeared around him, and he continued to smile wickedly at the wizard. Abbey and Adrian turned to each other with concern. Then they looked back at Faegan.

Beads of sweat had broken out along the wizard's brow, and his face clearly showed signs of strain. Finally he let out a long breath and he opened his eyes.

"What's wrong?" Adrian asked.

"I am able to call the spell, but not to use it upon him," Faegan answered.

The women were stunned. "But how can that be?" Abbey asked. "His powers don't begin to rival yours!"

Thinking to himself, Faegan rubbed his face with his hands.

"The two of you must have inadvertently made him immune to the particular set of calculations required to deeply enter his mind," he answered at last.

"How could that be?" Adrian asked.

"Tell me more about this serum that you made," he said to Abbey. "Did you use laurel seed?"

Abbey nodded.

"And mandrake?"

"Of course. You're an expert herbmaster. You know the formula as well as I. I had to recall it from memory, but I think I got it right. It calls for both of those herbs, plus several more."

"It's not your fault—neither of you," Faegan said. He shook his head. "What you didn't know is that when laurel and mandrake are mixed for this purpose, they must never be enhanced with an additional spell of the mind. To do so inures the subject against further such intrusions for all time. Adrian couldn't have known, because she has little or no knowledge of herb-mastery. And Abbey, you didn't know because you are unfamiliar with spells that your partial blood signature lacks the power to employ. Only a full wizard or sorceress who was also an herbmaster would know this. You both have much left to learn, but I commend you for trying."

"I'm sorry," Abbey said.

"Don't be," Faegan answered. "You did what you thought best." He trained his gaze back upon the Valrenkian.

"You knew, didn't you?" he asked.

Uther grinned. "Of course, you old fool! I knew what was going on the moment I saw the beaker of green fluid in your herb-mistress' hands. They obviously needed information, and any herbalist worth his salt knows that the formula for the serum contains both mandrake and laurel. You know as well as I that it's the laurel that gives the solution its distinctive color. And why else would a Sister of the Redoubt be there, too, unless it was to help augment the serum with a spell? I was fully aware of how this combination would inure me. Your servants have given me a gift that I could never have attained on my own. How ironic! I put on quite a show at the time, but I wanted this, wizard—and badly. Your women willingly gave it to me."

Abbey's face grew hard. Her hands were balled up into fists, her knuckles white. Then she thought for a moment, and looked to Faegan.

"Just because you can't enter his mind now, that doesn't mean that at the time of their application our efforts weren't successful, right?" she mused. "In fact, how could they not have been? For all we know, the map might well be genuine."

Faegan nodded. "Or a complete fabrication," he warned.

Traax stepped forward. "There's one way to find out!" he said harshly. "Leave me alone with this animal! I'll get the truth out of him!"

Swiveling around in his chair, Faegan looked at Traax. He knew that the warrior meant well, but he obviously hadn't thought his plan through.

"Don't you see?" the wizard asked softly. "That won't do any good."

"And just why not?" Traax demanded. He glared hatefully up

through the stone bars at Uther. "Just give me the chance. We Minions have many ways of being persuasive, I assure you."

"Oh, I'm quite sure that you do," Faegan answered. "And I can think of nothing just now that would give me greater pleasure. But tell me, no matter how he answers, how will you know—really know—it's the truth?"

Traax scowled. "I see your point." He sighed. "But surely there must be something we can do."

"There is," Abbey said.

Faegan smiled, for he already knew the answer. "Tell us."

"We fly around to the entrance, and we force *Uther* to lead us through," she answered. She looked over at Sister Adrian. "That was the other reason I brought him—in case all else failed."

"Well done," Faegan said. He looked at Traax again.

"I think we have no choice but to accept those volunteers of yours," he said. "They will, of course, have to come from the other side of the lattice. Limit their number to two. Uther is unable to use the craft, so only physical restraint is needed. I will keep the map with me. Tell your volunteers to make a mark on the wall at every turn." Then he grinned at the Valrenkian.

"What say you, Uther?" he asked sarcastically. "Are you game for a little walk?"

Seething, the Valrenkian snarled something under his breath. The wizard only smiled.

"I'll take that as a yes," he said.

He turned back to Abbey and Adrian. "Ask for two Minion volunteers from your side of the lattice," he ordered. "Once you have sent them in with Uther, come to the top of the bluffs near the maze opening on our side. We will meet you there, to wait and watch. Then it will be out of our hands."

As Abbey's group started to soar away, the wizard lowered his chair to the ground. Duvessa, Traax, and Ox walked over. Duvessa placed one hand upon the old wizard's shoulder.

"Is this really going to work?" she asked.

Faegan sighed. "It has to," he answered. "Because if it doesn't we're going to be here for a very long time."

As a group, the warriors and the wizard headed for the dark, square-cut portal in the bluffs.

CHAPTER LV

"ARE YOU QUITE SURE YOU WISH ... TO GO ALONE?" ALRIK asked. Trying to steady himself, he placed a meaty hand against the wall. Screwing up his face, he blinked. It was all he could do to remain standing. He let go a wet belch, then wiped his mouth with the back of one hand. Despite the fact that he had just been rude in the presence of the First Wizard, he laughed a little—something he would have never done had he been sober.

Wigg couldn't be angry with him. The impromptu feast that had been arranged in celebration of Tristan and Celeste's marriage had gone on for hours, and every Minion and Gallipolai stationed in and around the Recluse had gladly attended. Alrik had given a drunken toast that seemed to go on forever.

Tristan, Celeste, Wigg, and Jessamay had sat at the table of honor, and gifts had been presented to the bride and groom. For a time, at least, the dancing, drinking, and feasting had provided a welcome respite from their troubles. It was now nearly midnight, and everyone was asleep save for Wigg, Alrik, and a complement of patrolling—and sober—warriors.

"Don't worry, I'll be fine," Wigg answered. "I see you brought what I asked for."

Alrik nodded. After fumbling about, he clumsily produced the empty canteen. He put its strap around Wigg's neck, then smiled stupidly again. Another fragrant belch followed. Wigg winced.

"I can't understand why you want to go back down there alone, Wirst Fizard," he said numbly. "And with an empty canteen, of all things."

Wigg gave him a wink. "Wirst Fizard's business," he said. "I should be back before the *Jin'Sai* and his new bride awaken. If anyone asks, tell them the truth—that I went for a walk. When I return, the three of us will need an escort back to Master Faegan's portal. We must arrive there by high noon, when it is due to open."

Alrik tried to click his heels, but almost fell down. Clutching at Wigg's robe, he did his best to straighten up. His breath was awful. Wigg averted his face.

"I live to serve," Alrik said.

Turning awkwardly, the warrior walked back down the hall. The wizard smiled as he heard Alrik begin to belt out yet another Minion drinking song. The singing soon faded away.

Wigg pointed one hand toward the dark passageway and brought the radiance stones to light. Then he reached under his robe to make sure that the rolled-up parchment was still there.

He was tired, and the walk down and back would be a long one. He didn't relish going but knew it had to be done. The idea had come to him during the celebration. He wanted to take something of this place back to Eutracia with him, something that he thought would be of help—especially if things were about to become as serious as he feared. Taking a deep breath, he started down.

He was very pleased that Tristan and Celeste had married. But his heart was troubled over his daughter's worsening condition. He could see the changes rapidly taking place, and it was breaking his heart.

He had much to worry him. Jessamay had told him all she knew about the Well of Forestallments, but it wasn't much. The two of them had pored over parts of Failee's grimoire to learn the secret of Jessamay's altered blood signature, an aberration they were sure was of immense importance to the craft. And in his heart he was equally sure that the Orb of the Vigors continued its rampage across Eutracia. He could only hope that Faegan and the other members of the Conclave were having a better time of things.

He shook his head. It was all such a great riddle—the craft, Eutracia, Parthalon, the two orbs, and most certainly the possibility of Wulfgar's survival. Some of these puzzles were new, and some far, far older than he. He had already lived for more than three hundred years, been instrumental in the victory in the Sorceresses' War, and personally overseen the births of the *Jin'Sai* and the *Jin'Saiou*. Even so, sometimes he felt much more like a pawn in this amazing confluence of riddles than he did a figure of any great importance.

He finally reached the bottom of the stairs and crossed the first room. The silence was deafening. He stopped in the second room and looked around. He was relieved to see that everything was as he hoped it would be.

He produced the parchment and read aloud the incantation recorded on it in Old Eutracian, copied from Failee's grimoire.

A haunting azure cloud began to form in the air before him. When he finished the recitation, he rolled up the parchment and put it away.

Closing his eyes for a moment, the First Wizard took a deep breath. This would have to be done very carefully. He removed the canteen from around his neck.

The cloud beside him, Wigg set about his work.

CHAPTER LVI

"BIND HIS HANDS," ABBEY ORDERED. "WE CAN'T AFFORD TO TRUST him."

She looked respectfully at the two Minion warriors who had volunteered to enter the maze with the Valrenkian. Many had stepped forward; choosing two who might well be going to their deaths in the maze had not been a pleasant task. She hadn't been around their race for long, but she knew one thing for certain: the Minion warriors—both the males and the females—were the bravest, most selfless souls she had ever encountered.

Sister Adrian stood next to her before the entrance to the bluffs. Wall torches lit the hall into the maze, their combined glow streaming out of the square-cut entrance and into the night. The Minion phalanx that had accompanied the two women to Valrenkium stood nearby, watching, alert.

One of the warriors bound Uther's hands behind him. The Valrenkian seethed quietly.

When Abbey was satisfied that Uther was bound securely, she called for an unlit torch. A warrior came running with one and she handed it to the first of the volunteers.

"The torches in the maze are supposedly enchanted to burn forever," she said, "and Uther cannot use the craft. But take this along, just in case. Do you have flint and steel?"

The warrior nodded.

"Then it's time to go. Faegan and your fellow troops await you on the other side. Don't forget to make a distinct mark on the wall at every turn." She gently touched each Minion on the arm. "May the Afterlife be with you both."

The two volunteers nodded. With a dark smile, the first drew his dreggan and placed the tip against Uther's back.

"Move," he ordered gruffly.

But Uther turned to look at Abbey and Adrian. "Goodbye, you bitches of the Vigors," he snarled. "When we meet in the Afterlife, beware of me. I'll be waiting."

Abbey hesitated for a moment. Uther's words were unsettling—even more, she thought, than he intended them to be—but there could be no turning back now.

"If for any reason he refuses to do as he's told, kill him," she told the warriors.

The one holding the dreggan nodded. Then he poked Uther in the back, and the three of them entered the maze.

Abbey and Adrian walked to the entrance and watched the Valrenkian and the warriors grow smaller as they headed down the wide, high tunnel. When they arrived at the first intersection, Uther turned right. Nothing happened. The warrior without the sword used his dagger to mark the wall, and all three disappeared around the corner.

Adrian looked anxiously over at the herbmistress. "Is this really going to work?" she asked.

Abbey shook her head. "I have no idea. But it's too late to second-guess ourselves now." She cast her gaze toward the litter nearby. "Time for us to go back to Faegan," she said. Then she thought for a moment.

"Leave a dozen warriors here," she ordered Ottikar. "If Uther should somehow come back out the way he went in, I want him intercepted."

Ottikar clicked his heels. "As you wish," he answered.

Abbey and Adrian got into the litter. From where they sat they could hear Ottikar relaying Abbey's orders. Twelve warriors stepped forward to guard the entrance to the maze.

Bearers took up the litter and lifted it into the night sky. As the rest of the phalanx took flight, Ottikar led everyone back to the opposite side of the bluffs.

THE WARRIOR HOLDING THE SWORD TO UTHER'S BACK WAS NAMED Agrippa; the other was Flavius. They had been following the Valrenkian for nearly an hour, and so far everything had been quiet. Uther had not turned around or spoken since they had entered the tunnel, and he had successfully negotiated more than a dozen intersections. Flavius had marked the wall at each turn.

It was deathly silent here, the only sound that of their boot heels echoing against the cold sandstone floor. The enchanted wall torches were spaced about every twenty meters and gave off a deceivingly welcoming glow. As he wondered how many more intersections might await them, Agrippa shook his head. Asking the Valrenkian would do no good, for lying was his way of life.

As the three of them approached another intersection, Uther paused and looked around. There were seven different tunnels to choose from this time. Each branched off in a different direction, their torchlight enticing the travelers to enter.

Uther finally made his choice and began walking down one of the tunnels. The warriors held their breath. Nothing happened. Agrippa gave Flavius a nod, and they continued on.

"WHAT'S TAKING THEM SO LONG?" ADRIAN ASKED. FROM HER place atop the bluffs she looked down through the latticework at Faegan. "Do you think something has happened?"

Taking a deep breath, the wizard shook his head. "I can't be sure, but I doubt it," he answered. "I think that if the craft were to strike them, it would by necessity be strong enough that we would either hear what was happening or see flashes of azure. As for how long it is taking, remember that they are walking a maze. By definition a maze takes much longer to traverse than if one were simply walking in a straight line. We must be patient."

Faegan rubbed his face with both hands. He was trying his best not to show it, but he was worried. If the Valrenkian failed them in negotiating the maze, how could the accuracy of his map be trusted?

It was nearly midnight, and the cloudless sky was filled with countless tiny stars. Other than when someone spoke, the only sounds were the calls of the various night creatures. Faegan found the stillness and the waiting frustrating.

Shifting in his chair, he sighed and looked up at Duvessa. Smiling as best she could, she placed one hand upon the ancient wizard's shoulder.

FLAVIUS AND AGRIPPA WALKED SIDE BY SIDE BEHIND UTHER. AGRIPPA still held his sword, while Flavius clutched his dagger and the unlit torch. Two more hours had passed, during which Uther had successfully navigated at least eighteen more intersections. Since they had entered the maze, he had neither turned around, nor spoken to them. At every turn, Flavius had dutifully marked the walls.

Every new tunnel looked just like the last. *Of course they do,* Agrippa thought. *They were meant to. This worthless bastard could be leading us in circles, for all we know.*

Another intersection loomed up ahead; it looked to be the largest one yet. When they reached it, they saw that fifteen separate tunnels led away from it. Where the other intersections had been confusing, this one was totally overwhelming.

Uther turned to face them. He had the same haughty look on his face that he had given Adrian and Abbey. Ever alert, Agrippa widened his stance and raised the tip of his sword.

"This is the last of the intersections," Uther announced softly. "The exit is only a short walk from here down the correct tunnel." He smiled at Agrippa. "Choose one."

The warrior scowled. "What are you talking about?"

"I no longer care to live. As a farewell gesture I grant you the right to choose, because both of you are about to die with me."

The two warriors looked around warily. Nothing had

changed. The place remained deathly silent. The wall torches still burned softly.

Agrippa gave Uther a hard look. "I cannot choose," he said. "You alone can lead us to safety. The wizard Faegan has ordered it."

"Ah, but Faegan is not here. The wizard of the Vigors cannot help you now." One corner of Uther's mouth came up in a sneer. "Don't you see? No one can save you except me, and I choose not to." Then he took a long breath, and he seemed to make up his mind.

"Very well," he finally said. "If you want me to select a tunnel, I will. It's all the same, anyway. But you won't be happy with my choice." He gave them another strange look.

"Farewell," he said. Uther turned and ran down one of the tunnels as fast as he could.

The warriors immediately gave chase. When they caught up to him, Flavius dropped the torch, grabbed the Valrenkian by the neck, and threw him to the floor. Without the use of his hands to break his fall, Uther went down hard. It looked like his right forearm was broken. But instead of crying out in pain, he only laughed. Flavius pulled him roughly to his feet.

"Are you crazy?" the warrior growled. "Keep going! Trying to escape us will do you no good!"

When Uther looked back at them, there was victory in his eyes.

"You fools!" he said. "Don't you see? There is no escape. The process has already begun. And as I told your herbmistress and your acolyte, even I do not know what form it shall take."

Almost as soon as Uther had finished speaking, the shrieking began. At first it was soft and distant, coming from somewhere down the tunnel. Then it increased in volume. A strange cross between the sound of a woman screaming and the wind rising from the worst possible storm, the noise quickly flooded the passageway. A ferocious wind erupted and tore down the tunnel. Its force nearly knocked them down.

The wind extinguished the wall torches, and darkness descended. Flavius reached for his flint and steel to light the torch he had brought. But even if he could have struck a flame, it would have been unnecessary, for the passageway was soon bathed in a different kind of glow. From the far end of the tunnel, three balls of azure light careered toward them.

As they raced toward Flavius, Agrippa, and Uther, their light grew in intensity. They were each about half as tall as a fully grown man, and jagged bolts of white light careened to and fro within their depths. The closer they got, the louder they shrieked, and the wind intensified to the point that Uther and the warriors could barely stand. Then the rushing lights began to change.

The fireballs had morphed into demonic faces, with dark blue slanted eyes and mouths full of long, pointed teeth. As they sped down the tunnel, the awful mouths opened wider. Screeching and howling, the first of them took Uther up in its jaws.

It bit into him at his waist and picked him up as if he weighed nothing. As the thing's teeth crunched powerfully down into flesh and bone, Uther screamed. With savage, grunting sounds, the thing shook him back and forth as if he were a rag doll, then began to crash him against solid rock. Uther's head split open, and the demon dropped his corpse to the floor. Uther's blood dripped lazily from its mouth.

The beast looked at the two warriors, and let go a deranged laugh. Then it turned to look at the two other faces that waited there. As if giving its permission, it smiled. In a flash, the other demons set upon the Minions.

Flavius and Agrippa frantically swung their swords, but to no avail. The razor-sharp blades of their dreggans passed harmlessly through the monsters. The demons opened their glowing jaws and ravaged Flavius and Agrippa in the same manner they had Uther. Soon the tunnel floor was awash in blood, and three mangled bodies lay still in the puddles.

Their task complete, the demonic faces streaked back the way they had come. With their passing, the shrieking and the wind stopped, and the wall torches came alive again.

WHEN FAEGAN HEARD THE TERRIBLE SOUND AND SAW THE AZURE light flashing within the tunnel, he knew that something had gone terribly wrong.

"Everyone to either side of the entrance!" he shouted to the Minions crowded around him. "Hurry—your lives depend on it!"

But for many of them it was already too late. There was a terrible shrieking sound, and then three azure energy balls rushed out of the tunnel. Those troops that couldn't get out of the way were vaporized instantly.

After careening around the area for a few moments, the balls slowed and then vanished altogether. Faegan looked around. The occasional smoking boot or blackened dreggan was all that remained of many who had followed him here. The stench of burning flesh hung in the air. Closing his eyes for a moment, the ancient wizard hung his head.

Then his wizard's mind started working again, and he came to a stark realization. *How could I have been so blind?* he thought.

As he expected, the ground began to shake. It started gently at first, but it quickly grew to such intensity that the village's buildings started to collapse. The surviving warriors could barely stand. The wind began to howl, sending dirt and debris whirling into the air, blinding them all.

Thunder rumbled over the earth and lightning cascaded across the sky. To the Minions who had never experienced this phenomenon, it seemed that the world was about to end.

As the bluffs shook, the connecting stone latticework that had trapped Faegan and his warriors began to crack. The cracks grew quickly, snaking through the stone web and breaking it apart. Tons of certain death rained down upon the warriors.

Hoping to save as many of the Minions as possible, Faegan raised his hands.

CHAPTER LVII

"If the Jin'Sai's blood can truly be healed, and he and the Enseterat do endowed battle over the future of the orb, Faegan and I fear that tremendous, previously un-known forces will be unleashed. To our knowledge, a conflict of such massive proportions has never taken place upon the earth. In fact, Faegan believes that this

may have an effect upon the craft that will not be within our power to repair. . . ."

—FROM THE PRIVATE DIARIES OF WIGG,
FIRST WIZARD OF THE CONCLAVE
OF THE VIGORS

HER ARMS CLAMPED FIRMLY AROUND K'JARR'S NECK, TYRANNY looked back at the Black Ships pursuing them. Their dark sails full, they flew above the sea like huge birds of prey, ungainly but unbelievably swift. The sun would be up soon, and the privateer desperately wondered how long the Minions could keep up the blistering pace—especially with herself, Scars, and Shailiha in their arms. She knew that if they were ordered to do so, the fiercely loyal warriors would fly until their hearts burst.

But the craft is stronger than any Minion, she reminded herself as the wind tore at her. If they didn't reach the litter with at least a little time to spare, they wouldn't have a chance.

She looked over at Scars. He was being carried by Lan, who was having a harder time of it due to the first mate's great size. The warrior was clearly spent, every motion of his wings seeming to be another desperate effort to simply stay aloft. Scars and Lan would be the first to perish, Tyranny knew.

As for Scars, his expression told her that he was resigned to whatever fate awaited him. Since the day they had first met, he had always said that his life would end in a cold, watery grave. Closing her eyes, Tyranny hoped that this would not be that day.

Beside herself with worry, she turned away. Scars had been by her side since the earliest days of her father's fishing fleet—long before she had turned privateer, and even before she had vowed to hunt down the demonslavers that had killed both of her parents, and abducted her only brother. Scars had been with her during every decision, every battle, and every storm at sea. She couldn't imagine being without him.

Even more important, she and her little band had certain proof that Wulfgar still lived. *We have to make it home somehow,* she thought. *We simply have to. It can't just end here, over these cold, faceless waves.*

Just as Tyranny was about to give in and cause the litter to glow, Crevin cried out. Taking one arm away from Shailiha, he pointed out over the sea. At first Tyranny couldn't see anything. And then, suddenly, there it was.

To the northwest the lifesaving litter bobbed up and down peacefully. To her delight, she saw Micah was standing up in it and waving frantically, trying to get their attention. Tyranny couldn't see the captured demonslaver that Micah had carried away from the Citadel. But since the warrior had made it back, it was probably safe to assume that the slaver was in the litter with him.

K'jarr immediately adjusted his course. Tyranny looked back to see that the Black Ships were gaining on them. Reaching beneath her jacket, she nervously fingered the parchment hidden there. This was going to be a very close-run thing. She placed her lips to K'jarr's ear.

"Get everyone into the litter as fast as you can, and keep them there!" she ordered. "Under no circumstances are you to fly back and try to attack those ships! We *must* escape!"

K'jarr nodded and adjusted his angle of flight to start down. Once he was sure the other two were right behind, he folded his wings back and dove down into a nearly vertical free fall.

As the ocean rushed toward her, Tyranny was sure that she was about to die. The wind tore by her so fast that she could barely see, and she couldn't begin to understand how K'jarr might recover from his suicidal dive in time. Then she heard his dark wings snap open and felt his strong shoulders move up and down as he buffeted the sea air.

They were the first pair to half land, half crash their way into the litter. K'jarr had brought them down swift and hard. Tyranny was dazed but unhurt. The other two pairs came down in the same fashion. As Tyranny's head cleared, she saw the still unconscious slaver lying on the floor. The litter was cramped with all of them in it at the same time, but it couldn't be helped.

Tyranny snatched her spyglass from the floor, raised it to her face, and twisted the last cylinder. As the Black Ships came into focus, her mouth fell open.

With the dawn sun now glinting off them, the Black Ships looked even more ominous. The seven of them approached fast, each of their skeletal captains standing proudly in their bows, eager to begin the fight. They were so close now that as she looked through the glass, she could almost count the gold buttons on the captains' tattered waistcoats. Lowering the glass, she looked at Shailiha. There was no time to lose.

"Find the sextant and the map!" she ordered. For a few irretrievable moments, Shailiha scrabbled about in the litter. Then she found the items and handed them over.

The princess knew exactly what Tyranny meant to do. Before they had departed, Faegan had instructed them both regarding the spells and given a duplicate parchment to the princess. Tyranny was in charge of this seagoing mission, but if she were killed or incapacitated, Shailiha was to take over command and employ the necessary spells to see them all safely home. The princess was also fully aware of why Tyranny hadn't employed this last, desperate spell on the way here. It would have given them away. Now, that didn't matter.

Tyranny pulled the parchment out of her jacket. She scanned the list of incantations and found the one Faegan said they should employ only as a last resort. There were three shorter but equally important inscriptions listed just below the longer one.

Looking back to the east, she saw that the Black Ships were nearly upon them. This would be their last chance and it had to work. She gave Shailiha a questioning glance, and the princess nodded anxiously.

"You can do it!" Shailiha shouted. "I know you can! But do it *now*!"

Hoping against hope, Tyranny read the longest incantation aloud. The litter began to glow with the craft and rise from the sea.

But as it ascended it started to twirl violently. Tyranny was thrown hard against one of the warriors, and her sextant and map fell to the floor. Struggling to focus, she read the next passage aloud. To her utter amazement the litter stopped spinning.

They had risen only to about the height of the Black Ships' oncoming mainsails. Demonslavers swarmed over the enemy decks, shouting at them and brandishing their swords. They were so close now that Tyranny could see the eerie glow pouring from the captain's angry eye sockets.

"Hurry!" Shailiha screamed.

Tyranny read the second passage aloud as fast as she could. The sextant and the map started to glow. The map unfolded itself and hovered in the air. The sextant took its readings from the sun, then a beam of light shot from it to the map. The beam burned a direct course from their current position back to the *Reprise*.

Tyranny was about to recite the last of the incantations when she heard the unmistakable sounds of swordplay. She turned to look, and her breath caught in her lungs.

Their litter was literally bumping up against the mainmast of one of the Black Ships, and the demonslavers in the rigging were hacking relentlessly at Scars, Shailiha, and the three warriors. More slavers were climbing up, and it would be only seconds now before all was lost.

Scars reached out and grabbed one of the slavers by the arm. He gave it a short twist and broke it. Wasting no time, he tore the creature away from the rigging and threw him down to the deck. The screaming slaver hit hard, head first.

The rest of Tyranny's group was fighting wildly with their swords. But for every slaver that they cut down, two more rose to take his place. The glowing litter swung wildly back and forth, banging uncontrollably into the Black Ship's mainmast and threatening to send its occupants tumbling out at any moment. Several of the slavers began to swing shiny grappling hooks. Fighting the temptation to draw her sword, Tyranny looked back at the parchment and read the next incantation.

The litter shot higher into the sky. Finally free of the Black Ship's mainmast and rigging, it spun around to face northwest. Then it sped off, the amazing force of its momentum throwing all of the occupants crashing backward. Somehow, the sextant and the map stubbornly remained in place near the middle of the litter, guiding it on its way. Fighting the force of the oncoming wind, the exhausted passengers began to claw their way back to their seats.

Sheathing her sword, Shailiha looked over at Tyranny. Her face and arms were splattered with blood, but she was unhurt. Micah and K'jarr had suffered superficial wounds. Striving to work against the wind, Crevin did what he could to tend to them.

The two women looked east, back toward the Black Ships. To their relief the ships were already little more than dark bumps on the horizon. The privateer and the princess smiled at each other.

Tyranny looked down at the demonslaver still lying unconscious on the floor of the litter. Then she turned her gaze northwest again toward where the *Reprise* circled, awaiting their return. It would be good to feel the ship's sturdy, shifting decks beneath her boots again.

Suddenly she thought of the *Jin'Sai. We have what you sent us for,* she thought. *But how will you receive the news of your half brother?* Too tired for words, Tyranny closed her eyes and laid her head against the sidewall of the litter. As she did, the sun rose in earnest, bringing with it the promise of a beautiful day.

CHAPTER LVIII

DAX AND THE TWO WARRIORS FLYING ESCORT ON EITHER SIDE of him were glad to see the sunrise. They had flown throughout the cold, cloudless night; the sun would bring welcome warmth to their wings and to the air that filled their lungs. As the morning light improved, Dax looked down to get his bearings.

He was relieved to see that they were still on course. They were flying south, following the Sippora River, and were about halfway to Tammerland. Dax had left camp far later than he would have liked, as there had been important matters to attend to. Rufio had been well liked, and his fellow warriors had taken his death hard—especially since there had been no body to immolate. Dax's first order of business had been to oversee an impromptu memorial service in the slain warrior's honor.

He then told his troops about the azure wall barring the entrance to the pass and he assigned a group of warriors to watch over it. If it changed in any way, they were to report it at once. He also assigned fresh troops to monitor the orb and issued them identical orders. According to the latest report, the deadly sphere, having created the new pass, had turned south again, still hemorrhaging golden energy. Where it would go from there was anyone's guess.

It had been the dead of night by the time Dax had been ready to depart for Tammerland to make a report to the *Jin'Sai* and his wizards. As the only living warrior who had seen the azure wall, he felt it was his duty to make the report personally.

The young Minion captain stole a few moments to close his bloodshot eyes against the wind. The respite felt wonderful. He had been awake for nearly thirty-six hours, and he was exhausted. Bowing to the inevitable, he opened his eyes again and looked down to make sure that the Sippora was still below them.

To make his group a little warmer, he led them to a lower altitude. As his view of the river improved, his eyes narrowed. *I must be seeing things,* he thought. He blinked, but the scene remained the same. To his utter amazement, the normally mighty Sippora had turned black and looked as thick as tar. Its banks teemed with refugees and loaded-down beasts of burden, all walking south along either side of the river. The crowds seemed to stretch on forever. They weren't simply fleeing, Dax realized. They were moving permanently, and it seemed that they were all on their way to Tammerland.

Stunned, Dax quickly signaled to his warriors, and the three of them soared down to take a closer look.

There were no major cities in this part of Eutracia, but the Sippora's fertile banks were lined with small farming villages. The water table was notoriously low here, and wells had never been a viable option. But that had never mattered, because for centuries the majestic river and its hundreds of tributaries— supplied by the glacial runoff from the Tolenkas—had easily provided all the water these peaceful farmers could use, both for drinking and for irrigation. It had also granted excellent fishing and trapping, and its fast-moving branches could always be relied upon to turn the waterwheels that milled the farmers' hard-won grain. But now all that had changed.

Dax thought for a moment. If he and his escort swooped closer, he knew that they would frighten the people. But it couldn't be helped. He simply had to know more. Using hand signals, he ordered his warriors down. Buffeting the air with their dark wings, they came to land on the western bank of the river.

As the Minions set down, citizens screamed, scattering with their burdened animals as fast as they could. Dax had harbored a slight hope that he might speak with some of them. But it was clear that he wouldn't get the chance.

Accompanied by his warriors, he walked closer to the river and looked down.

The once beautiful Sippora had become a terrible sight. The water—if one could still call it that—had turned black. As thick as molasses, it moved at about one-third of its normal speed. At first its soft, pliable surface seemed unbroken. But occasionally it would crack open, hiss noisily, then send pent-up energy high into the air.

The Minions could easily feel the damaged river's intense heat, and see the steam that rose from it. Then the Sippora's awful stench reached them. It smelled like a cross between rotting fish and human waste. Everything the river touched, it turned black; the ground on either bank was scorched for quite some distance. In places where the banks had been dry, grass fires had ignited. Many still burned.

The river looked like death itself. Nothing could live in that, Dax thought. But what had caused this horror? Suddenly he understood.

The energy spraying from the ruptured orb had polluted the river, he realized. During the darkness of their night flight, he and his warriors hadn't been able to tell the difference. But in the light of day it was clear that the river's toxic flow was headed straight for Tammerland. When the stinking, super-heated mass finally reached the capital, the entire city would go up in flames.

Dax made up his mind. He looked over at one of his fellow warriors and he pointed to the river.

"Arius, see if you can take a sample of whatever that is," he ordered. "If possible, I want to take some of it back to the wizards. But be careful."

The warrior named Arius clicked his heels. He took up his water flask from one hip. Standard issue for each warrior, the flask was made of metal and had a leather strap. After dumping out its water, Arius walked to the river's edge.

The overpowering heat and stink nearly made him faint. He opened the flask and touched it to the top of the black, slowly moving mass. The flask began to hiss and melted away immediately; the strap burst into flames. Jumping back, Arius realized he had been lucky not to lose his hand.

As Arius walked back, Dax shook his head. Opening his own flask, he took a generous gulp of water, then handed it to Arius to replace the one that the river had just destroyed.

"I want you to fly back to camp and report this," Dax ordered him. "Tell the warriors to gather water only from the glaciers. Under no circumstances are they to approach the Sippora. Go now."

Arius clicked his heels again. "As you wish," he answered. He took several running steps and launched himself into the air. Climbing quickly, he turned northwest, back toward the camp. Soon he was merely a speck in the sky. Then he was gone.

As Dax looked back at the river, the refugees filed grimly past him and his remaining escort; their expressions cautious and hateful, they gave the warriors a wide berth. Many of them were wounded—either by the orb, Dax assumed, or by the strangely mutated waters of the Sippora. Some were hurt so badly that he doubted they would live to see Tammerland.

He shook his head. Tammerland was about to become a living nightmare. For a brief moment he wondered whether the refugees would blame this new calamity on the *Jin'Sai* as well.

There was nothing more the two warriors could do here. Dax nodded to his escort, and they both took to the air. As the Minion captain gained altitude, he cast his gaze southeast, down the length of the steaming, stinking river.

Even from this height, the refugees lined its banks for as far as the eye could see.

CHAPTER LIX

DEEP INSIDE THE REDOUBT, TRISTAN SAT ONCE AGAIN AT THE IN-laid table in the ornate meeting room. His dreggan and his sheath of knives hung over the back of his chair. Around him were the other members of the Conclave, a circle of long, discouraged faces.

The prince, Wigg, Celeste, and Jessamay had returned to Eutracia the previous day by way of Faegan's portal, which the wizard had been able to reopen once he had returned from Valrenkium. Tyranny's enchanted litter had finally reached the *Reprise* and then the group had eventually found the portal Faegan created for them. The return trip had been even harder on the privateer's already mangled flagship. Minion carpenters and Tyranny's crewmen were already hard at work to get her seaworthy again, but it would not be an easy job. The captured demonslaver they had brought back with them sat bound in a chair in another room, guarded by watchful Minions.

Exhausted and disheartened, Tristan wiped his face with his hands, then grabbed his wine goblet and took a drink. They had all been talking for a long time and it wasn't over yet. By now they had all told their various stories to one another, but they had come to no conclusions about what to do next.

Failee's grimoire of tooled red leather lay on the table before Tristan. He knew that Faegan was eager to plumb its depths, but so far the ever-curious wizard had managed to contain himself.

Tyranny sat on Tristan's left. Beside her sat Wigg and Abbey. Faegan—still wearing the Paragon around his neck—was next to Abbey. Adrian, Traax, and Shailiha rounded out the company. Everyone seemed unharmed, save for Traax, whose left arm was in a sling due to the dislocated shoulder he had suffered when some of the falling latticework struck him. Celeste sat

quietly on the prince's right. The toddler Morganna sat nearby
on the floor, gurgling and batting at some toys. Jessamay occupied what had been Geldon's chair, in between Celeste and
Shailiha.

Tristan still couldn't believe that the hunchbacked dwarf was
dead. Geldon had proved a good friend—staunch, loyal, and incredibly brave—and his death had left a hole in all their hearts
that would be a long time healing. Tristan hadn't known Lionel
the Little particularly well, but he knew the diminutive herbmaster would be sorely missed, especially by Faegan.

Faegan had told everyone of the assassin Satine: how she had
managed to breach the palace walls, do her dirty work, and then
brazenly walk right out again—or so they surmised. The prince
was stunned not only by her creativity, but also by her daring
and her skill. As he thought of her, his fingers tightened around
the wine goblet. It would be pointless to search for her now, just
as it would serve no purpose to scour Eutracia for the displaced
Valrenkians. Shifting his thoughts back to the present, he
looked over at Tyranny and Shailiha.

"You're both sure that it was Wulfgar you saw?" he asked.

Tyranny and Shailiha nodded.

"He was standing on the shore," the privateer said. "There
was a woman by his side. She looked pregnant, but I couldn't
swear to that. Another man stood there, as well. He wore the traditional dark blue robe of a consul. Far more demonslavers
guard the Citadel and crew Wulfgar's Black Ships than we ever
knew existed. I'm also sorry to say that a substantial demonslaver fleet still exists, patrolling the waters around the island."

Tristan sat back in his chair. For some time now he had suspected that Wulfgar might still be alive. He could even accept
Tyranny's report about the remaining demonslaver fleet. But he
was having a very hard time believing what the privateer and his
sister had just told them all about the Black Ships. Had anyone
else been spinning this tale, he would have thought them mad.

"You say that these vessels can not only run submerged, but
also fly above the waves?" he asked. "And that they are not only
crewed by demonslavers, but commanded by skeletons in tattered military uniforms?"

"That's right," Shailiha said. She shook her head, as though she couldn't believe it herself. "You simply have to believe us, Tristan. We saw what we saw. We were lucky to get away with our lives."

For the first time that day, the prince smiled.

"I believe you," he answered. Then he turned to Wigg. "First you mention the Black Watch, and now come the Black Ships. I'd say there's more than just a passing coincidence in the choice of names here, wouldn't you?"

"Indeed, First Wizard," Faegan chimed in. As was usually the case when he knew that he had Wigg in an uncomfortable position, Faegan's eyes lit up. "I'd say you have some explaining to do."

Wigg laced his fingers together. "The Black Ships once sailed in the service of the Directorate," he said at last. "They were the maritime branch of the Black Watch during the Sorceresses' War. Jessamay captained one of the vessels for a time. All of the captains were accomplished wizards or sorceresses whom we trusted implicitly. Like the Black Watch, the ships were manned by handpicked civilians. Some of those civilians were of endowed blood, although they were not trained in the craft." Pausing, Wigg looked around the table. When no one spoke, he went on.

"Failee had begun to form an armada of her own, and we needed to be able to strike back at her on the sea. The war was going poorly, the Coven's land forces advancing rapidly from the west. Tammerland was quickly becoming a fortress, its walls bursting with refugees. Famine and disease threatened. Worse yet, if the Coven gained control of the coast, they would be able to launch troops from their vessels, and we would suddenly be fighting a war on two fronts. We conjured the Black Ships to hold her off. The Tome had only recently been discovered, and the calculations for the vessels' conjuring were found within its pages. As the leader of the Directorate I oversaw not only the Black Watch, but also the Black Ships." He sighed and glanced at Jessamay again.

Faegan leaned forward in his chair, his eyes alive with curiosity. "I never knew about any of this," he said. "It must have all happened after the Coven captured me."

"Yes," Wigg said.

"Where have the Black Ships been all this time?" Abbey asked. "And can they really do everything that Tyranny and Shailiha claim?"

"Indeed they can," Wigg answered. "They are an absolute marvel of the craft." He shook his head, frowning. "Near the end of the war, all seven Black Ships disappeared while on a mission to engage part of the Coven's fleet. We assumed that they had been overwhelmed by Failee's armada and sent to the bottom of the sea."

Wigg rubbed his chin. "And now, it seems, they and their captains have resurfaced.

"Even the Black Ships cannot fly on their own. It takes one skilled in the craft to make each do so. The training is long and arduous—and was known only by a few."

Wigg looked grimly around the table. "Aside from Jessamay and me, everyone who knew how to fly a Black Ship is long dead—and yet there are these seven mysterious captains. Then there is this business about their uniforms looking eerily familiar. Our naval uniforms during the Sorceresses' War looked much like those worn by the late royal guard. Given all of that, who else could these captains be, eh? It all fits!"

Turning, Wigg looked into the aging face of his beloved daughter. Every time he gazed upon her now, his heart broke a little more.

"And now, too, we may at long last have a clue to the riddle of the Necrophagians," Wigg said. For several long moments the room was quiet.

"Please explain," Faegan said.

"For as long as we can remember, no vessel has been able to sail more than fifteen days into the Sea of Whispers," Wigg answered. "But when the Directorate banished the Coven three centuries ago, Failee found a way to cross—by way of her so-called bargain of tenfold times four. She promised that in the future she would pay forty dead bodies to the Necrophagians every time she wished to traverse the sea. But there has always been a part of this tale that bothered me."

"And what is that?" Traax asked. Wincing a bit, he adjusted the sling that supported his right arm.

"Why would the Necros agree, when they could have just as

easily devoured the Coven right then and there?" Wigg asked. "For all they knew, her promise was no more than a trick, and Failee might never return. Indeed, it took a full three centuries for her to prepare for Succiu's return to Eutracia to steal the Paragon and to kidnap Shailiha. By then, the Necrophagians must surely have thought they had been duped."

"So what is the answer?" Jessamay asked.

"At the time we banished the Coven, Failee already knew that the Necrophagians were there," Wigg answered. "And she must have had some kind of partial hold over them."

Slapping one hand upon the arm of his chair, Faegan cackled. "By the Afterlife, you've figured it out!" he shouted. "Finally— after all of these years! Well done, I say!"

Tristan scowled at them both. "Figured *what* out?" he demanded.

"It's really quite simple," Faegan answered, wiggling his bushy eyebrows up and down. "The current-day Necrophagians were at one time the captains and crews of Wigg's Black Ships. Failee caught them at sea and she used the craft to condemn them to an eternity deep below the waves, forever feasting on the dead for their sustenance. And that has been their punishment ever since. I'm right, aren't I?"

"Partially," Wigg said. "But how do you explain the fact that even long before the Sorceresses' War, no vessel could sail for more than fifteen days across the Sea of Whispers? The Necrophagians must already have been there; Failee only added to their numbers."

"But then how did the first Necrophagians get there?" Adrian asked.

Suddenly everyone heard Faegan take a quick breath. "But of course," he said. "It's all so clear now."

All eyes turned to look at him. Even he seemed stunned by his sudden conclusion.

"It's all a part of the War of Attrition that the preface of the Tome speaks of," he whispered. "The great struggle that took place aeons ago between the Heretics of the Guild and the Ones Who Came Before. There is a passage about that ancient war— one that had long eluded my comprehension. Now I understand."

Closing his eyes, Faegan called upon his gift of Consummate Recollection. The members of the Conclave watched and waited. Eyes still closed, Faegan began to recite a passage.

"During the War of Attrition, many of us practicing the Vigors were resigned to the sea by those who would seek to divide us and attempt to cause the rise of the dark side of the craft. Those vanquished souls were left with no recourse except to exist in the cold depths and to feed upon human carrion. But one day those of endowed blood—either of the Vigors or of the Vagaries—may acquire sufficient knowledge of the craft to bring them up and turn them to their cause."

Faegan opened his eyes. "Do you understand now?" he asked. "The original Necrophagians were members of the Ones who were captured by the Heretics of the Guild during the War of Attrition. Instead of being killed outright, they were condemned to eternal torture."

Astounded, Tristan sat back in his chair. Suddenly another thought hit him.

"And if the captains of the Black Ships can be recalled after three hundred years, then perhaps . . ." The prince didn't dare give voice to his suspicion.

"Then perhaps members of the Ones still suffer as Necrophagians to this very day," Shailiha finished for him. "They await their descendants of the Vigors to acquire sufficient knowledge to free them."

Wide-eyed, she looked first at Faegan, then at Wigg. "Could it really be true? Could there really be members of the Ones still living among us, albeit in an entirely different form?"

"Very possibly," Wigg answered. "But even if it is true, we do not have the knowledge required to free them."

"But Wulfgar was apparently able to free the captains of the Black Watch," Shailiha countered. "And despite the quality of his blood, he is still very new to the craft. So where did he acquire such training?"

"Presumably from the same source he has acquired all of his other gifts," Wigg answered. "The Scroll of the Vagaries. Remember, the Scrolls were written to supply 'shortcuts,' if you will, to one's training in the craft in the form of Forestallments. Your ability to commune with the fliers of the fields is a perfect example of this, Princess. You have never been classically trained, yet you are able to perform that feat. And unlike us, Wulfgar has an entire group of highly trained consuls to research the Scroll for him. While it's true that we have the acolytes to help us wade through the Scroll of the Vigors, their skills don't yet match those of the consuls. And don't forget that at least one-third of our scroll was burned when Wulfgar tried to pollute the Orb of the Vigors. There is no telling how many secrets turned to ash that night. I must say that I fear that Wulfgar is far ahead of us in his understanding of the Scrolls—at least the one in his possession."

Wigg gave Adrian a little smile. "No offense meant about your abilities, First Sister," he said. "The acolytes simply haven't studied and practiced the craft for as long as the consuls." Then he gave her a wink. "But your time will come."

Adrian smiled back. "No offense taken," she said.

"But some of this still doesn't make sense," Celeste argued. "Why bother to condemn the captured Ones to the sea at all? Why not just kill them outright? The Ones and the Heretics were mortal enemies, were they not?"

"I think I may have the answer to that," Jessamay said. This was the first time the sorceress had spoken during the meeting, and everyone turned to look at her.

"The Heretics wanted to protect the Citadel," she said. "It is supposedly one of the aeons-old birthplaces of the craft, is it not? I propose that it was upon that island that the Vagaries were first conceived and then perfected. What better way for the Heretics to guard their precious knowledge than to ensure that the Ones could never reach it? Unless they were in Heretic vessels, of course—in which case it's quite reasonable to assume that if they could create the Necrophagians, they could demand safe passage from them as well." She looked around the table.

"I agree with Wigg," she added. "The Citadel holds far more secrets of the craft than even Wulfgar may realize. True, he is the *Enseterat*. But his future powers—and even those still unrealized gifts of the *Jin'Sai* and the *Jin'Saiou*—may pale in comparison to what was once accomplished by the Ones and the Heretics. The truth is that we simply don't know."

Tristan was about to speak when an urgent pounding came on the doors. He looked over to one of the Minion guards and he nodded. They swung the double doors open to reveal Ox.

The giant warrior looked worried. Another warrior unfamiliar to the prince stood beside him. The second Minion looked totally exhausted. With a wave from Tristan, the two of them walked briskly into the room and they came to attention.

"This be Dax," Ox said. "He be the captain I leave in charge to watch orb. He fly all night to bring news."

Ox turned to look directly at his lord and master.

"All news very bad," he added.

Tristan and Traax both came to their feet and walked over to Dax. Tristan gave him a chair. Traax poured him a goblet of wine. The warrior drank deeply. After sitting down and taking a few moments to collect himself, Dax told his tale.

It was clear to everyone that Ox was right: The news was very bad indeed.

CHAPTER LX

WULFGAR WAS UNEASY AS HE LOOKED OUT OVER THE SEA OF Whispers. The sun was setting. Much of the demonslaver fleet and all seven of the Black Ships sat at anchor in the horseshoe-shaped bay, waiting for their lord to join them. The rest of the fleet dutifully patrolled the waters surrounding the island. Two days had passed since Tyranny's raid on the Citadel, and the *Enseterat* remained concerned.

Einar and Serena stood beside him. The seven skeletal captains of the Black Ships stood at attention to one side, awaiting their orders. Today Wulfgar and his forces would sail for Eutracia. And this time he knew he would not fail.

He wasn't particularly worried about the captured demonslaver. The slaver had been only one of many such guards of lower rank, and he did not possess information that would be of great use to the Eutracian wizards.

What concerned him was that the sanctity of his home had

been violated—the very place where he had vowed to keep his queen and unborn daughter safe. The demonslavers who had failed him had paid for their mistake with their lives. Extra precautions had been taken to protect the fortress, and he was reasonably sure that its security would not be breached again. Without informing his consuls, he had granted Serena's blood signature a host of additional Forestallments, should she need them in his absence. Even so, he had mixed feelings about leaving.

Yesterday the soothing voices of the Heretics had come to him again, bringing words that had slowly salved his concerns. He had been in the throne room with Einar and Serena, poring over maps of Eutracia and briefing them about the impending campaign.

Wulfgar had been in midsentence when he heard the chorus of voices. Recognizing their timbre, he walked to the edge of the room that looked out over the sea. Lowering his head, he went down on both knees.

"Wulfgar," the voices whispered.

"I am here," he answered.

"The wizards of the Redoubt have violated the Citadel. But remain strong of heart, for they have gained little. The wounded Orb of the Vigors has succeeded in cutting its way through the mountains that lie on the western side of Eutracia. When you reach Eutracia, you and a measure of your forces must immediately travel to the pass. Send another group under the leadership of your captains to find the orb and keep it safe from the Jin'Sai and his wizards. Nothing must be allowed to stop its decay. Allow the female assassin to continue her work, for it will prove useful. But if she is unable to kill the Jin'Sai and the Jin'Saiou, then that shall become your task."

The voices paused for a moment. Sensing that his mind should remain still, Wulfgar waited reverently.

"Under no circumstances are you or any of your servants to attack the capital until you have first secured the mouth of the pass. Proceed with caution, because the forces of the Jin'Sai guard it and they must be dealt with. Once the pass is yours, we shall again reveal ourselves to you. Do not be alarmed by what you will see there, for it will be wondrous and will further aid you in your cause. Go quickly, Wulfgar, and have faith. All will be revealed."

"I shall obey," he answered.

Stunned, he slowly walked back to Einar and Serena. They looked at him curiously.

"What troubles you, my lord?" Serena asked. She took his good hand. It felt cold, as though all of his blood had somehow left him.

Wulfgar cast his gaze westward toward Eutracia—the land that had once been his home. "The Heretics have spoken to me once more," he said. He told Einar and Serena the news and instructions.

"Is it true?" Wulfgar asked Einar, unsure he believed what he'd been told. "Could a pass to the other side truly exist? What wonders might await us there?"

Einar lowered the hood of his robe. He seemed as stunned as his master—perhaps more so. He considered the question for a moment.

"If the Heretics themselves have told you of this, then it must be true," he answered. "It must be a vision without equal in our history! How I wish I were going with you, my lord! How my eyes hunger to witness all that you are about to see! Even so, I know that in your absence my place is here, guarding your queen and your unborn child. But tell me—did the Heretics say what would be required of you once you reach the pass?"

Wulfgar shook his head. "Only that I am to crush the *Jin'Sai*'s Minions who guard it, then await their word."

Einar smiled. "Given your captains, the demonslavers still under your command, and the Earthshakers that have already been boarded upon the Black Ships, your dealings with the Minions should be swift. Also quite rewarding, I might add. Who knows, you may even face the *Jin'Sai* himself on the battlefield. I envy you the impending struggle. It will be glorious."

Serena moved her husband's hand to place it on her swollen belly. As though she could have somehow willed it so, the baby gave a gentle kick. The ravaged skin of Wulfgar's face contorted in a smile.

"Do not forget us," Serena said softly. "And do not forget the magnificent side of the craft for which we all struggle."

Wulfgar gave her a kiss, then turned his good eye back to the sea. As the sun sank below the horizon, the wind was freshening. They would make good time during this first night of their adventure.

He turned to his queen. "I have something for you," he told her. He reached into his jacket and produced a single red rose. She smiled as he handed it to her.

"Thank you, my lord," she said. "While you are gone I shall treasure it."

Wulfgar looked into her eyes. "It is more than a simple rose," he told her. "It is bound to the craft, just as you and I are. As long as I am alive, it will bloom. But should it wither and die, you will sense the change wherever you are, and know that the unimaginable has occurred."

Serena reached out to touch the ravaged side of his face. "I am sure that this flower will continue to bloom until the day you return to our shores," she said softly.

Wulfgar nodded. "Goodbye, my love," he said quietly. "Take good care of our child."

Having suddenly lost her voice, Serena tried to smile. As she did, a tear traced a path down her cheek. When Wulfgar kissed her, he tasted salt, like the sea he would soon be sailing upon.

"Guard my queen and my child with your life," he told Einar. Then he smiled wickedly. "While I am away, find a suitable place to display the heads of the *Jin'Sai* and his two wizards. I intend to bring them home with me."

CHAPTER LXI

As DAX FINISHED TELLING HIS TALE, A HUSH DESCENDED OVER the Conclave. Tristan looked first at Faegan, then at Wigg, but the wizards were at a loss for words.

For a long time no one spoke. Finally, Faegan broke the silence. His face stern, he trained his gray-green eyes upon the warrior. Dax could almost feel the power in the wizard's gaze burrowing its way into his own.

"The azure wall that guards the entrance to the pass," Faegan began. "What does it look like?"

"It is flat, and stretches from one side of the pass to the other," Dax answered. "It rises high into the sky, so high, in fact, that one cannot see its top because it stretches into the fog that always lies upon the peaks of the Tolenkas. White shards of light shoot about within its depths. It is not solid; instead, it is like a liquid, though its surface is as smooth as glass. My dreggan plunged through it as though it were made of water. When I pulled the dreggan out, the wall immediately sealed itself. It is the most amazing thing I have ever seen."

Scowling, Faegan sat back in his chair. Wigg looked at Faegan and then, when the crippled wizard nodded, turned to the prince and Shailiha.

"I need to ask you both a question of the utmost importance," Wigg said. "You will no doubt find my inquiry odd, but this is no joke, I assure you."

"What is it?" Tristan asked.

Pursing his lips, Wigg placed his gnarled hands flat upon the inlaid table.

"Have either of you been hearing voices?" he asked. "Voices carrying messages that you didn't understand, and were perhaps reticent to tell us about?"

After shooting each other puzzled looks, the prince and princess turned back to stare blankly at the wizard.

"No," Tristan answered flatly.

"Nor have I," Shailiha said. "Why would you ask such a thing?"

"Because of the sudden existence of this azure wall," Faegan answered. "The Tome contains a prophecy mentioning the appearance of such an edifice, an ominous prediction that Wigg and I have discussed many times. It was deemed of such great importance that for decades many of the late members of the Directorate attempted to research it further, but to no avail. This sudden appearance of the wall marks one of the greatest turning points in the history of the craft. And yet—and I believe I speak for Wigg as well as myself—it brings us no joy. The fact that no voices have come to commune with the prince or the princess does not bode well for any of us."

"What does the prophecy say?" Abbey asked.

Closing his eyes, Faegan began to recall the cryptic passage.

"With acts delayed activated within their blood, the Jin'Sai, *the* Jin'Saiou, *or any others of the same womb will one day be able to commune with either the Ones or the Heretics,"* Faegan recited. *"And should for any reason the mountains separating us somehow be breached, an azure wall shall arise to contain that breach. The wall shall be the ministrations of either the Heretics or the Ones. If the Ones bring the wall, it shall be employed so as to keep your side of the land safe from harm. But if the Heretics conceive the wall, they will unleash horrors from our side to yours—horrors such as have not been seen for aeons."*

"I still don't understand," Adrian said. "What does it all mean?"

"The 'acts delayed' are Forestallments," Wigg answered. "And we now know that the mountains the Ones speak of must be the Tolenkas. The Tolenkas have now been breached by the ruptured orb. Whether this was accidental or deliberate remains to be seen. And the azure wall has risen, just as the prophecy states it would. Even though Tristan and Shailiha have been imbued with Forestallments, except for the princess' ability to commune with the fliers, these spells have not been activated. Because the wall is already here and neither the prince nor the princess has heard voices, then only one conclusion can be drawn."

"Wulfgar has been imbued with the Forestallment that allows him to commune with the Heretics," Tristan said. "Worse yet, he will soon have control over the wall.

"He's coming back, isn't he?" he asked the First Wizard. "The wording of the prophecy implies that the Heretics—or at least their spirits—reside on the western side of the Tolenkas. Wulfgar means to breach the wall, gain the help of the Heretics, and take Eutracia."

Tristan's face grew hard. He didn't like secrets. And yet there seemed no end to the secrets the wizards had been keeping from him and the other members of the Conclave. Trying to calm him, his new bride gave him a sympathetic look, but he just glared at Wigg.

"You knew, didn't you?" he growled. "Both you and Faegan have known this all along! Why didn't you tell me?"

"In fact we did not know," Faegan answered. "Of course we assumed that the natural barrier the Tome refers to might be the Tolenkas, but we could never be sure. The barrier could also have been the Sea of Whispers, or the oceanic ice floes lying both to the north and the south, or the very sky above us, for that matter. But now we are much closer to the truth. The Heretics must still exist in one form or another on the western side of the Tolenkas. And they will very likely soon cede control of the azure wall to Wulfgar."

"I'm afraid it goes even deeper than that," Wigg said. "Wulfgar doesn't mean to only take Eutracia. He has other designs, as well."

"And what are they?" Celeste asked.

"You're forgetting the orb," the wizard answered. "Once he has landed on Eutracian shores, Wulfgar's battle plan will probably be threefold. First, he will divide his forces. He will lead one group to the pass to take control of the azure wall. A second group—probably under the control of his Black Ship captains—will search out the Orb of the Vigors in order to protect it from us at all costs. Wulfgar will turn his remaining legions south to Tammerland, to crush those of us who remain loyal to the Vigors. And as the polluted waters of the Sippora finally reach us, much of the city will go up in flames, only adding to Wulfgar's chances of success." He paused for a moment as he looked around the table.

"I doubt that even my powers combined with those of Faegan, Jessamay, and all the acolytes could effectively disperse the river's heat," he continued gravely. "As the refugees flood in and the city becomes a fortress, food and water will quickly grow short. Riots will break out. I know," he added sadly. "I have seen it all before."

His thoughts went back to those dark days when the Coven had nearly taken the capital.

"It seems that it is all about to happen again, old friend," Wigg said to Faegan. "We must prepare for a siege. If Wulfgar has already left the Citadel, we have little time to prepare. His

Black Ships can travel much faster than his demonslaver ships, or anything that Tyranny has in her fleet."

Taking a deep breath, Faegan nodded.

"I don't understand," Shailiha protested. "Wulfgar wants to *protect* the orb? And from *us*? What in the name of the Afterlife are you talking about? I thought Wulfgar and the Heretics wanted the Orb of the Vigors destroyed!"

Suddenly understanding, Tristan nodded his head. "They do," he mused. He looked over at his sister.

"Don't you see?" he asked her. "Wulfgar doesn't need to destroy the orb; it's accomplishing that task on its own. If your blood and mine only can accept the powerful Forestallment that will save it, then Wulfgar will do everything in his power to try to keep us away from it."

"That's right," Faegan said. "And that is why we must hit him with everything we have when his forces are divided and he is at his weakest. If he reaches the wall and parts it, I fear that no power on earth will be able to stop him."

For several moments the only sounds came from the wood burning in the fireplace, and the happy gurgling of Morganna as she played on the floor.

"These horrors from the other side of the Tolenkas," Tyranny said, "what are they likely to be?"

Wigg shook his head. "That is impossible to say," he replied. "The Heretics were the originators of the Vagaries, and we have always believed their gifts to be massive—far outstripping our own."

Tristan took Celeste's hand. Sighing, he looked down for a moment.

"So much of this is about me, isn't it?" he asked. "It all hinges on returning my blood to its original state. Supposedly only the Scroll Master can provide us with the calculations for the Forestallment that we need. But despite our trip to the Recluse, we're no closer to finding him than we were. The spell might be somewhere in the Scroll of the Vigors, but at least one-third of the scroll has been destroyed. For all we know, the calculations we need were destroyed with it that same night. Search the scroll as hard as we might, it could still all be for naught."

Faegan looked at Jessamay. "Do you have any idea what

Failee meant about the Scroll Master guarding something called the Well of Forestallments?"

Jessamay shook her head. "Not really. Only that the Scroll Master was supposedly the world's greatest keeper of Forestallments. I have no idea what that means. And I have no idea what the Well of Forestallments might be. Failee claimed that they both resided in Eutracia. But I don't think that even she knew where, because she said that once Eutracia was hers, she planned to search him out and torture his knowledge from him." She was quiet for a moment, her forehead wrinkled with thought as she searched her memories. "She did say one other thing: that the Scroll Master could be found via the River of Thought, whatever that is."

Wigg and Faegan exchanged glances.

"Are you sure that's what she called it?" Wigg asked quickly.

The sorceress nodded. "Reasonably sure."

Faegan leaned eagerly across the table. "Did she say anything else about it?"

"Only one thing," Jessamay answered. "She said that the basic calculations for the River of Thought carried with them many subdisciplines, all of which could be found in the scrolls. One of these was said to be particular to the Scroll Master—that the bearer of the Forestallment would be drawn to the Scroll Master. That's all I know about it."

Stunned, Faegan sat back in his chair. "I've seen it," he said quietly, half to himself.

"What!" Wigg exclaimed. "What do you mean, 'You've seen it'?"

"When I found the calculations in the scroll that allowed you to call the acolytes home," Faegan said, "I saw others listed as well. I paid them little heed, because I felt sure I had already found the one I needed. One of those subdisciplines must be for the Scroll Master!"

"Then our path is clear," Tristan said firmly. "You must immediately imbue my blood with this Forestallment so that I can search for him."

To his great surprise, both wizards shook their heads.

"We can't do that," Wigg said.

Tristan scowled. "And why not?"

"For the same reason that we cannot train you right now," Faegan answered. "As long as your blood is azure, we can't know what effects our use of the craft might have on you. Despite the desperate nature of our situation, we cannot risk losing the *Jin'Sai*. Especially now."

"But Failee was successful in granting Tristan Forestallments," Abbey countered. "If she could do it, then why can't we?"

"The prince's Forestallments were granted to him in the Recluse, *before* his blood changed to azure," Wigg reminded her. "No, Faegan is right. As tempting as it might be, we simply cannot risk it."

The First Wizard looked over at Faegan. "I'm sure that you will agree with me when I say that I should carry the Forestallment," Wigg said. "I have already employed the River of Thought, and I am familiar with its use. Therefore, augmenting my already existing Forestallment with the subdiscipline for the Scroll Master should be relatively simple—should one care to call it that. And then the prince will accompany me, as my blood searches out the Scroll Master."

After thinking it over for a few moments, Faegan finally nodded his agreement.

Wigg turned toward Tristan. "It seems that you and I are about to go on another adventure."

Tristan nodded, but he felt torn. He knew how important it was for him to go with Wigg. But with Wulfgar on the way, part of the prince wanted to remain here to lead the Minions into battle. And he hated the idea of leaving Celeste. Would she still be alive when they came home? He couldn't bear the thought of losing her—or of her facing death without him or her father by her side. Then he had an idea. With hope in his eyes, he looked at Wigg.

"We should take Celeste with us," he said. "Every moment is precious. If we are successful with the Scroll Master, then I could help her right then and there, without having to first return to the palace. This makes the most sense, does it not?"

"You must have been reading my mind," Wigg said with a smile. "Of course she should come with us. We will go together in a Minion litter."

"Begging your pardon, First Wizard, but taking a litter won't work," Adrian interjected. "You will need to go by horseback."

Wigg's right eyebrow arched upward. "And just why is that?"

"The flying Minions' pace will overcome the workings of the spell," she answered. "When you employed the River of Thought to bring the acolytes home, we found that we all shared something in common—an undeniable need to come as quickly as we could. Of course, that meant riding at a gallop. But every time we did, each of us seemed to somehow outpace the spell and we lost the feeling. When we slowed back down, the feeling reemerged. Flying Minions will be unencumbered by the lay of the land, able to fly in a straight line. Even bearing a litter, they will go too fast. And flying in circles just to slow down will end up exhausting them."

Wigg rubbed his chin. "Interesting," he said. "Very well, we shall go by horseback. But we should have a phalanx of warriors accompany us with a litter full of supplies. If we need to come home quickly, they can fly us back."

Tristan nodded, then turned to Traax.

"In my absence, I leave Faegan in charge of the Minions. You are to follow his orders as if they were my own. Should Faegan fall in battle, then Shailiha will take charge. Do you understand?"

Traax bowed his head. "It shall all be as you command."

Tristan could see that everyone was tired—especially Tyranny and Shailiha, who had returned home only hours earlier. Further plans could wait while everyone took a break. But first he wanted to make an announcement. He reached for Celeste's hand. She smiled at him.

"This meeting is adjourned for four hours," he said. "But before you all go, there is something I have to tell you." Taking a deep breath, Tristan smiled.

"Three days ago, in Parthalon, Celeste and I were married. We waited to tell you because we wanted you all to hear our good news at the same time."

After a few seconds of shocked silence, the group erupted with joy. Everyone immediately came to hug, kiss, and congratulate the newlyweds. Only Tyranny hung back, momentarily frozen in her chair. But then even she, face white, eyes suspiciously shiny, rose and went to give Tristan a quick kiss on one cheek.

As the hoopla died down, Jessamay unexpectedly raised her voice.

"I'm sorry to have to do this just now," she said, "but with the prince's indulgence, may I please ask that everyone sit back down for a few minutes? I would not ask if it wasn't very important. When you hear what I have to say, you'll understand."

After passing curious looks among themselves, the members of the Conclave returned to their seats.

"What is it?" the First Wizard asked.

Jessamay took a deep breath. "I have something to tell you all," she began. "It is something that only I could know—something that could make a great difference in the impending struggle. I learned of it only after my arrival here at the palace."

The sorceress paused for a few moments. As she did, Shailiha went to take up Morganna and bring the toddler back to the table to sit on her lap. A foreboding silence crept over the room.

When she knew that she had everyone's attention, Jessamay began her tale.

CHAPTER LXII

PUSHING WITH HER HEELS, SATINE CASUALLY ROCKED HER CHAIR back upon its two rear legs and took another sip of ale. It had gone flat some time ago, but she didn't care. Placing the pewter mug back on the table before her, she carefully looked around.

The tavern was a forlorn, ramshackle place. She sat by a window that looked out on to the street. A small fire burned in the fireplace to her left, occasionally sending the comforting smells of smoke and soot her way.

Other patrons—mostly men—sat at tables nearby, slowly

drinking their way into the evening. Although she had received several curious glances when she first walked in, none had approached her, and for that she was thankful. She didn't need any unnecessary attention just now.

Since she had killed Lionel, this was the first time she had departed the quiet, out-of-the-way inn where she'd been staying on the other side of Tammerland. Now she kept an eye on the archery shop across the street, waiting until she felt it was safe to venture out to see what word Bratach had for her.

So far she had seen nothing unusual. She had recognized none of the passersby in the street, and she had seen no one loitering about the shop. Several archery customers had come and gone, but that was to be expected.

She lowered the front legs of her chair to the floor. Pulling several low-denomination kisa from her pocket, she let them jangle to the tabletop. Then she pulled the hood of her cloak up over her head and walked out of the tavern.

Evening was falling and the air had become cooler. Leaning casually up against the outside wall, she looked up and down the street. She saw nothing to concern her. But there were still two customers inside the shop and she wanted them gone before she walked over.

To pass the time she watched a ragged lamplighter approach. Carrying a ladder, he trudged slowly along from one lamp pole to the next. Hunched over and ancient-looking, he was blanketed with soot.

He leaned the ladder up against the pole before the inn and climbed up to remove the globe. He lit the wick, and the lamp came alive, casting his shadow long across the ground. He replaced the globe, then climbed down, picked up his ladder, and slowly made his way toward the next pole.

What a fruitless existence, Satine thought as she watched him. *How much better it is to be a huntress. If I die, at least I will die quickly rather than slowly, from sheer boredom.*

She suddenly found herself thinking of Aeolus, and the Serpent and the Sword. She had not been back to see her onetime master since she had swung through the skylight and choked one of his students unconscious. She missed the old man, and hoped that he was well. She also missed the hard, ascetic life that the school had once forced her to tolerate, before she had come to love it. Often she wished that she could go back there for good and live in peace. *Perhaps one day,* she thought. *But only after all of this is over.*

At the sound of the archery shop door opening and closing, she turned to see the two last customers leaving.

Glad for the darkening night, Satine shifted her weight away from the wall and walked quickly across the street. She opened the door and stepped in, the little bell at the top of the door cheerfully announcing her presence. She lowered the hood of her cloak and looked around.

Ivan was alone, standing behind the counter. When he saw her, his expression darkened. He nervously pointed to the front of the shop.

"Lock the door, turn the sign around, and pull the shades!" he said anxiously. As Satine turned back to do as he asked, he growled, "We expected to see you here before this! Where have you been?"

Satine walked to the counter and gave Ivan a hard look.

"That's my business," she shot back. "Is he here?"

Ivan nodded and waved her around to the other side of the counter. He walked to the rear of the shop and parted the curtains. Cautious as ever, Satine place her hands loosely atop her dagger hilts and followed Ivan down the stairs.

Bratach sat alone at the shabby table. As Ivan and Satine descended into the basement, the consul looked up. He smiled.

"Take a seat," he said to them.

Ivan sat down. Satine turned a chair around to straddle it. Bratach lifted a half-full bottle of wine and held it out to her. Satine shook her head. He refilled his glass.

"Suit yourself," he said. "By the way, Lionel the Little, as he was called, is quite dead. He committed suicide in his own quarters three nights ago—and in the royal palace, of all places. It was a hanging followed by a disembowelment. What a mess! Just imagine the uproar it caused!"

It was clear that despite his sarcasm the consul was impressed—a rare occurrence. Holding the wineglass high, he tipped it in her direction. After talking a sip, he placed the glass back on the table.

"How on earth did you manage it?" he asked. "I half expected never to see you again. But here you are."

Leaning her forearms on the back of the chair, Satine smirked at him.

"No assassination is impossible," she answered. "I thought you might understand that by now. I told you I could do it, and I did." She flashed Bratach a look that was all business.

"I didn't come here to listen to something I already know," she said. "The sign in the shop window tells me that you have news. It had better be more than the fact that the gnome has met his maker."

Bratach looked at Ivan, then back at Satine. "Oh, my news is important, I assure you," he said. "But you aren't going to like it."

"Tell me."

"The wizards of the Redoubt know who you are. Worse yet, they have your description."

Her jaw set, Satine took a breath and sat back a little.

"How?" she asked.

"A captured Valrenkium told them. The prince's Minions took him from his village and the wizards forced him to talk. They also know about Reznik. We have no word that search parties have been sent out looking for you, but we don't know that they haven't been, either. How do you wish to proceed?"

Taking a deep breath, Satine looked toward the ceiling. This was the worst possible news. Still, she remained calm. She looked back at Bratach.

"I will continue with the sanctions," she said.

Bratach looked narrowly at her. "Very well—it's your neck. I needn't tell you that you must use extreme caution from now on. Wulfgar will be arriving soon. Because of that we have decided to up the ante, so to speak. This will only make things more difficult for you, but there it is."

"What do you mean?"

Bratach reached into his robe and produced a parchment, which he flattened on the tabletop. He picked up a knife and rammed it through one of the portraits depicted there.

"This is your next victim," he said. "I suggest you approach your task with care."

Satine recognized the face immediately. *They've upped the ante indeed,* she thought.

"What else can you tell me?"

"Very little, I'm afraid. As far as we know this person is still out of the country. We await word from our confederate inside the palace. When we have more information, we will tell you. Until then you must wait."

Looking around the dingy cellar, Bratach smiled. "Might I recommend that you hide here until we learn more? I know it's not much, but staying here would save you time."

Satine shook her head. This was the last place she wanted to be holed up. Now that the wizards had her description, she knew she needed to stay off the streets, but it wouldn't be here, in a dank cellar with Wulfgar's consul and his greasy lackey.

"I'll make my own arrangements," she said.

"Very well," Bratach answered. "But you must check the shop window every day—twice a day would be even better. We cannot be sure when your target will return to Eutracia. But when it happens, you'll have to move fast."

Nodding her agreement, Satine stood from the chair. "Is there anything else?"

Bratach shook his head. "Just make sure that you come into the shop the moment you see that we have news for you."

Satine walked to the door. As she opened it, its hinges creaked. It would be a long walk back around to pick up her horse, but it would be the safest way.

After giving the two men a final look, she entered the tunnel and closed the door behind her. The winding, dimly lit passage yawned before her.

She had been wise to refuse Bratach's offer to stay in the cellar. But she also knew that she could no longer risk staying at the inn she had chosen. After going back to collect her things, she would have to move on. As the sound of her footsteps rang out against the bricks in the tunnel floor, her mouth turned up into a slight smile.

The Gray Fox knew exactly where to go, but there were things she needed to do first.

IV

DELIVERANCE

CHAPTER LXIII

"Even if we find the Scroll Master and make Tristan's blood whole again, Faegan and I fear that his struggle against his half brother may alter the craft forever. But if the craft is to survive, the confrontation must occur—no matter the outcome . . ."

—WIGG

As Tristan entered the little room and saw the demon-slaver in the glowing cage, he couldn't help but have mixed feelings. Forced into slavery by the consul Krassus, then morphed into the nightmarish creature now glaring back at them, this being had once been a Eutracian citizen. *Did I once know this person?* the prince asked himself. *If I did, does it matter now?*

Wigg, Faegan, and the prince had come to this lonely chamber of the Redoubt just after Tristan dismissed the Conclave. Wigg, Tristan, and Celeste would depart Tammerland soon. If Wulfgar attacked before they returned, Faegan and the others would be left alone to defend the capital. Whatever information they might glean from the slaver could prove vital.

The cage Wigg had conjured to hold the demonslaver was fairly large. The azure bars shone brightly in the relative darkness of the otherwise empty room. A tray of uneaten food and a flask of water lay on the floor of the cage.

When the demonslaver saw them approach he charged angrily to the front of the cage, the black talons at the ends of his fingers curling tightly around the bars. Curling his lips back, he hissed at them, his pointed teeth and black tongue showing up eerily in the glowing light of the cage.

"Trying to get answers from him without the use of the craft will be pointless," Tristan warned Wigg. "I suggest we don't waste the time."

Nodding, Wigg looked over at Faegan.

"I agree," the crippled wizard said. "Let's get on with it."

Wigg closed his eyes. The demonslaver's eyes went wide, and his head snapped back and then came slowly forward again. His demeanor gradually calmed. He let go of the azure bars, and his muscular arms fell to his sides.

Wigg opened his eyes and looked at the demonslaver. "What are Wulfgar's battle plans?" he asked.

"I do not know," the slaver answered. "I am only a guard. We do not have access to such information."

"How many demonslavers does the *Enseterat* command?" Tristan demanded.

"Perhaps ten thousand. Many were lost in the sea battles with the prince's warriors."

"How many consuls reside upon the Isle of the Citadel?" Faegan asked.

"There are many there who wear the blue robe," their prisoner answered, "but I do not know their numbers. The most senior among them is named Einar."

Tristan saw a flash of recognition cross Wigg's face. "Do you know this Einar?" the prince asked the wizard.

Wigg nodded. "He is of highly endowed blood and an expert regarding the various calculations of the craft. Wulfgar could not have made a better choice to sit at his right hand."

"Is Wulfgar in possession of the Scroll of the Vagaries?" Faegan asked the demonslaver.

"I have no knowledge of such things."

"Who is Wulfgar's woman?" Tristan asked.

"She is Serena, his queen. She is pregnant with his daughter. She will give birth in two moons."

Wigg and Faegan exchanged grave looks. "What are Wulfgar's plans for the Black Ships?" Faegan asked.

"He will use them to crush the *Jin'Sai*. The Black Ships now carry great beasts—beasts too massive for demonslaver vessels to hold. That is why the Black Ships and their captains were summoned from the depths of the sea. But that is all I know about them."

His eyes alive with curiosity, Faegan wheeled his chair closer to the cage. "Tell us more about these beasts," he said.

"They are huge things, their backs so long that twenty of us can ride them at one time. Their tails end in massive, bony paddles. When they walk, the ground literally trembles beneath their feet. Our lord calls them Earthshakers."

Pulling thoughtfully on his beard, Faegan sat back in his chair. "What else can you tell us?"

"I know nothing more. I am only a guard. Guards are never made privy to our lord's plans, or granted access to the inner recesses of the Citadel."

Tristan looked at Wigg. "Can you tell whether he's hiding anything from us?"

Wigg closed his eyes again. After several more moments went by, he looked back at Tristan and Faegan and shook his head.

"I hate to say it, but I believe him," Wigg answered. "We'll get no more out of this one, for he has no more to give. Like the Minions, it seems that the demonslavers have a strict chain of command. Within the demonslaver cadres, this one ranks among the lowest of the low."

They heard a knock on the door. Tristan walked over and opened it to see Shannon the Small standing there, his ever-present ale jug gripped firmly in one hand. A puff of blue smoke rose from his corncob pipe. There was a sad look on his face.

"Please forgive the intrusion," he said, "but the others asked me to come and tell you that all has been made ready. Everyone is gathered and waiting."

Nodding, Tristan took a deep breath. "Tell them we will be there momentarily," he said.

"Very well," Shannon answered.

As the gnome walked away, Tristan shut the door. He looked across the room at the two wizards.

"It's time," he said softy. Then he looked at the demonslaver. "What about him?"

"There's nothing more that he can tell us," Faegan answered. "There is only one thing to do."

He looked at Wigg. "Do you agree?" he asked.

Pursing his lips, Wigg nodded.

"And does the *Jin'Sai* agree?" Faegan asked.

Tristan nodded. "But make it painless," he commanded. "Not long ago, this bastardization of the craft was a fellow Eutracian."

Wigg shook his head. "I cannot do this in any fashion—painless or otherwise. You're forgetting my vows."

Tristan nodded. He had forgotten the vows that had been made by all the members of the Directorate.

"Faegan," he asked, "will you—"

"Yes," the old wizard answered.

Faegan pointed at the demonslaver, who continued to stand there placidly, his mind still under the First Wizard's control.

There is something very wrong about this, Tristan thought. But he had to admit that there was also something satisfying—even righteous—about it. As he watched, the slaver's eyes rolled back in his head and he slumped to the floor.

Saying nothing more, the three friends left the room, each aware that their next task would be equally unpleasant.

Tristan quietly shut the door behind them.

TRISTAN, FAEGAN, AND WIGG EMERGED AT THE BACK OF THE palace. It was a clear night, and the three moons cast their combined glow across the ground. The air smelled clean and sweet, but the prince knew that it wouldn't stay that way for much longer.

By prior order of the *Jin'Sai,* the wounded had been moved out of the spacious rear courtyards. The other members of the Conclave stood waiting. When Celeste saw Tristan she gave him a sad but encouraging smile. Pursing his lips, he nodded back at her. The rest of the area was filled to overflowing with Minions; more of the winged warriors circled silently in the sky above, their numbers sometimes blotting out the moons.

The Acolytes of the Redoubt were also here, as were all of the palace gnomes. Crude wooden stands had been constructed for the gnomes to stand upon, so that they wouldn't become lost in the massive crowd. The ever-protective Shawna the Short held Morganna close.

A clearing had been preserved in the middle of the courtyard. In its center stood two tall funeral pyres, with a ladder against each. Geldon lay upon one pyre, Lionel upon the other. Around them, hundreds of standing torches had been lit, adding to the sense of solemnity.

The necropsy that had been performed upon Lionel's body had revealed it contained the same substances that Geldon's had: human brain matter, human yellow bone marrow, human red bone marrow, root of gingercrinkle, and oil of encumbrance. The only difference had been that Lionel's blood showed traces of honey, rather than derma-gnasher venom.

It was clear that despite the different ways in which Geldon and Lionel had taken their own lives, they had been poisoned by the same assassin. Every person here—human, Minion, and gnome alike—wanted the killer dead. For Satine, Eutracia was about to become a very small and dangerous place.

Traax walked slowly forward, holding a flaming torch. Going down on bended knee, he handed it expressionlessly up to the *Jin'Sai*.

Tristan took the torch and turned to face the crowd. The thousands of Minions suddenly went to one knee in the soft, dewy grass.

"We live to serve!" came the thunderous oath, its power so great that it seemed to shake the earth. Lifting his hands, Tristan beckoned them all to stand.

The prince knew that it had long been Minion custom that no eulogy should be given before the traditional lighting of the pyres. Like the Minions themselves, the philosophy behind the ritual was both solemn and simple. A disgraced warrior was never granted honorary immolation. The fact that these two bodies lay upon pyres tacitly told everyone all they needed to know.

Still, as he walked to the pyres Tristan found himself torn about whether to speak. He hadn't known Lionel well, but Geldon had been a close friend. His eyes filled with tears as he remembered the first time he had met the hunchbacked dwarf in the Ghetto of the Shunned in Parthalon. Physically, Geldon had been small. But the goodness of his heart and the quickness of his mind had more than made up for it.

Standing before the pyres, Tristan made his decision and raised the torch. Better to let everyone say goodbye in his or her own way.

Tristan touched the torch first to Geldon's pyre and then to Lionel's. The fire caught quickly, and he lodged the torch in Lionel's pyre before stepping back.

As the flames roared into the night sky, an idea came to him. *There is indeed one last thing that we can do to honor you,* he thought.

Tristan reached back and drew his dreggan, its curved blade ringing as it slid from its scabbard. Raising it high, he pressed the button on the sword's hilt. With a deadly clang the blade launched forward. Knowing what would happen next, the *Jin'Sai* kept his weapon high as he looked over his legions.

Thousands of dreggans immediately left their scabbards, the combined ring of their blades filling the courtyard. With one heart, the warriors all triggered their blades, the clang nearly deafening. His jaw set, Tristan looked back to the pyres.

We will find the one who did this to you, he silently swore. *And she will pay with her life.*

CHAPTER LXIV

TWO HOURS LATER, CELESTE STOOD AT THE WINDOW OF HER PERsonal quarters. Despite the sadness of the immolation ceremony, the night still seemed beautiful, peaceful. She silently blessed the fact that her view did not overlook the flaming funeral pyres.

The cool evening wind wafted gently into the room. The stars twinkled down at her as though she were the only person in creation. Normally these things would have given her great pleasure, but not just now. Another wave of awful pain came over her, and she was forced to go sit on the bed.

The first attack had come during the lighting of the pyres. The grinding, exquisite pain felt like thousands of tiny needles stabbing into the very essence of her being. It had lasted only a few moments, but that had been an eternity. As the pain recurred, she had done her best to hide it from the others, and she believed that no one had noticed.

As this latest attack subsided, her hands shook and she was bathed in sweat. Closing her eyes, she silently prayed that no one would see her like this—at least not for a while. If these attacks worsened with the progression of her illness, she knew she would not be able to keep them secret for long.

She had told Tristan only part of the truth about why she wanted to visit these rooms. As his new wife, she would take up residence with him in his quarters. She had told him that she needed to come here to collect some of her things. The rest could be delivered by the Minions later, she had said.

Her real reason was that she needed time to think. She was acutely aware of how guilty Tristan already felt about her condition—and how intensely worried he was about all of the other troubles plaguing the nation. She knew that if these attacks continued, soon there would be no way she could keep him from seeing them. Before that day arrived, she wanted to sort things out for herself—especially before she left with Tristan and her father to search for the Scroll Master. Once they departed the palace, she might never have the luxury of another private moment.

Standing on shaky legs, she walked back to the window. An idea had been brewing in her mind ever since she and Tristan had been told about her condition. She was aware that he was trying to be as supportive as he could. But each of them knew that it was what they did *not* say that somehow always seemed to negate whatever assurances they gave one another. A dark cloud hung over them that could be banished in only one of two ways: if they found the Scroll Master soon and he agreed to help them, or if she were to die.

She went to her writing table and sat down. She selected some paper and carefully dipped the quill in ink. Pausing for a moment, she gathered her thoughts.

Three false starts lay torn up on the desk before her note was finally finished. Folding the letter, she placed it into an envelope and sealed it with red wax. Almost as an after-thought, she walked the letter to her dresser and she sprinkled it lightly with myrrh. Then she packed the few things that she had told Tristan she had come for and hid the letter among them.

Her belongings in her arms, Celeste looked around the room for what she feared might be the last time. After blowing out the candle on the desk, she left the room, softly closing the door behind her, and walked down the hall to join her new husband.

CHAPTER LXV

"ALMS FOR THE BLIND," THE HAGGARD BEGGAR WOMAN PLEADED. "Won't someone please spare a few kisa for a poor blind woman?"

Two coins rattled into her cup. Gleefully, she snatched them out. One went into her mouth and she bit down on it. Then she did the same with the other. She smiled.

Feeling for the pocket of her tattered dress, she carefully deposited the two precious disks. Coins had already been stolen from her cup twice today, and she wasn't about to take any more chances.

She reached out again to find the hand of the one who had just been so kind, but whoever that person had been, he or she was gone. Just the same, the old woman thought she should give thanks.

"Bless you," she said to no one in her soft, cracking voice. She resumed feeling her way down the busy street. She moved hunched over, her gray hair hanging in snarled ropes down either side of her face. Her dress was in tatters. Her skin was gray; her eyes were sunken and without life. Every now and again she paused to cough raggedly. Then she once again took up the handles of the small, dilapidated handcart that held her meager possessions, and hobbled on.

The new day had broken clear and bright over Tammerland, and Evenger Street was as busy as it always was this time of the morning. Famous all over Tammerland for its bustling farmers' market, Evenger Street would soon fill with tavern owners, cooks, and wives come to haggle over the best selections. The woman knew the prospects for begging should be fair.

The shops here were all stalls, designed to be easily opened in the morning and then closed up again at night. Animals and birds were often slaughtered out in the open. Buckets of pig blood sat about, their contents to be used in the making of sausage. Piles of animal innards often blocked the way, black with flies as they dried in the sun.

The various chickens for sale were usually still alive, trussed up and flapping about noisily. The more valuable Eutracian pheasants resided anxiously in cages atop the stall counters. Upon their purchase they would be removed from their cages and their necks broken for transport home. Smaller creatures, such as rabbits, squirrels, and squab, usually suffered the same fate.

In the continued absence of the Royal Guard, cheating was prevalent. Wine was frequently watered, cheese was soaked in broth to make it look as if it had aged longer, and the flesh of bad fish was sometimes dipped in pig's blood to make it appear fresher. Although the markets on Evenger Street teemed with selections, true bargains were few and far between.

As she passed by the bakery she could smell the warm bread and hear the baker sliding a loaf from the oven with his long-handled wooden paddle. By law, the prices and weights of the loaves were supposed to be fixed, and each baker was required to stamp his loaves with his own seal. Bread was such an important staple that if a baker was found cheating, the citizens occasionally took matters into their own hands. The baker would then appear in the courtyard pillories, one of his underweight loaves firmly tied around his neck as a warning to his peers.

Guessing that cheating a blind person would prove far too tempting for any of these merchants, the beggar woman moved on, taking her growling stomach with her. Instead of soliciting at these stalls, whose proprietors saw many beggars like her, she decided to try her luck on a side street, where she could knock directly on doors. It would be harder for them to say no if she stood in the doorways of their homes, she reasoned.

Her first two solicitations yielded naught but slammed doors. The people behind the third door had been kinder, but they had been able to spare only a single kisa.

Tapping her way to the next door, she reached up to feel its surface. Eutracian custom said that the name of the family house was to be engraved on the doorpost. She ran her dirty fingers over the words and then knocked upon it.

This door opened and a man peered out. "May I help you?"

Staring at nothing, the woman held out her cup. "Alms for the blind?" she asked.

The man simply stared at her for a moment. "This is not an average dwelling," he finally said. "I understand that you are unable to see our sign, but we are not in the custom of giving our money away. I suggest you try the next door down."

The beggar woman thought for a moment. "Are you the master of the house?" she asked.

"No. Please go away."

She held her cup a bit higher. "If only I could speak to the master of the house," she pressed, "then perhaps he might grant me a few tokens of kindness. It is so little to ask."

The man scowled. "As I just told you, this place is not what you think. We never—"

"What is it, Caleb?" a deeper, more commanding voice interrupted. Another man joined the first in the doorway.

"It is only a beggar," Caleb replied. "I was just about to shoo her away."

The second man looked down at the ragged woman. Her gray skin told him that she was quite ill. A look of sympathy crossed his face.

"Let her in," he said. "I will see to her needs. You need to learn how to be more charitable, Caleb. After all, we have plenty to spare."

"As you wish," Caleb answered.

The older man took the woman by one hand and led her into the house, pulling her cart in after her. He led her to a nearby room and closed the door behind them. The simple chamber held little more than a bed and an adjoining washroom. As the man regarded her, he smiled.

"I knew you would come," he said. "But I didn't know when."

Standing up straight for the first time in hours, Satine stretched her back. After putting down her cup and her walking stick, she smiled at Aeolus.

"Thank you for letting me in. I worried that you might not recognize me."

Coming closer, Aeolus kissed one of her dirty cheeks. He beckoned her to a small table, where they both sat and he poured her a glass of water. She drank greedily. He looked her up and down while she emptied the glass.

"Forgive me, child, but are you ill?" he asked.

Smiling, Satine shook her head. "I'm fine."

"Then why is your skin so gray?" he asked. "And what happened to your hair? If I didn't know it was you, I'd truly think that you were at death's door! How did you manage this?"

"I swallowed one of Reznik's potions. It makes you violently ill for a while but the nausea eventually passes. It leaves your skin gray for a couple of days. As for my hair, I ran ash from a fireplace through it." She smiled again. "It is easily washed out."

Aeolus pointed at her pull-cart. "Are those your things?"

She nodded.

"So you need the Serpent and the Sword as a safe house after all," he said. "You're in trouble, aren't you?"

"Not exactly," she answered. "My situation had become more dangerous, but it's nothing I can't handle." She placed one hand atop Aeolus'. "Provided that you'll let me stay here for a while," she added softly.

"Of course," he answered. "You can stay here in this room. That door in the back wall opens into an alleyway. I'll give you a key so that you can come and go as you wish. But I think it would be wise that you do not wander about the school—especially without your disguise. You would surely be recognized."

"What will you tell your students?"

Aeolus smiled. "I'll tell them that I decided to take in a stray. It wouldn't be the first time. By the way, do you have a horse?"

"Yes. He's boarded in a stable not far from here. The fee is paid up for the next two fortnights."

Taking a deep breath, Aeolus nodded. His expression became grave.

"Have you heard the rumors?" he asked.

Satine shook her head. "I have been trying to speak to others as little as I can."

As he gathered his thoughts, Aeolus poured her another glass of water. "They're saying that a tragedy has befallen the Sippora. The rumor is that the river has been poisoned, and that a dark, superheated mass of some sort is approaching the city. If it reaches us, Tammerland is likely to be destroyed. There are bound to be riots for food and water. Only some act of the craft could cause such a calamity. Do you know anything about it?"

Satine sidestepped the question. "If it was caused by the craft, who do you think might be responsible?"

"I don't know," Aeolus answered. "It is said that the prince hosted a large meeting of townspeople in the palace to explain to them that he, his Minions, and his new Conclave are not the cause of our troubles. It is said that he went so far as to introduce them all personally—even the warrior who is second in command of the winged ones. But few were convinced. The wounds of the citizenry still run deep. Many lost loved ones to the very winged creatures the prince now claims to control."

Pausing for a moment, he looked into her eyes. "Are you still pursuing your sanctions?" he asked. Satine nodded.

"During your previous visit you told me that these were to be political killings," he added. "Is that still the case?"

"Yes. But please do not ask me again to desist in this matter, master," she said. "You may not like what I do, but I am a professional. Once I accept a sanction, I always follow it through."

His expression softening, Aeolus took both of her hands into his.

"You must hear me out on this," he said. "During his meeting with the citizens, the prince spoke of a great orb that rained destruction down upon the land. He also said that he and his Conclave did not create it. He claims that he and the princess have a half brother who is the real culprit."

"I know," she said softly. "I was there."

Stunned, Aeolus sat back in his chair. "You were?"

"Yes."

Aeolus looked hard at her. "Your sanctions are aimed against the prince and his Conclave, aren't they?" he asked. "The only reason you attended that meeting was to look them over."

Satine didn't answer. His eyes wide, Aeolus took her gently by the shoulders.

"What if the prince is telling the truth?" he asked.

"What if he is? That wouldn't change anything for me."

"Don't you see?" he protested. "If the Conclave isn't responsible, then other forces are—forces that want to tear this nation apart. And if that is the case, then the only hope Eutracia has is Tristan and his wizards!"

"And if Tristan *is* the cause of all this and I kill him, then who is to say that I haven't done the country a great service, eh?" she shot back. "Either way, I won't stop now!"

"Do you really want the fate of the nation in your hands?" Aeolus protested. "All for the sake of blood money that you will no doubt only use up to try to chase down your father's killer? Tell me, is it really worth all that? Where does your allegiance to yourself end and your duty to your nation begin? I taught you better than this! If Tristan is telling the truth, then he has found a way to put the death of his father behind him for the good of the nation. Can't you do the same?"

Satine looked down at the floor. "I didn't come here to debate you," she said. "I have to do what I have to do. But I must know right now. Are you going to turn me in?"

Aeolus shook his head. "I could never do that," he answered. "How could I betray the closest thing to a child I ever had? That would surely kill me as quickly as though someone plunged a dagger into my heart."

Satine let go a long sigh. "I would like to rest now," she said. She touched the sleeve of the old master's martial uniform. "But I want you to know that I will consider your words," she added softly.

Aeolus smiled. "You always were stubborn. I know I ask a great deal, but I also believe that I am right. Rest now, my child." He reached into a pocket and produced the key to the back door of Satine's room. He placed it on the table.

"In a few hours I will bring you some food and hot tea," he said as he walked to the other door. "In the meantime, you are safe here."

Once he was gone, Satine rose from the table and unpacked her things. She was glad to wash up and put on her usual clothes again. She hung the dual holsters that held her daggers over a bedpost so that they would be within easy reach. Then she removed one of the daggers from its sheath and she slid it beneath her pillow. Only then did she lay her tired body down upon the bed and close her eyes.

As sleep began to overtake her, she recalled what Aeolus had said. The more she considered his words, the more she began to wonder. For the first time since the death of her father, the Gray Fox felt uncertain about her chosen path. As sleep came to her in earnest, a lone tear slowly traced its way down one cheek.

Chapter LXVI

On the other side of Tammerland, Jessamay walked quickly along the street. It was still morning and the sun's rays were warm against her back. She wore a dark brown robe with its hood pulled up over her head. Her left hand tingled with the spell she had cast yesterday, the same spell that Faegan had granted Shailiha to hide her endowed blood from others of the craft. She flexed her fingers and smiled.

Pulling her robe closer around her, she carefully scanned the busy street ahead. The person she was following still maintained her quick gait, obviously sure of her destination and in a hurry. It was vital that Jessamay not lose sight of her, for the Conclave might never get another such chance.

Jessamay had taken no pleasure in informing the Conclave of her discovery the previous day. She had certainly not wished to intrude upon Tristan and Celeste's happiness. But her news had been so important that she knew it couldn't wait. Despite how impossible it might seem to the others, she was positive that Sister Vivian was a traitor.

She had first realized it just after returning to Eutracia with Wigg, Tristan, and Celeste. There had been many new people to meet. So many, in fact, that in some cases she found herself still trying to match the faces with the names.

But the moment she met Sister Vivian was one she would never forget. After more than three hundred years of being experimented on by Failee, Jessamay had finally been able to employ one of Failee's bizarre gifts: The first time she gazed into Vivian's light blue eyes, she knew that the acolyte's blood signature leaned to the left.

When she told the Conclave, everyone was stunned. When Wigg had called the acolytes home upon the River of Thought, he and Faegan had taken great pains to be sure that each graduate of Fledgling House was who she claimed to be and that none of them had in any way been tainted by the Vagaries. Their blood signatures had been matched to their birth documents in the Hall of Blood Records and also closely examined for preexisting Forestallments and the proper degree of lean to the right. Every woman had passed with flying colors.

Just the same, Jessamay had been adamant about what she had seen in Vivian's eyes. There could simply be no mistake. And so two intriguing questions bubbled to the surface. First, when had Vivian's signature been altered? It must have been at some point after she had been admitted to the Redoubt. And, second, who had accomplished this amazing transformation?

Surely no acolyte possessed the abilities to change the lean of a blood signature. Despite their combined skill and knowledge, even Wigg, Faegan, and Jessamay remained unable to do such a thing. They suspected that the calculations for the spell resided in Failee's grimoire, but so far none of them had had the time to research it. That left only one other person in the world whom they deemed capable of such a thing—the *Enseterat* himself.

At first the wizards had considered entering Vivian's mind to learn the truth. But that idea was quickly dismissed. Better to follow her discreetly, they realized, than to reveal their suspicions. More might be learned that way—perhaps even things Vivian herself did not yet know.

So now Jessamay followed her through Tammerland, eager to see where the traitorous acolyte would lead her.

Vivian slowed and came to stop at a street corner that faced a roundabout. A fountain danced and burbled in the roundabout's center. For some time the acolyte stood there looking around warily. Finally she walked to the fountain and sat down upon its edge. Several people sat near her, and three children played noisily in the area just to her left.

Jessamay settled down to wait on a bench before a shoemaker's shop, directly across from the fountain. She pulled the sides of her hood closer to her face.

Once the area cleared, Vivian looked around. Then she slipped a hand into the side pocket of her robe and withdrew something. Narrowing her eyes, Jessamay called upon the craft to augment her eyesight. As she waited and watched, the seconds ticked by. Suddenly, there it was.

For the briefest of moments an azure glow escaped from between Vivian's fingers only to vanish as quickly as it appeared. After looking carefully around again, the acolyte opened her hand. What looked like bits of golden grain drifted down into the water. Then the acolyte stood and walked away.

At first Jessamay was in a quandary about what to do. Vivian had obviously just left a message for someone. The device she had employed was called "the reading of the wheat," and Jessamay was well familiar with it. But was Vivian now going off to meet with someone else? Should Jessamay stay here on this bench before the shoemaker's shop, or leave to follow Vivian?

Taking a deep breath, Jessamay made up her mind to stay. Someone would come to read the message—of that much she was sure. The only question was how long it might take for Vivian's contact to arrive. Settling back against the unforgiving bench, Jessamay prepared for what could be a very long wait.

Hoping against hope that she was doing the right thing, she watched Vivian round the next street corner and vanish into the crowd.

TAKING A DEEP BREATH, JESSAMAY SHIFTED HER WEIGHT ON THE bench. Two hours had passed and she was beginning to wonder whether she had made the right decision. But there was little she could do about it now.

She was about to go buy a cool drink from one of the street vendors when she saw a man approach the fountain. Dressed in a peasant shirt, dark trousers, and scuffed knee boots, he was unremarkable. He looked around furtively and sat down on the edge of the fountain in the exact spot that Vivian had vacated.

Her interest piqued, Jessamay took a chance and strolled out into the roundabout. She stopped to stand directly behind the man on the opposite side of the fountain. Unless he turned all the way around, chances were he wouldn't notice her. If she was right about him, he would soon be too engrossed with the craft to bother. And if she wasn't, then it didn't matter.

From where she stood she could just see over the edge of the fountain and into the pool of swirling water. At the moment no one else was around. *If he's going to do it, now's the perfect time,* she thought.

As if he were cooling himself, the man casually placed one hand down into the water. Jessamay saw no evidence of azure. As if by its own accord, however, the water in the pool quickly stilled. The man looked down for a few moments and then withdrew his hand. Soon the water moved again. The entire procedure had been smooth and silent, but that hadn't fooled the experienced sorceress. She had her man and she knew it.

The fellow stood and walked purposefully across the square. Determined not to lose him, she followed. Suddenly he picked up the pace and rounded the next corner. Lengthening her stride, Jessamay went after him.

As she came around the corner, she nearly panicked when she saw that he had a carriage waiting. After shouting something up to the driver, the man climbed in and closed the door after him. The driver cracked his whip and the carriage-of-four charged up the street.

Frantic, Jessamay looked up and down the thoroughfare. Finally she saw a lone carriage about twenty meters up, its three passengers disembarking. She hiked up her skirts and ran to it as fast as she could.

"Take me up the street!" she shouted. "I'm in a great hurry!"

The grizzled driver looked down at her with distaste.

"That was my last fare for the day. I'm off duty. Find yourself another ride."

"But yours is the only one here!" Jessamay protested. Looking up the street, her heart sank when she saw the other carriage vanishing in the distance.

"I'll pay you anything!" she shouted. "You simply have to take me!"

"What are you, some kind of a crazy woman?" he shouted back at her. But greed and curiosity got the better of him. "How much ya got, anyway?"

Jessamay conjured high denomination kisa in her pockets as quickly as she could and began literally throwing the money up at him. His eyes grew as big as saucers.

"Get in!" he shouted.

"No!" Jessamay shouted back.

Using the craft to augment her strength, she jumped straight from the ground into the seat alongside the driver. His mouth agape, all the stunned man could do was to look at her.

Narrowing her eyes, she looked up the street again. She could just make out the other carriage rounding a far corner. She ripped the reins and whip away from him.

"I'll be the one driving!" she shouted. "I used to be pretty good at this, but it's been a while. I suggest you find something to hang on to!"

Jessamay snapped the whip, and the carriage charged up the street, the bewildered driver holding on for dear life. Keeping a reasonable distance behind the other carriage, Jessamay followed her quarry until it came to an abrupt stop in front of a tavern. When she watched the man jump from his carriage, run across the street, and enter the archery shop there, she knew that this was the place the Conclave had been searching for.

CHAPTER LXVII

FAEGAN LIFTED HIS EYES FROM THE PAGE HE WAS READING AND SHOOK his head in wonder. He had been sitting alone in the Archives of the Redoubt for most of last night and all of this morning. The half-eaten remains of the breakfast Shawna had insisted on bringing him rested near one elbow. Nicodemus padded about on the floor, purring and winding his way around the wizard's useless legs.

Faegan took another sip of tea, only to find that it had gone cold. Narrowing his eyes, he called the craft and heated the brew until it steamed again. This time it felt warm going down. Placing the cup down upon its saucer, he turned his attention back to the handwritten pages.

The book he was studying was Failee's grimoire. As he had anticipated, it was fascinating. Failee's elegant script was very stylized and she had written in dark green ink in a handwriting that was difficult to decipher, making the reading slow going. Worse yet, parts of the text were written in a code that Faegan had yet to unravel. But what he had been able to make out so far already had the wheels of his ever-curious mind turning.

The First Wizard, his daughter, and the *Jin'Sai* would be leaving within the hour. Late last night Faegan had granted Wigg's blood the calculations that would draw the First Wizard to the Well of the Forestallments, but the two wizards had not spoken since.

As he thought about the odds building against the Conclave, Faegan shook his head tiredly. He would have been far more comfortable about all of this if everyone were staying at the palace. Wigg's gifts in the craft were second only to his own, and he was sure that the Minions placed far more confidence in the prince than they did in him. He felt a deep need for Celeste to stay so that he could watch over her. But he also knew that Tristan was right. With Celeste accompanying them, they had a much greater chance of saving her life.

It was imperative that they find the Scroll Master. Absolutely nothing could be allowed to interfere with returning Tristan's blood to normal. Then the *Jin'Sai* might—somehow—repair the rent in the Orb of the Vigors and, everyone fervently hoped, save Celeste's life. But succeeding in these trials would be nearly impossible and the wizard knew it. As he looked back down at the grimoire, he couldn't help but think back to those days before the Sorceresses' War, when their world was still at peace and their early discoveries in the craft all seemed so wondrous and new.

Wigg and Failee had been married then, and at first they had seemed happy. For a long time Faegan had secretly envied Wigg's relationship with Failee. Not only was she beautiful, but her intelligence and skill in the craft were nearly without equal. That was why he and Wigg were both so stunned when she began to dabble in the Vagaries and to recruit others to follow her in her new cause.

But her imperfect use of the dark side of the craft had driven her mad. The result had been the Sorceresses' War, which had nearly torn both the nation and the craft asunder. Two centuries later, the Directorate learned that each blood signature had a discernible lean, and that Failee's angled far to the left. Such a trait inspired in her not only a desire to practice the Vagaries but a compulsion to do so—probably one beyond her ability to control. Had her crimes not been so heinous, one might even have been compelled to forgive her. *We fought hard to survive those dark days,* Faegan thought. *But how will we survive the ones that lie ahead?*

Suddenly he detected the presence of endowed blood. As it approached, he recognized that it belonged to Wigg.

The door swung open to reveal the First Wizard. Like Faegan, he looked tired and drawn. He had been this way ever since learning of Celeste's impending death. It was almost as if their lives and health were linked, one unable to survive without the other.

Wigg sat down heavily at the table. When he saw the grimoire, his brow furrowed.

"Shawna told me that I'd find you in the Archives," he said.

"But what I didn't know was that you'd been laboring all night. What on earth are you trying to accomplish down here, all by yourself?"

Not entirely sure where to begin, Faegan spent the next several minutes outlining his plan. Wigg listened politely, but the more Faegan spoke the more skeptical the First Wizard looked. "What do you think of it?" Faegan asked.

Wigg pursed his lips. "A very interesting notion, I agree. But the first part of your plan is clearly impossible. I don't know how we could ever accomplish such a thing; we simply don't possess that much raw power. And as for the second part, you mean to dabble in a discipline of the craft that we really know nothing about. That's why you've locked yourself away here in the Archives, isn't it? To research Failee's grimoire and try to discover how she managed to do it. But I needn't remind you that her work in this field was only half completed. To fully implement your plan, you would also have to first complete her calculations. Who knows how long that might take, even if it's possible at all! And I'm afraid, my friend, that time is one luxury we don't have."

Faegan sighed. "I know. But this seems the only way to proceed. If you have a better idea, I'm certainly willing to listen."

Wigg shook his head. "No," he said softly. "Nor will I be able to help you in your work—at least not until Tristan, Celeste, and I return from wherever the River of Thought takes us. There's no telling how far afield we might have to go."

"Have you tried to employ the additional spell that I imparted into your blood last night?" Faegan asked.

"Yes."

"And when you activate it, what does it feel like?"

Wigg thought for a moment. "I almost feel as though part of me has become a living, breathing compass. I am inexorably drawn in a certain direction. And although I cannot say for sure, I suspect that the closer I come to the Well, the stronger the feeling will become. I must also remember what Sister Adrian said. If I try to travel too fast, I will overtake the spell and temporarily lose the sensation. But finding the Well quickly is exactly what *must* be done. Even though we haven't departed yet, I can't begin to tell you how maddening this restriction already seems!"

Nodding, Faegan put one hand over Wigg's. "I can only imagine," he said. "Tell me. In which direction does the spell bid you?"

"Northwest."

Faegan scowled. "I needn't remind you that the ruptured orb lies that way."

"Of course," Wigg answered.

Deciding to change the subject, Faegan leaned back and placed his hands into the opposite sleeves of his robe. "Has Jessamay returned?" he asked.

"No," Wigg answered. "But she can take care of herself. She was one of the most powerful sorceresses of the Vigors that we ever knew. We are indeed fortunate to have her back."

"Are you quite sure about that?"

"What do you mean?"

"I'm talking about her blood signature," Faegan replied. "You said that it now has no discernible lean. But what does that mean for us? It would seem to make her more prone to want to practice the Vagaries, would it not? And to what degree? I do not need to tell you how dangerous it would be for such a person to be privy to the Conclave's plans. In fact, she may already know too much."

"I'm aware of your concerns," Wigg answered. "I have personally examined her signature. Since it shows no appreciable lean one way or the other, I am convinced that her past devotion to the Vigors and the basic goodness of her heart will win out. Besides, what other choice do we have? To forbid such a powerful sorceress to help us in this time of need would be inexcusable."

"I suppose you're right," Faegan said.

"When she returns you must make quick use of whatever information she brings you," Wigg cautioned. "If she has unearthed any link to Wulfgar's confederates or to the assassin Satine, you must deal with them quickly. But try to take at least one of them alive. The information they might provide could prove priceless."

As he recalled Geldon and Lionel's deaths, Faegan's look became harsh. No one had to remind him about Satine. Only she and the Afterlife knew how many more she had disposed of during the course of her grisly career. And his wizard's pride was still stung over the way Reznik had outsmarted him at Val-renkium. *This is far from over,* he thought. *But when all is said and done, I will be the one to end it.* He looked back to Wigg.

"Don't worry," he said. "Taking care of them will be my pleasure."

Wigg gave him a slight smile. "I know," he said.

Wigg reached out and ran his palm over one of the pages of the grimoire. The dry green ink and the wrinkled parchment felt dead, almost alien to his touch.

"Do you miss her?" Faegan asked.

Withdrawing his hand, Wigg sighed.

"I miss what she once was," he answered. "But certainly not what she became. For the last three hundred years I have struggled against everything that she believed in. And now here we are, trying to employ her tools to help the Vigors. It's ironic, to say the least."

"Indeed," Faegan answered. "This grimoire is a revelation, Wigg. I am only beginning to understand just how brilliant your late wife really was, and what an impact she has had on us all, right up to this very day."

Wigg stood abruptly, his face unreadable. "Tristan, Celeste, and the Minions who are to accompany us await me in the court-yard. But before I go, tell me. Are you completely in agreement with our battle plans?"

"Yes. Tyranny's fleet and what remains of the Minion fleet will guard the coast as best they can. She has been ordered to simply report the appearance of the enemy vessels—though if I know her, she will engage them, even though she has little or no chance against the Black Ships. Once we have learned when and where Wulfgar is about to land, Traax and I will hit him with everything we have. I seriously doubt that it will be enough."

"And the flask that I brought back from Parthalon," Wigg said. "You have it hidden in a safe place? If it fell into the wrong hands, it would be disastrous."

For the first time that day Faegan managed a slight smile. "Safe and sound, I promise," he said. "And by the way, I must compliment you. That was excellent thinking on your part. You will tell Tristan and Celeste about my idea?"

"Of course. It's only right that they be informed. But I must tell you again how slim your chances of success seem to be. Still, if there is anyone who can do it, it is you."

Faegan reached up to take Wigg's hand. "Even though I'm coming to see you off, I will say my goodbyes now, old friend," he said. "May you succeed in all that you are about to do."

"And you," Wigg answered.

The First Wizard released Faegan's hand, turned, and walked out the door. Leaving Failee's grimoire behind, Faegan followed along. As they traveled in silence back up to the palace, each wizard knew that he would need every bit of luck in the world.

As Tristan walked hand in hand with Celeste through the palace halls, he did his best to conceal his worry. The time enchantments that held her youth in place were clearly decaying at an accelerating rate. Her appearance had noticeably worsened.

When she rose this morning and looked into one of the mirrors in their personal chambers, her eyes had filled with fear. Taking her in his arms, Tristan had done all he could to convince her that they would soon find the Scroll Master, and that everything would be all right. But even to him his words sounded hollow.

Right before his eyes, the beautiful, vivacious woman Tristan loved was literally turning into someone else. Her once red, shining hair was becoming gray, brittle, and coarse. The crow's-feet around her eyes had deepened; folds had appeared in the skin of her neck. She was thinner. The brown jerkin and peasant's blouse she wore hung loosely on her frame, and she carried herself with less power and authority than she once had. Her gift with the azure bolts was fading, as well. It was almost as if she were wasting away from some disease.

In a way that is exactly what is happening, Tristan thought as he walked beside her. *She suffers with a disease of the blood— and it is my fault. If we cannot find the Scroll Master in time, I will lose her forever. My heart will never recover.*

As they approached the end of the hallway, the two Minion warriors standing guard snapped to attention. Tristan gave them a short nod. One of them quickly opened the paned glass doors, and the *Jin'Sai* and his new bride walked out into the sunshine of the rear courtyard.

Everything seemed to be ready. A phalanx of fifty warriors waited on the grass, a litter laden with food and water beside them. Ox waited nearby, holding the reins of three saddled horses, one of them Shadow, whom Tristan had brought from Parthalon. When he saw Tristan, the black stallion flung up his head and whinnied impatiently.

The other members of the Conclave and all of the palace gnomes had come to see them off. Tristan did not see Jessamay, and he realized that she must still be on her mission in Tammerland. Shawna stood front and center among the gnomes, Morganna in her arms. As they waited in the sun, each person seemed to display his or her particular brand of concern.

Looking past the litters, Tristan saw the charred remains of the funeral pyres. Smoke still curled lazily into the air, and from where he and Celeste stood they could feel the lingering heat. Turning away, he walked Celeste over to the waiting crowd.

Shailiha was the first to say goodbye. As she approached, Caprice fluttered gently overhead. Shailiha gave her brother and sister-in-law each a kiss on the cheek.

"I want you both to be careful!" she said with mock ferociousness. Then she smiled. "I have every intention of becoming an aunt, and soon!"

Tyranny walked forward to embrace them both. There was a rather tight smile on her face. As she hugged him, Tristan could sense that there was something brittle about her, and that was unusual. Given the circumstances, however, he decided not to pursue it. The privateer looked at Celeste, then the prince.

"You just go and do what you have to, and don't worry about us," she said. "If Wulfgar is foolish enough to enter our waters, Scars and I will give him a proper reception, I promise you."

"I know," Tristan answered. "We're counting on you."

The prince found Traax standing alongside Duvessa and beckoned him forward.

"Has there been any word from the warriors following the orb, or from those watching the pass through the Tolenkas?" Tristan asked.

"No, my lord."

"Or any messages from our outposts on the coast?"

Traax shook his head. "The land seems quiet, and that's what bothers me."

Taking a step closer, Tristan placed one hand on Traax's shoulder. He was pleased to see that his second in command was no longer wearing his sling.

"Do you remember your orders?" the prince asked.

"Yes, my lord. We will do everything in our power to stop them."

Movement at the other side of the courtyard suddenly caught the prince's eye. He looked over past Traax to see the two wizards approaching. As they came nearer, Tristan saw that Wigg wore the Paragon. Its bloodred highlights twinkled in the morning sun as it swung on its gold chain.

"Is everything ready?" the First Wizard asked.

Tristan nodded. "As ready as it can be," he said. "It's time to go."

The rest of the Conclave and all of the palace gnomes came forward to say goodbye. Abbey walked up to Wigg and gave him a long kiss on the mouth. Wigg blushed. As if he suddenly needed something to do with his hands, he quickly looked down and unnecessarily smoothed out the folds of his robe. Faegan cackled softly.

"That kiss was for luck," Abbey said. Smiling, she grabbed Wigg's robe and pulled him closer. "Come home safe, old man," the herbmistress whispered into his ear. "After being without you for nearly three hundred years, I wouldn't want to lose you now." Letting him go, she stepped back and wiped away a tear.

The three of them walked to their horses. Wigg climbed onto his bay mare, and Tristan helped Celeste mount the gentle gray gelding he had selected for her. He took Shadow's reins from Ox and swung up into the black, hand-tooled saddle. As he wheeled Shadow around, the stallion danced eagerly beneath him.

Tristan turned to give Shailiha a final look of farewell. She nodded back at her twin brother with a tight-lipped smile. Saying nothing more, the *Jin'Sai* trotted Shadow toward the rear gates, Wigg and Celeste following behind.

Minion warriors swung the heavy portals wide. Without looking back Tristan led Wigg and Celeste out.

Ox promptly shouted out a series of orders to the phalanx of waiting warriors, and they immediately took flight. A dozen more hoisted the heavy supply litter to their shoulders. A few moments later, they were gone as well. With a command from Faegan, the remaining warriors closed and locked the palace gates.

As the crowd dispersed, Abbey came to stand by Faegan's chair. She placed one hand on the wizard's shoulder.

"Do they really have any chance of success?" she asked him. "Does this Scroll Master even exist?"

His face grim, Faegan looked up at her.

"You are asking questions that I have no answers for," he said. "Just the same, Tristan and Wigg *have* to succeed. Our entire world depends upon it."

Saying nothing more, Abbey wheeled Faegan's chair from the courtyard.

As the *JIN'SAI* AND HIS GROUP PASSED BY, A HAGGARD OLD woman waited quietly on horseback, partially concealed by the foliage lining the road. In one hand she held the reins of a loaded packhorse. She waited until both the group on horseback and the circling warriors were out of sight, then she carefully walked her horse out into the road and followed along behind.

Realizing that one of her dagger sheaths was exposed, she covered it with the folds of her tattered dress and smiled slightly.

CHAPTER LXVIII

His FACE GRIM IN THE LIGHT OF THE FIREPLACE, FAEGAN PUT down his wineglass. The tavern was a shabby—perhaps even dangerous—place to be, but it suited his needs. The four people sitting with him were eager to take action. It was early evening in Tammerland. The light of day was being slowly replaced by the softer glow coming from the lampposts bordering the street.

"You and Scars are probably the only ones that they cannot identify," he whispered to Jessamay, who had returned only two hours earlier to tell her tale. "That's why you two are going in first. We have to know how many we're dealing with. When we see your signal, we'll come straight away. But remember, we want at least one of them taken alive."

Pausing for a moment, the crippled wizard placed a hand on one of Jessamay's. "Is your spell still in place?" he asked.

"My blood is well cloaked," she answered with a brief smile. "Just like the old days."

"Just like the old days indeed," he replied. Glancing across the street one more time, Faegan decided that his little band was as ready as they'd ever be.

"Go now," he said. "And may the Afterlife be with you."

Jessamay and Scars rose from their chairs, walked quietly across the tavern, and went out through the double doors.

As Faegan watched Jessamay and Scars walk toward the archery shop, his nerves coiled up. He knew that there were a thousand ways his makeshift plan could go wrong, but they needed to gain entrance to the shop today, before whoever was inside decided to close for the night. Further complicating matters was the fact that when they left the palace, Vivian had not yet returned. No one knew where she might be.

Taking a deep breath, Jessamay opened the door of the shop and walked in with Scars. As the little bell at the top of the door jingled, the two of them looked around, wary.

The place was empty save for the two men behind the counter. One of them was short and balding. Red garters held up the sleeves of his sweat-stained shirt. He looked like the type who would be perpetually nervous, regardless of the circumstances. The proprietor, Jessamay reasoned.

The other man was the fellow she had seen at the fountain. He had close-cropped hair, dark eyes, and a hawk-beaked nose. Seated in a chair behind the counter, he slowly whittled a piece of wood. When he looked up at her, she could sense his innate intelligence. Of the two men, he was clearly the one to fear. He looked back down at his whittling and casually blew the freshly shaven wood chips to the floor.

As Jessamay approached the counter with Scars, she felt the familiar tingle. Clearly, each of these men possessed endowed blood. But were they trained in the craft? Using the pre-arranged signal to inform Scars, she touched one finger to the side of her nose. Tyranny's first mate gave her a nearly imperceptible nod.

Jessamay gathered up her nerve for her final test of the two men. If it proved what she already guessed to be true, she and Scars would have to move fast.

Leaning his great bulk up against the counter, Scars looked the proprietor in the eye.

"I need a good deer bow," he said. He jerked one thumb over his shoulder at Jessamay. "The wife and I are leaving town to go live in the country. They say there's trouble brewin' here in the city. If you were smart, you'd think about doin' the same."

"A deer bow, you say?" the proprietor asked. "That will cost you. Deer bows are the most powerful, and it takes a long time to make a good one."

"Show me," Scars said.

The proprietor came out from behind the counter. Out of the corner of her eye Jessamay kept track of the fellow in the chair. Another sure, slow stroke of his whittling knife sent more fresh shavings to the floor.

The proprietor walked to the far wall and took down a bow. Scars walked over to join him. The man handed it to him.

"This is one of the strongest I have," he said. "Few men can even pull it. Why don't you give it a try?"

"Give me a broadhead," Scars said. "Pulling a bow with an arrow in place is the only way I can tell whether I'll like it."

After giving Scars a skeptical glance, the man provided him with a broadheaded hunting arrow. Scars notched it. He then extended his bow arm and easily pulled the arrow and string back to his chin. He looked as though he could have held it that way all day.

He turned to face the rear of the shop. Acting the part of dutiful wife, Jessamay turned to admire his strength. She gave him a slight nod. Time for the second test, she thought.

She turned back to examine the other man, who continued to whittle away. Steeling herself against whatever might happen next, Jessamay dropped the spell that cloaked her blood.

The man immediately stiffened, and stopped his knife mid-stroke. Without looking up at her, he simply did nothing for a moment. Then he leaped to his feet.

Jessamay turned toward Scars. "Now!" she shouted.

Turning back toward the front of the shop, Scars loosed the arrow toward one of the store windows. The front of the shop exploded in shattered glass. Faegan glided his chair across the street; Tyranny and Shailiha, their swords drawn, ran as fast as they could behind him.

"You bitch!" the man behind the counter screamed. "I'll kill you where you stand!" He raised his arms.

Jessamay knew that she would not be able to summon the craft before the man behind the counter could. A split second before he loosed his azure bolts at her, she dropped to her knees.

The twin streaks of pale blue light ripped across the top of the counter. As they passed they tore at her hair, and she felt their searing heat. To her horror, they streaked straight for Scars.

At the last moment, Scars dropped the bow and grabbed the proprietor, lifted him off his feet, and held him up as a shield.

The bolts struck the man in the chest and tore him apart. Scars angrily tossed the mangled body to one side.

Jessamay crouched on the floor. Faegan, Tyranny, and Shailiha raced up the steps to the shop. Jessamay peeked up over the countertop just in time to hear the man growl another epithet before disappearing behind a worn curtain. She sprang to her feet and ran around the counter to follow him.

She didn't want to rush down the stairs, but she saw no other choice. As she set foot upon the cellar floor, the man hurried toward a door in the far wall. Just as he entered the tunnel he loosed another bolt at Jessamay. It missed, obliterating the stairway behind her. Faegan lowered his chair into the room. The man ran into the tunnel, slamming the door behind him.

Jessamay and Faegan hurried to the door. The sorceress was just about to open it when Faegan shouted at her and roughly pushed her to one side. Positioning his chair against the wall on the other side of the doorway, he called upon the craft.

As soon as the door swung open, two more azure bolts tore from the tunnel and into the cellar. Had Jessamay been standing in the doorway she would have been killed instantly. The bolts streaked across the room and struck the far wall. Much of the brick edifice came thundering down, exposing the dirt behind it. As the smoke cleared, Jessamay saw Scars' strong arms lowering first Tyranny and then Shailiha down into the room.

Turning back, Jessamay saw that Faegan had situated his chair in the doorway. She hurried to stand behind him. In the distance she could see the man running down the length of the tunnel to freedom. When Faegan didn't immediately react, she raised her arms to stop the fugitive.

No!" Faegan hollered. "I want him alive!"

Taking careful aim, the old wizard loosed twin bolts. Jessamay held her breath as she watched them speed down the length of the tunnel.

The bolts flew over the fugitive's head and stopped directly in his path, where they split into multiple strands—a glowing azure spider's web stretching from the tunnel's ceiling to its floor, and from wall to wall. Before the man could stop, he ran straight into it. Suspended within its grasp like a fly waiting helplessly for the spider, he struggled mightily to free himself—to no avail.

Jessamay turned to see Tyranny and Shailiha looking down the length of the tunnel, their expressions awestruck.

Wasting no time, Faegan raised his arms again. More azure energy streamed from his hands. It snaked around the outer edges of the web, separating it from the wall and turning it so that the trapped fugitive faced them. Then more azure came, this time creating a transparent wall that separated them from the captive. Faegan lowered his arms.

Hearing a noise, all four of them turned to see Scars hanging by his hands from the damaged shop floor above. He let go and dropped safely into the cellar. Faegan motioned for the giant to come nearer. Scars' shirt was charred and partially burned away, and his massive chest was scalded.

"Hold still," Faegan said. Narrowing his eyes, the wizard invoked a spell of accelerated healing over the burn, and another to take away the pain.

"Better?" he asked.

Nodding, Scars sighed with relief. "Much better, thank you," he answered.

Faegan looked at the others. "Is everyone all right?" he asked. They all nodded.

Shailiha pointed down the length of the tunnel. "What is the purpose of the wall?" she asked.

Faegan gave her a wink. "It will help ensure that our traitor cannot try to hurt us again," he answered. "Follow along behind me, everyone. It's high time we got some answers. But be careful—we do not know what else he is capable of."

Faegan wheeled his chair down the tunnel to a spot just short of the azure wall. Hanging spread-eagled in the web, the man looked down in defiance.

"Very clever, Wizard," Bratach said. "But neither you nor Wigg will defeat Wulfgar. He is about to unleash a devastating force upon Eutracia, the likes of which you haven't seen since the Sorceresses' War."

"Why don't you tell me about it?" Faegan asked, his face hard.

Bratach spat at them in defiance, the spittle running down his side of the azure wall.

"You were once a loyal member of the Consuls of the Redoubt, weren't you?" Faegan asked. "But the son of the *Jin'Sai* altered the lean of your blood signature, and he turned you to the worship of the Vagaries. Yes, that's right. We know all about it. Tell me: How many more of your traitorous kind still roam Eutracia?"

Bratach remained silent.

"What is your name?" Faegan asked. "You might as well tell us now, for we can always glean it later on from your blood records."

The man's face was a mask of hatred and defiance.

"Very well. Suit yourself," Faegan said, deciding to try another line of questioning. "I will have all of my answers after I enter your mind.

"Where is Satine?" he asked. "She has already killed two of my friends. I have unfinished business with her."

Smiling, the consul shook his head. "You'll never find her," he gloated. "She's far too good at what she does. She's a killing machine. She'll go on and on until she's satisfied every sanction that she accepted, no matter what becomes of me. Whatever else the future might hold for you, from here on, all of your days are numbered."

Pausing for a moment, Bratach smiled down at them. "And as you are all about to see," he added cryptically, "so are mine. Surely you must understand that I cannot allow you to enter my mind."

Faegan took a quick breath. He suddenly understood what was about to happen, but he couldn't predict what form it would take. Without knowing the required counterspell, he was helpless to stop it.

Bratach narrowed his eyes. Almost at once, the glow of the craft surrounded him. His eyes locked upon Faegan's, he began to shudder. Soon he was convulsing madly as he hung in the azure web.

He began to bleed from his ears. Suddenly he convulsed even more violently, and blood began to run from his eyes, nose, and mouth.

Faegan knew what was happening. The yet-to-be-identified consul was committing suicide by enacting a Forestallment that caused him to bleed out, and there was absolutely nothing that he could do about it.

As she stood by the wizard's side, Jessamay understood it, too. Looking over her shoulder at Shailiha, Tyranny, and Scars, the sorceress shook her head.

The blood slipped down Bratach's face to the strands of azure webbing and dripped to the tunnel floor. His blood signature formed here and there, revealing dozens of Forestallments. For his use later, Faegan committed the shape of the signature to memory. Soon there was so much blood that the signatures were engulfed by a single, spreading pool.

Bratach's head slumped to his chest and a final rattle escaped his lungs. He hung there limply in the web, his skin blanched. Knowing he had been bested, Faegan looked down at the pool of blood. As he expected, areas still moved. Finally dying, the trained, endowed blood slowly stilled.

Faegan knew what was coming next. Lifting his head, he augmented his wizard's hearing. The phenomenon started almost immediately.

From the streets above, they heard the wind pick up and start to howl. Louder and louder it became, until the noise hurt their ears. Then the thunder boomed, and flashes of lightning illuminated the cellar. With so many powerful Forestallments dying at once, the wizard could only imagine what it must be like up above, on the streets of Tammerland. The citizens would be scared to death.

He looked back at the pool of blood that only moments before had held one of the greatest secrets of the craft. *Perhaps we will one day truly understand what happens when a Forestallment dies,* he thought. *And why the sky seems to break apart when it does. Perhaps Wigg and Tristan will learn the secret—provided they can find the Scroll Master and the Well of Forestallments.*

But for now all I have is another dead traitor upstairs, and his secrets will go with him to his grave.

CHAPTER LXIX

STANDING ALONE IN THE BOW OF HER FLAGSHIP, TYRANNY TOOK A final draw from her cigarillo. She lazily blew out the smoke and tossed the cigarillo's charred remains into the sea. The waiting was the worst part, she knew. Half of her wanted the impending conflict to start, and the other half hoped that it never would.

After what the traitorous consul in the archery shop had told them, the Conclave knew that Wulfgar's Black Ships were on the way. But given so much coastline to guard—and with only her twelve ships and the remainder of the Minion fleet with which to do it—the task before her seemed impossible.

For the last three days the *Reprise* and the other vessels under her command had dutifully plowed up and down the Sea of Whispers. Their mission was to patrol the waters between the coastal city of Far Point and the huge bay that bordered Farplain. So far, everything had been quiet.

Faegan had strongly advised her that when Wulfgar arrived, he would probably try to anchor his ships as close to the pass through the Tolenkas as possible. Reaching the azure wall in the mountains would be his first priority. That meant that the most logical staging point for his invasion would be somewhere along the coast that lay just north of Shadowood.

Only fifty-one Minion warships had survived the prior battles with Wulfgar's demonslaver fleet, and their captains were doing their best to help Tyranny patrol. As for the *Reprise,* her repairs had been hurried but adequate. Though all sixty-three vessels in the fleet were filled nearly to the sinking point with eager warriors, Tyranny shuddered when she thought of how much Eutracian coastline remained open to invasion. She hoped that Faegan's assumptions about Wulfgar's battle plan would prove to be correct.

She cast her gaze back out to sea. It was almost seven o'clock, and the sun had just disappeared below the western horizon. When she was aboard ship, this was always her favorite part of the day.

Tonight the sea was relatively calm, the winds were steady, and the fleet's pace was more than adequate. Unless a fog formed, the visibility would be excellent. The other vessels followed the *Reprise* in a line, at intervals of approximately one-half league. Just now they were in the midst of yet another northern leg of their patrol, and the mysterious area of Shadowood would soon come up along their port side.

At least K'jarr's scouts were keeping the vessels in some form of communication, however tenuous, she thought. Others continually patrolled as far to the east as they dared. This added great range to Tyranny's search, and she was thankful for it. But a squad of four such scouts had already perished when they had overestimated their endurance. She was determined to keep loss of life to a minimum, no matter what it took.

Hearing the sound of approaching footsteps, she turned to see Shailiha, Sister Adrian, and Duvessa walking toward her, the princess carrying an open bottle of red wine. Adrian held four glasses. Duvessa carried a stone jug of akulee. They were all smiling. Tyranny raised an eyebrow.

Shailiha and Duvessa held their bottles high. "Reinforcements!" the princess announced cheerfully. "At least that's what Tristan likes to call it."

Duvessa and Adrian laughed.

Shailiha poured out three glasses of wine, while Duvessa served herself a glassful of akulee. Tyranny accepted a glass from Shailiha, raised it in a silent toast, then drained it in one long, welcome draft.

"Bless you," she said. She held the glass out for a refill.

As she took another sip, Tyranny looked at Duvessa's body armor. Since that day in Valrenkium when Reznik's beasts had come snarling up out of the earth, all of the healers who had participated in the fight with Duvessa had been granted the additional distinction of the red feather. Embroidered into the leather, it crossed over the white one at a sharp angle.

When Traax had seen how well the women fought, he had immediately requested permission from the *Jin'Sai* to grant them warrior status—without the need for the customary rites of ascension. Glad to see that his vision of adding females to the warrior ranks was taking hold, Tristan heartily approved.

Upon seeing the honor of the red feather emblazoned upon the healers' armor more female Minions had requested warrior training. Even the stern Traax—who at first had harbored grave doubts about the prince's idea—now touted the concept every chance he could find. Duvessa found that amusing, but she did not chide him about it.

Ironic, Tyranny thought as she stared at the red feather. The Minion women were such wonderful healers, and yet now such accomplished takers of life, as well. Tyranny had requested that a small group of these new warriors be assigned to each of her sixty-three ships, and she was particularly glad to have their dual skills at her service.

Shailiha walked to the gunwale and leaned her arms upon the rail. She smiled to herself as she remembered that she no longer needed Faegan's spell to combat her seasickness. She was beginning to understand her brother's love of the sea.

But when she turned back around to the others, her face was worried.

"If Wulfgar catches us out here with his Black Ships, do we have any hope of stopping him?" she asked Tyranny bluntly. "Worse yet, can we survive it?"

Tyranny didn't answer. Striking a match against one of her scuffed knee boots, she lit another cigarillo. After taking a luxurious lungful of smoke, she shook her head.

"I don't know," she answered. "But if you put a dagger to my throat and force me to choose, I would have to say no. Faegan and Wigg seem to believe that the *Enseterat* will come with his Black Ships first, because they are so much faster. Then the demonslaver war frigates will follow. If the wizards are correct, in the beginning we will have superior numbers. But at the Citadel, you and I saw firsthand what the Black Ships can do. And don't forget about how huge those vessels are. They were built to carry something. But what could that be—more demonslavers, perhaps? Or will it be something even worse? We barely got away with our teeth that night.

"Remember that day not so long ago in my cabin?" she added. "After K'jarr had described what the Black Ships were capable of, I was practically ready to have him keelhauled! But in the end he was exactly right."

She took another sip of wine as she gathered her thoughts.

"And we still don't know what these seven captains of Wulfgar's are capable of," she added glumly. "Wigg and Faegan claim that they were once powerful wizards. But in their present form, can they still employ the craft? No one knows. But I needn't tell any of you about the kind of destruction seven full-fledged wizards could wreak upon our ships. We might never know what hit us."

Tyranny gave Sister Adrian a respectful nod. "That is why I petitioned Faegan so forcefully to allow us to have some of the Acolytes of the Redoubt along. If the seven captains of the Black Ships still command their powers, perhaps our ladies can pay them something back in return. I would have loved to have Jessamay here with us as well, but Faegan swore he couldn't spare her. Something about how she was the only one who could help him in his seemingly never-ending research, he said. Tell me. Does he *ever* stop studying the craft?"

Shailiha smiled. "I don't think so," she answered. "Sometimes it seems like—"

Two distinct sounds interrupted her. One of them was the peal of the warning bell in the crow's nest. The other was the sound of K'jarr and Scars running toward them.

K'jarr had just returned from a patrol. His wings drooping toward the deck, it was all he could do to catch his breath. Scars had that predatory look on his face that Tyranny knew so well.

"A patrol has found them!" Scars announced. "All seven of the Black Ships are approximately six leagues due east and coming fast, flying above the sea." The giant first mate's face turned hard in the growing moonlight. "Wulfgar's invasion has begun."

Tyranny shot a look at K'jarr. "Did you see any demonslaver frigates?" she asked.

Still trying to catch his breath, the Minion shook his head.

She nodded. *It seems that the crippled wizard Faegan was right after all,* she thought. *And unless we change course, the Black Ships will soon have the angle on us—in addition to their greater speed.* She turned back to K'jarr.

"Do you think they saw you?"

K'jarr shook his head. "I kept the patrol very high. But I'm sure of what I saw. The size of the Black Ships makes them hard to mistake."

Tyranny looked over at Adrian. "What are the odds that Wulfgar will sense us?" she asked.

"That is nearly impossible to say," Adrian answered. "The spell Faegan invoked over the Sisters and Shailiha to cloak our blood continues to hold, but this is the *Enseterat* we're dealing with, and in many ways his powers dwarf even those of Faegan's. There is simply no telling whether he will be able to sense our blood before he actually sees our fleet. I recommend caution."

Tyranny shook her head. "There will be a time for caution,"

she said ominously. "But now is not it. Tonight he sails only with his Black Ships. He is as vulnerable as he will ever be. If he isn't stopped before his demonslaver frigates arrive, or before he can breach the azure wall in the Tolenkas, he may never be defeated."

She looked east. She saw nothing except a calm ocean, but she knew that was about to change. For several moments she calculated the various distances, speeds, and angles in her mind. Finally she turned back to K'jarr.

"Order a messenger to fly to each of our other ships and inform them of the situation," she said. "I want the fleet divided. The northern half is to turn northeast; the southern half is to turn east for two leagues, then turn north. Each ship is to douse all of her lights and go on battle alert. Go now. And tell all of your messengers to hurry. Our lives depend upon it."

K'jarr bowed slightly. "I live to serve," he said. He was gone in an instant.

"What are you planning to do?" Shailiha asked the privateer.

After draining the rest of her wine, Tyranny rolled the glass back and forth between her hands. She looked up at Scars and the other three women.

"What I *must* do, if he is ever to be defeated," she said. "First we will surround him. Then we will attack with all sixty-three ships, and every crewman and Minion we can muster. We have to stop him here." Her jaw set, she looked to the east once more.

"And may the Afterlife save us if we fail."

CHAPTER LXX

CROUCHING ON THE DAMP FOREST FLOOR, SATINE LOOKED OUT over the glowing Minion campfires. The night was dark. She shivered with the cold. She hadn't eaten any warm food for three days. From this distance, she couldn't smell the cooking aromas that would be coming from the warrior camp in the small valley below, but she could imagine them.

The Gray Fox had patiently followed the prince, Wigg, Celeste, and the Minion phalanx for the last three days. Bratach and Ivan had told her that the *Jin'Sai* would be leaving the palace, but they hadn't known why. She still didn't know where the prince and his group were leading her, and she didn't care. All she wanted was to complete her sanctions.

The royal party's pace had been agonizingly slow, with the Minions continually circling overhead so as to not hurry on before them. At first she had been certain that the accompanying warriors would make her job all the more difficult, and she had cursed their presence. As time went on, however, she realized that by watching the warriors in the sky, she could follow from a far greater distance and still not lose track of her quarry. This advantage—coupled with her disguise—added greatly to her hopes for success.

Still, she hadn't found an opportunity to act. With so many warriors guarding the royal party both in the air and on the ground, nighttime would provide the best opportunity. She would follow them for as long as necessary to find the perfect moment to strike.

Tonight would not provide the chance she sought. These Minions weren't fools. Each night they made camp in an open spot where cover was scarce. Two tents always sat in the center of the camp, surrounded by the others. She was sure that those belonged to the *Jin'Sai*, Celeste, and the wizard. Tonight was no exception. Deciding that she would have to wait yet again, she retreated into the woods.

Her campsite was sparse, allowing her to move quickly should she need to. She had tied her gelding and her packhorse to a nearby tree. The saddlebags containing her food and weapons lay within easy reach on the forest floor. She had no fire, for she couldn't risk being discovered. A blanket lay on the ground, and her saddle served as her pillow. When dawn came she would rise, eat something quickly, and then set out again to find the warriors circling the sky in the distance.

She reached into a pocket of her tattered dress and removed a piece of folded parchment. She had been carrying it ever since

Ivan had first given it to her in the dank cellar of the archery shop. At the time, she had thought his self-important skulduggery silly. But now—two kills later—she had to admit that the traitorous consuls and their unknown confederate in the palace had been immensely helpful.

She unfolded the parchment and held it up to the moonlight, memorizing the address on it and its related code phrases.

She looked back up at the three magenta moons. It would be at least ten hours until dawn, so she should have plenty of time to visit the nearby village. *Besides,* she thought, *maybe they'll have some real food.* She refolded the parchment and hid it in her boot.

After changing from her disguise into her usual clothing, she strapped her daggers onto her thighs and put on her cloak. She made certain that her packhorse was securely tied to the tree, then she mounted her gelding and set off. It would be slow going through the forest until she came to the road, but it would give her valuable time to think.

So far, the *Jin'Sai* and his group seemed to be sticking to the roads, heading northwest. They had avoided the few towns along their route. Only three hours earlier the royal party had gone around a small hamlet called Morningshire—no doubt in order to avoid the Minions frightening the inhabitants. Satine had chosen to continue following the royal party, rather than risk losing them by detouring through the village, which her parchment listed as the location of one of the rural consular sanctuaries. Once the prince and his companions had made camp for the night, she would be free to double back to the village and check to see if there was a message waiting for her there.

Once she emerged onto the road, she memorized the spot where she exited the forest, then turned her horse southeast and spurred him into a relaxed gallop.

Half an hour later, she could see the lights of Morningshire. She slowed her horse and entered the village cautiously. Few people were out and about; those on the streets took little heed of her. Morningshire struck her as the kind of place that wanted little to do with the rest of the world, and that suited her just fine. She passed a schoolhouse on her right, and then a small inn on her left. As she continued, a livery, a general store, and a bakery appeared out of the darkness and then retreated again, each of them closed.

She recalled the address: 555 Everwood Lane. It certainly sounded innocent enough—hardly the kind of place that might harbor dangerous, endowed rebels against the crown. She finally saw a sign marked Everwood Lane, and turned her horse at the corner.

The sanctuary proved to be a modest, thatch-roofed cottage. Warm light could be seen coming through the front windows; a swinging bench hung beneath the porch roof. Hickory-scented smoke curled out of the chimney, reminding her how cold she was. And a wreath of wildflowers hung from the door, indicating that a message awaited her inside.

She climbed down off her horse and looked around. Everything seemed peaceful. She tied the gelding to the rail. Without a sound she stepped onto the porch and walked to the door. After knocking twice, she reached beneath her cloak and settled her hands on the hilts of her daggers.

The door swung open. An old man stood there. He had to be ninety Seasons of New Life if he was a day. He very much reminded her of Aeolus. Despite his advanced age, he stood erect. He was bald, dressed in simple peasant's garb, and his sharp eyes looked her up and down. In one hand he grasped a long-stemmed clay pipe.

"Can I help you?" he asked quietly. His graceful fingers guided the clay pipe into his mouth and he clamped down on it with his teeth. This old man didn't seem like the other two consuls she had met. Satine wondered if she had come to the wrong place.

"Pardon me," she said, "but I'm looking for the master of the house. Can you tell me if he's here?"

"You're looking at him, lass," the man said. His voice was strong and deep.

Surprised, Satine continued to size him up. He didn't look like a threat to anyone—much less like one of the vaunted Consuls of the Redoubt.

"I've been told that calmatrass berries are in season and that you sell them," she said, using the code phrase she had read on the parchment.

"Right on both counts," he answered. A whiff of smoke escaped his pipe bowl. "I sell them by the pound."

Upon hearing the proper phrase come back in return, Satine raised an eyebrow. "In that case I'd like to buy some," she answered back. "I want to make a pie."

With a wry smile, the man pushed the door open wider. Her hands still lightly on her daggers, Satine walked inside.

The cottage was modest, but it was warm and clean. On the far side of the room a fire danced in a fieldstone hearth. A stout, elderly woman with a bun of gray hair bustled about in the adjoining kitchen. The smell of warm food made Satine's stomach growl.

The man closed the door behind her. "How long has it been since the Gray Fox has eaten?" he asked. His endowed hearing had apparently not missed the rumbling of her gut. She began to relax a little.

"I've been three days without hot food," she answered.

The man turned to look at his wife. "Evelyn, please fix a plate," he said. "We have important company." Evelyn smiled back.

The man beckoned Satine to a table. She removed her cloak and sat down. She welcomed the warmth that had begun to seep into her bones. The man poured out two glasses of wine.

"What is your name?" Satine asked.

"I am Shamus," he answered. He smiled. "And I am well aware that there is no point in asking yours."

Satine took a sip of wine. "You don't look like a consul," she said.

Smirking, Shamus took the pipe from his mouth and he placed it in a bowl.

"Really?" he asked. "Tell me, lass. Just what is one of us *supposed* to look like?" He gave her a wink. "Don't make the mistake of painting us all with the same brush."

He was right. Her only association with consuls had been with the menacing Bratach and his greasy underling Ivan. This calm, married man in his neat little country cottage seemed worlds away from their kind. But if he was a consul, married or not, he was powerful.

Evelyn appeared with a plate of food. It looked like stew—mutton with rosemary, Satine's nose told her—and boiled red potatoes. A big hunk of aged cheese sat on one side of the plate.

Satine began to shovel the food in hungrily. Shamus remained silent for a time as he watched her eat. When she was done, Satine wiped her mouth and sat back in her chair. Shamus poured her another glass of wine.

"Thank you," she said. "Now then, what is the message you have for me?"

Shamus' face darkened a bit. "Let's the three of us go and sit by the fire," he answered.

Satine nodded, picked up her wineglass, and followed the consul and his wife to the fireplace. The three overstuffed chairs looked very comfortable. Satine sat and crossed one of her long legs over the other.

Shamus noticed that his pipe had gone out. He took a wax taper from the mantle and set it alight in the fire. Soon the pipe was smoking again. Waving out the taper, he looked at Satine.

"Forgive me," he said. "Would you like a pipe?" Satine shook her head.

Shamus sat down across from his wife, who took up her knitting as she settled into her chair.

Seeing that the fire was low, Shamus called the craft. A dry hickory log from the pile next to the hearth lifted into the air to gently land atop the ones already burning. Its smoky fragrance gradually filled the room. Apparently satisfied, Shamus turned his attention to Satine.

"Bratach and Ivan are dead," he said.

Satine took a quick breath. Leaning forward, she scowled.

"How?" she asked.

"Faegan," he answered. "It had to be. Bratach was found in the tunnel, hanging in a web of the craft. He had bled out. He could have been killed by the wizard, or it might have been suicide. There is no way to know."

"Why would he commit suicide?" she asked.

"He would have gladly taken his own life, rather than be forced to reveal information to the wizards of the Redoubt," Shamus answered. "We all would."

"And Ivan?"

"His body—or should I say, what was left of it—was found upstairs. It seems he was blown apart by a bolt of the craft. In any event, you will be receiving no more help from them. I strongly suggest that you never visit that archery shop again."

Satine sat back in her chair. She had never liked Bratach or Ivan, but she had come to rely upon the information they provided her. This would make her sanctions more difficult.

"How will you proceed?" Shamus asked her.

The Gray Fox thought for a moment. "I will keep going," she answered. "There are four more people on my list. I'm following two of them now. To the best of my knowledge, the other two remain in Tammerland. If I can dispatch the ones I'm following, then I can deal with the others at my leisure. But without benefit of Bratach and Ivan's information, things will be more difficult. When did they die?"

"One of our agents visited the shop three days ago," Shamus answered. "The killings had apparently just occurred. Consul riders from our network were immediately sent out with word to all of the other sanctuaries. The one who informed us arrived here yesterday. He stayed the night and then rode back."

Satine decided to take a chance. "What of the orb?" she asked. "On my way here I passed by a great canyon that had been gouged into the earth. I have never seen anything like it. The orb did that, didn't it?"

Shamus nodded. "The Orb of the Vigors is bleeding. These are wonderful times for us, my dear. But of course you must already know this; it is the reason you were hired. It is said that only Tristan or Shailiha can heal the orb. If you can kill them both, victory will be within our grasp."

"How did you and Evelyn come to live here in Morningshire?" Satine asked.

"I knew Wigg and the other wizards of the Directorate well," Shamus answered. "Later, I was also one of those who helped build the Gates of Dawn. Nicholas—Tristan's son—altered the nature of our blood signatures, bringing us out of the darkness and into the light. I was proud to serve him. Before that, Evelyn and I lived in Tammerland for many years. When the Gates of Dawn fell, the surviving consular network sent us here. It certainly isn't Tammerland, but I have come to like it. Each of us in the brotherhood must do his part, whatever and wherever that might be."

"Forgive me, but how do you make ends meet?" Satine asked. "It is my understanding that the Directorate never allowed the consuls to learn how to conjure kisa."

Shamus smiled. "The story about the calmatrass berries is true," he said. "I have a small patch out back that I harvest and sell. Evelyn cans the rest for sale in the winter, and she also sells her knitting. With a little help from the craft to make our work go faster, we get by."

Evelyn looked up from her knitting. "Tell me, Father," she asked, "does she remind you of anyone?"

"Of course, Mother," he answered. "I saw it the moment she walked in."

"What are you talking about?" Satine asked.

"You remind us of our granddaughter," Shamus said.

"Where is she now?" Satine asked.

Shamus' face grew hard again. "Clarissa is dead," he answered softly. "During the ill-conceived return of the Coven, she was raped and butchered by the very same winged ones the prince now commands. Her parents were also killed. Clarissa was a schoolteacher in Tammerland, and she was about your age. She knew nothing of the craft, or of my part in it all. Many of us have paid dearly to see the defeat of the prince and his wizards."

Silence reigned for a time, the only sound the occasional crackling of the fire.

Sensing that it was time for her to go, Satine stood. "I must leave," she said. "I want to thank you both for everything that you have done for me."

"Please stay the night, child," Evelyn said. "There's no reason for you to sleep out in the cold."

Satine shook her head. "I cannot afford to miss seeing the Minions when they take flight. That is how I have been following the prince and his group."

Shamus rose. "Suppose I arranged to have you wake two hours before dawn?" he suggested. "Would that give you enough time?"

Satine carefully considered their offer. The prospect of a warm bed was very tempting, and the odds of a roving Minion patrol discovering her campsite were next to nil.

"Very well," she said. "I accept. And thank you."

"It is we who thank you," Evelyn said. "It is good to have a young woman in the house again."

"I have a small barn round back," Shamus said. "I'll go and bed down your horse."

The elderly consul went to the door. Taking his overcoat from a peg on the wall, he walked outside.

Satine sat back down in the chair by the fire. Evelyn came to pour her another glass of the calmatrass berry wine.

The three of them talked for hours as the logs burned low in the hearth.

SATINE AWOKE WITH A START. AT FIRST SHE DIDN'T RECOGNIZE her surroundings and immediately lunged for the dagger beneath her pillow. Then she remembered that she had stayed the night with Shamus and Evelyn and she calmed down. She got out of the warm bed and dressed quickly.

The sleeping spell with which Shamus had gifted her had worked perfectly. She felt wonderfully rested and refreshed. Looking out the window of her room, she saw that it was still dark outside. She quietly opened the bedroom door and walked into the front room.

The fire had gone out, and a package lay on the table next to her cloak. A parchment note pinned to the package read: "For the journey." She opened it to see a wedge of cheese, a generous amount of jerky, and a small package of purple calmatrass berries.

She tiptoed to the other bedroom door and opened it a crack. Beneath a great, patterned quilt, Evelyn and Shamus lay asleep in each other's arms. A tear formed in Satine's eyes and she quickly brushed it away.

She walked back into the front room, put on her cloak, picked up the package, and headed for the door. She was just about to leave when she had a thought. She walked back over to the table and put the package down.

She looked around for something to write with, but she

couldn't find anything. Instead, she took a piece of warm charcoal from the hearth. She removed five gold coins worth twenty kisa each from her cloak and put them on the table. Using the charcoal, she wrote, "For your kindnesses" on the tablecloth. She took up the package again and left.

FOUR HOURS LATER THE GRAY FOX FOUND HERSELF AT A FORK IN the narrow country road. She was in disguise again, and she held the reins of her packhorse firmly in one hand. The Minions had dwindled to specks in the sky as they traveled west, following the branch of road that bore away to her left. The road to the right led east, toward the coast. The way behind her would take her back to Shamus and Evelyn's comfortable cottage, where she knew she would be welcome to stay for as long as she liked. She found it an oddly attractive prospect. Even though she had collected only half of her fee, she was already one of the wealthiest women in Eutracia. But Wulfgar's reach was long, and if she quit now, she knew that the specter of his wrath would haunt her forever.

Thinking to herself, she reached down into her boot and withdrew the precious piece of parchment. From here on, her sanctions would prove to be even more dangerous. If she were killed, she wanted no harm to come to Shamus and Evelyn as a result of her failures. Their names and address were at the bottom of the list.

Ripping their information from the page, she tore the small section into pieces then cast them to the wind.

Eager for his mistress to choose her path, the gelding danced beneath her. She looked at first one branch of the road, and then the other. She thought for a moment about Aeolus and Shamus. They were so alike, she realized. And yet also so different.

Finally she made up her mind. Her jaw set, the Gray Fox turned her horse and spurred him into a trot down the road leading west.

CHAPTER LXXI

FROM WHERE HE STOOD IN THE BOW OF HIS BLACK SHIP, WULFGAR looked out over the moonlit sea. His fleet was making good time. The six other Black Ships traveled abreast in a broad line. The ebony vessels and their cargo of Earthshakers and demon-slavers flew quickly and silently above the waves.

Miraculous, Wulfgar thought. They had traveled from the Citadel to the coast of Eutracia in only five days. The wizards of the Redoubt would rue the day that they created these mighty ships—he would make sure of that.

Suddenly Wulfgar stiffened. For the briefest moment he thought he sensed something, but then it was gone. Relaxing again, he returned to his previous thoughts. Suddenly the feeling returned. This time the sensation was unmistakable.

"What is it, my lord?" Captain Merriwhether asked. His eerie green eyes glowed brightly from within his dark skull. "Is something amiss?"

Wulfgar quickly raised his good hand, demanding silence.

"There is endowed blood out there," Wulfgar said after a time. "It lies to the west, not far off the coast. You will probably not be able to sense it, but I can. It is blood of a very high order. Its quality is slightly higher than my own, but not altogether perfect. That leads me to only one conclusion. It must belong to the *Jin'Saiou*. But the *Jin'Sai* is not traveling with her.

"I find that curious," he added with a smile. "After our first encounter, I would have thought him eager to meet me again. And someone is cloaking Shailiha's blood—either Wigg or Faegan, no doubt. They think that they can hide it from me, but they can't. The enemy fleet must be out there. They're coming fast."

He turned to look at Merriwhether. "Signal the other Black Ships," he ordered, "and alert them to the situation. For now, I want them to maintain this formation. Unless I miss my guess, the enemy will try to surround us. When I give the order, I want the other Black Ships to follow our actions to the letter. It is not my intent to crush the enemy fleet. Our primary goal remains to break through their lines and reach the coast intact. But if we can send a few of them to the bottom, so be it."

"Yes, my lord," Merriwhether answered. "But there is something that I don't understand. If you were unable to detect Shailiha's blood at the Citadel, how is it that you can sense it now—especially if it is cloaked as it was before?"

Wulfgar smiled. "Because I also sense lesser endowed blood out there," he answered. "The wizards are trying to cloak all of it at the same time, and it is taxing their meager gifts. That means that there are also Acolytes of the Redoubt aboard at least some of the enemy vessels. There are, without question, hosts of Minion warriors with them as well. I expected as much. They are throwing everything at us that they dare, while also keeping a suitable force in reserve at the palace. Even so, that will not be enough."

Wulfgar gave Merriwhether a hard glare. "Now stop questioning me and go and carry out your orders."

With a slight bow, the captain hurried away.

Wulfgar turned back to look westward. He would land his troops and Earthshakers on Eutracian soil this night, no matter the cost. And then he could begin the all-important journey to the Tolenkas, just as the Heretics had ordered him to do.

As the northern half of her fleet sailed up the coast, Tyranny searched the sea with her spyglass. She could see nothing but empty ocean.

She stood in the stern, next to the ship's wheel. Scars manned the wheel and Shailiha stood by his side. Duvessa had gone off to assemble her female warriors, and Tyranny had ordered Adrian into the crow's nest to use her heightened senses to search for the *Enseterat*'s fleet. The assembled Minion warriors aboard the *Reprise* were spoiling for a fight. K'jarr stood before them, ready to follow Tyranny's orders at a moment's notice.

Collapsing her spyglass, the privateer took a deep breath. The thirty-one vessels to her south were long gone by now, and they would soon be altering course to help intercept Wulfgar's Black Ships. At this point, she could only hope that she had done the right thing in dividing her fleet.

She was about to speak to the princess when another peal came from the warning bell in the crow's nest.

"I see them!" Adrian called down.

"Where away?" Tyranny shouted back.

Adrian pointed an arm out over the waves. "North by northeast and closing fast!" she answered. "Less than half a league away!"

Tyranny turned and raised her glass. At first she saw nothing. She twisted the cylinders to bring the image into better focus. Suddenly, there they were.

Seven huge moonlit forms flew eerily just above sea, closing in on her position with a speed that she couldn't match. Even at this distance their size was spectacular. She was glad to see that they were sailing in an arrowhead formation. They would be easier to surround, she thought. Perhaps her plan to stop Wulfgar here and now might work after all.

"Steer north by northeast!" she ordered Scars. As the giant spun the wheel, Tyranny called for K'jarr. He was by her side in a flash.

"Send thirty of your fastest messengers to each of our other vessels," she ordered him. "When they see *Reprise* turn due east, they are to do the same. Once our line has formed east to west we will turn due south, to trap the Black Ships against the other half of our fleet. Then the circle will close."

Worry crowded her face. "Go now. We have no time to lose!"

As K'jarr ran off to follow his orders, Tyranny stabbed another cigarillo between her lips and lit it. She raised the spyglass to her eye once more. This time the Black Ships seemed much larger, and she could almost make out their skeletal captains in their bows. Their course remained unchanged.

"Yes, that's right," she whispered, as she looked through the glass. "Keep on coming, you dark bastards. Soon you'll all know the sharp, unmistakable kiss of Minion dreggans."

* * *

UNLIKE TYRANNY, THE *ENSETERAT* HAD NO NEED OF A SPYGLASS. Enhancing his vision with the craft, he could easily see both the northern and southern lines of the enemy fleet as they advanced on his position. Soon they would close their circle and be upon him. Perfect, he thought.

"Your orders, my lord?" Merriwhether asked.

Smiling, Wulfgar shook his head. "The other captains of the Black Ships have been commanded to do exactly as we do, isn't that right?" he asked.

Merriwhether nodded.

"Then I have no additional orders," Wulfgar said softly. "Watch and learn."

The two lines of Tyranny's fleet started to close. Hundreds of Minion warriors launched themselves into the air from the enemy decks.

"Their warriors will try to board us," Wulfgar said calmly. "Make sure the demonslavers are ready to welcome them."

When the first Minions arrived, they were met by rows upon rows of battle-hungry demonslavers banging their weapons against their shields. The rising cacophony was deafening.

Wulfgar turned to Merriwhether and nodded. Then, slowly—almost lazily—the *Enseterat* and his dark servant raised their arms and began blasting Minion warriors from the nighttime sky.

WHEN TYRANNY SAW THE GLEAMING AZURE BOLTS STREAKING though the darkness, her heart skipped a beat. The nightmare they had feared was quickly coming to pass: Wulfgar wasn't their only enemy to command the craft. His skeletal captains did as well—and that could spell disaster.

Faegan had warned them of this possibility, and yet he had refused to come along, insisting that he stay deep in the Redoubt with Jessamay to continue their research. As Tyranny looked through her glass at the carnage, her blood began to boil.

Damn your eyes, Faegan! she thought. *We need you now!*

As the Black Ships approached, Minion warriors were blasted from the sky in staggering numbers. For each one who fought his or her way down to the enemy decks, four or five more burst apart in midair. Others were burned so badly that they crashed helplessly into the sea. As Tyranny looked down at the water, she felt her stomach turn. The sea had turned from black to red in the moonlight.

Looking up at the crow's nest, Tyranny was about to shout an order to Sister Adrian but the acolyte acted first. Twin beams shot from Adrian's hands toward the first of the Black Ships. The acolytes aboard Tyranny's other ships followed suit. The night sky turned bright as day.

The privateer and the princess held their breath as literally hundreds of the sisters' bolts screamed across the waves. Surely nothing can stand up to that, Tyranny thought.

But to her horror, as the azure bolts struck the Black Ships they flattened out and fell away, sizzling harmlessly into the sea—almost as if the enemy vessels wore some kind of endowed armor. Over and over again the acolytes tried, but each time it was the same. The Black Ships were so close now that Tyranny and Shailiha could see their skeletal captains without the use of the spyglass.

Tyranny's ring of ships continued to tighten around Wulfgar's small fleet, but even with their huge advantage in numbers, the Minions failed to take control of the enemy decks. The acolytes' use of the craft seemed little more than pinpricks against the onrushing Black Ships.

Her face grim, Tyranny looked over at Shailiha. The princess immediately understood. Both women drew their swords.

Tyranny turned to K'jarr. "Prepare to board the enemy vessels!" she shouted. "Gangplanks and grappling hooks at the ready!"

She looked out across the sea. Even without her glass, she could see the other half of her fleet taking a line on the port sides of Wulfgar's vessels. There was no going back now. She turned to Scars.

"Steer due south—hard to starboard!" she shouted.

With a massive groan, the *Reprise* came over hard, the vessels following her quickly doing the same. Tyranny saw her southern line of ships come to port and head north. She knew that in mere moments her vise would tighten its grip, and both lines of her fleet would be near enough to try to board the Black Ships.

As Tyranny's fleet closed, she watched with dread as Wulfgar, in the bow of the lead vessel, raised his hands.

The Black Ships rose higher into the air and their speed increased dramatically. The western ends of Tyranny's two rows of ships finally closed ranks, but to no avail: hulls gleaming in the moonlight, the seven incredible vessels literally flew over the mast tops of Tyranny's fleet.

As they soared overhead they blotted out the moonlight. Tyranny and Shailiha could do nothing but stand there and watch the spectacle in awestruck wonder.

Then, standing by the enemy gunwales, Wulfgar and his captains cast azure bolt after azure bolt down upon the westernmost vessels of Tyranny's fleet. The bolts tore though the ships' riggings, masts, decks, and hulls. Decks exploded, crewmen and warriors were launched into the air, and thick, choking smoke started to blanket everything.

The stricken ships immediately burst into flames. Crewmen and Minions jumped overboard to quench the flames that burned them. At least a third of Tyranny's fleet was ablaze. The privateer watched, aghast, as ship after ship disappeared beneath the waves. Determined Minions continued to hurl themselves against the Black Ships. But between the demonslavers and the azure bolts, the warriors died quickly.

Tyranny looked frantically down the deck of her flagship. The *Reprise* had been hit at least twice—once in the stern and once amidships. Both areas blazed, and much of the ship's rigging was gone. Pandemonium reigned as the warriors and crewmen desperately tried to save the beleaguered ship. Then came a terrible cracking sound.

With a tortured groan, the entire mainmast and all of her accompanying sails crashed to the deck. The mast bounced once and then split in two, crushing crewmen and warriors to death beneath its weight. The crow's nest and the top half of the mast exploded against the gunwale, to lie awkwardly over the side and droop toward the sea. Sister Adrian was nowhere to be seen.

Tyranny raised her spyglass to the sky. In the darkness she

could just make out the hulls of the fleeing Black Ships. They were on course in the exact direction Faegan had predicted they would go. They would anchor just offshore in the great bay that lay directly east of the pass through the Tolenkas. From there Wulfgar and his forces would march west.

Tired and beaten, the privateer and the princess looked out over what remained of their smashed fleet. Fire and smoke ruled the waves as still more of their vessels went down. The remaining ships hurried to help those in need. The water was crowded with Minion dead and dying, but there were very few demonslaver corpses to be seen. Tyranny ordered Scars to search for Sister Adrian.

The privateer sheathed her sword. The crew worked to bring the fires aboard her flagship under control, but it would be many days before the *Reprise* could be made seaworthy again. Tyranny looked back up to the spot in the sky where the Black Ships had disappeared. Some of the surviving warriors were chasing after them, but she knew that they would never be able to catch up.

A third of my fleet is either lost or disabled, she thought, and slammed a fist against the gunwale. *Not to mention the crewmen and warriors I've lost. And for what,* she wondered. *In the end, what had been the point?*

Looking west to the coast, Tyranny hung her head.

CHAPTER LXXII

As Tristan sat before the campfire, he absentmindedly poked at its blazing logs with a dry stick. His dreggan and throwing knives lay in the grass beside him. The fire was comforting, and the nighttime sky was full of stars. It would be a pleasant night for sleeping, he thought.

Two tents sat in the center of the clearing by the road. One belonged to Tristan and Celeste, the other to Wigg. The tents surrounding them were Minion quarters. The horses were picketed nearby.

Wigg, Celeste, and Ox sat there with Tristan, their faces highlighted by the fire. They had been traveling for three days now. That morning Wigg had told them that the pull from the River of Thought was growing ever stronger. He guessed that they would reach the Well of Forestallments in one more day, two at the most.

More than once the anxious wizard had tried to gallop ahead to test Adrian's warning that if he went too fast, he would outrun the effects of the spell. Sure enough, each time he tried, he quickly lost the sensation—only to have it return when he slowed down again. The necessarily slow pace of the journey did nothing to improve Wigg's mood. Like Tristan, he sensed Celeste's life quickly ebbing away, and his frustration and anger grew by the moment.

The remains of their roast venison dinner lay nearby. The Minions were good cooks, and Tristan shared their love of rare meat. Over the course of the trip the prince had begun to develop a taste for akulee, even though it was much harder on his head than the ale or wine he was used to.

After a good bit of cajoling, he had even managed to get the wizard to try some. Against his better judgment, Wigg had cautiously taken a sip. Then his face screwed up and he spat it out. Over the last three hundred years he had become accustomed to the best wine the palace cellars had to offer. After wiping his mouth on his sleeve, the First Wizard had proclaimed akulee to be the vilest concoction ever created. Tristan and Celeste had laughed at him, and the rare, comic interlude had done them all good.

Tristan looked over at Wigg. The wizard's hands were shoved into the opposite sleeves of his robe. The Paragon hung about his neck, firelight dancing in its bloodred facets. Lost in his thoughts, he stared into the fire.

"Can we beat him?" Tristan asked.

Everyone understood all too well that he referred to his half brother, Wulfgar. Celeste laid her head upon her husband's shoulder.

Wigg sighed. "Who knows?" he answered. "Maybe—but only if we can find the Well, if it exists at all. And then we must convince this Scroll Master to help us. But I would be lying to you if I said that the odds against us weren't long. And I fear that our time grows short."

He looked over at Celeste, his face rueful. "I'm sorry, my child," he said. "How are you feeling?"

As Celeste gathered her shawl about her, Tristan pulled her closer. He felt her shiver.

"I'm all right, Father," she answered. "Really I am." Looking up into Tristan's face, she smiled. "The two of you worry about me too much."

She's lying, Wigg thought. Just the same, he loved her for it, and his heart was breaking.

During the last two days Celeste's movements had become noticeably stiffer and her limp more pronounced. Her hair was grayer and she had lost even more weight. Using the craft, Wigg did all he could to ease her pain, but even he had been only partially successful. Yesterday's examination of her blood signature revealed that even more of it had vanished.

It killed him to see his only child wasting away before his eyes. Before long, she would look as old as he did. And he knew that Tristan was hurting for her just as much as he was, perhaps even more.

Wigg turned his craggy face back to the fire. *We simply have to reach the Scroll Master in time,* he thought. *So much depends upon it.*

He stood and brushed the loose grass from his robe. "I will be retiring," he announced. "I hope you sleep well."

The others bid him good night.

Celeste looked up at Tristan again. "I'm also tired, my love," she said. She stood with difficulty. "Are you coming?"

"In a little while," he answered. "It's a beautiful night. I'd like to sit by the fire with Ox for a while longer."

Celeste smiled. "I had almost forgotten how much you love being outdoors," she said. She looked over at Ox. "Goodnight," she said.

The warrior gave her a short smile. "Ox say goodnight, too," he answered.

Tristan watched her enter their tent, then turned back to the fire. Silence reigned between him and the warrior for a time.

"The wizard be very worried," Ox said. "Ox worried, too. We reach Well tomorrow, Ox hope. I no want see Wigg's daughter die."

Ever since the episode at the Gates of Dawn, Ox had considered Tristan his personal charge. During their first conflict with Wulfgar, he had come to feel the same way about Celeste and Shailiha. When he had learned that Tristan and Celeste had married, in his happiness he had consumed an entire jug of akulee by himself. Despite his great size, his head had hurt for the next two days.

"I know, my friend," Tristan answered. "I know."

Ox handed the akulee jug to the prince. As the tree frogs sang and the fire snapped, Tristan took another slow, welcome drink.

NESTLED SECURELY IN THE BRANCH OF A TREE, A FIGURE DRESSED in black leather watched the campsite. Satine had been forced to slither toward the tree very slowly. More than once, Minion patrols had nearly spotted her.

She took up the small spyglass that hung from a leather cord at her hip. Before she had begun the night's surveillance, she had carefully rubbed the instrument with dirt so that it would not shine in the moonlight. She had done the same to her face and hands. She lifted the glass to one eye, extended it, and twisted it.

The magnifying lenses brought everything into sharp relief. This was the second time tonight that she had viewed the campsite through the glass. The first time, she had watched her targets eating. Now she watched as the prince, the wizard, and his daughter finally retired, leaving a giant Minion guard alone by the dwindling fire.

Shifting her position in the tree, Satine stretched her back and lowered the glass. It would be a long night, but if she could just catch one of them away from the campsite, she would be that much closer to completing her sanctions. If the warriors continued to fly over the road tomorrow, she could sleep briefly in her saddle.

She looked up at the three moons. It occurred to her that they beamed down upon not only her and her targets, but also upon Aeolus, Shamus, and Evelyn. *The three moons bind us together in a way,* she thought.

She was also reminded of Wigg comforting his daughter, and of Tristan perhaps holding her close as he lay by her side. She thought of Shamus and Evelyn in their bed together, and of what the consul had told her, as well as what Aeolus had said just before she left Tammerland. Their contradictory messages ate at her, feeding the growing seeds of doubt.

She pushed her thoughts away and turned her dark eyes back toward the campsite.

TRISTAN STARTED FROM A FITFUL SLEEP. IT TOOK HIM A FEW moments to recognize his surroundings, then he relaxed.

Rising on one elbow, he looked over at Celeste. She slept peacefully. Given his restlessness, he knew that it would do little good to try to go back to sleep. What he needed was a walk. He kissed his wife on the cheek, then slipped from beneath the blanket, quietly took up his weapons, and stepped from the tent.

The night was crisp, the moons bright. Ox lay asleep by the fire, his snoring as loud as ever. Tristan smiled. One could have far worse friends, he thought.

He stretched his sleepy muscles, then strapped both the dreggan and his throwing knives into place across his back. He walked to the other tents and talked with some of the warriors just back from patrol. They were glad to see him and happily shared their akulee.

On the way back to his tent, Tristan suddenly remembered what it was that had been scratching at the back of his mind. He had been worried about Shadow. Late in the day, as they had neared the place where they were to make camp, the horse had suddenly developed a limp. Tristan could tell that it was nothing serious, but he had made a mental note to check the horse later, after the Minions had bedded him down. Now was as good a time as any.

He thought for a moment about asking a patrol to accompany him, but then decided against it. He would feel foolish about taking them on so short and simple an errand—and besides, he wanted some time to himself. Leaving the relative safety of the camp behind, he starting walking to where the horses were tied.

* * *

WATCHING THROUGH THE SPYGLASS, SATINE COULDN'T BELIEVE her luck. At last, she thought. She easily recognized the figure leaving the campsite. She even thought she knew where he was headed.

After securing her glass in her cloak, she looked around carefully. She could see no Minion patrols nearby. She descended from the tree. The grass beneath her feet was wet with dew, the better to muffle her footsteps.

As she moved toward her quarry, she reached behind her back and took up the tools of her trade.

THE HORSES HAD BEEN TIED TO A LINE THAT STRETCHED BETWEEN two large trees in the center of an open meadow. At the edge of the meadow, Tristan called softly to the lone Minion guard to alert him to his approach.

As he neared, the horses came to their feet, whinnying. Shadow's black coat shimmered in the moonlight as he turned his large, dark eyes toward his master. The prince gave him an affectionate rub on the neck.

Tristan had long thought that his former mount, Pilgrim, would never have an equal. But over the course of the last three days he had learned that in terms of sheer speed and endurance, Shadow had no match. A bond was growing between them that might soon eclipse even the one he had shared with Pilgrim. As he rubbed the horse's ears, Shadow snorted and shook his mane.

Tristan looked at the guard. "All is well here?"

The guard nodded. "Yes, *Jin'Sai*."

Tristan smiled. "Now then," he said to Shadow. "Let's take a look at that foot, shall we, boy?"

Bending over, he coaxed the stallion's right front hoof from the ground and placed it on his bended knee. It was difficult to perform an examination in the moonlight, but he eventually found the problem. There was a long bramble-bush thorn lodged between the horse's shoe and the frog of his foot.

Tristan took out one of his throwing knives. It wasn't a proper tool, but it would have to do. He bent down again.

There was an unexpected breeze, and he heard a dull thud. He coiled up and snapped his head around to see an arrow, its shaft still quivering, buried in the Minion guard's forehead. The warrior's face registered surprise, and then he collapsed to the ground, dead. In shock, Tristan realized that had he not bent over when he had, the arrow would have gone straight through his neck.

He ducked under Shadow's legs and rolled to the other side of the horse, where he stood again, using his horse and the bay mare next to him as cover. The sudden action startled the other two horses, and they danced about nervously, shaking their heads.

Tristan peered over the bay's back. He saw nothing unusual. The horses settled down, and everything was quiet once more. The meadow stretched innocently before him, its dewy grass shimmering in the moonlight. The only cover he could see was the woods that bordered the opposite side of the clearing. It would have been a very long shot with a bow from there, and only an expert archer could have accomplished it.

Hunching down behind the middle horse once more, he caught his breath and tried to decide what to do. His decision was made for him as another arrow sliced through the air and went through the horse's eye.

The mare screamed wildly and died in an instant, tumbling to the ground and leaving Tristan exposed. He caught a glimmer of reflected moonlight streaking toward him. He twisted to avoid the impact, but he was too late. The arrow buried itself in his left shoulder. Had he been a fraction slower, it would have taken him in his heart.

Holding his bleeding shoulder, he leapt toward the nearest tree of the picket line. Landing hard on his knees, he turned and sat up against the tree trunk.

His chest heaving, Tristan looked down at his wound. The arrow was lodged just below the collarbone; he was bleeding profusely, his glowing azure blood bright in the darkness. He needed Wigg, but there was no way he could cross the open meadow and get back to camp without being killed. Closing his eyes for a moment, he tried to control the pain as best he could.

He broke the arrow shaft in two close to his body. The pain nearly made him faint. Gathering his strength, he pulled out one of his throwing knives and peered around the trunk of the tree.

There was still nothing to see. He retreated behind the tree again, and did his best to stand.

If he tried to run he would be killed, he knew, his azure blood making him an easy target for his assailant. And if he stayed where he was he would soon bleed to death. He cursed his foolishness for having come here alone.

"They told me that you were good," a female voice shouted out unexpectedly. "But I have yet to see any evidence of that."

Satine, he suddenly realized. It had to be.

Peering around the trunk of the tree, Tristan saw a woman standing about ten paces away in the moonlight. She held a bow in one hand, an arrow notched upon its string. She was dressed in black leather. Daggers were strapped to either thigh, and the hilt of a sword was visible just above her right shoulder.

"Come to me," she said. "Your only other choice is to bleed to death. I promise that your death will be quick."

Knowing that he had no choice but to face her, Tristan emerged unsteadily from behind the tree.

He threw the dirk at her with everything he had. But given his blood loss, he couldn't put enough strength behind it. As he watched it go, he collapsed to his knees.

Satine saw the silvery blade flashing toward her in the moonlight and pivoted, her dark cloak swirling about her. The dirk twirled by, missing her cleanly. She dropped her bow, drew her sword, and approached the prince.

"If you still desire an easy death, do not try that again," she said.

As he sat on his heels, his azure blood running down his arm and chest, she walked around him the same way that a cat might toy with a wounded mouse. She took in his strange-looking blood, and the ingenious method by which he carried his throwing knives. She came full circle, to face him once more.

Fighting through the pain, Tristan reached back with his good arm and drew his sword. He had never known it to feel so heavy. Satine simply watched him without protest. As the dreggan cleared its scabbard he could barely point it at her. He swayed woozily. Finally the point of his sword fell to the grass.

He would be unconscious soon, he realized. Then Satine would either leave him here to bleed to death or finish him with her sword. Either way, he would never see Celeste again. Worse yet, the Orb of the Vigors would never be healed, and Wulfgar would win. He stared at her with hatred.

"I thought you preferred blow darts to swords," he said thickly.

Satine smiled. "My identity is no longer a secret," she said. "So, you see, apparent suicide is no longer required. Given your present circumstances, my sword will do the job as well as anything else."

"Why did you kill the gnome and the dwarf?" Tristan asked. Another surge of pain coursed through him and he shuddered. "I know why Wulfgar wants *me* dead, but why murder Geldon and Lionel? Surely they meant nothing to him."

Satine took another step closer. "To see you all suffer," she answered. "That is how your dear brother wants things done, you see. And I always follow my orders to the letter." She smiled again. "After you are sent to the Afterlife, you will be joined by your sister and the two wizards of the Redoubt. It may take a bit longer, now that they know who I am. But I'm a patient woman."

"I understand Wulfgar's motives," Tristan gasped. "But why are *you* doing this? Why do you serve . . . such a monster?"

"For the money," she answered. "I need it, you see, to complete a lifelong mission of my own. We all have our own hopes, our own needs."

"Don't you care about anything other than yourself?" he asked. "You work for Wulfgar. You must have met him. Couldn't you sense the rage and hatred within him? Is that who you want to rule Eutracia?"

Trying his best to remain conscious, Tristan looked up into her eyes.

"Don't you care about your loved ones?" he pressed. "Do you really want to see them and your entire nation suffer forever beneath the yoke of his oppression? His will be a darkness that will know no equal. Your actions here this night will forever be a part of that."

Something in her face changed. For a moment Tristan

thought she looked conflicted. Then her face darkened again and she stepped closer.

"Enough of this," she said. "It is time. Drop your sword."

Tristan shook his head. "At least let me die with my dreggan in my hand."

Satine thought for a moment. "I will grant that request because I understand it so well. If our positions were reversed, I would ask it of you. Besides, I doubt that you can even lift it anymore."

She placed one hand atop Tristan's head and pushed it down to expose his neck.

"No!" he growled. "If I must die, I want to see it coming!"

"Very well," she answered. She kept her hand in place to steady his head.

Satine lifted her sword. The edge of her blade glinted in the moonlight.

At the apex of her swing, her eyes caught his. All of the contradictory thoughts that had been collecting within her suddenly collided. For a split second, the Gray Fox hesitated.

Sensing his chance, Tristan reached up with his left arm and grabbed the wrist of the hand that supported his head. He pulled her down to him and raised the dreggan with his other arm. As she understood what was happening, Satine brought down her sword, but the die had already been cast.

Tristan rolled to one side and narrowly avoided the edge of her blade. Using the momentum of her swing against her, he pulled her down toward him and shoved the point of the dreggan into her chest. With his final bit of strength, he pushed the hidden button on the sword's hilt.

The dreggan's blade shot forward, impaling her and exiting through her back. A look of surprise crossed her face. She collapsed, her body sliding down the blade of Tristan's sword as she fell on him.

For the briefest of moments, Tristan thought he heard the flurry of Minion wings.

Then everything went black.

CHAPTER LXXIII

JESSAMAY WRITHED IN PAIN.

Faegan strengthened the spell that would help her cope with her suffering. *She's being so brave,* he thought. Then again, she always was.

Faegan finally stopped applying the craft and he sat back in his chair. He caused yet another drop of blood to rise from the open wound in Jessamay's arm and he guided it to land upon a parchment on a nearby table. It twisted itself into the sorceress' blood signature, then slowly dried up, and died.

Smiling, he looked back at Jessamay. He used a damp cloth to gently wipe the perspiration from her forehead.

"Are you all right?" he asked. She gave him a brave smile, but he could see that she was near the end of her strength for the day.

"The pain can be intense," she said. "This brings back such awful memories. At first I wasn't sure whether I could go through it again. But at least this time it's you, rather than Failee, trying to alter my blood signature. I feel safe with you."

"Do you need more help with the pain?" Faegan asked.

She shook her head. "I don't think we should risk it. We cannot be sure that it won't interfere with what we're trying to accomplish. We must succeed no matter the cost, and I fear we are running out of time."

"Very well," Faegan answered. "Just try to rest while I check the latest result."

Wheeling his chair over to the table, he positioned the signature scope over Jessamay's fresh blood signature and examined it. He was not pleased with what he saw. He sighed and looked over at her.

"Another failure, I'm afraid," he said glumly.

"I understand," Jessamay said. "We'll just have to keep trying."

Faegan wheeled himself back over to Jessamay, raised one arm, and removed the wizard's warp that enveloped her. Grateful to be free, Jessamay stood on unsteady legs. Faegan hadn't wanted to use a warp on her, but it had seemed necessary to keep her from moving in response to the pain as he applied the various spells.

She shuffled stiffly to the table and poured herself a glass of wine. As Faegan watched her drink he saw that her robe was soaked through with sweat, and he winced. She sat down heavily beside him, and they delved into their work once more.

Tristan, Wigg, and Celeste had been gone for four days. Since then, Faegan and Jessamay had been prisoners of their own research in one of the many Redoubt laboratories. Piles of reference books sat on several nearby tables, along with various parchments, charts of esoteric symbols, jars of dried herbs, and bottles of precious oils. A network of tubing carried colored, bubbling fluids from beaker to beaker.

Failee's red leather grimoire lay open on the table between Faegan and Jessamay. The Tome of the Paragon had been placed upon a pedestal in one corner of the room, the Scroll of the Vigors upon another. Sighing, the crippled wizard pulled the grimoire toward him to read more of Failee's elegant Old Eutracian script.

When Faegan and his group had returned from the archery shop, the acolytes had informed them that Sister Vivian had been found dead in her quarters. She had bled out, just as Bratach had done.

An examination of her body had convinced Faegan and Jessamay that Wulfgar had placed the same death Forestallment into Vivian's blood that Bratach's had carried. As for Bratach, his identity had been confirmed by documents gleaned from the Hall of Blood Records.

Their assumption was that Vivian's death Forestallment had been placed into her blood without her knowledge and that Bratach had been able to activate it at will—even from so far away as the archery shop. Faegan felt certain that when the consul activated his own Forestallment, he had activated Vivian's as well.

Clever, Faegan thought, as he turned over another page of the grimoire. *Imagine the ability to kill one's enemy with a single thought and from such a distance. Wulfgar has been one step ahead of us—right from the moment we thought we defeated him that night on the palace roof. How little did we realize . . .*

Faegan and Jessamay's research centered upon reestablishing the proper lean of Jessamay's blood signature. They did this not purely for Jessamay's benefit—although under normal circumstances that alone would have been reason enough. Rather, they both thought that if they could accomplish this feat, it might help them in their fight against Wulfgar. If any of the *Enseterat*'s traitorous consuls could be taken alive, the Conclave could perhaps change their signatures and return them to the Vigors.

But so far there had been no progress, and the stress that their experimentation placed upon Jessamay tormented Faegan greatly.

All they had ascertained so far was that Failee had concocted a formula that could change the lean of a blood signature. The grimoire clearly outlined the formula, which combined both the craft and the science of herbmastery. But even Failee had been able only to force Jessamay's signature to morph from right-leaning to neutral. The grimoire gave no evidence that she had accomplished the other half of her work—completing the shift all of the way to the left.

Faegan and Jessamay's goal was to change the lean back to the right—returning Jessamay's blood signature to its original state. But the research meant reversing the late First Mistress' work step by agonizing step.

Faegan shook his head. Aside from Failee's initial experiments, this work was entirely without precedent in the craft, he thought. It made him wonder whether this dark area of study was really the kind of thing into which the Ones Who Came Before wanted craft-users to delve. It was a true wizard's conundrum. If they succeeded, the implications of the murky ethics of their accomplishment would be staggering. If they failed, they might never save the world from the Vagaries. They knew one thing: They had to forge ahead, regardless.

Jessamay pointed to a crooked symbol on one of the parchments. "Look at this," she said. Faegan glanced over.

"This symbol is shown over and over again in both Failee's writings and the Scroll of the Vigors," she said with excitement. "I believe that—"

Suddenly there came an urgent pounding on the door. Angry at the interruption, the wizard scowled.

"Enter!" he called out.

The double doors parted briskly, and Abbey, Shailiha, and Tyranny tromped into the room. The privateer and the princess were dirty from head to foot. Faegan was grateful to see them alive, but he could also tell that they were in no mood for small talk.

They walked to the table, and Tyranny leaned her hands upon its shiny surface.

"I'll make this simple," she said. "At least one-third of the fleet is gone, as is half of the Minion cohort that sailed with us. The Black Ships went through us like we were made of parchment. By now they have no doubt reached the coast." She looked over at Jessamay.

"Wigg said that you once served aboard those vessels," she added. "During the battle, they did things we had no idea they could do, things we couldn't begin to fight against! I think you have some explaining to do."

Tyranny struck a match against one of her knee boots and lit a cigarillo. Given the immense value of the documents and dried herbs in the room, Faegan was about to protest, but when he caught the defiant gleam in her eyes, he decided against it.

Tyranny took the wine bottle from the table and she poured herself a glassful. She dropped unceremoniously into a chair, and threw a long leg up over one of its arms. Shailiha and Abbey sat down next to her.

"First, give me your report," Faegan said to her.

Before beginning, Tyranny took a deep draft of smoke, followed by another gulp of wine. They seemed to calm her.

"As I just told you, we were defeated. I had sixty-two warships at my disposal—far more than enough, I thought, to deal with the enemy. But I was wrong. I have never seen anything like what happened out there in my life."

For the next quarter hour, Tyranny described the sea battle. When she finished, Faegan looked over at Jessamay.

"When you served aboard the Black Ships three centuries ago, did they have these fantastic abilities?" he asked. "If so, why didn't you and Wigg tell us about them?"

Jessamay shook her head. She seemed as stunned by Tyranny's story as the wizard.

"No," she insisted. "The Black Ships could soar above the waves, but never fly so high or as fast as Tyranny describes. Nor could they absorb bolts of the craft without suffering harm. Had we known, we would have certainly told you." She thought to herself for a moment. "There can be only one answer."

Faegan nodded. "Wulfgar has enhanced their capabilities," he said. He looked at Shailiha. "Were you able to determine what cargo the Black Ships carry?"

Shailiha shook her head. "Other than the swarms of demon-slavers aboard, there was no way to tell."

"What about Sister Adrian and K'jarr?" Jessamay asked. "Did they survive?"

"Yes," Tyranny answered, "but just barely. Adrian was in the crow's nest of the *Reprise* when it came down. She was able to use the craft to break her fall. K'jarr was wounded in the arm, but he will recover. Duvessa survived, as well. But several acolytes of the Redoubt went down with their ships. Shailiha and I thought it best that we come ahead of the returning fleet by way of Minion litter, so as to make our report. Scars is bringing home what's left. It's not a pretty sight. They should be anchored off the Cavalon Delta by tomorrow morning."

Faegan looked down at his hands. Sensing his distress, Shailiha put a hand on one of his. "How goes your research?" she asked.

The wizard sighed. "It does not go well," he answered. "But we are hopeful."

"What we are being forced to do is essentially reverse all of Failee's original work," Jessamay told them. She turned to Abbey. "We have discovered that the answer must be a complex combination of craft calculations and herbmastery," she said. "We could use your help."

Abbey smiled. "Of course," she answered. "But tell me—has there been any word from Tristan and his group?"

"No," Faegan answered. "But we mustn't take that as a bad sign."

"And what about the warriors who watch the pass through the Tolenkas and those who follow the orb?" the herbmistress went on. "Have you heard from any of them?"

"No," Faegan answered. "But that does not mean bad news, either. If those at the pass haven't sent word, then that simply means that nothing has changed. And as for those who are trying to follow the orb—well, that was probably a wild-goose chase from the start."

"Why?" Abbey asked.

"The orb is in constant motion. In its natural state, it is invisible," he explained. "To be seen, it generally must be called into view by a practitioner of the craft—or, at least, that is how things used to be. But since the orb was wounded, it seems to be in view much more often. If it is randomly disappearing and reappearing, it must be giving fits to the warriors who were assigned to follow it."

"Wulfgar must be marching toward the Tolenkas by now," Shailiha said. "Only the Afterlife knows what havoc he is causing while we sit here and speculate. We have to do something!"

"Agreed," Faegan said. "We must send another force to attack him. Perhaps we can do on land what we could not do on water. I will have Traax organize the Minion forces and we will make a battle plan. If Wulfgar breaches the pass and unleashes the Heretic hordes, then nothing can stand in his way."

"Except perhaps for the blood of the *Jin'Sai*," Shailiha said softly. "Or mine. If we learn that Tristan is"—she faltered for a moment, then rallied—"dead, you must train me as fast as possible. I will do whatever it takes to stop Wulfgar and avenge my brother's death."

"Wulfgar would have anchored as deep as possible in the huge bay that stretches from Shadowood to Malvina Watch," Tyranny said. "Several Minion outposts dot that section of coastline, don't they?"

The wizard nodded. "Yes, and the outposts are already on alert. But given what I have heard here today, I can't hold much hope that they will be able to stop him by themselves." His face was very grave.

"May the Afterlife care for their souls," he said.

CHAPTER LXXIV

As Wulfgar stood on the Eutracian shore, the sea wind brought the stench of death to his nostrils. It was midday, and the Black Ships lay anchored in the bay. Six of the seven members of his macabre council remained aboard their vessels, awaiting further orders.

The sky was clear and bright, save for the pungent smoke that curled toward the heavens. Even though the Minion warriors had fought well, their outpost had fallen quickly. The *Enseterat,* his seven dark captains, and the crushing number of demon-slavers had overwhelmed the garrison easily.

The rough-hewn structure's four long log walls rose nearly twenty meters into the air. Numerous scorch marks and gaping holes were all that remained where azure bolts had exploded against them. Lookout posts stood at each of the four corners, and several crude buildings occupied the spacious grounds inside. Parts of the outpost still burned.

Wulfgar knew that the entire Eutracian coast was dotted with such garrisons. He would not bother to attack them; it was unnecessary. Nor would they be immediately alerted to his presence, for not a single Minion warrior had escaped to tell the tale.

The ground was soaked with Minion and demonslaver blood. Hungry flies had already begun to feast. Eleven surviving warriors hung nearby, tied by their thumbs to the horizontal beam that stretched across the opening where the outpost gates used to stand. One of them was Olaf, the commander of the garrison. Saying nothing, they all looked down at Wulfgar with hatred, their eyes glazed with pain.

Captain Merriwhether approached and gave his master a short bow.

"If my lord is interested, I have a suggestion about the survivors," he said. "I believe our troops would find it amusing."

"What is it?" Wulfgar asked.

"During our examination of the compound, our demonslavers found several barrels of pitch. I suggest that we put them to good use."

Wulfgar smiled. "You may proceed."

With another bow, Wulfgar's skeletal captain went off to give his orders.

Several demonslavers emerged from the compound rolling two large barrels before them. Two more carried ladles and brushes. When they reached the hanging captives they stopped and upended the barrels.

Using the hilts of their swords, they smashed open the barrel tops. After a sign from Merriwhether, they dipped the ladles and brushes into the barrels.

Wulfgar raised one hand, and used his power to lift the demonslavers into the air. Wulfgar guided them closer to the hanging warriors, and the slavers began slathering the helpless Minions with the dark, sticky pitch.

The prisoners screamed out curses and kicked uselessly at the slavers. When his servants had completed their work, Wulfgar lowered them to the ground and walked over to look up at Olaf.

The large, gray-bearded Minion commander carried more than enough scars to prove that his worth had been well tested. Olaf had served with the *Jin'Sai* during both the air campaign over Farplain and during the sea battles when Wulfgar had first returned to Eutracia to pollute the Orb of the Vigors.

Wulfgar only smiled.

"I have a request of you and your warriors," he said. "I want to hear you all scream."

Olaf looked down the line of warriors who were hung alongside him. To a man, their eyes carried the same defiance that his did. He looked back at his tormentor.

"Never," he said. "Minion warriors know how to die well, and perhaps this is as good a day as any. But mark my words, you bastard. When the *Jin'Sai* hears of this, he will kill you all."

Wulfgar reached up to touch the sole of the warrior's boot. Casually examining a sample of the pitch, he rubbed it between his fingers for a few moments. Then he narrowed his eyes and caused the pitch to vanish, leaving his fingers clean. He looked back up at Olaf.

"The *Jin'Sai* will somehow kill *me*?" he asked. "Oh, no, I don't think so. I have nothing to fear from my half brother—or his twin sister, for that matter. But you, on the other hand, have a great deal to fear from me."

Turning his back on the Minions, Wulfgar went to Merriwhether and asked, "Would you like to do the honors? After all, it was your idea."

As Merriwhether smiled, his white teeth showed brightly against his dark skull.

"Of course, my lord," he answered. He raised the blanched bones of one arm and pointed at Olaf.

"Goodbye, you winged freak," he said softly. "May your soul rot in whatever place you call the Afterlife."

He shot an azure bolt at Olaf's pitch-laden boots. The Minion's feet burst into flames. The fire fed quickly on the pitch and roared up his body and wings.

Merriwhether did the same to the others. In mere moments, all of the warriors were ablaze.

Wulfgar looked at Olaf, already smelling the sweet, sickly odor of burning flesh as the smoke darkened and took to the sky.

Olaf didn't scream or beg for his life. Nor did any of the others hanging there with him. They died as they had lived, warriors to the end. Eventually their charred carcasses proved too heavy for the burning ropes that suspended them, and what remained of their lifeless bodies crashed to the ground.

Wulfgar suddenly felt the touch of the Heretics on his mind. He turned toward the shore and went to his knees.

"You have done well," sang the heavenly chorus of voices. *"Now, release one of the creatures that waits in the hold of your ship and turn it against the remains of the Minion garrison. You have but to think of the command and it shall obey you—just as the others shall also obey your dark captains in your absence. It will be a paltry use of their formidable talents, but from this you shall learn their amazing gifts. Then send six of your Black Ships to lay siege to the palace. While they do that, you must go west, toward the azure pass through the mountains. From there you will turn south, to Tammerland. But you must hurry. As we*

speak, the Jin'Sai *and his First Wizard attempt to unravel the secret of his azure blood."*

Wulfgar raised his eyes skyward. *"It shall be as you command,"* he replied. He rose and walked back over to Merriwhether.

"Your orders, my lord?" his captain asked.

"Bring the ships," he said. "It is time to unleash one of the beasts. We are to finally learn the secret of their power."

Merriwhether walked to the shore and sent an azure bolt soaring through the air.

Almost at once, the ships' anchors were pulled up, and the ships rose above the waves, turned, and approached the shoreline sterns first.

The first ship finally crossed over dry land. As her massive hull settled, crushing all of the rocks and vegetation beneath her, she groaned and came to rest a bit toward her starboard side.

The massive ship's stern door lowered to reveal an impenetrable darkness.

From deep within the ship, one of the Earthshakers emerged. No demonslaver rode atop its back. First its great skull appeared, its long, dark horn protruding from the center of its forehead. Then the huge body followed. Finally came the massive, bony tail—a gigantic paddle that swayed back and forth as the beast stopped and stood upon the lowered stern door. For a moment the door threatened to buckle beneath the thing's great weight, but it held.

The creature looked around, saw Wulfgar, and let go a terrifying scream. Wulfgar held out his hands.

"Come to me," he ordered.

The Earthshaker stepped onto the shore and lumbered toward its master. As it walked, the ground trembled beneath its feet. It stopped about five meters away. Wulfgar pointed to the Minion outpost.

"Destroy it," he told the creature. With another earsplitting scream, the Earthshaker walked over to the garrison, lifted its tail, and gave it a mighty snap. The air erupted with a massive, sonic boom.

The wall exploded. Pieces of wood flew everywhere, and the

dust raised by the blast obscured everyone's vision for several moments. When the scene finally cleared, even Wulfgar was stunned by what he saw.

The entire wall was gone. Pieces of wood no larger than toothpicks rained down, covering everything. The monster screamed once more and lumbered into the compound.

With another swipe of the thing's tail, the first of the Minion buildings exploded into nothingness. Then another, and another. Soon nothing of consequence stood in the inner yard.

The creature walked to one of the remaining walls and, with another concussive blast, tore it apart. The other two walls and the remaining lookout posts quickly followed. Shards of wood drifted down slowly, and all became quiet once more.

"Come to me," Wulfgar ordered the beast.

The Earthshaker returned to its master, and Wulfgar affectionately rubbed the front of its face. The beast moaned softly.

"Return to the ship," Wulfgar ordered.

The Earthshaker walked slowly back to the vessel from which it had come. Once it was aboard, the demonslavers hauled the ship's stern door back up into place. Wulfgar turned back to look at where the Minion outpost had once stood. Nothing remained.

"Come here," Wulfgar ordered Merriwhether. The captain obeyed.

"I leave for the azure pass," Wulfgar said. "Take six of the Black Ships and make for Tammerland. Whatever remains standing, once the polluted Sippora has set the city ablaze, have the Earthshakers blast it to ruins. Make your way to the palace and begin the siege. I will meet you there after I have released the Heretic hordes and overseen the destruction of the orb. If you can take the *Jin'Sai* alive, then do so. He and I have unfinished business. But feel free to make an example of the populace in whatever manner you see fit."

Wulfgar took another step closer.

"Do not fail me, Merriwhether," he added with menace. "It was I who plucked you and your brothers from the icy depths of the Sea of Whispers, and I can just as easily oversee your return."

Merriwhether bowed his dark head. "Have faith, my lord," he answered. "Everything shall be as you order."

"Good," Wulfgar said. "Go now, and may luck be with you."

Merriwhether walked to the first of the great vessels and boarded, barking out orders. As Wulfgar watched, six of the massive ships slowly righted themselves. Their black sails snapped open and their hulls rose into the air, heading south over dry land, toward Tammerland.

Soon they were gone from sight, leaving the *Enseterat* with one ship, one captain, and a host of demonslavers. The remaining captain was Cathmore. As his dark heart beat within the tattered folds of his uniform, he smiled at the honor of escorting his savage messiah to the pass in the Tolenkas.

"Make way," Wulfgar ordered. "We leave at once."

As the ship lifted into the air, Wulfgar and Cathmore levitated themselves onto her black decks. Her sails snapped open and she turned toward her mission and her destiny.

CHAPTER LXXV

WHY DOES MY SHOULDER HURT SO MUCH? HE WONDERED. CAN'T they just leave me alone? I wish they would stop talking and let me sleep. Don't they know that I'm the Jin'Sai?

With a groan, Tristan opened his eyes. At first everything was out of focus. Soon things became clearer. Celeste's lined face looked down at him, and her gray hair brushed against his cheek.

Wigg and Ox's faces appeared behind her. Celeste and Ox smiled broadly. Wigg wore the typically condescending scowl that seemed always reserved for castigating him.

"So you have finally decided to return to us," the First Wizard said. "By the time we reached you, you had lost a great deal of blood. How do you feel?"

Tristan tried to sit up, but the pain in his shoulder forced him back down. He was in his tent, lying on several Minion blankets.

Wigg pressed a wooden cup against the prince's lips. "Drink," he said.

"What is it?" Tristan asked thickly.

"If you must know, it is ground root of canckleberry, sliced blossom of synthia, and boiled water. It will help you to recover your strength. It will also aid the spell of accelerated healing that I granted over your wound. Out here in the wilderness, it was the best I could come up with."

Tristan took a gulp of Wigg's potion; it tasted awful. He winced.

"Your cure is worse than my injury," he said.

Smiling, Celeste bent to kiss him. "We were so worried about you," she said. "For a time, I thought I was going to lose you forever."

Tristan smiled back and gingerly raised himself up onto his elbows.

Suddenly it all came flooding back. Satine, the fight in the meadow, his wound, her death . . . He twisted to look down at his left shoulder. The arrow shaft had been removed. Bandages had been wound around the joint, and spots of azure blood dotted the fabric. The front of his black leather vest was streaked with dried azure blood. Pain momentarily overwhelmed him, and he settled back down upon his makeshift bed.

"It was Satine," he said.

"We know," Wigg answered. "Her body matched the description given to us by Uther. We buried her in the meadow. I found some interesting items hidden in the lining of her cloak. Faegan was right about her methods of killing. I found something even more interesting in one of her boots," he added wryly.

"And what was that?" Tristan asked.

"A list," Wigg answered. "I haven't made complete sense of it yet, but I think it might be a list of safe houses. I recognize many of the names matching the addresses—all onetime Consuls of the Redoubt. It appears torn at the bottom, as though she wanted part of the list removed for some reason. I suppose we'll never know."

"She hesitated," Tristan said, more to himself than to the others. Then he looked up. "She had me dead to rights, and then she hesitated. Why would she do that?"

Wigg shook his head. "Perhaps it was a sudden lapse in resolve. Who knows? In the end, all that matters is that you survived and she did not."

"How did you find me?"

"I wake up by fire to see you gone," Ox said. "Other warriors say they see you go off to horses. I go to find you. Just as I first see you, you kill Satine. I call out for wizard and other warriors."

"What time of day is it?" Tristan asked.

"Midafternoon," Wigg answered. "Do you feel well enough to travel in a litter? We're losing valuable time."

Tristan raised himself up again. "I'll ride."

"Oh, no," Wigg answered adamantly. "I can't take the chance of your wound opening up again. Besides, we're down to Shadow and one other horse." He gave Tristan a critical look. "You managed to get my mare killed, remember?"

Tristan nodded. "Very well," he answered. "And I'm sorry about your horse."

"If Tristan travels by litter, then so do I," Celeste announced.

"Very well," Wigg said. "Let's go."

Wigg looked over at Ox. "Tell the warriors to strike the camp," he said.

As Ox went to follow his orders, Wigg and Celeste helped the prince to his feet.

THREE HOURS LATER, TRISTAN LOOKED DOWN FROM HIS MINION litter. They were traveling through the flat grasslands of Farplain, as they had been for the last two days. Wigg's spells had helped his shoulder greatly, but it still throbbed from time to time. As a precaution he periodically flexed his muscles to keep them from stiffening. The exercise hurt like the blazes, but he knew that later he would be glad he had done it. His weapons were back in place over his right shoulder. *At least the arm I rely on the most was spared,* he thought.

Ox flew alongside the litter. He looked over from time to time, as if he were expecting the prince to do something foolish—like dive out to the plain below, perhaps. One corner of Tristan's mouth curled into a smile. After the scare he had given them all last evening in the meadow, he really couldn't blame Ox for being so protective.

Celeste lay asleep on the floor. Her hair was completely gray now, and her skin was lined with wrinkles. Her face had an un-healthy pallor, and it was growing difficult for her to move. Even so, he loved her as much as ever.

Down on the ground and slightly ahead of the flying Minion cohort, Wigg led the way on Shadow.

Tristan cursed softly. He hated traveling so slowly—especially when every moment was so important to Celeste. He knew that Wigg felt the same way, but what else could they do? Every time Wigg tried to charge ahead, he lost the spell—only to have it return when he slowed. It was an agonizing frustrating way to travel.

His thoughts again found their way back to Satine. She had perhaps been the best adversary he had ever faced, and he knew that he was lucky to be alive. On their way from the camp, he had seen the simple stone marker that Wigg had erected at her fresh grave. He had used the craft to inscribe the single word "Satine" into its face, along with the date of her death. It was all that they really knew about her. Who was she, and who trained her so well? the prince wondered. He would probably never know.

Below, Wigg brought Shadow to an abrupt stop. For several moments the wizard did not move. Then he looked up and waved the warriors down.

Tristan's heart fell. The sun was setting, and the wizard had chosen this spot to camp for the night. This was the only reason they could be stopping—because there was nothing but grasslands for as far as the eye could see.

He looked down at Celeste as they descended, and closed his eyes against the pain he felt for her.

The Minions and their litters landed. Celeste stirred and sat up. Running one hand back through her hair, she blinked. Tristan helped her from the litter, and they walked over to Wigg. Her gait was even slower now, her limp more noticeable.

The wizard dismounted, handing Shadow's reins to a waiting warrior. He looked perplexed.

"What is it?" Tristan asked.

At first Wigg did not answer. He simply stared out over the vast grasslands as if searching for something.

"I've lost it," he said softly.

"Lost what?" Celeste asked.

"The River of Thought," Wigg answered. "Its pull upon me has vanished."

"But how can that be?" Tristan protested. "You weren't traveling fast enough to lose the spell."

Wigg sighed. "There can be only two explanations," he said. "The first is that the spell has been broken somehow—which would mean that we may never find the place we are searching for."

"And the other answer?" Tristan asked.

"The other possibility is that we have arrived, and the pull from the River of Thought is no longer required."

Tristan looked around. All he could see was waving grass.

"But how could this be the place?" he asked. "There's nothing here."

Wigg was about to answer when they all heard a rumbling. Almost simultaneously, the ground began to shake. Shadow and the other horse reared up and whinnied in fear. As they looked around, the warriors of the Minion cohort automatically drew their blades.

The rumbling sound grew louder and the earth shook more violently, making it difficult to remain standing. Tristan was about to order everyone into the air when he saw a pinprick of azure light form in the grass. He pointed it out to Wigg and Celeste. As the light grew in size and intensity, everyone stepped back.

Something emerged from the ground. At first they could see only azure light, but then another form started to take shape. It was like an arrow, with four sides extending down from its pinnacle. On and on it came, thundering up from the soil and tearing fresh sod loose as it grew. Its azure light was nearly blinding. Then it came to a halt. The rumbling sound died away, and the ground stilled once more.

Tristan gazed at it in amazement. A shimmering azure pyramid stood before him, its smooth shiny sides reflecting the dwindling daylight.

"I think it's safe to say that we have arrived," Wigg said softly.

Tristan was about to answer when a brilliant white door appeared in the pyramid's wall. The door slowly moved to one side, and a soft blue light spilled out over the threshold and onto the grass. Tristan looked over at Ox.

"Make camp here," he ordered. "Wigg, Celeste, and I are going inside. There is no telling how long we might be gone—or whether we will return. Under no circumstances are you or any of your warriors to follow us inside. You will simply have to wait for our return. Do you understand?"

Ox's face fell, but he knew his duty. "I live to serve," came the standard reply. "Luck with you."

Tristan looked over at Wigg and Celeste and they nodded back. He took each of them by the hand, and together they walked into the magnificent structure.

After several steps, by silent, mutual agreement the three of them stopped, breath held, eyes wide with wonder. The inside of the structure was far larger than its outside had led them to believe. Stunned, Tristan looked over at Wigg.

"How can this be?" he asked.

"Nothing is impossible within the purview of the craft," Wigg answered. "But I must admit that this comes close."

They stood in the middle of a huge foyer that branched off into several seemingly endless halls. The walls, floor, and ceiling were all constructed of what looked like azure glass. Soft light of the same color illuminated the place, radiating from everywhere, yet originating from nowhere. The only other color was a bloodred image of the Paragon, inlaid in the center of the floor. Silence reigned.

"What do we do now?" Celeste asked at last. Her voice, brittle and dry, echoed down the halls. Tristan took her withered hand.

"There can be only one answer," Wigg said. "We pick a hallway and begin walking. It seems to me that—"

He stopped in midsentence.

"What is it?" Tristan asked.

Eyes glued dead ahead, Wigg pointed. "Look," he said.

Another pinprick of azure light was forming in the air. As it grew in intensity it spun, and a form started to take shape in its midst. The form grew longer and wider until it was clearly identifiable as a boy. He glowed softly with the color of the craft. Tristan guessed him to be no more than nine or ten Seasons of New Life.

His hair was dark, his eyes were large and expressive. Completely naked, he stood there before them without shame.

Staring, Tristan realized that he could actually see through the boy, as if the boy was made of azure fog. It was like looking at a ghost. *Perhaps that is exactly what he is,* the prince thought. Suddenly the apparition knelt.

Not knowing what to do, Tristan looked over at Wigg and then back at the boy. "You may rise," he said awkwardly.

"So it is true after all," the boy said. "The *Jin'Sai* really is of this world. That must mean that the *Jin'Saiou*—she who was prophesied to be your twin sister—must now also have mortal form. Is that not true?"

"Yes," Tristan answered simply. "But how could you know?"

The boy pointed to Tristan's wound. "The dried azure blood on your vest. It is said that the true *Jin'Sai* or the *Jin'Saiou* might possess such blood." He paused. "So you have come to me at last."

He looked at Wigg. "It is also said that the watchwoman of the Chambers of Penitence recently oversaw the requisite trials of an ancient wizard who wore the Paragon. And that as a result of his trials, she provided his friend with herbs and oils that would help them in their struggle against the Vagaries. It was the reenactment of *your* greatest regrets that she oversaw, was it not?" he asked.

Stunned, for a moment Wigg couldn't find his voice. His time in the Chamber of Penitence was not long past, and it had taken all his strength to survive his experience there. Finally he spoke.

"That is correct," he answered. "But how did you know?"

"First of all, you wear the stone," the boy answered. "It was the nearness of the stone that alerted me to your presence and activated the structure in which you now stand. And, secondly, the watchwoman and I serve the same masters. We have done so for aeons. They see all."

"The Ones Who Came Before," Wigg said.

"Yes."

"But you are so young," Tristan said. "If what you say is true, then how is that possible?"

"I am aeons old, but for your benefit I have taken a form that your minds could understand and that you would find pleasing," the boy said. "But if this form doesn't suit you, I can take on another appearance.

"It is my task to watch over this place, this wonder left behind by the Ones. It is also my duty to serve those who come here bearing the stone and wishing to serve only the Vigors.

"There is far more history about our land and the craft than you know. Many others who have worn the stone have visited here, long before you. I helped them as well. Even so, our struggle against the Vagaries seems to know no end."

"Are you the one known as the Scroll Master?" Tristan asked.

The boy smiled. "Yes, among other things."

"And what is this place?" Wigg asked. "Is this the Well of Forestallments?"

"Yes," the boy answered. "But as is true with so many other wonders of this world, it too has another name, and another purpose."

"And what is that?" Celeste asked. Her voice was faint, and she clung weakly to Tristan's arm. The prince held her close.

"It is also known as the Abyss of Lost Souls."

"I don't understand," Wigg said.

"The craft is a vast universe, of which you have charted but a little," the boy said. "But you will understand far more by the time you leave here."

The boy gave Celeste a puzzled look. Gliding closer, he examined her, then looked at Wigg again.

"She is of your seed," he said. "And she is dying. What is left of her blood signature is vanishing as we speak."

"That is true," Wigg answered anxiously. "But how could you—"

"And you, *Jin'Sai,*" the boy said, interrupting the wizard. "I see your blood at work there. Did you not know that a union between your blood and hers would result in such a tragedy? Did your wizards not inform you of this? The warning was clearly illustrated in the Scrolls of the Ancients. Is this why you have come to me—to try to save the life of this woman?"

"Yes," Tristan answered. "But we have other reasons for searching you out, as well. The Orb of the Vigors has been wounded and it is bleeding. It wreaks havoc across the land. The *Enseterat*—my half brother—is returning to Eutracia to oversee its death throes. The Tome states that only the *Jin'Sai* or the *Jin'Saiou* might be able to heal the orb, but only after being granted the proper Forestallment. That Forestallment can supposedly be found in the Scrolls, but we had no time to search them out. So we chose to find you instead."

"Tristan, my love . . ." Celeste suddenly whispered.

Finally overcome with weakness, she fainted. Struggling against the pain in his shoulder, Tristan caught her and he lifted her into his arms.

Wigg rushed over. Lifting one of her eyelids, he looked into her eye. What he saw there turned his face ashen. He shook his head.

"She's nearly gone," he breathed.

As tears of desperation welled up in Tristan's eyes, he looked at the boy.

"Can you help us?" he pleaded.

The boy nodded. "You were right to search me out, *Jin'Sai*," he said. "I will do what I can. I know that you love her. But if the *Enseterat* has been loosed upon the world, the task before us has suddenly become far greater than the saving of a single life, no matter how dear she may be to you. Follow me."

With Celeste in his arms and Wigg by his side, Tristan followed the boy down one of the endless hallways.

CHAPTER LXXVI

THE OUTSKIRTS OF TAMMERLAND WERE IN FLAMES, AND SHAI-liha, Tyranny, Adrian, and Duvessa watched, aghast, from the Minion litter that hovered in the smoky, stinking air. Eight stout warriors bore their litter and another fifty flew guard alongside.

When the first Minion reports of the fires had come in, Faegan had ordered the women to go and investigate. Still consumed by their research, he and Jessamay remained ensconced in the Redoubt. But this time the women did not argue when Faegan told them that he and the sorceress must stay behind.

The black, stinking mass that had polluted the Sippora had finally reached the outskirts of the city and the damage it was causing was extraordinary.

For centuries, the Sippora had wound though the heart of the city the same way a major artery traversed the human body—and it was just as important. Although not suitable for drinking, its water was essential for washing, for use in many of Tammerland's hundreds of trades, and for the transportation of goods. Homes and businesses lined both sides of its banks. Many of the structures were wood. Most were old and dried out. It often seemed that little more than a stiff wind would send them tumbling into the water. They were simply no match for the superheated "waters" of the polluted Sippora.

Anyone foolish enough to try to save his or her home or business was quickly consumed. Scorched bodies lay at contorted angles on the banks; survivors screamed and ran for their lives. Even from where they hovered above the holocaust, Faegan's observers could smell the sickly sweet odor of burning flesh—both animal and human.

Shailiha lowered her head and closed her eyes. Tyranny put one arm around her shoulder. *Tristan, Wigg, where are you?* the princess found herself wondering. *We need you now!*

"Look there!" Adrian shouted. She pointed northeast, toward the heart of the city. Shailiha shifted her gaze to peer through the drifting smoke.

A crushing mass of humanity was fleeing the firestorm. Although some moved north or south to avoid the river altogether, the vast majority were running down the streets and byways alongside the river, carrying as many personal effects as they could bear.

But that will only take them deeper into the city and make things worse! Shailiha realized. *Can't they see that? What in the name of the Afterlife do they think they're doing?*

And then she understood. The terrified citizens were struggling to get to the royal palace, where they thought they might find safety, medical care, and food.

Shailiha's blood ran cold. The palace and its grounds were still crowded with the wounded who had first sought sanctuary from the rampaging Orb of the Vigors. She doubted that many more would fit—certainly not as many as were approaching its gates.

Shailiha looked over at the other women to see their sad faces turned toward hers—as though she might have some solution simply because she was of the royal house. She thought she understood now how Wigg and Faegan felt every time they were turned to for answers simply because they were wizards.

Wulfgar started this all, she thought. *But now we are doing these things to ourselves. Can't the people down there see that? What is to become of us?*

Leaning out of the litter, Shailiha caught the attention of the warrior commanding her group. "Take us back to the palace!" she shouted. "And hurry!"

With a nod, the warrior barked out orders and the litter turned for home.

"DRINK THIS," ABBEY SAID.

She handed the heady concoction to Jessamay, who was again seated in the familiar chair, surrounded by Faegan's azure wizard's warp. He relaxed the warp just enough for her to use her hands. She took the silver goblet.

A dense, greenish fog rose up and brimmed over the cup's lip to settle on the nearby floor and thread its way around Jessamay's feet. She glanced at the cup with no small degree of trepidation.

"How is it different this time?" she asked.

Abbey smiled. "We have added ground root of cat's claw, and a touch of widow-winkle," she answered. "It is the combination of the two that produces the sage fog. We have further refined the calculations taken from Failee's grimoire, and they led us to this particular combination of herbs." Her face became more serious. "How are you feeling? Are you sure that you have enough strength for another try?"

"Indeed," Faegan added from his chair on wheels. "I would prefer not to wait, but we could pause for a few hours if you wish."

Jessamay shook her head. "Time is precious," she answered. "You have both said so yourselves. And you can be assured that Wulfgar isn't resting as he travels toward the pass in the mountains. No, we must keep trying, no matter the cost."

It was evening in Eutracia, and Faegan and Jessamay had been at their work the entire day. Abbey had joined them, to contribute her knowledge of herbs. Everyone in the room was close to exhaustion, especially the sorceress.

Faegan felt sure that they were getting close to reversing Failee's work and moving the lean of Jessamay's blood signature back toward the right. They had made dozens of attempts, each bringing them a little closer to their goal, but it was maddeningly slow work.

Faegan also knew that it might take far longer to achieve their goal than they could afford—especially if Shailiha's impending report was as bad as he feared it might be. Worse yet, even if they succeeded in their efforts, it was imperative that Wigg and Tristan return home in time to help implement the rest of the plan.

He looked up at the ceiling and closed his eyes, willing Wigg and Tristan to succeed. Without them, and without the prince's blood returned to its natural state, the Vigors would be doomed. He looked back at Jessamay.

"Very well, then," he said. "Are you ready?"

Taking a deep breath, Jessamay nodded.

"Begin," he said.

As Abbey watched, Jessamay drank the potion and Faegan applied his most recent calculations upon her. At first the wizard could discern no difference from his previous attempts. But then things started to change.

Jessamay's eyes rolled back up into her head, and she convulsed with such force that Faegan found it necessary to enhance his warp. As Jessamay screamed in pain, her chair rose into the air. Despite his best efforts, Faegan found that he could no longer control it. As if it suddenly had a will of its own, the chair took the sorceress higher and flew manically around the room.

But it isn't the chair that's flying, Faegan realized. It is Jessamay, her blood signature going wildly out of control as it changes. Then he suddenly understood why Failee had kept her in a sorceress' cone for all of those years. It had been to protect her experiment by keeping this from happening. His mouth agape, Faegan watched Jessamay's speed increase as she soared about the Hall of Blood Records.

I beg the Afterlife, he asked himself in terror. *What have I done?*

"Stop her!" Abbey screamed. "If she smashes into one of the walls, she'll kill herself!"

But try as he might, the wizard remained powerless to stop Jessamay. He sat there, wide-eyed, as pieces of the room's furniture suddenly flew against the walls and smashed to bits. Hundreds of the alphabetized file drawers secured in the walls flew out; thousands of carefully categorized blood-signature records sailed about the room in a blizzard of parchment.

From the upper floors, ancient scrolls were sucked off from their shelves and unrolled, soaring down to the first floor to join the maelstrom of whirling paper.

Many of the jars and beakers holding herbs and precious oils suddenly burst, their colorful contents splashing into the air, spilling across the tabletops and floor. The oil chandeliers swung violently back and forth. Two of them smashed to the floor, threatening to start a fire among the growing collection of litter. Abbey rushed to quench the impending cataclysm.

Then things calmed. The wind died away, the drawers stopped opening, and the remaining scrolls on the upper levels stayed in place on their shelves. The parchments and other scrolls floated gently down until nearly every square inch of the floor was covered.

But to Faegan and Abbey's horror, Jessamay's chair continued to soar. Suddenly it changed course and crashed into a wall.

Despite Faegan's wizard's warp, the chair burst apart on impact. Jessamay tumbled out and landed in a heap near the center of the room. She lay there unmoving.

Faegan and Abbey hurried over. Faegan caused the warp surrounding her to disappear. He examined her for broken bones and could find none. Satisfied that she could be moved, he levitated her body to lie on one of the nearby tables. It had been his warp, he realized, that had kept her from being killed.

He was about to examine Jessamay further when she groaned. Her eyes opened.

He smiled at her. "How do you feel?" he asked.

Jessamay rose upon her elbows and looked in horror around the room.

"What happened?" she asked.

"You had a violent reaction to the last potion and spell," he told her. "In truth, that may have been exactly what we were looking for. Do you think you can stand?"

Jessamay nodded. Faegan helped her to her feet, secured a drop of the sorceress' blood, and caused it to fall upon a blank piece of parchment. The droplet twisted itself into Jessamay's blood signature and then died.

Faegan hurriedly placed the signature scope tripod over the blood signature and looked down. Several tense, quiet moments followed.

When he looked back up, he was beaming. Slapping his hand upon the arm of his chair, he let go a sharp cackle. Then he levitated his chair and soared around the room.

"We've done it!" he shouted. "We actually managed to change the lean of a blood signature!"

Jessamay shuffled weakly over to the scope and peered down through its crosshair lens. Lifting her face, she smiled.

It's really true, she thought, as Abbey walked over to embrace her. *I am myself once more. After three centuries of nearly becoming a slave to the Vagaries, my blood has finally been returned to its natural state.*

Just then the huge double doors parted. Shailiha, Adrian, Tyranny, and Duvessa stood there covered with soot. The four of them looked wide-eyed around the ransacked Hall of Blood Records and then at Faegan, who was still flying about the room whooping for joy.

Faegan lowered his chair to the floor.

"What in the world happened here?" Shailiha demanded.

Faegan smiled broadly. "We've done it!" he exclaimed. "Jessamay's blood signature has returned to normal!"

Then he noticed for the first time how filthy the newcomers were, and he remembered the mission he had sent them on. Shailiha's expression was not reassuring.

"It's bad, isn't it?" he asked.

Shailiha nodded. "I know this is a happy moment but, yes, the news is terrible." In quiet, measured tones, the princess described everything that they had seen.

Faegan's face fell.

"How long do you estimate before the throngs reach the palace?" he asked.

"Hours, at most," Duvessa answered. "By dawn the palace will be awash in refugees trying to gain entrance."

"And the dark mass of pollution in the Sippora?" Faegan asked.

"It moves far more slowly," Shailiha said. "My guess is that it will reach the palace environs in two days, perhaps three."

"By the time it reaches us, half of Tammerland will have gone up in smoke," Faegan said unhappily.

"What shall we do?" Tyranny asked.

Faegan pulled on his beard as he thought. "Wigg was right," he commented.

"Right about what?" Jessamay asked.

"Wigg said that in his absence we would have to prepare for a siege," he answered. "But now it is even worse than we imagined."

"Why?" Shailiha asked.

"Most of the population of Tammerland will be trying to smash down our gates to acquire what they believe will be greater safety and adequate food. They don't realize it, but if Wulfgar cannot be stopped, they will have chosen the worst possible place in which to find sanctuary. And it will all happen very soon now."

"Is there no way that you or the others can employ the craft to extinguish the fires?" Tyranny asked. "Or, at the very least, warn the people away from the palace?"

Faegan shook his head. "I wish that there were," he answered. "We could quash some of the fires, but surely not enough to do much good. And once the pollution reaches the most inhabited sections of the city, it will cause ten new fires for every one that we could extinguish. It would be like shoveling sand against the tide."

"What shall we do, then?" Adrian asked.

"What we have been doing, with a few notable exceptions," Faegan answered. He looked at Duvessa. "After Tristan and Traax, who is the ranking Minion officer?"

"A warrior named Ancaeus," she answered. "He is very capable. But Traax ordered that Ancaeus go with him to attack Wulfgar. Of the other warriors you are acquainted with, Ox is of course with Wigg and Tristan, and K'jarr is aboard Tyranny's flagship. What do you have in mind?"

Faegan thought for a moment. "The Minion captain named Dax, the one who first brought us the news about the Sippora being polluted," he said. "He impressed me. Do you know whether he is still attached to the warrior group defending the palace?"

"Yes," Duvessa answered, "I believe he is. Do you wish me to send for him?"

"All in good time," Faegan answered. "You and Dax are about to receive the promotions of a lifetime. Until either Traax or Tristan returns, you are both to be promoted to the temporary rank of field commander. You are to be in charge of the palace defenses—including the siege preparations. I know that you are both relatively inexperienced, but you can glean advice from others as need be. I want to be familiar with those giving the orders."

Duvessa's mouth fell open. She had never expected to have so much responsibility thrust upon her. She knew that Dax would be equally overwhelmed.

"As . . . as you wish," she whispered.

Faegan's face darkened a bit. "I'm afraid that your jobs will not be easy," he added. "As much as it pains me to say it, you must both harden your hearts. If Traax fails and Wulfgar comes, many of the citizens outside the palace are sure to die. If and when that day arrives, we will protect them as best we can, but you mustn't allow more of them access to the palace grounds, no matter how much they plead. Their added numbers will only harm our efforts to defend this place. I don't like it any better than the rest of you. But desperate days call for desperate measures. They always have."

He turned to look at the other women. "Adrian, I want you to select one acolyte to sail aboard each of Tyranny's vessels," he said. "Choose them wisely, for they will be helpful in battle. The remainder of Wulfgar's demonslaver fleet can be expected to arrive soon. When they do, we can only hope that our fleet of ships has been repaired and that they are ready to fight.

"Tyranny, I want you to go back to your fleet immediately and oversee the repairs. When you are ready and your vessels have been provisioned, do not wait for further orders from me. Take the remaining warriors still under your command and sail immediately."

"I understand," the privateer said. "We may be few in number, but with the Minions and the acolytes aboard, we will give the demonslavers a reception they will never forget."

"What about the rest of us?" Shailiha asked.

"You are to stay here and help Jessamay and me. And you can pray that Wigg and Tristan arrive home in time. Without the *Jin'Sai* and the First Wizard, everything else we do will be for naught."

CHAPTER LXXVII

WITH CELESTE STILL UNCONSCIOUS IN HIS ARMS, TRISTAN FOLlowed the Scroll Master down the brilliant azure hallway. Wigg walked beside him. The prince's shoulder hurt desperately, but he refused to give Celeste to her father. If he should lose the love of his life this day, he wanted to remember that it had been he who had carried her. The only sounds were their footfalls as they followed the hovering boy.

Soon, though, they began to hear strange sounds as they walked. The sounds, which seemed to be a bizarre mix of moaning and sobbing, grew louder and more distinct, and at first Tristan thought he was imagining things. He looked over at Wigg. The First Wizard nodded; he heard it also.

Another intersection loomed up ahead. It was circular, with still more hallways branching off from it. Dense, gray fog filled the space where a floor should have been and spilled out over the narrow walkway around the edge of the room. A white marble railing ran around the edge of the walkway.

As he entered the intersection, Tristan's nerves coiled up. Now he could recognize the sounds for what they were: the combined wails of a host of human beings. Not since the day of his ill-fated coronation and the attack of the Minions upon Eutracia had Tristan heard such a chorus of human suffering. But he could see nothing save for the marble walkway, gray fog, and circular railing that lay several steps beyond.

The young Scroll Master stopped and turned to face them. His face was serene, his manner calm.

"You may put the woman down," he said. "She will survive for the time being. There is something I must show you. If you follow my instructions, you will be safe. Disobey me, however, and harm will befall you beyond even my control."

Unsure of what to do, Tristan looked over at Wigg. The First Wizard nodded. Tristan gently lowered Celeste to the floor.

"Come with me," the boy said. "Under no circumstances are either of you to violate the boundaries of the rail."

Doing as they were told, they followed the boy to the rail. As they did, the rising gray fog slowly wound around their feet. Tristan looked down.

The breath rushed from his lungs, and for several long moments the prince was sure that he would become ill. Then his nerves began to quiet. As he had suspected, there was no floor beneath the fog. The circle was far larger than it had first appeared. Tristan now guessed it to be at least one hundred meters across. *But how can this be?* he wondered. *Somehow, the normal rules of space and distance do not apply here.*

About five meters down, billowing waves of black fog washed to and fro. They looked bottomless. The wails and cries were much louder now.

From amid the waves of fog, naked human beings rose and fell. Blood ran from their eyes. As if trying to save themselves from drowning, they fought their way to the surface, only to be sucked back down into the churning, swirling chaos.

As they cried out, sometimes they would claw, strike, and bite one another in their never-ending attempts to rise free. Some of them would scrabble at the smooth glassy walls, only to fall prey to the grasping fog once again and disappear. Their bleeding gazes stabbed their way into the prince's heart.

Tristan turned to the Scroll Master. "Is this the Afterlife?" he asked, horrified.

The young boy shook his head. "This is the Abyss of Lost Souls," he said. "It is for neither the living nor the dead. It is, rather, the place in between. Only certain souls suffer the misfortune of imprisonment here. Each of them is of endowed blood, and once one is cast into the pit, his life and his suffering become eternal. Those you see here died over the course of aeons in your world, but they did not successfully cross over into the Afterlife."

"I don't understand," Wigg said.

"The answer is as simple as it is complex, as crude as it is elegant," the boy said. "You see, each of these lost souls—were they one time of either the Vigors or of the Vagaries—once possessed Forestallments. But when they died—their blood signatures dying shortly thereafter—in your world no thunder rumbled across the sky, and no wind rose. They simply went into the void, to end up here."

"Why?" Wigg asked.

"Because their Forestallments were not collected successfully," the boy answered. "That is why they bleed from their eyes. You have by now learned that blood runs closest to the surface of the body in the white of one's eyes, have you not? And that if properly trained, one of the craft is able to detect the lean of a blood signature simply by looking into a subject's eyes?"

Wigg nodded. The boy turned to look at Tristan.

"You, *Jin'Sai,* will be the first human in all of history to willingly give up his Forestallments," he said. "Ridding you of the Forestallments that Succiu imparted to your blood is the only way that your blood can be changed back to red."

Stunned, Tristan looked back down into the Abyss of Lost Souls. "Why did you bring me here?" he asked. In his heart he already knew the answer, but he wanted to hear the Scroll Master say it.

"It is important that you see and understand this place," the Scroll Master said, "because if your Forestallments are not collected successfully, your body and soul will be condemned to this place for all of eternity. If that happens, then being the *Jin'Sai* will no longer have any meaning."

Tristan looked back down into the writhing mass of tortured souls. Closing his eyes, he hung his head as he contemplated such a fate. But, he knew, there could be no going back now.

"You say that his Forestallments are to be 'collected,' " Wigg said. "What do you mean by that? When a Forestallment dies, it simply vanishes into nothingness. Isn't that so?"

"No," the boy answered. "But I may only share the answer with the *Jin'Sai*—or the *Jin'Saiou,* should that become necessary. I am forbidden to reveal it to any other. Should Tristan survive, he shall become part of one of the most hallowed, most intricate of the many processes left behind by the Ones Who Came Before. He shall also be witness to one of their greatest constructs. They knew his blood might turn to azure should he somehow employ the craft without proper training. I was placed here aeons ago to help him should such a fate befall him."

"Are you one of the Ones Who Came Before?" Wigg asked.

"No," the boy said. "I am but one of their servants." He looked at Tristan again.

"What say you?" he asked. "Are you prepared to come with me?"

Tristan did not look up. "Yes," he answered softly. "There is no other choice."

He turned toward Wigg. "If I never return, tell Celeste how much I loved her," he whispered. "And tell Shailiha to be brave, for with me gone she will have to carry on the struggle to unite the two sides of the craft."

Tristan walked over to Celeste and took her into his arms. She felt cold and lifeless, as though she were already gone. A tear escaped from one of his eyes to land upon her wrinkled cheek. He kissed her gently on the lips.

"Goodbye, my darling," he said softly.

He carried her over to Wigg and placed her into her father's arms. Saying nothing, he touched Wigg gently on the shoulder and went to stand next to the boy.

Wigg watched as an azure glow surrounded them. As the glow brightened, the figures of Tristan and the boy slowly disappeared. Then the glow vanished, leaving nothing behind.

Wigg gently laid his only daughter back down on the floor and settled her head on his lap. As he cradled her, the wailing and crying continued from the Abyss of Lost Souls, and soon his own sobbing became no less plaintive.

CHAPTER LXXVIII

WULFGAR STOOD BEFORE THE NEWLY CUT PASS THROUGH THE Tolenkas, stunned by its raw beauty. Captain Cathmore stood by his side, his tattered uniform barely covering his skeletal frame and the dark organs within.

Wulfgar was fresh from his victory at the Minion outpost, and his Black Ship had crossed the fields of Farplain to reach the majestic Tolenkas in a single day. The journey to the pass had been uneventful. If any sizable Minion force searched for him along the way, they hadn't shown their hand.

The glowing azure wall climbed high into the fog lying quietly upon the peaks of the mountains. Its surface was as smooth as glass, stretching from one side of the pass to the other. White-hot flashes of raw energy shot to and fro within its silent depths. Wulfgar felt as though the wall was begging to be opened. He yearned to see the wonders waiting on the other side come streaming through.

Wulfgar turned and looked down the mountainous slope. The Minion warriors who had watched over the pass had. There had been fewer of them to contend with, and they had perished valiantly but quickly.

His lone Black Ship hovered over the grassy field below. Lit torches had been shoved into the ground, their flames highlighting the dark lines of the vessel and lending the scene a surreal, ghostly quality. The corpses of warriors and demonslavers littered the nearby ground. The surviving demonslavers milled about, watching the azure wall from afar. Some scavenged the bodies of the dead Minions for dreggans and returning wheels.

Smiling, Wulfgar turned back toward the pass. As he did, he felt the touch of the Heretics on his mind. The mixed chorus of voices was as lovely and commanding as ever. He went to his knees.

"Wulfgar . . ."

"I am here," he answered silently.

"It is time to reach deep into your blood and call forth the special Forestallment that allows you to breach the azure pass. Do not be alarmed by what emerges from its depths. They do not possess the intellect of your dark captains or even your demonslavers, but your new servants will be the blunt instruments of your eventual victory. The Old Eutracian word for them is K'ton. Unlike the Minions of Day and Night, they know no hierarchy within their ranks. Bring them now, Wulfgar. Bring them and watch their swift evolution take place before your eyes. Then you must leave this place and travel to Tammerland. As you near the city, we will speak with you again."

"As you command," Wulfgar replied.

He stood and raised his arms. Bolts streamed from his outstretched fingers. Streaking up the slope, they snaked over the surface of the wall to form a vertical line, separating the pass into two equal halves. He moved his hands apart, and the line split and moved toward either side, opening a dark gap in the wall. Then he lowered his hands, and he and Cathmore backed away.

Snarling, grunting sounds came out of the darkness, becoming louder as something neared the entrance to the other side of the world. Finally one of the K'tons walked through to stand and face the *Enseterat* in the moonlight.

Wulfgar held his ground as he looked at the first of his new servants. Standing at least seven feet tall, the K'ton had skin of the darkest black. It stood on two massive, humanlike legs; simple, black warrior's sandals adorned its feet. The massive arms and torso rippled with bulging muscles. Its head was huge—even in relation to its great body. Its dark, straggly hair fell down past its shoulders.

The K'ton's bright red eyes were small, giving its gaze a furtive look. Its nose was wide and constantly testing the air. Its thin lips and pointed teeth were covered with drool. The only garment it wore was a black, fringed warrior's skirt. As more K'tons appeared, Wulfgar saw that their only weapons were either short swords or huge, bulbous clubs with silver blades extending from the club heads.

As they gathered to stand before Wulfgar, the K'tons' collective snarling and grunting grew ever louder. As the night wore on, they continued to march out to stand in the torchlight. Wulfgar suddenly wondered how he could load so many aboard a single Black Ship. But then the monsters started to change and he had his answer.

One by one, they became surrounded by azure. Twisting and turning, crying out in agony, they sank to their knees or fell to the ground. The sound of ripping and tearing filled the air. As he watched, Wulfgar recalled part of the Heretics' last message:

"Bring them," they had said. *"Bring them, and watch their swift evolution."*

Wulfgar suddenly understood: Having been released to the world, the K'tons were changing.

The skin of their backs split open down the center. Fully exposed spinal columns rose to rest upon the surfaces of their backs. Then their shoulders split open. Appendages extended from within the fresh wounds.

As the new limbs exited the K'tons' bodies, Wulfgar smiled. The freshly formed appendages were wings. Dark and leathery, they looked very strong. The K'tons quickly snapped their new, wet wings into place behind them.

At last, Wulfgar realized, *the Minion advantage of flight is ours as well!*

The winged K'tons now covered the slopes of the mountains for as far as he could see. The azure glow slowly faded away, and the breach in the wall closed. The K'tons waited in the torchlight, their weapons at the ready.

Wulfgar walked up to the first of them and pointed at the Black Ship below.

"Walk to the ship," he ordered.

Its teeth curling back in a vicious grimace, the K'ton raised its head and gave a cry that was half scream, half snarl. Its red gaze held Wulfgar's for a moment. Wulfgar glared back. Then the K'ton turned and lumbered down the slope; thousands of others followed his lead. Their dark numbers were so vast that as they walked it seemed the entire hillside was moving. But as the first of the K'tons neared the recent battle scene, they slowed. Wulfgar tensed.

The K'tons at the edge of the field raised their heads. Their sensitive noses began testing the night air.

They've detected the blood of the fallen, Wulfgar realized.

The K'tons charged down into the killing field, roaring with delight as they grabbed up corpses.

Wulfgar smiled. He looked over at Cathmore; his captain smiled back at him.

"How marvelous," Wulfgar said softly. "Frankly, I was wondering how we were going to feed them all. Now I know."

Cathmore turned his glowing eyes back to the grisly scene. "Indeed," he answered.

When the feeding frenzy was finally over, Wulfgar and Cathmore walked down the slope to stand among the K'tons.

Not a shred of once-living tissue remained. Blood colored the ground. Minion body armor and weapons lay scattered over a wide area, as did the clothing and weapons of the fallen demonslavers who had vanquished them. The K'tons stood quietly, blood staining their hands and mouths. Even now they seemed unsatisfied.

Cathmore turned to look at his lord. "There wasn't enough for them to eat," he observed casually. "Such a pity."

Wulfgar nodded. "We'll just have to get to Tammerland faster. There will be lots of soft-bellied citizens for them to feast upon in the city."

Cathmore smiled.

"Even so, we must first deal with the orb," Wulfgar reminded his captain. "And it needs to be done on the plains, far away from the azure wall. Then we can join the rest of the Black Ships and take Tammerland."

Wulfgar walked over to the demonslavers. "Get aboard!" he yelled at them. "We leave at once!"

He turned to face the K'tons.

"Half of your number are to follow my ship by air," he ordered in a craft-enhanced shout. "The rest are to fly to Tammerland to join the other Black Ships. When you find them, follow the orders of Captain Merriwhether. Stragglers will be killed. We will join you there. In the capital there will be plenty of food for all!"

The K'tons in the front ranks snarled and beat their bloody

fists upon their chests. Soon all of them followed suit in a massive display of power.

Wulfgar raised one hand. Calling upon the craft, he caused a blank parchment to appear. He pointed at it and writing appeared upon its surface. When he was done, the parchment rolled itself up.

Wulfgar took the scroll from the air and walked it over to one of the K'tons. The drooling monster simply looked at it for a moment. Then it took the scroll from its master.

"Give that to Captain Merriwhether," Wulfgar ordered the K'ton. "Fail to do so and you will pay with your life. Do you understand?"

Raising the parchment high, the K'ton gave a fierce battle cry.

Satisfied, Wulfgar levitated himself to the foredeck of the ship. Cathmore followed. Wulfgar commanded the great ship to lower so the last of the demonslavers could enter the open stern of the ship's hull, and the door slowly rose up. The ship lifted into the air.

As the Black Ship sailed away, the K'ton throngs snapped open their wings and lifted into the night.

CHAPTER LXXIX

TRISTAN AWOKE TO FIND HE WAS STANDING UP, THE YOUNG Scroll Master beside him. As his vision cleared, the *Jin'Sai* looked around in awe. He had long believed that he would never see a room larger than the Hall of Blood Records, but what he saw here made even that great place seem small by comparison.

Like the others before it, this chamber was also constructed of glowing azure glass. The ceiling had to be at least one hundred meters high. Massive columns rose to meet it.

A seductive cross between the finest of choir voices and the gentle tinkling of glass wind chimes teased his hearing. Saying nothing, the young Scroll Master watched and waited as Tristan took in the scene.

Row upon row of glowing azure bookcases stood in neat

ranks, filling the hall from one side to the other. They seemed to stretch into infinity.

"What is this place?" Tristan asked with wonder and respect.

The Scroll Master turned to him. "Your wizards and sorceresses are wrong," he said, "about so many things. They always have been. But even without the direct guidance of the Ones, and with only the Tome and the Scroll of the Vigors to guide them, their advancement has been exemplary."

It was not lost on Tristan that the Scroll Master hadn't actually answered his question. "I don't understand," he said. "What have they been wrong about?"

"A great many things, I'm afraid," the boy answered. "Perhaps their greatest mistake of late has been their misguided theories regarding the art of Forestallments. But that is understandable. Wigg, Faegan, and Jessamay are little more than three centuries old. That length of time is but a single heartbeat in the life of the craft. They remain infants in the ways of magic."

Tristan was becoming impatient. "You haven't answered my first question," he said. "What is this place?"

"We are standing in the presence of one of the greatest achievements of the Ones," the boy said. "The Well of Forestallments. Come with me."

The boy floated toward one line of shelves. As Tristan followed along, his boot heels rang out against the floor, mingling with the comforting sounds that came from everywhere at once. They traveled a long way before stopping. Pointing to one of the bookcases, the boy indicated that Tristan should walk around to face it.

"Do not be threatened by what you see," the boy said. "Although it will be unexpected, it cannot hurt you."

Tristan was devastated by what lay before him. Taking a quick breath, he stepped back. He couldn't believe his eyes.

It was the face of Failee.

Failee—the mad First Mistress of the Coven and onetime wife to Wigg. The woman who had ordered the deaths of his parents and the Directorate of Wizards, absconded with both the Paragon and his twin sister Shailiha, and one of the Coven of Sorceresses he had killed with his first and only use of the craft. Memories flooded his mind as he stood there looking at the face of the woman he had hated for so long.

He finally realized that he was looking at only a death mask. He relaxed a bit. Taking a deep breath, he walked closer.

From the depths of the shelf, Failee's face hovered behind what seemed to be a curved pane of clear glass. Her eyes were closed. Azure light highlighted the contours of her face, and words in Old Eutracian were inscribed into the area just below the mask. He looked down.

The cubicle below the one holding Failee's likeness was also encased in glass, but what it contained fascinated Tristan even more.

Like tributaries snaking away from a river, dozens of azure Forestallments twinkled there. Many more words in Old Eutracian were inscribed below them. The Forestallments hovered vertically in space; amazingly beautiful, they sent out shimmering waves of azure as they rotated side by side.

Looking to the right, Tristan saw the death masks of Vona and Zabarra—two of the other sorceresses he had killed—along with two more cubicles of Forestallments.

Then his eyes fell upon the death mask of Succiu. He stepped over to stand before it.

He had never believed that he would see her face again, and doing so now gave him no joy. Under Failee's orders, she had raped him and imbued still-dormant Forestallments in his blood signature. She had also been the mother of Nicholas, Tristan's only child. As he looked at Succiu's beautiful almond-shaped eyes, a shudder went through him. Like those of the others, her Forestallments were displayed just below her death mask.

Overcome with curiosity, Tristan looked down the limitless length of this case. Death masks and their accompanying Forestallments lined both sides for as far as he could see. Then he realized that it was the slowly revolving Forestallments that were the source of the lovely tinkling sounds.

He turned to the Scroll Master. "Why would the Ones build such a place as this, only to record the expired Forestallments of the dead?"

The boy smiled. "Those persons who are represented here are quite dead, that's true," he said. "But the Forestallments that their blood signatures once carried are not."

"That's impossible," Tristan said. "When one of the endowed

dies, his or her blood signature and Forestallments die with them. That is why there is always an accompanying atmospheric disturbance—it is the craft's way of reacting to the passing of a collection of Forestallments. Wigg and Faegan are sure of it."

"No," the boy said. "Your wizards are wrong. Forestallments do not die unless they are dismantled by a proper spell of reversal. If their host dies before this is accomplished, they leave the host and travel here, causing the disturbances you describe. They do so because of a process of the craft that the Ones refined just before they disappeared, but it does not always succeed. If they are unsuccessful in their journey, their owners are condemned to the Abyss of Lost Souls.

"The words in Old Eutracian inscribed below the Forestallments identify them and illustrate the spells required for their conjuring and their dismantling," the boy went on. "Your wizards are right about one thing, though. The Scrolls of the Ancients were written by the Ones and the Heretics of the Guild. Collectively, they contain the spells required to both form and dismantle nearly every Forestallment known to man."

Stunned, Tristan looked around the chamber once again. "But that still does not answer my question," he said. "Why did the Ones build this place, and why are the Forestallment branches collected in this way?"

"Two reasons," the boy answered. "The first is the most obvious. A properly induced Forestallment is a precious thing. Here they would always remain safe from harm, as would the required spells."

"And the second reason?" Tristan asked.

"They built this place for the *Jin'Sai* and the *Jin'Saiou*," the boy said gravely. "They knew that it would help you in your struggle to combine the two sides of the craft. Once your blood is healed, the Ones have dictated that three of these preserved Forestallments are to be given to you and activated—and then three shall be selected for Shailiha, should you die or otherwise fail in your destiny. Your wizards were wise not to activate the Forestallments that Succiu imparted to your blood. Had they been brought to life improperly, they would have killed you.

"Do not be misled," he warned. "The Well of Forestallments

has existed for aeons. But it was not built with such care and so lovingly maintained for all this time for only you and your sister."

"Who else was it built for, then?" Tristan asked.

"It was built for the other *Jin'Sai*s and *Jin'Saiou*s who came before you and Shailiha—and for those who may have to follow you, should you both fail to join the two sides of the craft."

Tristan's jaw fell and the breath rushed out of his lungs.

"But *I* am the *Jin'Sai*!" he exclaimed. "And Shailiha is the *Jin'Saiou*! The Tome says so! How could there have been others before us?"

"Think for a moment," the boy said. "The Tome makes mention of a Chosen One who will be preceded by another. But does it say how many pairs of these twins there might eventually be?"

"As far as I understand it, no," Tristan said. He simply couldn't believe what he was hearing.

"And does the Tome mention you or your sister by name?" the boy pressed.

"Not that I have been told," the prince answered.

"Then how can you and your wizards be so sure that you and Shailiha have been the only ones?" the boy asked. "There have, in fact, been dozens of *Jin'Sai*s and *Jin'Saiou*s before you. Over the aeons they have always arrived in pairs—one girl child and one boy. So far, each pair has failed to unite the two sides of the craft. And like you and your sister, each pair thought themselves the only ones—unless they succeeded in finding me, as you have, and were informed about the true nature of things. But you, Tristan, are the first to use his gifts without the advantage of training. Your blood is the first to turn azure. When the Tome speaks of this, it is referring directly to you. We know that now."

"But how can that be," Tristan protested, "when so much of what the Tome prophesied about me has already come true? Are you saying that the *Jin'Sai*s before me also followed the exact same path as I have in life?"

"Of course not," the boy answered. "That would be illogical. But only in your case have so many of the prophecies come true—that is why hope runs so high that you shall be the one to finally succeed. Only time will tell."

Tristan shook his head in disbelief. "But the Ones hid the Tome and the Paragon in the Caves!" he protested. "During the Sorceresses' War it was Wigg who first found them and brought them to light. If that is the case, how could previous *Jin'Sai*s and *Jin'Saiou*s have learned about and employed the craft?"

"Because it was not Wigg who discovered the Tome and the Paragon," the young Scroll Master answered. "It was the previous *Jin'Saiou.*

"Her name was Elena. She was very old. Her twin brother had been killed defending the Vigors. She had also failed in her destiny, and her life was ending. A war was raging, just as another is about to begin now. Darkness ruled, and few practitioners of the Vigors remained. The dire circumstances of her times dictated that she hide the book and the stone while she still could. Ever since the appearance of the first *Jin'Sai* and *Jin'-Saiou,* the Tome and the Paragon have been passed down from one trusted practitioner of the Vigors to the next. Elena was the first and only one to hide them. She knew she was taking a terrible chance, but there was no other way.

"It was indeed fortuitous that it was Wigg who found them, many centuries later. Had it been a servant of the Vagaries, our lives would be very different now. During all of this time, the Vigors and the Vagaries have been at odds, with no clear victor. We can only hope that you and Shailiha finally succeed. And not all of the previous *Jin'Sai*s and *Jin'Saiou*s are represented here. For you see, the art of Forestallments was lost for centuries before it was revived by Failee."

Stunned by what he had just heard, Tristan suddenly needed to move. He absently walked away. The Scroll Master did not follow. The prince found all of this too mind-numbing to grasp. It was as if his entire world had suddenly been turned upside down.

After a time, he walked back to the Scroll Master, one question plaguing him.

"I want to know something," he said. "Were Nicholas and Morganna really our parents, or were they simply the vessels the Ones worked through to place us both here upon the earth?"

"Even I do not possess the answer to such a puzzle," the boy answered. "You are both of Morganna's womb. Even so, given the complex nature of the craft and the seemingly infinite powers of the Ones, that may mean nothing. But it is said that if you are successful in joining the two sides of the craft, you and Shailiha shall finally have all the answers you seek. We all hope for that day. I cannot answer all of your questions, but the Ones left others like me behind who may prove helpful—such as the watchwoman of the floating gardens who helped your wizards. Each of us was placed here for a specific purpose—to employ our particular skills to help the *Jin'Sai*s and *Jin'Saiou*s as best we could, should they come to us."

"How do I find the others?" Tristan asked.

"I cannot help you with that. The Ones dictated that we may commune with one another, but that we may never divulge our locations to each other. You will find them the same way you found the watchwoman and me—by way of careful research. Their existences are far too valuable to entrust to any other form of detection."

Taken up with all of this as he had been, Tristan suddenly remembered Celeste. "We must hurry!" he said. "Celeste is dying as we speak. My blood must be healed, so that I can go to her. I fear that we might already be too late."

"You are correct, *Jin'Sai*," the boy said. "But not for the reasons that you believe. We must hurry, but the greatest reason for doing so is that Wulfgar has landed, and his forces are on the move. He has already breached the pass in the Tolenkas and unleashed the Heretic hordes. They make their way toward Tammerland as I speak. But the Ones dictated that I show you this room and make the proper explanations before I tried to heal your blood."

The thought of Wulfgar's return to Eutracian soil made Tristan's blood run cold.

"How can you know all this?" he asked.

"I commune with the Ones, just as I'm sure Wulfgar now does with the Heretics. In many ways, *Jin'Sai,* the fatal chess match between good and evil has only just begun."

"And Celeste?" Tristan asked anxiously. "Do you know whether she still lives?"

"Yes, although she is fading quickly. But there is something else about Celeste that I have been empowered by the Ones to tell you. It is not something that you will wish to hear."

His face darkening, Tristan walked closer. "What is it?" he demanded.

"I know how much you love her, and we will save her if we can," the boy said. "But in the great adventure that is to be your life, in the end she is not to be your destiny. If Celeste survives, for both your sakes you must leave her. Another shall have the honor of being by your side. You will know her when you see her, and she will not be what you expect."

"You're lying!" Tristan exploded. He took another aggressive step toward the Scroll Master.

The boy raised one hand and the reigning *Jin'Sai* lapsed into unconsciousness. Before he hit the marble floor, the boy levitated his body. Keeping Tristan hovering by his side, he looked into the prince's face.

"No, *Jin'Sai*," the boy said softly. "I have told you the truth. But of all the *Jin'Sais* who have walked this earth in the pursuit of uniting the two sides of the craft, your journey shall prove the most difficult of all."

Another azure haze began to form, and the prince and the Scroll Master vanished.

CHAPTER LXXX

AS TRAAX RAISED HIS BLOODIED SWORD ARM, HIS DREGGAN FLASHED in the moonlight. The blade came down and split one of the awful thing's skulls. He watched his lifeless enemy tumble to the ground far below. Swiveling in the air, Traax looked for another opponent. With so many of the monsters surrounding him, it didn't take long.

It was well after midnight, the three Eutracian moons providing ample light as the airborne battle raged on. When Traax and his group had first seen the lone Black Ship sailing toward them, he and Ancaeus had thought their superior numbers would give them at least a fighting chance. But the Minions had no way of knowing that Wulfgar had already breached the azure pass and loosed the Heretic hordes.

This Minion attack was exactly what Wulfgar had been hoping for. Sure that the *Jin'Sai* would send the bulk of his forces north from the palace to try to stop him, he had ordered the K'tons to fly well behind the Black Ship as she traveled south. The K'tons' dark forms blended perfectly into the night sky. When the Minion warriors flying northward first saw the lone ship, they attacked immediately. The trap had been sprung.

At first Traax hoped that they might gain the upper hand, despite Wulfgar and Cathmore's azure bolts raining down on them with maniacal fury. But then the K'tons had caught up to the fighting, and the Minions quickly found themselves in dire straits. Even Traax, with all his battle experience, had never expected such a devastating onslaught.

The K'tons outnumbered the Minions, and they were proving as capable at dealing death as any warrior who ever lived. Those Minions who fought their way through the K'tons to land upon the ship's decks were cut down by the surging slavers or vaporized by azure bolts. The decks were slick with blood.

As the battle raged, Traax became sickened by what he saw. The Minions had been bred to be savage, ruthless warriors who would gladly die in the service of their lord. But there was no glory or honor in what he saw in this killing zone so high above the ground.

Some of the more confident K'tons actually paused in their fighting to consume a Minion conquest—whether the victim was alive or dead. Minion blood ran red down their chins and chests. More flew to the ground to pounce upon the corpses of both the Minions and the demonslavers littering the fields of Farplain. In their deep desire to feed, they saw no distinction between the corpses.

Bloodcurdling screams rang through the night air as the butchery and gorging went on. Traax was quickly becoming worried about his forces' ability to survive.

Looking around, he found the Black Ship. She hovered safely above the fray, allowing Wulfgar and Cathmore to shower the Minion forces with azure bolts. He watched in horror as two more deadly shafts streaked down to tear into a group of struggling warriors not fifty meters from him. Amid their awful screams, some were vaporized instantly. Others caught fire and lost arms, wings, or legs to the bolts as they crashed to the ground.

Traax suddenly realized that Wulfgar and his skeletal captain didn't care whether their bolts occasionally struck their own awful forces. *He has more of these twisted servants than he will ever need to take Tammerland,* Traax thought. *If he has to purposely waste some of them in order to smash my troops in a single battle, then he will. But not before I try to kill him myself. I owe that much to the* Jin'Sai.

Traax was about to soar up to try to board the Black Ship when Ancaeus flew up by his side. His second in command was wounded in one wing and was having trouble staying aloft. His hands and chest were covered with K'ton blood. Then Traax saw another K'ton coming straight at him. As it approached, its teeth flashed in the moonlight.

Traax twisted in the air and lifted his sword. As the monster soared by, he pushed the button on the dreggan's hilt and the blade jumped its extra foot, piercing the beast's wing and exiting the opposite side.

Gripping the dreggan with both hands, Traax used all his strength to hold it still as the K'ton soared by. The razor-sharp blade tore through the length of the K'ton's wing, sending it head over heels toward the ground. Satisfied for the moment, Traax shot a quick, questioning glance at Ancaeus.

"Battle status!" he shouted at the top of his lungs, but his voice was drowned out by the screams of friends and foes all around him.

"Ancaeus!" he yelled again. "What is our battle status!"

Ancaeus heard him this time and flew closer. As he did, another K'ton struck at him with a massive club. He dodged the blow. He was about to strike back when a warrior came up from behind the K'ton and took off one of the thing's wings with a single sword stroke. The K'ton screamed in agony. Ancaeus watched it tumble to the ground, smashing into Minions and K'tons alike on the way down. Safe for the moment, he turned to Traax.

"We are being defeated, my lord!" he shouted. Traax could barely hear him. "We must retreat! We cannot win; there are simply too many of them! We must save what forces we can for the defense of Tammerland!"

As the battle raged all around him, Traax tried to collect himself and decide what to do. His forces were dwindling, while the enemy seemed to keep coming and coming. If this kept up for very much longer, his army would be obliterated.

His blood boiling, he looked up at the imperious Black Ship. More azure bolts rained down. Wulfgar would have to wait, he realized. He looked back at Ancaeus and nodded.

"Sound the retreat!" he shouted. "We fly for home! But if they follow and we cannot outrun them, we shall turn to fight them again—no matter the cost!"

Ancaeus grabbed the battle bugle hanging around his neck and blew the retreat. Other buglers took up the call. Traax gnashed his teeth and turned for home. One by one, his bloodied warriors reluctantly broke off their fighting to follow him.

Looking down from the deck of the Black Ship, Cathmore smiled. He turned toward Wulfgar.

"They are in retreat, my lord," he said. "Shall I order the K'tons to pursue them?"

Wulfgar shook his head. "The Minions are of little importance now," he said. "We fought them this night only because we were forced to. We need to travel farther, so that I might call forth the orb before my dear half brother has a chance to intervene. When my business with the orb is concluded, we shall sail on to Tammerland, and the K'tons can gorge themselves on as many Minions and soft-fleshed civilians as they wish. Make our course south-southeast," he ordered. "I have unfinished business with the craft."

CHAPTER LXXXI

TRISTAN SLOWLY OPENED HIS EYES. AS HIS VISION CLEARED HE realized that he was still in the Well of Forestallments, but he had been moved to another area of the massive room. The Scroll Master hovered by his side.

Tristan shook his head. The chamber was even larger than he had first imagined. The huge distances covered by the book-cases made the angles between them so slight that he hadn't re-alized that the room was actually a great circle, as was the Abyss of Lost Souls. Like the hallways of the Redoubt, the cases were laid out like the spokes of a wagon wheel, with Tris-tan and the boy now standing at the hub.

"We are finally at the center of the Well of Forestallments," the boy said. "I used the craft to transport us here, because if we had walked, it would have taken several days. This is where I shall endeavor to change your blood back to red, should you still wish to endure the process. But before we begin, there is some-thing else you must know."

"And what is that?" Tristan asked. He was desperately impa-tient to get on with it and hurry back to Celeste.

The Scroll Master raised one arm. "Behold," he said.

The glow of the craft appeared in the center of the circle. It slowly grew brighter and denser, then abruptly vanished, to re-veal a shimmering, pure white marble altar.

Tristan shuddered. It was very much like the altar upon which Succiu had raped him and imbued his blood with Forestall-ments. Taking a deep breath, he did his best to push away the awful memories.

"What is it?" he asked. "Why is it here?"

"I told you that the Scrolls of the Ancients hold the spells for nearly every Forestallment in creation," the boy said.

"Yes."

The boy ran one hand lovingly over its polished surface, then looked back at Tristan.

"This structure contains the rest of them," he said, "those that are not contained in the Scroll of the Vigors. They are the most powerful of all Forestallments. Only the descendants of Queen Morganna might have blood strong enough to accept them. Unfortunately, Wulfgar carries two of them already, gleaned from the Scroll of the Vagaries."

"One of them must be the ability to summon the orbs and to move them about at will," Tristan mused. "But what is the other?"

"The second Forestallment allows him to commune with the Heretics," the boy answered. "This has been of great advantage to him as he has pursued his most recent plans."

"These potent spells of the Vigors were placed here in safekeeping by the Ones, in hope that their *Jin'Sais* and *Jin'Saious* would find me and make use of them. They considered these spells too valuable and powerful to be loosed upon the world, but the Heretics did not. The Heretics believe that chaos, not compassion, is the overriding principle of the craft. They placed all of their spells into the Scroll of the Vagaries, regardless of how powerful or destructive they might be. That scroll remains in Wulfgar's possession. Once identified, any number of Forestallment calculations may be imbued in his blood by his consuls. If you are successful in stopping the *Enseterat,* your next duty must be to recover the other scroll for the good of mankind. Our world will depend upon it."

"But Wigg and Faegan can also summon the orbs," Tristan countered. "And neither of them has visited this place before today. How can that be?"

"Your wizards unraveled the necessary calculations themselves," the boy said. "Despite their other errors, this was truly a great accomplishment. The wizard Faegan is particularly adept at such things, especially with his gift of Consummate Recollection. But they still have not deciphered the entire spell. They can call the orbs, but their lesser blood cannot move them at will. That was clear when you and Wigg nearly died in that litter as the Orb of the Vigors destroyed Brook Hollow, remember?"

Tristan nodded. Many things that had long puzzled him were beginning to make sense.

"You're going to do more than simply heal my blood, aren't you?" Tristan asked. He looked over at the altar once more. "You're going to rid me of my present Forestallments—the ones Succiu forced on me. Then you will replace them with others gleaned from within the altar." He looked back at the Scroll Master.

"I'm right, aren't I? And if my present Forestallments do not successfully transfer to these shelves, then my soul shall forever reside in the Abyss."

"Yes," the boy answered. "The Ones have said that it should be so. Still, unlike the Heretics, they also recognize and respect your free will. You have the right to refuse. Without you, your wizards and Minions stand no chance of defeating Wulfgar's forces. And Celeste's blood signature is now all but gone. When it finally vanishes, so shall her time enchantments. You know what that means. But even if successful, the process will invariably take a toll upon your body and your mind—and you may carry these burdens forever.

"And remember that of all the *Jin'Sai*s and *Jin'Saiou*s who have walked the earth, only you possess azure blood. What I shall attempt in your name has never been done before. The chances of failure are very high."

He looked at Tristan. "It is time to decide, *Jin'Sai.*"

"There is no decision to be made," Tristan said harshly. "This is one of the reasons I was placed upon the earth. We have to go forward. Our world requires it, no matter what happens to me." Pausing for a moment, he took a deep breath. "Do what you must," he said.

"Very well."

The boy pointed at the altar. A thin beam of light shot from his hand to strike its top. The boy moved his hand slowly. As he did, the beam of light cut a long, narrow slit in the marble. The light slowly vanished, and the boy lowered his hand.

Tristan heard a scratching noise. What looked like a sheet of transparent azure glass rose from the slit. Hundreds of Old Eutracian words and symbols were finely etched into its surface. It was immensely beautiful as it twinkled in the light.

"This glass tapestry holds the Forestallments meant only for the *Jin'Sai* and *Jin'Saiou*," the boy said. "I am not at liberty to tell you which of them will be granted to you until your blood has been healed. But what I can tell you is that one of them is the formula required to change your blood back to red, so that you may finally be trained in the ways of the craft, wear the Paragon, and read the Tome." Looking back over at the altar, the boy paused for a moment.

"The other Forestallments that I grant you shall last for only two days," he said. "Then they will disappear. It has been this way for every *Jin'Sai* and *Jin'Saiou* I have aided. Your nation is in crisis, and you must make the best possible use of them quickly, before they are no more."

Tristan walked over to the magnificent sheet of glass and reached out to touch it. It felt smooth and cold, like ice. He turned back to the boy.

"Why would the Ones wish their Forestallments to perish so soon?" he asked.

"Because of the quality of *Jin'Sai* and *Jin'Saiou* blood," the boy answered. "The Ones professed that granting a permanent Forestallment to one of you who has not yet been trained would be too dangerous. Should the lean of your blood signature be turned to the Vagaries, for example, the results would be disastrous."

Tristan closed his eyes for a moment. "As is the case with Wulfgar," he said.

"Yes," the boy said. "Now you are beginning to understand. But there is more—much more—regarding your destiny that we do not have the leisure to discuss now. It is time."

Tristan nodded. "Proceed, then," he said softly.

"Very well."

The Scroll Master pointed to the prince. Tristan felt a wizard's warp envelope him. He still stood but he could not move. Wondering what would happen next, he broke out into a cold sweat.

The boy pointed to the sheet of azure glass. The etchings representing the first of the four spells lifted silently from the glass to hover near the prince's head. His breath caught as they sparkled above him.

Tristan felt the soft, cool touch of the boy's palm on his forehead. Then waves of unrelenting pain coursed through him, and he screamed.

CHAPTER LXXXII

FAEGAN SAT IN HIS CHAIR ON THE PALACE ROOF, HIS HEART SADdened beyond measure. Jessamay, Shailiha, Abbey, and the remaining acolytes stood by his side. Duvessa, Dax, and a large host of Minion warriors were there as well. Safe in her nursery, Shailiha's daughter, Morganna, was being tended by the everprotective Shawna the Short.

Faegan had called the group together because he would need all of their services if his plan was to have any hope of success. But the early optimism he had felt as a result of his research in the Redoubt was dampened by what he saw from the rooftop.

Tammerland was burning.

It was well past midnight. The southwestern side of the city was engulfed in flames. The once-beautiful capital had become a raging inferno. Faegan could smell the stink of the polluted river and the smoke that was rapidly filling the sky. The terrible spectacle was almost more than he could bear.

The unexpected speed of the fire would make his group's task much more difficult—perhaps even impossible. If he underestimated the pace of the fire's progress, then all of their work would be for naught—as it would be anyway if Tristan and Wigg did not return soon.

The sound of screams alerted him to the fact that the first of the city's refugees had finally reached the palace. Earlier in the day, Faegan had steeled himself and ordered the drawbridge raised, and every other entrance to the palace closed and guarded. The dark, ominous forms of Minion warriors lined the tops of the palace walls.

Desperate citizens jumped into the moat and tried to scrabble up the palace walls. Minion warriors used their spears to gently but firmly push them back. Still more jumped in, crowding one another in a fury of desperation. Many drowned before Faegan's eyes.

Tears in her eyes, Shailiha turned to look at the wizard. "Is there nothing you and Jessamay can do to help them?" she asked.

Faegan shook his head. "Nothing. As much as I hate to say it, we are doing exactly what we should right now—that is, preparing to implement the first stage of our plan. I understand your feelings. But you all simply must trust me when I tell you that, this way, far more people will survive."

Shailiha took the old wizard's hand. "We all trust you," she said. "You know that. It's just so difficult to stand by and watch."

"I know, Princess," Faegan answered softly. "I know."

Turning his chair around, he surveyed the results of his group's recent labors. Hundreds of closed containers of every size, type, and color covered the rooftop. Several Minion litters sat nearby filled with yet more vessels.

"Do you all understand what it is you are to do?" he asked. They said they did. Faegan nodded.

"Under no circumstances are you to open the containers until you are sure of your surroundings," he reminded them. "Waste nothing, for your lives may depend upon it. Be sure to use it all. And above all, do not stray far from the palace. If you come too close to the fires, not only might you lose your lives, but all of our good work will go up in smoke. Be as surreptitious in your work as you can."

Pausing for a moment, he looked at them all with hope. "Go now," he said.

Faegan and Jessamay watched as the Minion warriors picked up the various containers and took flight, headed for the parts of the city that were still intact. Then Faegan's group took their places in the litters and the remaining warriors lifted them into the air. In a matter of moments, the wizard and Jessamay were alone on the rooftop.

Faegan watched as the litters grew smaller and smaller, their sides highlighted by the raging orange-red flames. He knew that if the warriors carrying them flew too close to the inferno, the intense updrafts of heat could cause them to crash. But the job had to be done. Even so, for the hundredth time he wondered about the wisdom of his actions.

"Can it really work?" Jessamay asked, interrupting his thoughts.

Faegan sighed. "The theory is sound. But when the craft is involved, there are a hundred ways for something to go wrong—especially when the theory has never been applied. We can only wait and hope."

CHAPTER LXXXIII

WHEN TRISTAN WOKE, HIS VISION WAS BLURRED, HE ACHED everywhere, and he couldn't remember why. Then his vision started to clear, and so did his mind.

He was lying on the floor in the center of the Well of Forestallments. His weapons were still with him. He stood slowly, testing his balance. His head swam as his senses returned to normal.

The white marble altar was gone, as was the etched glass tapestry. The Scroll Master stood nearby.

"We succeeded, *Jin'Sai*," he said. "You survived the ordeal. Your blood is red once more. It now also holds the three Forestallments the Ones dictated that I grant you. If you like, you may check to see that I am telling the truth."

Tristan took one of his throwing knives from its sheath, held the blade against the palm of his left hand, and made a small incision. He took a quick breath as he saw that his blood was indeed red again.

Several drops fell to the floor and began to twist and turn into his familiar blood signature. He wiped the knife on his trousers, placed it into its sheath, and bent down to look. Three crooked Forestallment branches led away from his signature, rather than the dozens that bristled from it when his blood had been azure. He stood in amazement.

"This cannot be," he said.

"And why is that?" the boy asked.

"Before now, the red water of the Caves had to be combined with my blood in order for my blood signature to form. The wizards said it was because my blood has not yet been trained. So how can my signature form on its own?"

"The Forestallments that I have granted you," the boy said, "enliven your blood to the point that the Cave waters are not necessary for your signature to form. Two days from now, when the Forestallments vanish, the Cave waters will again be required. Your blood will be as it was the day you were born."

The boy pointed to the three Forestallments and explained what powers each would grant the prince, and how to call them forth. Awestruck, Tristan listened intently to every word.

"There is something else that you must know," the boy added. "Even though you are the reigning *Jin'Sai,* and your blood now carries activated Forestallments, you still may not be able to beat Wulfgar. Doing so will take everything you have—perhaps more than you have. You may still fail."

Tristan's jaw hardened. "Why?" he asked. "The Forestallments you granted me come from the Ones, do they not?"

"Yes," the boy answered, "just as Wulfgar's come from the Heretics. He has had ample time to become proficient with them, and you have not. Be exceedingly careful, *Jin'Sai.* He means to kill you, and his gifts are strong."

So are mine, Tristan thought. Then he remembered Celeste. "How much time has gone by?" he demanded.

"Three of your hours have passed," the Scroll Master said sadly. "I'm afraid it is too late."

Tristan felt as though a dagger had been plunged into his heart. *"What do you mean!"* he shouted.

"Come with me," the boy answered quietly.

The Scroll Master glided over to one of the shelves and pointed. The breath rushed from Tristan's lungs, and he fell to his knees.

Behind another pane of glass, encapsulated in azure light, was Celeste's death mask.

Tristan wept, shaking uncontrollably. When he was finally able, he lifted his head again and looked into the face that he so loved.

It was Celeste as he would always remember her—young, lovely, and vibrant. Her eyes were closed, the generous bell of hair falling down over part of her forehead and cheek. The Forestallments she had possessed when she died twinkled in the case just below.

"I am sorry, *Jin'Sai,*" the boy said quietly. "Had you found me sooner, she might have lived. Even so, I told you she was not your destiny, no matter how much you loved her. I know how much it hurts you to hear this, but the fact that the two of you found each other and married is of minor importance in the forthcoming scheme of your life. In fact, had she lived, you would have gone on to hurt her far more than she might have been able to bear, for you would have been forced to leave her. You are meant for another—another whom you will love with an ardor even greater than you felt for Celeste. It is she who will become your queen and be the mother of your children."

The boy held out his hand. "Come with me, *Jin'Sai,*" he said. "We must return to your First Wizard. There is little time to lose."

Tristan looked at the floor. "So she has turned to ash?" he asked, barely able to get the words out.

"No," the boy answered. "I have granted her body the ability to hold its earthly form until you can hold her in your arms one more time. But even I cannot do so for much longer. Hold my hand, and I'll take you to her. Your mind needn't be stilled as we travel this time, for your blood is strong enough now."

Tristan took the boy's hand. The young Scroll Master felt cold and lifeless, like a statue that had been left outside all winter.

"Behold," the boy said.

The glow of the craft surrounded them. Tristan felt his body lighten, then cease to exist altogether. As the thousands of shelves and the endless hallways flashed before him, all he could think of was Celeste.

"WIGG . . ." TRISTAN SAID SOFTLY.

The wizard sat cross-legged on the marble floor. Celeste's head lay in his lap. He did not turn around. As he held his daughter's lifeless form, his body shook and he sobbed quietly.

Finally he looked up. Tears ran down his face, and for several moments his mouth moved but no sound came from it.

"She's dead, Tristan," he finally uttered. "Despite all my powers, I couldn't save her."

Tristan walked up to the wizard and placed one hand on his shoulder.

"I know," he answered. "In the end, I couldn't save her either. I'm sorry."

As Wigg pulled Celeste closer, confusion crossed over his face. "I don't understand why she has not turned to ash."

"The Scroll Master is preserving her form," Tristan told him. "But it will not last much longer."

Wigg looked up at Tristan again. At first he thought that his grief was causing his mind to play tricks on him. But the longer he regarded the prince, the surer he became.

Tristan had changed. The changes were subtle but definite. He seemed slightly older, more mature, and his demeanor was somehow more commanding. There was a slight graying of his hair around the temples, and his dark, penetrating eyes looked even more lustrous than before. Concerned, Wigg tried to put his grief aside for the moment.

"What have you done to him?" he demanded of the Scroll Master.

"Nothing the *Jin'Sai* did not agree to, and only what the Ones dictated that I do," the boy said. "All is as it should be."

Wigg finally eased Celeste's head and shoulders gently to the floor. As he stood, his knees shook. When he regained his footing, he looked carefully into the prince's face.

"Are you all right?" he asked with concern.

"Yes," Tristan answered. "But there is much to tell you."

Wigg reached into his robe. With a shaking hand he produced an envelope sealed with red wax. As he handed it to Tristan, the prince detected the scent of myrrh.

"This is for you," Wigg said. "She gave it to me just before she died. In the event that you did not see each other again, she wanted you to have it. She said that you would understand."

Tristan took the envelope from Wigg. He broke the seal and removed the letter. It read:

My darling,

If you are reading this, my love, then I am dead. As I put quill to paper, it is nighttime at the palace. It is the night we lit Geldon and Lionel's funeral pyres, and I have come to my chambers to collect my things so that we might be together. There is so much that I want to say to you—and so much that will, of necessity, remain unsaid—but I will try.

You must not feel guilt over my passing. If the Afterlife has claimed me, then it was meant to be and you must accept that. But also know that all that I suffered I would have gladly endured again, if it meant reclaiming even the brief months that we were able to share. They say that lovers can live a lifetime in a matter of days, and you and I proved them right. Please look after Father for me, as I know you will. The two of you will need each other more than ever now.

And, lastly, know that from wherever my spirit shall come to rest, I shall continue to love you. You were the light of my life, and the spark that you lit within my heart shall never die.

Goodbye, my love,
Celeste

As the tears streamed down his face, Tristan handed the letter to Wigg. The First Wizard read it slowly, then placed it back into his robe. Trembling, Tristan looked down at Celeste. The Scroll Master came to stand by him.

"It is almost time," the boy said. "You must say goodbye to her before it is too late."

Tristan nodded.

Kneeling, he took her into his arms. She looked even older, her face more wrinkled, her hair whiter than when he last saw her. But to his eyes she seemed as beautiful as ever. He pulled her to him and kissed her cold cheek for the last time.

"Goodbye, my love," he whispered.

With that her body turned to ash and slipped between his fingers, falling lightly to the floor. He covered his face with his hands, and sobs wracked his body.

After a time he looked down again. Something caught his eye, twinkling in the gray ash. Reaching down, he plucked her wedding ring from the ashes and placed it into his worn leather vest.

"You and your wizard must leave now, *Jin'Sai*," the Scroll Master said. "Your destiny awaits you."

"Her ashes go with me," Tristan said. As he turned to look at the boy, there was no compromise in his eyes. "I know it is in your power to make it so," he added.

"As you wish," the Scroll Master answered.

The boy waved one hand and a golden vase appeared. It settled gently to the floor. Celeste's ashes collected, whirled into the air, and flew into the vase. The vessel's top sealed itself. Tristan picked up the vase and cradled it in his arms.

"Thank you," he said softly.

The boy nodded. "Farewell, *Jin'Sai*," he said.

Tristan and Wigg heard the door in the wall of the pyramid slide open. Night had fallen. Several surprised warriors—Ox among them—stood there, gaping.

Without looking back, the *Jin'Sai* and the First Wizard walked through the door and into the night.

CHAPTER LXXXIV

AS CAPTAIN MERRIWHETHER LOOKED OUT OVER TAMMERLAND from the bow of his Black Ship, he couldn't have been more delighted. It was nearly midday and the sun was high. The captains of the five other Black Ships stood beside him at attention.

Thousands of K'tons had arrived only moments earlier to join Merriwhether's waiting fleet. They had flown all night to reach him. Their speed had been astonishing; they could certainly outpace any Minion warrior who had ever lived. Their numbers darkened the sky for as far as he could see, and none appeared tired. Satisfied, he raised his spyglass and looked out over Tammerland.

The southwestern sections of the city already lay in ruins. Merriwhether had directed his airborne fleet to swing around and approach the city from the opposite direction in order to avoid the fires. The part of the capital that lay before him was as yet untouched, and he relished the idea of unleashing his servants upon it.

He would march his forces southwest, trapping the royal palace between his army and the raging fires. The flames continued to burn, and Merriwhether could smell the stench even from here.

Only moments before, he had read Wulfgar's message, brought to him by a drooling K'ton.

Merriwhether:
   The creatures that I have sent to you are called K'tons. Until I arrive with more, these are yours to command. When I have concluded my business with the Orb of the Vigors, my K'tons and I will join you, and victory will be ours. In the meanwhile, start at the outskirts of the city and destroy everything in your path as you make your way to the palace. Leave nothing standing; leave nothing alive—except the two wizards and the Jin'Sai *and* Jin'-Saiou. *Leave them to me. I have scores to settle with them all.*
                                                                    Wulfgar

Smiling, Merriwhether read the message to the other five captains.

"Do you understand your orders?" he shouted.

They all nodded.

"Very well!" he said. "To your ships, then! Wait for my command!"

Merriwhether watched as the other dark captains went to take command of their respective vessels. He then raised one skeletal arm and waved the K'tons on ahead to begin the attack.

WHEN THEY SAW THE DARK SWARMS FLYING OVER THEIR CITY the citizens panicked, but there was nowhere to hide. Tens of thousands of K'tons landed in the streets, their hungry eyes glaring about as more of their kind darkened the sky above. They immediately began kicking in doors and windows in their search for fresh meat.

Men, women, and children poured from buildings, only to find hungry K'tons waiting for them. The lucky ones fell prey to the monsters' weapons and died on the spot. Others were scooped up into the beasts' arms to be devoured alive. The air was soon thick with the screams of the dying.

Through his spyglass, Merriwhether watched as the northeastern section of Tammerland erupted into chaos. He turned to his lead demonslaver.

"Signal the other ships," he ordered. "We're going down."

"Yes, my lord." The slaver ran off to carry out his orders.

As each of the huge vessels landed on the outskirts of the city, their stern doors slowly lowered.

The first of the Earthshakers lumbered out. It wore a massive bridle, and a demonslaver sat on its back. Free of its confines after so long, the beast raised its head and gave an earsplitting scream. The others soon followed.

Once assembled, they headed into the city. Demonslaver troops poured from the dark hulls to follow the huge monsters, short swords drawn. Merriwhether gave the order to ascend again, and the fleet rose into the air.

In the wake of the K'tons, the Earthshakers destroyed every structure in their path with mighty swipes of their massive tails, the earth trembling beneath their every step. Walls, roofs, and glass exploded into shards of shrapnel. Whatever remained alive in the swaths cut by the K'tons and the Earthshakers was systematically butchered by the demonslavers. The six Black Ships sailed over the destruction left by their servants.

The army of the Vagaries moved inexorably forward, leaving nothing standing, nothing moving, nothing living. Only black, charred rubble and thousands of corpses, blood, and body parts remained.

Merriwhether raised his arms to loose azure bolts, but then he stopped himself. Looking down, he smiled. His use of the craft was unnecessary, he thought. His servants were doing the job well enough on their own. By this time the next day, they would be at the palace walls.

Merriwhether watched as his fleet sailed silently over the carnage. He smiled again. Soon his lord would arrive, and he would be pleased with his servants' work.

* * *

AS HE SAT AT THE WAR TABLE ON THE PALACE ROOF, FAEGAN EXAM-
ined the scale model of Tammerland. Using his gift of Consummate Recollection, he had conjured the model the previous
night while waiting for his group to return from their secret
labors.

Blessedly, everyone he had sent out had returned safely, their
tasks performed as well as possible. Now they all stood by his
side, their faces clouded with worry.

The fire and smoke choking the city grew closer to the palace
with every passing moment. According to the status reports
brought by the Minion scouts, the situation was deteriorating
rapidly. If Wigg and Tristan did not return soon, all of his work
and planning would be for nothing. Wulfgar would be victorious, and the Vagaries would rule for all time.

Faegan also worried about the fate of Traax and his war party.
There had been no word from them, and that only made the situation more desperate. Without Traax's warriors, he knew he
couldn't dare deploy those Minions that remained at the palace.
Few as they were, they constituted the last line of defense. He
had therefore ordered the scouting parties only to observe, not
to engage, any enemy forces they might discover.

Duvessa and Dax had worked tirelessly to make the castle secure. But Faegan knew that if Traax hadn't stopped Wulfgar,
only hours remained before all was lost.

A scouting party landed upon the roof. Their leader quickly
walked over to the table, a worried look on his face. He came to
attention and clicked his heels.

"Your report," Faegan said.

Looking down at the model, the scout pointed toward the
northeastern section of Tammerland.

"There," he said darkly. "Six Black Ships have arrived. Tens
of thousands of flying monsters followed and even more are
coming. As the beasts began attacking the city, the ships landed
and unloaded huge creatures that are destroying every building
they approach with their massive tails. Had I not seen it with my
own eyes, I would never have believed such a thing to be possible. Demonslaver forces were also deployed from the ships. As
the great beasts and flying monsters do their dirty work, the

slavers follow along behind, killing off survivors. The Black Ships sail along overhead."

Faegan looked down, then back up at Jessamay. There could be little hope for them now, despite all of his planning and preparation. The look on the sorceress' face told him she understood.

"There is something that the two of you aren't telling us," Abbey said. "What is it? We have the right to know."

"Earthshakers," Jessamay said.

"What?" Shailiha asked.

"Earthshakers," Jessamay repeated. "Massive beasts that Failee and the Coven used three centuries ago during the Sorceresses' War. Wulfgar must have found the formula for their conjuring in the Scroll of the Vagaries."

"Is there no way to defeat them?" Shailiha asked.

"Azure bolts can harm them," Faegan said, "if enough are loosed against them. But even if Jessamay and I were able to get close enough to try, the captains of the Black Ships would quickly defeat us. Six against two are odds that even she and I can't overcome."

He looked back up at the scout. "There were only six Black Ships, you say—not seven?" he asked.

"Six, my lord."

"Did you see Wulfgar aboard any of them?"

"No."

Faegan remained silent for a time as he looked back down at his model.

"What are your orders, my lord?" Dax asked. The young Minion officer was clearly spoiling for a fight.

Before answering, Faegan raised one hand and burned away the northeastern section of the model, as the scout had described. In size, it roughly matched the other destroyed areas that lined the Sippora. By the wizard's reckoning, one-third of the capital already lay in ruins. He could only assume that an equal proportion of her inhabitants were now dead.

The *Enseterat* had planned exceedingly well, and his strategy was plain to see. Traax had not stopped him; the flying beings that the scout referred to must surely be the Heretic hordes. And since the scout made no mention of Wulfgar, that could only mean that the *Enseterat* was searching for the damaged Orb of the Vigors.

With the Sippora doing part of the work, and the attack of the Black Ships and their creatures coming from the opposite direction, the pace of the destruction would now double. Together they would close in on the palace. When the Earthshakers arrived, even the thick castle walls would bow to their fury. Faegan balled his hands up into fists and banged them down on the arms of his chair.

"Like it or not, we must wait," he said softly, defiantly. "I know how badly you all want to take action, but we cannot. We need Traax's forces, and Wigg and Tristan. Until they arrive, sending our small force of warriors out against the invaders would be sheer suicide. I simply won't do it. We have to trust in the *Jin'Sai,* and hope he and the First Wizard arrive in time."

Chapter LXXXV

THEY WERE MAKING GOOD TIME. STANDING IN THE BOW OF HER flagship, Tyranny scraped the common match against the side of her scuffed knee boot. She cupped her hands and lit the cigarillo dangling from her lips. Blowing the smoke out through her nose, she shook out the match and cast her gaze out over the Sea of Whispers.

It was midday and the weather was favorable. Bright blue sky stretched overhead, with just the occasional trace of a passing cloud. The easterlies were strong, forcing her fleet to tack back and forth as they made their way north, up the coast. They sailed behind her in an arrowhead formation. A red image of the Paragon adorned each of their mainsails, bright and brazen for the world to see. Looking up, she silently blessed the good weather, for it would help her Minion scouting parties perform their searches.

She looked eastward. Her gut told her that the remainder of the demonslaver fleet was out there somewhere. Scars was fond of saying that she could smell a demonslaver from fifty leagues away. She smiled to herself. *Perhaps he's right,* she thought. *But right now all I smell is salt air.*

Tyranny was far from confident about the hurried repairs that had been made to her ships. Even as she plowed through the waves, the sturdy *Reprise* groaned in ways her skipper had never heard. But Tyranny had to believe she would hold together, just as she had done so many times in the past.

Despite the ramshackle condition of her fleet, Tyranny was hopeful about their prospects. If they met the enemy, this time wouldn't be like the last. There would be no massive Black Ships to sail blithely over her lines. And if there were no one of the craft aboard the slaver vessels, there would be no azure bolts to contend with.

This time it would be Tyranny's turn to use the craft at sea, and she relished the opportunity. Each of her ships carried an Acolyte of the Redoubt, handpicked by Adrian for her superior abilities. Tyranny had counseled them carefully about how and when to strike. And K'jarr's Minion phalanx was rested and spoiling for a fight. She could see it in their dark eyes and mannerisms, in their eager talk with one another about the battle to come, and in the careful way they sharpened their dreggans.

She felt exactly the same way. All in all, even if they found themselves outnumbered, this time they would have a fighting chance. She would not shrink from this battle, but boldly claim it for her own.

As the *Reprise*'s hull groaned and the waves split against her bow, Tyranny thought of Tristan and what he might be going through. She closed her eyes for a moment. She was worried for him—more than she ought to be.

He's not mine, she thought as she tossed the spent cigarillo overboard.

Scars approached, his massive frame casting a long shadow over her. Tyranny put away her thoughts of the prince and turned to look at her first mate.

"Your report?" she asked.

"Steady as she goes," Scars answered. "The other ships report no difficulties and the winds remain brisk. The fleet is ready for battle." He gave his captain a conspiratorial wink. "All we need now are some demonslavers to kill."

"Indeed," Tyranny answered. "It's almost *too* quiet out here. I'm starting to think that—"

Her sentence was suddenly interrupted by the sounds of boot heels striking the deck. She and Scars turned to see a scouting party landing. K'jarr hurried over to greet them.

The warriors talked animatedly among themselves. Then K'jarr turned to her, smiled broadly, and Tyranny knew. He and the leader of the group ran over to her and came to attention.

"They've been spotted!" K'jarr exclaimed.

"Where away?" Tyranny demanded.

"Due east," the other warrior answered. "I estimate them to be no more than six leagues from our current position."

"How many ships?" Scars asked.

"Thirty," the warrior answered, "and each of them loaded to the sinking point with slavers. We saw no humans among them. They sail in an arrowhead formation, just as we do."

"Do you think you were seen?" Tyranny demanded.

"I do not know," the scout said. "I sent one of us lower to determine whether there were any humans aboard. Given the clear weather, he might have been noticed. If he was, the slavers gave no indication of it."

Tyranny looked at K'jarr. "Prepare your warriors," she said. "We're going into battle."

K'jarr clicked his heels. "I live to serve," he answered. He turned briskly and hurried away.

Scars grinned at Tyranny. "Your orders, Captain?" he asked.

"Signal the other ships," she said. "I want them in a straight battle line. If the enemy has not broken their formation, then we shall know that we haven't been detected. Damn this good weather! I would have preferred to attack suddenly from a fog bank, but that can't be helped. This will be a straight-up fight." Pausing for a moment, she looked back out to sea.

"Once our line is formed, make our course due east," she said. "We must make the most of our first pass."

Scars smiled again. "Aye, Captain," he answered. "And may the Afterlife be with us."

Tyranny looked east once more. Soon they would be outnumbered by more than three to one. As she felt the *Reprise* rise and fall beneath her, she took a deep breath.

May the Afterlife help us indeed, she thought. *I fear we are going to need it.*

CHAPTER LXXXVI

FROM WHERE HE STOOD IN THE MINION LITTER, TRISTAN GAZED northward. The wind tore at his clothes and hair, but he paid it no heed. As he watched the distant horizon, he firmly clutched the gold medallion hanging around his neck.

Wigg could tell that Tristan was a changed man. But the *Jin'Sai* had yet to confide in him about what had transpired between him and the Scroll Master. Nor had they spoken again about Celeste's death. The silence between them was deafening and unnatural.

After exiting the azure pyramid, they had watched it sink back into the earth. The displaced sections of loose sod had smoothly closed over, leaving the ground looking as though it had never been disturbed.

Without first conferring with Wigg, Tristan had ordered the warriors into the air and given them a course to follow. For the last hour he had silently looked north—as though his destiny lay out there somewhere and he was searching for it.

Wigg looked sadly at the golden vase bearing his daughter's ashes, nestled at the prince's feet. He didn't blame Tristan for Celeste's death. He had no doubt that Tristan had done everything in his power to save her. But Wigg still did not know what Tristan had meant when he had said he had been "too late."

He saw Tristan stiffen and lean forward to wave to Ox. When the giant warrior flew closer, Tristan shouted out another course change. The entire group turned slightly to the east.

More relaxed now, the prince sat down beside the wizard and placed an affectionate hand upon his shoulder. There was a compassionate look in his eyes.

It's almost as if we have traded places, Wigg suddenly realized. He now seems to be the master, and I the student.

"It is time for us to talk, old friend," Tristan said. "There is much to tell you. You have been patient with me, and for that I thank you."

"Where are we headed?" Wigg asked.

"To the Orb of the Vigors," Tristan answered. "Part of Wulfgar's forces march toward Tammerland. In fact, they may already be laying siege to the city. But before we engage them, we must find the orb. We near it as I speak."

Wigg gave him a curious look. "How can you know where the orb is?" he asked.

Tristan looked back out toward the horizon. "I can sense it," he answered. "It is almost as if the orb calls to my blood."

Wigg's mouth fell open. "But that's impossible!" he protested. "The best any of us has ever been able to do is make the orbs appear, and even then, we were not always successful. No one has ever been able to sense the location of the orbs and go to *them*!"

"Until now, perhaps," Tristan answered.

Wigg scowled. "Even assuming that you can find the orb, why not simply call it forth, rather than go to it?"

Tristan's expression darkened. "Wulfgar," he said. "In the interests of time, I am both racing to the orb while also calling it to me. I want to draw the *Enseterat* near and tempt him with my presence. It is for that reason I ask you not to cloak our blood. Nor is his cloaked; I can sense his approach. He is twelve leagues away and closing quickly."

"But no one can sense endowed blood from such a distance!" Wigg said.

Tristan took one of his throwing knives and made another small cut in his hand. He allowed several drops of his red blood to fall to the floor of the litter. They twisted into his familiar blood signature, complete with the Forestallments granted him by the Scroll Master.

Wigg raised an eyebrow. "So you succeeded after all . . . ," he said.

Tristan smiled slightly. "Yes," he answered. "There is little that is impossible within the purview of the craft. Isn't that one of the things that you have been so fond of telling me all these years?"

Tristan took a deep breath. "I need to explain some things to you," he said. "They have to do with both our past and our future.

You will find them difficult to hear, and even more difficult to believe. But you must accept what I now tell you, just as I am trying to do."

He looked sadly at the golden vase. "Much of it has to do with Celeste," he added softly, "and my destiny without her." Tears began to form in his eyes and he brushed them away. He looked back at Wigg.

"You must listen to me with your heart, as well as with your ears. To fully understand these things, you must accept them in your soul as well as in your mind."

While Wigg listened, Tristan told him about his experiences with the Scroll Master. The First Wizard hungrily absorbed every word. As the sun sank toward the western horizon, their litter soared on toward their destiny.

WULFGAR LOWERED HIS HANDS, STYMIED. FOR THE FIRST TIME since receiving his Forestallments, he had encountered a force of the craft that was his equal.

Then he sensed the distant presence of the *Jin'Sai*'s blood, and he knew.

His Black Ship and the accompanying horde of K'tons sailed south over the fields of Farplain. For the last several moments he had been trying to summon the orb. But the opposing force was strong—as strong as his own. The Heretics had told him that he must put distance between himself and the azure pass before calling the orb, and that much he had accomplished. But the orb would not appear. Then, in the midst of his frustration, he heard the choir of voices again.

He went to his knees and bowed his head.

"The Jin'Sai *approaches. He, too, tries to call the orb. His blood is now red, and also carries Forestallments. We did not foresee this development. His blood is strong, but so is yours, and you command far more Forestallments than he does. There is a way to beat him, our son. Hear us as we tell you how . . ."*

As he listened to the Heretics, Wulfgar began to smile. When they had finished speaking, he stood and turned to look at Cathmore.

"Halt the Black Ship," he ordered, "and order the K'tons to the ground. Allow them to rest. Tell them that when the order is given, they are to rip into the approaching Minions. But under no circumstances are they to attack the *Jin'Sai*."

Pausing for a moment, he rubbed the damaged side of his face. He thought of Serena and their unborn daughter waiting for him at the Citadel. Very soon now the *Jin'Sai* would be dead, and the world theirs to command.

"I will deal with my half brother myself."

Cathmore gave his lord a short bow. "As you wish," he said.

The Black Ship slowed to a stop, then hovered in the air. The K'tons landed in the fields, their vast numbers darkening the ground as they milled about anxiously, swords and clubs at the ready.

The *Enseterat* smiled. With a wave of one hand, the Black Ship, everyone aboard her, and all the waiting K'tons vanished.

Raising his arms he again tried to call the orb, knowing full well that by doing so he would continue to attract the *Jin'Sai* and his forces.

Come to me, you bastard, he thought. *It shall be a clash of the two sides of the craft like no other. Let us finally finish what we have begun.*

AS THEY SOARED THROUGH THE SKY, TRISTAN STIFFENED AGAIN and walked quickly to the front of the litter, all of his senses alert. With a shout, he ordered the warriors to stop and hover in place.

The easterly breeze that had fought them all day suddenly calmed, as though someone had just commanded it to do so. There was no sound other than the beating of Minion wings. To the west, the setting sun was just beginning to sink behind the Tolenka Mountains. The sudden quiet was eerie and unexpected.

Tristan narrowed his eyes and cocked his head to the side as if listening. Then, his face grave, he urgently motioned Wigg forward to join him.

"He is here," Tristan whispered. "Place the strongest possible wizard's warp around our litter, and do it now! But don't let an azure glow appear—I want the warp transparent. And don't raise your arms as you conjure it."

His face locked in concentration, Wigg was silent for a moment. Then he looked back at the prince.

"It is done," he said.

Tristan stared intently out into the air. "Turn slightly to your right, and tell me what you see."

The wizard did as he was told, but he saw nothing out of the ordinary.

"There is nothing here," Wigg protested.

"Yes, there is," Tristan countered. "There is a massive distortion in the sky. Its edges waver, like that of a reflection in a rippling pond. It hovers directly before us, about fifteen meters away. Listen to me well: No matter what happens from here on, you must not interfere. The very future of the craft hinges on what I alone must do."

Wigg looked out into the air. "But I see nothing," he protested. "Are you quite sure that—"

Azure bolts suddenly streaked toward them, born of nothingness. Twin beams of light exploded against Wigg's warp, threatening to send both the wizard and the *Jin'Sai* tumbling to the ground. Several warriors supporting the litter died immediately, torn apart by the blast, their bodies tumbling to the ground.

But Wigg's warp held, and other warriors quickly took the places of those who had died and righted the litter.

Suddenly the Black Ship materialized before them. Dark forms appeared in the sky and pounced upon the unprepared Minion warriors. In the first few moments, the K'tons' surprise attack cost at least one-third of the Minions their lives. As the airborne battle began in earnest, Tristan and Wigg saw how badly outnumbered they were.

Tristan looked back to see Wulfgar standing in the bow of his Black Ship. For the first time, the prince took in what had become of Wulfgar's face and left arm. The scarring, he realized, was the result of that night on the palace roof, when they had thought they had defeated him.

The two half brothers glared at each other. Finally Wulfgar spoke.

"So you and your wizard live." He smiled, the pink skin of his destroyed face contorting grotesquely. "Frankly, I'm surprised that Satine hasn't killed you by now. She's very good at what she does."

"She won't be carrying out any more of your orders," Tristan answered. "I killed her myself."

Wulfgar smiled again. "Such a pity," he said. "Tell me, Brother, how many of you did she manage to dispose of?"

As he thought of Lionel and Geldon, Tristan's blood rose hotly in his veins. But he would not rise to Wulfgar's provocation.

He turned again to the fighting. The battle had spread out in the sky, but his warriors were losing badly. Soon the fighting would be over, and every Minion in his phalanx would be lying dead on the ground below.

He looked back at Wulfgar. If he was going to take action, it had to be now.

"I know why you have come," Tristan said. "You wish to oversee the final destruction of the Orb of the Vigors. You must know that I cannot allow that to happen—and that I will go to my death, if need be, to stop you."

He held his hands out to his half brother.

"Surrender to me!" he said. "Call off your creatures and allow my wizard to enter your mind. I promise he will not harm you. Come with me back to Tammerland, my brother, I beg of you. Allow us one final chance to bring you to the light. Refuse, and I will have no choice but to destroy you."

Wulfgar laughed. "Look around, *Jin'Sai*," he shouted back. "Can't you see that you're losing this fight? No, it is *you* who must surrender to *me*!"

Tristan took a deep breath. "I will grant you a final chance," he said. "Either come with me now, or perish. You have been turned to the Vagaries, but that is not your fault. Let us help you. I have no wish to see my brother die this day."

Tristan stretched his hands out farther in a gesture of goodwill. His expression was almost compassionate.

Wulfgar stared at Tristan for several long moments. As the *Jin'Sai* and the *Enseterat* regarded each other, Wigg realized that he was witnessing a pivotal moment in the long history of the craft. Frozen, he held his breath.

"I cannot do that, Brother," Wulfgar finally said. His voice had become quieter, almost friendly. "My blood will not allow it. Only you and I truly understand that, eh? What will be, will be. It is ordained."

Tristan nodded sadly. "For the first time in my life, I know that," he said. "Then proceed as you must, Wulfgar. Just as I shall."

The *Enseterat* wasted no time. As the battle raged all about them, he raised his arms. Aghast, Wigg watched as Tristan did nothing to try to stop him.

The Orb of the Vigors materialized to the west. The huge, golden sphere seemed to take up the entire sky. It still shrieked in pain. Offshoots of the palest white radiated from its center, broke off, and fell toward the ground. Some of them landed on the fighting Minions and K'tons, killing them instantly.

The jagged tear in the orb's lower half continued to drip a golden, living energy. As that energy reached the ground, it created an ever-deepening crater in the earth and set grass fires that quickly spread. Choking smoke rose, and both Wulfgar's Black Ship and Tristan's litter shook violently as the first of the orb's shock waves struck them.

His heart pounding wildly, Wigg watched Wulfgar prepare to hasten the destruction of the orb. He had to remind himself that Tristan had told him not to interfere.

Twin bolts shot from Wulfgar's outstretched hands and headed straight for the gash in the orb. Tristan raised his hands with blinding speed and responded in kind.

The energy that streamed from Tristan's hands was the brightest Wigg had ever seen. More white than azure, it screamed toward Wulfgar's onrushing bolts. Wigg raised one arm before his face, fearing he might be struck blind by its awesome power. But he watched just the same, his need to know overshadowing his sense of personal safety.

With a massive explosion, Tristan's blinding energy slammed into Wulfgar's bolts, stopping them in midair. The two opposite manifestations of the craft flattened out against one another, each battling for supremacy.

Tristan's brow was covered with beads of sweat. Suddenly there was another explosion, and Wulfgar's bolts disappeared.

Stunned, Wulfgar looked at his one good hand and what was left of the other. Now both hands were hideously burned, as was the rest of his face. Screaming in agony, the *Enseterat* suddenly realized that he would not vanquish the *Jin'Sai* this day.

Amid all of the noise, death, and confusion, Wigg saw Wulfgar wave his damaged arms, wildly giving the order to retreat. The K'tons broke off the fight and returned to surround the Black Ship as she turned her great bulk in the air and sailed away. Wigg quickly went to Tristan's side.

"You mustn't let him escape!" Wigg shouted.

As the Black Ship shrank in the distance, Tristan turned to look at Wigg. Despite the recent strain, his face was calm.

"I know," he said. "Even though he is my brother, he must not be allowed to walk the earth."

He cast his gaze back to the Black Ship. Its dark form and the thousands of K'tons flying alongside would soon be lost from view. The *Jin'Sai* raised his hands.

At once, the Orb of the Vigors started to move again. As it rained down destruction, Tristan sent it in pursuit of the Black Ship.

Wigg's jaw dropped in awe. In more than three centuries, he had never seen anyone manipulate either of the orbs like this.

Tristan raised his hands higher. The orb obeyed his will and gained altitude. It was over the Black Ship in a matter of seconds.

The orb's golden energy poured down upon the Black Ship and the accompanying K'tons. When it struck the ship, the masts, sails, and decks began to melt away. Wulfgar, Cathmore, and the demonslaver crew were instantly vaporized. The hull of the great ship broke in two, each half a raging fireball plummeting toward the earth.

Unable to understand what was happening, most of the K'tons hesitated, and it cost them their lives. They screamed as they burst into flames and followed the Black Ship's broken hull as she went down. A smattering of K'tons escaped. Dazed and confused, they hovered tentatively in the air.

The burning hull hit the ground with a massive explosion; the earth trembled. Great shock waves shook the *Jin'Sai*'s litter even at this distance. Then the Black Ship's ruins burst into nothingness.

Ox appeared in the air by the litter. Tristan pointed at the surviving K'tons.

"Kill them," he ordered.

Bloodied but joyful, Ox and the surviving warriors beamed at Tristan with delight, then flew off to tear into the K'tons.

Tristan turned to look at the orb. A pitiful thing to watch, it still wailed with pain.

"Come to me," Tristan said.

At Tristan's verbal command alone, the orb obeyed. As it neared, Wigg could feel its blazing heat, and their litter rocked violently again.

Tristan held out his arms. "How you have suffered because of us," he said quietly. "But now your suffering shall end." He pointed at the base of the orb.

A delicate, ethereal glow flowed from Tristan's hands to touch the gash in the orb. The orb's wound began to close. Wigg stood spellbound as Tristan healed the orb. When the great rent was finally closed, Tristan lowered his hands.

Almost at once the orb glowed more brightly, and its wailing stopped. Then Wigg saw something he would remember for as long as he lived.

The orb came a bit closer. Its majesty regained, it dipped and revolved one time, almost as if paying homage to the prince. Tristan lowered his head.

"You are free to go," he said.

The orb vanished, leaving nothing in its wake except the terrible destruction it had caused.

Wigg took a careful look around. Save for the sounds of the distant battle between the Minions and the K'tons, silence reigned once more. The ground below them was strewn with the dead, the green grass soaked red with blood.

He walked over to Tristan. They were both sweating and covered with soot. Wigg put one hand on Tristan's shoulder.

"It is finished," he said.

Tristan looked at the wizard, his expression grave.

"You're wrong," he said. "The rest of Wulfgar's forces are attacking Tammerland. There is still a war to fight."

Ox returned to the litter. Bloody and exhausted, he made his report.

"Battle finished, my lord," he said. "Rest of flying monsters dead."

With so many of the K'tons killed by the orb, Tristan had

known that the results of the battle would be a foregone conclusion. But he hadn't expected it to come so quickly.

"So soon?" he asked Ox.

Ox beamed and pointed to the sky above them. "We get help," he said.

Tristan and Wigg looked up to see Traax's vast phalanxes hovering high above. He could just make out Traax victoriously waving his dreggan. They were indeed a welcome sight. Smiling, Tristan looked back at Ox.

"Tell Traax to have his forces follow us," he said. "We make for Tammerland with all possible speed. Our struggle isn't over."

Ox nodded. "I live to serve," he answered.

While the faithful warrior climbed into the sky, Tristan took a final look down at the carnage on the ground.

So many dead, he thought. *And still so many yet to die.*

As the sun set behind the Tolenkas, the litter and the Minion army headed south.

CHAPTER LXXXVII

WHIRLING AROUND ON THE BLOODY DECK, TYRANNY HELD HER sword high as another demonslaver came at her, thrusting his trident toward her abdomen.

She spun and parried at the last second, but the blade of her sword became entangled in the tines of the monster's weapon. With a victorious sneer the slaver twisted his trident. Tyranny's sword was torn from her grip, and rattled to the bloody deck of the *Reprise.* Losing her footing in all the fresh blood, she fell hard to the deck. Suddenly defenseless, she watched the points of the trident descend upon her.

Then she saw two familiar hands wrap around the slaver's neck from behind. She scrambled to her feet as the fingers squeezed the slaver's throat. The monster desperately tried to reach behind him, but it was no good. His eyes soon bulged and his tongue protruded from between his black teeth.

With a loud cracking of bones, Scars broke the thing's neck. The slaver died instantly. Scars picked him up over his head and tossed the corpse overboard.

Tyranny retrieved her bloody sword. She gave Scars a nod of thanks and watched him hurry off in search of another slaver to kill.

The battle had been raging for nearly two hours. The sun was setting and darkness would soon fall. All around her, weapons clashed; Minions, crew members, and demonslavers screamed; and massive explosions rocked the heavens. Azure bolts streamed across the waves. Catapults launched fireballs from the demonslaver ships.

Tyranny's orders to her ships had been simple: sail close enough to the slaver vessels so the acolytes could hit them with their bolts, but not so close that they could be boarded. The result was a deadly, seaborne game of cat and mouse, with Tyranny's twelve ships deftly weaving between the more numerous slaver vessels. Even so, some slaver frigates had managed to come close enough to throw grappling hooks and board their warriors. Four of her vessels—the *Reprise* included—now swarmed with slavers.

Tyranny's Minions had boarded the enemy vessels and fought for their lives. The sea was littered with bodies and the debris of battle. The smoke rising from the strikes of the azure bolts and the demonslavers' fireballs was so thick that Tyranny could barely see.

She had told the acolytes to aim first for the enemy masts to render their vessels dead in the water. Only then were they to try to blow holes in their hulls. Five of the slaver vessels that she knew of had been sent to the bottom; without their masts, many of the others wallowed aimlessly at the mercy of the sea, the slavers aboard them helpless to join the fight.

Three of Tyranny's ships had already gone down. Some of her other vessels desperately tried to save what was left of their surviving crewmen before they drowned, but amid all the smoke and confusion it was a nearly impossible task.

Then she saw another orange fireball launch from a nearby

slaver ship. Trailing dark smoke, it was following a high, deadly trajectory straight for the *Reprise*. Helpless, Tyranny held her breath as she watched it come.

The fireball fell short, but it trailed showers of sparks that landed on the mizzen sail. In mere moments the sail was ablaze. Aghast, Tyranny searched the deck for crewmen not engaged in the fighting. She finally found two and sent them aloft with buckets of water. If the *Reprise* caught fire, she was done for.

But as Tyranny looked back out to sea, her face lit up with joy. As far as she could tell, every surviving demonslaver ship was finally without its masts. Minions and slavers still fought aboard her ships, their weapons flashing as the moons rose. But without the ability to maneuver, the slavers would no longer be able to aim their fireballs with any kind of accuracy.

The fighting aboard the *Reprise* waned. Scars supervised as the crew lined up the surviving slavers. Blessedly, Tyranny saw no other fires on board, and her crewmen had nearly extinguished the burning mizzen sail.

The battle won, Tyranny's fleet regrouped around her flagship, leaving the slaver ships to wallow helplessly in the sea.

Exhausted, Tyranny placed the tip of her sword against the deck and leaned upon its hilt. She had won, but only by a whisker. Things could just as easily have gone the other way, she knew.

She heard the flurry of Minion wings and she looked up to see K'jarr coming to a landing beside her.

The warrior's wings drooped to the deck and his sword arm was covered with blood. Coming to attention as best he could, he clicked his heels.

Tyranny smiled at him. "Your report," she said.

"Thirteen slaver vessels have been sunk," he said, as he tried to reclaim his breath. "The remaining are without their masts and cannot maneuver." His face covered with soot and sweat, the warrior smiled. "The acolytes did very well," he added. "But desperate fighting still rages aboard many of the enemy vessels."

Tyranny looked out to sea where the enemy vessels bobbed aimlessly like so many children's toys afloat in a bathtub. She turned back to K'jarr.

"Order the warriors to break off and return to their ships," she ordered. "There is no sense in losing more of them. I have a feeling we'll need them in Tammerland. Go now."

K'jarr gave her a short bow. "I live to serve," he replied. He quickly returned to the air.

"It is a great victory," a female voice said. "You have my congratulations."

Tyranny turned to see Adrian standing there. The young acolyte's fingertips were scorched, and she looked past the point of exhaustion. Her face and dark red robe were speckled with soot.

Smiling, Tyranny embraced her. "And no small thanks to you and your sisters," she answered. "We could never have done it without you." She gave Adrian a conspiratorial wink. "I might just ask the *Jin'Sai* to assign some of you to my fleet on a permanent basis."

They suddenly heard a scream and turned to look. Scars and several of the Minion warriors were beheading the slavers who had survived the struggle aboard the *Reprise*. Lined up in rows on their hands and knees, they awaited their fates in terror. As they were killed, Scars and the Minions threw their heads and bodies overboard.

Adrian turned back to Tyranny. "Does it have to be this way? It seems so brutal."

Tyranny whipped her head around. *"Brutal?"* she repeated venomously. "You think this is *brutal*? Are you mad? Do you have any idea what would have become of us had we been captured? For all we know the Citadel is still crawling with these monsters. You are still new to the horrors of war, sister. Out here it is kill or be killed. Besides, it is my sworn duty to dispose of them. Wherever and whenever we encounter them, they are to die. It is a standing order from the *Jin'Sai*."

"Very well," Adrian answered. "If that is how it must be."

Tyranny gave Adrian another harsh look. "Steel your sensibilities further, sister," she warned. "I want to question one of them first, and no matter what you see me do, you are not to interfere. They are a very tough lot, and the harshest of incentives need to be applied. Do you understand?"

Adrian nodded. Tyranny sheathed her sword, and the two

women walked over to Scars. He had his sword held high over his head and he was about to bring it down again.

"Hold!" Tyranny shouted.

Scars turned to her, startled. "Captain?" he asked.

"I want to question this one," Tyranny said. She looked over at one of her bloodied crewmen. "Go below and bring me a bottle of wine."

The crewman went below. He soon returned with an amber-colored bottle.

Tyranny took the bottle from him and allowed herself one long, luxurious draft. She casually lit a cigarillo and blew the smoke out her nose.

Then she poured the rest of the wine onto the deck. She walked over to the gunwale and smashed the empty bottle on it. Reaching down, she picked up two sharp pieces of glass. She walked back over to the demonslaver who kneeled before Scars. She looked at her first mate.

"Open his mouth," she ordered.

Scars took the slaver by the throat and lifted him to his feet. The slaver tried to wriggle free but to no avail. At Tyranny's signal, two warriors walked over and used a sharp dagger to force the slaver's jaws apart.

Tyranny turned to the next slaver in line. He gave her a defiant stare.

"On your feet," she said.

With a snarl, the slaver did as he was told.

Tyranny didn't particularly approve of what she was about to do. As much as she hated the demonslavers, this would be difficult, even for her. But she was embroiled in an all-out war—one that consumed her on both a personal and a national level—and she meant to help win it, no matter the cost.

Thinking of Tristan, and of her parents' hideous deaths at the hands of these abominations, she steeled her heart and came closer. She looked the slaver in the eyes. He glared back at her hatefully. No one on deck spoke; no one moved. Her eyes still locked on the slaver's, Tyranny pointed to the one whose jaws were being held apart.

"Watch and learn," she said.

Reaching up, she placed the two razor-sharp shards of glass

into the other slaver's waiting mouth. With a nod from their captain, the two warriors forced the monster's mouth closed.

"Put him back on his knees," she ordered.

Blood ran from between the slaver's lips and down his chin as Scars shoved him back down to the deck. Tyranny took another step closer.

Without warning she lifted one foot, and kicked the kneeling slaver in the chin.

The blow knocked him over onto his back. He writhed and choked for a time, then died as his own blood slowly filled his lungs.

As the final death rattle escaped him, Tyranny walked over and picked up two more shards of glass. She walked back to the other slaver and held the shards before his face.

"Answer my questions truthfully and you won't suffer the same fate," she said. "Now then, how many more slaver ships guard the Citadel?"

His hateful arrogance withered; the slaver bowed his head. "None," he answered. "Sure of his victory, our messiah sent them all."

"And the number of slavers?" she asked.

"They all came with the fleet."

"Then the traitorous consuls constitute the only remaining defense of the Citadel?" she asked.

"No," the thing said. "There are now others there, too. They are human, like you, but they are not consuls. They arrived just before our lord departed for Eutracia. They asked for his sanctuary and he granted it. He seemed glad to have them there."

Concerned by this unexpected news, Tyranny took another step closer. Her eyes narrowed. "Who are they?" she demanded.

The slaver shook his head. "None of us know," he answered. "They remain largely out of sight."

"Can you tell me anything else about them?" she asked.

The slaver shook his head again. "That is as much as any of us knows."

Rubbing her chin, Tyranny backed away. She took a final draft on her cigarillo, dropped it to the deck, and crushed it beneath her bloody boot. She looked over at K'jarr.

"Have our troops returned from the enemy vessels?" she asked.

"Yes," the warrior answered.

"Good," Tyranny said. "Have all of the surviving slavers taken back to their ships. That is where they shall meet their fates."

She turned back to K'jarr. "As this is being done, order all of our remaining vessels to form a line in the sea, with the *Reprise* at the center."

K'jarr clicked his heels. "As you wish," he said.

The demonslaver that Tyranny had questioned glared at her harshly. Struggling to break free of Scars' grip, he spat at her.

"What about me, you bitch!" he screamed. "You said that if I talked, you would spare me!"

Tyranny barely glanced at him. "No, I didn't," she said.

She nodded at her first mate, then looked at Adrian. "Walk with me," she said.

As the two women strode to the gunwale, Scars wrapped his hands around the protesting slaver's throat, and the screaming died away. The privateer looked out to sea.

"The slaver's information is disturbing," Tyranny said. "What do you make of it?"

Adrian shook her head. "I have no idea," she answered. "But the *Jin'Sai* and *Jin'Saiou* must be informed immediately."

At the mention of Tristan, Tyranny felt the familiar pain go through her heart. "Indeed," she said. "Provided they are still alive."

Silence reigned as the two women watched the Minions fly the slavers back to their vessels. As ordered, the remainder of Tyranny's fleet began lining up on either side of the *Reprise*.

By the time the ships had deployed as ordered, the sun had set and stars twinkled above.

"What will you do now?" Adrian finally asked.

Tyranny turned to her. "I'm giving you command of the fleet," she said.

Adrian's jaw dropped. "Wha-what?"

"You heard me," Tyranny said. "My job here is done. Both the warriors and I can be of far greater use in Tammerland. I shudder to think of what we might find when we arrive. We will leave straightaway."

"What are your orders?" Adrian asked tentatively.

"Have the acolytes blow holes in the hulls of the slaver ships until each of them is sunk," Tyranny answered. "And make doubly sure that each and every demonslaver has drowned. Then and only then are you to order the fleet back to the coast. Many of our vessels are in a bad way, but the voyage is short. I will leave Scars here to help you. Anchor off the Cavalon Delta, then report to the palace."

Tyranny gave the acolyte a wry look. "You have acquitted yourself well out here, Sister Adrian," she added. "This shall be your first command, but I have the feeling that it won't be your last."

"I will do my best," Adrian said.

Tyranny looked over at her giant first mate. "Scars!" she shouted. "Have my litter made ready! And tell K'jarr that all of the warriors are to accompany me back to Tammerland!"

Scars nodded back. Tyranny turned to Adrian again.

"Good luck," she said. "And don't lose any of my ships!"

"And good luck to you," Adrian answered.

Tyranny walked to her litter and climbed in. Adrian watched her give some final orders to Scars; the first mate nodded. In a matter of moments the litter and the entire host of warriors had taken to the nighttime sky.

As her litter climbed higher, Tyranny heard the muffled echoes of explosions. She turned to watch the Acolytes' azure bolts shooting across the dark sea to smash into the hulls of the slaver frigates. One by one the ships went down. She let out a long, tired sigh. *Perhaps the time of the demonslavers is finally over,* she thought.

Tired and bloody, Tyranny closed her eyes and leaned back in her seat. The nighttime air felt fresh and clean against her face.

As her litter turned toward Tammerland, the privateer dreaded what she might find there. But she was sure of one thing: The *Jin'Sai* would need her sword, and she would give it.

CHAPTER LXXXVIII

As Tristan and Wigg's litter was carried over Tammerland, they could hardly believe their eyes.

The western half of Tammerland was destroyed. The superheated mass in the Sippora still moved slowly along with the river, setting fire to everything nearby. The streets were filled with a writhing, crushing flow of humanity. Demonslavers and K'tons systematically slaughtered the refugees as they fled. Blood slicked the streets. The fires roared high into the night, sending choking smoke up to greet them, and even from their altitude, Tristan, Wigg, and Traax could easily hear the cries of the dying.

Behind the demonslavers lumbered giant beasts the likes of which Tristan had never before seen. With sweeps of their incredible tails, they were destroying building after building, sending walls and roofs high into the air. Behind and above them sailed the six remaining Black Ships, their skeletal captains raining azure bolts down upon anything that still moved.

Horrified, Tristan turned to look at Wigg. The First Wizard's face had gone ashen. Tristan quickly guessed that this was not Wigg's first encounter with these monsters.

"You know what those things are, don't you?" he asked.

Wigg nodded. "Earthshakers," he said. "They are abominations originally conjured by the Sorceresses of the Coven. Unless they are stopped, they will smash through Tammerland until nothing is left. If they reach the palace they will surely destroy it. And with the upper levels gone, the fires might easily find their way down into the Redoubt. If they do, three hundred years of records and research in the craft could be destroyed forever."

Tristan shuddered at the prospect of the craft's written history gone in a single night. He took the wizard by the shoulders.

"Can your plan defeat them?" he asked anxiously.

Wigg shook his head. "I don't know," he answered. "Perhaps. But only if Faegan and Jessamay have been successful in their research. Right now, our priority is to reach the palace without being seen. Only then can the three of us do what we must, while you go on to follow the dictates of the Scroll Master."

"Agreed," Tristan said.

Ox was flying nearby. Tristan shouted out a series of orders to him. Because they had flown in from the northwest, they had not yet been spotted by the enemy. But if they didn't change course, they soon would be. It nearly drove the prince mad that they would have to take such a circuitous route, but there was no other choice.

Their litter banked hard to the left, and the two of them held on tight.

Tristan breathed a huge sigh of relief when he saw that the palace was still intact. Its lights shone brightly, providing a beacon visible through the rising smoke. Faegan and the others milled about on the roof. They looked up eagerly when the shadows of the arriving warriors fell over them.

As the litter descended, Tristan could see that the grounds were still littered with the wounded. At least the Orb of the Vigors would cause no more harm, he thought. He leaped from the litter, Wigg quickly following him.

Shailiha was the first to greet him. She took him into her arms, a question in her tear-filled eyes.

"Celeste?" she asked.

Tristan shook his head.

Shailiha hugged him tighter. "I'm so sorry," she said.

"I know," he answered.

She looked back into his face and studied him. "What has happened to you?" she asked. "Are you all right?"

Tristan caressed his sister's cheek. "Yes," he answered. "My blood is finally healed."

He was about to speak again when they all heard a massive explosion. As a group, they ran to the edge of the rooftop and looked over.

To their horror, part of one of the walls surrounding the palace had been smashed to bits by an Earthshaker. Raising its head in triumph, the monster gave an earsplitting scream. Demonslavers followed, eagerly waving their swords.

His hands balled up into fists, Tristan burned with rage. His worst fears had been realized.

With a swipe of its tail, the Earthshaker destroyed another section of the wall. The drawbridge tumbled down to crash headlong into the moat. Demonslavers quickly lifted it to span the water, and in a moment they were pouring through the entrance, while hungry K'tons descended into the palace grounds.

Soon the entire place was alive with the sounds of battle. The wounded victims of the orb tried to run for their lives, but there was no place for them to hide. The K'tons pounced on them, tearing them limb from limb and devouring them greedily.

Tristan looked over at Faegan. The wizard nodded; they were ready. Tristan then hurried to Traax.

"This is the most desperate battle of our lives, but I cannot lead you," he said. "My place is here this time. You know that."

Traax bowed his head slightly. "I understand, my lord," he answered. "No matter what happens, it has been an honor to serve by your side."

Another explosion rocked the palace. Tristan looked over at Duvessa, Dax, and Ox and waved them to him. They were by his side in an instant, dreggans drawn. He looked at each of them for what he feared would be the last time. With the same thought in his heart, Traax gently wrapped his wings around Duvessa.

"Follow Traax's orders to the letter!" Tristan said. "There are too many of the enemy to defeat by yourselves. Most, if not all, of you may die this night. But you have to buy us time, time for the wizards to work the craft. Above all, you must somehow keep the enemy from taking this roof. Go now!"

The four of them came to attention and raised their dreggans high. Their blades flashed briefly in the firelight.

"We live to serve!" they shouted, then ran to the edge of the roof and launched themselves.

Another explosion shook the building. Fire began to lick at the inner ward of the palace. Tristan looked over the edge.

Most of the surrounding walls were gone. The Black Ships

were fast approaching, their dark hulls looming in the nighttime sky. Unaware that their leader was dead, the captains rained azure bolts down upon the beleaguered city with abandon, killing anything in their path. Soon the Black Ships would sail over what was left of the walls and the battle would be over.

Tristan ran across the shaking rooftop to join Wigg, Faegan, and Jessamay. The three mystics were huddled together, talking urgently.

"Are you ready?" he pleaded. He turned back to see that the first of the Black Ships was already passing over the shattered palace walls. "It must happen *now*!"

Faegan gave him a weary nod. "We will try," he said.

Wigg and Faegan went to the very edge of the roof. Jessamay stood to one side. The two wizards raised their hands and closed their eyes.

The resulting explosion was deafening, filling the heavens with a thunderous roar. For a split second, a spot of azure light appeared high in the sky, directly over the center of the city. Far brighter than any star, it burst apart, sending brilliant, concentric circles of light cascading for leagues in every direction. As they spread and fell, the circles gradually vanished. In their place a massive azure dome formed, covering the entire city of Tammerland. Its sheer beauty and raw power resonated everywhere at once.

Tristan took Shailiha's hand. Together they stared in wonder at the awesome work of the craft. The trap had closed. There was now no way out for any of them, friend or foe.

As Wigg and Faegan held the dome in place, Tristan turned toward Jessamay. The future of their world now rested upon her abilities alone.

Stepping to the edge of the roof, Jessamay raised her hands and closed her eyes.

Across the city, glowing, liquid azure appeared, dripping slowly from the surviving houses, their roofs, and even from the remains of the palace walls. As the precious seconds ticked by, Tristan looked east toward the sections of the city that were still intact. The oozing stuff was showing up everywhere; already eerie, winding rivulets snaked down into the streets and alleys, forming countless, glowing pools. The mission Faegan had sent the other members of the Conclave out on two nights earlier had been successful.

From the first of the glowing pools, a creature took shape. As its head came up to take living form from the enchanted, primordial ooze that gave it birth, it turned to examine the bloody scene with its slanted, yellow eyes.

The first of the Wingwalkers rose.

The Wingwalkers, Tristan thought, as yet another of the Earthshakers' explosions rocked the palace—the same terrible breed of beings that had nearly killed him, along with Wigg and Celeste, in the bowels of the Recluse. Failee's onetime servants, born again from the fluid that Wigg had risked his life to gather in Parthalon. Faegan's attempts to magnify the volume of Wingwalker fluid had been successful! Now tens of thousands of the creatures were rising to the aid of the palace.

Or were they? Tristan's blood ran cold as he suddenly remembered the other, equally important half of the wizards' plan.

Had Faegan and Jessamay been successful in *all* they had needed to accomplish? Which side of the craft now owned the Wingwalkers' allegiance—the Vigors or the Vagaries?

Tristan held his breath as he watched multitudes of the dreadful things soar up toward the palace roof. As Wigg and Faegan used all their power to support the azure dome, Jessamay raised her hands higher. Thousands of Wingwalkers gathered before her, their number growing by the moment. Legions of slanted, yellow eyes stared at her.

Jessamay's gaze was as hard as granite. Lowering her arms, she pointed down into the palace courtyard.

"Kill," she said.

The Wingwalkers didn't hesitate. At Jessamay's command they turned and tore into the *Jin'Sai*'s foes—those who served the Vagaries and possessed blood signatures that leaned leftward.

With their talons and long, pointed teeth, the Wingwalkers were an equal match for the demonslavers and K'tons. But merely being their equal would not win the Wingwalkers the day, Tristan knew. Their victory would be in their superior numbers. Turning to look back at the northeastern section of the city, he saw thousands upon thousands more rise to join in the fray.

Breathless, he watched as the Wingwalkers descended upon an Earthshaker, digging in with their talons. Screaming in agony, the Earthshaker shook its huge head wildly as the creatures bit great hunks from its flesh. The demonslaver astride it also screamed as the Wingwalkers plucked him from the Earthshaker's back and tore him apart.

Each of the other five Earthshakers met the same fate. One by one the great beasts fell, the ground trembling as they hit. In their death throes, their great, bony tails flapped up and down, smashing against the ground. With each great blow, more of the palace walls came tumbling down.

The demonslavers and the K'tons fared no better. Massively outnumbered by the Minions and the Wingwalkers, they died by the thousands. Tristan watched in awe as the Wingwalkers defied gravity to scurry sideways along the walls, hang upside down beneath roof alcoves, then spin and cartwheel deftly in the sky to strike down their prey. Bit by bit, the Minions and the Wingwalkers—both onetime servants of the Coven—gained the upper hand.

Some of the K'tons attempted to flee, but were vaporized when they tried to break through the azure dome. Undeterred, still more of them suffered the same fate.

And then the six Black Ships finally entered the grounds of the palace. The six skeletal captains rained bolt after bolt down upon the Wingwalkers and Minions. Many fell, and for a moment Tristan feared that all would be lost despite their valiant efforts. He felt Shailiha's grip on his hand tighten.

But then another great horde of freshly born Wingwalkers descended upon the scene, turning the tide. They swarmed darkly over the vessels' captains and demonslavers, killing them all.

Without their captains to guide them, the great ships careened out of control. Tristan watched, his mouth agape, as the first nosed down to plow along the ground. As its hull tore across the earth of the inner ward, it took down countless hastily erected hospital tents; the people who had been hiding inside of them went screaming and running for their lives.

With a loud groan, the great ship lay over on her port side, but inertia kept her barreling straight for the entrance to the Great

Hall. Sending up clumps of ragged earth in all directions, her bowsprit tore through the chamber's double stained-glass doors. With a mighty crash, the ship came to rest.

The other five ships crashed in a similar manner. One by one they banged into the earth and skidded across the palace grounds. Tristan felt the palace quake beneath him as two more ships rammed into its walls.

As the fighting in the courtyard died down, Tristan looked out over Tammerland again. Some of the Wingwalkers and Minions soared over the smashed palace walls to chase down and kill off the demonslavers and K'tons still ravaging the city. New fires were still erupting, and the courtyard resounded with the screams of the wounded and dying.

Tristan and Shailiha went over to join the others. Wigg and Faegan continued to support the azure dome with the craft. Jessamay and Abbey stood staring in horror at the carnage. Wingwalker, Minion, and demonslaver bodies seemed to lie everywhere, as did the dead and wounded who had first come to the palace seeking refuge from the Orb of the Vigors.

As he looked down at his traumatized subjects, Tristan lowered his head. He recalled that day not so long before when he had addressed many of them in the Great Hall and asked them for their trust.

But how will I ever gain their allegiance now? he wondered. *How can they trust me when, yet again, the craft has brought them nothing but pain and death?*

Then he thought about the three Forestallments remaining in his blood, and the muscles in his jaws tightened.

Hearing the flurry of approaching wings, Tristan turned to see Traax, Duvessa, and Ox land on the roof. They were all worn out and splattered with blood. Dax was not present. Tristan hurried over to them.

"Dax?" he asked anxiously.

Traax shook his head. "No," he said. "But he died well."

"And the state of the battle?"

"Our scouts tell us that it is over," Traax answered. "The wizards may dispense with the dome."

Wigg and Faegan gladly lowered their arms. They both looked past the point of exhaustion. The azure dome surrounding Tammerland slowly faded and then vanished, releasing the smoke that had collected beneath it.

"It is now time for you to complete your part of it," Tristan said to Jessamay.

The sorceress nodded and walked over to the map table. She picked up Failee's red leather grimoire. A golden bookmark extended from between its pages. As everyone watched, she went back to stand at the edge of the roof.

Opening the grimoire to the marked page, she balanced the book in one hand and raised her other. She looked down at the swarming Wingwalkers.

"Come to me," she said.

Almost at once the horrific creatures obeyed. Soon the night sky was black with them. The entire multitude hovered in the air before Jessamay, their numbers so vast that they blocked out the stars and the three Eutracian moons.

Taking a deep breath, Jessamay looked down at the grimoire and started to recite a spell.

Tristan stared sadly at the throngs of Wingwalkers. They had proven invaluable in the defense of Tammerland, but his mind was made up: though they were truly little more than killing machines, and despite the fact that their blood signatures now leaned to the right, they could not be allowed to live.

And so, Jessamay recited the secret words in Old Eutracian—the same spell that Wigg had tried to find that day in the bowels of the Recluse, but could not—and the leathery skin of the Wingwalkers burst into flames. As they cried out in pain, Tristan couldn't help but feel a touch of remorse. Steeling his heart, he put one arm around Shailiha and watched them die.

One by one they fell to the earth, dead. Their bodies burned until only their skeletons remained.

Tristan looked down into the courtyard and out across the city to see the streets piled white—as if it were the Season of Crystal and it had just snowed. Stunned citizens, their clothing and faces black with soot, stared in wonder.

Jessamay turned to look at the *Jin'Sai*. "It is over," she said wearily.

He shook his head. "You're wrong," he answered. "There is still much to be done."

Tristan looked down into the city that he so loved. From the west, the fires were fast approaching the palace. Surviving citizens had formed bucket brigades, but their efforts accomplished little. Soon the entire city would be lost.

He looked at the bend in the Sippora River where it curved to flow near the palace. He then looked upriver. Because of the smoke and the darkness, at first he couldn't find what he was searching for.

Then he finally saw it. He was quickly running out of time, he knew. If he didn't play his part now, the final act of this tragedy would soon open.

Tristan called Ox to his side and pointed to a spot on the ground just outside the smashed walls.

"Fly me there!" he ordered.

Without hesitation Ox picked up the prince, ran to the roof's edge, and took flight. As they went, Tristan gave Shailiha a final look. Panic and confusion gripped the princess as she watched her brother go.

Then they saw Tyranny's litter and her host of warriors cross before the three moons. As quickly as the litter touched down, the privateer came running to Wigg. Shailiha ran to join them, and she and Tyranny looked at the wizard with trepidation.

"What is Tristan doing?" the princess asked.

"What he was born to do," Wigg answered, placing his hands into the opposite sleeves of his robe. There was a worried, resigned look on his craggy face. "And may the Afterlife see him through it."

Wondering what was about to happen, Shailiha and the others could only stand and watch as Ox and Tristan soared away.

Ox landed and lowered Tristan to the ground. Tristan looked around urgently. The place he had chosen was deteriorating rapidly. New fires were erupting all about them, and the heat was unbearable. He knew that he and Ox wouldn't be able to stand this for very long. He looked into the faithful warrior's dark eyes.

"You must leave me now!" he ordered. His voice was nearly drowned out by the roaring flames.

No sooner had he finished speaking than another building fell, its walls collapsing only meters from their feet. When the blast of heat hit them, it nearly knocked them down.

Despite Tristan's order, the huge warrior seemed locked in place. Wondering why Ox hadn't obeyed, Tristan steadied himself, then grabbed Ox by his massive shoulders.

"Fly back to the roof!" Tristan commanded him. "You must go now! Even I am not sure of what is about to happen! What I must do here, you cannot be a part of!"

As the flames roared all around them, Ox looked sadly into Tristan's eyes. He opened his mouth to speak, but then closed it again. Then Ox did something that no Minion warrior had ever dared to do.

Taking a step forward, he embraced his *Jin'Sai* in his wings.

Both honored and surprised, for several precious moments Tristan embraced him back. Saying nothing, Ox released Tristan and took to the air.

Tristan looked around. He was near the banks of the Sippora, about thirty meters upriver from the palace. Buildings as yet untouched by the approaching inferno stood nearby, the fires' shadows crawling along their walls—a haunting portent of things soon to come. The stinking heat and choking smoke were nearly overpowering. Feeling faint, Tristan placed one hand before his face. He couldn't go any farther or he would die before he did what he had come here to do. And so he was forced to wait for the awful thing to come to him.

Finally, the dark, stinking mass of superheated pollution in the Sippora drew closer. The ever-changing cracks in its surface shot poison and hungry flames high into the air. In moments it would be alongside the palace. It was time to act, Tristan knew, and there wasn't a moment to lose.

He reached over his right shoulder and took one of his throwing knives from its scabbard. Just as the Scroll Master had instructed him, he made a small incision in his left palm. He replaced the knife, then braved the heat to struggle to the edge of the river. He held his wounded hand out. Making a fist, he squeezed the wound until his blood dripped into the water. He stepped back from the bank, looked at the blood, and narrowed his eyes.

Almost at once the blood expanded, billowing outward, and began to flow upstream, against the current. As if it had a life of its own, it sought out the dark pollution coming its way.

The two substances touched.

The clouds of red blood slowly snaked their way around the mass. As Tristan concentrated with all of his might, the blood formed red tentacles that left the water and, like a spider's web, reached up and around the mass. Once the mass was encased, the tentacles started to squeeze. As the mass flowed down the river, an azure haze formed around it.

The explosion that followed ripped through the heavens. Blinding rays of pure white light burst upward, illuminating the burning city. The mass disintegrated, cracking and splintering noisily. Its remaining fragments rained down harmlessly on the river and its banks.

And then it was gone. Amazingly, the river had returned to its natural state.

Exhausted, Tristan lowered his hands. The Scroll Master had been right, he realized. But there were still two Forestallments that remained to be employed. As he stood there among the flaming ruins, he could feel them calling out to him, begging to be released.

Turning to face the river, he raised his hands again. The Scroll Master had warned him that, due to his growing fatigue, each of the two successive Forestallments would be progressively more challenging to dominate. If he lost control, they could turn on him, killing him. Wondering whether he was about to die, Tristan looked to the water and concentrated all of his newfound power upon it.

Slowly, agonizingly, the waters of the Sippora started to rise. The plume that was being generated soared high into the sky. As the onrushing river water continued to feed it, the whirling maelstrom of water flattened out at its top until it reached from one end of the city to the other.

Tristan's body shook and the flames licked at his boots. He tried with all his might to enlarge the whirling plume. As he felt the power slipping away from him, he knew that it was time. He dropped his arms.

The plume broke apart, sending a torrential downpour

crashing into the city. It flooded through buildings, rushed down the streets, and fell upon every fire. Jubilant citizens rushed out of hiding places to lift their arms and embrace the downpour.

In every part of the great city, the fires went out. Steam plumes rose into the air, blanketing everything for a time. Much of Tammerland lay in ruins, but the eastern half of the metropolis had been spared. And the Sippora River—once destined to annihilate everything it touched—now flowed clean and strong again, just as it had for untold centuries.

Trying desperately to see through the rising steam, Shailiha searched for her brother. At first she couldn't see him. Then some of the haze lifted, and there he was. She stared in horror.

Curled up into a fetal position, Tristan lay unmoving on the bank of the river. His eyes were closed, and it was impossible to tell whether he was dead or alive. It looked like his hands were badly scorched from his untrained use of the craft.

Mad with worry, Shailiha turned to Ox. "You must take me to him!" she shouted. "He could be dying!"

Ox was about to obey when Wigg stopped him. His expression held no room for compromise.

"It's true that he may be dead," Wigg said, "and no one dreads that more than you and me. But under no circumstances are we to go near him. The Scroll Master warned Tristan of this, and the prince explained it to me. His wishes must be obeyed to the letter. If the *Jin'Sai* still lives, then what he must do, he must do alone."

Putting one arm around her, Wigg looked sadly into Shailiha's glistening eyes. "I'm sorry, Princess," he said. "At this moment in the history of the craft, we are but pawns in the struggle between light and dark. The *Jin'Sai*'s destiny shall be what it shall be. We must accept that."

TRISTAN'S MIND WAS FEVERISH AND HIS BREATHING WAS IRREGUlar, as his body fought to stay alive. Time after time his consciousness struggled to resurface and join the world, only to be dragged back under again. And then—for the first time in his life—Tristan heard the voices of the Ones Who Came Before. They revealed themselves to him gently, soft tones in his mind.

"Tristan . . ."

His breathing shallow, his heartbeat slow and weak, Tristan did not move.

"Tristan," they called again, more insistently. *"You must rise, our son. As the reigning* Jin'Sai, *you have done well. But you must discover whether you still possess the strength to perform this last deed. The release of your last Forestallment will bring you the acceptance and trust of your subjects that you have so long desired. Rise up,* Jin'Sai. *Rise and employ this last Forestallment, to take your rightful place in your world."*

Groaning, Tristan moved slightly. With a supreme effort of will, he raised himself up to his knees. He was exhausted. His body and clothing were both soaked with rain and charred and dirty from the fires. But he bowed his head and answered the call of the Ones Who Came Before.

"I am here," he told them silently.

"You and your sister are the strongest Jin'Sai *and* Jin'Saiou *ever to walk the earth,"* the voices said. *"Our hopes run high that it shall be you and she who finally join the two sides of the craft. But, in truth, your travails have only just begun. If you live through the application of your final Forestallment, you know what your next deed must be, for the Scroll Master has told you. Do not tarry in that mission,* Jin'Sai, *for there is so little time."*

"It shall be as you say," he answered silently.

Tristan got wavering unsteadily to his feet. He pushed his dark, wet hair away from his eyes.

Trying to reclaim his senses, he again drew a knife. He hardly felt the fresh cut he made in his palm. No longer caring what became of the knife, he let it slip from his hand and fall to the wet ground. He closed his wounded fist to squeeze more of his blood onto the ground.

Raising his arms, he closed his eyes.

With the release of his final Forestallment, the small pool of blood on the ground began to glow with the aura of the craft. The azure pool grew larger and larger. It soon split into crooked lengths that looked like lightning branches. There were hundreds of them now, their ends starting to snake through the streets of Tammerland. Other tendrils traveled across the surface of the moat and invaded the palace grounds.

Raising his hands higher, his body trembling and his mind pushed to the limit, Tristan silently ordered the branches to search out their targets. Their speed increasing, they obeyed. Lightning tore across the sky. Thunder cracked, and a stiff, cyclonic wind overtook the city, its ferocity sending the charred, wet debris from the fires whirling high into the air. One by one, the azure branches reached not only the citizens of Tammerland, but his own Minions of Day and Night as well.

The terrified citizens tried to run. But the azure branches were too fast. The exhausted Minions held fast, most of them trying to strike down the snaking branches with their dreggans. But their blades caused no damage. Pandemonium reigned again.

As those on the palace roof watched, they soon realized that the branches were not seeking out all of the people and warriors, but only some of them. Finally understanding, Shailiha's eyes went wide and she looked at Wigg. With a smile, the First Wizard nodded back.

The branches were only seeking out the wounded and dying!

With each caress of the craft, the wounds healed. Burns and gashes closed, bleeding stopped, and broken bones mended themselves. Cries of jubilation rose in the city as the lame walked and the blind saw again. Crutches were cast aside, and tearful mothers and fathers held each other as they watched their stricken children become whole once more.

As the citizens and the warriors came to understand what was happening, they embraced one another. As if they had suddenly found a common thread of humanity that had never before existed, the citizens began to shed their sense of fear, and the warriors gradually cast off the guilt they had felt for so long about what they had once done to these people. Even the stern warriors shed tears.

Unfettered happiness engulfed the city in ways that the fires and the *Enseterat*'s forces had not been able to do. Someone climbed one of the city's still-standing towers and began to ring its bells in celebration. Joy commanded the night.

With tears in his eyes, Wigg looked down at Tristan. The *Jin'Sai* was still struggling to hold his arms wide. At last, sensing that his work was done, he lowered his arms. He watched weakly as the azure branches faded, then disappeared.

Tristan fell to his knees and hung his head. Citizens and warriors rushed toward him with gratitude. With the end of his final Forestallment, the thunder and wind died away, leaving only the sounds of celebration.

But his heart was not gladdened. Although he was grateful that he had succeeded, the merriment meant little to him. As the crowds formed around him he ignored them, his mind imprisoned by his own grief.

Celeste, he thought. His tears came freely.

His mind turned to the stark image of her azure death mask, hovering in space with so many others in the Well of Forestallments. *Was her soul content?* he wondered. *Did she indeed forgive him from wherever she had gone to rest?*

Reaching into his leather vest, with a trembling hand he removed her wedding ring.

Then he lost consciousness and fell to the ground.

EPILOGUE

"WE HAVE BEEN SUMMONED," EINAR SAID.

Looking up from the ancient text he had been studying, Reznik turned to stare at his visitor. His expression said that he did not appreciate the interruption. He sullenly looked back down at his work.

"Can it not wait?" he asked. "I am at a critical juncture in my research, and—"

"Now," Einar insisted.

Removing his spectacles, Reznik sighed. "Very well."

He stood up from his work stool, brushed off his clothes, and followed Einar from the room. The door closed heavily behind them.

The walk was long but pleasant. Colorful birds flew about the inner ward; fountains danced and burbled happily, and the sky was clear. They crossed the grounds, then navigated a series of labyrinthine hallways. Finally, the men stopped before a pair of double doors. Einar knocked. A voice bade them enter. A servant opened the doors, and the two of them walked in.

Serena stood at the far end of the throne room, facing the sea. When she turned to look at them, they could see that she had been crying again.

It was known throughout the Citadel that she had lost her child two days earlier. The baby girl had been both premature and stillborn. It was rumored that in her grief Serena had enchanted the little corpse to remain fresh, and that it lay in state in her private quarters, but no one knew for sure. Nor did anyone dare ask.

Despite her recent loss, the queen of the Citadel remained as beautiful as ever. Brunette ringlets hung to her shoulders, and her wide blue eyes regarded the men calmly. Her black mourning dress was tailored to perfection. Since Wulfgar's departure for Eutracia, her demeanor seemed to have become even more commanding.

"You called for us, your grace?" Einar asked.

Saying nothing, Serena turned and walked to one of the two black marble thrones that overlooked the sea. She sat down and arranged the hem of her gown. Without being told, the two men came to face her.

Serena reached to one side and took up a small, leather-bound journal. She opened the book and produced a flower that had been pressed between its pages.

The single red rose was withered. Even so, it did not give the appearance of having been dead for long. Serena held the rose up to them.

"This rose has died," she said, "and with it many of my hopes and dreams."

"I do not understand," the first man said. "Does this flower bear some significance?"

"Before he left for Eutracia, Wulfgar plucked this rose and bound its life to his own," she answered. "As long as he lived, so, too, would the rose."

Pausing, she took a moment to collect herself. She closed her eyes and pressed the withered blossom against her breast.

"The *Enseterat* is dead," she said.

Stunned, the men looked at each other and then back at their queen. *First her child and now her husband,* one of them thought, *and both dead within the space of only two days.*

"We can only assume that our invasion of Eutracia has failed," she went on, "and that our armies have been annihilated. Worse yet, the Black Ships may remain intact and in the hands of our enemies. Only the blood of the *Jin'Sai* could have defeated my husband. That means that his blood is red once more, and that he can, therefore, be trained in the craft. He is now without question the most dangerous man in the world.

"We must also assume that the assassin Satine is dead, and perhaps Bratach as well," she added. "In addition, our entire network of consuls scattered throughout Eutracia may be in jeopardy. Buoyed by his recent victory, the *Jin'Sai* might even try to come and take away the Scroll of the Vagaries. He must be stopped at all costs."

Still trying to digest the awful news, the two men simply stood there for a time. Finally Einar spoke.

"My greatest condolences for your losses, your grace," he said.

"And mine," said the other.

Serena nodded. "There is more to tell you," she said. "Before he left for Eutracia, Wulfgar granted me dozens of additional Forestallments to my blood signature, and trained me in their use. I am now a fully empowered sorceress of the Vagaries." As she paused for a moment, her expression turned grim.

"You are my senior consul, Einar," she said. "In many ways, your talents are equal to Faegan's and Wigg's. I shall need your expertise in the days to come."

"As you wish, your grace," Einar answered.

Serena turned her gaze to the other man. She took in his bloody butcher's apron, bald head, and wrinkled face. She found him an unpleasant creature, but his gifts might prove useful, so she tolerated his presence.

"And you, Reznik?" she asked. "I trust that you and your Corporeals are as comfortable here as you were in Eutracia?"

"Yes, your grace," Reznik answered. "It was wise of your late husband to bring us here after Faegan first discovered Valrenkium. We have settled in nicely. The fruits of our labors shall be yours alone."

Serena lowered her eyes. "Yes," she said softly, her gaze far away and her thoughts on her stillborn child. "The practitioners of the Vigors will soon rue the day they killed my family." She looked back at her two servants.

"Leave me," she ordered. "I wish to be alone. Soon—very soon—our new work will begin."

Bowing, the two men left the room. The heavy double doors closed behind them.

Alone once more, Serena allowed herself the luxury of tears. As they traced their way down her cheeks, she walked to the edge of the throne room and looked west, toward Eutracia.

Lowering her head, she pressed the withered rose to her breast.

GAIUS WAS UNUSUALLY FAIR FOR A MINION WARRIOR. He was clean-shaven, with light brown hair and green eyes. Recently promoted to the rank of captain, he commanded the eleven warriors stationed near the magnificent azure pass that had been carved into the rugged Tolenka Mountains. Eager to impress his superiors, he took his first command seriously.

Seated by the campfire with five fellow warriors, he looked up at the mountainside. He could easily see the pass shimmering in the night. Six more warriors were camped up there, watching it. Even from its great distance up the mountainside, the pass's magnificent rays flooded the plains below.

Gaius and his troops had been stationed here for nearly two months, but the pass had yet to relinquish any secrets. As he looked back down at the fire, he wondered whether it ever would. Those were riddles for wizards to unravel, and far beyond a warrior's knowledge.

Tristan, Wigg, Faegan, and the sorceress Jessamay had arrived in Minion litters to view the pass just after the *Jin'-Sai* and his forces turned back Wulfgar's invasion for the second and final time. Ox and Traax had accompanied them. Although his written reports to the *Jin'Sai* had said little since his posting here, Gaius still sent them along at regular intervals.

By now it was widely known that the *Jin'Sai* was a widower. During his visit, each of the warriors had expressed his or her heartfelt condolences. His face grim, Tristan had thanked them, then ordered that his group be taken to view the pass. Gaius had climbed aboard and directed the litter bearers up the mountainside.

On reaching the site they all disembarked. They walked to face the glowing pass while the wizard Faegan levitated his chair on wheels, following along behind. The entire mountainside had been scorched black and barren. Even now, warm cinders crunched beneath their boots. There were no trees, no brush, and no grass—just the strange pass, shimmering brightly against the face of the granite mountainside. Because their habitats had been decimated, all the forest creatures had fled.

They'll never return, Gaius thought as the group approached the strange phenomenon. *The craft is at work here, and somehow they know it.*

When they saw the group coming, the six warriors guarding the pass came to attention. At first no one spoke. As everyone stood before the pass's wondrous presence, it was almost like there could be nothing left to say.

The deep gap was barred by a brilliant azure wall, its aura so bright that it hurt everyone's eyes. It stretched silently from one mountain sidewall to the other—a distance of about twenty meters. Looking up, they could see no limit to its height, for it disappeared into the dense fog that always crouched atop the mountain peaks.

The pass's flat surface was smooth as glass. As the visitors gazed into its depths they could see white shards of light shooting to and fro, as if begging to be released to the outside world. It was a wondrous, awful thing. No matter how many times Gaius came here, he was stunned by its majesty.

Knowing that his place was with his troops, the captain stayed behind as he watched the inspection party approach the glowing wall. He saw the wizards point at it and speak anxiously to one another. Tristan said something to the wizard in the chair, and the mystic nodded.

Gaius watched the *Jin'Sai* unsheathe his dreggan. As the blade cleared its scabbard, for several moments its unmistakable ring filled the air. With another nod from Faegan, the prince walked closer.

Gaius held his breath as the prince drove his sword directly into the glowing wall. The blade disappeared effortlessly, like it had entered the still surface of some countryside pond.

As the prince steadily held his weapon, the light shards on the pass's other side started gathering around it. They danced to the dreggan like it was a lightning rod, but they did it no harm. With another nod from the wizard, Tristan withdrew the blade and sheathed it. Again the wizards and the sorceress huddled together, talking in urgent tones. Finally turning away from the pass, the *Jin'Sai* ordered a return to the base camp.

The royal party stayed the night, and everyone feasted. As the smell of roasted venison filled the air, much akulee—the dark, bitter brew of the Minions—was consumed. Although they spoke little about what they had seen, Wigg, Faegan, and Jessamay had been sociable enough.

But the *Jin'Sai* was another matter. He had eaten little, then gone off to be alone at the camp's far edge. He sat there for hours before finally falling asleep, holding the gold medallion around his neck and drinking akulee while he stared into the darkness. The two wizards and sorceress had looked at him often.

At dawn the inspection party had thanked Gaius, then flown back to Tammerland. Before leaving, the *Jin'Sai* had instructed Gaius to keep the reports coming, no matter how sparse they might be. The captain had answered with a smart click of his heels.

His thoughts returning to the present, Gaius again looked up the mountainside. The pass's azure rays pass still flooded the ground around him. He had no idea how long he and his warriors would be stationed here, but they would gladly do their duty until ordered otherwise.

Gaius took a last pull on the akulee jug, then wiped his mouth with his forearm. Lying down by the fire with the others, he finally fell asleep.

AS THE PASS THROUGH THE TOLENKAS CONTINUED TO SHIMMER, three of the six warriors stationed nearby lay asleep by the fire. The other three sat on camp stools playing at cards. It would be dawn soon. Then they would sleep while the others stood guard.

Being posted to this desolate place had quickly become tiresome, even for diligent Minion warriors. The wall of azure light never wavered, never threatened. Silent and beautiful, for them it had become nothing more than what it appeared—a seemingly harmless construct of the craft. Even the usually wary Minions had begun taking its harmlessness for granted.

Without the warriors noticing, a thin white line started silently climbing up the middle of the azure wall. Starting at the ground, it soon stretched as high as the eye could see and disappeared into the fog. Still the three warriors did not turn around. The line quickly parted the wall into halves, revealing a space that was dark and endless.

As an intruder came through the gap, still the warriors did not notice. A mounted black stallion stepped silently forward to a place about five meters from the fire. The vapor from the stallion's nostrils streamed in the cool night air.

The warrior named Eranan was the first to jump to his feet and draw his sword. Startled, the other two quickly followed.

Without hesitation the rider raised one arm. With a muffled explosion, Eranan's insides burst through his chest and abdomen. His fellow warriors watched in horror as his vitals slipped wetly from beneath his body armor and fell to the ground. Without saying a word, Eranan dropped his sword to fall facedown, dead where he lay.

Drawing their dreggans, the other warriors ran to attack the intruder. Before they could near him, they died in the same hideous fashion as had Eranan. Rising sleepily from their places by the fire, two more warriors perished before they grasped what was happening.

The lone surviving Minion charged, swinging his dreggan for all he was worth. Surprisingly, the murderer did nothing to stop him. Sure that he was about to take the intruder down, the Minion smiled menacingly.

The dreggan blade came whistling around, slashing into the rider's right shoulder. But as it did, the warrior felt no resistance against it.

Doing no harm, the dreggan flowed through the intruder's body, then down through his mount as though they were ghosts, burying itself into the trunk of a nearby tree. The warrior frantically struggled to free the blade, but could not. His eyes wide, he looked up at the miraculous opponent who had just bested him. The being's face was hideous, terrifying.

"Who are you?" the warrior demanded.

Staring down at his bewildered enemy, the being atop the horse smiled. He raised one arm.

"I am a Darkling," he said quietly. "But you won't live to tell anyone."

The warrior's organs exploded like those of his fellows, and he fell dead to the ground. His dreggan—still caught in the tree trunk—glinted softly in the light of the three red moons.

Saying nothing more, the rider guided his horse down to where Gaius and the five other Minions were camped. The dark gap in the pass sealed itself, leaving no trace of the exit that had just formed.

In the end, the sleeping warriors at the bottom of the mountainside would fare no better than their brothers.